11/96

NECROSCOPE:
RESURGENCE

ALSO BY BRIAN LUMLEY

Brian Lumley

NECROSCOPE: RESURGENCE

THE LOST YEARS: VOLUME TWO

TOR®

A Tom Doherty Associates Book
New York

NECROSCOPE: RESURGENCE

A Tor Book
Published by Tom Doherty Associates, Inc.
175 Fifth Avenue
New York, NY 10010

Tor Books on the World Wide Web:
http://www.tor.com

Tor® is a registered trademark of Tom Doherty Associates, Inc.

Library of Congress Cataloging-in-Publication Data

Lumley, Brian
    Necroscope : resurgence / Brian Lumley, — 1st ed.
        p.   cm. — (The lost years ; v. 2)
    "A Tom Doherty Associates book."
    ISBN 0-312-85948-1
    1. Vampires—Fiction.   I. Title.   II. Series: Lumley, Brian.
    Lost years ; v. 2.
    PR6052.U45N43   1996
    823'.914—dc20   96-22941
                                                              CIP

First Edition: November 1996

Printed in the United States of America

0 9 8 7 6 5 4 3 2 1

For
Sylvia Starshine—
who provided an item
of fascinating information
—my thanks and undead
gratitude.

CONTENTS

Necroscope:
The Lost Years

A Résumé

HARRY KEOGH IS A YOUNG MAN IN ANOTHER MAN'S BODY: HIS MIND HAS RE-animated the brain-dead Alec Kyle. Recently he has had to get accustomed to the idea—to the feel and looks of his new self—which would be problem enough without the additional complications of being Harry Keogh. For Harry is the Necroscope, the man who talks to dead people in their graves! Moreover, employing the formulae of the long-dead mathematician and astronomer, August Ferdinand Möbius, he has learned the secret of instantaneous travel in space and time. He's a teleport.

But since his "death" and metempsychosis the Necroscope's problems have been unending. His wife, Brenda, traumatized by past events and faced with the prospect of life with a "total stranger," has taken their infant child and vanished off the face of the earth. The agents of E-Branch—the British, London-based ESPionage agency Harry worked for—cannot find her, and despite his skills Harry, too, is at a loss as to Brenda's whereabouts . . . or perhaps not. He knows his son's powers are at least as great as his own. It is possible that the baby has taken his mother and hidden her away. But where?

In order to devote himself to the search, Harry has left E-Branch and returned to his home outside Bonnyrig, near Edinburgh, Scotland. Unknown to him, however, Darcy Clarke, Head of E-Branch, has taken certain measures to ensure the Necroscope's unique skills can't be put to use by alien powers. For British E-Branch isn't the only parapsychological intelligence organization in the world: Red China and the Soviet Union have long followed similar lines of research and run similar covert agencies. Clarke couldn't simply let Harry walk, and take a chance that he wouldn't be recruited or coerced by some foreign agency or criminal organization. Indeed, the Necroscope's wife and baby may well have been stolen away by such an agency! Which is why, before Harry left E-Branch, Clarke had him drugged, hypnotized, and his mind seeded with post-hypnotic commands forbidding him to divulge or display his powers to anyone else.

That was three and a half years ago. In some ways Clarke's scheme has worked out in Harry's favour; in others it has added to the complications of his rehabilitation, his coming-to-terms with the weirdness of his situation . . .

In Scotland, lonely and plagued by nightmares—residual "echoes" of Alec Kyle's precognition, inexplicable glimpses of future events—Harry has developed a romantic relationship with Bonnie Jean Mirlu, a "wrong-headed girl" who helped him out of trouble on a case in London. With a staff of attractive girls, B.J. runs a wine bar in a seedy area of Edinburgh. But the bar is a front, and B.J. Mirlu is more than she seems.

In fact she is a two-hundred-year-old vampire thrall who all her life has kept watch over an ancient horror from a monstrously alien parallel world. Her Master is Radu Lykan, whose lair is an inaccessible cavern complex in the high Cairngorms. Waiting out his time in suspended animation—as he has waited for six centuries—Radu is Wamphyri! The first of the Wamphyri were banished into our world almost two thousand years ago. There were four: Nonari the Gross Ferenczy, the Drakul brothers, and the dog-Lord Radu Lykan, a werewolf. And they brought with them a blood-feud that was already hundreds of years old.

But our world was different. Its teeming tribes were warriors who had their own bloodwars, in which the Wamphyri might easily get caught up and crushed. It was a far cry from their home world, where they had only one real enemy— themselves! At first they failed to adjust; the times were many when they came close to extinction, before learning the golden rule for survival: that longevity is synonymous with anonymity.

Then, gradually, they began to blend in. With their metamorphism it wasn't difficult to play the roles of men; in their own world they had *been* men before they were Wamphyri! Now they must be men again, find positions best-suited to their skills, use them to build their power-bases in this new world. So the banished vampire Lords went their diverse ways.

They became sparing in the dissemination of their evil; they chose their egg-sons carefully and made fewer bloodsons. Mainly they settled in remote areas, and kept themselves secret from the affairs of men. The Drakuls built their redoubts (or aeries) in the Transylvanian Mountains, where in nine hundred years they became powerful *Boyars.* Nonari Ferenczy fled east from the dog-Lord Radu Lykan; he changed his name, became a citizen of Rome and eventually the Governor of a small province on the Black Sea. He got vampire sons out of comely slave women; these made lives of their own in the gloomy east-facing mountains, which Asiatic invaders were loath to climb.

Generally the Drakuls and Ferenczys would remain covert in their ways; they desired that the legends arising out of their earlier days on the Danube and the wooded hills of Dacia—terrible legends of blood-sucking beasts and loping man-wolves—be forgotten by men in the wake of all the bloody wars that had washed across those parts. And in the main they *were* forgotten.

But as for Radu Lykan:

With that of a wolf in him, he was the wild one. Initially Radu ignored the tenets of the rival Lords—he would not hide himself away but go out in the world, become a mercenary, revel in the reek and roil of warfare! Which he did with tremendous enthusiasm. And as the other vampire Lords established themselves in their various places, Radu and his pack became warhounds caring nothing for isolation or anonymity but lusting after the spoil of sacked cities. They fought as mercenaries for personal gain—as well as for the sheer joy of it!—under human warlords whose knowledge and skill in battle was varied far beyond that of any vampire Lord in the world of Radu's origin. Thus he became an artful warrior in his own right.

But eventually, following an act of human treachery, Radu knew it was time to take stock. Returning to Romania, the dog-Lord determined to isolate himself in a mountain "den." Except he must find a livelihood, and the only way he knew was by the blood which *is* the life. Wherefore he built an aerie, and set himself up as *Voevod*—a warlord protector—to the mountain-dwelling peasants of the eastern Carpathians. But the Drakuls, long-established in the western arms of the Carpathian horse-shoe, knew his plan. They swept down on him to murder him and destroy his manse. Radu wasn't to house; but when he returned and saw what was done . . . he knew who to blame.

There was nothing he could do about it; yet again his pack had been decimated, and Radu hadn't the manpower to fight back. But at least the Drakuls had shown their true colours, and from now on Radu would know where he stood with them. Indeed, he had always known, but this was in effect the first actual "declaration" of war. A bloodwar, aye!

Down all the centuries from that time forward, no quarter would be given or expected by the rival Wamphyri factions. Drakuls and Ferenczys, their descendants and thralls, Radu and the pack: they formed a far-flung triangle of mutal animosity, of a hatred and loathing far beyond the passions of any merely human adversaries. From time to time they might come into contact—though usually they would find it prudent to avoid one another—but in the right place at the right time . . .

. . . Blood will out. And blood will be *let* out!

Keeping his band small and fighting in many of the ancient world's great battles, Radu went on as a mercenary. When times allowed he would return to Romania, which he considered a home of sorts. But he knew that the Drakuls continued to Lord it in the mountains, and that his worst enemies, the Ferenczys, were still abroad in the world. He begged of his mistress moon that eventually he would meet up with them to right the wrongs they had worked against him. And in a way—though not entirely as he had wished it—his prayers were eventually answered . . .

Time went by; the world changed; a new terror came ravaging from the east. No conquering Mongol horde this time, but a horde of rats! The Black Death had come to Europe—and vampires as well as entirely human beings were dying from it.

In the Vampire World there'd been only one human disease that the Wamphyri feared: leprosy, which infected their metamorphic flesh faster than their leeches could repair or replace it. Now in this world there was another. It seemed grotesquely ironic: that where the Wamphyri were the greatest parasites of all, this plague was spread by the very smallest—the fleas that infested the Asiatic rats!

The last Drakul (Egon, a Starside original) lived in Poland for the duration of the terror; Poland suffered little or no plague mortality. As for any remaining Ferenczys: at least one may have seen out the plague years on some easily-defended island, for at that time they were powerful in the Mediterranean. But Radu Lykan was ever the mercenary, the adventurer and wanderer. And he was caught out in the open.

Fleeing west through a panic-stricken, plague-ridden Europe, Radu was attacked, wounded, and infected with the plague. Overburdened with Radu's strenuous physical life-style and the disease in his blood both, his parasite grew weak and began to fail him. So that by the time he and the survivors of his pack reached Scotland, he felt exhausted and had but one recourse.

For a long time the dog-Lord had pondered the preservative, perhaps curative powers of resin. Now he would take refuge in a resin "tomb," immerse himself in a great vat of the stuff, and place his trust in the tenacity of his leech. Relieved of some of its burden, his parasite would have an opportunity first to cure itself, then to work on him. And it would have ample time in which to perform its duties.

Radu had a skill other than his hypnotism and mentalism; he was a scryer on future times, which he glimpsed in oneiromantic dreams. Scanning the future, however, is a dubious art. The events witnessed may not come to pass *exactly* as foreseen. But the one thing Radu "saw" quite clearly was the duration of his planned "sleep"—more than six hundred years! It came as a blow at first, but as the dog-Lord got weaker so he resigned himself to the idea. In the high Cairngorms he prepared a lair and set watchers over it; when all was done, he consigned himself to the resin . . .

That was then and this is now.

The centuries are flown and the time is right; Radu will return. Except first he awaits the coming of a certain "Mysterious One"—a "Man-With-Two-Faces"—whom he has scried close at hand in the imminent hour of his resurgence. And B.J. Mirlu has brought just such a one to her Master's attention: the Necroscope, Harry Keogh.

Radu communicates telepathically with B.J. from the resin vat in his Cairngorms hideaway. When she attends him, they converse as if he were up and about. He has ordered her to present Harry at her earliest opportunity. He wants to know the Necroscope's mind, to see if this is indeed the man of his dreams of the future. But Radu is not merely curious. Since his mind is mainly "divorced" from his physical body by virtue of his long period of suspended animation, he cannot be sure that his body is fit and well and that his leech has beaten off his disease. However, and even in a worst-case scenario, he believes he may still survive resurgence by use of metempsychosis: mind transference—to the body of Harry Keogh. In which event the Keogh identity would be entirely subsumed, and Harry would *be* Radu!

Bonnie Jean knows Radu's plan and is in two minds about it. Soon to be

Wamphyri in her own right—if indeed she has not already "ascended"—she would have Harry for herself. For the moment, however, she is under Radu's spell no less than the Necroscope is under hers. She *must* obey her Master, even though her every fiber cries out against it.

Perhaps if she knew Harry's history, his esoteric skills, she would be of a different mind. But she can't know, for despite that B.J. is a powerful beguiler, second only to Radu himself, E-Branch got to the Necroscope first. Even twice-hypnotized he is forbidden to reveal his talents. Radu's hypnotism, on the other hand, is of a different order. It is possible he can even use it to enter Harry's mind. Indeed, to achieve metempsychosis he will have to do just that! Thus Harry's secrets may yet be discovered . . .

Radu is not the only Great Vampire who survived the turbulent centuries. The only *original*, yes, but not the last. On Tibet's Tingri Plateau, Daham Drakesh, a Drakul, is the self-proclaimed High Priest of a monastery where he is breeding an army of vampire thralls. Ostensibly he is in league with a parapsychological unit of the Chinese Red Army, based in Chungking. But in a region as desolate and inaccessible as the Roof of the World, Drakesh is left much to his own devices. He knows that Radu Lykan is still "alive," and that he'll soon return as a power in the world. Drakesh emissaries, vampire disciples, are searching for Radu's lair, to destroy him before he can re-establish himself.

Likewise the last Ferenczys, twin brothers, have risen to the status of Dons of Dons in Sicily. They are not part of the Mafia as such, but they are "advisers" to the heads of all the Families on a world-wide scale; also, they are part-time advisers to the KGB, the CIA, and other intelligence organizations. Their "oracle," the source of their information, is the vastly mutated Angelo Ferenczy—great-grandson of Nonari the Gross! Some three hundred years ago Angelo's parasite suffered a metabolic breakdown; his metamorphism overran him, reducing him to a freakish, lunatic Thing who is now confined to a pit under Le Manse Madonie, a "villa" in the Sicilian mountains of the same name. His bloodsons, Anthony and Francesco, feed him, extorting the information that keeps them in business. For, paradoxically, Angelo's vampire talents have been enhanced by his disorder; he is a scryer and seer of extraordinary power.

Being Wamphyri, however, and mad, Angelo's solutions, his answers, are seldom direct: he obfuscates and plays word-games to keep his bloodsons guessing. But he has warned them of Radu Lykan's imminent return, and of what the dog-Lord will do *when* he returns: that he'll seek them out to destroy them!

Recently then, both Daham Drakesh and the Ferenczys have set to with greater determination to find Radu and kill him in his lair before his planned resurrection. They have discovered his keeper, B.J. Mirlu, and know that she has the assistance of Harry Keogh. Except they believe *him* to be Alec Kyle! Also, it would appear that this same Kyle has somehow contrived to break into the Ferenczys' treasure vault at their "impregnable" manse, and make off with millions in negotiable currencies.

Daham Drakesh—who has kept himself secret even from the Ferenczys—is playing *agent provocateur;* he has sent disciples into Scotland to take out Bonnie Jean Mirlu and stir up additional trouble between Radu and the Ferenczys. Drakesh's plan has backfired; protected by the Necroscope, B.J. has survived; Drakesh's bloodson and a thrall have paid the ultimate price.

At Le Manse Madonie, the Ferenczys are furious over their own losses; they believe the break-in was a "pre-emptive strike" by Radu's people, to discover their weaknesses before the dog-Lord's return and the commencement of all-out war. In addition, they are now aware of a third player; for one of their thralls, a "sleeper" in Scotland, has witnessed something of the death of Drakesh's disciples at the hands of Harry Keogh.

But while Drakesh's losses are considerable (and while he has inadvertently shown his hand in things), he still plans to be the ultimate *agent provocateur*. In possession of a means to set not only vampires but nations at each other's throats, the last Drakul is simply biding his time while continuing to plot against his own kind and humanity in general . . . and B.J. Mirlu and "Alec Kyle" specifically.

There are desperate, dangerous times ahead for Harry and Bonnie Jean—not least because the Necroscope's mind is under her control. Already, many of the things that have happened to him are blank spaces in his memory, missing from his life like pages ripped from a book.

As such, they are part of the lost years . . .

Prologue

TWO OF THEM WAITED IN THE SNOW, BOTH PREDATORS HOWEVER DISPARATE in means and motives. The first was a man, while the other . . . was *Other*. It was other than wholly human. That of humanity was in it, but there was a great deal of something else. It was part-human female, and part *Other*.

Though the man was unaware of the Thing's presence, it had been here for some time, watching him put the finishing touches to his lair. This was something that it understood well enough: the compulsion to build a lair, a base of operations, a secret, private place to call one's own. Indeed, far to the north, inaccessible in a mountain fastness, the Thing knew of just such a lair: not its own, but that of a Higher One.

Normally at this time of the year, the month, the thirty-day cycle—at this oh-so-dangerous time—the she-Thing might even be there, attending her Master in his lair. But not this time. For this time one of her own was threatened, which meant that she herself was threatened. And this was her response: to watch and wait, for the moment, while the human predator prepared his lair.

But there are lairs and there are lairs . . .

The man's lair wasn't intended as a permanent structure. Scarcely a structure at all, it was . . . a hollow, a burrow, a low cave scooped out of the snow drifted against the side of a knoll at the foot of the hills, like a play-place such as children might make; except it wasn't a play-place, and he wasn't a child. Its roof was the hard, crystallized snow that crusted the drift, layered now with the grey, camouflaging cover of a fresh fall; its floor was of hard-packed snow, compressed by the body weight of the man during the process of excavation. The cavity was eight feet long, four and a half wide, three and a quarter deep. A fragile, temporary place at best, yet still a lair. The den of a monstrous human beast. And the beast had completed his work on it a full ten minutes ago.

Something less than one hundred and fifty feet away, and seventy higher up the steep hillside in the lee of a rocky out-crop, the Thing sat, watched, scented—generally *sensed*—the man's activity. She knew what he had done, the preparations he had made and those he was making even now. Her eyes, of a penetrating feral yellow with crimson cores, yet alive with a sentience far beyond the ken of the wild, a more than merely animal cunning, gazed down on the snow-capped knoll and the man's lair at its base. She watched the soft outlines and silhouettes disrupted by his work gradually regaining their bland white anonymity, as the snow continued to fall.

Penetrating eyes, yes: they saw the faint red glimmer of a torch switched on, even through the cave's ice-crystal roof; and a second torch, to lend the lair a sensual, blood-hued illumination. At last all grew still, except—to the Thing's *differently* intelligent mind, her alien perceptions—a sense of the man's actions inside his lair, his final preparations. At which she knew that the human predator intended to go through with it.

Then, maintaining a low profile—her chest ploughing the snow, which tumbled before her in a small, silent avalanche—the Thing came down from the hillside. Where the ground was uneven she wriggled; where the snow was thin she slid on belly and paws; but on a weathered snow-covered scree saddle between the hillside and the knoll she halted, crouched down low, listened, and continued to sense. She was now less than sixty feet from the man's lair and only twenty feet higher.

As yet, the Thing's telepathy wasn't of a high order—it could scarcely be compared with the "mentalism" of her Master in his northern lair—but there are other arts, and the human predator wasn't unknown to her. For which reason she attempted to reach out to him across the distance of two dozen paces and implant this message in his mind:

You were given a warning. There is still time to heed it. What you do now is of your own free will, and its result will be as you *willed it.*

Perhaps something of it got through to the man; he switched off a pen-light torch, paused in his pig-eyed scrutiny of grotesquely lewd photographs in a wallet of pornographic poses, cocked his head on one side and adopted a frowning, listening attitude. But there was nothing to hear—except in his head, like a memory: *This one is not for you. To pursue and take her will place you in extreme jeopardy!*

No, not *like* a memory, it *was* a memory—but from where, from when? Some thought he'd had? Some premonition? The customary lump in his throat as the final phase of an operation moved toward its inevitable conclusion? An attack of . . . what, conscience? Scarcely that! His "good" side, then (did he have one?), telling him this need not be inevitable?

But it was! It was, and he *must* have her! (A glance at the luminous dial of his wristwatch . . . 7:30 P.M.) By now she would be on her way, coming. Soon he'd be coming, too! Then her blood coming . . . *hot spurts from the raw red gash of her throat, gradually slowing, like a well drying up: the well of her life. Her hot breasts cooling, elastic for now but slowly stiffening. Her face pale as the snow, eyes glazed as the ice on the beck.*

He shuddered. It was awful . . . and it was wonderful! Like being a strange dark god: the power of life and death. But not really, for a god has a choice and the man had none. Afterwards . . . she *must* die. Only let her live and she'd talk; it would be the end of everything. They would find him; she'd identify him; they'd crucify him! Not like the son of a god but like a beast. Not on a cross but in a cell, behind bars, forever—or for as long as the other inmates allowed him to live. Strange how even the most vile and violent men hated his sort . . .

He had been to the place where she worked. (Funny, but he couldn't remember much about it.) A darkish place, and red like his snow cave of red light. So she'd lived and so she would die—like a temptress. All who lived as she had lived, luring and teasing and promising, but never living up to the promise, took their chances. So she'd taken hers.

And he had taken his, just going there, to the place where she worked . . . but of course he must in order to know all about her. He'd gone there two or three times, yet couldn't remember a thing about it, except . . . it was dark, red-lit, with dark-eyed Loreleis serving drinks.

The Lorelei . . . a legend out of Germany . . . it was associational. There'd been places like it in Hamburg: low music, low lights, lowlife . . .

He had been a Sergeant then, but his rank had given him no special privileges with the nightclub girls. Oh, the men in his platoon had had them—whores galore!—but the only way he'd been able to get it was to pay for it. How he'd hated that: the fact that they rarely took him a second time, not even for his lousy "geld." There'd been something about his eyes, something . . . cold, in his eyes.

Cold, yes. For other men it was heat that went with lust, but for him it was the cold that turned him on. Six years ago in the Harz Mountains, on a winter warfare course (before various misuses of rank and privilege had come to light, sufficient to see him reduced from a promising middle-ranker to an out-of-work bum in a society with little or no use for the specialized skills of a commando), he remembered being holed-up for a week on a snow-covered mountain, allegedly acquiring survival skills while in fact fantasizing about sex with hot, quivering, naked women. That was where the notion had first occurred to him: in the Harz, in Germany . . .

. . . But snow is snow the world over, and women are women: good for fucking but small use for anything else. Except a man can't be a "real" man without he at least has the use of a woman's body; but *only* the use, since the permanent possession of a woman, the burden of ownership, will very quickly reduce him to *less* than a man! That was the lair-builder's understanding of male/female relationships, anyway—a paradox where the man always came out the loser. And it had seemed to him that there ought to be an alternative.

Well, and so there was, and this was it. But since it served only the needs of a minority of one (namely himself) it was unacceptable to the majority. So . . . *fuck* the majority! How he wished he could, except from his point of view the society that rejected him had its own predators. They were called police and *he* was their prey; or would be, but he was wily and they hadn't caught him yet. Almost but not quite, not yet.

There are predators and predators, known and unknown. Even among the known sort you are only a small creature of the kind, while among the unknown *things you are a speck, a mote, a miniscule! So back off now, while yet you may . . .*

What? Talking to himself again? That recurrent dream he'd been having: of something awesome stalking him? Not conscience, no, but guilt pure and simple. For *he* was the stalker, the Awesome One. He shrugged off the feeling of eyes where there were no eyes, and warning voices where there couldn't possibly be.

A short distance away, the Thing crouching at the crest of the scree saddle sensed the man's rejection of her—her what? Her reminder? Its suggestion? Sensed, anyway, the human beast's resolution, his determination, the fact that he would indeed go through with it. So be it: it was of his own free will.

Beyond the knoll, the narrow road was an icy black ribbon chopped two feet deep through the snow. Maintained by the snow-plough team that serviced the local villages, the road had last been cleared two hours ago. Since when it had furred over again with a pelt of fresh snow, through which the tarmac's black ice glittered like jet. In these parts conditions such as this were common; the weather would have to be a lot harsher to close the roads completely. And in any case, this was only a service road to the hamlet. The main highway, to Perth in the north and Dunfermline and Edinburgh in the south, lay a mile and a half away through a pass in the Ochil Hills.

The tiny hamlet itself, Sma' Auchterbecky, lay in a valley or re-entry in the Ochils. This was the only road in; it came to an abrupt halt at a wooden footbridge over the currently frozen beck. Where the road ended a blacktopped rectangle served a dual purpose, as a turning place for vehicles and as the hamlet's communal car park. The squat, humped, anonymous shapes of jacketed cars, three of them—Sma' Auchterbecky's total vehicular complement—crouched on the parking area like a trio of oddly frozen mammoths on some Siberian tundra.

No longer black—but grey-topped under a layer of snow, the rectangle turned briefly to glittering white as the light of a full moon penetrated the threatening cloud blanket. Only a momentary effect—a churning of leaden, snow-laden clouds, allowing just one blink of the silver Cyclops eye—still the Thing felt it like the jab of a cattle prod. Magnetized by the moon, a ridge of erectile fur stiffened along her spine; lured by the Lunar orb, a *sound* died unborn, aborted with difficulty in her throbbing throat. But at the same time a need was born in her belly.

The crimson cores of her eyes expanded, driving back the feral yellow; her jaws dripped saliva; her head turned, muzzle twitching, from the safely sealed vault of the sky back to the cyst in the snow that was the man's lair. All of her awareness was now centered on the cavern of the beast—the human beast—where he lay on his back, masturbating by red torchlight to a pornographic centerfold ripped from a men's magazine. The Thing smelled his sex, heard his pounding heartbeat and sensed the coursing of his rich blood. But this was scarcely the climax of the man's activity, merely a part of it. The last part as he . . . *readied* himself. For everything was now in position and the predator was poised. Only one thing was missing: the prey, and she was coming.

It called for one final effort on the part of the Thing; for to simply let this go ahead—to encourage it, if only by non-interference—might in the long run mean endangering herself. Indeed, in any other scenario but this one, the man might even be considered her ally, her cover! But not when he threatened one of her own. Wherefore:

You are making a mistake. There is great danger here!

But despite all the effort she put into it the man heard nothing—or if he heard anything at all it was only an echo from that dream again:

Of the red-lit darkness . . . of the Loreleis taunting, and flaunting their flesh . . . of the Awesome Stalker, not himself after all but some other, or rather some other's voice in his head, questioning, whose simple questions he couldn't refuse but must answer. That was what really stalked him, gnawed at him: the idea that he might have told someone (some thing?) his innermost thoughts. But . . . in a dream?

It returned, as dreams are wont to do, unexpectedly. Finally he remembered it, something of it at least:

He stood on a black road on a black night and gazed into the yawning throat of a black tunnel cut in a black mountainside. And he was frozen there, bereft of will, unable to move a muscle as something (a vehicle?) approached, bearing down on him in dreadful, inexorable slow-motion out of the tunnel. Its yellow headlights shone on him, fixed him in their blinding glare, froze him like a rabbit in his tracks. Then, from the utter darkness behind the dazzling yellow lights, a question:

"Why?"

And he knew the meaning of it, also that he must answer.

"Because I want her."

"For her body?"

"Yes."

"Only for that?"

"And for her life."

"Why?"

"I can't leave a trail. Can't leave any tracks."

"Tracks?"

"I mean, she would talk."

"You've done it before . . ."

(But since it wasn't a question, there was no requirement to answer that one.)

"Have you done it before?"

"Yes."

"How often?"

"Three times."

"Murder?" (A question this time).

"Not for the sake of murder, but for the sake of my needs . . . at first, anyway."

"You've killed innocents?"

"They weren't innocent! Shaking their backsides, flashing their tits! They were *asking* for it!"

And all the while the yellow headlights expanding, coming ever closer; and the darkness behind them and surrounding them growing darker yet . . .

"When?"

"Soon. When it snows good and deep."

"Where?"

(Hesitation. He shouldn't be telling this, not even in a dream, not even to himself. But he couldn't refuse to answer.) "I'll do it where she lives."

"How?"

"I'll wait for her, and do it in the snow." *A long pause, and then:*

"Of your own free will, aye. But I warn you: this one is not for you. To pursue and take her will place you in extreme jeopardy! But if you must—so be it . . ."

Then:

The headlights sweeping upon him, expanding to envelop him! The darkness opening, as if to swallow him whole! A rumbling growl that wasn't *the thunder of an engine. And the headlights . . . the headlights! Not yellow but—*

—Red?

The man gave his head a shake, snapped out of it. He had been daydreaming, staring at his red torches where he'd rammed their tubes into the soft snow walls. Staring as if hypnotized by them. Hypnotized? Had he been hypnotized by someone, somewhere? He blinked, then issued a snort of self-derision.

Maybe he was losing it. Maybe he was mad! (Well of *course* he was, had to be—a homicidal maniac!) But it didn't change anything. Neither did his dream, already slipping away, fading into the mists of his twisted mind. Nothing had been changed. His course was set. He *was* going to do it.

So be it!

Hidden in the shadow of the hillside, the Thing slid and tobogganed on her chest and belly down the slope of the saddle to level ground. She was only fifty feet or so from the predator's lair now; his man's scent hung heavy in the sharp, otherwise clean night air, which pulsed with his vibrations. He was a strong one, just as she remembered him. Good!

And his timing was perfect.

Headlights on full beam sliced the night, cut twin swaths through the silently falling snow, swung like searchlight beams towards the hamlet across the frozen beck but without reaching it. Myriads of drifting snowflakes diffused the light, reducing its penetrative power; likewise the sound of the taxi's engine, muffled by the snow. Maybe this was what the predator had been dreaming of: the arrival of the taxi, its lights and the purr of its engine.

And out from his lair he crept, invisible in a white nylon track-suit and parka, the hood zipped to the neck and his face hidden behind a white stocking mask.

Meanwhile the taxi had slowed, turned, halted on the hard-standing; a female figure was getting out, standing in the pale glow from the driver's window. The oval of her face was visible inside the fur-lined hood of her coat; she fumbled with payment for her ride.

Then the taxi's door slammed; it pulled carefully away in a *crump* of crushed snow and a puff of exhaust smoke. And clasping the neck of her coat close to her throat, the girl tramped fresh-fallen snow towards the footbridge. But before she could reach it—

—Out of nowhere, the predator was there before her!

Her instinctive, involuntary gasp galvanized him to violent action. As her eyes went wide and she tried to jerk herself out of reach, he stiff-fingered her deep in the stomach. And as the air she'd drawn to scream whooshed uselessly out of her and she folded forward from the first blow, he hit her again; this time in the throat . . . but not hard enough to kill. Not yet.

Choking, she crumpled; her feet shot out from under her on the icy surface. If he hadn't caught her she would have fallen. And with his right arm under her neck, breast, and armpit, and his other hand in her hair, he dragged her writhing form back across the road to the side of the knoll.

He was tittering now but couldn't help it—little girl's laughter that bubbled up in his throat to spill from his mouth in short bursts—hyena laughter, excited but muted: the call of a wild dog to the pack as it tracks its wounded prey. Hooting and giggling, but softly. And between each crazed burst, a guttural, frothing spray of obscenity: "Fuck, fuck, *fuck!* Fuck, fuck, *fuck!*" And his flesh hard and throbbing under the zipper of his track-suit trousers.

The girl was making a recovery. She fought harder as he dragged her round the foot of the knoll to his snow-cave's low entrance. He paused to grip her throat and crush it, shake her head like the head of a rag doll until she went quiet. Then he was dragging her into his den . . . his red-glowing lust-lair.

Inside, he hauled her up alongside, kneeled over her. She moaned and clutched her throat, trying to breathe as he showed her his mad smile, his teeth, his pig eyes. He wrenched at his zipper and his steaming meat jerked and nodded into view. Smelling it, her eyes went wide with knowledge; she knew his intention, what he would do! Her coat was open; his hand raked down the front of her blouse, caught at her bra, popped buttons and ripped material. Her breasts lolled out, hot and quivering.

"For you!" He waved his swollen, throbbing penis at her.

"Ur-ur-*urgh!*" She gurgled and choked, trying to rise up on her elbows. He backhanded her—not too hard, just a slap to let her know who was boss here, which rocked her head back and stretched her prone—then reached down, snatched up her short skirt and groped between her legs for her panties. God! He'd be into her in a minute . . . biting her tits . . . shooting his spunk! A whole year's worth into her hot, slimy little—

—His obscene giggling and mouthings were cut short in a moment. For holding her neck, looking down between her legs, looking back at the burrow entrance . . . *someone was there!*

He recognized the scene immediately, the prescience of it falling like a hammer blow on his mind, so that he jerked back from it as if shot. His dream, but no longer a dream! The dark tunnel and yellow headlights; except, as he now saw, the headlights were eyes! Great yellow eyes, triangular, unblinking, hypnotic, and oh so intelligent! And the voice when it came—that soft burr of a Scottish brogue, more growled than spoken, but hinting of a monstrous strength—no longer the suppressed *memory* of a conversation but real, immediate, now!

"You were warned, were ye no? *I* warned ye!"

"Wha—? Wha—? Wha—?"

"I warned ye: this one was no for ye. To pursue her would place ye in jeopardy most extreme! Aye, but ye ignored mah warning! So be it . . ."

"Wha—? Wha—? Wha—?" He groped for his knife, found it; the blade gleamed red in red torchlight. But the Thing inching forward in the tunnel wasn't in the least afraid.

And suddenly: *it was as if the predator were really there, back in his dream! Once again he stood on a black road gazing into the yawning black throat of a tunnel, and as before he was frozen, unable to move a muscle, as something awesome bore down on him in a dreadful, inexorable slow-motion. Its yellow eyes shone on him, freezing him rigid, while the darkness surrounding those eyes grew darker yet . . .*

It had never been a dream (he knew that now), but it *was* a nightmare! The headlight eyes expanding to envelop him. The darkness opening to swallow him whole. The rumbling growl that wasn't the roar of an engine. But the eyes—those awful eyes—no longer feral yellow!

The face emerging from the darkness wasn't human. It was triangular. Ears pointing forward, pointing at the man; bottom jaw yawning open; great yellow headlight eyes . . . turning luminous red. As red as blood!

"Eh?!" said the man; simply that. It scarcely qualified as a question, and wasn't even close to a scream—no more than a squeak or a whimper—as a hand, a paw, something, reached out of the tunnel, arched for a moment like a great grey furry spider over his leg, and drove home inches deep through track-suit trousers and flesh to scrape the bone of his thigh.

Then he screamed, dropped the knife, tried to hang on to the girl where she had finally managed to sit up . . . and where she sat there *smiling* at him! But there are smiles and there are smiles.

And her eyes were as yellow as the Thing's had been just a moment ago, rapt on him, watching him being dragged into the tunnel; and her ears seemed to reach tremblingly forward, like the Thing's ears, eager for his panting, bubbling screams and the terrible *rrrip!* of his clothing and flesh, as talons sharp as razors opened him up the middle like a steaming, screaming joint of meat.

After that, amid all the slobbering, snarling and panting, it was as much as the girl could do to cram herself in a corner and so avoid the hot red splashes.

Knowing the Thing the way she did, she knew how dangerous it would be to try to take her share.

Well, not for a little while, at least . . .

PART 1

The Sleeping and the Undead

I

INSPECTOR IANSON INVESTIGATES

IT WAS TEN IN THE MORNING, BUT AT THIS TIME OF YEAR, IN THIS PLACE, IT might just as easily be four in the evening. Under a heavy blanket of lowering snow clouds and in the shadow of the hills the time made little or no difference: everything looked grey . . . except that which now lay exposed, with the snow shovelled back from it, under the canopy of a scenes-of-crime canvas rigged up by the local police. That—what was left of it—was not grey but red. Very red. And torn . . .

"Animal," said old Angus McGowan, giving a curt, knowing nod. "A creature did it, an' a big yin at that!"

"Aye, that's what we thought," Inspector Ianson returned the old man's nod. "A beast for sure. That's why we called you in, Angus. But now the big question: what *sort* of a beast? And how a beast . . . I mean, up here in the snow and all?"

"Eh?" Angus McGowan looked at the Police Inspector curiously, even scathingly. "Up here in the snow and a'? Why . . . where else, man?"

Ianson shrugged, and shivered, but not entirely from the cold. "Where else?" He frowned as he pondered his old friend and rival's meaning, then shrugged again. "Just about anywhere else, I should think! The African veldt, maybe? The Australian outback? India? But Scotland? What, and Auld Windy, Edinburgh herself, little more than seven or eight miles away? No lions or tigers or bears up here, Angus—not unless they escaped from a zoo! Which is the other reason I called you in on it, as well you know."

Angus glanced at him through rheumy, watering eyes. The cold—and, just as the Inspector himself had felt it, maybe something other than the cold—had seeped through to the old vet's bones. But then, the sight of bloody, violent, unnatural death will have a similar effect on most men.

Inspector Ianson was tall, well over six feet, and thin as a pole. But for all that he was getting on a bit in years, George Ianson remained spry and alert, mentally and physically active. Homicide was his job (he might often be heard complaining, in his dry, emotionless brogue, "Man, how I hate mah work! It's sheer *murrrder!*"), and this was his beat, his area of responsibility: a roughly kite-shaped region falling between Edinburgh and Glasgow east to west, Stirling and Dumfries north to south. Outside that kite a man could get himself killed however he might or might not choose, and his body never have to suffer the cold, calculating gaze of George Ianson. But inside it . . .

"Africa? India?" Angus echoed the gangling Inspector, then squinted at the tossed and tangled corpse before shaking his head in denial. "No, no, George. She was no big cat, this yin. Nor a dog . . . but *like* a dog, aye!"

It was Ianson's turn to study the other: dour old Angus McGowan, whom he'd known for years. A living caricature! Typically a "canny old Scotsman," hugging his knowledge as close to his chest as a gambler with his cards, or a rich man with his wealth. His rheumy grey eyes—the eyes of a hawk for all that they were misted—missed nothing; his blue-veined nose seemed sensitive as a bloodhound's; his knowledge (he'd been a recognized authority in zoology for all of thirty years) brimmed in the library of his brain like an encyclopaedia of feral lore. Quite simply, as the Inspector was gifted to know men—their ways and minds and, in his case especially, their criminal minds—so Angus was gifted to know animals.

Between the two of them, on those rare occasions when the one might call upon the other for his expert knowledge, it had become a game, a competition, no less than the chess game they played once a week in the Inspector's study at his home in Dalkeith. For here, too, however serious the case, they vied one with the other, trying each other's minds to see which would come closest to the truth. The beauty of it was this: in chess there's only one winner, but here they could both win.

"*Like* a dog?" Ianson looked again, deeply into McGowan's watery eyes, his wrinkled face. Old Angus: all five foot four or five of him, shrivelled as last year's walnuts, but standing tall now with some sure knowledge, some inner secret that loaned him stature. Nodding, and careful to avoid the bloodied snow, he went to one knee. Not that it mattered greatly—no need to worry about the destruction of evidence now; the scenes-of-crime men had been and gone all of an hour ago—but Angus didn't want this poor devil's blood on his good overcoat.

Looking up at Ianson from where he kneeled—and had the situation been other than it was—the slighter man might well have grinned. Instead he grimaced, tapped the side of his dripping nose with his index finger, and answered, "Shall we say—oh, Ah dinnae ken—a dog *o' sorts?* Shall we say, a dog, or a bitch, o' a different colour? Like maybe, grey?"

A great grey dog. Angus could mean only one sort of beast. Ridiculous! Except he wasn't given to making ridiculous statements. Wherefore:

"From a zoo?" Ianson gripped McGowan's shoulder as he made to straighten up. "Or maybe a circus? Have you heard of an escape, then? Has one got out?"

"One what?" The other was all wide-eyed innocence.

"Come now, Angus!" The Inspector tut-tutted. "A wild creature of the snows, like a great, grey, handsome dog? You can only be hinting at a wolf, surely?"

"Hintin', is it!" the other chuckled, however drily, and was serious in a moment. "Ah'm no hintin', George. Ye want mah opinion? This *was* a wolf, aye! An' one hell of a wolf at that! But escaped frae a zoo . . . ?" He shook his head; not in denial, more out of puzzlement. "Ah've never come across a beast this size—no in any zoo in England, Scotland or Wales, at least. And as for yere circuses—what, at this time of year? Certainly no up here! An' so, well, Ah really canna say; Ah mean, Ah wouldnae *care* to commit mahsel'."

"But you've done exactly that," the Inspector pointed out. "The piece is moved, Angus. You can't put it back."

"Wolf, aye!" the other snapped, more decisively now. "But as for how she got here, her origin . . ." He offered a twitch of his thin shoulders, stamped numb feet, blew into cupped hands. "It's your move, George. It's your move."

"Me . . . I say we move in out of the cold!" Ianson shook himself, both mentally and physically, breathed deeply of the wintry air, deliberately forced himself to draw back from the morbid spell, the dreadful fascination of the case—for the moment, anyway. For if McGowan was right, which in all likelihood he was (or there again not, for after all, the Inspector did have information to the contrary), then it was out of his hands. Murder by a man is one thing . . . but by a dog, a wolf, or some other wild creature, then it becomes something else: a savaging, a misadventure, simply a killing. (And what of a man *and* a dog?) But *if* McGowan was right, then they'd need to call in a different kind of hunter with a very different brief: to kill on sight!

Old Angus guessed what he was thinking—the latter part of it, anyway—and was quick to say, "But first we must try to prove it, or narrow down the suspects, at least."

"Back to the house?" Ianson ducked out into the open with his small friend close behind. The house he referred to was one of a picturesque cluster standing some three hundred yards away across the footbridge. Once a great farm with outbuildings, now Sma' Auchterbecky housed a small community, scarcely a hamlet, in the very lee of the mountains.

"Ah can make a few calls frae there, aye," Angus nodded. "D'ye see the telephone wires?"

"And I've a few more questions for the girl," the Inspector replied, turning up the collar of his coat. He scanned the land all about, noted that it had started to snow again: great fat flakes that fell straight out of a leaden sky. In the lowering atmosphere there was little or no wind.

"A pretty enough place in the summer," McGowan commented. "But in the winter? A hell o' a place for a man tae die. *Huh!* An' a hell o' a *way* for one tae die, too!" They stood side by side a while, scanning the valley between the hills. Nearby, a police Land Rover hunched on the verge at the side of the road, also a squad car fitted with snow chains, and an ambulance with its rear doors open, waiting. The blue lights of the vehicles, silently revolving, loaned eerie, intermittent illumination to the handful of stamping, arm-flapping uniformed policemen and paramedics in attendance. Exhaust fumes from the Land Rover went up in a blue-grey spiral, mimicking the smoke from the cluster of near-distant cottage chimneys.

Ianson signalled the paramedics forward; now they could take the body—its remains—out of here. The forensic lab in Edinburgh would be its next port of call, then the morgue. But there wouldn't be much gutting of this one. He'd had more than his fair share of that already.

"A hell of a way to die?" The Inspector echoed his companion curiously, enigmatically. "Or maybe a weird sort of . . . I don't know, justice, maybe?" There was that in his voice which caused old McGowan to glance at him sharply. Something he'd not been informed of, then? Oh, the vet would stand by his claim to the bitter end, that this was the work of a wolf. For he'd seen (indeed he had sensed, *felt*) evidence which to him was indisputable. But Ianson was the policeman after all, and a damned good one! Anyway, it wouldn't do to press the point; a man can't be seen to know too much, or he might have too much explaining to do. A hunch is one thing, but an assertion needs proving.

"Justice?" Angus let his sharp tone reveal his own suspicions. "Somethin' ye've nae told me, George?" It was hardly surprising; this was the way their game usually went.

Ianson's smile was grim. "Oh, a lot to come from this yet, Angus . . . not least from you! Nothing's solved until everything is known." And before the other could question further: "Let's get on over to the house now. We can talk as we go . . ."

"I know him," Ianson admitted, as they crossed the footbridge.

"The victim?"

"Victim, villain, whatever," the Inspector shrugged. "John Moffat's his name. I wouldn't have known his body—who would? But I recognized his face. Moffat, aye: prime suspect in a murder case in Glasgow just a year ago. Then, too, he'd done it in the snow; a park on the outskirts of the city, in the wee small hours of the morning. The same *modus operandi:* he dug a hole in a snowdrift, chose a prostitute on her way home and dragged her in. He raped and murdered her. Slit her throat ear to ear. He'd been seen in the park earlier. There were one or two other bits of inconclusive evidence . . . not enough to pin it on him."

"He walked away frae it." McGowan nodded.

"But not away from this one," Ianson's voice was grim. "So it's one down . . . but it's still one to go."

"Ye're saying that this was . . . what, revenge? Which means ye believe it was a man. A man and his bloody big dog, maybe?"

Ianson glanced at him out the corner of his eye. "Maybe," he answered. "Which would put the whammy on your wolf theory."

The other made no reply. It suited him either way. He knew that Ianson wouldn't have asked him along if he hadn't at least suspected a large canine or some other animal. The Inspector had admitted as much.

"I only know that someone protected the girl," Ianson went on. "Except he did too damn thorough a job of it!"

"Someone close to the Glasgow prostitute, maybe?"

"Eh? Aye, possibly. Close to that one, anyway."

"Oh? Has there been more than one, then? Unfair, George!" McGowan tut-tutted. "A man cannae play if the lights are out! Ah have tae know all yere moves."

"One more at least," Ianson said. "Gleneagles, two winters ago."

"In the snow again! And no too far away, at that. A prostitute, was she?"

"Aye. We didn't find that one until the first of the warm weather when the snow melted. She'd been there a month or more. Any evidence had been washed away. Our wee man back there could have done it, though. Again, same *modus operandi*. But of course we didn't know him then. He didn't come into the picture until the Glasgow thing."

"And that's it?"

"That's it for the prostitute murders . . . well, as far as I'm aware. Of course there could be others we *don't* know about. People disappear and are never found—as well you know." And again he gave that sideways glance.

"But if our man John Moffat wasnae linked to the Gleneagles murder, and if who or whatever killed him was somebody out for revenge, then this new killer can only be someone who knew the Glasgow girl, surely?"

Ianson frowned. "Or someone who knew John Moffat, what he was doing—someone close to him, maybe?—who thought it was time he was stopped."

"No just someone protectin' this girl especially, then?"

"Eh?" Ianson paused and stared hard at the other. "When I said she'd been protected, I meant by accident; by someone just happening on the scene, as it were."

"Ye hadnae thought o' the other sort o' protection, then? That this one's pimp might have been lookin' out for her?"

"Pimp?"

"Well, it follows that if yere man only kills whores, the girl must be one. And if so, she probably has a pimp. Someone—and his dog?—who was waiting for her when she got dropped off last night!"

The Inspector started, then grinned and took the other's arm above the elbow. Frail as old Angus seemed, the resilience of his flesh never failed to surprise Ianson; he felt the muscles move under the man's clothing, bunching at his unexpected grip as if resenting it. "Now see!" Ianson said. "What a grand team we make! Why, it's possible ye've just hit the nail right on the head!"

McGowan freed himself and said, "Maybe. But it's like ye said: nothing's solved until everything is known." And now it was time to change direction again: "Personally, well, Ah still opine tae a big animal. On its own. A wild thing come down out o' the hills tae hunt."

"I thought we had discounted the wolf theory?" The Inspector was making for the houses again.

"No, *you* had," McGowan told him. "But me, Ah have several theories. See, if ye'd no told me about they other murders, or that this John Moffat was a suspect, Ah'd still be thinkin' in terms o' a wild yin. And deep down inside, Ah still am."

"A wild one? How long ago since there was a wild wolf in Scotland, Angus?"

"Two hundred and fifty years, that we know of," the other answered. "But

Scotland's a big place, and plenty of wild country still. All over the world the wolves are stealin' back down frae the north, so why not here?"

"Because we're an island, Angus, that's why!"

"Is that so? Then explain the big cats on Bodmin Moor, and Dartmoor, and other places. Sheep killers, them—and real!"

"Not proven," Ianson said.

"Proven for mah money!" McGowan snorted. "Ah was down in Devon and Cornwall, remember? They called me in on it. No, Ah didnae see the beasts in question, but Ah saw their handiwork! Big cats, George. Take mah word for it!"

"My God, you'll be swearing an oath on Nessie yet!" Ianson grinned. "They called you in on that one, too, didn't they?"

"That American team? Three months' work there, George. It was the easiest money Ah ever made in mah life! What? A summer holiday on the banks o' Loch Ness, with all found and money in the bank?" McGowan chuckled and smacked his lips, and then was serious again. "Anyway, Ah was only a 'technical adviser.' Ah didnae have tae believe . . . no as long as they *thought* Ah did! But a wolf is no a plesiosaur, George. They big yins have been gone a long time, but there are still wolves in the world."

"Not in Scotland," the other was stubborn.

"Ah, but there could be soon enough!"

"Eh?"

"There's talk o' stocking a sanctuary somewhere up north. They'd have tae cull them, o' course, or shoot any that strayed too far. But there's a study on it."

"Really?"

"Well why not? The wolves have been here just as long as we have. And there are still foxes, after all. Even the cities have foxes! Ah mean, is it no ridiculous? The Irish have their Irish wolfhounds—and never a wolf to be found!"

"Except here?"

But Angus only shrugged. From now on he would take a back seat and only do or say what was expected of him. He had talked of men and he had talked of wolves, but he'd not once mentioned the creature in between. Nor would he. Unlike the Loch Ness Monster, who really didn't exist, that would be just too close for comfort. But in the final analysis—if and when it should come to it—it would be no bad thing for Inspector George Ianson to have a wolf on his mind . . . or even a werewolf. For as a legend the creature was far enough removed from certain *other* myths to make it unique in its own right. No one in his right mind would confuse an isolated case (or even an outbreak) of strictly medical or pathological lycanthropy with vampirism. It might alert humanity to the one type of monster in its midst, but the other would remain obscure as ever . . .

While the Inspector talked to the girl, Margaret Macdowell, old Angus spent the time on the telephone. When both were done they thanked the girl for coffee and sandwiches, then walked back to Ianson's car. It was snowing again and the path was white under foot.

On their way into Edinburgh, they talked:

"No whore, that lady," Ianson said. "She sells booze, not her body. Works at a wine bar in Edinburgh. That's why she was late home: late opening hours. It might easily have been later still, but her boss lets her off early if the forecast is bad. As you probably overheard, Moffat had been frequenting the bar, chatting up the other girls, too, but paying particular attention to Margaret Macdowell. She knew his first name, that's all. She did recognize him, however—barely, or briefly—during the attack, after he'd dragged her into his . . . what, his den? And she knew that he would kill her. Before she passed out she sensed that someone was there. And she woke up to . . . all that mess! She thinks she remembers snarling and savage motion, and something of Moffat's gibbering. And that's about it."

"Ye spoke to her before the police drove me up here," old Angus was thinking out loud. "Didnae ye get any o' this then?"

"She was tired, shaken, shocked," Ianson shrugged. "Still is, but refuses treatment. Can't say I blame her. She has a few bruises, that's all. She's young and the shock won't last. Yes, I got something of it, but the stuff about the snarling is new. She may remember more as she settles down."

"So, no whore," McGowan mused.

"But easily mistaken for one," the other returned. "A bar girl—all long legs, a backside like an apple, and a half-bare bosom—decked out in a short dress, black stockings and garters, serving drinks to a mainly male clientele. Oh, our Mr. Moffat could easily get the wrong idea, I'm sure."

"A modern Jack the Ripper," McGowan grunted.

"Except this one got ripped," Ianson reminded him, grimly. "And no surgical instruments did *that* to him, be sure."

"A man and his dog," old Angus mused. "But no tracks . . ."

"The snow," the Inspector grunted.

"So, what's next?"

"For you? I expect you'll carry on contacting and checking out all the zoos and wild-life parks in the area," Ianson glanced at the smaller man. "So that we can be absolutely sure that there's been no escape. I'd certainly appreciate it, Angus, for they'll talk more easily to you than to me. As for me . . . I'll need to be talking to the other girls at Margaret Macdowell's place of work: B.J.'s Wine Bar, in town. But I've little doubt they'll corroborate all she's said."

"So why bother?"

"Oh, routine," Ianson shrugged. "Who knows, maybe they can tell me more about John Moffat? Did he have any enemies or such that they might know of? That sort of thing."

"Like a man and his dog?"

"Just so . . ."

Or, the Inspector wondered, *maybe a woman and her dog?* On that point, there'd been several occasions when the old vet had mentioned a "she" in connection with his wolf. Like "she" was a big yin, and so forth. And anyway, why had Angus strayed so far from his argument, his original conclusion? Had he or hadn't he given up on his wolf theory? What about his telephone calls?

"Who did you speak to, Angus?" Ianson glanced at him. "The zoo people in Edinburgh?"

"They're on mah list. Ah have tae do it, ye understand, if only tae settle it in mah own mind."

"But in fact you've given up on it now?"

Old Angus merely shrugged.

"Well?"

"Murder by dog. It seems more and more feasible . . ."

The Inspector was mildly concerned. McGowan was saying so very little now; probably because he was . . . what, hiding something? This was usually how he was before making some surprise move on the chess board. Maybe Ianson should look more closely at the case from old Angus's point of view—wherever that was coming from! Since he now seemed to be making light of his wolf theory, perhaps the Inspector should pay more attention to it.

Except, if Angus *was* onto something, Ianson felt certain he wouldn't get much more out of him just yet. Wherefore a second opinion might be in order. And if his memory served him, he knew just where he might find a lead to that second opinion: in the unsolved files at Police HQ in Edinburgh . . .

After dropping McGowan off at his place in a sagging, decaying district east of the city, the Inspector called in at Police HQ and made a request to Records: for a list of attacks, savagings by animals, of people and livestock, occurring in the last five years. Then a quick call to New Scotland Yard for more information, and by the time he was through Records had run off some stuff for him. Too much stuff: the incidence of animal attacks, usually by "pet" dogs, was surprisingly high.

He spoke to the clerk in charge and asked him about older cases: "Some thirty years ago? I was new on the force, but seem to remember a case somewhere up north that made a big splash at the time. A sighting? A savaging, at one of the wildlife parks, followed by the resignation of a local policeman. He quit after his report was rubbished and he was ridiculed. Do you think you could dig it out for me?"

The clerk, a man thin and tall as Ianson himself, wearing spectacles, squinted at him and said, "Thirty years ago? That's a hell of a memory you've got, Inspector! But I'm afraid those old files aren't on microfiche. It could take a while. However, I'll make a search if that's what you'd like."

Ianson nodded. "Yes, go ahead. If you find the file, you can contact me at home."

He took the sheaf of papers home with him to his spacious garret flat in Dalkeith, made himself a light lunch, then took his food and work both into his study and sat with them at his desk under a huge sloping skylight. Ianson liked natural light best, even when it was the dim grey light of winter. His chess board stood on a small table to one side of the room, with the pieces in position just as he and old Angus had left them some nights earlier. They would get to finish the game eventually, but now there was bigger "game afoot."

Munching on chicken salad sandwiches, the Inspector began scanning the pages of information printed out for him from Police HQ's microfiche files. But after a minute or two, realizing that it would take a while to separate out the stuff that interested him, and because tonight he intended to visit B.J.'s Wine Bar in the city, he paused to make a telephone call and reserve a little time with the boss of the bar now.

Margaret Macdowell had given him the number; using it, he found his call answered by a female voice with a soft Scottish burr. He asked for the proprietor, and was told:

"That'll be mahsel'—Bonnie Jean Mirlu."

"Miss Mirlu—or is it Missus?—perhaps you're already aware of the attack on one of your girls last night?" And following that up quickly, in case she hadn't heard: "I'm talking about Margaret Macdowell—but I'd like to reassure you that she came to no harm. I'm the Inspector on the case."

"It's Miss," the voice told him. "Just call me B.J. And Ah've heard, yes—Margaret called and told me. Is there somethin' Ah can do for ye, Inspector, er . . . ?"

"Ianson. George Ianson. I've a question or two you could perhaps help me with, routine stuff. Perhaps tonight, opening hours? I'll make it brief as possible and try not to keep you from your business."

"But what could Ah possibly know? It was miles frae here, and he wasnae even a regular customer. Just a pest to the lassies, that's all."

"You knew him, then? I really must come to see you, B.J."

She sighed and answered, "Well if ye must ye must, but Ah cannae see what ye're hopin' tae learn frae me."

"How many of you are there . . . in the bar, I mean?"

"Four, all girls, and mahsel'. But ye'll surely no be wanting to question us all, now will ye?"

"Probably. But only a few minutes each, I promise."

"Verra well, then," she agreed, grudgingly. "Say, eightish?"

"That'll do nicely," he told her. "Until tonight, then."

But after putting the phone down, the Inspector sat frowning to himself before returning to his papers. Something about her accent, he thought. Oh, it was a very good imitation, but it wasn't the real thing, wasn't the genuine article. Or maybe it was *too* genuine.

He pondered it a while longer, then snapped his fingers. That was it! B. J. Mirlu's accent wasn't phony at all; it was simply out of date, not quite the modern vernacular he was used to hearing in the city. She sounded more like something out of the last century—out of the Highlands, maybe—like Granny Ianson, God bless her, when George was a lad. Maybe this B. J. Mirlu was from up north, then, and the high-faultin' accents of Edinburgh still alien to her tongue. It was something he would have to ask her, if only to satisfy his own curiosity . . .

It took the Inspector some two hours to sort through the photocopy files. Closed cases (prosecutions mainly, brought by individual complainants on their own behalf, or by the parents of children savaged by "pet" or domesticated dogs, and a number of cases where enraged farmers had shot dead strays found worrying their flocks) went into one sheaf, and open cases into another. Then this second sheaf was sub-divided into attacks on animals, on people, and sightings; the latter because there was no lack of reports of large, generally unspecified creatures wandering in the wild. Just such cases as interested Angus McGowan.

But the Inspector would have nothing to do with the likes of Bodmin Moor wildcats, great hounds of Dartmoor or Nessie o' the Loch. His monsters—the monsters of his calling—were invariably human. Or in this case, maybe a bit of both. A man and his dog, aye. Or maybe a woman and *her* dog . . .

Before Ianson could look at the relevant parts of the sub-divided paperwork, his phone rang: a call from a friend at New Scotland Yard, in Criminal Records. "George, we got your request," Peter Yanner told him. Yanner was an ex-Inspector seeing out his time to retirement behind a desk. "And I saw the morning's sitreps. You'll be working on that case at, er, Auchterbecky?"

"Sma' Auchterbecky," Ianson corrected him. "Nasty stuff, Peter. One case closed, and another opened."

"Indeed," said the other. "And I suppose you'll be torn two ways: glad to see the one go down, but unhappy that a new one's come up. Like the gang wars down here. We're never too unhappy about it when a bad lad gets hit, but there's always the question of who did it. A pity they can't *all* kill themselves off, eh?"

"Murder is murder," Ianson replied. "John Moffat's paid his dues, but who to?" He shrugged, if only to himself, then asked: "So what have you got for me?"

"I'm just trying to clarify things," the other answered. "Big dog attacks, you said: animals. But what about lycanthropy?"

"Eh?"

"We had this bloke who thought he was a werewolf. A cop-killer, too! That was three, maybe three and a half years ago. We got him . . . but the whole case was weird. There were a lot of threads left dangling, you know? But when the Home Office puts the cap on something, that's it, case closed."

"So?" The Inspector's mind had begun to switch elsewhere as soon as lycanthropy was mentioned. He couldn't see any connection with the current case; he had taken in very little of what he'd been told. "No big savage dog, then? No *genuine* big dog, anyway."

"Well that's why I phoned you," the other explained. "I mean, you can't get much bigger than a werewolf, now can you?"

Finally Ianson's mind focused. He knew that this wasn't for him, yet his instincts told him to follow it up. "You say the case is closed? You got him? So what makes you think that I'd be interested? I mean, lycanthropy, Peter? What's on your mind?"

"It's just funny, that's all . . ."

"Funny?"

"Not ha-ha, just funny. OK, you're probably not in the picture, so let me explain. This thing with the werewolf: the guy was killed with a crossbow, with silvered arrowheads."

"What? The police used a crossbow?" Ianson was lost again.

"No, whoever killed him did."

"We had outside help, then. The SAS?"

"No."

"Secret service?"

"Not that I know of. Just someone out to get him, as far as I know." And before Ianson could question further: "Then, a couple of months ago, we had this other case up in your neck of the woods."

"What case was that?" (His neck of the woods? The Inspector's attention was suddenly riveted.)

"Murder, up on the Spey not far from Kincraig? You surely remember those Tibetans who got killed, George? Sectarian warfare or some such? Two dead up there in a wrecked car, and a whole bunch of them got tossed out of the country."

Ianson frowned. "I remember the headlines but I wasn't on the case. It was outside my jurisdiction. Anyway, what does it have to do with attacks by big dogs—or lycanthropy, for that matter?"

"A possible connection, that's all," Yanner told him. "It was the same kind of murder weapon: a crossbow. The same silvered arrowheads, too . . ."

"Boltheads," Ianson growled, more to himself than to the other.

"What's that?"

"A crossbow doesn't shoot arrows but bolts."

"Whatever," Yanner answered. "But a silver bolt killed our werewolf nut, and likewise one of these Hari Krishna types. The other one fried in the wrecked car. It might not mean anything, I don't know. I just sort of connected it up, that's all. A so-called werewolf, and a crossbow with silvered arrowheads—er, *bolt*heads! And your request for stuff on dog or big animal attacks: Scotland, murder, and silver boltheads again. A bit of a tangle, I know, but that's how my mind works."

Ianson licked his lips, then shook his head despite that Yanner couldn't see him. "But what is there to connect the murder last night and these killings on the Spey? I mean, how does our John Moffat fit in? I don't see it, Peter."

"Me neither, but that's not what I'm paid for. I only keep the books. You're the man on the ground. Anyway, maybe I should have kept my nose out. I'm sorry if I've confused the issue."

"No, no, not at all. In fact you've interested me greatly. Let me have all you've got on this lycanthropy thing, will you? I mean, as well as the routine stuff?"

"Sure."

"And the case is closed, you say?"

"Yep."

"Without a murderer? A *second* murderer, I mean?"

(An invisible shrug). "The guy was a cop-killer, George."

"And everyone involved was satisfied with the conclusion?"

"Apparently."

"Weird!"

"That's what I told you . . ."

"Peter, thanks for calling."

"You're welcome. And this stuff will be on its way ASAP."

"Cheers . . . " And slowly, Ianson put the phone down.

After that the paperwork was boring . . . for a while. Until the Inspector began glancing through the "sightings" list. At first he would read, shake his head and muttering disbelievingly to himself put the report aside. These so-called "sightings" covered just about every eventuality.

"Nessie" was in there, of course (as reported by a drunken gamekeeper to the police station in Drumnadrochit). Also feral cats in an attack on a chicken farm at Aboyne; stray dogs worrying sheep at Braemar near Balmoral, and also at the foot of Arthur's Seat in Edinburgh itself. And . . .

. . . And wolves seen at Newtonmore, Blair Atholl, and in the Pass of Killiecrankie. Also at Crianlarich under Ben More, and at Carrbridge and Nethybridge on the Spey! Great grey wolves, by God! Half a dozen cases. Too many bloody wolves by far!

So, perhaps old McGowan did know something after all. But if so, why wasn't he saying anything? Or could it be (the Inspector gave his head a worried shake) that he, George Ianson, was simply letting himself get tangled up in this thing—in a load of hogwash, that is? And what the hell, weren't there *always* boogy men in these out-of-the-way places? And wouldn't there always be a Nessie lurking in the loch? Well, yes. Just as long as there were tourists there would be, for sure!

A great grey dog with eyes like lanterns seen padding the road on a misty night at Newtonmore . . . a wolf? Not a bit of it, just a big dog. And the pair spied in the Pass of Killiecrankie? Rationalization: a man out walking his Alsatian dogs steps into the bushes for a pee. His dogs stand waiting; they maybe rear up a little, and draw back onto the verge as a car passes. The motorist— with a dram or two under his belt, no doubt—sees their eyes turn to flames in his main beams. As for the valley of the Spey: why, a man could swear to seeing anything on a misty, moonlit night, on those winding wooded lanes and rocky hillsides! Damn, it was only a year ago that they'd been seeing flying saucers! And the same down in Sussex, and crop circles in Devon and Dorset!

So what was it that was bothering him, Ianson wondered? And a moment later believed he had the answer. He hadn't been able to remember much about it at Police HQ, but now recalled it clearly enough. These damned silly reports had jogged his memory: about that constable who had quit his job some thirty years ago over just such a sighting. But there'd been more to it than that. Not *just* a sighting . . . but a killing, too! Not of a man but an animal! And not just any animal but a bison! A creature as big as that, gutted!

As for the location . . .

. . . It had taken place at the Highland wildlife park near Kincraig. Then the park had been the merest nucleus of what it was now; indeed, it hadn't opened properly until sixteen years later. Even so, it had been stocked with a canny complement of "Highland" creatures, many of which had vanished from Scotland centuries ago: brown bears, beaver, reindeer and the like. And bison, yes.

Kincraig. On the River Spey. And these Tibetans had died there, too. And then there'd been those sightings up at Carrbridge and Nethybridge. But as for wolves—and bloody werewolves, by God!—why, Ianson could almost break out laughing at himself. But he didn't, and wouldn't. Not until he checked with the wildlife park that they didn't have wolves, too!

Was that what old Angus had been hinting at? Had he been laughing up his sleeve at Ianson when he'd told him there was a scheme afoot to re-introduce wolves into some wild place up north? Had he known that they had *already* introduced them? In which case he was cheating! What, old Angus? *Huh!* His "A man cannae play if the lights are out!" And, "Ah have tae know a' yere moves, George." The canny old devil!

It should be easy enough to check out. A call to the park could settle it right now. Except the Inspector knew that something else was bothering him, something out of myth and legend. He snapped his fingers as suddenly it came to him: silver! Silvered crossbow bolts! And you'd need a silver weapon to kill a werewolf, wouldn't you?

So, just what *sort* of outside help had the Metropolitan Police called in that time to deal with their lycanthrope; or rather, their lunatic? And whoever the hunter was, why had he used a silvered crossbow bolt? Not for the "obvious" reason, surely? Or was he some kind of lunatic, too . . . ?

The Inspector sat there a long time, just thinking . . . or not thinking very much at all. Sometimes things worked themselves out better that way.

The light was fading. Short days, long nights, and a full moon rising. Ianson remembered it from a night or two ago when he'd sat in here with some case or other: the moon nearing its full, hanging low over the horizon. So last night . . . would it have been full?

Now what was he thinking? What the *hell* was he thinking?

He stood up, stretched, glanced at his watch. God, it was 4:45 already! The afternoon had flown. And going to the window he looked out across the rooftops of Dalkeith, to where a full moon was three-quarters free of the grey evening haze . . .

He turned on the lights, headed back towards his desk, and jumped like a shot rabbit when the phone rang. It was the records clerk at Central HQ. "I'll be shutting up shop in a couple of minutes," he said. "Just thought you'd like to know, I found your case file—that business at Kincraig nearly thirty years ago? Will you call in for it tomorrow, or what?"

"No," Ianson told him. "I'll be in town tonight. Leave it with the information desk, will you? I'll pick it up there."

"Very well, as long as you'll sign for it. And one other thing. That constable you mentioned who resigned? I traced him through the pay office . . . a disability pension for some small injury he got as a serving officer. He's Gavin Strachan: a Kingussie man, but he moved down here shortly after quitting."

"Down here?"

"One of those coincidences. Lives not far from you in Dalkeith. A ten-minute walk along the Penicuik Road."

The Inspector was grateful and said, "Thanks. That takes a lot of the effort out of it."

"You're welcome. And goodnight."

"Goodnight," Ianson answered automatically. And glancing at the moon again through his window, he hoped it would be. It had started out good, anyway . . .

Since it was too early to eat, and much too early to get ready for his appointment at B.J.'s Wine Bar, Ianson checked through the reports again. Now he was looking at cases covering attacks on people. And though five years was a long time, still, in his opinion—based on the number of savagings alone—there were far too many Rottweilers and Dobermanns around! As for the incidence of people bitten in the face . . . it was horrific! Worse, several of these attacks had been fatals.

What the hell is it in a dog, the Inspector wondered, *that will make it bite a child in the face?* And what the hell was it that caused them to carry on even after they'd reduced the victim to a bundle of red rags? The wolf in them, he supposed. The only good thing was that in almost every case where a rogue pet dog had savaged someone, the beast had been easily tracked back to its owner. And nine out of ten such animals—the dogs, that is—had been destroyed. Ianson had never been much of a dog-lover, and he didn't go a lot on their owners, either.

And then there were the unsolved cases . . .

But the Inspector's eyes were tired; the rest of the reports could wait; he would take a break from the paperwork and try contacting ex-constable Gavin Strachan instead. He was in the book—several of them were, in fact. Ianson matched addresses with the one he'd got from the records clerk and gave his man a call.

"Eh?" said a rough voice at the other end of the line.

"Good evening, sir," Ianson answered. "Gavin Strachan?"

"Aye. What is it?"

"Ex-constable Strachan?"

"Eh? No for a long time, it isn't! Anyway, what of it?"

"Inspector Ianson," Ianson told him. "We never met, but I would certainly like to."

"Why?" (Strachan's voice was rough as sandpaper, and full of suspicion.)

"Oh, routine," (Ianson's stock answer). "A case you dealt with up in Kincraig thirty years ago—something that happened at the wildlife park . . . ?"

For a moment there was silence, then: "Some kind o' joke?" Strachan's voice was harsher still.

"Joke? Not at all. I'd just like to hear it from you what really happened that night. What you think you saw."

"Think, is it? But Ah told them what Ah think thirty years ago—told the newspapers, too. *Hah!* Tellin' mah story was like pissin' in the wind. Aye, and it pissed mah career away, too!"

"Mr. Strachan, I—"

"Fuck ye!" the other cut him off, and slammed the phone down . . .

II

STRACHAN, BONNIE JEAN, AND ... McGOWAN?

IF THERE WAS ONE THING GUARANTEED TO GET GEORGE IANSON'S BACK UP, IT was someone talking to him like that. Very well, maybe the man had cause, or thought he had. He'd *better* have or, by God, Ianson would see to it that his bad manners brought him a great deal of trouble! Easiest thing in the world to have him called in to the local police station, and there let him cool his heels for an hour before seeing him. Aye, and the law was on Ianson's side all the way. Judge's Rule number one: "Whenever a Police Officer is endeavouring to discover the author of a crime, there is no objection to him putting questions in respect thereof to any person or persons whether suspected or not from whom he believes useful information may be obtained." *So fuck ye, too, Gavin Strachan!* Ianson thought as he knocked solidly on the door of the man's ground-floor flat in the Penicuik Road. *We can do it the hard way or the easy way, it's up to you.*

His knock was answered by a tall, surly-looking, stocky man in his mid- to late fifties. He stood straight, but still had to look up a little at Ianson. And he recognized a policeman when he saw one, by which the Inspector knew that this was indeed his man. One copper can spot another a mile away; even an ex-copper.

To prove the point, Strachan squinted at him through red-rimmed eyes, and grunted, "Inspector Ianson. Well now, and is it no strange Ah was expectin' ye." It wasn't a question.

"Gavin Strachan," Ianson replied, "I need to talk to you. What's more I *will* talk to you, here or elsewhere, in my time or yours, it's your choice."

"And have Ah done somethin' wrong?"

"Not that I know of. I was hoping you'd want to do something right, that's all. It could be you can't help me; if so this won't take very long and I'll not bother you again. It's only on an off-chance that I'm here. But . . . here I am."

The other grunted, stood aside and let him in. *"Huh!"* he said. "Ye may have gathered that ah'm no well pleased tae see ye. Polis? Aye, ah was one, and a good yin—much good it did me! So it's bad enough tae have tae entertain ye without that ye have tae revive a' that stuff up at the wildlife park."

"But I do have to, Strachan, I do," Ianson answered. And there was that in his voice that made the other turn sharply and peer at him.

"So . . . what's happened?"

It could do no harm to tell him. In any case, the story was in the newspapers. "A killing's what happened, like the one up at the wildlife park. But this time it wasn't a bison. Murder, Strachan. It could be—it probably is—that the two cases are unconnected. But it's one of those things I have to check on. That's why I need your story. I remember some of it from the time—from the newspapers, yes—and I'll be reading up on the case file tomorrow. Until then the details have sort of faded in my memory. Though not in yours, I suspect."

While he had talked to the man, the Inspector had looked him over. Gavin Strachan looked gritty, tired and bitter. The bitterness had been there a long time; it was etched into his face like coal dust in the pores of a miner. Behind their red rims, his blue-grey eyes seemed trapped, while the bags under his eyes spoke of sleepless nights. And in his every word and move there was a whole world of suspicion, just as Ianson had detected it during their brief telephone conversation.

On the other hand, the Inspector had always considered himself a judge of character, and it had to be said that he could find little to actively dislike in Strachan—well, apart from the man's obvious dislike of him! And even that seemed to be on the wane now, as finally Strachan waved him into a chair in his drab sitting-room and said, "Coffee? Might just as well, for as ye say, ye're here now."

Indeed Strachan had appraised his visitor, and the Inspector's open attitude and honesty had stood him in good stead. For a policeman—and a senior one at that, used to at least a modicum of respect—he was a hard man to dislike. "Coffee will be fine," he answered.

"With a little somethin' in it, maybe?"

"Just a touch," Ianson answered. "Thanks."

"What, on duty?" Strachan had gone into his tiny kitchen. The Inspector couldn't see him, but he could hear the genuine note of surprise in his voice. "Are ye sure?"

"This isn't official, Gavin, if I may call you that. I'm here on spec, as I said."

The other came back out of the kitchen, stood facing him. He had a bottle of good whisky and two glasses that he placed on an occasional table close at hand. "Guid!" he said. "For if ye're wantin' me tae go back over a' *that* business, Ah for one will pour mahsel' a dram! Ye can join me or no, as ye will."

And why not? One shot couldn't hurt. The kettle whistled as Ianson poured himself a drink, and Strachan went off again to fix their coffees. And by now the atmosphere was much more relaxed. Except . . . the Inspector could feel a definite tension in Strachan, when finally the man sat himself down facing him. And:

"So," said Strachan, in a tone that said he was resigned to it. "Now we get tae it." He picked up his glass and poured a double shot straight into the back of his throat.

Ianson watched his gasping mouth reform, then said, "Is that what it takes?"

"George," said the other (which surprised the Inspector, that Strachan had remembered), "if ye spend thirty years trying tae forget somethin', and when it still comes back tae ye in yere dreams, it's no easy thing tae talk aboot when ye're conscious. Ye've asked me what happened that nicht up at the wildlife park, and Ah'm goin' tae tell ye. But ye'd best hang on mah words, man, for Ah won't be repeatin' them—ever!"

Then, forcing himself to relax a little in his chair, he lay back and half-closed his eyes. And sipping alternately of whisky and coffee, he unfolded his tale for Ianson's inspection . . .

It had been one of those nights.

Ask any policeman anywhere in the world, he'll be able to tell you about that one night when right out of nowhere everything decided to happen all at once. *Just* such a night, then, when Constable Gavin Strachan got caught up in the occurrences at the Kincraig wildlife park.

But in the Highlands? And the night not even a Friday or Saturday, when you might expect a bit of trouble from the lads at the various socials and community dancehalls, with a couple of drinks too many in them and their bright young eyes full of the other fellows' girlfriends?

In fact it was a Wednesday, wintry even for the middle of May, the sort of night when anyone with tuppence worth of sense would be home toasting his feet in front of a warm fire. Anyone but a policemen on duty, that is. And over the past three-month Strachan hadn't covered anything worse than a bad traffic accident on an icy road. So he certainly hadn't been on the lookout for anything big going down midweek on a night as wild as this.

So maybe it was the full moon . . . but whatever, he hadn't stopped moving from the moment he woke up the day-shift man at the tiny Police Post in Kingussie and relieved him of his duties. That had been about 6:00 P.M., and of course there'd been nothing for the day-shift constable to pass on; the Daily Occurrence Book showed a blank page. Like yesterday, and the day before that, and the nights in between, too.

Ah, but this had been one of *those* nights.

Strachan had no sooner got settled in, made some coffee, opened a book to the first page of a science fiction thriller, when the phone rang—a break-in at the museum at Newtonmore. A three-mile drive along the Spey road, an hour spent examining a broken window and recording statements, and three miles back again. But before he could enter the details in the book, another call-out to the Aviemore Holiday Centre, where a guest was drunk and wrecking the hotel bar!

Ten miles each way this time, and Strachan righteously annoyed and fully prepared to arrest the man—except he was sleeping it off when he arrived, and the manager of the hotel wouldn't put him to the trouble. Besides, he was sure he could recoup his damages in the morning. Er, but in the event there should be any problem . . . well, maybe the constable would like to make a note of the breakages now, while he was here?—And that had taken another hour. But at least Strachan was given a wee dram on the house, just the one, to warm him up a bit.

Which should have been ample for one "quiet" night in the vale of the Badenoch. But no, the phone was ringing when Strachan got back to Kingussie: a traffic accident at a bad bend on the Coylumbridge road. Damn it to hell, but he'd only been a mile or two from the site up at Aviemore! If he'd known, he could have gone out onto the road and waited for it to happen! Except that was a bit of Irish, and he was a Scot, and a policeman's lot is not a happy one.

But it wasn't all that bad. Two cars had glanced off each other. One of the drivers, a young woman, had scraped her knees and shaken herself up a bit when she'd run off the road and hit a tree. Strachan had dabbed her pretty knees with an antiseptic swab (no, not bad at all!) and as always when there was an accident, he'd taken along a brandy flask. So he'd given the drivers a tot each, and one for himself, then let the male driver of the other car go off while he and the young lady sat in his police vehicle and waited for the tow-truck. She was a pretty wee thing; far better than sitting there with some grumbly old codger.

By the time he'd set off again to drive back to Kingussie it had been something after eleven-twenty, and a cold mist coming up off the Spey to shroud a full moon hanging low over the valley. Which was when it happened . . .

Level with the wildlife park, suddenly there was someone on the road! A man with a torch (thank God, else the constable might easily have hit him), wreathed in mist, desperately waving Strachan down. It was old Andrew Bishop, the owner of the site and keeper of the park. His eyes were wild and fearful as Strachan pulled off the road and drew to a halt on the verge.

And as he got out of the police car, Bishop was on him in a frenzy. "Is it Gavin Strachan?" he panted, as he glanced back over his shoulder at the misted park outbuildings and wire-mesh enclosures. "Gavin, lad! Thank goodness ye're up and aboot!"

"Eh? What's up?"

"Up? My God, up? I'll tell ye what's up. Somethin's in wi' the animals!"

Strachan caught at Andrew's arms, tried to hold him still. "Where are the boys?" (Old Bishop's sons.)

"No back frae the dance in Dalwhinnie. And Liz is locked in the bedroom, at the hoose."

"Locked in? Yere wife?"

"Ah locked her in mahsel'! Have ye no a weapon, Gavin?"

"A weapon? Now Andrew, what would Ah be doing wi' a weapon?"

Bishop was fairly dancing in his anxiety. "Ah have a shotgun in the hoose," he cried, "but Ah'm out o' shells. Oh, hell! Oh, damnation!"

Now Strachan held him tighter still. "Andrew, now come to yere senses, man! What on earth's wrong wi' ye? Somethin's in wi' the animals, ye said."

"Aye, Ah did," the other wrenched himself loose. "And more than one somethin', Ah fancy! Mah deer are oot and runnin' wild frae whatever it's that tore its way in tae the pens!"

"Come on," Strachan said, making for the track to the outbuildings, barns and pens. "Let's see what we've got here." But old man Bishop at once dragged on his arm.

"What? And will ye go in there wi'oot a gun?"

Which stopped Strachan in his tracks. The quaver in Bishop's voice, where the constable never before heard a tremor in all his life. The fact that he'd locked his wife safely away in a bedroom—but safe from what? And in that same moment, Gavin Strachan knew there was something terrible here . . .

Then, distracting him, even unnerving him, there came the furious, frenzied squawking of terrified chickens.

"Mah hens!" Bishop gasped. "They're in wi' mah poor chickens!"

"Let me get mah licht," Strachan quietly growled, taking a heavy-duty torch from the back of the car.

"And yere truncheon," Bishop whined. "But by God—a gun would be a sight better . . . !" Already the mad fluttering, squawking and screeching was dying down.

They were on the track, approaching the outbuildings, when a different sound brought them to a halt. But there are sounds and there are sounds. This one was a cry: eerie, ululant, electrifying—and unmistakable.

"Dog," Strachan breathed, hurrying forward again. "Out in the woods back o' the house. A big yin, probably, returned tae the wild." Even as he spoke the howl was answered, from closer at hand. And when the sound had died away, Strachan added, "Or dogs. There's been some sheep worrying south o' here."

"Ye say?" Old Bishop seemed to breathe a sigh of relief. "Dogs? Ye think?"

"Why, what else?" Strachan moved forward again. "Yere animals must o' smelled 'em."

"Smelled 'em, heared 'em, seen 'em, probably," the old man seemed steadier now. "God, they've been howlin' this last half-hour! Put the wind up me and Liz, Ah can tell ye! We saw one o' they frae the upstairs window. But Gavin," again he clutched at the constable's arm, " . . . ye can damn mah eyes for liars if they didnae see him stand up on his hind legs! And big . . . man, he was one *big* yin!"

There came a rustling from the nearest enclosure—and a moment later a squawk. "Mah hens!" Old Bishop aimed his torch, sprang forward, skidded to a halt in swirling ground mist where a hole had been torn in the high wire-mesh boundary. And Strachan saw that the wire was of a heavy gauge. Then:

"Dogs," Strachan whispered again, his own beam flickering this way and that, but nervously now. "Big yins, aye."

Old Andrew turned to him and his mouth was slack. "God—they chewed through this wire like it was cheese!"

And again it was the old man's voice that did it to Strachan, got through to him like nothing else could have. And yet again he asked himself, just exactly *what* had Bishop seen that caused him to lock up his wife and run dancing down the road? An old stoic like Andrew Bishop? Why, there wasn't a more down-to-earth man in all the Highlands! And so far (Strachan suspected) old Bishop had been entirely too reticent, like he hadn't wanted to destroy his salt-of-the-earth image.

Strachan checked himself; he was now as nervous as the old man. It wasn't good enough. "Two of us," he said. "Which should be more than enough for a couple of rogue dogs. And anyway, the birds are quiet now. In we go." He climbed in through the large hole in the wire, with old man Bishop right behind him.

The enclosure was a big one, free range, with hen-houses on both sides and a boardwalk up the centre. But as the beams of their torches sliced deeper into the swirling mist they saw that the houses had been wrecked, wrenched apart. And the carcasses of dead birds were everywhere. Old Bishop picked one up in a trembling hand; not a mark on it. It was as if the creature had died of fright. But others were bloody, and some were without heads.

Various alternatives passed uselessly through Strachan's mind. Uselessly because they didn't work. This could have been done by foxes—indeed the wanton destruction of so many birds was precisely the fox's *modus operandi*—but foxes would have dug *under* the wire, not through it; they couldn't have chopped through it. As for wildcats: they would never come this close, and certainly not at this time of year, when there was plenty of food in the wild.

"Well, whatever he was, he's out o' here now," the constable croaked, and cleared his throat. "The birds would tell us if he was still here."

Old Bishop was wandering among the shattered hen-houses, gathering up corpses. "What birds?" he said, his face a fearful mask in Strachan's torch beam. "There's no a one o' they left!" And he went stumbling to the far side of the enclosure.

"What about the deer pens?" Strachan was acutely aware of the eerie silence, and he didn't like it. "Ye told me the deer had been scared off?"

"Stampeded, aye. Me and the wife saw them scattering away intae the woods. Ye'd think the place was on fire, by God! But Gavin, it's time ye knew. Ah don't think the things Ah saw oot here were dogs. Ah'm no sure, Ah cannae say what they were . . . but no dogs, they yins."

Before he could continue, there came an uproar of chattering and screeching from a large cage set well apart from the other enclosures. "The pine martens!" old Bishop gasped.

"Quick! Back out through the hole," Strachan husked.

But: "No!" came Bishop's answer. "This way'll be better."

Strachan stumbled to him across the shattered boards of a wrecked hen-house, and found him shaking like a man in a fever beside a second hole in the wire-mesh. His eyes stared fixedly at a trail of bloodied feathers, wings, and bird debris in general that led off into the night and the mist.

"Enough o' this!" Strachan was furious with himself, disgusted at the fear that the situation and the old man's obvious terror had inspired in him. "Let's see what the *fuck* this thing is!"

They went through the hole in the perimeter and ran stumblingly towards the pine marten cage, where it was at once seen that the animals had only been complaining about—or warning of—the presence of outsiders and possible danger. But despite the fact that the cage wasn't damaged, certainly *something* had been here. The pine martens' fear was manifest in the way they clung close together, spreadeagled on the wire-mesh ceiling of their cage.

The mist was thicker now, swirling knee-deep and sending tendrils up into the trees bordering the park. "This mist," old Bishop complained, and shivered uncontrollably, "man, it *clings* tae ye!"

It was true: the mist seemed alive, like the thick breath of a beast. They moved through it, torch beams stabbing ahead, towards the next enclosure: a small corral containing Bishop's five prized bison of a species long absent from the Highlands proper. Which was when things livened up again, and in a single moment the night became a nightmare.

First the agonized bellowing of a beast from beyond the corral's four-bar fencing; then the fence itself splintering outwards as a pair of stampeding bison smashed into it, hurling boards and then themselves in Bishop's and Strachan's direction; and a moment later the sound of breaking glass, and a cry—a scream—from the dimly visible, dark silhouette of the old man's house:

"Andrew! Andrew! *Andrew!* Let me out . . . oh, *let me out!"*

Sent flying as the wild-eyed, fearful bison went thundering off into darkness, the two men picked themselves up—only to stumble aside as two more animals came snorting and kicking through the break. Then old Bishop was off at a run, heedless of life and limb, towards the house. "Liz!" he shouted. "Ah'm comin', lass, Ah'm comin'!"

And Strachan was on his own, fairly certain that whatever was plaguing the beasts was in the corral. But all he could see through the break was a lake of mist, with milky tendrils lapping outwards from some central disturbance. Then—

—The black and crimson hump of a thrashing animal's back heaved up into view, breaking the surface . . . *and other things reached up to pull it under again!*

Strachan wasn't sure what he'd seen; it had happened too quickly. But an afterimage, of thick white ropes—or arms?—fitted with grapples or claws—or taloned hands?—burned on his riveted retinae. He stood there as if nailed in position, smelling hot blood and listening to tearing sounds . . . and the bison's panting and bellowing, quickly dying away.

And then the snarling, and slobbering of frenzied—what, gluttony?—as the ripples of mist continued to swirl outwards from that deadly central area . . .

How long? Difficult to say. Minutes that felt like hours, before Strachan could think again. Or before he was galvanized to activity, as the knee-deep mist began swirling and rippling in his direction, and vague *outlines* were seen within the mist, with eyes like lamps that burned on him!

He had no weapon but a torch. Glancing this way and that, he saw pieces of shattered fence at his feet and snatched up a two-foot length of inch-by-four sharpened to a splintery point where it had broken along the grain. There were three pairs of luminous eyes in the mist. Three—whatever they were—were in there; they spread out as they moved towards Strachan.

But seen out of the corner of Strachan's eye, coming from the direction of the house and heading for the woods, a figure. Not Bishop but . . . a *figure* that leaned oddly forward, upright like a badly formed man—or woman—loping through the mist. And its eyes were luminous, too . . .

. . . Then old Bishop was back, and a double-barrelled shotgun in his trembling hands. "Ah found a couple'ay shells," he found time to pant . . . before the scene at the corral impacted on his mind. And cursing as he pointed his gun—without even bothering to aim—he let fly with both barrels. There came a flash and a roar both dazzling and deafening, which for a single second blew apart the menacing dark and stunned silence.

Half-blinded by the flash, Strachan threw up an arm before him as the mist erupted! He was bowled over—*something* bowled him over, and raked at the sleeve of his jacket in its passing. Then there was a blur of sinuous motion, an angry snarling receding rapidly into the woods behind the animal park, and an urgent howling ringing down from the foothills beyond the trees. Almost as if . . . as if *they* were being called off.

And there was a gasping and sobbing from old Andrew Bishop, stretched prone on the earth. "It's mah damn leg!" the old man groaned. "Mah bleddy leg! It has tae be broken. But did ye see, Gavin? Did ye *see?*"

"No." White as a ghost, the constable went to him. "Nothing that makes sense, anyway."

"But . . . dogs?" the old man pressed.

And as their eyes met Strachan was obliged to admit: "No, Ah cannae say they were dogs."

"What, then?" Bishop's voice was a whisper.

Strachan could only shake his head. The sleeve of his uniform and shirt had been sliced as by razors down to the skin, but by some miracle his skin was unmarked. And no matter what he might *think* he had seen, what he thought he'd seen couldn't possibly have done that. Not unless it—or she?—had a handful of razor blades . . .

At the house Liz Bishop was in a bad state of hysteria. Shuddering and almost incoherent, she told a story that night that she could never repeat to any court, nor ever commit to paper. Her husband wouldn't let her, and he himself would later deny all knowledge of anything but "an attack by wild or rogue animals, probably dogs, on the creatures of the park." Perhaps he feared ridicule, but Strachan thought not. Knowing Andrew Bishop's character, it seemed more likely he believed that in denying what he *truly* believed, he might make it go away—like a man whistling in the dark. And later, the constable might have wished that he had taken a similar course.

As for Mrs. Bishop's story:

Alarmed by the squawking of the chickens and the frenzy of the pine martens, she'd gone to the window of her upstairs bedroom and looked out. Immediately beyond the window, a balcony overlooked the park; and down below, there was the mist, of course: a milky lake lapping between the trees and various enclosures. But also down there, crouching by the wall of the house and staring up at her . . .

. . . Something wild and naked and awful, and human! Or perhaps not human.

For as its yellow triangular eyes met hers, the creature had snarled, sprung upright, bounded all of fifteen feet into the air to grasp the balcony rail and vault over it. And its *face* had stared at her through the window, as its lips became a muzzle that drew back from teeth like bone daggers! At which she had picked up a chair and smashed it at the thing through the window, then screamed for her husband, and for her life.

But when next she had dared look the thing had gone, and all Mrs. Bishop could remember of it was that, "It looked like . . . Ah could swear . . . Ah mean, it wasnae *all* animal, Andrew! Am Ah mad, or what? It looked something like . . . Ah mean, it *reminded* me o' . . . a lassie? But what sort o' lassie, Andrew? What sort?" And her last few words had been spoken in little more than an awed and frightened whisper.

That was what she'd said that night, but the next day she was in too bad a way to record a statement, and old man Bishop too busy looking after her. Meanwhile:

"**M**ah report had gone in," Strachan finished. "Ah was young and eager; Ah would hae made a good cop; Ah tol' it the way Ah saw it. Big mistake. When finally they Bishops did speak about it, *huh,* it was animals did the job. No specific creature, ye ken, but most likely dogs. Me? Ah was left holdin' the bleddy baby! *And* it came out how Ah'd had a couple'ay wee drams that night! So that was that. As for the rest . . .

". . . Ah got no peace frae then on in—until Ah got out! What an idiot, eh? For like Ah said, Ah tol' it the way Ah saw it, and Ah tol' *what* Ah saw. That was mah error."

"But what *did* you see?" Inspector Ianson pressed, fascinated by the sweat on Strachan's brow, despite that his flat was cool.

The other nodded. "Hear me well," he said, "for it's the last time, Ah swear. Ah had seen *wolves,* George! White wolves, or things that moved, crept and snarled like wolves. Certainly Ah had seen *one* wolf—the one that came frae the house, after scarin' Liz Bishop half tae death. But the hell o' it is that as the thing made for the trees, just before old Bishop let go wi' that double blast, it looked more like a lassie! Aye, just like the old lady had said. But wolf, bitch, girl or some sort o' weird mixture—whatever it was—it stood on its hind feet, George, upright! Now how can ye explain that?"

The Inspector believed he had evidence that *might* explain it. "What if she wasn't a dog?" he queried. "Or a she-wolf, if you insist. Could it be that what you saw was a mad woman *running* with rogue dogs? How about it, Gavin? Could I be right?"

"Eh?" Strachan licked his lips, frowned, and finally said: "There's more tae yere visit than meets the eye. Now how about you tell *me* a story for a change? Like, how it is wi' this case ye're workin' on?"

"There are—might be—similarities," Ianson admitted. Then, sighing, he said: "OK, it's a deal. I'll tell you something of it, on the understanding it's for your ears only."

"Done! But let's go through intae mah study . . . Well, Ah *call* it a study. As for *what* Ah'm studyin'—what Ah've been readin' intae for years—Ah've learned better than tae put it on open display."

He got up, crossed the floor and opened a door to a room scarcely bigger than a closet. There was space for a desk, two chairs, and bookshelves built into the walls; and there was one small, high window to let in a little light in daylight hours. That was all.

As Strachan saw Ianson seated, and went off to fetch his bottle and glasses, the Inspector stared at the shelved books, so close at hand, and read off some of their titles to himself. And because of recent events and conversations, it didn't take him long to recognize the nature of Strachan's obsession. Lycanthropy: werewolves. Anything and everything in literature to do with them. But there were also a good many books on predators—real-life predators—in general, but mainly wolves . . .

"Even comic books, aye," Strachan said grimly, as he entered, sat opposite his guest and poured a drink. "If it's tae do wi' the beast, Ah probably have it. An obsession?—maybe." He offered the Inspector the bottle but Ianson turned it down.

"Thanks, no. I've other people to see tonight. But Gavin, are you telling me that all of this springs from that night up in the wildlife park?"

Strachan's nod was his answer, qualified by: "So maybe Ah really am as daft as they say, eh? Anyway, now ye know what Ah dream of nights, and why Ah'm reluctant tae talk about it. And now it's yere turn tae talk."

Ianson had spotted a book he recognized. Its subject was nature's meat-eaters, its predators of course, but the Inspector was more interested in the author. If only because he knew him. And as he told Strachan some of the details of the murder at Sma' Auchterbecky, so he took the book down, opened it, and idly flipped the pages. *Wild Dogs, Big Cats,* by Angus McGowan. This was an earlier printing than the one Ianson had seen previously at Angus's place during a rare, rare visit; it was an old and shoddy copy, strained at the spine and badly thumbed, with creased and discoloured pages throughout. Later editions contained a lot more information, the Inspector knew.

It was definitely McGowan's work, though; despite that the paint had flaked out of the spine's stamping, still the lettering clearly displayed his name. And then there was his picture on the inside back flap.

Finally Ianson finished telling Strachan about the murder. And putting down the book (frowning as he rapped his fingers on it; something bothering him that he hadn't as yet pinned down), he said: "So now you see why I remembered that business at the wildlife park and wanted to talk to you. Even now the connection may be weak to nonexistent, but however remote the chance, still I had to look into it."

Strachan nodded. "Oh, Ah see well enough. But now tell me, George, and honestly, mind: do ye believe mah story?"

The Inspector thought about it. "I'll tell you what I believe," he finally answered. "I believe there are some things we simply don't know, can't understand. But I also believe that fear is contagious, and that when people are afraid they become victims of their own imaginations."

Strachan said, *"Huh!* So ye don't believe even now, eh?"

Ianson shrugged. "What does it matter?" he said. "I certainly believe that *you* believe! And also that when you left the force we lost . . . well, 'a good yin.' "

He glanced at his watch. It was time he was on his way.

But at the door he paused, frowned again, and looked back in the direction of Strachan's small study. Strachan followed his gaze, lifted an eyebrow and asked, "Is there somethin'?"

"Do you mind?" the Inspector said. He crossed to the tiny room, entered, and picked up McGowan's book again. And turning to the opening pages, he checked something. Then, frowning yet more deeply, he said. "May I borrow this? And when I return it, can we talk again?"

"As ye will," the other shrugged. "As long as we can talk about *yere* case, not mine."

The Inspector agreed, and taking the book with him went to keep his appointment with Bonnie Jean Mirlu.

But first he called in at Police HQ to pick up the file on Strachan's Highland incident, and some photographs of John Moffat, plus one or two other pieces of information that had begun to trickle in. For one thing, the Inspector's investigators had tracked down Moffat's address, and for another they'd found his car in a snowdrift half a mile from Sma' Auchterbecky. At least the frame of the jigsaw was taking shape, if not the finer details . . .

The street was awash in snow turning to slush as the Inspector was let into B.J.'s just ten minutes ahead of his appointment. But she was ready to see him. And:

"As ye see," she said, in the bar-room, "business suffers a bit on nights like this. Who in his right mind wants tae turn out for a drink on a night like this, eh? So Ah'm sorry, but as ye can see no all mah girls are in tonight. Margaret's no in—Ah've given her a few days off—and no point bringing all four of the others in tae sit around doing nothing. So there's only mahself and these two. And besides, as Ah told ye on the phone, Ah can't see how we can help anyway."

Ianson's coat was taken from him by one of the girls, and as he gave the place a cursory once-over B.J. said, "We'd best talk upstairs in mah rooms. It being so quiet, Ah don't expect we'll be disturbed." She was right: there were only two men in the place. One was at the bar chatting to the second girl, and the other at a table, head down, nursing his drink.

So now the Inspector could concentrate more fully on B.J. Her accent puzzled him face-to-face no less than on the phone. It was antique, yet modern, too—"stage" Scottish. When she used it, it sounded unreal: a sort of "designer" brogue. Maybe she had an upper-class background while her assumed tongue was that of the lower- to middle-classes, as befitted her position. For what was she in reality but a barmaid? Ianson told himself that this wasn't his own snobbish attitude but merely a factual observation. And perhaps that was the essence of it: *she* didn't want her clients thinking she was "a posh yin."

As for the girl—or woman—herself:

Well, her age was hard to gauge, as witness Ianson's indecision. But then again (he was obliged to ask himself), what *is* the difference between a girl and a woman anyway? And has age got anything to do with it, or is it a matter of experience? As for his own experience: Ianson had never been much of a one for the girls. Having never married, he had to admit that his knowledge was limited.

B.J. was undeniably attractive. Tall and well-formed, her figure was all curves and her posture self-assured as any model's. Her hazel eyes were interesting. They had an almost Eurasian slant, and yellow flecks in their cores that loaned them a golden gleam in the bar's muted lighting. One might even say she had feral eyes. Her ears were large but not obtrusive; they lay flat to her head and seemed elflike with their pointed tips. B.J. was probably sensitive about them, however, for she kept them not-quite-hidden in the swirl and bounce of her shining, oddly neutral hair. Her nose was tip-tilted and a little flattened, and her mouth too ample by far, yet perfect in the curve of its bow. And her teeth were as white and well-cared for as any the Inspector had ever seen.

Thus he captured her description, as years of practice had taught him to do, while she took him upstairs and made him comfortable in her living-room over the bar. There she offered him a drink, which he politely refused, and when she was settled he quickly got down to it.

"Did you know the man who attacked Margaret Macdowell? His name was John Moffat and he lodged on the other side of town." He showed her a photograph taken from Moffat's lodgings.

"Ah recognize him, yes," she answered, staring at the picture. "But did Ah know him?" Now she glanced at Ianson. "Not at all. The girls get tae know some o' them, but Ah steer clear."

"Your girls—I mean your staff—form romantic attachments?"

"No such thing!" she bridled. "They get tae know the regulars, that's all, just as ye'll know all the crooks."

"I see. But he did used to come in here. A frequent customer, was he?"

"As Ah said, Ah recognize him. He was in once, maybe twice a week. But it has tae be said, he did fancy Margaret."

"She didn't encourage him?"

B.J. sighed—patiently, Ianson thought. "Mah girls are no like that, Inspector. Ah pay them tae work, not flirt. And just in case ye're wonderin' if this is a whorehouse, Ah can tell ye now it's no! Ah run a wine bar, nothin' more than that."

"I never once thought differently," Ianson could afford to be truthful with her, for in fact he hadn't formed any opinions as yet. As was his wont, however, he now pulled something right out of the blue. "How about dogs?" he said, his eyes riveted to B.J.'s face.

She blinked, just once, and her expression registered surprise if not alarm. "Dogs?"

"Do you have one, Miss Mirlu? A big dog? A guard-dog, maybe, to look after downstairs after you lock up?"

"I never considered it," she shook her head. "I've always thought the place was reasonably secure. Anyway, I don't especially like the smelly things!" And Ianson had to smile, if only to himself. For while she'd retained her composure, that accent of hers had vanished into thin air.

"And your girls? Does one of them have a big dog? Margaret Macdowell, for instance?"

She shrugged. "Not that they've ever brought here, no."

"So what is it that upset you when I mentioned dogs?"

"Eh?" She looked confused, startled. "What's that, ye say? Ah appeared upset?" And the accent was back again.

"You're not from these parts, are you?" Ianson's smile was open this time.

"My, how ye jump about!" She managed to smile back at him, however tightly. "One minute it's dogs, and the next ye're wonderin' where Ah come frae!"

"Your accent," he told her. "Me, I'm an Edinburgh man. But I try to keep my accent under control. I only fail when I'm excited. Not that I'm ashamed of it, you understand, but it's my nature to be precise. But *ye* . . . are no *frae* Edinburgh. An' no amount o' 'frae's and 'ye's can convince me otherwise!"

"And is it part of your investigation, to discover my origins?" She was just a little bit angry now. "Well, to put your mind at rest—and so that we may get on—I'm originally from the Highlands. My parents were from Garve and Strathpeffer, but we moved to London when I was a child. So you're right, my accent is phony—or not quite phony, but necessary. My customers like to think I'm a 'wee Jock,' so if only for their sake I'm a wee Jock. Are you satisfied now? And if there's nothing else—" She made as if to stand up, but Ianson caught her hand, applying just enough pressure to hold her in place.

"A policeman," he explained, "develops certain habits, not all of them good. I apologize, Miss Mirlu—"

"—B.J.," she cut him off. "Well, to my friends, anyway."

"—For my devious methods," the Inspector continued. "But you see, it looks like John Moffat was killed by a large dog or hound. And I have to satisfy myself—"

"—That someone from here wasn't protecting her? Inspector, to my knowledge no one even *dreamed* such a thing might happen! Bad snow was forecast and I let Margaret go early. That's standard procedure if we're expecting bad weather; I always let the girls from outside the city off early. I myself called the taxi for Margaret, and it took her right off the doorstep." (It was a lie, for in fact B.J. had already been on her way to Sma' Auchterbecky; she knew, however, that her girls would stand by her alibi to their last breath.) "Then, the next thing we know, the poor girl has been attacked." She held up her hands. "What else can I tell you? That's all there is to it."

"Well, not quite all," Ianson frowned. "Her attacker *was* murdered—or should we say killed?—after all. And murder is murder, B.J., whether it's done to or by a beast." That wasn't entirely correct, but it accurately described his feelings.

He tried a different tack. "Could John Moffat have known she'd be let off early?"

"He'd been in often enough, yes," B.J. answered. But suddenly she was frowning. "A great hound," she murmured. "Someone with a big dog. Hmm! Like, how big?"

"Oh?" Ianson leaned towards her again. "And is there perhaps something I should know?"

"I don't know," she said. "I'm not sure."

"Well tell me anyway, and I'll decide. Who is it you know who has a big dog, B.J.?"

"Oh, Ah dinnae *ken* him," she fell almost naturally, with a sigh of relief, as it were, back into her brogue. "Ah only wish Ah did, so's Ah could tell ye his name! All Ah know is, he watches mah place."

"He watches this place?" Ianson's voice had tightened in a moment. "Someone has been watching you, and your girls? Someone with a dog?"

"It . . . it's probably nothin'. Ah mean, Ah *hope* it's nothin'!" B.J. answered. "Sometimes he has his dog with him, others he's on his own." She stood up, said, "Come on, Ah'll show ye."

She took him upstairs to the top floor, her bedroom, then to a small window that looked down at a shallow angle on a recessed doorway across the road. "That's where we saw him first," she said. "Him and his dog, aye." She was lying, about the dog at least, but the Inspector couldn't know that.

"How long ago?" he queried.

"Oh, years!" she answered. "Ah used tae think it was maybe the father of one o' mah girls—lookin' out for his daughter, if ye take mah meanin'. Or maybe a detective on the trail o' a wayward husband . . . Ah mean, Ah'm bound tae get all sorts in here, tae ogle the girls and a'."

"But this has been recurrent?" Ianson was eager now.

"On and off, aye."

"Recently?"

"About a fortnight, the last time."

"But . . . why didn't you speak of this before? On the phone, for instance, or when I first mentioned a dog?"

She shrugged easily, maybe apologetically. "It slipped mah mind. It didnae connect until now. Oh, Ah worried about the wee man at first, but nothin' came o' it. He watched but didnae try tae do anythin'. And we . . . sort o' got used tae him."

"We?"

"Me and the girls, aye. Oh, and there's somethin' else: he has been known tae follow them once or . . . once or twice!" Suddenly she gasped. Her hand flew to her mouth, and her eyes grew big and round. "Do ye think . . . ? Mah God! That wee man, and his big Alsatian!"

"Describe him," Ianson snapped. And as B.J. drew back from the force of his voice, in a gentler tone: "Please, as best you can, tell me what he looks like." And she did . . .

Later, standing at the kerb outside the wine-bar, breathing the cold night air and feeling the slush turning to ice, the Inspector waited for his taxi and thought through the way events were shaping up. There were some odd circumstances and queer coincidences here, and George Ianson had never quite believed in the latter. His years on the force had taught him otherwise.

B.J.'s description of the watcher had been a good one; too good to have been conjured out of thin air, even if it had been her purpose to deceive (and why should she want to?). But as it was, the description had been so real it could even fit one or two persons of Ianson's acquaintance . . . and one in particular. Ridiculous to attempt to match it with the latter, however—

—Wasn't it? And yet . . .

The Inspector could feel Angus McGowan's book weighing in the large inside pocket of his overcoat. That old edition, probably a first (according to its date, anyway), but wrapped in a dust jacket from a more recent edition—surely? Well, that was possible; it must sometimes happen, Ianson was sure. Yet to the best of his knowledge the later editions—one of which he had handled at Angus's place during a rare visit—didn't have the old vet's picture in the back. And it was that photograph that concerned him most.

For if the jacket *did* go with the book, if they were both originals . . .

He was tempted to go back inside and show it to B.J. Mirlu. He would, if he didn't feel so stupid about it. But he did feel stupid about it, and rightly so. What, a bloody book that was twenty-eight years old, embellished with a photograph that looked like it had been taken yesterday? But it was the price of the book that really stymied him. The price on the *replacement* dust jacket, if it was a replacement.

Just seven shillings and sixpence, which nowadays wouldn't even buy you a paperback . . .

III

DEAD SERIOUS TALK.
BONNIE JEAN'S DILEMMA.

ON AND UNDER THE RIVERBANK, IT WAS DARK, COLD AND INHOSPITABLE. Above, the cold was the natural chill of a winter's night, and the grass was glazed and brittle with rime. If not for a recent melt up-country, the release of a torrent to stir the water and keep it liquid, there might even be a treacherous skim on the river itself. Without a doubt the water *was* treacherous in that place. But in a small backwater where the current was subdued and the ripples sluggish, the ice had more of a chance.

There, under the overhanging bank, under the water itself, in the deep mud of the weedy bottom, the cold was *un*natural, a "dead" cold. For in and around an unmarked watery grave (but a very important grave, of someone taken before her time) it was the cold of death itself. And she was Mary, the mother of the Necroscope, Harry Keogh.

There she lay, all mud and bones and weed, and to all intents and purposes, to everyone except Harry himself, it was as if she had never been, because there was nothing physical left of her to remind anyone. She was dead and departed, almost but not quite forgotten. But forgotten by the living, anyway.

For the living cannot know and wouldn't care to be told, and if they were told they would want it proved, and even then they still wouldn't believe . . . that death isn't like that. It isn't The Absolute End that most men in their hearts believe it to be, not entirely. The flesh dies, but the mind goes on; the Great Majority *go on,* in their fashion. Great thinkers continue to think their great thoughts, to be shared among their teeming dead colleagues. Great architects build fantastic cities of the mind which may only exist *in* their minds, for their voices have been silenced except to the Necroscope, Harry Keogh. Great mathematicians and astronomers continue to puzzle out the nature of a universe whose secrets they can never expose, except to those gone down with them into the earth. And to one other. Or maybe two others . . .

Thus, while on the surface the waters of the pool in that small bite of a bight might seem relatively calm—rippled by a mournful wind and awash with stars reflected on the darkly mobile mirror—and the night silent bar the wind itself—and the ether void of all evidence of life . . . underneath was less than calm, was indeed unquiet, where the dead conversed.

And maybe seventy-five yards up-river, set back from the water behind a high wall and a long, wild garden, and standing central between two sagging, derelict companions, an old house gloomed out across the ruffled ribbon. Upstairs, a pair of dim lights behind matching windows were like bleary close-set eyes: Harry Keogh's bedroom, where the Necroscope had fallen asleep with the lights still burning, and now lay dreaming.

This time Harry dreamed in sounds, not pictures, and the voices in his pillow were quiet and secretive as whispers, and shielded so that he wouldn't overhear them—or if he did, so that he would know he was *only* dreaming . . .

*M*ary, *can we really afford to take that chance? Dare we do, or not do, as you advise? Surely you know how we ache from our inactivity? Why, it's been years that we've lain here doing nothing! But it's Harry, Mary, Harry himself! And your son has done so very, very much for us. So why won't you let us at least try to do something for him?*

The dead voice was Sir Keenan Gormley's; Harry would know it anywhere, any time. And yes, it had been years, three years at least, since he had been in London and talked to Sir Keenan. For there could be no mistaking the fact that the teeming dead were talking about him. And because his mother was close (and her voice, too, so very familiar), he could separate out these individual sources from the background "static" which he alone knew to be the murmur of a million voices, the private conversations of the Great Majority.

But this time that static was far less evident, and Harry knew why: across a vast swath of land—or under it—the dead in their graves weren't talking but *listening* to this same conversation. And if for that and no other reason, he knew it must be very important to them. But he must listen carefully—like an eavesdropper, yes, despite that he was the subject of their conversation, or because he was—else they would sense him and close him out.

Do you think I don't want to help, don't want you to help? (His Ma's voice brimmed with her frustration.) *Can you think of anything I wouldn't do for him? Can you name anything I* haven't *done for him?* Indeed not, for there'd been a time when she had even risen from the river for him.

But—

No buts, Keenan Gormley! I gave him life, remember? While it was you and yours who took it from him! For it was the work he did for you that killed him in the end.

Unfair, said another voice when Gormley failed to answer; and the Necroscope knew this one, too. It was his old physical training instructor, Graham "Sergeant" Lane, speaking from his grave in a Harden cemetery. *Oh, Harry's your son, Mary Keogh—but you only had him for a few short years. Me, I watched him grow up. I saw the grit in him, and I knew how special he was. He's a fighter, that one! I know it, for I've had the privilege of fighting with and through him. We all know it, which is why we can't bear to see him crash now.*

And unfair in another sense, too, Sir Keenan at last put in. *It's true that his work with E-Branch got him in trouble. But he knew what he was getting into. And always re-member, if Harry hadn't learned what he did when he was with E-Branch—about the Möbius Continuum—then when he died he would have stayed dead! His metempsychosis wouldn't have been possible. We wouldn't be talking about him now but to him—and in our own medium, on our own level! He died, Mary, yes, but now he lives again. And we want to keep it that way.*

Harry's Ma let him finish, but she was still considering what Sergeant had said before him. *Crash?* (Her voice was even more a whisper.) *How crash? Do you mean die, and join us here? What, and are we to ignore all the talented people we've lis-tened to?* And lifting her dead voice for everyone to hear: *What of our precogs, Keenan Gormly, who have told us that my son is to go on?* And singling out Sergeant: *How can you even* think *to presume to know my son better than I? We're of one flesh. Why, even when he's silent—when he shuts himself off from me—still I know what he's thinking!*

But we've all known something of that, Mary. (It was Gormley again, but gen-tler now, for he felt something of her fear).

No, (Harry sensed the incorporeal shake of his Ma's head, and her face-less but unforgotten, indomitable smile), *not like that at all. I mean . . . the* feel-ings *at the very core of him. I mean all the aches and hurts and moods of his heart. I know him like . . . like a mother?* And who else could have put it better than that?

And we know him as the one shining light in our darkness, Sergeant was as rough as ever, but a rough diamond for all his bluntness. *Which we aren't about to see blown out!* A babble of ready agreement went up from at least a dozen more dead voices that Harry hadn't recognized as yet. *Yes* (Sergeant continued, cutting them off), *our precogs tell us that Harry will go on. But it's the future we're talking about, and that's an inexact science. Who can second-guess tomorrow? Who wants to risk it? So Harry is going to live, going to go on, is he? But who or what as? Himself . . . or something else?*

Knowing the depth of Sergeant's feelings—that he, too, had come to Harry's rescue in the past, as all of them would if given the chance—Mary Keogh wasn't overwhelmed or outraged by his passion; she merely tut-tutted, and qui-etly inquired of all the rest: *So, what would you have me do? What would you* do, *if you were closest to him? What advice would you give him?*

We would simply tell him the truth, Sir Keenan answered. *And we would want to know why he hasn't seen it for himself! I mean, we* know *he's in trouble again; things have come into our world that are not human, things that were human but have suf-fered a change, things that "lived" between life and death. And even truly dead, still they are evil and the Great Majority of us hold them at bay, ostracised. The Necroscope . . . sent them here—but we can't blame him for that. They're a plague that had to be cut out of a world where our children and loved ones still live.*

So, you'd tell him the truth, Harry's Ma was patient. *And how would you go about it? "Harry, we know there are still evil creatures in your world. We know, because you keep sending them to our world. So tell us: what is it that's caused you to team up with one of them? And not just a vampire, Harry, but a shewolf—a werewolf—too!" Is that what you'd tell him?*

Something like that, yes. But Sir Keenan was cautious.

Listen to me, all of you, she said then. *My son is in as much danger from himself*

*as he is from them. It's been a long time since he spoke to me—or to any of us—but the
last time he did he asked me if I thought he was going mad. He thought he might have a
drink problem, not of his making but one passed on to him in his new body. He thought
he might have inherited something of Alec Kyle's talent, too. His dreams were insane, nightmares in the truest sense of the word. And even awake, during a conversation with me,
he saw strange visions; portent of things to come, I'm sure, but far beyond his understanding. And beyond mine—and in life I was a psychic in my own right!* But *because
I was a psychic, and* because *he's my son, I heard more than his spoken words. I understood more than he was trying to convey to me. And I knew that* he *didn't know what
was wrong with him.* She paused to clear her thinking, see her way, and then continued:

*So I spied on him, in his waking hours and sleeping hours alike, to see if I could
discover what was wrong. And I discovered more than I had bargained for. This female*
Thing *who holds him in her spell: she, this Bonnie Jean, has caused him to live in two
different worlds, even different minds. In one of these, he knows what she is, and it hor-
rifies him! But yet he is bound to her, in thrall to her—but no, thank God, not as a vampire thrall! Yet in his other mind he's also enthralled, but . . .* differently. *Which any
man who ever loved will understand. Complicated? Oh, but that isn't the half of it. Don't
you see what's become of him? He is, literally, a split-person if not a split-personality!*

*But even before B.J., his difficulties defied description. What, his mind in another
man's body? His wife and child, fled from him, gone off to a place where even he, where
even* we *(and again I thank God, that they haven't come among us!) can't find them?
In his search for them, my son has discovered vampires in his world—but he can't admit
it or do anything about it until B.J. lets him. She has . . .* hypnotized *him, absolutely!
But more than that, I suspect there's something else wrong with him that neither he nor
I understand. Something that interferes with his talents, his use of the Möbius Continuum, even his willingness to talk . . . to talk to his own mother! Now tell me: don't you
think Harry has problems enough?*

She fell silent, and for a while the Great Majority could feel her anguish
like grief . . .

Then Keenan Gormley asked her: *What's your point, Mary?*

My point? She repeated him. *But isn't that obvious? If my son is on the brink of
madness, wouldn't telling him the truth push him over? Would he accept the truth, or
deny it? Would he accept his self-deception and try to put it right—or escape into the unreality of madness? Quite simply, how much can his mind take? It was heavily overburdened before, but now . . . ?*

Which is why we can't *tell him, because we don't know all the answers. But even
though you don't seem able to understand that, this B.J. knows it only too well. And she
keeps him on a tight leash. She wants him sane, for her own purposes, and for herself! I
hate it, hate to admit it, but she may well be his salvation. This . . . she-thing anchors
him, and while she keeps him safe, she keeps him sane. For that reason we've got to let it
be, for now at least . . .*

All of them let her words sink in, until Sergeant clarified the situation with:
You mean, we do nothing? From his tone of voice, the idea disgusted him.

But then another dead voice came to the force. *Well, maybe not exac'ly
nothin'.* And the dreaming Harry knew this one, too. It was R. L. Stevenson
Jamieson, indebted to the Necroscope as a result of some work they'd done to-

gether down in London. R.L. Stevenson's brother had been the lycanthrope (just a very sick person, *not* a werewolf) that Harry and his team had dealt with at the time he'd first met Bonnie Jean Mirlu. In the main, R.L. owed his acceptance by the Great Majority—the respect they gave both him and his name—to Harry, and he wasn't about to forget it.

How do you mean, R.L.? Sir Keenan wanted to know. *Is there some way we can help Harry, without jeopardizing his sanity?*

Well I sure can! came the answer at once. *See, I has obi. That's obeah to you. It's in my blood, come down to me from my Poppy. But here in this place I has no great use for it, excep' to keep my brother Arthur Conan in check. Not that A.C.'s much trouble, not any more. Now, I wants you to understand, my obi's the gentle kind like Poppy's before me: white magic, you'd call it. See, Poppy wouldn't a harmed a soul. He was just happy with his charms and love potions, over in Haiti where I was brung up. He never once messed with poisons or dead folks . . . er, I means the zombies, beggin' your pardon. My Poppy was more into protection, yeah! And in that line, well, he did have somethin' more than the simple stuff.*

Heck, he coulda used it to make himself a big man. Why, in Haiti whole governments has stood or fallen on stuff such as my Poppy's obi! Yeah, for he had the power to look into a enemy's mind and so know his every move. And me, I has it too, only not so strong now that I is dead. See, when a man don't use his obi he loses it. It grows strong with practice, and shrinks without it. And down here among the dead folks, well I haven't had much use for it. Not too many enemies, down here . . .

But I knows the Necroscope; *we worked together to put some stuff right—I mean with my brother Arthur Conan. And I knows that if Harry coulda found a different way . . .* (R.L. sighed, and the dead sensed his incorporeal shrug.) *But there you go: A.C. couldn't give a damn for anyone else's life, so in the end his own was forfeit.*

Anyway, I know Harry's aura. So in a way I guess I'm somethin' like his Ma. It's not just that I hear him *when he talks to us, but I also knows how he feels. I can feel for him, and I can feel out his enemies, too! Oh, I'm not one for gettin' into their heads like A.C. could, but I knows when they's around and how many they is and where they's comin' from. Stuff like that. I couldn't—I wouldn't—tell him who they is, but I could at least let him know that they's there. So . . . what you think?*

And Harry's Ma said, *Good! Yes! It's a start. Down inside, Harry knows he's in trouble, and R.L.'s obeah can emphasize the truth of it without being specific. After that it will be up to Harry to work it out for himself, step by step, stage by stage.*

But Sir Keenan Gormley wanted to know: *And is that all? We can't do anything else?*

Oh, we could probably do a lot, Mary answered. *But slowly, and very carefully. For if it comes to it, well, eventually we may have to do an* awful *lot—I mean our very utmost.*

And each and every one of the teeming dead, they knew what she meant . . .

But in a while, frustrated beyond measure, Sergeant—who was once a man of action—said, *And meanwhile we're even forbidden to advise him? I mean, there's no other way to help him, except by leaving him alone?*

Only if he asks for our advice, she answered, *and only if he asks for our help. For that will be the first sure sign that he's coming to terms with it and is ready to fight back. I remember when I was a girl, my mother used to tell me: "No one can help the man who won't help himself." I've lived by that maxim, and so has Harry—and he'll go on doing it. There you have it. We daren't show him the light but must wait till he sees it for himself.*

And when he does . . . he's going to be one mad Necroscope! (Sergeant's incorporeal nod of agreement.) *Not crazy, just mad as hell! So maybe you're right and it's for the best.*

Oh, he'll be a lot madder than hell, (Sir Keenan's short, grim forecast). *Hotter, too. And I fancy that will be his main problem, for that's when he'll need to be at his coolest. Then, when Harry Keogh is cool . . . well, just watch. You'll see hell itself freeze right over . . . !*

All talking done, their meeting concluded, they could go their own ways now, and withdraw to the only places they knew: their graves in the lonely earth, where they lay in their dust and decay and the endless night of death. But in that interminable darkness, a lonely candle flickering; one source of light and warmth, one heart still beating.

One Necroscope, tossing in his tumbled bed . . .

The telephone was ringing.

The voices of the dead receded, took on the form of "genuine" dreaming, metamorphosed into the periodic clamour of the phone.

Harry knew he should try to hang on to his dream, but was afraid to and so let it slide into limbo. Then the voices were gone and any significance to events in the Necroscope's waking world gone with them. He woke up.

Br-rrring! Br-rrringgg!—nerve-janglingly. With which, the last ring echoed into silence. But the answering machine had clicked on, and a red light glowed to indicate a message.

What? Who? Harry scrambled to reach for the monitor, and almost tumbled out of bed. His mind was fuzzy; he'd only been asleep for an hour or so, and he'd only gone to sleep to kill some time until B.J. called. If she called.

And now? This could be her! He grabbed the monitor—too late. The answering machine clicked off.

He sat up, breathed heavily, ran his fingers through his hair. Time? Just before ten. He'd been dreaming, and he'd wanted to remember his dreams . . . hadn't he? And then the phone.

He played back the message:

"Harry, mah wee man. Call me back, will ye?" B.J.'s husky voice coming out of his answering machine had a weird effect on him:

On the one hand he shuddered as a mournful howling came echoing out of nowhere (in fact from the deepest vaults of his mind), while a wolf's head in silhouette angled itself sharply against a full and shining moon, its throat throbbing with its song. And on the other he recognized and was helpless to fight against his dependency, his desire for B.J., and the fact that he hadn't seen her for over a week now.

Then the howling was gone into limbo (along with a dream he knew he should remember) and all that remained was the fact that B.J. had called and he'd missed it. As indeed he'd missed B.J. herself for the last six or seven days. Too long by far.

He blinked his eyes, rubbed at them, forced himself more fully awake.

Which wasn't easy. His mind was buzzing with half-memories, dreams and fancies—and fantasies? Almost as if he hadn't woken up at all. Or wished he hadn't.

Six or seven days . . .

Well, the last couple of days without her were only to be expected; it was her time, when she would—or should—have been up in the Highlands doing her own thing, hunting and living off the land. *What, even in this weather?* . . . But the Necroscope didn't even give that a second thought. It was one of the many things he wasn't allowed to question, something that *might* from time to time register, until his mind made an automatic compensation. For until she said otherwise, B.J. was "an innocent." And even then—despite that in a hidden place inside he knew something of who and what she really was—still Harry was in thrall to her, beguiled by her, in love with her.

He shivered, because in his hidden place he did know what was behind her, yet took pleasure in her voice—even her recorded voice—and thrilled to her reality. For his dependency was as much physical as mental: the addiction of her body, her companionship, and the fact that she was all he had.

. . . All he had, yes.

It was true, and the Necroscope felt obliged to admit it: he seemed to be shutting himself down. He'd long since severed his connections with his friends at E-Branch—his only real, *living* friends—cut himself off almost entirely from the real world, and even neglected the dead. Including his beloved Ma.

Something of his dream came back again, fleetingly—only to dissolve into atoms a moment later.

As for Brenda . . . but who was Brenda? She'd been gone so long now that her face, its memory, was only a blur. Harry only remembered her as she had been: as a girl, his childhood sweetheart. And the child, Harry Jr. . . . would be four years old now! He'd be walking, talking, and doing . . . whatever he did. Except that wouldn't be what other infants did. Not him, for just like his father he was a Necroscope, too. He could talk to the dead, and knew all the secrets of the Möbius Continuum.

"He can go wherever he wants," the Necroscope told himself out loud. "They can hide . . . anywhere!" Or be anywhere, as long as he wasn't there. And he knew that if they wanted to be found he and the whole professional army of investigators that he had bought would have found them. Well, they obviously didn't want to be found, and so were gone. But because it was his obsession now, he had to keep on looking.

It was unreal, everything—except B.J., whose number he was already dialling.

I chase around after her like a puppy, he thought—then laughed, however drily, because it seemed such an accurate analog or simile—then stopped laughing, because he didn't know why it seemed accurate. A puppy?

The phone was answered by one of her girls: Zahanine, he recognized her slow, sultry voice. "B.J.," he said, and Zahanine didn't even ask who it was. Then B.J. was on the phone.

"Harry?" (That might be a note of anxiety in her voice.)

"Aye," he mimicked the brogue he knew she affected. "It's yere wee man." (*Yere wee fucking puppy.*)

And after a moment's thoughtful silence: "But are you . . . angry about something?" The note of anxiety had turned to curiosity now.

Harry shook his head, blinked his eyes, thought: *Well, am I?* Or was he just blaming her (again) for something that wasn't her fault? Something he didn't understand but which couldn't be her fault anyway, because she was innocent?

"No," he said, "not angry. Just fucked up."

Another pause, and: "Something you want to talk about?"

"Radu," he said, almost automatically. The word, or name, slipped off his tongue as easily as that, popped from the forbidden limbo of subconscious mind into his real thoughts like a champagne cork teased too far, too soon. And for the life of him, Harry couldn't understand why he'd said it! But deep down inside, something churned. *The champagne,* he thought. *But long since turned to vinegar, to bile.* And now he felt sick to his stomach, still without knowing why.

On the other end of the line, B.J. was in the bar. Two of her girls were with her, tidying up. Catching their attention, she put a finger to her lips. And when they were still:

"Forget what you just said to me, Harry," she told him, as naturally as she could. "You're not to talk about that, or even think about it. If it's bothering you, you can tell me why when you see me. In an hour's time, maybe? Is that OK?"

"See you tonight?" he replied after a while, sounding distant and dazed. "I've . . . I've really missed you, B.J."

And with that she believed she knew what had happened. It had been some time since she last reinforced the post-hypnotic commands separating his two levels of consciousness, and a week since she'd had contact with him. But this was no ordinary man; left to its own devices, Harry's mind had been trying to bridge the divide. However slowly, things were beginning to leak from one level to the other. If the process should speed up and the two flow directly into each other . . . it was possible he could even go into shock, catatonic withdrawal.

Harry, a cabbage! B.J.'s Harry!

No, she corrected herself, *Radu's Harry,* Her Master's Man-With-Two-Faces. And her tilted eyes narrowed to feral slits as a growl sounded deep in her throat.

"B.J.?" Harry's voice sounded tinny and more distant yet, sad, lonely, and lost. Suddenly fearful—for him and nothing else, despite that there was plenty to be worried about—she said, "I'll be with you as soon as possible. So why don't you just take it easy now and rest, and wait for me?"

"Yes," he said. "OK." And a moment later, "B.J.?"

"Yes?"

"I think I may have been dreaming."

"We'll dream together," she promised. "Soon." And she listened for the click as he put the phone down . . .

Driving west for Harry's place along lonely country roads outside the city, B.J. thought: *So, it's finally beginning to get to him. He's wondering what's wrong with him* *and openly admitting that he's fucked up. Well so he is, because of me. But at least he has something, someone, to believe in, to hang onto—even if it's only me! But what do I have?*

And like a stab of pain felt deep inside, coming out as a cry: *Oh, Harry, mah wee man! You can take it from me, ignorance is bliss! Knowing what's happening could be far worse than not knowing, and it wouldn't solve or change a thing. It hasn't for me, anyway. Hah! And you think that you're fucked up?*

It was true, she was. And just as she had done it to Harry, so he had done it to her. Differently, but in the end it worked out the same. Not so long ago, he'd been just one small part of a big equation, one small cog in a vast wheel. Now he was a big spanner in the works, the one part of the equation that refused to work out. Harry's mind was a computer, and she had put a bug in it. Two bugs, in fact. One was a lie and the other was love. He had become her personal toy. But the love-bug had been virulent and it had escaped back into B.J.'s system. Harry Keogh, her wee man? Not any longer, and not for quite some time now.

"Mah wee man" was the phrase she used to activate Harry's post-hypnotic implants and change his mental "mode." Employing it as an opening, she could tell him—impress upon his mind—anything she desired him to know. And before closing she could delete anything deemed undesirable for him to know or remember. But as well as a trigger, the phrase now seemed to be mutating into a term of endearment, and in so doing it had lost some of its potency. B.J. had to reinforce it, for his sake as much as hers, before his two halves clashed and destroyed each other.

Her Master Radu Lykan had once told B.J. that he would need a strong man in the hour of his resurgence, not a sot. That was after she had used an ancient, addictive wine to weaken Harry's resistance. And the dog-Lord had further pointed out that there were other ways to enthrall a man than by poisons. He had meant her body, her woman's wiles, which in the course of two hundred years she had learned to use very efficiently.

But love and sex are two-edged swords, and Harry Keogh was something of a beguiler in his own right. A "wee man?" Scarcely that! For it now seemed more than likely that he was indeed the man of Radu's dreams of the future, in whom the dog-Lord might yet rise up again, resurrected from his vat of resin. All well and good . . . if B.J. didn't want Harry for herself.

But she did. Except . . . nothing was that straightforward; everything was convoluted; B.J. *was* "fucked up," yes.

Without the gradual encroachment of the Ferenczys and the recent declaration of war on the part of the Drakuls (if those red-robed Tibetan vampires had not chosen to come on the scene at this late and difficult hour), then things might be easier and B.J.'s choice less fraught . . .

(Her choice? Between Radu's resurrection and Harry's continuity? To even consider that there was a choice seemed sheerest madness! Yet she considered it. Oh, she was fucked up, all right!)

. . . But at last the enemy had shown his hand, and B.J. had realized her own weakness. For all that she was a werewolf she was no warrior, not by Wamphyri standards. As for Harry Keogh: while he would appear to be both a skilful warrior and tactician—or maybe a reckless madman?—still he was *merely* a man. Despite that he'd been lucky once, B.J. knew that in the long run he would be no match for the Wamphyri. Dealing with enemies as terrible as Drakuls or Ferenczys was to have been (and would still be, surely?) the dog-Lord's province.

The dog-Lord Radu, her "Master." B.J.'s thoughts skipped this way and that, contradicting themselves as they went . . .

Radu Lykan: he had become the bane of B.J.'s life and no small threat to Harry's. And she was still amazed at the speed of her conversion—which was something she scarcely dared to think about even now. Bonnie Jean Mirlu, the guardian of Radu's lair for more than one hundred and seventy years. His "minder," as it were, whose every effort had been towards his safety and eventual resurrection. B.J.—a traitor to his cause? Not yet, not physically, but the thought had been there, certainly. And not only the thought but now, with Harry, the motive, too.

What was it with Harry, she wondered? What was his attraction? He was only a man . . . yet the first man who had ever put his life in jeopardy for her, which had perhaps been the turning point. So that now, even thinking such things, she in turn was putting hers in jeopardy for him!

But was it only Harry, his natural attractions, or was it a different kind of nature entirely? *Was it her own nature, as the change more surely shaped her? Was it something—some physical thing—inside her, deflecting her devotion to Radu and pandering to her own gratification?*

And again her thoughts switched tracks, perhaps to escape the inevitable conclusion . . .

Radu, who had burned so brightly in her mind: like a god, the creator and father of his own species! A sleeping god, aye, and B.J. the one who watched over him in his undead tomb. That was how it had been for as long as she could remember, so that it was no easy thing to consider the termination of everything that she'd worked so long and so hard for, the efforts and aspirations of a lifetime. Not a life as long as B.J.'s had been, or one as long as it might yet be.

The past passed before her in short order:

At first, as a girl, Radu's cause had been hard work; but in the course of a century it had become an almost unbreakable habit, and in the next fifty years a binding duty. She'd lived her entire life so that her Master might live his again; which now, if she would go *on* living, it seemed he must. For without the dog-Lord, sooner or later her enemies must surely take her out. They knew her even now (she had more than enough proof of that) and would have moved against her long ago, but they were greedy and wanted her Master, too.

So much for the past and the present, but what of the future? What would it be—how *could* it be—without Radu? Would she even have a future? What, with Harry? But he was only a man . . . and so she was back to *that* again!

So many uncertainties, and B.J.'s life in the balance. And Harry's too. Harry: why was he always there, in the back of her mind? She could do without him, didn't actually *need* him in her life . . . did she?

Well, *did* she?

Perhaps not . . . but it seemed certain she would need Radu; his guidance when he was up again. She would need to learn from him—all the secrets he had promised her—in order to understand the nature of the Wamphyri, and so understand herself. No less important, she would need his protection. Thus for all her dithering, the dog-Lord was her safest route.

Safe? *Hah!* The truth of it was that she was Radu's thrall and feared him! She even feared her own wayward thoughts: that he might discover a germ of treachery in them—or more than a germ—and find her wanting.

So the dog-Lord's cause lived on—if only through revulsion and fascination, fear and need—and B.J. continued to be torn two ways: between loyalty to a nightmarish creature from an alien world and a past time, and love of a man who was very much of this world and ahead of his time. But it was true that her loyalty to Radu wasn't what it used to be, else there were no contest in the first place.

Oh, upon a time she had worshipped him with the fervour of a dozen thrall forebears before her, moon-children in their own right. But that was *all* they had been: Radu's thralls and caretakers. While Bonnie Jean Mirlu . . . was Wamphyri!

There, it was out, she had come down to it at last. Like the dog-Lord himself, B.J. was of that same High Order of vampire, and must soon ascend to a Lady.

How this had come about was hard to say. By the regular, voluntary transfusion of B.J.'s blood into Radu's system? But surely that was impossible; she had always understood it to be a one-way transfer. And in all her time in Radu's service B.J. had never had physical contact with him, *except* through fluids which had already left her body. How could she possibly, while he lay in a vat of semi-solid resin? Ah, but even the Wamphyri couldn't know everything about their . . . *condition*. Its mysteries were diverse as life itself . . .

Perhaps B.J. was a throwback then, through genes as tenacious as the Wamphyri themselves, to Starside in a vampire world. Or could it be that Radu had inadvertently issued a spore, to surface gradually through the resin and pass into her system? But whichever, she knew she was possessed of a leech and that her parasite was rapidly maturing.

She knew, felt it as surely as she felt the powerful beat of her own heart, or the breath going in and out of her lungs. And if ever she doubted it, there was always the corroboration of her vampire metamorphosis, which she had had for full forty years now: the change at or near the full of the moon by which she'd be transformed into something else, something *other* than a woman. In addition, there was this burning desire in her: a need to howl, to run with the pack wild in the moonlight—and to hunt! The feel of emotions, of passions that rose way above the merely human scale; a raging, ravaging love of life, and a lusting after the blood which *is* that life! Wamphyri passions all. And one other trait that indentified her species like a fingerprint and made it undeniable: B.J.'s territorialism.

For almost two hundred years the mountains over the long, wooded valley of the Spey had been her territory, which she had protected. Her small "pack"—the girls she'd recruited to make them moon-children, replacing them as and when necessary—were hers. Even the dog-Lord's cavern lair was more familiar to B.J. than it had ever been to him. To Radu it was merely a refuge, a hideaway, a tomb. But to B.J.—an aerie, her seat, the secret heart of her operations when at last she ascended and became a fullblown Lady of the Wamphyri!

Perhaps it was an idea that had been in her head for some time, even decades, as the year of Radu's re-birth loomed ever closer. So that she had often wondered: *How will it be when my Master is up again, when he is back? What will be allowed, and what disallowed?* And she had thought: *What if he should return to Romania, and take back his horseshoe mountains now that the Drakuls and Ferenczys are no longer there?*

If so, he might even leave B.J. behind, to watch over the lair in the Cairngorms and become a true Lady in her own right. Then he and she would be equals—an incredible concept!

Once (oh, a long time ago), when she had been delirious from letting too much of her blood drain down into Radu's vat, she had even broached the subject. And now she remembered his answer:

Ah, my Bonnie! But think, just think! If I am a dog-Lord, *and the female equivalent of a* vampire *Lord is a Lady . . . what would that make you—a* bitch-Lady? *Or would you be more bitch than Lady?* And then his coughing, barking laughter had sounded in her mind . . . but behind his laughter, the deep and thoughtful rumble of a growl, too.

She hadn't understood, but he had brushed it aside, saying: *Let it be, my Bonnie. For in any case it's all a hundred years away. But you, Wamphyri? First be a wench,* then *a witch—or a bitch, whichever . . .*

That had been only the first time that Radu denied B.J.'s destiny, but there had been many times since. He hadn't wanted her to think along such lines, and B.J. believed she knew why. For in the dog-Lord's vision of a future world there wouldn't be room for other Lords—or Ladies . . .

The headlights of an oncoming car flashed in B.J.'s eyes, and as the car swept by her mind was drawn back to the present. Giving herself a shake, she sat up straighter behind the steering wheel and tried to concentrate on where she was going, who she was going to, and why. The present was more important than the past, and what she had been thinking about was long before Harry's time. Now, even more than she worried about Radu's future or even her own, she worried about his . . .

Need him? What sense was there in fooling herself any longer? Of course she did, even loved her "wee man." *Madness, aye!* And again B.J.'s mind went off at a tangent:

Radu had warned her against contaminating Harry; she could seduce him by all means, but on no account let anything of herself get into him. The dog-Lord wanted him pure, and of course she knew why. If Radu's vampire leech had failed to cure him of the plague in his blood, then he would attempt metempsychosis: the transfer of his entire personality into the body of another—into Harry's body! For Radu had dreamed oneiromantic dreams of a Mysterious One, a "Man-With-Two-Faces," who would be there at the hour of his resurgence. Harry Keogh was just such a man, with survival skills worthy of the Wamphyri themselves.

In one way the idea was intriguing, while in others it was appalling. The thought of Harry with the awful strength of Radu appealed to B.J.; his longevity assured, and with the skills of a special agent, he would make the perfect mate. But she knew that would not be the way of it. For he would have Radu's mind and eventually his metamorphosis. And B.J. knew how Harry would look then: as Radu Lykan looked now! He would be as clay in the dog-Lord's hands, to be rebuilt in Radu's image. And picturing her so-called "Master" in his great vat— his grotesque man-dog outline as seen through the semi-opaque resin crust— even B.J. shivered.

No, she couldn't even contemplate that, not for a moment. And yet in three months time, in the spring, she would have to do just exactly that. For that was when Radu had determined to be up. He might even be up now, but had wanted to see Harry in advance of the event. He *should* have seen him three months ago, and barring the intervention of a Drakul lieutenant and thrall would have done so. It had been then that Harry Keogh had once again demonstrated his talent for survival—and his feelings for Bonnie Jean, that he would protect her with his life—for now those Drakuls were no more.

And half-way to Harry's place near Bonnyrig, B.J. remembered what little she had seen of the Drakul attack, and how it had been afterwards . . .

IV

LET SLEEPING DOG-LORDS LIE—COVERT SURVEILLANCE— AULD JOHN'S REPORT—THE LIMBO INTERFACE

B.J. HAD TAKEN HARRY NORTH FOR A LONG WEEKEND'S CLIMBING, HUNTING, living off the land and generally roughing it in the Highlands. So she'd told him, anyway. But in fact they'd been going to see the sleeping dog-Lord in his lair. She had had all kinds of misgivings about it; she'd grown inordinately fond of Harry, too fond, perhaps. He'd aroused emotions in her other than the grand passions of her kind, and she had known that to let Radu see him, "talk" to him, would mean simply giving him up to the dog-Lord. But in any case they hadn't made it.

On the unseasonably warm autumn morning scheduled for the climb, as B.J. and Harry headed for the starting point in Auld John's car—then the Drakuls had launched their attack.

There had been two of them, red-robed "priests" in a station wagon that they used as a juggernaut, trying to force B.J. off the road. She had "switched Harry on," told him that these were two of the enemies she'd warned him about. But as soon as she had gained a little distance, rounded a bend and so passed out of sight of their pursuers, Harry had asked to be dropped off. She had done it, and a minute or two later when the Drakuls failed to catch up she'd gone back for him.

Somehow he had caused them to crash; their station wagon had left the road over a wooded gorge and fallen to earth nose-first through trees which had scarcely broken its fall. One of the occupants, the driver—a lieutenant by his looks, and by the way he later died—had got himself skewered on his steering column; the other, a thrall, was uninjured. B.J. had come on the scene barely in time to prevent the latter's attack on Harry. She had put a crossbow bolt through the thrall's heart, and Harry had set fire to the petrol leaking from their shattered car. Both of the Drakuls had burned, melting down in the furnace heat as B.J. and Harry backed off.

That had been a horrific thing, but it had served to confirm that the driver was a lieutenant:

Through the envelope of blue-shimmering heat, his blazing figure had been plainly visible where he tried to lift himself off the steering column. Failing, he'd then looked out through the wall of fire with eyes like peeled grapes. A moment later, his torso had burst open and put out corpse-white tentacles or feelers to lash in the super-heated interior of the car. Twining together, the tentacles had blossomed outwards through the stripped-away roof and upward into the fiery slipstream, where they floated in the incendiary updraft like the arms of a crippled anemone.

Other tentacles had uncoiled like worms from the open car door. They pissed an orange fluid all around that smoked where it fell to earth. Then the lieutenant's vampire had submitted, and he had withdrawn his molten appendages, crumpled down into himself and begun to slop out of the door around the shoulders of his companion. As for that one: he had sat there lifelessly with B.J.'s bolt through him.

And it had been over . . .

They had driven to Dalwhinnie, and during the journey B.J. had cancelled the episode from Harry's mind. He'd seen things that just didn't fit the "innocent" image he had of her, things out of her dark side that he wasn't ready for. And from then on—from Harry's point of view, at least—they had simply been on a climbing and hunting trip, which for reasons of her own B.J. had cried off. Nothing more complicated than that . . .

But of course Harry was thinking and acting under hypnosis, and for B.J. it wasn't that easy to throw off. Indeed she daren't forget a single detail, for it was life and death.

From Dalwhinnie, she had phoned Auld John in Inverdruie and told him to see to Radu. Unlike B.J., who was Radu's lieutenant, Auld John was merely in thrall to the dog-Lord. Though he had been a moon-child all his long life, he would never run with the pack under a full moon; it wasn't in him to be a werewolf. But he was a very capable climber, and he knew the way to the lair. Indeed, as a gamekeeper, in the protected preserve of the Badenoch valley, John had guarded the routes to Radu's lair for most of his life. And of course he would attend to the dog-Lord in B.J.'s absence. That is to say, he would see to Radu's feeding—and to the feeding of his creature . . .

And doubtless Radu would probe John's all too eager mind, to see what had gone wrong.

The plan had worked; two days later Auld John had called B.J. at the wine-bar to tell her all was well. But as for "Him in His high place," well, he "wasnae verra pleased!" His time was fast approaching, and his resurgence could not be delayed. Come hell or high water, B.J. would present the Mysterious One to him when next duty called her to the Cairngorms lair. Which should have been this past weekend.

The three months' reprieve had flown, and despite that the weather had worsened dramatically—and that she was less inclined than ever to part with her "wee man"—there'd seemed no putting it off. But at least (B.J. had told herself anxiously) this would only be Harry's initial audience; after that, there would still be six months left before Radu's actual resurgence.

Then, with less than two weeks to go before the scheduled visit, things had started to happen . . .

In fact a variety of things had been happening all along, ever since the failed attack of the Drakuls. For just a day or so after the release of the story of a "fatal Spey Valley accident" in the newspapers, B.J. had been pleased to read how the Home Office had issued expulsion orders on "several members of an obscure Tibetan religious order, believed to have been engaged in inter-sectarian warfare in the British Isles." Not only were they being expelled but others of their order—the "Emissaries of Drakesh"—had been refused entry . . . This had gone hand in hand with the story of a firefight, and the discovery of weapons and evidence of their use at the scene of what was previously and mistakenly considered a traffic accident.

It all fitted, especially that reference to these Emissaries of Drakesh. But a religious order? *Hah!* An order of Drakuls, no less! And in no way engaged in sectarian or any other kind of warfare (not until they had met up with B.J. and Harry Keogh, anyway), but in spying and building up their numbers in advance of the dog-Lord's resurgence! Well at least Radu would now know where to look for them—or for *him,* "D.D.," the last of his line. In Tibet.

But if this sneaking Drakul in his far-distant monastery hideaway knew of Radu's imminent return, then what of the Ferenczys? For a long time, even decades, B.J. had suspected that she was being watched; just as she had watched out for, and on occasion even tried to *seek* out, others of her own and the dog-Lord's kind. Some years ago she had lost one of her girls, mysteriously vanished in London. Radu's opinion had been that it was the work of Ferenczys, who were seeking him out in anticipation of his rising. Since when B.J. had been doubly careful, but not watchful enough. Or perhaps familiarity had bred contempt, and time had worn down her vigilance.

It had been Harry Keogh who first brought to her attention the fact of a secret observer, the little man she had told the Inspector about. For on Harry's first visit to B.J.'s Wine Bar, he had seen this strange figure lurking in a shop doorway across the street, apparently taking pictures. But it was only after Harry had described this watcher to B.J. that she realized she'd seen him, too . . . frequently over the years, in and around the city and the rundown district of her wine bar. But only at night, or when it was cloudy and overcast.

Then B.J. had remembered a hundred occasions when she'd sensed eyes on her in a crowd, or heard soft footsteps sounding behind her in quiet lanes, or glimpsed pin-pricks of gold in the shade of a vaguely familiar broad-brimmed hat. And not only B.J. but most of her girls, too . . .

So, was this watcher a Ferenczy spy such as Radu had warned her about? It seemed more than likely. A spy—a "sleeper," sent to Scotland thirty or more years ago—with no orders but to establish himself, seek out the dog-Lord's thralls and minders, and through them find Radu himself in his secret place.

Well, so far he had failed, B.J. felt reasonably sure. Her base was so far removed from Radu, and her precautions when she paid him her quarterly visits so strict—and the climb to his lair so arduous, with Auld John to watch the routes for strangers—that Radu's safety seemed assured. But she herself, and the pack, her girls . . . they had been discovered long ago.

So, why had this Ferenczy scum waited? A hundred or more times he could have put a silver bullet through B.J.'s head—yet hadn't. The answer seemed simple: to take her out would be to alert Radu's *other* thralls, if any such existed, jeopardizing both the watcher and his Masters, wherever they were! Also, the Ferenczys could afford to wait, for while Radu was down he was no real threat. And obviously this "D.D.," the last Drakul, felt the same: let the sleeping dog-Lord lie, and while he lay investigate his thralls, discover his lair and find out everything there was to be known about him and his.

Then, in the hour of his resurgence—strike full force, before his strength had time to flow back into him!

It all made sense, or would do if the Drakuls hadn't preempted things. So what had caused them to jump the gun? And as for Harry . . . he had seemed edgy from his first glimpse of the red-robed "priests." What was it with him and them? Or was it simply coincidence, or B.J. reading too much into too little?

But that aside, in the quarter gone by since the Drakuls' failed attack, Ferenczy surveillance on the wine-bar, on B.J.'s girls, and herself, had gone up one hundred per cent. It was no lie when she'd told Inspector Ianson about the observer; since alerting her girls to his presence, the furtive little man had been spotted a dozen times. The only lie had been in regard to his "great dog." No such dog existed but a wolf, a great white she-wolf . . .

As for the Drakuls themselves:

B.J. had read in a third newspaper report how the police were looking for four more members of the sect, believed to be hiding out in the country. It made sense: originally the group had been six members strong. So, four of them were still here, and probably not too far away. Well, no way they could sneak up on B.J. now, not in their red robes, anyway! And be sure that she and her girls would avoid Asiatics of *any* description; or, if need be, strike back at them a second time.

So then, all these reasons to let Auld John stand in for her again, put off her quarterly visit to Radu in his den, and so for a second time delay his meeting with Harry—a meeting which would surely seal the latter's fate. All these reasons—and not one of them good enough. The dog-Lord would doubtless tell her that since she knew the problems to be overcome, she must simply take greater precautions, that was all. Worse, he would probably wonder at her reticence, too.

Then, with only a week to go, the reprieve, when fate had delivered a pair of far more acceptable excuses: the fact that one of her girls, Margaret Macdowell, had been threatened—a matter which B.J. must attend to herself—and severe weather conditions, making any kind of Cairngorms venture more treacherous yet. Despite that she'd had Harry in training (she would protest), he was by no means the expert climber; she certainly wouldn't want to lose him on some icy, vertiginous face on the route to the dog-Lord's lair! Better far if his first audience with Radu were delayed a further three-month, when the weather should be improved and the climb so much easier.

So her excuses were finally sufficient, and she'd called Auld John in Inverdruie and told him her decision. And because she took time to list all of her reasons, impressing them into John's memory, she could be sure that when Radu used his mentalism to dig them out again—which he surely would—he would know that Bonnie Jean Mirlu was his true and devoted servant.

But in fact B.J. knew what she was—treacherous! And she knew why she was; *because* she was Wamphyri!

Wamphyri, aye, and devious to a fault, as every Great Vampire before her. And yet devoted too, to Harry . . .

B.J.'s jumbled thoughts returned to the present.

She was driving across an old stone bridge. A quarter of a mile away along the river, silhouetted against a threatening sky, Harry's house stood like an old, watchful but bleary-eyed owl between two sleeping brothers.

Watchful but tired, yes . . .

It was only then that B.J. paused to consider how anxious and tired *she* was, and her actions since Harry's call. For the first time in a long time she hadn't bothered to take any precautions against being followed. But it had been a week since she'd last seen Harry, and he was feeling down and troubled in his mind. And what with all of B.J.'s other worries, not least the Inspector's visit, and the fact that she was still waiting for a call from Auld John in Inverdruie to confirm that all was well with Radu—well, little wonder she wasn't quite with it! And anyway, what the hell? Who would be out following her on a night as cold and dark as this?

They would, that's who.

But too late now to cry over spilled milk. And anyway, the odds were that they already knew about Harry. On the other hand they would also know he was only a man, her human lover, and of no great concern to them. The Ferenczys would think so, anyway. And the handful of Drakuls were still in hiding. So, there was really no way she could have seriously compromised anything.

Still, as she pulled up outside the old house and dimmed her lights, B.J. narrowed her slanted eyes and looked long and searchingly into her rearview— and finally sighed her relief. There was nothing back there but the dark ribbon of the river, suddenly silvered by moonlight as a gap opened in the low cloud ceiling. Moonlight, aye, but two days past its full. In another moment the gap had closed and it was dark again.

B.J. got out of her car, locked it, and almost ran up the path to Harry's front door . . .

. . . **B**ut across the river and roughly opposite Harry's place, on the grass verge of the country road and hidden beneath the overhanging branches of tall trees, a second car sat in darkness and silence, with only the occasional *tick, tick* from an engine that was already cooling in the frosty night air.

The car was an old but reliable Volkswagen Beetle, whose driver had known from several previous visits the best place to park. For the next half-hour or so he would simply sit and watch, and wait for the lights to go out, then take his departure. But at first light he'd be back in time to see the girl leave. Nor was this any kind of weird long-distance voyeurism but simply his sinister job. For B.J. Mirlu's habits were all-important to him—especially in connection with the man she was visiting . . .

. . . **A**nd two hundred yards back up the same road, on the same grass verge, a third vehicle sat in darkness and silence; but Inspector George Ianson was here for a very different reason. Not to spy on the girl—not at all—but on the spy. And to wonder what in hell old Angus McGowan thought he was up to!?

The Inspector was here by virtue of a series of coincidences, which was odd in itself because he'd never believed in them. His street was a no-parking area, wherefore he garaged his car the best part of a mile from home. Ex-constable Gavin Strachan lived only a short walk away but in the other direction; wherefore on leaving Strachan's place, Ianson had taken taxis to and from B.J.'s. But on his way home—still wrestling with this thing about old Angus's book—he had decided to pay the vet a visit.

It was rather latish, true, and McGowan didn't much care for visitors at any time, but Ianson knew him for a night-owl and hoped he wouldn't mind. Also, he could disguise the real purpose of his visit by asking the vet about his zoo queries, how he was getting on with them . . . though why he would *want* to use such a subterfuge he couldn't quite say.

So he had taken the taxi to his garage, then driven himself to McGowan's place east of the city towards the sea. But as he'd driven into the poorly-lit street of tall dark houses where his quarry lived, he had been barely in time to see the man himself leaving in his battered Beetle.

It was the car that gave McGowan away (though again, why Ianson should think of it in those terms was anybody's guess). Unless it was the way McGowan was crouched over his steering wheel, intent on his driving, staring straight ahead . . . his furtive attitude in general. Or not even *his* attitude but Ianson's, the way he was beginning to feel about this whole damn business. A gut feeling, yes: a hunch. The instinct that sometimes makes a good policeman great— and sometimes the thing that makes him feel guilty, too.

Be that as it may, Ianson had turned his car around and used covert pursuit techniques learned twenty-five years earlier in the Metropolitan Police to follow the vet through Edinburgh's wintry night streets. Mercifully, there had been just enough traffic that he could stay two or three cars back out of sight without losing McGowan. Fortunate, too, that Ianson's seven-year-old car was an anonymous brown model of which there were hundreds in the city.

But in a little while it had dawned on the Inspector that he was backtracking much the same route his taxi had taken from B.J.'s Wine Bar— returning in fact *to* B.J.'s Wine Bar! A wild guess, but it had proved to be an accurate one. And as he drove into the bar's district, Ianson's gut-feeling had begun to knot into something else inside him.

Once there, McGowan had found a space in a line of parked cars some little distance from the bar. While he was engaged in manoeuvring into position, Ianson had taken the opportunity to overtake and find a space of his own, from where he'd been able to keep an eye on his rearview and watch both McGowan's car and the street in front of the wine-bar. Then for some fifteen minutes he had sat there rubbing his hands to keep the circulation flowing, and hoping that the heater wasn't running his battery low. But mainly he'd been wondering what was going on here.

What, old Angus doing some investigating of his own? That wasn't acceptable . . . McGowan was a vet, not a policeman! What was more, he so perfectly fitted B.J.'s description of a watcher who had been seen on several occasions *before* the attack on Margaret Macdowell.

Deep in thought, the Inspector had been very nearly taken by surprise when a party of girls exited from the recess leading to the wine-bar's entrance. They were well-wrapped against the cold and too far away for him to identify any of them, and in any case they had quickly split up and gone their own ways into the night.

It was approximately an hour since the Inspector had left the bar; obviously B.J. had closed early. Well, that was self-explanatory; she had had little in the way of business to keep her open. But as the girls dispersed so old Angus's Beetle had pulled out and driven away in some haste, so that Ianson must hurry to keep up with it.

And now where was the little man going? His route lay west on a fairly major road out of the city, so that once again Ianson was able to sit back behind a car or two as he followed the distinctive shape of the Volkswagen to whatever was its destination. But as the flow of traffic dropped off and the night grew murkier yet, the Beetle turned onto a farm track, reversed and came to a halt. And its lights went out.

Two hundred yards behind his quarry, Ianson hadn't thought that the track would lead anywhere. Perhaps McGowan had feared he was being followed and pulled off the road to test the theory. So the Inspector had turned in through an open gate onto a lesser track, turned about and pulled forward for a quick exit, and waited. The glint of the Beetle's windows had been visible through a near-distant hedgerow . . .

And by then there had been only a few vehicles on the main road, most of them heading into Edinburgh . . .

The next five minutes had passed slowly, until a silver-grey car had come speeding along the main road from the directtion of the city. As it passed McGowan's farm track so the Volkswagen's dipped lights had come on, and McGowan had turned back onto the main road. Following him, Ianson had driven on dipped lights, too . . .

. . . **A**nd now he had been sitting here in this place for half an hour, and he was still wondering what was going on and what it was all leading up to. But there was old McGowan down the road, out of his car now and leaning on its curving rear end—doubtless for the warmth from the engine—and gazing through binoculars at the lighted windows of the house across the river.

Well, enough of this. Ianson had just made up his mind to move on, go home, ask Angus about it tomorrow, when the lights in the house were suddenly turned down low. A moment later and Angus had got into his car and switched on the sidelights. And it was as much as Ianson could do to squeeze down in his seat, out of sight, as McGowan turned the Beetle about on the narrow road and headed back his way. But as the car went by he couldn't resist it: the urge to lever himself up a little and look directly at the driver. Angus McGowan, absolutely. But—

—In that same moment McGowan looked back at him . . . and it was a different McGowan! How different, Ianson couldn't say. He couldn't even say if the other had recognized him, probably not. And he had only recognized McGowan because he *knew* it was him. But that *look* on the little man's face: the suspicion in those rheumy eyes—those feral yellow eyes. The evil, aggressive, thrust of the man's jaw . . .

For a good three minutes after the car had gone the Inspector sat there, then finally gave himself a shake, started his car and crossed the river by the old bridge. On the far side he parked and walked as quietly as he could along a rutted service road to where the silver-grey car stood in front of the middle house. Just one car, the one McGowan had been following. Ianson memorized the number plate, checked that he knew his exact location, went back to his car and drove home . . .

Half an hour earlier:

"I'm sorry I'm late," B.J. breathlessly told Harry in his bedroom. "I had to see to the takings, talk to the girls, lock up. I got here as quickly as I could."

Harry was fully awake now but still hollow-eyed. The last week had been a trying time; in fact the last three months had been trying, even if he didn't know why. But there'd been this feeling of an impending *something* that had worked on his nerves like sandpaper. And looking at B.J. he knew that it hadn't been easy on her, either. Whatever it was. But:

She should level with me, he thought, again wondering why.

B.J. wasn't a telepath. The germ of the talent was in her, as it was in most of the Wamphyri to one degree or another, but it wasn't an art yet by any means. Still, perhaps she got something of what was on his mind.

"Harry, I'm sorry—" she started to say, and bit her tongue. "—I mean, I'm sorry that you're feeling down."

"Sure," he said, but without conviction. And changing the subject: "Did you go away this last weekend? Did you go north?"

"Er, no," she shook her head. "I was busy, and—"

"—The weather?" He sought excuses for her. "And the new year just in? We didn't have much of a Christmas, B.J."

Christmas? That was scarcely B.J.'s time! But still: "Er, no," she answered, "we didn't. And I'm sorry. But you know how busy the bar is in . . . the silly season . . ." She tapered off.

"It's been a week, B.J.," he said then. "And a week before that, and before that, etcetera. In fact it's been this way for months. And when we're together you're always looking over your shoulder, avoiding my eyes, having . . . second thoughts?"

She had been standing there looking at him. Now her heart gave a mighty lurch as she flew into his arms, and said, "Second thoughts? Not about you, Harry! No, not about you!"

"Then say it," he held her tightly, mumbled into her hair.

"Say it?" She wasn't thinking straight—couldn't, not now that she was in his arms again.

"Call me yere wee man, and put everything right," he told her. *Put it right, even if it isn't.*

Well, and she would have to switch him on if she wanted to use the phone in his presence. Else there'd be things she said to Auld John that he wouldn't understand.

"Harry, mah wee man," she said—and at once felt him reel a little, the sway of his upper body . . .

. . . *As the full moon blazed down and the great wolf lifted his head in tribute, howling from a throat that pulsed with the power of his song.*

Then B.J. felt Harry tighten up a little in her arms, and released him. "It's all right," she said, fixing him with those hypnotic eyes of hers. "But I have to call Auld John."

Harry nodded. "To see how *he* is, yes?"

She nodded. "And then we can talk."

"Real talk?"

It's always real, Harry, always! For me, anyway. But B.J. knew what he meant, and said: "Real talk, yes."

She leaned towards him and gave him a quick kiss, and he didn't try to draw back. But neither did he respond. Then B.J. sat at the side of the bed, and phoned Auld John . . .

At his cottage in Inverdruie, Auld John was just done wrapping his wrist when the phone rang. His bleddy wrist! Man, if only his wounds would heal like the Wee Mistress's. But they wouldnae. He still had scars frae three months ago, where on Bonnie Jean they'd be quite invisible by now.

And the telephone was ringing, even as he tied a knot and tugged it tight with his teeth. This would be the Wee Mistress hersel' no doubt. But it wasnae his fault he'd no called. He'd been down and out for twenty-four hours, aye. A full nicht and a day. And even now he wasnae feelin' too guid.

"John Guiney," he barked into the phone, using a strong voice to disguise the fact of his physical weakness. "Wha' is it?"

"It's me, John," the Wee Mistress's voice came back, and he could almost taste the relief in it. "I was worried—you didn't call me."

"Ah would'a done it this minute!" John protested, trying not to whine. "But it's no gone easy wi' me, Bonnie Jean. The climb took it out'a me. And Him up there . . . oh, but He was a *hungry* yin, lassie!"

"John, are you all right?" She was anxious now.

"Ah am the noo," he told her. And: "Hush, hush now. Ah'm well enough. But He bled me good. No, no—it was mah own stupid fault. Like a bleddy auld fool, Ah fell asleep! And it was Himsel' shoutin' in mah head who woke me. Then mah wound—it wouldnae heal, and the climb down was sheer *murder!* That's why Ah've slep' like the big bairn Ah am this day and a half, and missed callin' ye. Forgive me, lass, for a bleddy fool."

B.J.'s sigh, and: "Nothing to forgive, John, as long as you're all right. But you sound so weary!"

"So Ah am, but never ye fear. Ah'm stoked tae the brim on guid broth. Another nicht shid see me fine and dandy. And down inside Ah feel stronger than ever. For think, Bonnie Jean, just think! It's *mah* blood that sustains Him the noo!" But a moment later the excitement ebbed from his voice. "Excep' . . . " And he paused.

"Except?" she prompted him. "Is there something, John?"

Trembling, Auld John sat down with the telephone. "Bonnie, He wasnae pleased. No, not this time, and far worse than last. Ah tol' Him a' ye said Ah shid; it wouldnae do. He spoke tae me—in mah head, ye ken—and oh He was angry! No so much wi' ye as wi' they *others,* they Ferenczys and Drakuls! But angry anyway. Ah could feel it boilin' in Him! And it's the Wee Mistress He needs, no this auld sod—if ye'll excuse mah language."

"What did you tell him? What did he get from you?" B.J.'s tone was anxious again; John could almost hear her heart pounding.

"Why, only what ye'd tol' me!" He trembled again, his old head swimming in a sudden dizzy bout. "Excep' ye ken Ah didnae tell Him anythin' much, but He took it right out o' mah head."

"Yes, yes," (he sensed B.J.'s nod of understanding). "But what did *he* tell you?"

"Oh, Ah've a message for ye, be sure," John answered. "No more putting it off, Bonnie Jean, no any more. Neither Ferenczys, Drakuls, disaster, nor even death—*nothin's* tae stand in yere way. Ye'll attend Radu in person next time, or it's over and He's done wi' ye! As for yere wee man, that Harry Keogh—he's tae be wi' ye. Aye, for he's *verra* important, that yin."

For a moment there was silence on the line, only a faint crackle of static in Auld John's ear. He could hear a log hissing sap in his grate, and the wind in the eaves. Then at last B.J.'s voice again, but faint as a whisper. "Will he . . . is he . . . does he think he'll be up?"

"Eh? The great wolf? Up, ye say? No, no, that wasnae mah meanin'. Six months, He said. But that's why He must see yere Harry next time, so that He may know the way of it. But Ah'm no the clever yin, Bonnie Jean, as well ye ken. Ah wasnae too sure what He meant . . . "

No, but on the other end of the line Bonnie Jean believed she understood only too well what the dog-Lord meant! Sitting beside her, drawn and hollow-eyed, Harry Keogh might well have understood it, too, if he'd heard. He hadn't, however, and:

"Don't worry about it, John," she told her old friend. "I can sort things out." And she was at once concerned again, for him: "But what about the climb? Was it really that bad?"

"Oh, aye, but Ah took the easy route up, and killed a fine beast along the way for His creature. That yin's . . . well, he's comin' on, ye ken?"

"Yes," she agreed. "I know . . . "

Auld John heard the dubious note in her answer, very much as his query had sounded dubious. "Lassie, is a' well?"

"As well as it can be," she answered. And before he could question that, too: "John, we have—*He* has—enemies here. I hope you were careful not to be followed. Are there any strangers up your way? Have you noticed anything odd?"

"No one, and nothin'," he answered. "But ye know me. Ah'm no the one tae take chances. Why, even when Ah answer the door, mah gun goes wi' me! Ah reckon it was sheer luck they picked ye up that time. And as for mahsel'— why, Ah'm just a cranky old gillie, as anyone hereabouts will be pleased tae confirm!" And sensing her grin, he smiled. Then she said:

"Take care, John. We'll talk soon. But don't you call me, I'll call you. Look after your . . . *wound.* Make sure it heals."

"Oh, it will. But it was only mah duty, ye ken . . . "

And after he heard the click as she put the phone down, Auld John sat and listened to the purring receiver in his hand, and stared at his bandaged wrist where a thin red line was showing through even now. His duty, aye—but it hadnae gone unappreciated. And then he remembered what else Radu had told him, which he hadn't dared repeat to Bonnie Jean:

You are second in line, John, after the Wee Mistress. Ah, but she is only a lassie after all, and weak as all women are. I fear that when my time comes she may bend, or even break. So mark these words, which are for you alone: keep my secrets and serve me well, John, as your ancestors before you. And who can say? . . . One day you could be first in line!

The dog-Lord's promise! It ran through Auld John's veins like wine and sang to him! It gave a new meaning to existence, and was well worth every extra drop of life's blood that he'd let flow down the funnel to the great hound-like thing in the vat. Worth, too, the lie he'd been obliged to tell B.J.—but that had been on the orders of Radu himself, and who was Auld John to defy Him in His high place?

Aye, for Radu was quickening and He had *needed* that extra drop or two. Up in a six-month? Ah, no . . . try four! But Radu had told John that he couldn't tell Bonnie Jean; indeed, that he must *lie* to her! For John was to be His confidant now that the Wee Mistress had shown herself to be . . . well, just a wee lassie after all.

It wasn't her fault, though, John was sure. (And he frowned and felt concerned for the ex-Wee Mistress.) More likely it was all down to that Harry Keogh, aye! Ah, but the dog-Lord had plans for him, too. Up in just four more months, and then we'd see about this Harry! And here's B.J. worrying about John contacting her. Well, he wouldn't. But Radu would, be sure!

Three moons from now—just thirteen weeks, that was all—and then she'd hear His call. That silent howling in her head, that drew her like a magnet. She'd get her instructions then, aye. And a month later, the one who'd caused her to stray from the path . . . *he* would get his comeuppance!

"His wound?" Harry had overheard one or two things after all.

"Hmm?" B.J. looked at him.

"You told him to take care of his wound."

"He cut himself on the rock face," she lied.

"Oh?"

"Is this the real talk you wanted?" She began unbuttoning her blouse. For there are other ways to beguile a man, and better ways to ease his pain, too. And hers.

"You tell me," he said.

"Very well, you can think and speak normally." And at once he was himself, those warm eyes disguising a cold and calculating brain.

"B.J., did something happen that time, when we were up in the Highlands? We went up to Auld John's place in Inverdruie to climb and hunt, but you cried off. And this last weekend, again you cried off going. Well, OK—for after all it's the middle of winter now—but what about the last time?"

"Have you been reading the newspapers, Harry?"

"No," (but E-Branch had contacted him that time three months ago, about some weird shit in his neck of the woods?) "Why? Was there something I should have read?"

B.J. shook her head. She'd cancelled the episode from his mind and didn't want to let it surface now, which obviously it was trying to do. "Have you been having bad dreams, Harry? You said on the phone that you'd been dreaming."

"Dreams, half-memories . . . anxieties and feelings I don't understand. You name it." He shrugged, despairingly she thought. And then, out of the blue: "B.J., why don't you level with me?"

"Level with you?" Her blouse was off now, and her breasts proud and stiff-tipped where they begged for Harry's attention. Almost automatically, she wriggled out of her skirt. "Ask your questions. If I can answer them, I will."

"I don't know all of it, do I?"

"No."

"Why not?"

"I can only tell you what he'll let me tell you."

"Radu?"

"The dog-Lord, yes."

"But he's a liar!" Harry snapped, his voice suddenly harsh and full of hate. "He's Wamphyri, and they're *all* liars!"

Again B.J. was taken aback. "But . . . did I tell you that, that he's Wamphyri?" *Had she?* Well of course she had, that time when she'd "explained" her purpose—and Harry's eventual role in things. She'd been thrown, that was all, by the vehemence in his voice, the knowledge in his eyes. But damned if she remembered telling him that the Wamphyri were all liars!

B.J. couldn't know it but Harry, too, had been thrown into a state of confusion. He'd almost trapped himself, tripped over his own tongue. For the Necroscope wasn't the only one who "didn't know it all." There were quite a few things that he hadn't, or couldn't, tell B.J., too.

"Yes," he said, "you told me. Radu is Wamphyri—a Great Vampire—and he has enemies opposed to his return: the Ferenczys and the Drakuls. And that they are full of lies."

She nodded, and thought: *He's sweating. Why does he sweat like that? What's on his mind? That oh-so-deep mind of his?*

Harry didn't know either—not what was *on* his mind—only that something swirled there beneath the surface, secret information hidden in its own mental limbo.

B.J. had the power to unlock it. But . . . he didn't *want* it unlocked!

If she knew he had been to *those* places, she would want to know when he was there, and why, and what route he'd taken!

She would want to know about the Möbius Continuum: how he had discovered it, and how he'd used it to *go* to those places!

. . . But *what* fucking places?

Then it happened. For several seconds it was what his Ma and B.J. had both feared, if not exactly as they had imagined it, when suddenly Harry's two levels of consciousness and knowledge interfaced:

He stood in the open, in bright daylight, and craned his neck to look up and up, at dramatically stark yellow and white cliffs and at the squat white-walled castle, mansion, or chateau that was perched there on the edge of oblivion. The scene was Mediterranean, and he knew it well! Knew the castle, too!

Le Manse Madonie!

Sicily!

The Ferenczys!

Wamphyri!

Jesus God!

His mind whirled . . . and Harry whirled too. He was whirled away from there, whirled elsewhere—

—To a frozen monochrome landscape, the Roof of the World, and a gaunt range of mountains marching against grey skies that went on forever. It was biting cold, and the snow slanting down like a million white spears, forming an ever-thickening, freezing crust on him where he leaned into the blast. And seen like a flickering old film on or through the dot-dash screen of hissing snow, the long snaking wall of a city like a small version of the Great Wall of China. While in the other direction, hewn out of a sheer cliff at the foot of the mountains, a great carved face as grim and as cold as its location.

At the head of carved steps, the yawning mouth in the face was the entrance to . . . what? A temple of sorts? A monastery, yes, but dedicated to what ancient and evil religion?

There came a distant tinkle of tiny golden bells, growing louder even as the hiss of lancing snow faded.

The scene faded with it, but the bells were louder still, sounding sinister now, as the Necroscope was once again transported, moved by his mind to yet another forbidden memory . . .

. . . He seemed to be in a glade where the light was dappled as it fell through the trees. B.J. was with him, and they were standing beside a car, looking back along a track like a leafy tunnel at a station-wagon standing some fifty feet away. Leaning on the vehicle's open front doors, a pair of red-robed Asiatics looked back at them. One of these "priests" had a gun in his hand, and both had grins on their faces.

But there are grins and there are grins. In the dappling of the trees, their eyes were feral, full of yellow, shifting light. And their grins were vacuous, like those of crocodiles or hyenas, and full of malice!

Drakuls!

B.J. had a crossbow and knew how to use it. Her eyes were feral, too, as she aimed and squeezed the trigger.

There came a thok! *sound, and a feeling—entirely physical—with it . . .*

. . . Then B.J.'s worried voice: "Harry! Harry!"—as he was jarred out of it, back into reality, however confused. His head had smacked against the bed's headboard when he'd jerked out of her arms and toppled over.

And: "It's OK," she told him. "It's OK," time and time again, as she lay his head back on the pillows, held his frantically if aimlessly waving arms, and riveted his pin-prick eyes with her own hypnotic ones—until finally he began to believe her. That it was OK.

Then she was turning the lights down low—her voice, too—as she began to reverse the process that had started within him, to once more separate his two levels of being . . .

In a little while it was as if Harry had been asleep; indeed he *had* been in a deep sleep induced by B.J., in a night-dark place where there had been absolutely nothing except her voice insisting that it was OK. And as he came out of it, it *was* OK.

Her cool fingers were on his brow, soothing away the last traces of fever; her body scent—masked or mingling with some subtle hint of perfume—was in his nostrils; her breasts were within easy reach where she knelt over him.

"What—?" he said.

She gave a little snort and said, "Some talker, you!"

"Talker?" Harry was baffled, but he was him again. Or the him she wanted him to be, at least. As if to prove it, he instinctively lifted his hands and gentled the marble, hard-tipped globes of her free-hanging breasts.

She threw back her head, stretched to the sensation of his hands on her, and sighed, "We were to have a 'real talk'—but you fell asleep! Some talker, you. And some lover!"

"Knackered," he said. "I must have been. But I'm OK now. Except . . ." He paused and frowned. She had left him in switched-on mode. He knew about her, Radu, everything she *wanted* him to remember, but everything else was safely back in limbo. It had to be that way, at least until she could check that her hypnotic adjustments had taken.

"Except?" she prompted him.

"Just one thing," he said. "Just one . . ."

"Real talk?"

"Yes," he nodded, stood up (a little shakily), and quickly stripped out of his pants and shirt. "Real talk—about Radu."

"Oh?" B.J. tried to remain calm. Despite the fact that his actions as he prepared for love had cushioned the impact of his query, still his words had seemed cold and calculating.

"He's in his vat, deep in a resin bath—yes?"

"In a sleep of centuries," she nodded.

"But he'll be up soon?"

Again her nod. "Has to be if I—we—are to survive. We can't fight his enemies on our own. Afterwards I . . . don't want to know about Radu. Only about us." That last was straight from the heart. If only it could be so.

He shook his head. "This isn't only about Radu, B.J. It's also about you."

"About me?"

"He's in his vat, deep in the resin. He hasn't . . . touched you?" It was as if those soulful eyes of his were looking right into her. Soulful but bottomless, and sometimes as cold as some unfathomed ocean floor. B.J. thought she knew what Harry meant, and believed she understood his concern. He was asking if Radu was more than merely her Master, wondering if perhaps he'd been her lover, too. And maybe, in one sense, B.J. was right to interpret his question thus.

But in fact it was deeper than that, and there were parallels here that only the Necroscope recognized, which he could never explain to B.J. because he'd been forbidden to do so. For example: the necromancer Boris Dragosani had also been the guardian of a vampire's tomb in his time, and at first he, too, had been an "innocent" in his fashion. Dragosani's fate, however . . .

. . . Was something Harry must steer clear of as best he possibly could. He daren't think too deeply about it, despite that it had prompted his question. For the idea simply wasn't acceptable, it wasn't tenable, not in tandem with B.J.'s situation.

"Touched me?" She contrived to look puzzled. "But Radu was down in the resin centuries before I was born, like a great fly trapped in amber! How could he possibly touch me, except in his capacity to speak to me through his mentalism?"

It was the truth, and it was a lie. A white lie. And what difference did it make anyway? For it was the cure.

Harry expelled air in a great sigh, as if he'd been holding it in his lungs forever. A single word came bursting like a bubble from his lips: "Innocent . . . !" And B.J. knew he meant her innocence, the only facet of her post-hypnotic façade that she'd forgotten to reinstate. So Harry had done it for her. It had been that important to him.

Now he was satisfied, and so was she. She switched him off with four simple words, "Harry, mah wee man," then switched him on again, with her body . . .

Afterwards they slept, but the Necroscope's dreams were uneasy and from time to time lurched into grotesque nightmares.

Twice in the night he started awake, fancying that B.J.'s breasts were too many, and that they felt like flaccid, hairy dugs in his hands . . .

V

THE WATCHER: UNMASKED

IT WAS A LATE NIGHT FOR INSPECTOR GEORGE IANSON, AND AN EARLY MORNING. A late night because he contacted Police Central and requested a vehicle registration check on the silver-grey car, then waited up until he had the answer; which had taken all of an hour, because they were busy. And an early morning because he didn't sleep too well (too much on his mind) and wanted to do an occupancy check first thing on Number 3, The Riverside.

What was on his mind was B.J., the fact that it was her car old Angus had followed. But why? Surely the old fool knew better than to go carrying out his own investigations on B.J. and her wine-bar? He had his own kind of investigations to do, for God's sake! And then there was that look on his face when he'd driven away from the place on the river. If there was an explanation for *that*—well, for the life of him the Inspector couldn't think what it might be.

At 9:15 A.M. he phoned B.J. at the wine-bar. He couldn't be sure she would be home yet, or even if she planned on returning home today, but he had to try anyway. He got her first go, and without ado asked, "B.J., didn't you fancy someone might be following you last night?"

He heard her suck in her breath—and then something that he really hadn't wanted to hear: "Last night?" (All innocence.) "When, last night?"

So, did she have something to hide? "Come, come, B.J. When you left the wine-bar—and went to see Mr. Keogh?"

"Oh!" But in any case, B.J. had realized her mistake the moment she made it. Stupid to play dumb with Ianson. He was no fool, this one.

"A big secret, is it?" he asked her softly, and heard her sigh of resignation.

But on the other end of the line she was doing some fast thinking. "Harry . . . is a married man," she finally said, "but separated. He doesn't even know where his wife is. She walked out on him. That was some time ago, years even, but . . . "

"I see," Ianson said. "You're still being careful."

"Inspector," (now she was pouring it out), "I thought it might be possible that the man who has been watching my place was a private detective employed by Harry's wife. But believe me, I wasn't trying to throw you a red herring. That's why I didn't tell you about him immediately—the watcher, I mean. But when you came to my place and mentioned a big dog, and what with Margaret being attacked and all . . . suddenly it all seemed to connect up."

"I understand," Ianson said. "But now tell me: does Harry Keogh have a dog?"

"No, nor even a budgie! But what are you thinking? Please believe me that—"

"—I'm *trying* to believe you, B.J. But no more red herrings, accidental or otherwise, OK?"

"No, of course not. But about last night . . . was I really followed? By you?"

"By . . . someone," he told her. "But it just happened that I was following him. It was quite accidental, I assure you. No one is investigating you. Well, not the police, anyway."

"Who, then?" she said. "I mean, if you were following him . . . does that mean you know him?"

"No," he lied (for old McGowan's sake. He'd known him for years and had to give him the benefit of the doubt . . . for now, anyway). "But you might be able to help me. I have a picture of our suspect. If you can identify him as your watcher, I'm sure I can trace him again, maybe even tie him to the murder at Sma' Auchterbecky." Then, too, it would be up to McGowan to explain what he was doing watching B.J., her place, and her girls. And doing it since a time *before* the attack on Margaret Macdowell.

On her end of the line, B.J. saw it as another chance to throw a spanner in this Ferenczy scum's works, get him off her back. "A picture?" she said. "A photograph? Any time you like, Inspector. I'll be only too pleased to identify him, if I can."

"Good!" Ianson told her. "Let's do it now, then. I can be there in half an hour."

"Very well, I'll be expecting you."

"And B.J.?"

"Yes?"

"Don't worry. You can be pretty sure that this isn't someone acting on behalf of your Harry's wife."

No, indeed . . .

Three of B.J.'s girls were there. Along with Bonnie Jean herself, they corroborated what Ianson had hoped *not* to discover, that McGowan—or someone who looked just like him—was the watcher who had been plaguing their lives. And he'd been doing it for a very long time, yes. Now Ianson must hope it was simply a case of mistaken identity, that the old vet had a double. But quite apart from that, there was this other thing that was weird beyond explanation.

Old Angus's book: the photograph on the dust-jacket. But once again, until all the facts are known, nothing is known . . .

* * *

The publisher was a one-man Edinburgh-based outfit, small potatoes in the vast world of books, that specialized in safaris and travel in remote regions, zoological and ecological topics in general. Its offices were in a quiet tree-lined cul-de-sac just outside the city proper towards Linlithgow.

It had turned out to be one of those rare bright and invigorating winter mornings when Ianson parked his car outside Greentree Publishing, Limited, and was seen into the main office—indeed the only office—by the head of the firm himself, Jeoffrey Greentree. The Inspector had thought that perhaps the firm had been named for its subjects, and had opened by saying as much. And in fact:

"Oh, it has, it has!" Mr. Greentree told him, beaming. "It was sheer good fortune that my name fits the subjects too. Conservation, Inspector. The creatures of the wilds and the woods, and the trees themselves, of course. Green trees, Mother Earth, Gaia! We only use recycled papers, you know? The pages may tend to brown, but the forests stay green. That should be our motto! What can I do for you, sir?"

Beanpole meets bean! Ianson thought, but not unkindly. *The odd couple!*

Jeoffrey Greentree was small and in his sixties, slightly hunched and round-shouldered, soft-voiced and twinkle-eyed. His chin sat forward almost on his chest. A bean of a man, yes. But for all that he'd worked with fine print all his life, his eyes were still alert if a little watery. His hair was very thin on top, but his mobile, bushy eyebrows somehow made up for it.

And Greentree's office was . . . something else.

Ianson had been in solicitors' offices that were far less cluttered. One entire wall looked like a vertical maze of allegedly "alphabetically arranged" pigeon-hole shelving. Spilling out of the various compartments were dusty packages of letters, old manuscripts, contracts, proofs . . . and photographs. Ianson was prompted to refer immediately to the reason for his visit.

"You can perhaps help me with this," he said, placing McGowan's book on a typically cluttered and dusty desk, and opening it to the back flap that showed old Angus's picture. "Or if not you yourself, then whoever edited this book for the author, or anyone else who might know something about it. It's quite an old book, I know, and it's been in print—and probably out of print—for years, but . . ."

"Sit down, Inspector, please sit," Greentree waved him to a chair (dusty, and covered with page proofs, of course), took up McGowan's book and sat down behind his desk. "And what have we here? Ah, yes! It's been some time since I happened upon a first edition—other than my own copy, that is."

"Definitely a first edition? The whole thing, wrapper and all?"

"Hmm?" Greentree blinked at him questioningly. "Oh, very definitely, yes. And rare, too! But as I said, I do have my own copy. I keep at least one copy of everything I do. It should be on the shelves there, er, *somewhere!*" He waved a hand, and returned to studying the book.

The shelves he referred to covered the wall opposite the maze of documents. Ianson stood up, went to then, and tried in vain to locate Angus McGowan's name on the spine of any one of nine hundred to a thousand titles. But:

"You might have a little difficulty," Greentree told him. "People refer to a book, and eventually return it to the shelves . . . but rarely in the right place. I gave up long ago. Ah, but that doesn't mean I don't know where they are!"

He joined Ianson at the bookshelves. "But you haven't yet told me, Inspector. Just what is it that interests you in *Wild Dogs, Big Cats,* anyway?" And with a marksman's aim, almost casually, he reached up a surprisingly long arm, and took a duplicate copy from one of the higher shelves. Blowing dust off it, he offered it to Ianson.

"Oh, the author's a friend of mine," the Inspector answered absent-mindedly. "Angus McGowan, I mean." He returned to the desk and compared this pristine copy with Strachan's. Condition apart, they were identical.

"Indeed? Well, I've only met the man twice myself, though I did speak to him on the phone more frequently. But that was a long time ago. An odd sort of man. I do remember thinking of him, er, that he held his years very well . . ."

Just why that last statement should hit Ianson the way it did wasn't hard to say: it was the very reason he was here. At the same time, however, Mr. Greentree might well have produced the answer—the very *ordinary,* commonplace answer—that the Inspector had been seeking to what had become an extraordinary question, if only in his own mind. No mystery here at all, but simply the fact that McGowan "held his years very well."

Oh, really? Then why were alarm bells clamouring even now in the back of Ianson's mind? "When did you last see him?"

"Why, it must be twenty years ago," Greentree replied. "We were reprinting his book—this book, yes, which was ten years out of date—and Mr. McGowan came in with a new chapter and a handful of revisions. And a request."

"A request?"

Greentree nodded. "He wanted us to replace his picture on the back flap of the jacket with some extra copy he'd prepared. That picture, yes." He pointed to the photographs that the Inspector was comparing. "It seems he wasn't very enamoured of his features. That's when I noticed that in ten years his looks had scarcely changed at all! So I suppose he's a lucky fellow—or maybe not. I mean, it probably isn't for me to say, but Mr. McGowan isn't a particularly handsome man. But at least he seemed to recognize that fact."

Old Angus's looks hadn't changed in ten years? Ianson felt a shudder run up his spine. *Well try the next twenty, my friend, try the next twenty!*

And that would make thirty in all!

But Greentree was right for a fact, and now that fact came back to the Inspector more forcefully than ever. He'd known McGowan for three decades—and never seen a change in him! *What?* (Ianson asked himself). *Am I blind or something?* Or had he, too, been telling himself all along that McGowan "seemed to hold his years very well?" Familiarity, was that it? The fact that scarcely a week passed that they didn't meet for a game of chess or a drink or whatever?

But I have changed, Ianson thought. *I have grown old, and plenty of my colleagues with me. Yet "old" Angus was old when first we met! Jesus God in heaven—what's going on here!?*

"Something wrong?" Mr. Greentree was looking concerned.

"Yes," said Ianson, numbly. "No . . . I don't know. But you can be sure I'm going to find out!"

Grimly determined now, he sat down with Greentree at his desk and took up one of the books. And for the sake of clarity—and probably for sanity's sake, too—he said: "Now I want to be one hundred per cent sure about this. You're certain that this is a first edition?"

"But of course!" Greentree looked mystified. "I mean, I *am* the publisher, after all! The date is clearly shown on the data page: 1952. Seven years since the war but I was still using the same low-grade paper to satisfy government restrictions. And as I told you, I've been using it ever since."

"And you published a new edition some ten years later?"

"Exactly ten years later. Would you like to see it?"

"Please." Ianson sat and waited while Greentree went back to the bookshelves and returned with much the same book but in the more recent edition that the Inspector remembered seeing at McGowan's place that time. And: "This is the edition that doesn't carry his picture, right?"

"Just as I told you," the other nodded. "But why not open it and see for yourself?"

Ianson did so and checked; there was more copy on the back flap but no picture—"Because he wanted more space for copy on the jacket?"

"And because he'd decided that the picture wasn't entirely flattering, as I told you, yes."

Or maybe (the Inspector told himself, getting to his feet) *because he didn't look any older? And he didn't want the—the what?—anomaly, mistake, repeated down the years in case someone should eventually notice?* This was crazy!

"Oh, and one other thing," Greentree frowned. "All of this was some time ago, as you'll appreciate, but now it comes back to me."

"What does?"

"Well, the fact that Mr. McGowan is something of a perfectionist."

"Go on."

"I do believe that he so disliked the earlier book that he bought up a good many copies and destroyed them. Though not for the photograph, I'm sure. No, it could only be that he was dissatisfied with earlier work that he considered incomplete. It's no rare thing; I've heard of several authors doing it. Professional pride or some such . . . "

"That would explain why you haven't seen a copy for such a long time—I mean, apart from the one on your shelves?"

"Exactly." Greentree saw the Inspector to the door.

"Mr. Greentree," Ianson shook his hand, "it was very good of you to give of your time like this—"

"Not at all."

"—But now I'd like another favour."

"Well, fire away."

"Don't mention this to anyone. If things work out, I promise I'll get back to you. But in the meantime . . . not a word."

"Well, it's all very mysterious, but very well. After all, you are a custodian of the law."

"Indeed," said Ianson, smiling. But his smile was forced. And in the back of his mind he was thinking: *A custodian of the law? Yes, and for the last thirty years, of God only knows what else!*

... **O**r, it had to be a mistake. There had to be an explanation. But with this case—this *murder* case, Ianson must keep reminding himself—absolutely nothing seemed to be making any sort of sense.

But tonight it would, or it would start to, at least. And it would start with Angus McGowan . . .

The Inspector had work to do at Police H.Q. Nothing connected with this thing, but work nonetheless. It kept him busy until mid-afternoon, when he drove home. Then he called McGowan and waited while the telephone rang and rang. It had always been the same: the little man invariably took his time answering the phone. But eventually:

"Aye?" came his rasping voice.

"Angus, it's George," Ianson told him, trying to keep his voice as casual as possible. "We've a game of chess to finish, as you'll recall. It's half-played out on the board, just waiting for us to pick it up where we left off. Your move, I think. So, I was wondering: how are you fixed for tonight? Oh, and of course you'll want to bring me up to date on your zoo-quest—that business at Sma' Auchterbecky?"

For a few seconds there was silence, then: "And Ah expec' ye'll be wantin' tae fill me in on yere own progress. Am Ah no right?"

The Inspector tried to imagine himself talking to McGowan face to face, and thus keep the conversation natural. But there was a certain something in the other's voice, a very wary something, that told him it wouldn't be that easy. Perhaps honesty would be the best policy after all. "Well it's true there have been one or two interesting developments—" he began.

But when he heard old Angus's dry, rasping chuckle in response—why, he could almost see the little vet grinning like a Cheshire cat! And that familiar chuckle of his, it was so reassuring that Ianson found himself wondering where all his doubts had sprung from. "Developments, is it?" the little vet queried. "Aye, and much the same at mah end, too. In fact Ah fancy Ah'm ahead o' the game, George."

That stopped Ianson dead. Damn the man! He *had* been investigating on his own, against all the rules, and obviously knew a lot more than he was saying. With which, all of the Inspector's remaining doubts flew right out the window. For this was sly old Angus as usual, playing his word-games and hugging his knowledge tight to his chest like a miser with his hoard. This oh-so-clever, *irritating* little man, this friend of George Ianson's for so long that the accumulated years couldn't possibly be brushed aside on a mere whim or set of weird circumstances. But aggravating? Absolutely!

"So, ahead of the game, are you?" he said. "Well you were last night, anyway—or *behind* it, certainly. And I was right behind you!" It was the Inspector's way: a shock statement like that right out of the blue. But if he had hoped to surprise the other, no such luck.

"Aye, so ye were," old Angus chuckled again. "Ah suspected it was yeresel'—

even in that nonedescrip' heap o' old junk ye call a car! But are ye no ashamed
o' yeresel', George? Hidin' in the bushes an a', as if yere old pal was up tae no
good!" Then, for good measure, he made *tsk, tsk* noises so that Ianson could
picture him shaking his head disapprovingly.

He had to smile. And it was good to smile, for he'd been down in the dumps
for some time. But now, almost audibly sighing his relief, he said: "Well, just
what *were* you up to, Angus? If I hadn't recognized your Beetle, I might even
have suspected I was following the murderer!"

There came another, longer pause, then McGowan's rasping voice again,
its tone more serious than Ianson could ever remember hearing it before. "Ah,
but ye *were* followin' just such a murderer, George. Ye were!"

"What!"

"Not me—and Ah'll *never* forgive ye if that's what ye've been thinkin', even
though ye may have had cause!—but the no so wee bonnie lassie hersel'. Aye,
Bonnie Jean Mirlu—and her pack!"

Ianson's brain whirled. "Angus, what in the—?"

"Big dogs, George! D'ye no remember?"

"Well of course I remember, but . . . "

"And what about big bitches, eh?"

Ianson shook his head, for all the world as if he thought McGowan could
see him. "Bitches? I'm not with you." But at the same time he recognized a not
so vague connection with ex-constable Strachan's story. And more, he remembered one of McGowan's comments at Sma' Auchterbecky, at the murder
scene: about a dog or a bitch of a different colour.

"Not wi' me, George?" old Angus repeated him. "Are ye no? But ye'd be a
damn clever policeman if ye were! Or maybe a madman, eh? There's *weird* here,
mah friend, and that's puttin' it mildly. Ah've been gatherin' it for years, and
now Ah have it a'! But there's a hell o' a lot o' it, and it's no the sort o' stuff a
man shid talk about on the telephone."

"A lot of what, for God's sake?"

"Evidence, man, hard evidence!"

"Angus, now listen—"

But he wasn't listening. "Will ye come?"

"To your place, now?"

"Aye, the nicht. The sooner the better. The noo!"

The Inspector made up his mind. Old Angus was eager; whatever he had,
he seemed ready to spill it all and delight in his cleverness. Which would be his
right if he really had stumbled onto something, and if it was as big as he appeared to think it was. But: "Bonnie Jean Mirlu?" McGowan's accusation had
finally sunk in. "Are you telling me that—?"

"Ah've said a' Ah'm sayin' on the 'phone, George. So?"

" . . . I'll come as soon as I've eaten," Ianson told him.

"As ye will, but don't keep me waitin', George. Ah mean, the game's afoot—
and it's *big* game this time!"

With which the Inspector was finally convinced—at least that there was a
lot he was yet to be convinced about. And so: "I'll be there in about an hour,"
he said.

"Guid!" said the other. "But drive careful, George. They roads are awfy treacherous wi' the slush freezin' on 'em. Aye, and a man can never tell who's followin' behind him—ye ken?" And in the moment before the phone went down, Ianson was annoyed yet again to hear the little vet's irritating chuckle . . .

It was barely five but already dark when Ianson reached old Angus's place and parked his car behind the vet's Volkswagen. He had been here before—well, on occasion—and so wasn't at a complete loss. But as he left the street through a complaining wrought-iron gate, climbed a short flight of steps to the arched-over entrance, and went to ring the bell, so the stout oak door gaped wide and Angus was there, waiting on the threshold.

At that precise moment some vehicle must have gone by in the road and sent a glancing headlight beam to strike the vet's eyes, which for a second burned yellow with reflected light. It wasn't the first time that the Inspector had noted this effect. Perhaps it was the contrast, for behind McGowan the hall lights were out; in fact the entire house seemed to be in darkness.

The little vet was dressed for outdoors: a raincoat over his street-clothes and his customary wide-brimmed hat. He took Ianson's arm and greeted him with a whispered, "No, George. It willnae do tae park just there—Ah'm probably bein' watched! So come on, we'll put yere car in mah garage by the sea."

He led the way back to Ianson's car, and directed him to a row of garages set back from the dark waterfront a quarter-mile away. His garage was spacious but damp, built of rotting bricks on waterlogged foundations. "Ah'm told they're comin' down in a year or so," he said. "A lot o' they crumblin' old houses, too. A new promenade or some such fancy scheme. For the tourists an a'." And then they walked back in silence to his place.

But as they reached the house and McGowan turned a key in the door to let them in: "Angus," the Inspector took his elbow. "Man but you're mysterious tonight! I mean I really don't know what to make of all this. You're being watched, you say?"

"Aye, it's more than likely," the other nodded, glancing back out into the street. "So we'd best no be standin' around out here, eh?" But as Ianson made to enter McGowan blocked his path. And: "George," he said, staring hard at his guest. "What Ah'm about tae tell ye—and maybe show ye—isnae for common men. Why, it can change ye forever, and it's no mah desire tae be the one ye'll be blamin'!"

Ianson shook his head in bewilderment. "Angus, if I didn't know you better," he said, "I'd have to take this as being some kind of joke. I can't *imagine* what you're into!"

"But ye do want tae know?"

"Of course I want to know. I have to know!" Irritated now, and with his patience quite exhausted, the Inspector brushed by him—and McGowan let him pass.

"Of yere own free will, then," he whispered, as he locked the door behind them.

The passageway leading past the gloomily climbing staircase to the living-room was night-dark ahead. Ianson knew the way, however vaguely; in any case it was McGowan's turn to take his elbow as he ushered him deeper into the house. But at last some welcome illumination—even if it caused the Inspector to stagger a little and blink in the sudden glare—as his host switched on the lights.

Ianson had never much cared for McGowan's house, nor even for the district in which it stood. The area was too old, cold, and too close to the sea. Only a few of the houses were habitable, and as Angus himself had pointed out they were being demolished street by street. But it was possible there'd be a government subsidy in it if and when he had to move out. So maybe that's what had kept him here all these years.

The houses were tall, narrow, terraced Victorian affairs, with gabled attic windows. They must have been handsome enough in their day, but the area had long since fallen out of favour with estate agents; much of the waterfront just here was dilapidated to the point of ramshackle. Ianson was fairly sure that was why old Angus never asked him round much: because he was a little ashamed of the district. But in any case the Inspector's bright and spacious flat had seemed more suitable for their occasional get-togethers. And come to think of it, it would have been just as suitable for this meeting tonight.

"Why here?" It was a trait of Ianson's—the hallmark of years of police-work—to ask leading questions. And sometimes it could be an error, too. "I mean, why couldn't you have come to my place? And since you fancied I had been tailing you, why didn't *you* call *me,* to put both of our minds at rest?"

"Ah was waitin' for ye tae admit defeat," McGowan grinned. "Ah was wantin' tae see how ye'd get on with yere 'man and big dog' theory. Oh, but never fear, Ah'd a' called ye for sure if ye'd taken much longer tae call me."

The living-room was L-shaped and high-ceilinged, draughty, yet damp-smelling, too. McGowan lit a gas fire in a converted hearth, fetched a whiskey bottle and glasses, saw Ianson comfortable on an ancient leather couch and seated himself opposite. And: "George, it's time Ah confessed," he said. "Ah didnae do mah job. Ah've no checked up on local zoos and what a', and Ah dinnae intend tae. But desertion o' duty? Never! And why not? Because Ah ken only too well where our murderin' beastie comes frae where she lives—and it's no a zoo or a wildlife park! Am Ah goin' too fast for ye?"

Ianson took his glass, stood up and moved to a bookshelf. "No," he answered, "because so far you've told me exactly nothing! You said or hinted that you had evidence of something far-reaching—but all we have so far is meaningless words. You're obviously talking about B.J. Mirlu—and it's also obvious you think she's guilty of something. Murder, you said. Well, maybe she is," he shrugged. "I won't know until I know it all."

McGowan had followed him. "So, ye're ready tae hear me out, are ye, George? Guid! But are ye open-minded enough? Ah told ye it was weird."

The Inspector had found what he was looking for. The book he'd seen once before on these very shelves—the second edition of *Wild Dogs, Big Cats,* by Angus McGowan. He took it back to the couch, and laid it on an occasional table close to hand. McGowan again followed him, looked at him in a curious fashion, and at the book, and said, "Well?"

"I'll hear you out, aye," The Inspector nodded.

"Verra well. But no interruptin', mind. Mah tale's a long yin, and once Ah'm started Ah'll want tae finish. It's *how* tae start that's the problem."

"Try the beginning," Ianson advised. And after old Angus had topped up their glasses, he did . . .

"**H**ere's a word for ye tae conjure wi': lycanthropy! Say nothin', George, just listen. Now, ye ken Ah've been interested in wild creatures a' mah life. Why, they books on mah bookshelves there tell it a'—that the diseases and hurts o' wild things have *been* mah life, Ah mean literally. But mah interest hasnae confined itsel' tae broken bones and ailments; it's the *nature* o' the animals theysels that fascinates me—zoology, aye. And Ah've awiz had a verra special interest in predators, big dogs or cats. But especially dogs. For y'see there's this tradition in mah family that certain ancestors o' mine—kith at least, if not kin—were killed by wolves. That was here in Scotland, of all places, but more than three hundred years ago.

"Ye'll no doubt recall mah passion for myths and legends? How Ah cannae resist a guid story in the papers about beasties killin' sheep on Bodmin Moor, or Dartmoor, or in the Highlands, or just about anywhere else? Aye, and even the *really* big-yins—though often the no-so-real yins, indeed ye might even call 'em bogus beasties, if ye take mah meanin'—in the lochs and such? How Ah pack mah bag and go off tae check such things out, and sometimes how they even pay me tae do it!

"Well, when Ah was younger Ah was very well-travelled. Ah got about in this big wide world, and learned a lot o' strange stuff. Ye've no doubt heard o' beast-children, George, brought up frae bairns by creatures o' the wild? Wolf-children in India and Nepal and Russia, dingo- or hyena-people in the Australian outback or the African veldt. Whenever Ah heard o' that sort o' thing Ah'd be off again, tae see what it was a' about.

"Most o' these 'marvels' are faked, o' course—'tourist attractions,' for want o' a better description, much like auld Nessie hersel', Ah fancy—but in Hungary and Romania Ah did come across the odd case or two that simply defied explanation. And in Sicily . . . oh, a' *sorts* o' rumours in Sicily and the Mediterranean in general! But in fact it was in Sicily that Ah met up wi' folks o' similar persuasions, people who were interested in trackin' down the same kind o' legends as mahsel' . . .

"Where was Ah? Oh, aye: Romania.

"Why, it's only thirty years ago in a place called Dumitresti in Romania that they had a spate o' wolf-killings—murders, mah friend!—by the light o' the full moon! The local folks knew what it was. They waited a month 'til the moon was full again, then sent out hunters intae the mountains wi' rifles and silver bullets tae kill the beast. They knew where tae find him, too: near a Gypsy encampment. Because they'd made a connection, d'ye see? That whenever the Romany folk came this way, the bleddy werewolf came wi' them!

"Romany, 'Szgany,' George; that's what they call Gypsies in they parts. And these were the Szgany Mirlu! Eh? And did ye no think tae ask that bonnie Bonnie Jean where she hails frae? Or if not the lassie hersel', her people before her?"

Oddly enough, Ianson *had* asked B.J. that selfsame question, though in a different connection and because of her accent, not her name; but as he opened his mouth and stumblingly went to make some comment that he hadn't quite thought out:

"Ah, no, dinnae gawp and wave yere arms!" McGowan seemed excited now. "Dinnae start yappin' on about 'coincidence' and such but hear me out! D'ye think Ah'm stupid, George? Ah mean, d'ye think Ah dinnae *ken* how a' this must sound? Well, Ah ken well enough, but first let me tell it a' and then make up yere own mind. For Ah'm no the luny here. Ye can take bets on that!

"Aye, and there's another good word for ye. Lunacy! Moon madness! The madness o' a creature who howls to his—or her—mistress moon, and whose foamin' mouth contains a bite that's contagious and carries a fever! A fever o' *change,* aye! What, impossible? D'ye think so? And what about rabies, spread bite by bite, that'll change a creature—even a man—tae a ravin' monster? And doesnae cancer change the cells o' a man's body? And malaria change the colour o' his skin? And acromegaly his verra *shape!?* So tell me, who's tae say lycanthropy cannae do the same?"

By now the Inspector was more than a little concerned for McGowan; in fact, he was downright worried. Despite the "logic" of certain of the contents of the man's—what? his "dialogue," or harangue?—they seemed to have no connection with Ianson's view of reality. Indeed, the little vet appeared to be outlining some peculiar obsession, something that he had kept hidden, bottled up inside him for a long, long time.

But as yet there was no sense of danger here; in fact if anything Ianson was starting to feel drowsy, lethargic, lulled by the vet's whisky. This despite the fact that old Angus himself waxed ever more excited, more animated.

"As for the 'myth' o' the silver bullet," he went on now, "—but isnae lead a metallic poison, too? Or mercury? Or plutonium? Or a dozen others? Different chemicals affect different species, George. One man's meat, as they say . . .

"So, what am Ah ravin' on about? But by now it's surely obvious, even tae a down-tae-earth bawbee such as yersel'. But hold yere fire a while longer, and Ah'll say on.

"Excep' Ah see ye've run dry. So let's top up yere glass a wee. There—and a drop for me, too." As he poured, so Ianson found strength of will to reach inside his pocket and draw out McGowan's first edition of *Wild Dogs, Big Cats,* placing it face-down on the table beside the other book. There was no hidden threat in this, no intention to surprise or startle; he merely intended to ask McGowan about the photograph and didn't want to forget, that was all. For surely someone—Mr. Greentree?—must be seriously in error here. Indeed, a great many things seemed in error here.

As in a dream, the Inspector opened the back flap of the book to old Angus's picture, which seemed to float up off the paper at him. Then he let his hand fall into his lap where it lay trembling, exhausted—apparently from the effort of handling the book!

McGowan's eyes darted from the book to Ianson's face and back again. He pointed at the photograph, and his pinched face gave an involuntary twitch as his thin lips drew back a little from teeth that were sharp and white. The Inspector had always thought they were false, those teeth. And surely they must be?

But: "Longevity!" McGowan had burst out, without any recognizable sense of continuity. "Another key word, aye! And Ah can see ye've been worryin' about it. But o' course, ye wouldnae have any *reason* tae check up on that sweet young thing at the wine-bar, now would ye? Well, we'll get tae that—eventually. But for now . . .

" . . . Where was Ah?" (McGowan's voice was rough and rasping as always, but angry, too, Ianson thought; his eyes kept straying to his photograph in the book on the table.) "Aye, Ah remember now," he pulled himself together. "Thirty years ago in a place called Dumitresti, in Romania. Werewolves, George, werewolves! They hunters Ah mentioned—they shot theysel's a wolf! A great grey monster o' a beast that had one o' they men's left arm off at the shoulder before they killed it! Then the authorities had them a' up for trial . . . for murder. For o' course it was the same auld story: they hadnae shot a beast but an innocent Gypsy lad, a youth frae the Romany caravan site. Oh really? So why were they *acquitted*, George? Set free—turned loose—wi' never a stain on their characters!

"A backward land, ye say, and even today full o' monsters in their own right—such as its bleddy government! Well it's true enough. And that's the noo. But Romania *thirty years* ago? And so Ah'm obliged tae agree, it's no fair o' me tae base mah argument—or shall we say, mah dissertation?—on alleged occurrences taken place in such a barbaric hellhole. So let's take a look at a more enlightened society, shall we? Like, how about England? Or even closer to home, Scotland maybe? What about the Highlands, just thirty years ago? Aye, just about the same time as this incident in Dumitresti. Ah, but it would surprise me if by now ye hadnae done yere homework, George. Indeed, Ah'm certain sure ye ken what Ah'm on about.

"So then, what about it, eh? That incident at the wildlife park on the Spey, eh? . . . *Eh?*

"Ah see it in yere eyes, George: how would auld Angus ken a' about that? But have ye no been listenin'? Man, this is *mah* field; it's a part o' me no less than police-work is a part o' yeresel'!

"But thirty years ago? Well let me tell ye that was some weird time! It was a phase o' the moon, somethin' different, a time o' unrest among a' the world's lycanthropes. Romania, Hungary—aye, and Scotland, too—it was everywhere. They couldnae control theysel's; they ran wild for however brief a spell. The moon held a' the wolf-folk in her power, and the bloodlust ran high as the highest tides . . .

"So, now let's get tae Bonnie Jean. But first . . . will ye no have another nip? What, it's gone right tae yere head, has it? Just a couple o' wee drams? Ah, well, it happens like that sometimes, when a body's a mite weary. Maybe it's a' this *detective* work ye're doin', George. Aye, for some o' us are no as young as we used tae be. It's gettin' time for ye tae quit, Ah fancy . . .

"But where was Ah? Oh, aye: Bonnie Jean Mirlu. Ah've been watchin' that yin for some time now—"

"For too long," Ianson gurgled, finding his tongue floppy in his mouth. "From a time . . . a time *before* the murder at Sma' Auchterbecky!" The moment after he said it, he could have bitten his tongue off. But too late, and it had probably been too late anyway. The doctored whiskey, and the fact that old Angus—*very* old Angus—had scarcely touched a drop. The Inspector could not possibly know or even make a guess at what was going on here, but he sensed that he was in serious trouble. And his fear must have shown in his eyes.

McGowan sprang to his feet, agile as a youth. "So, Ah was right!" he snarled. "Ye've tumbled me! Oh, ye've no proof positive as yet—no enough for George bleddy Ianson's oh-so-orthodox, down-tae-earth mind, anyway—but good enough tae start investigatin' me, eh? Well, Ah'm sorry, mah old friend, but it cannae be. And Ah'm *done* the noo wi' a' this blether!"

But the *look* on his face: Ianson had seen it before, when McGowan had driven away from the house on the river. That look of sheer bestial loathing! Was the man insane?

"Angus!" the Inspector tried to speak, but could only mumble. Quick as the vet himself, he too had *tried* to spring erect—only to go sprawling when his legs failed to obey his brain! Or maybe his brain wasn't sending or receiving the right information, for everything was beginning to swim before his eyes.

"Seein' me at that bleddy house outside Bonnyrig was bad enough," McGowan rasped. "Knowin' that Ah've been watchin' the wine-bar and B.J. Mirlu since long before she slaughtered that *other* damn animal at Sma' Auchterbecky is a lot worse. But now ye've found this bleddy book o' mine—mah one error—and me hopin' a' these years it would never come up again! Well, it's a' too much, and ye've *done* for yeresel', George."

He came around the table; Ianson could see his feet floating towards him, coming closer, expanding to the size of barges in his poisoned vision. Then, however numbly, he felt the vet's arms lifting him—but picking him up like a child—into the fireman's lift position. The strength of the man!

"In a way, it's opportune," McGowan was speaking as much to himself as to the Inspector. "They'll know ye were investigatin' the murder. When ye don't show up, they'll probably speak tae the girl again; that'll keep her busy. But they'll no' give me a second thought. What? But auld Angus McGowan was yere pal! And Ah'll be properly upset when Ah learn how ye've up and disappeared. But no as upset as yeresel', George."

Ianson felt himself carried out into the corridor, turned inward, into the house, borne along in darkness. Motion ceased momentarily when McGowan paused to grasp his hair, tugging his face round to look him in the eye. And old Angus's eyes lit up the darkness like yellow lamps, like lumps of raw sulphur burning in his face, with the fires of hell raging in their cores!

"Oh, but it has tae be a *terrible* thing, mah friend," he said, "tae stumble on such truths as these. And even then, *not* tae be able tae believe them! But ye will, ye will . . . "

There was a door, with stone steps descending to a cellar that Ianson had never known was there. But then, why should he? Nitre-streaked walls brushed the Inspector's thigh and dangling arm, as the stale smell of dampness—and of something else—came wafting from below. Then McGowan must have tripped a light switch for the darkness was driven back a little, but not much.

"These auld houses," McGowan commented, shaking his head as he put Ianson down on a wooden table. "When the tides are high, why, sometimes ye can smell the salt sea down here! But twenty-five years ago, Ah dug down two or three feet under the foundations—for sanitary reasons, as ye'll see." He jerked Ianson's head on its side and pointed. "Y'see that pipe there: that's an auld sewer, still runnin' out tae sea. Ah cut intae it and put a cover on it; mah verra own disposal unit . . . for the wee bits o' rubbish Ah've no more use for. *Yere* bits, too, George, when Ah'm done wi' them. Ah, but it'll be a guid wee while yet afore Ah'm *completely* done wi' ye! Oh, we'll share many a guid square meal taegether first, eh, George?"

The Inspector lay there and gurgled. He desperately wanted to cry out but couldn't. He made noises like a man nightmaring, trying hard to wake up. Except he *was* awake and knew it . . . but that didn't mean that this wasn't a nightmare. It was the worst possible nightmare!

And McGowan, wandering about in this loathsome subterranean den, muttering to himself and causing unknown but terrifying things to happen: the *hiss* of pressured gas, and *crump!* of sudden ignition; the clatter of tools taken up and laid aside, and the high-pitched yet sinister *whirr* as some sort of electrical apparatus powered into life. And the numbness, spreading into every part of Ianson's body until he could no longer feel his arms and legs. And his eyes blurred as if they were filmed over. They probably were, for he was incapable of blinking to clear their lenses.

And as for what little he *could* see, maybe he'd be better off if he couldn't.

There was a bench to one side, where McGowan seemed to be selecting certain tools from a rack on the wall. And if Ianson focussed his vision in the corner there . . . a stove? And cooking utensils? And . . . and what, a blowtorch? With its flickering blue tongue of near-invisible fire beating on some kind of flat-flanged branding iron, until it was beginning to radiate an orange heat of its own?

Finally the small man was finished with his . . . his *preparations,* whatever they were. Returning to Ianson, he began to undress him. And the Inspector managing to gurgle, "Whaaa . . . ? Whaaa . . . ?"

"Aye," McGowan told him, "ye're still firm-limbed, George. No quite the auld dodderer yet, eh? But that's more a problem than a compliment. See, that stuff Ah gave ye will soon enough wear off, and Ah cannae be around a' the time. Man, ye'll soon be mobile again! And we cannae have that, now can we?"

In a while Ianson had been stripped naked. Moving back to the bench and its rack of tools, McGowan called out to him: "They knockout drops Ah put in yere drink: guid, are they no? Mah bosses in Sicily swear by them. And so should ye, George, so should ye. Why, ye'll no feel a thing! Later, perhaps, but no just the noo."

He brought the sinister whirring thing back to the table and showed it to Ianson: the blurred silver-gleaming disc of a surgeon's circular saw! But as McGowan held the terrible thing close and grinned at his victim's frozen expression, so Ianson found himself far more fascinated and horrified by the little vet's face, mirrored in the fan of bright motion:

Oh, it was McGowan all right—old Angus himself—but it wasn't human. Not all human, anyway. Perhaps other than human? Or more than human. Or a lot less:

That gaping mouth, convolute snout, and red-ribbed throat that matched the cores of McGowan's feral yellow eyes! And his teeth—no longer perfect in their shape—but like shards of white glass sprouting from the crimson of his gums! And behind those teeth his tongue: deeply cleft and hideously mobile, and lashing like a crippled lizard in his mouth!

"Now then, see if ye can guess this wee riddle, George," McGowan rasped as he passed from view and the whirring of the saw became a rubbery vibration—*sensed* (or felt?) rather than heard—which seemed to physically move Ianson and blurred his vision more yet. "Where might a man expec' tae find a limbless police Inspector, eh?"

The vibration stopped, and McGowan's face swam back into view . . . except it was spattered red, and the saw was whirring again as it sprayed a fine pink mist all around! "What? Dinnae tell me ye've given in a'ready?" McGowan grinned.

But indeed Ianson had given in, fainting in the moment he recognized the red-dripping thing that McGowan held aloft. So that he never heard the little man's answer to his own riddle, as he went to fetch the white-hot iron, to cauterize the first of the Inspector's stumps:

"Why, where ye *left* him, o' course . . . !"

PART 2

The Other Players

DAHAM DRAKESH

I

T WAS SOMETHING AFTER SIX IN THAT NIGHTMARISH CELLAR IN EDINBURGH, Scotland. But some seven thousand miles away on Tibet's Tingri Plateau it was well past midnight, and the stars frozen in their orbits seemed so close you could pluck them right out of the firmament. So thought Daham Drakesh, Wamphyri, the last Drakul, where he stood tall and skeletally thin on the roof of the so-called "Drakesh monastery," in fact his aerie.

He stood on the high-domed skull of a monolithic head and face carved into the rock in the lee of the gaunt mountainside, and with his red robe fluttering behind him in a breeze off the plateau contemplated or more likely adored the night. But while the yawning—or perhaps shrieking?—face in the rock was huge it was merely a façade, and the gape of its great jaws only the entrance to the cavern complex proper.

As for the warren within: it was a many-layered labyrinth of tunnels, storerooms, accommodations, and . . . *other,* darker, and yet more secretive halls and chambers. These latter places, situated mainly in the lower levels, were forbidden to the majority of the aerie's inhabitants, where only Daham Drakesh himself, the High Priest, as it were, might venture with impunity. Even the most long-lived, most trusted and experienced lieutenants were loath to tread there, and then they trod lightly.

The project—the building of the aerie, by slave labour, by vampire thralls "recruited" from a nearby walled city—had taken fifteen to twenty years in all. Almost seventy years ago it had been finished, the entire complex excavated by hand from the ancient volcanic rock; or Drakesh had taken advantage of and expanded upon the many natural cysts, cavelets, and fissures in the riddled strata. The last of his line, the last Drakul—and by his lights deserving of an aerie of his own—he had personally supervised the work from beginning to end. By which time the once-prosperous walled city from which he'd taken his workforce had been as dead and forbidding as the greater expanse of the plateau itself.

The last Drakul, aye . . .

The last *true* Drakul, certainly, now that his chief lieutenant and bloodson, Mahag, was dead in Scotland by Lykan hands. But Daham had a vampire leech, and his parasite would doubtless have its egg; there could be another Drakul—and another, and another—well, given time. That time was not yet, however, nor would it ever be until the Lykans and Ferenczys were eradicated entirely from the world.

For unlike his forebears, Daham was a firm believer in an immemorial Wamphyri maxim—that anonymity is synonymous with longevity. His ancestors, however, had forgotten or chosen to ignore this simple rule; they had made blood- and egg-sons indiscriminately, so spreading their plague abroad . . . but where were his ancestors now? And where his egg-sire, Egon, last-but-one survivor of an alien parallel world, and brave defender of Wallachia since a time when the horseshoe mountains were known as Dacia? Gone the way of all and even vampire flesh, aye! But not Daham.

And not the Ferenczy Brothers, Anthony and Francesco, now the "Francezcis," grown rich and strong in their Sicilian fortress. Nor the dog-Lord, Radu Lykan, the last true survivor out of olden Starside, who *six hundred years ago* had gone to earth—gone to sleep, hypnotized himself into a state of suspended animation—in some far hyperborean lair.

Which was why Drakesh had sent Mahag and a party of "disciples" into Europe (and eventually into the British Isles) in the first place: to seek out the lair of the sleeping dog-Lord and destroy him before his planned awakening. It had been part of an even grander scheme; Drakesh had seen his opportunity to play *agent provocateur,* to set Radu's people and the Ferenczys against one another in an all-out bloodwar. Then, when all was finished, he would step in and pick off any survivors—all as a prelude to his Final Solution:

The total conquest, the vampirization, of planet Earth!

This had been Drakesh's burning ambition ever since learning of the death of his egg-sire, the so-called "Count" Drakul, all of ninety years ago: to make himself the undead, blood-red Emperor of a vampire world . . . but *not* while his ancestors' enemies were still alive in it. And so for half a century he had used his "emissaries"—the thralls he sent out into the world ostensibly as "ambassadors" of his sect—as spies to seek out other pockets of Wamphyri infestation. That was how he had discovered the Ferenczy Brothers in their Sicilian manse, and the *approximate* location of Radu Lykan in his Cairngorms lair. And so his greater plans had been stalled for a time.

As to the detail of those plans:

The Drakesh Monastery stood close to a junction of many lands, in a place which one hundred years ago had been mainly inaccessible. But distance and cold and inaccessibility, what are these for obstacles? Nothing, to the Wamphyri! Territorialism, on the other hand, is everything! When finally Daham decided to expand, it would be the very simplest thing to send out a handful of chosen lieutenants north into the heart of mysterious Tibet, China and Mongolia; south, into Nepal, India, Burma and Bhutan. And when they were established . . . the rest of the world would be waiting. By now, the first of these outposts—all masquerading under Drakesh's "religious" banner, of course—should be in place. But some twenty-four years ago, even as the last Drakul was making ready his expeditionary forces . . .

. . . The Chinese Army had intervened. And Drakesh had seen at first hand how the Wamphyri are not alone in their lust for territory, even for a land as desolate as this.

Tibetan cities were swept under; monkish orders were brutally suppressed and temples fell; the Dalai Lama himself fled to safety in the west. But the shunned "monastery" on the wind-swept Tingri Plateau survived. For Drakesh had long been aware of the Red Army's feasibility studies in parapsychology—and of its experimental ESP-Unit, the Sino-equivalent of the Soviet Union's and England's E-Branches—and had deliberately courted the attention of its controller, Colonel Tsi-Hong, at his headquarters on Kwijiang Avenue, Chungking.

He had been called to Chungking, been "studied" for over a year, had allowed them to learn what he desired them to know about him: his alleged "philosophy," his longevity, immunity to disease, tenacity for life—but no more than that. And Colonel Tsi-Hong had even visited him here at the monastery, to see for himself the extent of Drakesh's weird abilities in his own environment.

Drakesh had let himself be frozen into a block of ice and had melted it from within. He had demonstrated his night-vision—sharper than Tsi-Hong's, even when the Colonel was using his British nitelite binoculars!—and scarcely needed to point out the benefits of a possible military application. He had fasted, and after a month was fit and well enough to walk out ten miles into the snows to meditate.

Tsi-Hong had brought scientists, geneticists and mutationists, with him. They had taken away samples of Drakesh's sperm, frozen for future experimentation. And ten years ago, finally they had experimented with it, to produce, as it later turned out, monsters! All of which was precisely as Drakesh had warned the Colonel it would be—that Tsi-Hong could not hope to grow orchids in a paddy field without they come up pale and twisted. But if they were tended by caring gardeners, watered by familiar rains, and reared in their natural, their *native* soil . . . ?

The Colonel hadn't listened, not then. For how might this man—even with all his weird talents—father the nucleus of an invincible mutant army in such an inhospitable and unyielding wilderness? But Drakesh was more than a man, he was a Lord of the Wamphyri! By sheer *force of will*, and the laws of alien genetics, he had passed on his instructions to the very sperm that Tsi-Hong's scientists had taken from him.

And in Chungking, his children had been born. Fifteen of them had been deformed, destroyed at birth. But fifteen out of fifty? It scarcely surprised Drakesh; according to Egon Drakul, freak births and grotesque malformations had been common among the Wamphyri of Starside. But as for the others, they had survived—for the time being. And left to his own devices in his aerie, Daham had waited for his prenatal, genetic triggers to trip.

Two years ago they had.

Major Chang Lun, military commander of the army garrison at Xigaze, some ninety minutes away by snow-cat, depending on the weather, had brought him the news. Now he remembered Chang Lun's words, and how the Major (no great admirer of Daham Drakesh) had relished them:

"The last half-dozen escaped. Only eight years old; apparently perfect except for their accelerated growth-rate, but they murdered their keepers and instructors. They not only bit the hands that fed them . . . but fed *on* them! Drinkers of blood, cannibals, homicidal maniacs! In only eight years they'd grown to men, and sexually voracious women! Finally they were hunted down to the last one, and eradicated. But it wasn't easy . . . "

Drakesh had known no pain, no parental anguish, for he had *known* what the outcome would be. Indeed, he'd arranged it. Colonel Tsi-Hong's people had tried to teach his blood-brood to be human—albeit human machines, soldiers, warriors. But the *next* brood would be under their vampire father's instruction, and he would not fail. Nor would *his* warriors belong to China.

Nor were human beings, men, the only kind of warriors . . .

Earlier, before coming up by internal causeways and claustrophobic, flue-like chimneys onto the dome of the skull where it sloped back under the overhanging cliff, Drakesh had paid a visit to the *other* kind of warrior; three of which were waxing, as they'd waxed for five years now, in the vast stone vats of a lower level. For the moment he controlled their growth, delayed their emergence, waited for the right time. But when finally he allowed them to be "born," brought up out of their stone wombs, they would be mindless killing machines such as once were bred by the Wamphyri of Starside. And despite that these were *other,* still they were kin to those anomalies born of his frozen seed in Chungking. For these, too, were his "children," the produce of his undying vampire flesh.

He thought back to his visit:

Down there in the dark of a reeking cavern, Drakesh kept metamorphic protoplasm—the living or undead *material* of his warrior creatures, grown of his own flesh, spittle, sperm, and sweat—in a cell apart. Human flesh, fluids, teeth, and bone, when they are shed from the human body, die. But vampire flesh lives on until it is destroyed or ossifies. The last Drakul's flesh was especially tenacious; its . . . *extruviae* lived on the offal, tripes, skin and bone left over from the aerie's provisioning. But despite that it was mindless, it "knew" its father and Master. Some residual instinct in the alien DNA played the part of a primitive brain.

Drakesh himself fed the—creature? He must; it would be too dangerous for a lieutenant to even attempt it. Entering its cavern cell with a pan of offal, he'd sat down on a flat-topped rocky outcrop in the centre of the dark place, and waited. Dark or light, it was all the same to the vampire Drakesh. His feral eyes turned to blood in the darkness, and lit like lamps in his face. The cave appeared to be empty, but the thing was here, he knew.

At his sandalled feet the earth was loose, churned up. The *Other* was a creature of darkness, as Drakesh himself. It burrowed in the earth as if hiding there—or as if lying in wait? And feeling the first, tentative tremor beneath his feet, Drakesh smiled grimly to himself and kept his thoughts guarded, his identity shielded. It was a grand amusement, a game he liked to play: to tempt the thing, and then to deny it.

And with the pan of vile stinking offal in his lap, in the utter darkness, he sat there smiling and feeling his creature's presence. Then—

—A soft sound, as soil crumbling, behind him. The thing would sneak up on him. Oh so slowly, Drakesh turned his head on its scrawny neck and looked back and down. A mound of dirt was forming, pushing up from the loose, lumpy floor. And in a moment a small eruption, as a leprous grey-green tentacle or pseudopod pulsed up into view. It thickened, rising like some weird beanstalk, and formed a watery, rudimentary eye. What the thing saw—if it "saw" or "recognized" or "remembered" anything at all, in the accepted sense of those words—Drakesh could not say. But what it sensed was food! The food in his lap, or perhaps Drakesh himself.

The tentacle thickened more yet, and Drakesh felt a shuddering in the earth all around. The eye dissolved, reformed into faceless gaping jaws and twin rows of teeth that elongated into fangs even as he watched. And as the dry soil at his feet erupted in a dozen places and put up writhing pseudopod extensions of the thing, caging him in, as it were, so the main "body" or limb-like tentacle swayed towards him, its gaping jaws drooling a yellow, seminal bile.

. . . At which the Master Vampire opened his mind, revealing his identity. And:

Enough! he said. *Thus far, and no further!*

It was as if the thing had been electrocuted. The writhing tentacles were withdrawn, snatched back down into the earth; so rapidly indeed that one of them snapped, spurted bile, and left its tip like some weird blindworm snaking on the floor. Drakesh kicked at it and it quickly wriggled down out of sight, to join up with the greater mass. Behind him, the principal thigh-thick pseudopod slumped, melted down, poured back into its hole, and disappeared with a squelching sound like squashed ripe fruit or a thirsty drain. In a matter of seconds, all that remained was a puff of exhaust stench from the trembling, collapsing mounds, and two or three snaking runs, like panicked mole tracks in the floor. Then all was still again.

And Drakesh still smiling, for he sensed the thing's fear. Which was only right.

Then, upending the pan to slop its vile contents onto the dry earth, he said: *Know me. For I am the Drakul, your Master, and I am kind. You have no sense, knowledge or intelligence. I am all the intelligence you will ever need. You have no direction, but I give you purpose. You may not live without the sustenance I bring you, or die without my approval. But you may yet be more than you are now. Your brothers—grown out of you, as you were grown out of me—are stirring even now in my vats of metamorphism. I have elevated them, and may yet elevate you . . . or destroy you. If you remember little else, you would do well to remember these things.*

He moved to the exit, paused and looked back. *Now feed and be grateful. So be it.*

But as that mindless *octopus*, that living or undead *cancer* of metamorphic tissue oozed up out of the floor and fell like a mantle on its food:

Now hold! Drakesh sent a whiplash thought—and the thing froze at once, as if turned to stone. *And remember: this place is yours. But beyond this place* (he used his sandalled foot to draw a line across the mouth of the cave), *belongs to me. Thus far, and no further . . .*

And then he visited his vats of metamorphism, great baths excavated from the solid bedrock of a nearby cavern as dark and even darker than the place of the protoplasm. They prospered in darkness, his creatures; especially these creatures, which were or would be the *true* warriors. Hybrid monsters waxing in their vats, these were to be the first of Drakesh's many Guardians of the Curfew, securing the dark, shattered city bottoms and dust-bowl valleys in the long worldwide winter of nuclear aftermath, so that survivors of the wars and the vampire plague both could not scathe among his network of rearing aeries in the dangerous hours of daylight.

But in any case, there'd be little enough of daylight in that world. That, too, was part of his plan—it would be the first part—when finally Drakesh was ready to be Lord of All. For what good to set out to conquer a world of light, when the light *itself* must conquer in the end? But in a world where the light is weak, filtering through swirling clouds of radiation, and groping blindly in the rubble of man's greatest works . . . ?

Drakesh was mad, of course, and knew it. But perverse as every Great Vampire before him, he revelled in it. For if the Emperor has the last say, and if his word is law, then who is to say that the rest aren't mad and the Emperor sane? And one day, he would *be* that Emperor!

The vats of metamorphism . . . Drakesh stood at the rim of one such and looked down into it: the gelatinous surface of a liquid womb, surging with long slow ripples. They waxed, his warriors. They could be brought on quickly if need be, or lie here another hundred years just waiting to be born. And as he gazed the ripples quickened to wavelets—as if the inchoate *inhabitant* of the vat sensed him there—and something churned just beneath the surface. Then the outline of a grotesque head appeared, languidly turning, plated with what was as yet a softly translucent, grey-gleaming chitin. And for one brief moment a great vacant eye rolled in the gluey liquid.

"Strong!" Drakesh murmured to himself, nodding his skull head. "And faithful to the death." It was true. Bred from his own metamorphic flesh, from the burrowing thing in the other cave, these creatures would have no mind but his, no thoughts but those he gave them . . .

Then he looked at the trough-like conduits that serviced the vats, rust-coloured runnels carved in the rock, umbilical sluices to feed the freely-given blood of the brethren to the foetal abnormalities being bred here. Blood-beasts!—and that fool of a Colonel in Chungking, Tsi-Hong, would have him breed *human* warriors? Well, so he would—so he *was*—as witness the pregnant Chinese and Tibetan women who worked the stony fields and tended the farm in the walled city. But as for the monastery's priests, its brotherhood:

The Colonel knew nothing of them, that they were Drakesh's children, too. And what of these other warriors waxing in their vats? Why, Tsi-Hong would suffer a stroke and die if he knew of them! He *would* die, aye . . . would have to, even if Drakesh must attend to it himself. For to know of *them* would be to know that the High Priest of this place was not a man; another reason why he had built his aerie here in the first place: because of its seeming austerity, its isolation. Because it was less than welcoming. And because in the main (and apart from the prying eyes of Major Chang Lun, that other fool in Xigaze) Drakesh was left much to his own devices here. So that even when the Colonel and his so-called "scientists" came to visit, which they must eventually, they would only visit the city. For the monastery was a "holy" place, where Drakesh might grant them audience, however briefly, but where they could never expect to lodge. But then, who would want to? The place had not been designed for the comfort of strangers . . .

Turning these and other things over in his pit-deep mind, Drakesh had followed a tortuous route up onto its roof. Now he stood here, face to face with the night under a canopy of brilliant stars, and felt the fluttering of his red robe blown back against his spindly body. One night—soon, perhaps—he must test his talents to the full, shape his body to an airfoil, and fly out from here. For in their time the Drakuls had been grand flyers, and his father, Egon, a pastmaster. To have seen that one, circling like a great black bat over the high battlements of his Transylvanian castle . . . it had been awe-inspiring!

"Yours, in time," the Count had told him. "All yours. Only be my true son and keep my place in my absence, and you too can be Wamphyri!" And sealing the pact, before leaving for England, he had passed on his egg in a fond fatherly kiss. Then, a brief moment of unbearable agony . . . and when Daham had regained consciousness his egg-sire had been gone. And in the space of ten days, Daham, too: fled out of Romania en route for this place, with a handful of Szgany thralls, a pouch of gold, and a parasite leech—the very seed of greatness—growing within him.

Then for a while he had feared his father's revenge. What would the Great Drakul do when he returned to Romania to discover his egg-son flown from his castle and his trust betrayed? And it had been a relief—not to mention a delight!—later to learn of Egon's demise, his true death, at the hands of a vengeful Doctor, a student of such "legends" as vampirism . . .

Again the wind blew against him; he instinctively lifted up his arms and leaned into it, was tempted to launch himself, and denied the temptation. All in good time.

But for now:

The plaintive cry of a yak, thin in the gnawing bite of the plateau's night, was blown to him on the blustery breeze, some three miles from the old walled city. This was what Drakesh had been waiting for. For thoughtful master as he was, he tended the needs of all his creatures and familiars.

And: *Up now, you true flyers,* he sent. *Come!*

And from various cracks and crannies in the carved dome of the aerie— up from their colony in the darker recesses of the labyrinth of caves—the true flyers, they came . . .

With regard to Drakesh, Major Chang Lun had his instructions, his orders— such as they were. "Make periodic visits to the walled city." Stupid orders, ridiculous orders! Yet that was what he had been told to do, *all* he had been told to do: make periodic visits.

But how periodic? Frequently, infrequently, or what? And what to do or to look for when he went there? What, should he fondle the rounded bellies of Drakesh's enforced whores? Compliment them on their successful couplings with that creature? But no, nothing about these things, just that he should visit. *Hah!*

Oh, Chang Lun knew the problem well enough: lack of self-discipline and organization in a largely civilian, self-managing, covert and "experimental" branch of the military. It was that this . . . this so-called "Colonel," Tsi-Hong, in Chungking—this dreary, dreaming metaphysician—did not *himself* know what to do with or about Drakesh and his alleged sect. But on the other hand, it might also mean that Tsi-Hong didn't trust him, or was himself suspicious. In which case Chang Lun might read his orders very differently. Such as:

"Spy on the walled city. See what you can find out about it. But whatever you do, do it carefully, for we've spent time and money here and we don't wish to alienate this foreign charlatan in case he really does have something we can use." Chang Lun would know exactly how to interpret such orders as these. Much as he was interpreting them now.

He and his driver had come out from Xigaze a little after 10:00 P.M. The weather forecast had been good; bitterly cold, of course, but clear with little or no wind, and no snow forecast. Chang Lun's official visits (he had been obliged to devise his own roster) took place once every six weeks. This was not one of those.

The driver he used was his usual man, a Corporal, whose name didn't matter. But he knew every crevasse and boulder en route, and that was important. Over terrain as rugged as this, and at night, it would be only too easy to make a fatal mistake. Some of the cracks in the earth around here seemed to go down forever! But the snow-cat had given them no trouble, and they had got here safely a few minutes after midnight.

"Here" was a spot in the lee of outcropping rocks on the south-facing slope of a hillside to the west of the old walled city. As an observation point, the place was ideal. A climb of two hundred feet from where they'd secured and camouflaged the cat, and snug behind a wall of rocks they'd built during previous visits, Chang Lun and his driver could even brew up army-rations tea on a disposable stove, slice canned meat or cheese onto bread, and make a meal of sorts. And from here a man with a good pair of nitesites could keep watch not only on the ancient city, its gates and wall, but even the leering façade of the Drakesh Monastery three miles away across the valley.

The one drawback was the awesome cold. Even the best winter warfare clothing couldn't keep it out. It would find a way into your bones, and chew on them like a bad cramp. The strong tea helped, but not much. So that time and again Chang Lun had told himself to hell with this! This would be the last time he came out here, no matter his hatred for the unnatural, perverted bastard who ran the monastery.

Hatred: a strong word, and one that Chang Lun didn't use lightly. But he had hated Daham Drakesh from the first time he saw him and all the time since. And being Tsi-Hong's messenger, as it were, he'd had more than enough contact with the man. But to call him a man . . . well, as far as Chang Lun was concerned, even that was a matter for conjecture. And he remembered Drakesh as he had seen him on some four or five (but still far too many) previous occasions.

The physical appearance—the very *presence* of Drakesh—had never failed to impress Chang Lun, but never favourably. It wasn't just his height (six and a half feet, as compared to the Major's sixty-eight inches), but an over-all sense of something alien about him, complemented by grotesque distortions of human shape and proportion. Thin to the point of emaciation, he nevertheless managed to convey the impression that his pipestem body contained an awesome strength. His hands and feet were freakishly long and tapering, their sharply pointed digits tipped with thick yellow nails hooked into claws. His shaven skull was thin at the front and lantern-jawed, long at the back and bulbous as the head of an insect on his scrawny neck.

But his eyes . . . ah, his eyes! They were the worst or perhaps strangest of Drakesh's features. In daylight—what little ever filtered through into the monastery—they looked glassy, even transparent, as if all natural colour had been leeched out of them. But in the dark or semi-dark of the monastery's corridors and caverns, they were as luminous and yellow as molten sulphur. Their gaze was literally penetrating; turned upon a man, they seemed to stare right through him, as if their target were more ephemeral than Drakesh himself. And when they smiled . . .

. . . Chang Lun shuddered where he leaned on the low wall of piled stones and gazed through his night-vision binoculars. He was cold outside from the sub-zero temperature, but colder in his soul from letting himself dwell too long on Daham Drakesh. Even the simple mechanical act of focusing his glasses on the monastery's leering-face façade, to bring it closer, seemed in a way to draw Drakesh closer, too. And Chang Lun knew this sensation—this feeling of dread—that in keeping watch on Drakesh he had given the man power to keep watch on him. Almost as if his binoculars worked in both directions, so that while he looked out, some unseen Other looked in . . .

"That yak," said Chang Lun's driver, causing the Major to start. "He's noisy all of a sudden." The Corporal's binoculars were trained on the city.

Chang Lun thought to reprimand the man (mainly because he had been caused to start, not because his driver had forgotten the usual courtesies, the privileges of rank) but let it pass. And in any case, it was too cold for all that customary bowing and scraping. Back in the barracks they were Major and non-commissioned officer—"Sir," and, "You! Get your arse over here!"—but out here they were just two men in the cold waste.

"The cold," Chang Lun replied. "Tethered out there in the place of bones, full in the face of the wind blowing round the base of the township's wall, you would cry out, too!"

"Why have they put him there?" The Corporal wondered out loud. "Simply to die in the cold?"

The Major shrugged, kept his glasses focused on the monastery. Was that some kind of motion on the roof of the place? White smoke or steam going up? And was that a twig-like figure up there, obscured in a swirl of—well, what-ever it was? For all the cold, still Chang Lun's skin crawled. Absentmindedly, he answered his driver's question:

"Maybe the animal was diseased, infectious. They've separated it from the herd, that's all. Obviously it's what they do with all suspect beasts: tether them in the boneyard to die."

"Well, it's true there has been some disease in the local animals," the Corporal agreed, "but I was one of the drivers on several of the details when those animals were driven out here. They all seemed healthy enough to me—not that I'm an expert. But they were the best for many miles around. They always are. Only the best for the Drakesh township . . . "

"Sir!" the Major snapped, suddenly irritated. "Call me 'sir' when you speak to me."

"Yes, sir!"

But what he had said was true, and it had been an inordinately large number of animals at that. All for the fifty women in the ancient city? Well, possi-bly, since half of them were pregnant and well on their way to spawning. When Chang Lun thought of Drakesh siring children—especially out of criminals such as those women he'd been given—"spawning" was the only word that came read-ily to mind.

As for "the boneyard," the name that the Major's driver had given that place outside the city wall, when they'd first discovered it on a previous visit, it was simply that: a pile of bones littered around a tethering post. There had been one occasion when some of the women were out gathering the grisly remains, to grind them down for fertilizer, Chang Lun suspected. The thin soil of their farm could use the sustenance.

"But he—I mean the yak—is *very* noisy now." the Corporal uneasily, un-necessarily stated. For Chang Lun could hear it well enough for himself: the neighing bleat of an animal in distress. "He's kicking, jumping, trying to free himself!"

Silently cursing his gloved hands, Chang Lun focused his own binoculars just a fraction more—not on the city but the monastery—and suddenly his view of the domed roof, the carved skull, sprang up in much clearer definition. And there *was* a figure up there, yes, antlike at this distance but very definitely there. But doing what? The stick-figure's arms seemed raised in . . . supplication? Or invocation? Then Chang Lun felt his mouth go dry at the thought that he knew that figure, that he had recognized the skeletal frame of Drakesh himself.

And as for the cloud of "smoke" (not smoke at all, as the Major now saw, but something else, something a lot more solid): its spiral around the distant figure on the roof of the monastery was rising, widening, behaving far more sentiently, as its members headed in a certain direction—straight for the an-cient city, its walls, possibly this very vantage point!

The yak's nerve-rending shrieks had now risen to an almost human pitch. And the Corporal gasped, "That creature must soon strangle itself! See how it leaps, kicks, hauls on its tether. Surely you were right, sir. The thing is mad or diseased—or something is tormenting it, driving it out of its mind!"

But Chang Lun only thought: *Or the yak knows, senses, is somehow aware, of something that we can't possibly understand.* Or maybe the Major did understand. And trying to hold his binoculars more firmly in suddenly trembling hands, he followed the line of flight of the weirdly purposeful cloud; not heading his way at all, or only roughly so. But very definitely heading for the boneyard.

"Kill the stove," he husked at once, as he felt the short hairs stiffening at the back of his neck.

"Eh?" The Corporal didn't move; fascinated by the frantic activity of the yak, he couldn't look away.

"I said kill the fucking stove!" the Major elbowed him in the ribs. "Put the fire out. And do it quietly—do everything very quietly!" His last few words were a hiss, as he fixed his line of sight on the leading flyers. And without knowing why—or not exactly why—Chang Lun found himself terrified. Not of the flyers so much as the *fact* of them, that they were here at all, and the fact that Daham Drakesh had . . . what, called them up? Up from the depths of his blasphemous monastery.

Flyers, yes: great bats! The way they swooped and flitted, they could only be. But *white* bats, albinos, and by the Major's lights far larger than any bat has a right to be. With or without binoculars, these things were just too damn big! Chang Lun knew something about zoology, was fairly sure that these monsters were way out of place here. They were like the giant *Desmodus* bats of middle and South America, and . . .

. . . And *Desmodus* was a bloodsucker, wasn't he? A damned vampire, yes!

Meanwhile, the Corporal had killed the stove's chemical fire. A final wisp of smoke—real smoke—went up, which he dispersed by flapping his arms. Then he returned to his place at the wall of stones, took up his glasses, and quickly focused them on the tethered yak. But in a hoarse, uneven whisper Chang Lun warned him: "It seems to me you're a sensitive man. That being so, don't watch."

"Don't watch, sir?" What could the Major mean?

Chang Lun himself didn't know just what he meant. But he had this idea in his head and it wouldn't go away. He would do anything if it would, but it wouldn't.

And now the Corporal was training his binoculars in the other direction, to see if he could spot whatever it was that Chang Lun was concerned about. The Major felt him give a jerk as he too saw the bats. "What the devil . . . ?"

And Chang Lun nodded and answered. "The devil, indeed!"

Both men shrank down, huddling low behind their wall of stones, staring a moment at each other, wide-eyed and fearful. And as their eyes went back to the yak, each felt his own private pang of relief to note that the poor animal had given up the ghost; or if it wasn't dead, that it had collapsed in exhaustion. And as the stream of great albinos flew overhead not too far away, for a moment they heard the leathery flutter of membrane wings.

While in the ancient city . . .

. . . Lights were coming on. Dim lanterns were being lit in windows in the walls and towers, and pale faces were flitting as eerily as the bats themselves from window to window. Drakesh's women had come to . . . to what?

"They're watching!" The Corporal whispered, as if in answer to the Major's unspoken question. "Those women are going to watch!" He was omitting his "sirs" again, but his superior officer no longer cared. Chang Lun knew that no less than himself, his driver had guessed what was about to happen. Anywhere else, it would be . . . *unthinkable* to even think such things, but not in this place. Here in this place—which both men had come to loathe—it seemed the only thing *to* think.

And those women: they way they ghosted about the city smiling their sick smiles. But what could they have to smile about in a place like this? Oh, they were under their master's spell, no doubt about it. But what sort of spell? Criminals, convicts they might well be, but what could have happened to them—to their spirit, their humanity—that they could watch something like this?

The column of great bats spiralled down, plummeted out of the night sky to their unprotesting target, fell as forcefully as stones and clamped like leeches to the head, neck, body and limbs of the yak where it lay shuddering on its bony deathbed. They clustered to it, turned the grey mass of it white . . . and then red!

Red in a moment! From the blood that escaped their ravenous mouths, or spurted from arteries bitten through!

"Sir!" the Corporal choked, turning his glasses away.

"Didn't I tell you so?" Chang Lun growled. "That bastard in his bloody nightmarish 'monastery,' he breeds things. Even as he's breeding things now, in those hellish women. I suspect he even bred these bats! And for no good purpose, you can stake your life on it." With which it suddenly dawned on him that in being here they may already have staked their lives on it.

But no, that hideous travesty of a man on the roof of the monastery didn't know they were here, didn't know what they had seen. Viciously, the Major swung his glasses back to their original angle and quickly realigned them on the dome of the carved skull. The stick-figure was still there, and Chang Lun supposed he'd be looking in this direction. And:

You can't see me, Chang Lun thought to himself, *but I can see you. And I promise you this, Daham Drakesh: that if the day ever dawns when I can bring you down, then I'll do it. And with pleasure!*

Then . . . the air was suddenly electric! In the next moment Chang Lun remembered that earlier feeling: that weird sensation of some Other peering back at him through his own glasses. Utterly impossible, of course, and yet—

It was as if the figure on the dome of the monastery grew large in a split-second, as if Drakesh expanded in Chang Lun's binoculars—and in his mind—to a giant! They stood face to face, and Drakesh's eyes were blood red, fuelled in their pupils by the molten-sulphur fires of hell.

Aha! said a voice in the Major's mind, and there could be no denying that he recognized it immediately and knew its owner. *And so you spy on me. A mistake, Chang Lun, for I too have my spies, my watchdogs; but greedy dogs, such as they are, and ever hungry. Eh? What? You think I am threatening you? Ah, no! For my dogs are obedient and would never harm you—not without my permission. Indeed I shall have them see you home, back to Xigaze. And when you report the result of this, your latest mission, to Tsi-Hong in Chungking, be sure to give him my best regards . . .* With which Drakesh's sinister, sibilant telepathic "voice" rapidly devolved to a peal of fading laughter, and was gone. Likewise the spindly red-robed figure on the dome of the carved skull.

"Sir . . . *sir!*"

Chang Lun snapped out of it, and knew his driver had been yelling in his ear for several long seconds. He closed his gaping mouth, blinked his eyes and said, "Eh? What?"

"Sir, a wind is coming up, blowing stronger now. It might bring a little snow. And those bats are on the move."

The Major scarcely needed his binoculars to know that the Corporal was right. He could feel the wind and see the albinos rising up in a spiral from their feast. Also, the dim lanterns in the windows of the ancient city had been smothered, put out, so that now the place resembled nothing so much as some vast, sprawling necropolis; in which instinctive or automatic analogy Chang Lun was very nearly correct, except a necropolis is a city of the *truly* dead.

"Quickly now," the Major husked. "It's time we were gone from here."

The Corporal needed no urging; he was on his feet, making to collect up the stove and any other evidence of their having been here. But: "Leave it be," Chang Lun told him. "It doesn't make any difference. They'll know we've been here anyway." And the moment he'd said it he knew it was so, that he hadn't just been dreaming it when he'd heard Drakesh speaking in his mind. What was more, he knew that Drakesh's "threat"—to have him escorted back to Xigaze—hadn't been an idle one.

"Those bats," the Major's driver muttered. He was directly ahead of Chang Lun where they went sliding and bumping down the frozen slope of the hillside. "They seemed to be heading—"

"—This way," the Major cut him short. "I know."

And then they *both* knew, for certain, as the air overhead thrummed with the *whup, whup, whup* of leathery wings.

"Oh mother! Dear father!" Fearfully, the Corporal looked skywards, tripped, went tumbling head over heels to the bottom. But by the time Chang Lun was down he was up on his feet again, stripping the camouflaged canopy from the snow-cat.

"Easy! *Easy!*" Chang Lun told him, with a lot more bravado than he felt, as his driver yanked again and again on the starter. "Don't flood the fucking thing!"

But soon the cat was ticking over, then purring into life, and the two men were clambering aboard as if the vehicle were a life-raft and their ship was going down behind them.

"The bats! The bats!" The Corporal moaned, and slewed the cat dangerously, tiltingly, as he turned her about.

"For the last time, take it *easy!*" the Major yelled. "Do as I say or I'll shoot you and drive the fucking thing myself! The bats won't attack us. They'll just . . . follow us along the way." *At least, that is, I mean . . . if that bastard Drakesh is good as his word.*

Great white bats—two or three dozen of them, and two and a half feet across wing-tip to wing-tip—flitted, swooped, and side-slipped directly overhead. Their excited staccato chittering was clearly audible; they communicated with each other. And perhaps with someone else? For certainly that someone had communicated with them!

"But what in all that's . . . what the hell are they *doing?*" the Corporal shrilled, when a pair of flapping pink-eyed nightmares danced for a moment or so in front of his windshield and caused him to swerve. "What do they *want?*"

"Nothing," the Major shouted back, and prayed that he was right. "They're just seeing us away from here, that's all. They . . . they're our escort." Which sounded like something a madman might say, but Chang Lun believed it anyway. He couldn't rationalize it, but he had to believe it. For his sanity's sake.

And apparently he was right.

For even after it started snowing, still he and the Corporal knew that the bats were with them. They could feel, sense, occasionally sight them through the slanting, stinging, softly hissing snow, and when the wind was right they could even hear the *whup* of membranous wings in the whirling air all around . . .

Something less than two hours later—when the snow stopped at last and the wind eased off, and the dully flickering lights of Xigaze and the garrison blazed on the horizon—their "escort" fell back, seemed eaten up in distance and darkness.

Then, finally, Major Chang Lun felt he could begin breathing again. He'd been breathing, of course, but it scarcely felt like it. Likewise his Corporal driver: he, too, eased up a little and relaxed his tense, nervous grip on the controls.

Which was entirely the wrong thing to do.

They came up from nowhere, as if out of the very earth, a white, shrilling, sentient cloud of them. The bats! The vampire bats! Pink-eyed and needle-toothed, with their convoluted noses wrinkled back, flat to their wet-gleaming leathery faces. Three of them whirled, hurled themselves in a suicide attack directly at the windshield.

The screen was of clear plastic which cracked on the first impact, splintered on the second, flew apart as the third great bat came right through it in a welter of gore-spattered fur and torn leather, straight into the driver's face! Two more hit the Corporal from the side, while behind him another pair attacked the Major. Their massed impact was such that the cat rocked on its skis and teetered, so that the driver must yank on his handlebars in an attempt to straighten up. But at the same time he was fighting for his life as the great bats clung to him, wrapped membrane wings about him . . . and bit!

One of them was biting at his face, his lips, nose, eyes! He screamed and let go the controls, heard, *Crack!—Crack!—Crack!—*like explosions in his ear, as the Major sobbed, cursed and pumped shot after shot into the things that were battening on him, then rammed the snout of his gun into the white-throbbing creatures clustered to his driver's head and upper body and blew them away, too.

But the snow-cat had slewed aside, and now its riders saw where the bats had come from, that indeed they had come up out of the earth: up from the chasm that yawned directly ahead!

The Corporal cried out and yanked on the handlebars. The cat slewed again, then toppled sideways in a seeming slow-motion. And over and over the wildly revving machine went—and down and down—with Chang Lun and his man hanging on for dear life, and for death, all the way to the bottom.

But in the seconds before they hit:

Farewell, Chang Lun, said that faint, mocking voice in the Major's mind. *You'll go no more a-spying for Tsi-Hong, I fear! Oh, ha-ha-ha!*

"Liar! Liar!" the Major sobbed, still twirling.

And coldly: *Always, Chang Lun,* the voice agreed. *Always!*

With which the Major's world went out in a single tearing shattering roar that lasted the blink of an eye . . .

II

THE FRANCEZCIS

THE RITUAL AT LE MANSE MADONIE HAD BEEN SIMPLE AND SOLEMN. THE funereal weather—a damp, blustery breeze off the Tyrrhenian, that snatched the women's veils this way and that, first obscuring or masking their pale sad faces in black net, then framing them in stark, monochrome relief— had seemed entirely in keeping. Frequently disturbed, but never quite disrupted, by Julio Sclafani's agony—his pitiful but entirely forgivable bouts of wailing, and wringing of sweaty hands—so far the interment of his daughter had gone smoothly, entirely as planned. Its organization had been immaculate in every detail.

But then, in the company of such esteemed fellow mourners, in such a place, and since the Francezci Brothers were themselves responsible for the arrangements, perhaps this was only to be expected. It had been out of necessity, of course—in order to avoid untoward complications—that the brothers had settled for stark simplicity. And thus far no complications had arisen.

Only at the end—when gaunt Francezci bearers in black-banded top hats and tails took up the young, beautiful and now tragically deceased Julietta in her box, to carry her from the courtyard into the darkly shadowed manse—only then did her father, Julio, lose control completely.

"I must see her!" he cried, staggering forward, squeezing his way into the house proper through the varnished Mediterranean pine doors, and putting himself in the path of the bearers. "I must!" he implored. "I've seen her but once in a whole year! But now, this one last time, I *must!* Oh, God! Her sweet mother in heaven would never forgive me, if I let her go to her grave without seeing her one last time!"

"Julio!" The Francezcis were on him at once, each holding fast to an arm. The rest of the mourners had been left outside, and the doors were now closed on them. "Julio, Julio!" Anthony Francezci said again, shaking his head and sighing. "Please try to believe me, we *know* how it is for you, how it must be. Julietta, in these—what, four years? But the time has flown!—she has become a little sister to us. Why, just look at Francesco! How gaunt, how sad! No one was more fond of her."

"But . . . " Julio turned to him, clung to him, fat, weak and trembling against Tony's lean, implacable strength.

"*But* . . . this is Le Manse Madonie!" Francesco Francezci's voice was harder, and Julio glanced at him through red-rimmed, tears-blurred eyes. "It is what it is and what it has been for generations," Francesco went on, but in a gentler tone now. "A private place, Julio. And your Julietta had become like one of us. You could even say she was . . . *family*. Which in turn makes you family. That being so, please don't make things any harder for us than they already are."

"But to see her. Only to *see* her this last time. Why not? I beg of you! Before she goes down to the vaults?"

The brothers looked at him, then at each other, and came to a mutual, unspoken agreement. Then, letting Sclafani disengage, they nodded silent instructions to the six bearers where they stood patiently waiting. And:

"On the long table there," Tony told them. "But be gentle, be careful. Don't . . . disturb her."

The great hall was suitably still and shadowy. The walls with their arched-over recesses or entranceways into secondary rooms—the stairways, fixtures, furniture and hangings—were barely visible in the gloom. If Julio Sclafani noticed this at all it was only to find it well in keeping. He scarcely remembered that on the two or three occasions when he'd been invited to visit Julietta, Le Manse Madonie had always been gloomy. He couldn't know that it always was, or *why* it was that no chink of sunlight was ever allowed to filter in here, where even the sullen light of Sicilian winters was held at bay behind thick, dusty curtains . . .

As the draped box was lowered to the polished table, Julio gave a strangled cry and stumbled forward. The brothers at once got in his way and again took his arms. "We . . . we supposed you would want to see her." Tony explained. "That is why the coffin has a window of glass. But Julio, you *know* the circumstances of her death . . . "

"A wasting disease, yes," the fat man moaned. "A . . . what did you call it? A pernicious anaemia. 'Pernicious,' indeed! A dreadful, terrible, murdering anaemia, more like! Your private doctor, the very best, could do nothing."

"All true," Tony nodded. "Which means that . . . well, that she isn't the Julietta you knew. This thing was like a cancer. It ate at her. It had its own peculiar odour that can't be . . . masked. And Julietta may not be touched, or kissed. Hence the glass."

"But . . . I *will* know her?"

"Of course. Our only wish was that you should remember her as she was."

"Still, I must see her."

"So be it," said the brothers together, and released him.

Sclafani wobbled to the head of the coffin, slid back the grey silk cover, looked down on the face beneath the glass. It was dim; the glass was touched with a trace of dust; its sheen obscured the features of the pallid face within the frame. Sobbing, Sclafani clung to the edge of the table for support, and blinked his puffy eyes to improve their focus. And as the Francezcis silently took up flanking positions beside him, his Julietta's beloved features seemed to swim up at him. Being short, his face was quite close to hers; on the other hand, the Francezci Brothers were like trees, shading him and Julietta both.

Still, Julio could see her fairly clearly now. And though her eyes were of course closed, she was—

"—Smiling?" The word trembled from his lips.

"The pain-killers," Francesco murmured. "At the end there was . . . oh, a deal of pain. Mercifully, we were able to relieve some of it. But at the *very* end, your Julietta spoke of you . . . and smiled! Ah, yes, she died with a gentle smile on her face, Julio, just thinking thoughts of you!"

Sclafani's eyes had made the adjustment now. They saw more clearly. But in all honesty, he couldn't say he liked what they saw. "Thinking of me? But . . . this smile is like a grimace!"

"The pain," Francesco said again. "Despite the medication, she . . . " And he paused. "But she hid it well."

Sclafani kissed the glass over her lips; his tears fell on the dusty surface, acting like tiny magnifying glasses to blur and diminish the detail. "Just four short years ago, she looked like a girl!" he groaned. "She was—she *is*—a girl! Yet now she looks like some strange pale woman."

"Four years," Tony repeated him. "She grew up, Julio. Your Julietta grew up, and was changed . . . "

"Changed, yes. So waxy and sunken in." Sclafani hugged the top of the box.

"Depleted," said Tony. "The anaemia—like a cancer."

"And yet her lips are full and red!"

"And all wasted," Francesco put an arm around the grieving Sclafani's shoulders. "Our efforts, I mean. Still, you have the comfort of knowing she never shamed you, never knew a man."

"A comfort? It scarcely comforts me, Francesco! Where are my grandchildren? And would it have been so shameful? What, in this day and age? Her mother *loved* to love, even a man unworthy as myself! But Julietta, she is untried, denied such knowledge. Wasted, you are right. To be beautiful, and never have a chance to give of your beauty!"

"There, there," said Francesco, clasping his shoulders and turning him away, while Tony slid the silk back into position.

Sclafani struggled for a moment, then finally surrendered to the inevitable. "But I will be able to visit?"

"This place, where she spent her last years?" (Francesco seemed unsure.) "Well, we shall see. To walk where she walked, in the grounds of Le Manse? Perhaps. But the vaults? Alas, no. Not even now. The Francezcis are there, Julio: private in life and death both. We were ever proud, and proud to have Julietta, too. We had hoped that you would be proud knowing she is here. Perhaps in this we have elevated ourselves, but . . . "

"No, no!" the other protested. "I didn't mean to—"

" . . . But if so, then we elevate Julietta, too. Not to mention your good self."

"You have been . . . too kind to me and mine throughout."

Francesco saw him to the door and outside into the courtyard, hugged him, shook his hand and gave him over into Mario, their chauffeur's care. He watched him driven slowly away in the stretch limo. By then the other mourners, mainly Franceczi people, had already dispersed.

Then Francesco returned to where his brother was speaking to the bearers.

"Quickly, now," Tony told them. "Take her down to the pit and wait there for us. But don't go in until we're there." And as they left he turned to Francesco. "That all went very well."

"Hmmm? Do you think so?" Francesco seemed distant, absent-minded; his thoughts were elsewhere.

"What?" Tony frowned at him. "But what's this? Don't tell me you're actually missing her!"

The other stood straighter. "Perhaps, perhaps not. I don't know. But one thing is for sure: she's sleeping the last sleep, the Sleep of Change. My fault, I know. But whether I 'miss' her or not isn't relevant. What is relevant is that we can't afford another Ferenczy in the house—and certainly not a Lady!"

"Good!" Tony nodded, and his eyes were feral in the gloom and glowed red in their cores. "For a moment there . . . why, I thought you'd gone soft on me!"

Francesco smiled, however grimly. "Soft? Ah, no. Julietta was just . . . so *accessible.* Having her here made it all so very easy. I suppose I'm basically lazy, that's all. But miss her? I shall miss fucking her, be sure. She was so very good at it!"

"But then, you taught her," Tony chuckled.

"Well yes, there's that, of course!" Francesco laughed.

With which, they followed the bearers down to the pit . . .

In the lowest levels of Le Manse Madonie—in the very bowels of the place, mainly a natural cavern, but in part carved from the bedrock—the mouth of the pit was like a well, with walls of old hewn masonry three feet high. Indeed, it had been a well in the early days of Le Manse, many hundreds of years ago, when it had drawn water from an old cyst in the volcanic rock all of eighty feet deeper still.

Now the Franceczis stood at the rim of the pit and paused to consider what they were about. And quietly, a little uncertainly, Tony said: "Our Julietta—or rather, *your* Julietta—is hardly pure."

"Pure?" Francesco shrugged. "Who is, these days? Show me a good-looking virgin in Palermo over sixteen years old, and I'll show you a liar!"

"Well, true," his brother mused. "But still, you know how he likes them. And she's not even clean—not scrupulously—as he is used to them."

"What?" Francesco was short-tempered at the best of times, and this wasn't the best of times. "What are you suggesting? We should have purged her, perhaps? Put her through the usual ritual and chanced waking her up prematurely? I mean, in case you hadn't noticed, brother, our Julietta—or mine, if you will— is Wamphyri! She could do severe damage! I'm not worried about us, you and I, but the men, our lieutenants. The last thing we want is to lose someone at this stage of the game."

"What stage of the game is that?" Tony was suddenly pessimistic; unusual, for he was normally the optimist. "Has there been some subtle yet remarkable change in the last two or three years? Did I miss something?" . . . Pessimistic, and sarcastic.

"Yesss!" his brother hissed, rounding on Tony, glaring at him from eyes as red as hell. "The time has changed, narrowing down to *his* fucking time! Radu Lykan's time! And the grotesque *thing* in this bloody pit has changed: Angelo, our dear father, more unreliable, and more demanding than ever. And our fortune has been depleted, which we still haven't done anything about. And worldwide the Families are . . . they're *laughing* behind our backs! I don't know about you, but I can feel it! And since we started asking questions about this British E-Branch, and this Harry Keogh, and this fucking Alec Kyle—questions about *dead* men, for fuck's sake—the CIA, and the KGB, and everyone else we used to use don't want to know us! Then there's this Drakul 'sect' in England and Scotland, and our man's report more than three months old now; and we still haven't done anything about *that* either! *What?* And does it amuse you to ask has something *fucking* changed?"

"Calm down, calm down!" Tony sighed. "All right, so things have changed. But that's not what I meant. Or maybe it is. It's just that I'm sick of the inactivity . . . of that and everything else: all the things you mentioned. Yes, that's right: I'm just as sick and frustrated as you! And as if that weren't enough, I now have to talk to *him,* try to get some sense out of *him!*"

"Huh!" Francesco grunted, at least part-mollified. "Well, I have to admit I don't envy you that. But that's the way it is. He won't even acknowledge me!"

"Which is why I wondered if giving him Julietta will do us any good."

"Then stop wondering," Francesco answered. "Instead, just ask yourself this: what good will she do us undead? For that's what she'll be if we let her wake up—*and* Wamphyri! So then, it's settled: she's Angelo's. And all that remains—"

"—Is the bargaining," Tony nodded. "Yes, I know."

"And anyway, it's probably best this way." In a rare show of *camaraderie*—a show, at least—Francesco actually put his arm across his brother's shoulder, which Tony at once shrugged off.

"What's best?" he asked, suspiciously.

"That you're the one Angelo talks to. I mean, he was ever difficult, our father, but never more so than now. Let's face it: my temper is too short; I haven't the patience to . . . well, *play* with him. But you were always good at his word games. And anyway, he likes you."

"Huh!" Tony grunted. "That's a compliment, is it?" Plainly he was nervous; the way he licked his lips, kept glancing into the deeps of the well, or more properly the pit. "That's supposed to make me feel better about it, eh?"

Francesco narrowed his eyes and said, "What is it? You're afraid? But what of? I mean, this is hardly the first time that you've—"

"You just don't understand, do you?" Tony glanced at him, cutting him short. "No, this isn't the first time, or even the tenth or twentieth that I've had to talk to him like this. But recently . . . every time is worse than the last time. Don't you realize that when I go into Angelo Ferenczy's mind, or let him into mine, the kind of jeopardy I place myself in?" And before Francesco could answer, if he would: "Yes, you're right: I was always closer to him. I was able to 'get on' with him, and he seemed to be genuinely 'fond' of me. But do you think I don't worry about that, too? Well, I do, Francesco. I do . . . "

"Eh? How, worried?" Francesco frowned. "That he could harm you in some way? But if there's one of us he might want to harm it would have to be me. I honestly believe he hates me! And anyway, he can't hurt either one of us from this pit."

"Well, at least you're consistent," Tony sighed patiently, shaking his head at what he obviously saw as the other's naivety. "For more than three hundred years you've never thought of him as anything other than a monster in a pit."

"Wrong!" Francesco answered. "I've also thought of him as our father—and I've loathed the idea that we were spawned of *that* thing! But what happened to him was bound to happen. Why, even his twin was a monster, smothered at birth and burned as a freak. And do you know what has preyed on my mind these centuries, brother? It shouldn't be too hard to guess. That we are of the same flesh! And is it waiting for us, too? Given time, will our metamorphism also run rampant, reducing us to so much lapping, filthy protoplasm?"

Now Tony gripped his arm. "Almost!" he snapped. "For a moment there you almost had it. But you left out one very important word. So much lapping, filthy, *sentient* protoplasm! And one other thing, Francesco: the fact that he's Wamphyri!"

"Eh?" Again Francesco's eyes were wide, puzzled, staring.

"And what are the traits of the Wamphyri?"

The other's expression changed at once. "A word game," he sneered. "This has to be a word game! Why, you're as bad as he is! We can't even hold a simple conversation without . . . "

"Indulge me," Tony insisted. "The traits of the Wamphyri?"

Francesco shook himself loose. "Very *well*, if it's the only way we can go on from here. According to that thing in his pit, the Wamphyri were known for their greed, lust, lies and territorialism."

"And?"

"Eh?"

"And their *tenacity!*" Tony snarled. "Now do you see? It's what I meant when I said you almost had it. For you pointed out that he had 'spawned' us—without mentioning that we were only his bloodsons!"

Francesco shook his head. "I still don't underst—"

"—He still has his leech!" Tony cut him short.

"His leech? But by now . . . surely that, too, has devolved to so much—?"

"No, for if that were so he simply wouldn't want to go on. His leech *is* his tenacity, the only thing that keeps him going. And his leech still has its egg!"

"Is that what concerns you? But you are *already* Wamphyri! Angelo's leech or egg can't, couldn't possibly, get into you."

"I know, I know," Tony was pale now, paler than ever. "Yet just recently, whenever I'm obliged to talk to him—like now—I get this feeling that he's . . . waiting."

"Waiting?"

"Waiting, planning, watching! Don't ask me what for. I'll tell you something, though: I think we were damned lucky to get him down into this place in the first place."

"*Huh!*" Francesco snorted. "He was the lucky one. A hundred and more times we could have done away with him during the final years of his devolution. And for that matter, we could do it even now! Send down a fifty-gallon drum of kerosene, a stick of dynamite . . . no more Angelo Ferenczy to get concerned about!"

"And no more oracle," Tony answered him. "No more power-base. That's the logic of the defeatist, brother. Ten minutes ago you started raving when I asked you what had changed. All right, I was being flippant. But you pointed out that the Families were starting to laugh at us behind our backs; also that various intelligence agencies are backing off from us. But how much more rapidly would they desert us without Angelo?"

"Except for one small detail," Francesco answered, "your logic is impeccable. That small detail being that we're *already* 'without' him! When was the last time our father uttered a single useful word? Or one that made any kind of sense? He's gone, Tony, slipped beyond the pale. He's no longer of any use to us. Well, except on this one occasion, as a means of disposal."

"And possibly as our mindspy on whatever it is that's happening out there."

"Yes. One last chance to pin-point Radu Lykan's lair, and learn the hour of his resurgence. One last opportunity to scry on this damned Drakul's Tibetan aerie and maybe learn something of his plans. And if we're lucky—if Angelo feels like co-operating, assuming he's capable of it—one final glimpse, into our own futures."

"The first two, maybe," Tony was thoughtful now. "But not the last. How can we hope to learn that from him if he isn't a part of that future? He won't advise us to bring about his own demise . . . "

Francesco's jaws cracked open and his eyes lit in a monstrous grin. "And at last I see what a fool I was to have doubted you!" he said.

"Oh?" Tony looked at him cooly.

"You *have* considered putting an end to him!"

"Out of pity, if nothing else."

"What? But a moment ago you feared him!"

"And are the two so incompatible? Fear and pity? He is our father."

"He's a monster!"

"And are we any less?"

"You *are* playing word games!" Francesco flapped his arms.

"We go round in circles," Tony's tone was sharper; he was done with this now. "We've talked too much, said too much. And we've done it in the wrong place."

"What, do you think he might have been eavesdropping? And if so, that he would have understood? And then that he'd care? Nothing matters to him anymore; well, except that he raves and babbles to his victims, the minds that share his hell."

Tony's answer was to put a finger to his lips, glance once into the pit, and whisper, "Well, he isn't babbling now . . . "

It was true: the psychic aether seemed breathlessly still. But the pit's miasma—the breath or *effluvium* of the thing it contained—went up as ever: a stinking mist that vaporized on contact with the electrified iron-mesh of the hinged cover that sealed the throat of the old well.

For long seconds the brothers looked at each other, until Francesco said, "I don't envy you, as I said. But . . . "

" . . . It has to be done, I know," Tony finished it for him. "And yes, I have thought of doing away with him. For after all, he's the only thing that ties us to this place, and I fancy Le Manse Madonie has had its day. We could be elsewhere, as other people, doing other than we do now. You have suggested a fifty-gallon drum of kerosene and a stick of dynamite. But what if I were to suggest sufficient high-explosives to blow this entire place off the face of the mountain?"

"I would in every instance agree with you!" Francesco answered. "And to the world let it seem that we went with it."

"Except even if we were to leave this place in ruins, that wouldn't solve our problem—the fact that we are known to the dog-Lord's people and probably to this Tibetan Drakul, and that sooner or later we must run into them. For you can be sure that *they* would not believe we were dead!"

"Besides which," Francesco snarled, "I don't like the idea of backing off while this secret intruder—this Harry Keogh or Alec Kyle or whatever his bloody name is—goes unpunished. And we actually *know* where he is! That's the most galling thing!"

"We know something of what he can do, too." Tony was quick to remind his brother. "Which is also galling. This man goes up against vampires! He and the Mirlu woman, they took out a Drakul lieutenant and thrall. And our man in Scotland seems of the opinion that Bonnie Jean Mirlu is now Wamphyri. Indeed he would swear to it, for he's seen at least one of her kills."

"Our men are in position," Francesco was growing ever more heated and impatient. "We should go ahead and do it: order our lieutenants to kidnap, interrogate this E-Branch hypnotist, and our sleeper in Scotland to take out the Mirlu woman, along with any clever help she may have enlisted."

"None of which will help us find Radu Lykan," Tony's pessimism persisted. "The woman *must* be taken alive."

"And if she really is Wamphyri?"

"It would mean that we must . . . well, do it ourselves."

"And if all went in our favour?" Francesco seemed eager to get something, anything, going.

"Then blow this place to hell," Tony answered, but without his brother's fervour. "And the old creature in his pit with it. After that, set up again somewhere else. And eventually find a way to run this cringing Drakul to earth."

"No more Francezcis," Francesco nodded. "Ferenczys, maybe? And why not? It's a common enough name in Romania."

"That would do it!" Tony was in agreement. "Romanian dissidents—old aristocracy, even—fleeing from the madman Ceausescu's tyranny. But where to? America, perhaps?"

"Why not?" Francesco laughed out loud, and the echoes came bouncing back from the cavern's walls. "New York is nothing so dreary as this place. And there are plenty of penthouse aeries on 5th Avenue, believe me!"

"So good they named it twice!" Tony chuckled, however drily. "The Big Apple—just waiting to be bitten into!"

"And of an evening," (Francesco added), "we could stand on our balcony and watch those electrical rivers of light and life flooding through the canyons of the city!"

"Poetic," said Tony. "You know, brother, why, I've always suspected there was a poet in you? But rivers of life? Are you sure you don't mean rivers of blood?"

"But the blood *is* the life, dear brother," said the other. And as he finished speaking—as if invoked by all their talk of blood and life—a low moan sounded from close at hand.

The brothers' smiles fell away; their heads turned as one to stare at Julietta Sclafani in her coffin, whose glass-panelled lid now lay to one side. Julietta, whose head had turned a little as if to look at them, her too-pale face no longer smiling but frowning. One of her hands had slipped from her bosom where they had lain crossed, but her eyes were still closed and there was no breathing—as yet. Perhaps the bearers had jolted her when bringing her down here. And perhaps not . . .

"No more talk now," said Francesco, his tone serious in a moment. "Well, not to each other. Instead I suggest you talk to *him.*" He inclined his head to indicate the pit. "Try to start a conversation while I see to this." Switching off the current to the hinged grid covering the pit, he commenced cranking it open. But Tony's expression was more serious yet—even drawn—as he caught at his brother's arm and said:

"One more chance! We give our father one more chance. I'm pleading for him, yes. Oh, I know you're right: he's no use to us the way he is. But let's make this—our success or failure on this all-important occasion—the deciding factor. If Angelo comes through for us, if he can prove his value now, when we're most in need of him, then we carry on as before. We stay here, tend his needs, and use him as our oracle as long as he continues to function."

Francesco freed the cradle from its mooring, lowered it to the natural rock floor. "Help me with Julietta," he said. And a moment later: "I thought it was too good to be true: your suddenly seeing the light—your urge for flight, to throw off the shackles of this place. No, not you. You're much too much of a home bird."

And as they took Julietta from her box, placed her unprotesting body on the platform, and slid her loose cerements from her clay-cold, undead figure: "Well?" Tony demanded. "How is it to be?"

Swinging the arm of the hoist out over the pit, they waited until it found its equilibrium and stopped gyrating. Now all was in place; it only remained for Tony to speak to, or bargain with, the thing in the pit. And finally Francesco said:

"I say that one way or the other I'm out of here. There's a big wide world out there, brother, and for far too long I've felt confined to one little corner of it. So, I'll take what's mine to take and go. You can come with me or stay here, as you will. For let's face it, we may be brothers but we're also Wamphyri! And the Wamphyri are loners. We've had a good run as the Francezcis, and managed to keep from each others' throats, too. But all good things must come to an end eventually."

"Do you mean it?"

"Every word. My cards are on the table. And you?"

"If our father comes through for us," Tony answered, however slowly, " —if *we* come through whatever's coming—then I'll stay here in Le Manse Madonie and care for him. I'm used to this place. I like the idea that it is or will be . . . mine. Mine alone."

"Wamphyri territorialism," Francesco told him. "Stronger in you than in me. Do you see what comes of being a home bird, brother? You've grown kennel-proud—like a dog kept too long in a cage! Only let someone step over your threshold . . . why, you'd even bite the hand of your keeper! But I was always the one who was out and about in the world. And I will be again."

In answer to which Tony could only shrug and say, "Perhaps you're right. If so, then so be it . . . "

Anthony Francezci was no great telepath. Several centuries ago his father Angelo had told him that in the Ferenczys the talent was sporadic. It skipped entire generations, but given sufficient time it would generally resurface even in the most "insensitive" family member; which would appear to imply that Tony and his twin were entirely insensitive! This could be because they were more nearly a part of the modern world and in large part—especially in their thinking—divorced from their origins. In this world they had not required the art to combat alien, enemy vampire influences; thus it had failed to develop in them. Now that they did need it, it was too late. Unused, the metaphysical "muscle" had simply atrophied. Between each other, however, some vestigial telepathic awareness remained. And between them and their father, whose ESP was incredibly powerful, there was or could be a very strong link, even as strong as common speech . . . if and when Angelo allowed it. He knew his powers, however—knew that they alone were the reason he had lasted so long—and so guarded them jealously.

Recently it had been more than ever difficult to establish contact with him. He required bribing; the only bribes he would accept were of the human variety; the thing in the pit had little or no use for any other sort. He was what he was: a mass of ungovernable metamorphic vampire flesh, a monster of many parts in control of none of them. Not even his mind . . . not entirely. A madman, then. Or a mad mutant thing, certainly.

"Crazy," Tony muttered to himself where he leaned over the wall of the deactivated shaft. "His mind goes in circles. There is such *knowledge* in it! But all confused, jumbled, filled with the static of his multi-minds, which spills over into his consciousness. Yet he won't abandon them, extrude them, and let them die. They are his incorporeal 'thralls,' all he has left of connection with the material world, all that remains of power. And even in that respect his power is limited; he can't control the multi-minds, except to close them out. How can he threaten what he may not hurt? Terrible: to have such awesome talents and yet be trapped down there in his pit. He can spy on a world, but is confined here; he can discover almost anything he wants to know, but cannot *use* such knowledge except to pass it on to us. Frustration . . . hunger . . . and madness. Oh, our father is crazy! But then, who wouldn't be?"

"Crazy?" Francesco's nervous grunt sounded from close at hand, where he stood with his arms folded on his chest trying to appear relaxed. "He's that, all right—crazy like a fox!"

"*Shhh!*" Tony cautioned him. "His mind is stirring, attempting to concentrate. He . . . he *feels* me reaching for him, opening my thoughts to him. Look down there . . . "

Francesco took a single pace forward and looked down into the reeking well, whose fumes were rising thicker now. And from deep in the darkness of the lower regions of the shaft where it expanded into the old volcanic cavity, his father's eyes stared back at him. A great many eyes, unblinking, red, and hateful in the smoky reek of the pit.

Tony had to concentrate. Without so much as a glance at his brother, he felt him step falteringly back again. For all Francesco's bravado, he feared the old Ferenczy. Not without cause, for:

Treacherousss! came that single whispered or hissed accusation, as if their father had breathed the word out in a stream of cold air over the shrinking contours of their brains. And in the next moment, strengthening: *You, my son. Yesss, you, Francesssco—treacherous as ever! And infectious. Why, your poisons have even infected your brother!*

But: "Not yet, Father," Tony told him, speaking out loud, trying to keep his voice even. "And in any case, is it treachery to consider an act of mercy? Your misery has been long and long . . . "

There was a moment of stunned silence, until: *Oh? And you know that for a fact, do you? That I am miserable? So that you would deem it a mercy to consider releasing me from my burden? But how* kind *of you. How* thoughtful—*you murderous bastards! Your mother died giving you birth. But if she'd known the scum she gave birth to, it would have killed her anyway!*

"Listening!" Francesco grated. "And didn't I tell you so? Crazy like a fox! Now hear me, Tony: don't play his word games but put it to him straight. Our beloved father has a choice to make. So let him make it now."

"Be quiet!" Tony rounded on him at once—but immediately, anxiously, turned back to the pit. And over his shoulder: "He's not only listening but *speaking,* too! He's making sense at last—so let him."

Ah, Anthony, my little Anthony! But is this the same small boy I bounced on my knee in the cool shade of Le Manse Madonie? So guileless—well, within limits—and full of questions? The son who was so near and dear to me, so eager for knowledge, who would learn from his father's lips and witness in his deeds the ways of the Wamphyri? Why, in those days it was as if my every word was a revelation to you, to be soaked up as a sponge soaks water. And I knew you for a true bloodson, aye . . .

"Nothing has changed, Father," Tony answered. "For here we are as always, you and I. And still I come to you with my questions, ready to drink up your answers. Except you rarely answer any more."

Oh yes, I know. (Angelo Ferenczy's mental voice sounded full of self-pity in Tony and Francesco's minds. But it was all affectation, they knew. *I was listening, it must be admitted. Listening to you and Francesco . . . which might well have been a dream, for all I knew. Or a* nightmare! *Praying for some word of comfort. Seeking some act of solace, however small—or hoping, perhaps, for some sweet tidbit with which to relieve the unrelenting boredom of this hellhole? But what I heard . . . was none of these things.*

"You heard the words of angry, despairing, even desperate men, Father," Tony answered. "For we are at a loss."

And do you say that nothing has changed? (The thing in the pit continued as if he had not been interrupted.) *Ah, yes, and I recall you said it to Francesco, too. And that he also denied it. But* I *am changed, to this creature who is less than a creature. And* you *are changed, into ruthless men. And* the times *are changed—until they are charged with great dangers!*

Eagerly now, Tony leaned out more yet. He gripped the wall of the pit's coping with one hand and leaned his weight on Julietta's swaying platform with the other, so securing himself at the rim. "And do you know of these dangers?" He aimed his query directly into the shaft. "Can you speak of them? Are we threatened? For always remember, Father: what threatens us threatens you."

Aye, and you are full *of threats, you and your brother.*

"Now hold!" Francesco could no longer contain himself. He stepped forward and glared down into smouldering darkness. "If you were listening you must know that Tony championed you. Oh, I can be bitter. I can worry about what is happening out there in the world—of which we would have knowledge, if you would only apply yourself. Yes, *and* I can make dire threats, if only out of frustration, and despite that there can be no substance in them. But when it comes down to it, as always, Tony champions you. If you were eavesdropping, surely you heard him elect to remain here and care for you?"

For two or three seconds there was total silence, a stillness both physical and metaphysical. But in the next moment the atmosphere in the cavern took on the weight of a thunderstorm. The spotlights illuminating the mouth of the pit seemed to dim; Angelo Ferenczy's effluvium, his "breath," streamed faster and colder from the mouth of the shaft, and the darkness in the pit itself appeared to seethe. Then:

He doesn't want to talk to you! It was some other's voice, not their father's. The voice of one of his long-absorbed victims, his multi-minds, who were as mad, and more so, than Angelo himself. To spite Francesco—to ignore and refute his presence—Angelo had deliberately relaxed all constraint upon them; and now the rest joined in . . . a lunatic babble of denial, all different, but all directed into Francesco's buffeted mind:

He won't talk to you!

Muuurderer! Kin-killer! Do not invite conversation. Do not force it upon him. He can turn your dreams, turn your mind. You visit him now to torment him. But if he were to visit you . . . ?

RUN! OH, RUN! WOULD YOU BE A VESSEL TO HIM, AS HE IS NOW A VESSEL TO US?

He turns his back on you. Go now, before he turns his face towards you!

You are all cursed, you Ferenczys, but Francesco above all others!

OH, HA HA HA! YOU HAVE YOUR METAMORPHISM NOW, BUT HOW LONG BEFORE IT HAS YOU?

The sins of the father, Francesco . . .

Your father is glad that you are cursed!

HE WON'T TALK TO YOU.

Not to you, Francesssco . . .

The voices tailed off a little. And:

"Get away!" Tony half-turned from the pit, hissed at Francesco where he backed off, his face pale, his hands held up and forwards, as if ward off the unseen mental presences. "Get back from the pit, away from him. That temper of yours . . . you place yourself, place both of us, in danger! I know he'll talk to me. I can feel it. But you're right: he'll have nothing to do with you. And damn you, I don't blame him!"

"And what are you, his fucking keeper?" But still Francesco backed away, his features writhing. "Well, you can have him. *Burn* the useless, frothing old bastard, that's what I say! I'm finished with him! Fuck him, and fuck you, too!"

He turned and flowed with the eerie motion of the Wamphyri to the exit shaft, turned and looked back. Still dressed in funereal clothes, the change that had taken place in Francesco was even more apparent, and to any normal person appalling. For his blood was up and his vampire leech fuelled his metamorphism.

His eyes like scarlet lamps; his nostrils gaping wide in a convoluted, batlike flange of a snout; his mouth a fanged gash in a leaden-grey mask of a face! And: "Damn you both to hell," he snarled. "For you're two of a kind, you and my 'dear father' both!"

And the parting shot from his "dear father" was a sinister mental hiss:

But we are already damned to hell, Francesssco! And son, if I were you—which I thank my stars I am not—I would keep a tight rein on my metamorphism. For we are of one blood, Francesco, and Wamphyri blood runs true. Whose pit will you occupy, I wonder, and whose oracle will you be, in one or two or three hundred years' time? Oh, ha ha ha ha haaaaa!

But Francesco had already left, and only the fading echoes of his footfalls on the stone stairs came back to the cavern of the pit. Where eventually, breathlessly Tony asked:

"Can we talk now? And will you answer truthfully, to the best of your knowledge?"

His father's thoughts at once came groping, like fat cold graveworms in his head—and paused, startled. *What? But what have we here? Have I discovered . . . some other?*

Tony was still leaning on the wall of the shaft, with one arm outstretched, steadying the suspended platform. He frowned, pondering his father's query . . . which a moment later he understood only too well.

"Eh?" Julietta's first, gasping breath—her waking query—was like a sharp stab in Tony's awareness. Julietta! Awake! Wamphyri!

He snatched his hand away and felt her fingers scrape the skin from his knuckles where she had almost caught hold of him. Then she jerked erect—bending at the waist—sitting up like a corpse waking in its coffin. An accurate simile: to return to consciousness, to life, to undeath, on a swaying platform over a nightmare pit! But Julietta had never been down here in her life before, and for a moment she was disorientated.

Then she saw Tony, his expression—

—And her eyes widened as, with a vampire's understanding, she knew! Knew that this was to have been, and might still be, her end. The tenacity of the Wamphyri. Julietta's slender arms, marble-grey, with fine blue veins, reached for him; their inch-long painted nails crooking like claws to hook into his flesh.

But they never reached him. Tilting with her sudden movements, the suspended platform tipped her into the abyss. Bulge-eyed, she slipped from view; her hair floated over her head as she plunged; her shriek—of outrage more than terror—echoed in the throat of the shaft. And:

Mine!—came that guttural grunt of sheerest lust from the depths of the well. *A tidbit after all! From my Anthony to his ever-loving father!*

Tremblingly, Tony cranked the wire-mesh grid into place over the mouth of the pit. Only then, as he activated the current, and heard the hum and buzz of the field re-establishing itself, did he begin to breathe more normally. And to Angelo:

"You knew that she was here, of course. Francesco and I, we spoke of her when you were listening."

But Angelo was no longer listening. Now it was his son's turn to listen. To the obscene, disbelieving shrieking of Julietta; her panted, tortured, ignored denials as the thing that was Angelo Ferenczy *explored* her. Then to the splitting sounds. The sounds of suction, rending, finally of flesh exploding outwards as Julietta's screams echoed into silence. And Tony reeling at the rim, as he realized how close he, too, had come to being dragged shrieking into the pit.

And if he had been, would it have been any different for him?

Probably not . . .

Almost an hour later, when Tony climbed up from the bowels of Le Manse Madonie to its saner levels, he found Francesco waiting for him. Tony was exhausted and made no effort to hide it. Without comment, Francesco drove them in the Land Rover across the brutal terrain of their scrubby plateau to a rocky promontory looking out over the Tyrrhenian. Parking on the far side of an outcrop that shielded them from Le Manse, finally Francesco lit two cigarettes, passed one to his brother, and said:

"Well, how did it go?"

"Very well," Tony nodded. "Good cop, bad cop. A good idea. It *worked* very well indeed."

"*Hah!*" his brother laughed. "Good! And now who watches too much American television, eh?"

"It went well," Tony said again, but without emotion—as if he were *drained* of emotion—and showing never a sign of his brother's elation. "Which in turn presents its own problems."

"Eh?" Francesco stopped chuckling. "Come again? What problems?"

"Problems aplenty," Tony answered. "If we can believe him. And I think we can."

"Tell me about it."

Tony's face was grey in the gloomy light. A breeze off the sea blew a lock of his black hair across his sunken cheeks. "To start with, it will be soon," he said. "So little time. Radu's resurgence—only three months, until all hell breaks loose!"

"Our father has foreseen it?" Francesco gripped his brother's arm. "And you have faith in his predictions? How can he be sure? How can *we* be sure? Angelo is a madman, after all."

"But 'mad like a fox,' the last time we spoke," Tony reminded him. "And when did you ever know him to be wrong? Also, he isn't *predicting* anything, not this time. He overheard it."

"He what?"

"For the last two or three years we've taken his silence, his moods, his increasingly complex nature and general unwillingness to co-operate—in short, his apparent lack of mental equilibrium—as symptoms of a swift degeneration into madness. But as I've so frequently asked before, who wouldn't go mad in our father's circumstances? Put yourself in his position. When he is lucid, in control of his talents, he can scry—or spy—on the world! He can, or could, scan something of future times. He can locate a single man out of a million ten thousand miles away, and report on his circumstances. He was our oracle, from whom we profited for more than three centuries. And he was amazingly successful! It was as if, when his metamorphism ran out of control, confining his body to that place, it gave his mind far greater freedom . . . "

Francesco gave an impatient nod. "Now tell me something I don't know. Tell me about our intruder—who he *really* is, and how he's linked to B.J. Mirlu and Radu Lykan. Tell me about the dog-Lord: his location, the names of his thralls and the extent of his power. Then tell me about this lone Drakul in his Tibetan monastery: what *he* is all about and why he's chosen to show his hand now. If you can tell me some of these things, *I* might begin to have a little faith in our father, too."

"Some of these things," Tony answered, narrowing his eyes. "I can tell you some of them. For that is precisely what Angelo has been working on all this time, since the intruder—whoever or whatever he is—broke into the vault and robbed us."

"What? Did I really hear you say 'whoever he is'?" Francesco's voice was full of a biting, furious sarcasm. "Are you telling me we don't already *know* who he is? Has Angelo changed his mind? And did you also say 'working'? Has our dear father been *working*, then?" He paused as he noticed Tony's expression—the reddening of his eyes and angry flaring of his dark nostrils—sighed and changed his tack. "As usual, I'm short on patience," he gruffly excused himself. "Very well, tell it your way."

And between deep drags on his cigarette, Tony told it.

"He has located B.J. Mirlu's mind, and gained limited access. She is definitely Wamphyri and he daren't go too deep. She would know it if he was less than discreet. But one thing seems sure: she has a thrall or an assistant—help of sorts—in a place called Inverdruie, in the Cairngorms. It fits: it's where she and her E-Branch friend, our intruder, took out the Drakul lieutenant and a thrall. As to what the Drakuls were interested in: the dog-Lord's den, obviously. They came too close to finding him. Inverdruie is a hamlet, a country cross-roads, a scattered handful of houses. We can have our men check the place out house by house if necessary. If B.J. Mirlu's perhaps man is there, we'll find him.

"There are other thralls, too: a few, perhaps in Scotland. Like B.J. herself, they're descendants of old Szgany clans who came through from Starside in the old times. None of them are changelings but they are of the blood. 'Moon-children,' Angelo calls them. They are sleepers, and the woman can call on them for help as and when she needs it. And of course, we also have it from *our* sleeper and lieutenant, Angus McGowan, that all of the girls working at B.J.'s wine-bar in Edinburgh are in thrall to her—as was the one we gave to Angelo that time. But Angus can't be sure of their status. Simple thralls, at a guess.

"As for this E-Branch type: he's definitely our intruder. Goes under the name of Harry Keogh—who we know to be a dead man! Convenient, eh? But in fact he's Alec Kyle—who by all accounts should likewise be dead! And yet here . . . well, it has to be said that Angelo is confused, undecided; and under-standably so. There's something about this one's mind. Angelo can't get into it, or doesn't want to. This man is different in more ways than one. He's ex-E-Branch, yes . . . allegedly. Or perhaps he's still with them: a double agent work-ing for Radu Lykan's downfall? If so, he has B.J. Mirlu fooled. They're lovers. But as I said, Mr. Keogh is a tricky one; our father simply doesn't know what to make of him. He talks of him 'coming and going,' whatever that means, and still insists that he 'talks' to dead men! Which is something of a coincidence in itself. For if you remember, the KGB told us that the real Mr. Keogh was some sort of necromancer. Myself, I don't know what to think; I give up on it; but Angelo maintains that Harry Keogh is the very worst of our enemies, and I tend to agree with him. Assuming he *was* our intruder: anyone who can get in here sight unseen, and get out again with millions—*and* go unpunished for as long as he has—has to be special!

"So much for the dog-Lord and the people around him. But these are strong leads, you'll agree, which we must follow up. And soon. And personally. Then there's this Drakul . . .

"Angelo has been into his mind, too. Touched upon it, at least. Enough to learn that Daham Drakesh, as he calls himself—or the last true Drakul—knows more than enough about us. Which makes us a future target, obviously. But talk about madness? Francesco, compared with this Drakul, our father is the sanest of men! Drakesh plans to engineer a nuclear war—just how is un-certain—and in the aftermath will set up a network of aeries in the rubble of the cities, under cover of the last long winter! Indeed the apparatus, the trig-gers for this devastation, are already in place, and our father is still trying to dis-cover what the catalyst will be.

"So, troubles enough, you'll agree. And a vastly tangled skein for us to work our way through. But work we must, if we want to survive. And we have to start without delay."

Francesco had listened to all of it in a sullen silence. But despite his volatile nature he was wise enough to realize that Tony was deadly serious in everything he said, and sensitive enough to feel the winds of change blowing over the mountains of Le Madonie. Yes, and they blew far more ominously than the winds off the grey Tyrrhenian. And finally, now that Tony was done:

"So, what's next?" he asked, his tone sombre. "Is it time we got involved, do you think? I mean, in person?"

"Haven't I said as much?" Tony looked at him. "One of us, at least, with a handful of our men. In Scotland, yes."

"One of us?" Francesco raised an eyebrow. "Meaning me?"

"Unless you'd prefer to stay here and care for Angelo, and look after our other interests."

"No," his brother shook his head, flicked away the stub of his cigarette. "You were ever the home bird, while I'm far more at ease out in the wider world. And as for that loathsome thing in his pit: I would probably let him rot! So I'm the one who'll have to go."

He started the Land Rover's engine, reversed into the open, and headed for Le Manse. Then: "About Julietta," he began—

—But his brother cut him short: "She was . . . gratefully accepted," he said.

"Really? Despite that she'd been mine?" Francesco made no attempt to hide his surprise, perhaps even his chagrin.

"*Because* she had been yours," Tony told him, and shook his head in silent reproof. "You never heard a single thing he ever told us, did you? For if you had you would know it's one of the traits of the Wamphyri. Where blood and sex are concerned, we've always preferred our own. And when it was finished, Angelo told me he could smell you on her, and your essence *in* her."

"Huh!" Francesco grunted.

"Oh, yes," Tony grinned, however mirthlessly. "And there's one more thing you should know. Our father also told me his one regret was that it wasn't you yourself . . . !"

III

"THE OPPOSITION," E-BRANCH, AND OTHER AGENCIES.

IN MOSCOW, TURKUR TZONOV, A YOUNG MAN DESTINED FOR A MEASURE OF greatness—and one with the capacity for an even greater measure of evil—made report to Yuri Andropov's office in a coldly austere government building on Kurtsuzov Prospekt. His footsteps were sure on the marble flags of the echoing, high-ceilinged, unwelcoming corridor whose offices were the nerve-centre of Andropov's organization; which in itself said a lot for Tzonov's self-assurance. Few men, when they were summoned here, would arrive with their heads held high and their consciences clear. But in fact Tzonov had been expecting Andropov's call and it scarcely disturbed him. On the other hand, what he would report might well disturb the head of the Komissia Gosudarstvennoy Bezopasnosti, the KGB.

At the end of the corridor, Tzonov came to a halt at the closed double-doors of the last office. Flanking this terminal room, two lesser rooms stood with their doors open. These were secretarial offices, momentarily unoccupied. Tzonov could hazard a guess why: the clerks had been sent away. There are some secrets that even secretaries shouldn't share.

He knocked twice on the doors and a thin, cold voice from within said, "Come." Tzonov narrowed his eyes, and immediately composed himself. As he was well aware, that voice was a perfect match for the mind and soul that issued it. He entered the room, and his eyes were at once drawn to the figure of one of the most powerful—some would say *the* most powerful—men in Russia where he was seated at his desk. Comrade, or more properly Direktor, Andropov.

Andropov didn't look up but studied paperwork on the desk before him. Grey light from the frosted glass of large, bullet-proof bay windows framed him in a misty silhouette, turning the lenses of his spectacles, the larger dome of his polished head, and the lesser gleam of his chin to an ankh-like design of silvery ovals. But as Tzonov approached his desk he offered him a cursory glance and said, "Good morning, Comrade. Please sit."

Slightly inclined to the angle of the great desk, a large leather chair waited for Tzonov. Answering, "Good morning, Comrade Direktor Andropov," he sat down, put his briefcase on the floor, made himself as comfortable as possible . . . and waited. For much like Andropov himself—and despite the natural enthusiasm of youth—Tzonov wasn't an impatient man.

Eventually Andropov was done with his papers; he shuffled them aside, put his elbows on the desk and steepled his fingers before his face. In that face, only the ovals of his spectacles were visible against the haze from the windows. And:

"Well," he said eventually, his voice cold, measured and emotionless. And twice more: "Well, well! But such a young man, which was my opinion when first we met. Yet so persistent, and full of such large ambitions. The reorganization of a branch of Soviet security which on at least two occasions has proved itself an absolute liability to the system. Furthermore, a branch which in the past stood in direct opposition to my own rather more orthodox, er, institution and methods."

"Not only that," Turkur Tzonov spoke up, "—not only to reorganize ESP-Branch—but to run it. Er, with your guidance, naturally. That was my proposal when first we met five months ago, and it still is. As you required at that time, I have now procured evidence of my credentials for the job. Direktor Andropov, I was only eighteen years old when the ESP facility at the Chateau Bronnitsy fell and the Branch more or less ceased to be. Perhaps fortunately, I had been too young to be of service as a field agent, and instead had been ordered to attend a four-year course of studies to prepare me for my duties . . . "

Tzonov paused and waited, and when Andropov nodded, continued: "Even after Bronnitsy fell, I continued with my studies and six months ago passed all necessary examinations with honours. Since when, I and a handful of other Bronnitsy survivors have stood idly by waiting for a decision from . . . well, let's say from a higher authority. That decision has not been forthcoming. And we don't know if we're coming or going. But we do know that our talents are going to waste—or have been."

While Tzonov spoke, the head of the KGB was not only attentive to everything he said, but he also took the opportunity to scrutinize his visitor minutely. And what he saw didn't entirely displease him. For in just a few months this precocious youth seemed to have become more properly the man.

Turkur Tzonov was part Turk, part Mongol, all male. There could be no question but that he was an "Alpha" male, a future leader, an outstanding mind in an athlete's body. His penetrating grey eyes were the sort that could look *at* or *into* a man; and indeed that was his alleged talent: he read minds, through eye-contact with his subjects. Which was also the reason that Yuri Andropov had arranged his office this way. He wanted the light in Tzonov's eyes, for the moment at least. For Andropov must first let his visitor commit himself before he would show his own hand. If this man was as good as the reports Andropov had read on him, he certainly didn't want him in *his* mind! Not just yet. And probably not ever.

"But you came to see me five months ago," Andropov deliberately leaned back in his chair, diffusing the silhouette and contours of his face more yet in the light from the bay windows curving around him. "Somewhat pre-emptive of you, wasn't it? The 'higher authority' you refer to can only be Premier Leonid Brezhnev himself—the man who instigated this mindspy organization in the first place. And by seeing me, did you hope to jump the gun on Brezhnev? Did you think it likely I would be willing to risk going over his head? And what made you believe I might be prepared to reinstate ESP-Branch in the first place? For after all, the Branch was a thorn in my side. What is more, its first Direktor, that old warhorse Gregor Borowitz, was an actual pain in my arse!"

And while Tzonov thought about that, Andropov continued to study him.

The youth's eyebrows were slim as lines pencilled on paper; upward slanting, they were silver-blond against the tanned ridges of his upper orbits. From the eyebrows up he was completely hairless, but this was so in keeping with his other features as to make it seem that in his case hair was never intended. Certainly this premature baldness wasn't a sign of ill health; the bronze dome of Tzonov's head glowed with a vitality matched by the flesh of his face, where the single anomaly lay in the hollows of his eyes. Deep-sunken and dark, they seemed bruised as if from long hours of study or implacable concentration. A symptom of his telepathy, apparently.

Turkur Tzonov's nose was long and straight; his mouth was well fleshed if a little wide, over a chin that was strong and aggressively square. His cheeks were very slightly hollow, and his small pointed ears lay flat to his head. The overall picture was of a too-perfect symmetry, where the opposing halves of his face seemed mirror images. In a majority of people it would be a disadvantage, Andropov thought. The physical attraction of a face, its "good looks," are normally defined by imperfections of balance. Tzonov was the exception to the rule, for paradoxically he was a very attractive young man. "Talented" remained to be seen, but definitely outspoken.

Meanwhile, Tzonov had thought over what Andropov had said to him. Now, in an even voice he answered, "Comrade Direktor, it wasn't a case of my hoping you would go over the Party Leader's head. Indeed, I can't see how anyone could be accused of that. For to my knowledge there isn't anyone—or any-*thing*—inside that head! Let me try to explain. As soon as my studies were at an end I went to see Brezhnev, on behalf of that handful of Bronnitsy survivors. I spoke to his secretary, who knew of the Premier's interest in the Branch. I was granted an appointment. Two weeks later I was driven to a dacha at Zhukovka, where he was supposed to be 'resting.' But something had happened to him between times, for while Leonid Brezhnev was there, wrapped in a blanket and hunched on a couch, he was not really . . . *there*. It was an aide who did all of his talking for him."

Andropov held up a cautionary hand. "What are you saying?" His voice was quite emotionless.

"It is also an aide who signs his daily round of papers for him," Tzonov went on. "Articles of state, that is. And an aide who props him up when he appears on television. And probably another who imitates his voice . . . fairly difficult, that last, for to me it always seemed like the Party Leader was eating cabbage! And there must *definitely* be another aide to wipe his backside when he has been to the toilet! So what I am saying is that he's a zombie, Comrade Direktor!"

Andropov sat up straighter and his face became more visible, but still his eyes were silver ovals. "Treason, then," he said. "If what you say is true, it is treason. You understand that, don't you? You're undermining the security of the State. And if it is not true, still it's treason. Your youth is no excuse. Do you agree?"

"No," the other shook his head. "I don't think so. Oh, it would be reason if I said it to anyone else . . . especially to a foreign power! But not if I *report* it to the head of the Komissia Gosudarstvennoy Bezopasnosti. To gather intelligence—to be aware of everything—is your job, after all. And surely this is important intelligence."

"Do you presume to tell me my job?" Andropov's tone hadn't changed in the slightest degree. "Anyway, it wasn't *your* job to gather such intelligence."

Tzonov shrugged. "I made no effort to gather it. I merely observed it."

"And how accurate were these . . . observations? Sufficient to provide proof that Leonid Brezhnev, the Russian Premier, is on death's doorstep, kept alive—well, more or less—until someone else can be elected in his stead?"

"To my satisfaction, yes."

"And by virtue of your . . . talent?"

"Yes."

Andropov leaned back again, his face dissolving into misty white light. "This is the proof you would offer me that you are fit to head a revamped ESP-Branch of Soviet Security, right?"

"Not all of it."

"But some of it?"

"Some of it, yes."

"Then why didn't you tell me these things on the first occasion of our meeting?"

"Because I would not presume to tell you what you already knew. You are the head of the KGB. Of course you knew. You are probably responsible for this continuing—and very necessary—subterfuge."

"Twenty-two years old," Andropov mused, "and already deep as a well. I believe I may have work for you. In what capacity I can't yet say. A revitalized ESP-Branch? Well, perhaps, but I really do not think so. To date its Direktors have been . . . shall we say, less than co-operative? They seemed to develop a lust for power—all of them! It is a power thing, after all, the gathering and control of information. And as for esoteric information . . . ? I want no secrets kept from me."

"You would know everything that I learned the very moment I learned it!" Tzonov assured him.

"I would put one of my own in charge," Andropov continued to muse, "so as to have my finger on the pulse. And if and when your loyalty was proven, then you might one day replace him."

"Only give me the opportunity."

"And is that it?" Andropov's face came back into focus but his eyes remained invisible. "Are we done here? Is this what it boils down to: you could not get what you wanted from a failing Brezhnev, and so turned to me? But why me? After all, I'm only a special policeman."

"*Very* special," Tzonov answered. "According to my colleagues, at least."

"Your colleagues? The other survivors?"

"Futurologists, hunchmen, locators . . . "

"Psychics!" Andropov snorted, finally displaying something of emotion. "Borowitz was convinced, and he convinced Brezhnev. But where is Brezhnev now? What good did it do him? Similarly, Felix Krakovitch and Ivan Gerenko were true disciples of these . . . these 'metaphysical mysteries,' and they're dead, too! And the Chateau Bronnitsy—which was home to all such 'spirit mediums'—is a gutted shell."

"You have no faith in us." Tzonov smiled . . . and Andropov didn't like it.

He leaned closer across his desk, and his spectacles lost something of their opaqueness. His eyes were now part-visible, but not enough. "I have faith in proven systems," he answered. "Show me some respect, and show me the benefits—*real* respect, *real* benefits, *real* proof—and I'll give you what you want."

"I'm not lacking in respect," Tzonov told him in an even voice. "I would never have dared to come here without it. Nor without real proof. As for the latter, and the benefits: you must be the judge."

"What benefits? Are you talking in riddles?"

"Moscow is still standing, still secure. Isn't that benefit enough?"

"Moscow is still . . . ?" Andropov was obviously mystified. "Explain, and quickly."

"For the last four years, in my spare time, I've kept my group together," Tzonov answered. "Not difficult. They were at a loss what to do with themselves; the State had lost all interest in them; some of them even took mundane jobs. And . . . I have continued their training. I've kept them up to scratch."

"You have been operating a mindspy cell?"

"I've been gathering proof of their effectiveness. Isn't that what you asked for the first time we met?"

"We only met five months ago!"

"At which time I didn't *have* the proof—not the kind of proof that would sway you—not quite."

"What has all of this to do with the fact that Moscow is—what? Still standing, still secure? I am growing impatient now. You had better let me see the whole picture."

"It's a complicated picture."

"Show me anyway."

"Do you remember the Parapsychological Convention held in Moscow two years ago? I fancy it was a brainchild of Brezhnev's, though at the time he pretended to stand aloof from it. It was his last attempt to reinvent ESP-Branch, and he wanted to know what we were up against in the rest of the world."

"I do remember, yes," Andropov replied. "Psychic *détente*, ostensibly. Spoon-benders from Israel, and water-diviners from Egypt! Mentalists from Mongolia and scryers from Syria! Even a couple of futurologists from England—probably from their own E-Branch—and other metaphysicians from places diverse as Chicago and China!"

"And Tibet," Tzonov remained cool.

"Eh?"

"Tibetans, part of the Chinese delegation. Would-be saboteurs, as it has since turned out."

"Saboteurs?" Andropov growled. "And what were they trying to sabotage, pray?"

"Moscow," Tzonov told him without further ado or emphasis. "That for a start, anyway. Moscow and world peace, and but for my team they would have succeeded."

"Explain." Andropov moved out of focus again.

"Myself and several of my people attended the convention, naturally. Brezhnev required it."

"I remember something of that, yes."

"Well, we were there to spy on possible mindspies, to see how good they were. I was the group's telepath, of course. But there was also my precog, and a hunchman."

"*Your* precog . . ." Andropov's frown wasn't quite visible in the haze of light but Tzonov felt it all the same. "And—what did you say—a hunchman?"

"It's difficult to explain in layman terms," Tzonov said. "A hunchman is a special kind of esper who makes clever guesses—except it's not just guesswork but his talent. He's aware of—oh, all sorts of things. About what's going on in general. If he can pinpoint a British nuclear submarine in the Barents Sea, then we call him a 'locator.' If he dreams or nightmares about someone's death in a week's time, and seven days from now that someone dies, then he's a futurologist or 'precog.' At the convention, I had a precog *and* a hunchman with me."

"Go on."

"The Chinese attendees were paramilitaries, from the ESP-Centre on Kwijiang Avenue in Chungking. We've known about them for a long time. They were doing what *we* were doing: seeing if they could find out what the opposition was up to and how good we were at it. Nothing strange about that: apart from all the, er, 'spoon-bending,' and Zener card reading, it's what we were all there for. But these Tibetans were something else . . .

"There were six of them, sect members of an obscure monastery somewhere. They had shaven heads and wore red robes, usually with the hoods up. They moved together, always, almost as one man. One of them, their leader, I supposed, had tiny bells sewn into his sleeves.

"My hunchman told me he thought they were up to something. When he concentrated on them, all he got was a kind of smog, a mental smokescreen. The same sort of thing, incidentally, that we occasionally experience with British espers. My precog was similarly confused and very nervous in their presence. He preferred to be nowhere near them. Precogs are generally peculiar in that respect: they fear to 'see' too much, and are never or very rarely interested in their own futures. They say that the past and future are immutable. Since they can't *change* the future, they prefer not to *know* it, at least not with respect to themselves. It must be an awful thing to know you are going to die, when and how, and not be able to do anything about it . . .

"I was curious and tried to read the minds of these Tibetans. I pride myself on my skill, that it's almost undetectable except to other, skilled telepaths. But somehow the red-robes knew it. They accepted—far more readily than anyone else at the convention—that I was the genuine thing, and avoided me like the plague. But what little I did see . . . was very worrying. They were definitely hiding something.

"If you recall, Comrade Direktor, the convention accommodation was the Central Committee Hotel, in the Sivtsev Vrazhek district of the city, and the convention rooms were right here on Kurtsuzov Prospekt—which I imagine made it easy for your men to watch the comings and goings of foreign attendees. Easy to collect their fingerprints and other details, too."

Andropov nodded. "I believe we got them all, yes. A few dozens, to go with the many thousands already on file."

"Indeed. And if you didn't, my people did . . . "

Again Andropov's face was drawn back into view, and his frown—of disapproval?—was plainly visible. But before he could say anything, Tzonov continued: "The convention was inconclusive; there were too many fakers; the cause of parapsychological research was not furthered. But we did learn that there are many budding talents in China, that the British are probably leaders in the field, and that the Tibetans, whom we supposed to be working hand in hand with the Chinese, were up to . . . something.

"So, the convention ended and I made report to Brezhnev. By which time he was far more interested in Russian successes—and infuriated by our failures—in the Olympics! The American boycott seemed to have upset him greatly. I think it was about then that his slow decline first became noticeable. But in any case, he commended me for my efforts before sending me back to my studies . . . "

As Tzonov paused, Andropov put in: "I sincerely hope all of this is going somewhere? I have other things to do with my time, young Tzonov!"

"It is going somewhere," the other assured him, and went on:

"I have a locator, a man whose speciality is the detection of fissionable material. In his time under General Borowitz he tracked the flight paths of American bombers, also the movements of their mobile missiles, kept watch on NATO's nuclear capability in West Germany, and Great Britain's atomic submarines in waters around the world. His talent was largely dependent upon the critical mass or amount of fissionable material with which he was . . . sympathetic? For example: the many Trident missiles in the belly of a nuclear sub made it easy to find, while a single test bomb was far more difficult. In General Borowitz's time, however, he had noted an ammunition dump of bombs in Chungking, and had recorded its size. Likewise he had records of many other such dumps worldwide.

"But in the eighteen months following the convention, my locator was a puzzled, even a worried man. He had not attended the convention, because his talent would have had no application there. Yet now he felt himself drawn to—or repelled by—a certain district of the city. This city. Moscow . . . "

This time when Tzonov paused, Andropov immediately nodded and said, "Yes, go on, you have my attention."

"Finally," Tzonov continued, "three months or so after we met, you and I, for the first time, my locator came to me with his problem. By which time his inexplicable repulsion with regard to a certain district had become a morbid obsession."

"Tell me the district," Andropov cut in.

"The Sivtsev Vrazhek district, Comrade . . . "

"Go on."

"I went with him to the Central Committee Hotel, and we stood outside together looking at the place. For the locator, simply being there was a terrible ordeal! He wanted to be *anywhere* but there. The implications were obvious but proving our suspicions without causing a panic—a gigantic panic—would not be easy. Fortunately, an uncle of mine in Krasnoyarsk was scheduled to pay me a visit. He had good connections, was able to book himself in at the hotel."

"Cut it short!" Yuri Andropov's hands were pressing down on his desk now. He had thrust his face forward, and his staring eyes were more than ever visible.

"Once inside the hotel, access to the cellars—and from there to the substructure—was easy. We went down there when the hotel was sleeping, in the middle of the night. And after my locator had pinpointed the spot—"

"—You dug there!" Andropov said.

"Indeed. I had to, for my locator was now useless. I saw what was in his mind: a glaring ball of light, a nuclear furnace burning bright, sudden death by atomization. But my futurologists had foreseen no such disaster. So . . .

"I am no atomic physicist, Comrade Direktor, but I think it is safe to say the device is a crude one. The most surprising factor lies in its compact construction. Those six Tibetan 'monks' could easily have brought its components in as part of their luggage. Like all the other attendees, they had been met at the airport by officials and seen through customs. You will recall that at that time we were being 'helpful' to foreigners and trying to improve their opinion of us? It needed improving, for it was the same bad attitude that had impacted so badly on our Olympics. We were trying to mend our bridges, as it were."

Andropov was stiff as a rod now, bolt upright behind his desk. "Tzonov, do you know what you are telling me? That there was an atomic bomb under the Central Committee Hotel for over two years!?"

"Was," said the other. "That there *was* one, yes."

"You . . . moved it? *My God!*" (Which came as a surprise to Tzonov, because he would never have considered the Direktor of the KGB a believer.)

"Not a problem," he said. "The device was equipped with a radio receiver—a trigger. It would have to be detonated remotely by a prearranged series of signals. Remove the receiver and the bomb would be made safe. I removed it myself . . . "

"My God!" Andropov breathed again, then slumped down into his chair. He waved a loose hand. "How . . . how long ago?"

"Five weeks."

"You've waited five weeks to bring this to my attention?"

"To *anyone's* attention! To know that this thing was done was one thing, but to prove who did it . . . took longer. But it would have been totally impossible in the confusion that would follow an actual detonation . . . with Moscow reduced to so much rubble, and every nuclear power in the world blaming everyone else. A beautiful piece of sabotage, *especially if this wasn't the only bomb!*"

"What!?"

"Ah, no, Direktor," Tzonov read his mind the hard way: by *guessing* what he was thinking. "Not here in Russia but in some other part of the world."

"Explain!" Andropov was sitting up straight again, leaning forward, and his eyes were like windows to Tzonov so that he could look right into his soul. Except right now there was nothing in there but shock, confusion.

Tzonov reached down and picked up his briefcase. Placing it on the edge of the desk, he opened it—and Andropov immediately leaned away from it. But Tzonov only grinned with that too perfect face of his, and took out a small piece of electronic apparatus: a black box with a coiled wire antenna, attached to some kind of meter with a dial and flickering needle behind a small glass window. At one end of the scale the dial was painted red.

"The trigger," he explained, as he placed it in front of Andropov, and watched until the needle jerked to a standstill. "I had the meter wired to it in order to know when the signal had been sent—and 'received.' When that happens, the needle will swing to red and freeze there. And the time will be recorded. The time when you and I and Moscow were supposed to die, and World War III begin!"

"Chinese *bastards!*" Andropov's usually pale face was now chalk white. "Knowing that we'd be mainly interested in them, they used the Tibetans to do their dirty work for them!"

But: "No," Tzonov shook his head. "The Chinese knew nothing about it. The Tibetans were the ones who brought the bomb in and planted it; their fingerprints are all over the weapon parts and that receiver there. But . . . there are fingerprints and fingerprints."

"Explain."

"My locator 'sniffs out' the type of nuclear fuel. Every batch has its own distinct 'smell.' The dump in Chungking was the *source* of the device, yes. But why would the Chinese want to sabotage themselves?" And quickly: "Let me go on . . .

"The dump in Chungking has been depleted by three times the amount of fissionable material in that bomb. Three bombs' worth, then—"

"—Wait!" Andropov picked up his telephone, dialled, and in a moment said, "Sergei? Yuri. Are we on scramble? Good. I remember our listening station intercepted a report concerning the theft of three nuclear devices . . . Chinese, yes. It was—I'm not sure—two to three years ago? But I do remember that heads rolled among the higher echelon in the Chinese Army. Dig out a copy of that report for me, will you? Good." He put the phone down and looked at Tzonov. "I'm sorry. Go on . . . "

"So," Tzonov said. "The final piece in the puzzle. China overran Tibet, destroyed many of the monasteries, and created all kinds of havoc. Now the Tibetans would have their revenge, and safe on the roof of the world watch the rest of us destroy each other. It makes sense."

"Tell me now, where are the other bombs?" Andropov's face was grim now. "I take it your locator has found them for you?"

"By their psychic fingerprints, yes. But Comrade Direktor, can't I tell it my way?"

"Call me . . . oh, Yuri! But yes, go on, go on!"

"Locating the bomb in Moscow was easy, because we don't get much nuclear stuff in here. Even the missiles in our annual parade are dummies; they have no live warheads. Of course not. No sensible government wants this stuff in their highly-populated cities. Especially centres of commerce and control."

"That's where your man looked for them? In the cities?"

"Yes. There is one 'hotspot' in London . . . Hyde Park, we believe—or 'Jekyll and Hyde Park' as we refer to it now."

"And the other—?"

"—Lets the Chinese off the hook, very definitely. For it didn't move too far. It's still in Chungking. Not far from a certain address on Kwijiang Avenue!"

"Their ESP-Centre?"

"Yes. The same signature. And now we see it all."

"Really? Then be so good as to 'see it' for me!"

"At some time in the near future—maybe a time of high tension between East and West, or problems on the Sino-Soviet border—one of the bombs would be detonated. The world would go into shock, briefly, before the accusations started to fly. Then, say thirty-six hours after the first bomb, the second—retaliation, obviously. Confused messages—of peace, *détente*, commonsense, pleading, and threats, of course—are flashing all around the world. But those rubble-strewn centres of commerce were also the centres of communication! Now those communications are down. And in any case, no one is listening! Bomb number three follows in short order . . .

" . . . And numbers four, five, six, seven. China throws in all she's got. And her bombs are crude, dirty. *One* British sub wrecks Russia! France strikes at our satellites. The Americans decide to make it final and finish what they started at Hiroshima and Nagasaki. And we—what's left of us—reply in kind. And the Tibetans count beads, bang gongs, and begin rebuilding their monasteries. It's God's will after all, for he said he'd destroy us by fire next time . . . "

"We must tell the British, of course," Andropov was sweating now.

"Oh?"

"But of course! They would *certainly* blame us—as would the Americans! And it's as you said: afterwards, there'd be no proving who did it."

"Not so. There would be an atomic signature, too—pointing at China."

"And a war with China? On our doorstep? And China our next satellite, once she runs out of steam? No, it can't be allowed. We've come too close to nuclear war in the past. The purpose of these things is to *stop* us killing each other!"

"Of course."

"Therefore we *must* tell London . . . and China." (But Tzonov saw how Andropov was less enthusiastic about that.) "As for the British: they'll owe us a big favour. And it will give us a massive bargaining chip with China! Tzonov—er,

Turkur?—you've done extremely well!" The head of the KGB was on his feet now, coming out from behind his desk, holding out his hand.

Tzonov took it, shook it, said: "I'm glad you're pleased." And he looked Andropov directly in the eyes.

"Not only am *I* pleased, but the Politburo—and Brezhnev, who has been giving me a hard time—will also be pleased. He may even stop blocking my right . . . " He stopped, freed his hand and began to turn away. But too late.

" . . . To succession? Oh, I assure you he will, er, Yuri. He must, and soon, I think . . . " Again Tzonov looked deep into the other's eyes.

Andropov went back behind his desk, sat down again, faded to a dark blot against the haze of light. "Your precog?"

"Did I not tell you my people consider you a very special man?" Tzonov answered. "I'm sure I did . . . "

There was a long pause then, but as Tzonov took the electrical apparatus and replaced it in his briefcase, so Andropov said: "If—and I mean *if*—it comes to pass that I am elected to the Presidency, you have my word that I shall reinstate ESP-Branch. And you, Turkur Tzonov, shall be the head of that branch, responsible only to myself."

"I shall be forever in your debt," Tzonov answered. "But a debt that I'll repay many times over, be sure."

"Oh, I am," Andropov smiled thinly. "And now I have much to do."

"Likewise," Tzonov answered. He brought his feet together, bowed slightly from the waist, walked to the doors.

"And Turkur . . . not a word!"

"Of course not."

"I'll be in touch."

"Yes, Yuri. Except . . . "

Andropov leaned on his desk, looked at Tzonov across the room where he had paused at the doors. "Yes?"

"When *exactly* will it be? I mean, I read it in your mind, you understand? And I agree it has to be done. For we must have a strong leader, after all—especially in times like these—and Brezhnev is little more than a vegetable. It's almost like doing him a favour. So when, exactly, in November, will it be?"

Andropov thought about it for a long time, before slowly answering, "You realize, of course, that while I now accept your weird talent—and those of your group—parapsychology is not generally accepted? And certainly not in evidence."

"Oh, yes. I'm aware of that."

Andropov nodded. "Then *you* tell *me* when, exactly, in November, Brezhnev will die. For after all you read it in my mind."

"The tenth," Tzonov answered at once. "He'll be given the final dose on the morning of the tenth."

"Very . . . clever," said the slightly shaken voice of the figure in the haze.

"And on the eleventh, I shall be head of ESP-Branch."

But Andropov's silhouette only nodded and said, "Good day, young Turkur Tzonov."

Outside Andropov's office, Tzonov narrowed his eyes, gripped his brief-case and commenced walking the marble flags to the stairs. And on his way he thought: *You'd better keep your word, you arrogant bastard!* Having delivered ter-rific power into Andropov's cold hands, he wanted something of it back—and soon. It would have to be very soon, yes. For, as Tzonov was only too well aware, Russia's Premier-elect wasn't destined to last all that long himself . . .

Three days later, at E-Branch HQ in the centre of London, Ben Trask had just spoken to—or rather confronted—Darcy Clarke in his office.

"Just how did this come up?" Darcy asked him, when he was through.

"I had a little time to spare," Trask told him. "I'd finished with the police case I was working on and thought I might catch up on some old files. I never had read everything in connection with that case up in Scotland—those Tibetan monks—and I'd never been too happy with the result of that telephone con-versation you talked me into having with Harry Keogh, to see if he'd had any-thing to do with it. You said it had to be done, but I didn't like it anyway. Hell, we're all on the same side, you know?"

"Were," Darcy told him. "We *were* on the same side. Except Harry left us, remember? Oh, I know the argument—we don't spy on fellow mindspies, etcetera; our own, that is—but I had my reasons, believe me."

"Stuff you couldn't talk about?"

"It was all on a 'need to know' basis," said Darcy. "I needed to know, and you didn't."

"And even now, there's still something you're not telling me," Trask ac-cused.

"Security," the Head of Branch answered. And: "Look, Ben, I like the Necroscope as much as you do, as much as we all do, but when he left the Branch . . . "

"He became a security problem?"

"Could have become one . . . which is as much as I'm going to say." Darcy knew Trask's talent for getting at the truth of a subject—the fact that he was a human lie detector—and so tried to change the subject, or at least divert it. "So, what did you find in the files?"

"Something that the police had covered up, from the general public any-way," Trask answered. "Probably because they'd been asked to do so, and prob-ably by us." Looking at Clarke's face—his changing expression—he knew that he was right. He read the truth of it in the other's frown, the way he blinked his eyes.

"The crossbow bolts," Clarke said.

"Right," Trask answered. "Silvered bolt-heads. One buried in the door of that burned-out station-wagon, and another in the heart of a Sunday roast that used to be a man. The same kind of bolt-heads that were used in the garage that time. The same ones that Harry used, or so we believe. But we never did find the actual crossbow."

"You've a good memory," Clarke told him. "But didn't you ever stop to think I might be covering up for Harry?"

"Does he need covering up for? The way I see it, he did a good job that time. He *always* did a good job!"

"That's how *you* see it," said Darcy. "But the police see it differently. To them, murder is murder unless it's a state execution, and we stopped doing that a long time ago."

"What are you saying? That because Harry had quit E-Branch, because he no longer had our cover, the police could have dragged him in for the Scottish job?"

"Maybe," Clarke shrugged. "If he'd left clues to tie him to it."

"And did he?"

"No, just those bolt-heads—which tied the job to us instead, because the police knew it was one of *our* agents who'd put the whammy on that auto-theft gang!"

Trask cocked his head a little and pursed his lips. Darcy Clarke was telling the truth, he knew, but he still wasn't telling all of it. And that galled. "So," Trask mused, "since you already knew that the Necroscope was involved with these Tibetans—in fact that he'd taken them out—why did you require me to check him out? What else were you worried about, Darcy? And what are you still worried about?"

Clarke slumped a little behind his desk. "Is it that obvious?"

"To me, yes. Has been for more than three years now, ever since Harry walked—or 'went'—out of here. But especially in the last three months or so, since this incident with these Hari Krishna types. I mean, why can't you talk about it? Is it the old Department of Dirty Tricks again?"

And even before Clarke could answer, his expression said it all, said yes, it was *that* department again.

Trask nodded. "Now tell me about it," he said. "Because I really do 'need to know.' I need to be reassured that I'm working for the right side. Or at least the best side!"

Clarke sat up straighter and sighed. "All right Ben, I'll tell you. But since you expect straight answers from me, first let me ask *you* something. Do you really think that if you or I or any one of us should decide to leave the Branch it would be as easy as that? I mean, like snapping your fingers? What, you should be allowed to walk out of here—knowing all we've done, something of what we still might do, and everything we're capable of doing; with all the weird stuff you have seen and still got stuck in your head—and no questions asked?"

Trask saw it at once. "We 'fixed' him," he said, and his jaw jutted a very little. "How was it done?"

"Ben," Darcy said, "Think it over, will you? Without getting too excited? We're not just talking about an ordinary man or talent here. There *are* no ordinary talents, not in E-Branch. But we are talking about the most extraordinary talent of all—the Necroscope, Harry Keogh. He can go . . . anywhere, instantly! He talks to . . . to *dead* people, for God's sake! Of which there are a Great Majority who'll do just about anything for him. And we could just let him walk? Well, maybe we could, but there are others higher up the ladder who couldn't."

"How was it done?"

"Ben," Darcy was reaching the end of his tether. "I'm the one who's had to live with it. Why can't you leave it at that? Put it this way: this was the soft option . . ."

For a long moment there was silence, until Trask exploded, "I don't believe it!" But the trouble was he did, because he of all men knew it was the truth.

"We recruited him, remember? Keenan Gormley recruited him. And if he could do it nicely, then someone else might try to do it nasty. And anyway, it's no big deal," Darcy felt like he was lying, but had no choice. "Harry's lost nothing, except he just can't talk about it anymore. He can still do his thing, but no one else is ever going to get to know about it."

And now Trask understood. "Hypnotism!" he said.

And Darcy nodded. "The soft option. But still, and as you yourself pointed out, I've worried about it ever since."

And Trask saw the truth of that, too. "It's been on your shoulders like a tangible weight."

"An *extra* weight," Darcy answered. "A few extra ounces on top of the ton or so that's already there."

"You knew it was wrong—or that it wasn't right—and I sensed it in you. You felt that you'd lied to Harry . . . "

" . . . No," Darcy said. "But that I hadn't told him the whole truth? Yes."

"The reason I felt it was because it wasn't you. The moment Harry's name entered a conversation, you didn't read quite right."

"All right, so I'm guilty!" Darcy snapped. "And what about you, if or when it's your turn to run the show? Do you think it will be any easier for you? With your talent? Well it won't be. It'll be hell, Ben!"

The other thought about it, and said, "And there's nothing we can do about it? We can't put it right?"

"No . . . yes! Not for Harry, no. But for me? You've already done it, Ben. A load shared is a burden halved. Now you'll have to carry it, too. But you'll get used to it. And at least we'll be able to tell ourselves that Harry's still alive!"

For a moment they glared at each other, then gradually relaxed . . . and Darcy's intercom came cracklingly alive. "Sir?"

Darcy thumbed the Duty Officer's button. "Yes?"

"Minister Responsible. Urgent. Do you want it on screen?"

"Yes. Thanks."

A moment later his desk screen came alive, flickered for a second or two, got angry with itself in a crackle of static, then snapped into sharp focus. It displayed this legend:

> Origination: MinRes.
> Destination: Director INTESP.
> Duty Officer INTESP.
> FOR YOUR EYES ONLY! Message follows . . .

Trask had come round to Darcy's side of the desk. "I better not look, right?" The way he said it, Darcy felt the edge of sarcasm in his voice. And:

"Oh, don't be fucking silly!" he snapped.

The message followed:

For public consumption (Press, BBC, ITV, etc.) "A treasure-seeker with a metal-detector has found a World War II bomb in Hyde Park. The area has been secured and all buildings in the immediate vicinity are being vacated . . . "

Mr. Clarke: this isn't as it's made out to be. A man from my office has been fully briefed. He and other experts are on the scene right now. Take some of your best men and get down to Hyde Park. I shall need your first impressions and best opinions.

Good luck—
MinRes

"Good luck?" Trask murmured. And: "What the hell . . . ?" as a PS printed itself under the message:

Mr. Clarke, in the event that I or any other Minister should be required, the usual Whitehall telephone numbers will not suffice. You may contact me on:

Followed by a number. But there was something about the number that Darcy Clarke didn't like. Or if not him, his talent.

He waited until the screen cleared, punched in the number and queried it. The computer asked him for his security clearance, the first time *that* had ever happened!

He punched that in, too, and finally got his answer:

An allegedly "decommissioned" nuclear bunker in Uxbridge, fifteen miles out of the city.

"Christ!" Darcy gasped, as he felt the short hairs rising on the back of his neck. "It's clean underpants time again!"

"That bad?" Trask's query—his tone of voice—said it all: the other stuff was over and done with and he was Darcy's strong right arm again.

"Worse," Darcy answered. "A hell of a lot worse, Ben!"

But they had to wait until they got down to Hyde Park to find out just how bad it really was. Or how bad it might have been . . .

IV

RADU: HE DREAMS ON

RADU DREAMED HIS OLDEN, RECURRENT BUT FREQUENTLY FADING DREAMS OF blood. As ever, he strove to restructure and reinstate them in the eye of a memory occasionally filmed over by six centuries of sleep, his undead hibernation. He dreamed of ages past and the life he'd known then, and of the many lives he'd consumed since then. Crimson dreams of his beginnings in a vampire world; of his conversion to something other than a man; of his eventual banishment into a new, entirely different world, and his everlasting and soon to be on-going bloodwar against those who had dared to rape and ruin what little he had loved.

Less than vivid, his dreams, unless they were recounted, reinforced, revisited over and over to bring them into nightmare definition in Radu's yet more nightmarish mind. For these were things that he desired to remember forever. They were his one recourse, his only means of keeping his hatred alive while he waited out his time in a resin tomb, sleeping but not dead.

He recalled names from the swirling mists of a far-distant past: Giorga, Ion, and Lexandru Zirescu; and the Ferenczys, Lagula and Rakhi. In another time and world, the Zirescus had been his direst enemies, and the Ferenczys were Olden Lords of Starside. Now they were all long dead, and Radu relished fond memories of how he had dealt with them . . . and thoughts of how he would *next* deal with any survivor or descendant when once more he was up and abroad in a changed and ever-changing world. For the dog-Lord knew that there were such descendants, definitely . . .

. . . Abroad in the world, aye. And indeed, upon a time, he and his various packs, his pups, had been "abroad." Sufficient to start, or certainly to reinforce, legends as old as mankind itself: of the werewolf and the vampire—or of both. For Radu Lykan *was* both—Wamphyri!

His dreaming mind went back, back, back . . . to how it had been in those earliest days of his coming here . . .

In Starside he had been found guilty of treason. As punishment, Shaitan the Unborn, self-styled High Magistrate of all the Wamphyri, had had Radu and a handful of his retainers—a lieutenant or two and a few thralls—thrown into the so-called Hell-lands Gate, from which no one ever returned.

It had been like a long, slow fall into some weird white hell, and for a time Radu and the others had thought that this was all there was to it: to drift downward (or sideways, or up? . . . the Gate was a strange place!) forever, or until starvation put paid to them and they shrivelled to husks. But that wasn't to be the way of it.

The real hell began where the Gate opened into this world, in a subterranean cavern carved by an underground river. Lit by the glare of the Gate, the cavern's narrow ledges were cold and damp; the river was in flood and rushed through its borehole in a frenzy of black water. Along the course of the river where it left the cave, the walls bottlenecked and there was scarcely a gap between the water and the ceiling.

Black, rushing water: the Wamphyri feared it! Not for any superstitious reason (for contrary to certain myths, they swam as well as any creature); but deprived of air, buffetted against stone walls, and crushed by unfathomed depths, how *long* may a man or even a vampire survive? Flesh softens, fails, and is sloughed away. And when body and brains fall apart, all that remains is naked bone, to be broken up and rounded to pebbles. Perhaps this was the nature of these hell-lands.

Radu had a choice, but not much of one: brave the rushing waters, or stay safe on a ledge or crammed in some crevice till he had no strength to move but got cemented in place by layers of dripstone. And:

"Do as you see fit," he had told the others with him. "This river may run downhill forever . . . in which case it's goodbye Radu! But somewhere out there is moonlight, which I would feel silvering my neck again—or my ruff if the moon is full!" And with that he had jumped from the ledge and been borne under.

The other Lords and their men had followed suit, likewise Radu's lieutenants and a few thralls; some of whom survived to surface in Dacia near a Roman barter camp on the Danuvius. The year was AD 371, and the moon was indeed full. From which time forward the place would always be known as Radujevac . . .

That had been a time! (Radu's dreams sped fleet before the eye of his mind.) Night-skirmishes with legionnaires along the Danube and in the Dacian hamlets; piracy on the merchant shipping; blood-feasts by the light of the full moon. And as for the men of that era: they'd been naive as children when first Radu and the others came among them. Their sciences were young, superstitions many, and their blood sweet as any in Sunside in the far vampire world of Radu's origin. But as compared with the Szgany of Sunside: their numbers were vast, their races diverse, their courage unbelievable and their skills in battle phenomenal!

Still, in the first hundred to two hundred years the werewolf had flourished . . . *and* the true vampire! For the dog-Lord Radu was not the only Lord of the Wamphyri banished by Shaitan. Indeed, several great rivals had come through the Gate with him, at or about the same time. Such as Nonari "the Gross" Ferenczy, and the Drakul brothers, Karl and Egon. In Starside the Drakuls had been Radu's allies against Shaitan; here, they were simply rivals. And as for Nonari:

Nonari had made a blood-oath: to wipe out the dog-Lord and every last trace of him for the alleged "murders" of his father Lagula and his uncle Rakhi. But in Radu Lykan's eyes these were never murders but the putting right of a great wrong; for Rakhi and Lagula had been members of a foul Szgany gang who had raped his sister Magda of innocence and life. *Hah!* The Ferenczys were survivors no more—except in Lagula's son, Nonari. But savage as that one's blood vow had been, it was equalled and even surpassed by Radu's. For him there'd be neither peace nor respite until the very *name* Ferenczy was forgotten as if it never existed.

Their blood-feud came with them into Earth; it might have been settled there and then, in Dacia on the banks of the Danube. But this was a new world and strange, and survival was ever the first rule of the Wamphyri. So the Drakuls went up into the stony mountains (later the Carpathians), to find or build their aeries; Nonari fled east from Radu's wrath and took a new name; the dog-Lord crossed the river with his small pack, spread out into the lands around, and eventually became an adventurer and mercenary in a war-torn world.

But while that Classical World was vast beyond the dreams of any vampire Lord who had ever been, still it could never be big enough . . .

Radu's life (and with it the history of a world) passed in pageant over the buffed and slippery boards of his memory.

The history of a world. Of wars. And of men.

The Romans. But the Empire was on the wane, at least where the dog-Lord and the others came forth. Aye, for the Goths were coming, who were the merest harbingers of what *else* was coming! Such wars, such battles, such blood!

But . . . hell-lands? Ah no! It had been more like some Wamphyri heaven . . . for a time. But already Radu had noted how men reacted to the presence of the Wamphyri: fearfully at first, in a world rife with superstition—but then they fought back! For while men may suffer their lands to be stolen, their wives seduced away and their children eaten, when finally there is nothing left then there's nothing to lose. Unlike Sunside's Szgany, not all of these men of Earth were farmers or hunter-gatherers. Great armies of warrior tribesmen were sweeping the world, and sweeping all before them. And as for fear of the Wamphyri:

Frequently these eastern invaders had not even known they went up against vampires; they were merely murdering rich Dacian landowners in their gloomy castles, or hairy halfling creatures in foothill keeps, caverns and lairs. Also, these warrior hordes knew how to destroy their enemies: how a lance or arrow through the heart would kill a man, and how his *head* on a lance would guarantee that he was dead! Then how to reduce his castle and its contents to ashes, until nothing remained. Such was the way of the barbarian warrior, by no means reserved for the Wamphyri. But did these methods *work* against the Wamphyri? Be sure they did. Indeed they were the only ones that could! The stake, the sword, the fire . . .

And because of the times—times of change, tumult and crisis—the legend and *fact* of the Wamphyri, of the blood-crazed vampire and werewolf, was *almost* eradicated. What need for monstrous myths in a world that was in reality a bloodbath? Forty years after Radu's advent the Visigoths had sacked Rome itself! And forty-five years later it had fallen again, to the Vandals; except then Radu had been *with* the Vandals. For like every vampire Lord before him he was unable to resist blood—certainly not in such copious amounts.

War, to which Radu was drawn like a moth to the flame, and which singed him much the same. Or if not the wars, the commanders he fought under, who were treacherous to a fault. But *such* wars to be warred as nothing conceived by even the mightiest of the old Starside Lords! And down all the decades and centuries, the dog-Lord was a bloody mercenary washed hither and to by the red tides of conquest.

Gifted to some degree in oneiromancy, Radu used his dreams to scry on future battles. By this means he would often know in advance which side to join. Likewise, he stayed alert for portents and signs of those olden enemies who came through the Hell-lands Gate with him. And time and again he cursed himself that he'd not dealt with them then, when they were at their weakest. But then, he had been at his weakest, too.

And naive? Aye, he'd been that. To have sold his services to warlords, and think he would actually get paid and accepted as their equal.

Gaeseric of the Vandals had been the first to use and misuse him. After the sack of Rome, Radu had made his camp in the *Colli Albani* twelve miles out of the fallen city. Of course it was necessary to keep his "men" from the common soldiery; they were not only mercenaries and guerrillas but moon-children; he knew that fraternization could only lead to discovery, and one of the prime tenets of the vampire was that longevity was synonymous with anonymity. If men should guess what Radu was they would do away with him and his at once! And because of the dog-Lord's preference for night-fighting by the light of the moon, Gaeseric had already dubbed him "Radu, Hound of Night." And so it were best that the full *extent* of his wolfishness remained a secret.

Be that as it may, still Gaeseric had tricked him, turned on him. For what was he after all but a scurvy, hairy mercenary with a handful of howling berserks, like wolves of war? But the city had fallen now and Radu and his lot had been paid off. And having paid him in gold—having let him take women, wine, and other booty out of the city—

. . . By now he'd be drunk up in the hills, and all that gold gone to waste.

Or perhaps not.

By means of a lie—an alleged counterattack by a fleet of the Eastern Empire—the dog-Lord's forces were split into two contingents and dispatched to "defensive positions," where Vandal ambushes reduced his men to ten out of a hundred and fifty. His women were ravished and slain, his gold stolen, his den in the *Colli Albani* destroyed. But Radu and his handful had survived to head north for the Appenino heights that stretched the full length of Italia. In a land awash in Vandals, the rugged mountains would be the safest route out.

As for the treacherous Gaeseric: the dog-Lord must add a second blood-oath to his list. And where the Vandals as a race were concerned . . . from that time forward Radu would always be on the lookout for a way to take his revenge . . .

Fleeing Italy, Radu took his time; took his much-reduced band back to the Danube, then east through the woods and mountains, and eventually down into familiar Dacian territories. This was barbarian country now, but south of the river the people were mainly Christian. Radu had only one religion: blood! The various faiths and superstitions of locals and invaders alike made little or no difference to him, except it was safer to journey among the Christians.

Finally he headed north again, into the mountains of what would much later become Wallachia. For as in Italy, he believed that in taking the high ground he'd be secure from the tides of war washing all around. He needed some time to think and formulate his plans.

On his way from Rome to Dacia he had "accumulated" monies from Roman citizens fleeing the vandalism, and from small parties of the Vandals themselves still scathing in the land around. And on the Danube there'd been a last handful of Roman travellers and traders. Now, since for the time being the dog-Lord had had enough of war, he decided to put his gold to use.

Thus in the year AD 467, he and the pack wintered down in what would be their lair for the next sixty years: a great cave in the mountains of western Moldavia. He employed refugees from the Moldavian plains, which were still suffering under sporadic attacks from Asiatic warriors on horseback, to make his crag or aerie habitable. And he recruited (in his way) the strongest of these workers for his lieutenants.

And because day by day, year by year, fresh refugees were fleeing the warfare, climbing the mountains, reduced to scavenging in the heights, there was a steady turnover of workers and no lack of . . . provisions. Also, there was never any trickling away of Radu's gold, which he would steal back from anyone foolish enough to attempt desertion. And while work was in progress to make the cavern liveable, he was not remiss in seeing to its defences; he disguised its appearance externally, until it was simply a part of the crags all around.

It took time, even years, before Wolfscrag was finished to Radu's satisfaction, following which he had no more use for his workers from the Moldavian steppe. Or at best—or worst—only one more use . . .

During all of this time the dog-Lord and his men had gone without their "comforts": good wine and woman-flesh, which even as mercenaries under entirely human commanders they had come to expect as their right. No one ever grumbled, however, for Radu was known to deal with complaints in short order. He did understand the problems, though, for he shared them equally with his lieutenants and thralls.

There were now trappers in the mountains; Radu killed or recruited them, and took their women for his own. And from now on, any who entered that region of the Moldavian heights would suffer the same fate. And now Wolfscrag was more truly a home, or an aerie, for him and his.

Earlier, aware that the Huns had had the run of the steppe for decades and wondering if their supremacy was still holding, Radu had sent scouts east to discover the state of things. Others had been sent west along the twin spurs of the Carpathians, and spies into various makeshift hamlets clinging to the flanks of the mountains not far removed from Wolfscrag.

Eventually these scouts returned; the dog-Lord learned how the ramshackle hamlets of Moldavian refugees and the more distant Carpathian villages were ripe for conquest. The people were pacifists, isolationists who had cut themselves off completely from Dacia's war-torn regions and the great battlefields under the mountains.

Radu couldn't say he blamed them, but in any case his intentions didn't run to conquest—not yet, anyway. Or at best a very subtle conquest. Instead he would offer these people his services as a mercenary warrior, a *Voevod* against who- or whatever might brave these mountains to attack them. And in fifty more years he did just that.

But as well as hard information, his spies and scouts had brought back rumours, too. One of them had heard it that a Ferenczy was in league with the Vandals! Good luck to him, whoever he was, be it Nonari the Gross—if he yet lived—or an alleged egg-son, one Belos Pheropzis. For if that bastard Gaeseric dealt as badly with all of his mercenaries as he had dealt with Radu . . . well, that was at least one Ferenczy that the dog-Lord needn't bother to hunt down . . . !

Meanwhile, in the twin spurs of the Western Carpathians, the Drakuls had gained apparently impregnable footholds. Throwing caution to the wind—ignoring their own tenet that longevity is synonymous with anonymity—they ruled openly and by terror. People *knew* of them, and their works. True vampires, they flew—and slew, and converted—by night. Radu had sent spies to seek them out and learn the locations of their aeries; his men never returned. That should have been warning enough of Drakul superiority, but . . . Radu was safe in Wolfscrag. Or so he reckoned.

But eventually Drakul incursions into territory that Radu considered his own became too much and he determined to strike back. They had many advantages. Masters of metamorphism, they could shape their bodies for flying. Long-established in their places, their aeries were allegedly impregnable. But they had some disadvantages, too. Children of the night, they could not go out in daylight; every morning must find them safe in their beds of soil out of Starside. And they were very well aware of the dog-Lord's ruthlessness and savagery: that if he did come upon them there would be no bargaining, no quarter, no mercy.

Then on the eve of Radu's strike westward, a fresh rumour, but one that he couldn't possibly ignore. He went down into the steppe, to Bacau where this whisper had origin. And the truth was learned there:

How the Emperor Justinian had commissioned a fleet under Belisarius, to strike at the Vandals even across the Mediterranean, in north Africa and other parts. In short, to take back the Western Empire.

The Vandals! And Radu's old vow unfulfilled! And a Ferenczy among the treacherous scum at that! Old Gaeseric had gone the way of all or most flesh sixty or more years ago, but the Vandal kingdom remained and at least one Ferenczy! Well, even after all this time any surviving member of the Ferenczy dynasty was far and away Radu's direst enemy, spawn of the original destroyers of his dearest love in another world, another time, but all of it like yesterday to Radu.

Torn two ways—between attacking the Drakuls, and joining Belisarius as a mercenary and an expert in Vandal tactics—he returned to Wolfscrag in the heights . . .

. . . Only to find that the Drakuls had paid a visit in his absence. The place had been destroyed utterly, and most of his men and women, thralls and lieutenants, with it. No choice now but war on the Vandals, for to go against the Drakuls with his remaining handful were madness.

But later . . . ?

There would always be a later. And Radu, who was ever the opportunist, saw at least one distinct possibility:

Join with Belisarius, distinguish himself in the field of battle, eventually return to these desolate heights as Voevod of all Dacia . . . all with the Emperor's approval! *Then* see to these damned Drakuls, with an entire legion, perhaps, to back him up.

It was a good, even a grand scheme. And irresistible . . .

Radu's expert knowledge of the Vandals at war served him well. In Plika on the Black Sea, he broached that very subject to a squat, yellow, scar-faced and slant-eyed Hun *condottiere*, the son of the son of an Asian invader who had settled the steppe sixty years ago. Commander of a force of two hundred, now Tok Heng had had enough of farming and was returning to his grandfather's trade. But in fact, and as he admitted to Radu where they swilled wine in a tavern, he had never left it. His land had been stolen *for* him by warrior ancestors; the Romans had stolen it back *from* his father, and given it to peasants; Tok had stolen it a third time—with the result that the Romans had put a price on his head. Since he couldn't beat them he'd decided to join them; there was a pardon in it for him and his men—and a promise of citizenship and of land—if he would join Belisarius's force and fight the Vandals in the Mediterranean and Africa. Now he was waiting on ocean transport to take them to Constantinople.

But Tok was fifty men short of the contingent he'd promised to Belisarius's recruiters; perhaps Radu and his lot would care to join forces with him and make up his numbers? Certainly the fact that Radu had knowledge of Vandal battle tactics would be an advantage. The dog-Lord laughed at that. He fought under no man's colours but his own. Maybe Tok would care to join him? Or perhaps they could agree on a form of shared leadership?

No, Tok Heng wouldn't have it. But . . .

It was the time of the full moon; that night Radu converted the Hun and thus became leader of his mercenary band . . .

* * *

As for mixing in with the "Romans":

In Constantinople it was observed how Belisarius's army of fifteen thousand—ten thousand foot soldiers and five thousand cavalry—was composed mainly of mercenaries under *condottiere* commanders. Of actual Romans . . . there were a few. This was the best that Justinian's general could muster. And so there was no trouble at all mixing with true Romans, only in finding them!

Radu was allotted ten vessels with crews out of a fleet of five hundred, and was obliged to take horses on board, too. But since horses didn't care for him or his, he made sure that his "command" vessel was kept free of them and that they went with Tok Heng's people, who understood them. Thus a majority of the dog-Lord's original party, survivors of the massacre at Wolfscrag, travelled with him.

And Radu looked forward to killing Vandals. Nor was there long to wait . . .

The best of the Vandal fleet and soldiers were in Sardinia putting down a revolt; thus Belisarius's army was able to disembark without trouble near Sousse. Gelimer the Vandal King mustered what remained of his forces and met Belisarius head-on at a place called Decimum . . . well-named, for there Gelimer's forces *were* decimated! The survivors fled into Numidia, and Belisarius marched into Carthage mid-September, AD 533.

Gelimer had not fallen at Decimum. He recalled his troops out of Sardinia, mustered what remained of the Vandals locally, bought the services of Moors, and finally, in mid-December, offered battle on the approach route to Carthage. But weakened by recent losses, and in any case enervated by a century of "civilization," the Vandals were no match for Belisarius.

The Byzantine cavalry charged . . . and swept them away!

The weather was warm even for mid-December. The dog-Lord's moon-children played the same part in the final battle as they had played at Decimum: leaving Tok's Huns in support of Belisarius's cavalry, they went forward as advance scouts on the eve of battle (during the night, of course), and in the following night ranged far and wide to seek out any survivors who might try to form pockets of resistance—

—While Radu himself sought someone, or something, else. A Ferenczy was here! He could *smell* him! Disguised as a Vandal, or a Moor, or whatever, a Ferenczy *was* or had been here!

Who, why, how? Radu couldn't say. He could have been here for fifty years, or a hundred; he might even have stood off and witnessed the conquest of these parts by the Vandals. But hearing of the battle at Decimum—and perhaps fearing a Roman *re*-conquest—*he* had come down from his high place to join in the fighting, or simply to observe and so know the result at first hand. But which high place? For Radu knew that a Ferenczy—no less than a Drakul, and far more than any dog-Lord—*must* have his aerie.

Radu had checked charts of the land around. Sure enough, there was a peak mightier than any Starside stack near Zaghounan. Why, from up there, at night—looking east through his vampire's eyes, and employing Wamphyri "intelligence," senses more than the usual five—this Ferenczy would have known or even "seen" the approach and landing of Belisarius's fleet! Be *sure* he would have known that Radu was part of that fleet!

And cowled against the last rays of sunlight, in the evening after the battle while his men ranged abroad, so Radu had scoured the smoking field of combat like some strange, carrion dog. He found some that *might* have been the Ferenczy's—some that seemed dead but yet moaned, or were full of weird, creeping motion—and showed the men he had taken with him how to deal with them. Hun scavengers were also in the field; perhaps they thought it odd that Radu's escort were beheading and burning dead men, but they said nothing . . .

Later, Radu went up with a lieutenant and some thralls into the peak near Zaghounnan. This rearing knoll was or had been on the very border of Vandal territory, with Berber lands to the west. In short, it was neutral territory, no-man's-land.

Near the top, they found earthworks and ancient fortifications; and within the mounds and ramps, an aerie. The place was only recently deserted; there was evidence of an urgent departure. The aerie itself . . . took the dog-Lord back more than four hundred years, to Starside in a now alien world. It was unmistakable: that ultimate spire of the mountain, like a great fang thrusting for the sky. No windows faced east, just sun-bleached rock; all hollow within and tunnelled beneath, with roots going down into darkness. Radu and his men descended spiralling stone steps. There were vast, echoing chambers down there, and mighty stone vats, all unfinished. This Ferenczy would have bred monsters here—which gave the dog-Lord pause. The time might come when he must breed them, too . . .

A thrall lookout called down: a cloud of dust was approaching out of the west. It was a party of camel-riders, Berbers, heading this way. Radu let them come, and as dusk fell emerged from a jumble of rocks behind them where they climbed a frequently used track. The Berbers had three beautiful black girls trussed like chickens, doubtless for trading with this unknown, fled Ferenczy. Radu traded death for them, but not until he had tortured the Berbers to find out more about the Ferenczy. Waldemar Ferrenzig was his name—a German! Well, and so were the Vandals; but they had been here ten or more years *before* Waldemar. This the Berbers knew from their fathers before them.

So, it seemed that Radu's earlier information (with regard to a Ferenczy having sided "with" the Vandals) was only partly right. Sixty-five years ago—perhaps only a few years before Radu himself had arrived in the Moldavian heights—Hun invaders had driven this Waldemar, this son of Belos Pheropzis (himself the son of Nonari "the Gross" Ferenczy), out of his Moldavian keep. Under the assumed Germanic name of Ferrenzig, he had been accepted by the Vandals and allowed to settle here. Presumably he was rich, for he'd been able to trade with the Berbers and buy their friendship. But now that the Romans were back he had fled again.

Hah! But it pleased the dog-Lord to believe that the Ferenczy *had fled from him,* and perhaps on both occasions! And so he was a cowardly, scummy Ferenczy, like his ancestors in Starside before him, and more recent forebears in this world. Well, it wasn't over yet; their tracks might cross again, except the next time Radu would have better luck . . .

He questioned the terrified girls. They were "princesses," they said. Daughters of a nomad Sheik, they had been stolen by the Berbers for ransom or trading. That last, at least, was as Radu had suspected. He kissed all three (merely *kissed* them), gave them the Berber camels and sent them on their way. Waldemar Ferrenzig would have dealt ill with them; wherefore, contrary to his nature, Radu dealt well with them! Any other time he would have used them, and fed them to his pups . . .

The dog-Lord would have gone back with Belisarius to Constantinople, to witness the general's triumph. But already rumours were circulating as to his nature. It was AD 534, and the Mediterranean was broad and deep. Radu determined to be a pirate for a while.

But in Carthage, where the Roman fleet mustered and provisioned prior to setting sail for Byzantium, he learned more of this Waldemar Ferrenzig:

A fisherman told him how a ship had sailed by night from Tunis only weeks after the destruction of the Vandal army, and how a "great dark lord"—the commander of this Numidian vessel—had tried to recruit him as a crew-member. The fisherman had seen charts; he knew his sea lanes; the ship would be heading north for Sardinia, past Corsica and so to the mainland.

So, by now a Ferenczy was back on the Mediterranean's northern seaboard, perhaps heading for those same Moldavian mountains "beloved" of his father, Belos, and his grandfather, Nonari the Gross, before him. Or maybe Waldemar had determined to become a pirate, too, in which case Radu might yet come across him during his own voyaging.

And maybe not . . .

The first night out from Carthage Radu called a mist up out of the sea, a vampire mist like slime against the skins of Belisarius's crews. By the time his mist dispersed the dog-Lord had sailed away, and now he commanded a fleet of ten ships . . .

In Radu's memory the past speeded up as if a wind were turning the pages of history; sequences of events became blurred; they began to overlap. He was like a dying man, recounting his life in the moments before true death. That was a thought that disturbed him even in his sleep. For indeed he might well be dying, if the seeds of the plague were still alive in him and working on his vampire flesh. But the pages of history were still turning, and he couldn't ignore them.

. . . The Vandals were no more, their kingdom destroyed forever. Thus one of the dog-Lord's blood-oaths had been fulfilled at least. But again he had had enough of human commanders, and it was time he moved on to other things.

For a hundred and twenty years Radu was a corsair, a seawolf; his standard was a wolf's head against a full moon. Time and time again he replaced his aging ships with the vessels of traders and their escorts, or vanquished ships of war sent out to hunt him down. But he lost ships, too, till finally his ten were down to three.

Then in AD 654, near the island of Rhodes, he was engaged by a fleet of Arab warships out of Alexandria. Two of his vessels went up in smoke and flames; they sank just before nightfall; Radu was left to limp off to Crete to make repairs, and finally on to Sicily. By which time he had known that the Mediterranean was no longer a safe hunting ground. Islam was now a power, and the dog-Lord would do well to look to his future. But in any case, he had had enough of sea battles. On land it was one thing to engage in hand-to-hand combat—when with a shield and sword, or tooth and claw, he'd be the equal of any ten normal adversaries—but on the sea it was an entirely different thing. To have your enemy stand off and use his hurling-engines to lob sizzling balls of fire at you . . . to stand on a burning deck in the heat and the reek, and feel your ship sinking under you! . . . What was *that* for a fair fight? Not that he had ever cared much for fairness . . .

For a hundred and sixty years Radu was a bandit chief in the mountains of Corsica, from which he raided on the coastal towns and villages. A wolf, he was impossible to track over the rugged terrain—and who would want to track him? None who set out after him ever returned! And so he was first in a long line of Corsican outlaws. But the Saracens were still coming; Muslim pirates out of Sicily quickly became a far greater scourge than the dog-Lord; eventually he must move on.

Radu and his small band stole a ship and sailed north for the land of the Lombards, landed and loped east for Bulgar territories, and down to the Danube which he knew so well—

—And at once up into the Carpathians, when he discovered how fierce were the Bulgars! Ah, but the Drakuls had discovered it, too, as the "myths and legends" of Bulgar grandams at their hearth-fires were wont to confirm:

How two hundred years ago, brave ancestors had sought out the *obours*, the wampyrs in their mountain castles, and hounded them from the land. The *obours* were blood-sucking creatures who lived on bairns and virgins, and could shape themselves as bats to flee into the night. Though some of them had escaped in this fashion, their thralls and odalisques had been discovered in hiding. Hissing like snakes, they had been crucified and burned to ashes. And the castles of the *obours* had been razed to ruins . . .

Well, good! But in his heart of hearts Radu knew that the Drakuls themselves were still alive. Their power may have been destroyed—for the moment, at least—but *they* had survived. For there was a pain in him which would not go away until they had suffered the true death. Preferably at his hands . . .

When times were quiet he sent out spies to learn the way of things, and as always he stayed alert for word of the worst of his olden enemies, the Ferenczys—for he assumed that Waldemar would produce offspring. *Huh!* It would be a further fourteen decades before he heard of him and his again . . .

And meanwhile, as ever, the world was in flux . . .

It seemed no time at all (but in fact was seventy years) before Magyars occupied the fertile western plains. Since they were horsemen, the dog-Lord felt safe in the mountains . . .

Safe and bored! But while the Magyars were on the plains Radu would stay in the heights—until sixty years later, when in a dream he saw the next great battle, in which these savage horsemen would suffer their most decisive defeat. If it should come to pass, the plains and horseshoe mountains, and the Danube itself, would be up for the taking! And still Radu considered these lands his own, as he had from the beginning.

It was sufficient to send him and his pups north to skirt the plains, then west into Germany, where they joined Otto the First's forces at Lechfeld in the year 955. Then Radu's oneiromantic dreams were seen to be accurate in every detail. Loaded down with loot, their mounts exhausted, the Magyars were swatted like flies. Offering little or no resistance, their blood mingled with their spilled gold on a steaming field of battle. And when the fighting was over, their leaders were executed to a man.

Radu and his band were mercenary foot soldiers. Paid off—but remembering other payments, not to mention harshly enforced *re*-payments—he retreated at once back into the east, back to the mountains . . .

. . . **W**here a few years later he learned of a "great Boyar" with a castle in the Khorvaty north of Moldavia, a man called "Valdemar Fuhrenzig!" Now *surely* this must be that same Waldemar who had fled from the Romans, or from Radu, in Africa; that son of Belos Pheropzis, and grandson of Nonari "the Gross" Ferenczy? Aye, *and* Radu's immemorial enemy—and a blood-oath still outstanding!

But . . . in the Khorvaty, east of the mountains? A friend of Kievan Russia, then, this "Valdemar," with an aerie within its borders? A Boyar, he would have land and men and probably the protection of the Russian Prince. And what was Radu but a bandit in the hills? And if the dog-Lord had knowledge of this Valdemar, presumably Valdemar had knowledge of him. *Damnation!*

There was no putting it off: it was time Radu was on his way again.

Piracy! It had had its good points, and could have again. Anyway, the Saracens were in Radu's debt—a debt of blood—and it was high time he collected. When he learned from travellers how men of Western Christendom (chiefly free-booters out of Pisa and Genoa) were fighting Saracens on what the Arabs now considered their own "great lake," in Ligurian and Tyrrhenian waters, the dog-Lord was finally decided and knew what he must do.

A further hundred years of sea battles . . .

. . . Radu was with the Byzantines when they took back Crete and Cyprus from the Saracens . . .

. . . He was a pirate out of Pisa when Corsica, Sardinia and the Balearics fell . . .

He was rich on Arab gold beyond dreams of avarice, and a legendary sea-wolf . . . when, in 1118, fortune went against him and his boat was attacked by the Saracens off Syracuse. Fished from the sea burned, gouged, and half-drowned—taken hostage by the Saracens, who had learned to respect him—he was held for ransom in Ascalon for five of his longest years. But who was there to pay for his freedom? No one knew or would accept him; eventually his jail-ers must weary of feeding him and simply dispose of him. Also, his prison was thought to be inescapable, and in any case he was in no fit state to even try for an escape. Thus he spent the time healing himself—

—Until the Venetian naval victory of 1123, when in the panic and hysteria of the time he finally broke jail.

Having learned the Muslim tongue, and indeed *looking* like a long, loping Arab (and thus fearing to approach the Venetian crews where some of their ships had landed), Radu, a man alone now, took to the deserts and the high ground and made his way north . . .

. . . For years he fished the Sea of Galilee . . .

. . . He became a "holy man," a seer who read the future in dreams, in the Monastery on the Great Peak at Talat Musa . . .

. . . Eventually the real holy men were no more; Radu had a new lair and by night was leader of a fine pack; while in the daylight, thick monkish robes kept him from the sun . . .

. . . For long and long his leech continued to heal him. He had *suffered* that time off Syracuse, and his convalescence had its ups and downs . . .

. . . Time sped by. As ever, the whole world was at war. The Fourth Crusade came and went, and became part of the past however recent . . .

Territorial as every Lord of the Wamphyri before him, Radu had "adopted" Arabia, and "adapted," as best possible, to its arid climate. With the coming of the Mongols, however, it was time for him to shuck off his ill-fitting monkish robes.

Again the dog-Lord went to war, this time for two reasons. One: the Mongols were a threat; certainly if they succeeded in their expansion, he would be uprooted again. And two: with the extermination of the Assassins and the fall of Baghdad in 1258, rumour and evil dreams had forewarned of at least one Wamphyri mercenary among the Asiatics fighting for Hulegu. His name—

—Was "Fereng the Black!"

Fereng? Ferenczy, more likely! But who? Waldemar? It seemed unlikely for by Radu's lights he was a coward—if he was still alive! Some blood- or egg-son then? But what matter? He was a Ferenczy, and that was *all* that mattered! Yet Radu's dreams had hinted of more than one Lord, and in more than one dream he had seen a bat-like figure falling out of the sky towards the field of battle. What, a Drakul? A Ferenczy *and* a Drakul, together on the side of the Mongols? Well, why not; it had happened before, more than a thousand years ago in Starside. And then as now the pact had been sealed in order to face down an even greater foe, Shaitan the Unborn. Or . . . perhaps this time it was to gang up on a weaker one.

Radu tried to work it out:

What if this Ferenczy and this Drakul had both been established in the Wallachian mountains, as they were known now? News of Mongol attacks and overwhelming victories in the east would have reached them even as it had reached Radu. And the brilliance—the sheer ruthlessness—of the Mongol cavalry armies would have seemed to make them invincible. Surely the best way to ensure survival must be to join with them, at least until the tides of war had once more swept by?

Thus (he reasoned) Fereng the Black and this unknown Drakul had themselves reasoned. But he knew they had got it wrong! Radu's oneiromancy had forecast a turning point in Mongol fortunes which would be realized—at Ain Jalut!

In Cairo the Mameluke Sultan was massing his well-trained army. Radu joined them near Jerusalem, and in the last days of August 1260 marched north with them on Ain Jalut . . .

V

RADU: THE REST OF HIS HISTORY . . . HIS AWAKENING

T HE BATTLE AT AIN JALUT! BUT THERE ARE FIGHTS AND FIGHTS—AND THERE are massacres. The Sultan, Qutuz, was totally committed. Earlier, receiving a Mongol envoy who demanded his submission, Qutuz had flown into a rage and had the envoy executed. Now he *must* win, else disembowelling were the least of his torments.

The Mongol forces were split between several fronts many hundreds of miles apart. Their cavalry army riding south on Ain Jalut numbered "only" ten thousand. Led by Kitbuga, a Christian Turk, it was outnumbered more than ten to one by the Mamelukes. Moreover, the Mamelukes had knowledge of the Mongol advance and of the territory; they set up an ambush in foothills flanking a fertile plain. The plain was an historic invasion route not far from Nazareth; to ensure that the Mongols would come this way, a party of Berbers was deployed on camels to attract their attention and so lure them into the Mameluke trap.

"Ain Jalut," the Egyptian commander of Radu's group told them where they hid in the evening-shadowed hills looking down on the plain. " 'The Spring of Goliath.' Goliath was a giant of a man, a warrior who was brought down by a stripling boy. This time we reverse the process. This time *we* are the mighty, and the stripling—in the shape of these Mongols—is the pagan enemy of the faith. But *this* time he shall not prevail."

The trap worked. Where the valley narrowed between steep hillsides, the Berbers dismounted behind ditches and old earthworks, turned and defended themselves with bows and long spears. Meanwhile the Mamelukes came swarming down out of the foothills and engaged the Mongols from the flanks, and a reserve group of cavalry and infantry as strong as the entire Mongol force came sweeping from behind the hills to cut off any retreat.

Radu and his "monks," despite that they were on foot in the lower foothills, were among the first to engage the milling Mongol army; which was work they might have been born for! To hack and hew among that *mêlée* of reeling, astonished flesh! The raging, the shouting and screaming! The blood of hamstrung horses and skewered men! The scarlet deluge *erupting* into the green valley, to turn it red . . .

The last rays of the sun were striking the western mountains as the Mongol army fell before the Mameluke onslaught. In the twilight before the night, when the sunlight had faded entirely, Kitbuga's screams were his last when he was captured and quartered. After that—

—No birds sang over that field of blood, only a cloud of kites on high, biding their time, and wolves (but true wolves) in the hills, waiting. Which was when Radu and his party went among the fallen.

It was the same as in Africa that time; Radu knew what he was looking for, and wasted no time. His men found life in bodies where there should be no life, and stilled it with fire and steel. And aye, there were a good many thralls—even a lieutenant or two—among the "dead." Then, a strange thing, though not so strange to the dog-Lord. In a gulley between steep-sided spurs of the hills on the northern flank, a pocket of mist . . . where no mist should be! He sent out a vampire probe, his mentalism, into the mist and felt its *texture*, the way it clung—and knew it for what it was . . .

The sun was down now. Radu took two lieutenants, two pups, with him into the gulley, into the heart of the mist, and found it already thinning. But sensing a fierce presence, he climbed a rock above the level of the vampire mist and looked up. There on the sheer wall of the cliff, moving like a lizard toward the high rim, a manlike figure. Except, adhering to the naked rock in that weird fashion, this was no ordinary man. Wamphyri!

But who? Not a Drakul, surely? For since the sun was down a Drakul would have transformed himself for flight. A Ferenczy then—"Fereng the Black"—fleeing the consequences of a lost cause. Cowardly, treacherous spawn of Nonari the Gross! Treacherous, aye, like all of them before him.

Then, in the next moment:

"Radu!" a lieutenant called to him, cautiously out of the thinning mist. The dog-Lord had been on the point of hurling a question after the climber: WHO? A question the Ferenczy would not have been able to resist; it would have surprised him, and Radu would have read the answer writ large in the confusion of his mind, doubtless confirming his suspicion. Cursing, because that time was past and the stranger had vanished over the rim, Radu got down from the rock and loped to his men gathered near the foot of the cliff.

"What is it?" he barked—then stood in stark amaze, for it was obvious what it was. "Treacherous," he'd called the fleeing Ferenczy, and now the full extent of that treachery could be seen.

A body—a "man," all bloodied and broken, but not dead—lay in a cluster of rocks, where tomorrow's sun must doubtless find him . . . if Radu had not found him first. And the dog-Lord knew him, remembered him at a glance, of course—Karl Drakul! An original Starside Lord no less than Radu himself. But less than Radu now, certainly.

He lay in an ungainly tangle, sprawled on his back like a spider struck by a stone. And even as Radu watched, so the unconscious Drakul's naked body commenced a complex metamorphosis. Thick webs of rubbery grey flesh like the hairy, membranous airfoils of a bat—which joined his arms to his trunk down to his thighs, and also formed an elastic "V" between his legs—*shrank back into him!* And as his pipestem limbs thickened, so his body firmed out and put on a little extra weight.

And oh, this was Karl all right. The fleshy lips and bald dome of a head; the purple orbits of his deep-sunken eyes; the squat nose, showing only too clearly its convolutions. And in the lolling cave of Karl's mouth, the split tongue of a lying Lord of the Wamphyri. And those teeth, and those hands like a beast's claws.

Radu's lieutenants had seen *something* like this before—in their master, at that—but never to this extent. One thing to instantly develop the aspect and mannerisms of a great wolf, but another entirely to emulate a great bat! They drew back a pace, muttered and glanced at each other. But Radu stepped forward and, snarling, said: "He was preparing for flight when the *other* bastard struck and cut him down. So much for pacts!" And with an oath and a kick he turned Karl Drakul face-down in the bloodied dust.

Then the worst of it was seen: the sword slash along this undead creature's spine, and the ragged flaps of flesh wrenched aside to expose the knuckles of the spine itself. They were ribbed, warped, notched, those bones, with grooves and small drilled holes where something had clung like an alien organ. Karl's vampire leech, Radu knew—which Fereng the Black had torn out and probably eaten!

"One has escaped," Radu told his men then. "I saw him on the cliff face, climbing like a lizard. The pair of them, Drakul and Ferenczy, they came together to side with the Mongols and join the bloody butchery. For the hell of it? Possibly. To befriend this marauding Asiatic scum, and save their own miserable skins? Probably. Because they knew I was at liberty in the so-called 'Holy Land'? . . . Ah, very *likely!* But when the battle went against them they tried to make their escape. The Ferenczy . . . maybe he was injured and unable to transform? But he could not *bear* the idea of being left behind while the Drakul made a clean getaway! Or perhaps they had argued? Whichever, while the Drakul was preparing for flight, Fereng the Black cut him down and tore out his leech. Good, for it saves me the trouble!"

Karl Drakul's shirt, breeches and cloak were nearby. Radu brought them together and piled them on the shuddering shape of an ex-vampire Lord. But when he would have struck fire, Karl's no longer scarlet eyes snapped open. Turning his head this way and that, he saw his predicament. And:

"So," he gurgled, his forked tongue flopping in his mouth. "It is you, Radu. Well, better you than that other dog, the one who brought me to this."

"Time is short," Radu told him. "Doubtless there'll be an uproar when you burn. The Sultan's troops could find us at any time, and I would not want them to see . . ."

The Drakul managed a ghastly sharp-toothed grin. "Anonymity is synonymous—"

"—With longevity," Radu nodded. "But mine, I fear, not yours."

"Will you make it—ah! *Ahhh!*—quick?" Karl squirmed a very little, then lay still, panting.

"If you'll answer me truly."

"Ask away, but quickly. I'm a husk, drained . . . I have no leech . . . I hold my pain at bay, but not for long. It is quite . . . *unbearable*. My screams, such as they would be, would doubtless attract attention."

Radu nodded in his grim fashion. "But if you do scream it will be quicker still. Very well, let's get to it. Who is he?"

"Now? Fereng the Black," Karl answered. "Before that his name was Faethor. Great-grandson of Nonari the Gross Ferenczy. And . . . he's a one to watch out for."

"That seems obvious," Radu said. "How many of you remain?"

"Wamphyri?"

"Drakuls. First Drakuls."

"Myself only."

"Liar! What of Egon?" Radu looked deep into Karl's eyes, and when he would turn them away grabbed his large fleshy ears to hold his head still. Karl could not resist him: Radu's eyes penetrated into his very mind, even his soul, if he'd had one. And: "Ah! He lives!" Radu let go Karl's ears, sat back on his haunches. "But no egg-sons, nor bloodsons—not yet, at least. Perhaps when he learns of this—"

"—He will, in the moment of my passing."

"You will . . . communicate?"

"He will know. We Drakuls are special that—ah! *Ahhh!*—that way."

"Now the Ferenczys," Radu growled. "How many?"

Karl's eyes were starting out and grey sweat oozed on his face and bald head. "I think I want to die now," he said.

"I am in total agreement," Radu answered. "But I want to know how many Ferenczys. Do you not *want* me to know? For after all, it was a Ferenczy did this to you. He could have finished it, but left you to fry in tomorrow's noon sun. And even these rocks would not have sheltered you then."

"Three, that I know of," Karl coughed out the words. "Waldemar, Faethor's father, had two sons. The one is gone and only this bastard Faethor remains. But he, too, has two sons, called Thibor and Janos. Ask me no more. My time is come."

"What do you know about them, Faethor's sons?"

"You are cruel. *Hah!* Ridiculous! Of course you are, as am I. We are Wamphyri! But still, in these circumstances, you *are* cruel."

"No," Radu denied it. "*They* were cruel—the Ferenczys—to me and mine, and now to you. Now tell me what I would know, and all of this is at an end."

"You—*ahhh-h-h!*—you must know that you are damned?"

"Yes, but you first. And your brother, and most of all the Ferenczys. Now tell me."

"Thibor is Faethor's egg-son. A fierce Wallach even before Faethor took him, he's now a *Voevod* for the Wallachian and Russian princes. Janos is

Faethor's Szgany bloodson. He has been a *corsair* ever since the Great Crusade. As for—oh! *A-ah-ohhh!*—Faethor himself: he is in thick with the Mongols. Look for him there."

"There?"

"Wherever they are. It is all I know. But whatever you do—ah! *Arghhh!*—kill him for me!"

"No," Radu shook his wolfish head. "For myself." He stood up. "Now hold still." He stepped astride Karl and stood on his hands, then signalled to his lieutenants, one of which carried a curved Saracen sword. His other man lay on Karl's lower body to hold it in place, while the one with the sword raised it on high. It was all very quick. And:

"*Ooohhhaaarrr . . . !*" Karl's great cry commenced, but got no further. His head flew free. Then—

—His lower trunk burst open and the man who lay on him was tossed aside! The dog-Lord jumped nimbly clear of the confusion, and the lieutenant with the bloodied sword backed off. But before matters could further deteriorate, Radu got down on one knee and struck sparks to silk. All went up in flames.

His men piled dead branches, but from a distance, because Karl's uproar was monstrous. Mindless leprous tentacles lashed the night as at first his metamorphic flesh refused to succumb. For, despite that his leech was no more, Karl's flesh had been Wamphyri for long and long. *He* willingly gave way to his agony and passed beyond it, but his body would not—until the heat became too much for it, and the great twining anemone of alien flesh began to melt. Then in a little while, all that remained was the smoke, stench, crackling and popping.

And the dog-Lord's smile was grim and terrible as the commotion died down, and he approached and warmed his hands by the fire of Karl Drakul's passing. For by his reckoning Karl should be happy. He'd lasted sixteen hundred years, after all! No mean feat, not even for a Lord of the Wamphyri.

That was the way of it, at Ain Jalut . . .

Radu slept on, but now he was like a man between dream and waking, caught in the limbo that precedes reality. Except for him his dreams *were* reality: memories out of a past that continued to direct his future. And the pages of history were still turning.

. . . Large contingents of Qutuz's army commenced a withdrawal into Egypt, and Radu and his party went with them; for his part in the defeat of the Mongols he was offered citizenship, Mameluke protection, land if he desired to stay. He told Qutuz that he would make his home in Tunisia, in an ancient redoubt which he knew to exist high in the mountains.

The Sultan warned him that Tunisia was now Hafsid territory, and, in the hinterland, Taureg! The Tauregs were notorious dogs of the desert who could not be trusted by any man. If Radu wished it, however, Qutuz would arrange an escort to see him to his chosen destination; for there were bandits on the land and pirates in the sea, and this was no fit time for an honest man to be journeying abroad.

Indicating his "pups," Radu told Qutuz he had dogs of his own, but he would appreciate an escort nonetheless.

As for Radu's plan:

Since he could not return to Wallachia (because of Thibor, who as a *Voevod* would have an army behind him), or to pirating (for once bitten, twice shy), or anywhere north of the Mediterranean, where the Mongols were still a power despite that they were on the wane, instead he would try his luck in Africa.

The African routes were opening up, and Radu had heard of fortunes in gold and ivory and slaves. And where there's great wealth, there's also the need to protect it. Also, he felt limited in his wanderings; the world was a big place and this was his chance to explore a large part of it.

Given fine Arab horses by Qutuz, Radu and his men spent a six-month "taming" (but in fact "training") them, getting them used to their new masters. No easy task; the horses sensed the wolf in Radu and were reluctant to accept him, but finally they succumbed. Then it was time to head west.

His sea-escort disembarked Radu, his men and horses on the African coast south of Tunis. The dog-Lord had been here before of course, with Belisarius. He knew where he was going, and how to get there. Radu's pack was made up of just three lieutenants and fifteen thralls; they looked very grand in the ornate saddles of their white Arab horses, protected from the sun beneath silk-tasselled canopies. In their black pantaloons and flowing, gold-fringed robes of black silk—with their curved swords in jewelled scabbards, and their fingers dripping gold—they must surely be the emissaries of some rich eastern Sultan or Turkic king.

So thought a large scouting party of black, brown and yellow-clad nomads who had seen them land from camouflaged observation points. What the nomads had *not* seen was how fierce were the eyes of these rich strangers, burning above their heavily-veiled lower faces.

Evening was turning to night as Radu's escort saluted him and set sail; shadows were already shifting on the land . . . and some of them moved most oddly. Radu smiled in his grim fashion. "Now we have a second escort," he passed the message on to his men. "Be at the ready, but make no sudden move. Let's see what this is about, and who these people are."

Zaghounan was twenty-five miles inland to the west. After twelve miles, when it was night and a half-moon had risen, and the ground turned hard and stony, Radu made his camp. Though a watch was scarcely necessary (the ears of his men were acute as those of watchdogs), he posted a guard. He knew that if he did not—and if his silent "escort" took it as a sign of weakness or stupidity and decided to attack—then he would have a fight on his hands. Since these were probably local people, it would be a bad start. It was important that Radu be allowed to set up his base here as Waldemar Ferrenzig before him, in the ruins on the mount. Then when he was properly established, he would strike out into the heart of Africa itself.

But as Radu sat with his men around their fires, reports began to come in from his watchdogs (wolfish lieutenants) who were ranging the land around. Their "escort" outnumbered them by a handful. They had camels and some ponies, and were probably Tauregs. Even so, they could still be local; in any case, they were bandits. And they were gradually closing ranks, encircling the camp.

Radu decided to pre-empt matters. Loping out a little way into the rough land around, he stood tall, threw back his head and howled long and loud to the half-moon. And when the echoes had died away, he called out:

"I know you are there, you desert wolves. But as you see, I am a wolf myself, and all my men. So if you want to die this night, why keep us waiting? We have nothing against dying. But if you are merely curious, and if you would talk, I have nothing against that either! The night is chill, and we have warm fires. Your chief and his guard would be welcome. So come forward . . . unless you are cowards. I am one man, as you see. Do not fear, for when you walk with Radu you are safe."

(Well, scarcely. But for the time being, anyway . . .)

A minute passed, and another. Then shadows grew up out of the night. Three of them. Veiled, cloaked, dark . . . only their eyes shone, but never as yellow as the dog-Lord's. He met them, held his arms wide in peaceful greeting, escorted them into his camp, to a fire. They sat, threw back their hoods, showed their faces. Blacks, with some Arab in them. Not Tauregs but a breed apart. And:

"Who are you?" Radu inquired. "You know my tongue . . . "

"We know many tongues," their leader, the tallest of them, answered. "This land has had many visitors, a great many conquerors." He shrugged. "They come and go. But we . . . are a tribe. We were always here."

"And were you here more than seven hundred years ago, when the Germans, the Vandals came? And when the Romans under Belisarius destroyed them?"

The other was taken aback. "You know history, stranger. I was not here, no, but my ancestors were. Numidians, Berbers and blacks out of the southern forests and savannahs. We have something of all of them in us. We are nomads, but *not* Tauregs." He spat into the fire.

"One of my ancestors was here, too," the dog-Lord told him "He had my name, Radu, and he fought for Rome, killing Vandals. And where are the Vandals now? Gone forever. But you and I are still here. I think it would be good if, after tonight, we were *still* here . . . "

"Perhaps," said the other. "But you are travelling in the wrong direction. There is a mountain, and we hold it dear. You must skirt it, keep well away, else we may not be . . . *friends,* any longer."

"I know the place," Radu nodded. "It is my destination."

Again the other was taken aback. "You know it? Does your ancestor speak to you across the centuries then? Does he guide your feet? And did I hear you say that his name was . . . Radu?"

"Indeed—a man like a great wolf. I have seen representations of him; his characteristics are evident in me, his descendant. But does he speak to me? Alas, no. But I am a scholar and he left a legend and writings. I have learned about him in my journeys. He was here, in this place—and upon your mountain, I think—in the long ago. Which is why I would visit, and perhaps stay . . . "

"Wait!" (Radu's night visitors, especially their leader, were agitated now.)

They argued briefly in a tongue he didn't know, but obviously about him, and then—

—Their leader reached out and tore away the strip of black silk from his mouth! Radu had kept it there because of his wolfishness, which was pronounced—especially at night and under the moon. And:

"*Ahhh!*" said the three as one man, as the dog-Lord's men stepped up close and felt for their swords. But he waved them away, and said:

"Now say, what is this?"

"Stand up!" said the leader, himself standing.

Radu did so, and the other saw his height as if for the first time.

"Now smile," said the visitor. And Radu showed him that wolf's smile in a grin that made him look even more the monstrous dog.

At which his visitors shrank a little, and their leader said, "Will you come with us?"

"Where?"

"Will you trust me?"

Well, would he or wouldn't he? But . . . so far he read no harm in them. Only astonishment and more than a little awe. So finally he shrugged and said: "So be it."

Mounted on his horse, alone of his party and side by side with the leader of the nomads, and flanked by his men, Radu rode out into the night. They rode west, direct for the mount Zaghounan. As the peak rose up to blanket the sky, they skirted its southern flank to the winding ramp of access. And all along the way no word was uttered. Then they were there, and the ruins stood stark against the moon.

"Just as I read of it," said Radu. "This is the place. It is as if I remember it." (Which of course he did.)

"Indeed it is the place!" said his guide. "Get down from your horse and see here."

The party dismounted and the nomad leader showed Radu a great rock, part of the mountain's fang, outcropping from the desiccated earth. He struck fire to a torch, jammed it in the loose soil, and by its flaring light they gazed upon the face carved in the rock—

—Radu's face, grinning!

Even the dog-Lord was startled, but in a moment he knew what this was. "Now let me guess," he said. "Your people are rare among the men of this land. You are tribal, nomads, aye, but probably a matriarchy. You revere your queens, your princesses. And seven centuries ago in this place, three sisters, princesses, mothers of your race, were set free from bondage by the man on the rock."

"Yes, *yes!*" the leader of the nomads whispered. "His name was Radu. And then . . . ?"

"He tortured and killed the men who held the three princesses captive. Then he gave them camels to ride back to their people, and sent them on their way."

"But first?" The other breathlessly pressed him.

"Eh?" Radu cocked his head. "First?"

"There was something else he did, this Radu."

"Ah! He kissed all three . . . like a blessing. Is that what you mean?"

"Indeed," said the nomad, and took Radu's hand and kissed it. "A blessing, no less than this." He stepped back, and said, "That Radu, that grandfather of your grandfathers, was the saviour of our race. The three princesses were the mothers of our mothers. This is our legend: that they returned with a man who worked stone, and described to him their saviour—whose likeness was then chiselled into the rock. Since when this is like a holy place. Or perhaps a place that has been waiting?"

"It need wait no longer," Radu said. "I shall live here—if it please you?"

"It would please my mother!" said the other.

"Oh?"

"She can trace her line back to one of those sisters that your ancestor saved. Without him she would not have life—nor any of us!"

"Then all is well," said Radu.

"I would bring my mother to see you!" The nomad was eagerness itself now.

"When we have made this place worthy," Radu told him. "But meanwhile, give her this. Tell her it was made for me by a Sultan of the Egypts." Which was true enough. And he took a golden ring from his smallest finger. Its crest, when the nomad turned it into the torchlight, was the head of a howling wolf . . .

Radu never did scathe among the People of the Rock, who claimed all the land and watering holes for twenty miles around. Rather he "befriended" them, and from time to time protected them from other nomadic tribes and Tauregs alike. And in their turn, they showed him the routes south into Niger and Chad, and south-west into the "rich" kingdoms of Mali and the Hausa Traders. He took slaves for trading, hired himself out to protect caravans along the trade routes, was rarely to house on the rock of Zaghounan. The sun was ever a curse, of course, but the dog-Lord took precautions; whenever possible he travelled by night, sleeping out the days in the inner heart of his great black tent whose walls were thickly draped. Mercifully, he had never been as susceptible to sunlight as the great majority of Wamphyri Lords . . .

In his various ventures Radu covered many thousands of miles by horse and camel, mainly the latter, and learned all the Saharan routes from Wargla to Taghaza, Ghana, Gao, Timbuktu and beyond. It took years, even decades, but it was an adventure and earned him a fortune in gold. In 1324 he organized an endless relay of escorts for King Mansa Musa on his pilgrimage to Mecca, and was in control of eleven hundred men to fight off Tauregs and other bandits along the two-thousand-miles route from Kumbi Saleh to Augila, where he handed over to the Mamelukes. Paid off in such gold that he couldn't carry it all, still he knew it was a pittance to Mansa Musa. Later, in Cairo, the spending-power of the King's retinue—in solid gold—was so great as to depress the local currency!

But this was one of the dog-Lord's last great ventures. He had lived too long in one place; he'd become too prominent; the People of the Rock had grown wary of him, and during one of his long absences they even went so far as to deface his "portrait" on Zaghounan.

The dog-Lord's dreams had been bad for long and long. His oneiromancy—frequently a gift of great benefit—now seemed a curse. He couldn't go to his bed without recurrent nightmares plaguing him. Nightmares *about* plague, famine, blood and death. His death, or at least his suspension from life.

Once, waking with a cry, he tore the amber bauble that he wore about his neck loose and hurled it away. He had dreamed of the bauble—but in place of the fly trapped in its golden core he had seen himself! Himself, but the merest husk of the man he was now, sleeping but not dead in a resin grave!

Radu paid off half of his pups. There were a great many of them—moonchildren all, if not actual werewolves—but they would get by. If not . . . well, too bad. Some of them dispersed into Egypt, others the Mediterranean. The ones he kept, however, had a special mission: to buy (or steal) large quantities of resin from the Greeks and the peoples of the northern Mediterranean shores, and bring it to their master wherever he determined to settle. He gave them money to buy ships and sent them about their business.

Then the dog-Lord and his coterie went down into Sousse where he purchased a fine vessel. His plan was a simple one as always: to buy himself back into those old territories which he had always considered his own. For the horseshoe mountains were Hungarian now, and Radu believed that with his wealth he could sway the authorities and become a *Boyar* and a power there.

In Sousse, however, the atmosphere was strange; he sensed unease and panicky stirrings—the first real intimations that his oneiromantic nightmares were about to come true. It was the late autumn of the year AD 1347, and the Black Death was visiting itself upon the Mediterranean.

Ships out of Sicily, Sardinia, Corsica, were being refused entry into the ports. But plague ships had already run aground; the rats that infested them had swarmed to dry land; local people were falling ill, developing hideous black pustules, dying.

Radu was immune to human diseases by virtue of his vampire leech . . . so he thought. Likewise his men (certainly his lieutenants and inner coterie), *should* be immune through his blood. Yet even before setting sail for the Adriatic and Hungary some of his men fell sick, and Radu expelled them from his company. It had been the same in Sunside/Starside some fifteen hundred years ago, even before Radu was Wamphyri: if a man contracted leprosy, the Szgany expelled him. This new disease, this hideous Black Death, seemed so much like leprosy inasmuch as vampires were not immune to it. Maybe even Radu himself, Wamphyri, was not immune to it.

Radu's dreams returned, to "plague" him, but now they were more than mere dreams. In them he saw a great rock rising from a canopy of trees; but the climate was cold, "northern" in the true sense of the word. He dreamed of a den in that high place, and of a massive stone coffin within the den which he knew was his . . .

And meanwhile news was finding its way ashore from "clean" ships. The Ottoman Turk was dying in his thousands. The Mediterranean Islands, and even Marseilles on the northern mainland, were pestholes. The plague was spreading into Bulgaria, Serbia, Wallachia and Hungary. It advanced day by day and ate up entire towns and villages. It raged out of control, like a monstrous brush-fire blown by a relentless wind out of the east. Suddenly Hungary was out of the question, and the sooner Radu sailed—for whichever destination—the better. At least there'd be no plague aboard his ship!

The plague came from the east; Radu sailed west, for Barcelona in Aragon. At the entrance to the harbour, plague inspectors came aboard. The dog-Lord paid a heavy bribe, was cleared for landing, and sold his vessel at a great loss. He purchased horses, carts, caravans—everything at a premium, for plague-fear was at its height—and set out north-west for the Bay of Biscay and English Bordeaux. But his arrival in Aragon had not gone unnoticed; nor had he failed to observe a ship out of Sicily, whose veiled, secretive, closely-escorted master was given an especially difficult time by the "dedicated" port officials, and doubtless paid a crippling bribe for the privilege of being allowed ashore. Indeed just seeing that ship—sensing a definite *aura* about it that had nothing to do with any plague, or at least, not the Black Death—Radu was keenly interested.

So much so that he sent a lieutenant to follow this Sicilian party, with instructions to join up with him later and report on his findings. Except his man never did join up with him later, nor ever returned . . .

The journey between ports was three hundred miles; it took thirteen days and exhausted Radu's animals. Also, enroute, the dog-Lord was given a rude reminder that he wasn't the only one determined to prolong the centuried blood-feud with other Wamphyri factions. He had half-expected it, ever since seeing that ominous-seeming ship in Barcelona; but still, under the circumstances, it came as a surprise.

It was January 1348, and in Toulouse they were beginning to bring out their dead. Carts loaded with the bodies of plague victims came trundling out of the central district to block the approach roads, which determined Radu to skirt the town. But in the confusion as he turned his small caravan off the main highway into a forested region—

—Suddenly he was under attack!

What they were was obvious: vampires. As for their leader: Wamphyri! How it happened:

Radu was seated in the one small box-coach he'd been able to purchase. The sky was grey, overcast; a drizzly rain fell; a ground mist swirled up from the forest floor. And there was . . . this feeling. The forest way was narrow and Radu's coach was at the head of his column. A plague-cart had sunk to its axles in the mud. And as Radu's driver manoeuvred his vehicle around it:

Ho, great dog! These words, totally unexpected, seemed to burst in Radu's brain. *We almost met in Ain Jalut some ninety years ago. You were fortunate that time, for I had suffered a trivial hurt. Alas, this time you are* un*fortunate, for I'm fit and well. But* your *injury will not be so small!*

The identity of the sender rang clear as a bell in Radu's mind: that Ferenczy last seen lizarding up the sheer wall of a gorge in the so-called Holy Land! But so close at hand.

"Closer than you think!" Someone was right outside Radu's coach. He heard the neighing of a horse, yanked open the curtains and tried to get his sword from its scabbard. But trapped in the close confines of his box, he knew that his life was in jeopardy; he was the perfect target! To the right, the plague cart blocked his exit. And to the left . . .

. . . A great black horse pranced in the trees! Its rider—cowled, tall in the saddle, and dressed in black head to toe—leaned forward, drove his slender sword through the dog-Lord's driver. And kicking the howling thrall out of his way, he clambered from his horse up onto the driver's platform. Radu's door was half-open, but the bole of a tree blocked the way. He yelped for his men!

The Ferenczy looked inside through the view slit and saw him—and laughed from a mouth like a mantrap! And: "What use to cut you?" he shouted. "You would only heal. Why, I might as well stab dead men, eh?" With which he leaned down and speared the bloated belly of a corpse in the plague cart, and drew out his sword all slimed. Then Radu shrank down as he saw what was in the other's mind. And:

"Oh, ha ha ha!" cried that one, his eyes ablaze . . . as he drove his wet blade through the view slit at an awkward angle, yet still managed to stab Radu in his side. The dog-Lord stifled his pain, drew a knife, thrust it again and again through the view slit. But the Ferenczy was gone; only his sword thrummed there where he'd left it, jammed in the slit.

Radu's men came swarming—too late! The Ferenczy was up onto his horse; others joined him out of the mist; they wheeled about and were gone. And only Faethor's mocking mind-voice came back to taunt: *May you rot slowly and your death cause you awesome agonies, Radu Lykan. Then at the last, when even your Wamphyri flesh crumbles, remember who did this to you—the* ghazi *warrior, Faethor! My Ferenczy forebears are finally appeased!*

Radu commanded his leech: "Heal me!" . . . and immediately collapsed shuddering to the floor of his coach, which served to drag the sword from his side. But his shudders weren't from the pain, which he had already stilled. Rather they sprang from the sure knowledge that indeed the plague lived in him now, and the torment of knowing who had put it there, without his being able to return that favour. But mostly it was the uncertainty of his vampire parasite's ability to drive it out. Nevertheless:

Ferenczy, he sent a snarl, but no hint of hurt, from his telepathic mind. *If it were at all possible—even if it meant trying a little harder—you should have made sure I was dead this time around. Too late for that now, though. So run as far and as fast as you can, and hide where you will, it will make no difference. The next time you lay eyes on this "great dog," he'll sink his teeth in your throat and rip it out, be sure!*

Then he let go, and lolled and shuddered the rest of the way to Bordeaux . . .

The rest of Radu's journey—to a dreamed of but as yet unrecognized destination, the great rock rising from the trees—was a nightmare of several anxieties. The wound in his side healed less readily than the norm, and he began to experience an unaccustomed malaise, a weariness springing from deep within, as if a hidden part of him fought an unequal battle. And he believed he knew which part.

Several of his men took ill in Bordeaux; he gave them some money, sent them on their way, then hired a ship and again fled the plague—for England. Other men fell sick aboard; Radu had them put out of their misery, disposed of them in the sea.

London in March seemed a quagmire of mud, mist and stench. If ever a place was ripe for the plague, London was it. But it certainly wasn't the high northern territory of the dog-Lord's prophetic dreams. He made arrangements for a brief stay in the best possible accommodations, made known his location telepathically so that those parties he'd dispatched from north Africa in search of Greek resin would know where to find him, studied maps of the times until at last he found what he believed to be the refuge he sought. Then:

Disguised as the retinue of a rich political refugee from France, his party headed north and in Newcastle boarded another ship bound for Gascony— which of course, wasn't Radu's destination. No sooner out of port, he took command of the vessel, sailed north, and eventually wrecked on the wild coast north of Edinburgh. The healthy crew members became part of Radu's pack, strengthening it, and the party in its entirety became ostensibly the retinue of a rich Boyar out of Hungary.

At last, however briefly, Radu seemed to have outdistanced the Black Death. But his strength was fast failing, and he knew he must soon retire to a lair, go down into the resin, and give his leech a chance to combat the disease within him without the complications and additional effort of keeping up with his external, physical activities.

His Mediterranean pups found him; they wrecked their ships in the Moray Firth, joined Radu where he camped and recuperated in the wild, wooded country under the Cairngorm Mountains. And this was it: these mountains were the great stone of his dreams rising from the woodlands of the misty Spey valley.

Radu's people became "gypsies" now; all their rich robes were put aside for rags, their golden rings came off their fingers and out of their ears; and through the spring, summer and autumn of 1348, and all through '49 they guarded the foothills and found routes up into the high places, to the massive labyrinth of caves which they had discovered there.

Their labours were enormous on the dog-Lord's behalf, but there was game in the land, local clans not too far afield, and loners or people fleeing the cities, who were wont to come this way; so that provisions were never scarce. And by the autumn of '49 Radu's lair was ready. Oh, it was a rude place, be sure, but secret and high, and his moon-children—and their children—would always be here to tend him through his long sleep.

A long, *long* sleep, aye. Of more than six slow centuries.

Eventually it was the summer of 1350, and as the creeping evil of the Black Death tightened its grip even in the sparsely populated Highlands, the dog-Lord could no longer deny that his parasite was losing its—and his—fight for survival. And so he went down into the resin . . .

But that was then and this was now. And as the conscious world called to him, so Radu's dreams of other times receded. Stirring, though it was mainly his mind that quickened, he knew his confinement and felt the oppression of dense, glutinous, ever-thickening resin weighing on him.

Thud . . . !

Now what was that? The sound had not been threatening, at any rate. His own heartbeat, perhaps? Maybe that of some other? Not Bonnie Jean's, for it wasn't her time. He hadn't called for her. Whose, then . . . or what's?

He drifted a while, his thoughts gradually clearing.

Thud . . . !

Radu was "awake" now, or awake as he had ever been in six hundred years. At least his *mind* stirred—consciously, under his control—if not his physical body. And he knew that from now on he must *stay* awake, and that because he was out of practice it would have to be a question of mind over matter: self-hypnosis, to achieve resurgent, reliable and continuous mobility, activity, in a body wasted and atrophied by centuries of slothlike torpor, suspended animation.

But awake, really awake, *Radu longed to breathe!* He gagged and fought down the near irresistible urge. He couldn't breathe, not yet, and didn't need to . . . for he was Wamphyri! But in any case, his metamorphic body put out hair-fine filaments into his resin matrix and the pale sac of softer fluids surrounding him, to siphon off minute traces of oxygen directly into his sluggish bloodstream.

It gave the dog-Lord ease, and he thought: *Air! It will be so good to feel it on my body again! And blood . . . I could lie in it, and soak it up, and bloat to bursting in it!* Could—and would! The blood was the life, and it would renew Radu's life. But first he must stay awake, concentrate, instruct his leech, regain his strength. If only he didn't feel so weak . . .

. . . At which he remembered.

Remembered his dreams—which were nothing less than his previous life—which was in fact the problem. Radu was Wamphyri; he was undead, but had never been truly dead. Even now his mind was alive and well. But what of his body? He had put himself down into the resin sure (he had *had* to be sure) that his leech would heal him. But he'd been so long "disconnected," as it were, that even now he didn't know.

Or perhaps he did. He felt so weak.

Thud . . . !

The dull reverberation in the rocks, the resin, the otherwise emptiness, came from a distance. Always the same distance; it neither approached nor retreated. A heartbeat, yes—and the beat of a *great* heart, at that—but static in space and uneven in time. A fumbling heartbeat, not yet ready to burst into life full-fledged. But burgeoning, definitely. With which Radu knew what it was.

His creature! His warrior, created here, of his own piss, sperm, plasma, and metamorphic flesh—and part of the brain, but a very small part, of one of his lieutenants—before the dog-Lord had gone down into the resin. His creature lived! Why, of course it did! Hadn't the treacherous Bonnie Jean Mirlu, and later that cretin of a thrall Auld John, told him as much? And hadn't they nurtured it, even as they'd nurtured him? He knew they had, and recalled now how he'd heard that great heartbeat before during Bonnie Jean's and Auld John's visits. But if his warrior lived—and since it was made of his flesh and fluids—surely Radu himself must be clean. Surely his parasite had won its centuried fight with the Black Death that Faethor Ferenczy had stabbed into his system.

Thud-d-d! But dully this time, shuddering, uncertain. And as quickly as that, Radu's mood changed and he, too, was uncertain. His warrior was not . . . not *perfect* after all. And since it was built from his flesh and fluids . . . ? His earlier conclusion must stand reversed.

But nothing was proven as yet, nor would it be until he was up or ready to be up. And if he couldn't be up in his current body, well . . . those arrangements were covered, too.

His thoughts flowed faster and faster, also his blood, as he strove to connect up the two, mind and body. He was hungry and thought to call on Bonnie Jean, a mental howl that all of his moon-children near and far would hear. But it wasn't time and he wasn't ready. And in any case she was a traitor, or at least she contemplated treachery. What, with Harry Keogh? But it was ridiculous! He was only a man, and she was Radu's. She *belonged* to Radu.

Ah, but he wasn't *only* a man, he was *the* man! Radu's Man-With-Two-Faces, his Mysterious One—his new body, if need be! But patience, patience. Time was narrowing down, and after so *much* time what was a week or two, or three . . . or even seven? Seven weeks. It was down to that now, and Radu had work to do.

His blood ran faster still; his limbs felt the cold, life-sustaining liquids around him; *his* heart gave a single, solid-sounding *thud* deep in his chest, as he sent telepathic probes out into a world that was entirely strange to him, apart from what little Bonnie Jean and Auld John had managed to convey.

His mental probes went out, while the demands of his body, his parasite, sent physical probes—in the form of tubeworms of metamorphic flesh—up through the resin to find cracks in its crust. Air! It was drawn into his body with or without the involvement of his conscious will, its oxygen filtered out and pumped directly into his quickening bloodstream. And:

Thud! His heart gave another lurch, and after several long seconds a third *Thud!*

Two hearts beating now, his and his creature's, but both of them unsteady as yet. Radu laughed deep inside, bayed like the great hound he was—for a moment . . .

. . . And paused abruptly as his mind-probes came into sudden collision with others of a like nature. Vampires, if not Wamphyri! Thralls then, or lieutenants, but Drakul or Ferenczy Radu couldn't say; the contact had been that brief before he'd snatched back his probes and clamped shut his mind. But just *touching* upon them had been an electric experience, so much so that his metamorphic siphons had automatically drawn back down into him through the resin, leaving a trail of tiny bubbles to rise to the canopy of crusty resin, get trapped there and form into yellow froth.

But vampires! They were there—they were *here*, right here in Scotland—and they were listening! For him, obviously. And when finally he called for Bonnie Jean, they'd hear that, too. Except by then it would be too late for he'd be ready. And she too would know that they were there, which should make her put aside any . . . *plans* she may have made in her own right. And oh yes, Radu was sure she would have made plans—for Bonnie Jean was Wamphyri! And no matter how often she had dwelled upon the fact and he had denied it, by now she would be sure.

Wamphyri, aye, but inexperienced and no match for the Masters who were out there searching for the dog-Lord's lair even now. Bonnie Jean would have come to that conclusion, too: that if she would survive to live out her span, she needed the instinct, the expertise, even the merciless guile and savagery of someone who had *already* lived ten times her fragile lifespan! And so she must remain "faithful" to her dog-Lord even to the end. Which she would, Radu knew, for survival was everything to the Wamphyri.

Everything to him, anyway. As for Bonnie Jean: she wasn't worthy.

She was expendable.

She was blood.

She was meat . . .

PART 3

The Darkness Gathers

VISIONS AND VISITATIONS

I

THIS TIME IT WAS A FORTNIGHT SINCE HARRY HAD SEEN B.J. HE HAD MISSED her—and he hadn't. The last time he had been with her was when he'd woken up in a sweat, thinking he was lying with a hairy dog-bitch, whose multiple teats had felt like pulpy dugs in his hands.

Perhaps the nightmare was why he hadn't missed Bonnie Jean as much as he might: because he did *not* want to dream anything like that ever again, not about B.J., but was aware that recurrent nightmares were part and parcel of him now. He had wanted to get it out of his system, that was all. And maybe he'd succeeded at that, for it hadn't come back. Not in the last fortnight, anyway. Not while he'd been sleeping alone.

In that same period she'd contacted him only three times, sounding nervous and jumpy on the phone as if she were taking care not to say too much. Harry had likewise called B.J. three times, asking her when he would be seeing her again and hoping—because of the nightmare—that she wouldn't say tonight.

But the dream had stayed away and so had B.J. And a fortnight is a long time. Also, certain things she had said to him during their last phone conversation continued to bother him:

"Harry, it could be that we, the girls and I, will need to be moving on from here pretty soon now. There are people watching my place. Not just *the* watcher, the little man you saw that time, but people. People—and some who probably aren't people. Asiatic types, I mean, but no longer dressed in those lying red robes of theirs. They're difficult to spot, until they're right on top of you! And there's also a pair of shady types who just might be policemen, but I don't think so. I did have some dealings with the police but that was before I last saw you, since when I've heard nothing. I'm pretty sure that no one suspects me of . . . well, anything! So these strangers could be Ferenczy thralls, or simply ordinary men in their pay, or just my imagination. But when I'm out I find I'm frequently followed—the girls, too—and we can't stay cooped up forever. We feel like we're trapped, and as time goes by it gets worse. So maybe now you understand why I can't be with you as much as I would like—because I don't want to put you in jeopardy."

Harry had been switched on at the time, capable of holding a "normal" conversation. B.J.'s "wee man," he'd known exactly what she was talking about; more than Bonnie Jean herself would have believed. He'd felt her fear, not only for herself but for him—indeed *mainly* for him—and that had put everything right and made him want to tell her oh so much . . . Except he couldn't possibly, because it was forbidden.

But by whom forbidden? By what? By something inside him, was all Harry knew. Something that restricted his powers until they were all but useless to him. He couldn't talk about them, daren't display them, felt less and less inclined towards using them— even for his own protection.

But for B.J.'s?

"Why don't you turn me loose?" he had asked her then.

"What?" (As if the thought hadn't occurred to her—which in fact it hadn't. She loved him, and you don't unleash the one you love on things that would gladly eat his raw, smoking heart right out of him! Moreover, he would have to be there at Radu's resurgence. First to see him up, and then to put him down! B.J. knew that now: that somehow she must find a way to use the dog-Lord to destroy their enemies—before destroying Radu himself. It was the only way, if she and Harry were to survive and go on together.)

"I know about them," he'd told her then. "You told me all about them— that the time might come when we would have to go up against them. I've accepted that and I'm ready. So don't try to fight them alone, B.J. Also, what good can it do to run from them when you know they'll only catch up with you? And you even know *where* they'll catch up—in the lair of the dog-Lord! Why leave it until the last minute?"

It was as if he had read her mind. But B.J. knew that in fact he was only remembering what little she'd let him retain. Yet still he seemed to know so much, and to accept it so readily.

"Harry, you listen to me!" she had snarled then, in something close to panic. "You'll keep *out* of it! Oh, you're good, I know—but not that good. We were very lucky that time, up there in . . ." But there she had paused in sudden confusion. For it was something she'd erased from his mind: the failed attack of the Drakuls. Or at least she *thought* she had erased it. Yet when she'd mentioned Asiatics, "no longer in their red robes," he hadn't queried her. It had been a slip of the tongue on her part but he hadn't picked it up. It was as if he knew! So what the hell was going on here?

And again it was as though he had read her mind:

"Those Tibetan priests," he said, in an oddly neutral tone that defined her hypnotic influence on him (but how *much* of an influence?) "I felt there was something strange about them the first time we saw them. They've been on my mind ever since . . . "

At which Bonnie Jean had let out an audible sigh of relief, so clear that Harry heard it over the line. And he, too, sighed his relief, albeit *in*audibly, for once again he'd protected his powers. And:

"Anyway," B.J. had gone on, after a brief pause to get her thoughts in order, "that's what we're up against. The Tibetans—who I believe are Drakuls—and the watcher and his friends, who are probably Ferenczys. Lieutenants or simple thralls, or a mix, we don't know. Mostly thralls, I would guess. And their intentions: we can't be absolutely certain except that they're looking for Radu." But in fact *she* could be sure, for the Drakuls had tried to kill them that time. Harry didn't know that, however (or he couldn't remember), which was how she preferred it. She didn't want his two levels of awareness merging again, and certainly not at a time like this.

"You should let me help you," he'd told her. "Don't switch me off. Let me come to you, protect you. Two of us together, we have to have a better chance than one. And B.J., you're right: I am . . . *good* at this sort of thing." Then, hurriedly, as if to clarify what he'd said: "It's what I used to do, remember?"

"I've seen what you can do," she'd told him then. "I have lots of evidence as to what you can do. But you don't know what *they* can do! Anyway, it's decided. Pretty soon we'll be out of here . . . out of B.J.'s Wine Bar, I mean. And Harry, it might be a good idea if you got out of there, out of your house. If they decide you're a threat—if they suspect you're more than just my lover . . ."

"Am I?" He had cut in. "Am I your lover? And are you mine, B.J.? Do you love me?"

"Don't you know it?" She'd sighed again, this time a very different sigh, as human a sound as she'd ever made. "Love you? Harry, I love the sight of you, the air you breathe, the ground you walk on, the touch of you inside and out— the very thought of you! I don't know why, but I do."

"But you won't let me help."

"No, I forbid it. And when I switch you off you'll remember that, Harry: that you're forbidden to get any more involved than you are already. And that you won't act except on my word, or in order to protect yourself in my absence. Is that clear?"

"Yes," and his tone had been vacant, robotic again. "Perfectly clear. But if you're moving out, and if I move out, too, how will I know where to find you?"

"One of my girls will be watching, following you. You'll know her but you mustn't try to talk to her. And don't go anywhere too far or too fast; I mean, don't lose her. For when it comes to losing people, well you're *too* damn good at that, Mr. Harry Keogh! And if she loses you we may have trouble finding you again. But if we do somehow get separated, as a last resort you can always try my place. I can have someone watch out for you."

And when he said nothing: "Well?" B.J. had queried.

"That's it, then?" he had finally said, in a wavery, misunderstanding tone of voice that made her heart want to cry out loud. A tone that spoke all too eloquently of his tangled emotions, damaged personality and bewildered psyche all in one. And a tone that he really shouldn't be capable of, not while he was under her influence like this; not even while conversing "normally." Still and all, that was why she loved him: because there was no one else like him, not who B.J. had ever met before. But whatever else she did, she knew she mustn't weaken now.

"That's it, yes. Until we're together again. But Harry, I want you to remember this, too: that we *will* be together again. As for the rest, the usual rules apply."

"The usual rules?"

"Forget about the Drakuls, the Ferenczys, the vampires we are up against. Unless you come under threat, forget them. But if or when you are threatened, then you'll remember everything I've told you about them and be able to act against them. It's for your own good; I just can't have you fighting them on your own and getting yourself killed. For you see, I don't think I could bear that, Harry . . . mah wee man."

After a long pause he said, "I'll . . . remember?" And that was that . . .

And he *had* remembered—if only what "the usual rules" allowed him to—and wondered and worried about the rest of it. He remembered that B.J. would soon be moving out of her place in the city, but didn't know why. Also that she'd advised *him* to move out, too. (But that had been more in the *way* of advice, not an order.) And he was vaguely aware that certain enemies were closing in even now but that he couldn't go against them until she said so or until he himself was threatened directly. He remembered too that she loved him, that they would be together again, and that despite all the seeming ambiguities she was innocent.

She was innocent! . . . innocent! . . . innocent! The shout of an idiot in an empty church, echoing in the Necroscope's aching head. Aching because of all the strange stuff that was in there trying to find its way out, and all the natural— or unnatural—stuff that was the real Harry Keogh, that he no longer dared to *let* out.

All of which further served to remind the Necroscope that his life was screwed up and being screwed tighter all the time, perhaps to a fatal degree, and that someone or someones was or were responsible. Like—maybe Bonnie Jean herself? But no, for she was an innocent. Then who? And how?

If only he could get a look—take a peek, a single glimpse—at the picture on the box, then he might be able to work it out for himself, the whole bloody jigsaw puzzle. But all he had was the frame, and a twisted frame at that, and no picture at all. Or at best a jumble of pieces that wouldn't interlock, because they worked in three dimensions and Harry was working in only two of them (was only *allowed* to work in two of them), and then not at the same time . . .

The conversation with B.J. had been yesterday morning. In the afternoon, the Necroscope had got out his bicycle and pedalled it furiously five miles and back. His fitness programme (or so he told himself), and God he was *fit!* In his body anyway. Then, leaving the bike in the yard out front, Harry had gone through the house into the back garden—no longer an utter wilderness but *something* of a garden at least—and walked the riverbank to the tiny bight that was his Ma's grave. And for a long time he had stood there in silence, looking at the ruffled water.

He would have loved to talk to his Ma but couldn't . . . or wouldn't. She knew all about her son's weird talent, naturally, and he knew she wasn't about to betray him even if she could—but it was this *thing* again. Someone might be watching him, and someone might guess what he was doing: talking to dead people.

Crazy! Who in hell would ever guess he was doing something like that!? But nonetheless, Harry had looked all about, up and down and across the river, to see if anyone was there. And damn it if someone wasn't! A parked car, gleaming in the pale afternoon sunshine, maybe a hundred and eighty yards up-river on the grass verge of the road that ran parallel with the water. And a blurred figure at the steering wheel, whose breath was steaming the windows.

Then back to the house with his heart beating just a little faster, walking briskly, but trying not to act or look too concerned about anything (and wondering just how fast is a bullet anyway, and why would anyone want to shoot him in the first place?) and up to his bedroom, where he had tried to focus his binoculars through a chink in his curtains, only to be frustrated by his own breath on the windowpane.

And then there'd been nothing else for it . . .

. . . But a Möbius jump to the deserted country road some two hundred yards "downwind" of the suspect car, where the Necroscope had stepped out of his metaphysical door behind a shielding clump of bushes. There, peering through fringing foliage, finally he'd got his glasses focused on the car.

Zahanine's car! One of Bonnie Jean's girls. The gorgeous black girl with the legs that went up forever—well, almost. And Harry had *almost* chuckled: that in his situation, whatever it was, he was still capable of thinking along such lines. But not quite, because the sight of the girl standing there out of the car now, training binoculars of her own on his house, had served to bring back the rest of his conversation with Bonnie Jean. Some of it, anyway:

That she would have one of her girls follow him, keep an eye on him . . . protect him? And something else, about the girl herself. And about all of B. J.'s girls. A question he knew he should ask himself, without knowing what the question was. But ridiculous anyway, because they were all as innocent as B.J.

—Weren't they?

What, innocent? Zahanine, too? Really? With a body like that? And this time he *had* chuckled, albeit wryly, as he conjured a door and returned to the house—where the telephone in his study had been ringing, ringing.

But for how long? His answering machine wasn't switched on, and this could be B.J.! Flying across the room and snatching the phone from its cradle, he had almost tripped, before stumbling to his knees beside his desk. And:

"Hallo?" he had panted into the mouthpiece. And in a moment, when there was no answer, "This is Harry?"

Still no reply, only silence. Or at best, the merest suggestion of a shallow, somehow sinister breathing. And, "Harry Keogh?" he had felt obliged to prompt the caller, wonderingly, before stopping himself and pausing to think it out.

But in the next moment, kneeling there before his desk, he *had* started to think, and thought: *This isn't B.J.!*

Who then? And anyway, his number was listed. Not that that meant anything; there were ways round that, if someone was determined. But having called him, why the silence? For what good, or bad, reason? Shit, how he'd wished that the answerphone was on!

Perhaps the unknown caller had heard his gasp, for a moment later the telephone had gone *ch-click!* and started to purr at him. And staring at the dead plastic thing in his hand, the Necroscope had felt a weird panic rising in him as he wondered if *that* was back again:

His fear and loathing of the telephone.

But no, surely not, for it had been a long time now since anything like *that* had happened.

Which in itself had been like an invocation!

The ground had seemed to move under his feet; Harry actually felt his body swaying to compensate, clutched at the desk with his free hand, tried to throw the telephone away from him. For he'd known what was coming—known at least that *something* was coming—and that when it got here he wasn't going to like it too much.

It was in the sudden gloom that swept through or over his study—in the fading light that turned the garden beyond the patio windows to night, as if someone had switched off the sun—and in the blurring of reality as the vestigial talent of a dead mentality surfaced like a drowned thing from the swirling deeps of Harry's id, or the contours of his re-inhabited mind. It was Alec Kyle's prescience which, as applied to the Necroscope, could only manifest itself as a curse!

He had *tried* to hurl the telephone away. But the yellow hand that had squeezed itself out through the speaker to grip his wrist and sink its long curved nails into his flesh until they drew blood wouldn't let him! And the basin of the speaker was expanding, warping out of shape as the fingers of a second hand, twin to the first, came writhing up onto the rim, clawing their way to freedom. Then both hands elongated out of the telephone, and while the one continued to clasp Harry's wrist, the other went for his throat!

At first paralysed, the Necroscope's jaws had fallen open, and apart from a spontaneous spasm as he had tried to jerk away from what was happening— an instinctive recoil from the horror of it—he hadn't moved but an inch or so. But then, galvanized by terror, he had fought back. And it was as if he'd fought for his life, for the strength of this thing was supernatural.

And even knowing that this couldn't possibly be happening, still it had looked, felt, and even *smelled* like it was happening. Smelled like it, yes: the acrid stench of alien sweat, and a poisonous reek that had struck the Necroscope an almost physical blow as someone or something breathed directly into his face.

It had come from the telephone, its speaker grown to the size of a great fleshy pipe, a hugely convulsing vulva, as out from between the spindly, rubbery, reaching arms a bald, domed yellow head dragged itself into view. The thing was all froth, bubbles, sweat, and mucus; it was as if the mutating telephone had tried to give birth and squeeze this loathsome anomaly out into Harry's study.

Half out, the thing had squirmed in its own juices as it used Harry's straining against it to drag itself from the collapsing tube of the telephone. But then, in the next moment, as if the effort had been too much for it, *it* too had collapsed!

The hands on Harry's wrist and neck had turned to so much mush and bone. Pulsing yellow eyes had fallen in on themselves, sucked back into the madly wobbling head. And in that same moment, before complete katabolism, Harry had seen that the yellow face wasn't so much horrifying as horrified. And even as a rotting tongue wriggled between crumbling lips, he had heard his visitor's choked or whispered:

"H-h-h-*help meeeeeee!*"

And then the awful *gurgling* and *slopping* of the thing as it melted like a black and gold candle under a blowtorch . . .

With which dim daylight had flooded Harry's room, and a bird had chirped sleepily in the garden as his tottering universe warped back into something of focus, however unclear.

There had been no blood on his wrist, no slime on his clothing, no marks or hurt to Harry's throat. But still he'd slumped there in the coils of the telephone's spiral cable, leaning on the solid reality of his desk for long, long moments, satisfied simply to listen to the great pounding hammer that was his heart.

And it had taken him as long again to get to his feet and find the strength and spit to swallow . . .

That had been yesterday afternoon . . . following which he'd decided to take B.J.'s advice (that maybe he should get out of the house) a lot more seriously. And indeed he had determined to do just that. But his frustration—that he wasn't able to grasp the meaning of such occurrences—and his ever-increasing irritation or obsession with his own patently flawed faculties, his reasoning and recall processes, plus his naturally stubborn nature, had served to keep him at home for at least one more night. Perhaps he had been hoping that the telephone would ring again, if only to defy the thing or maybe learn something from it now that he knew it wasn't capable of physical harm.

But despite that he had deliberately left his answerphone disconnected, his sleep hadn't been disturbed except by recurrent nightmares, the substance or bulk of which, as usual, he couldn't remember on waking . . . except for one thing, one face, one fear-filled visage in his mind's eye that continued pleading with him even after he was awake:

"H-h-h-*help meeeeeee!*"

The yellow man, or youth, as Harry now seemed to remember him from his—what, precognitive?—visitation. But was that really what it had been? Was that *all* it had been? Alec Kyle's talent resurfacing again after all this time? Some kind of warning presence? Somehow Harry didn't think so, not this time.

Yellow men . . . Tibetan priests or monks . . . The monastery on the frozen plateau . . .

And the leader of those red-robes in London that time, taking pictures at the scene of the bombing in Oxford Street . . . And the same group, or another just like it, in the Forest of Atholl.

All of these things, yes—

—But what *else* did Harry know about them?

And his Ma: she hadn't come to his rescue or "interfered" this time. When the telephone had been a wolf—(*God!* But the Necroscope felt dizzy! Whirled along on his own wild thoughts, he could hardly believe he was turning such stuff over in his mind, having this conversation with himself!)—but *when* the telephone was a wolf his mother had come on like the cavalry! So why not this time? What if she hadn't been *able* to on this occasion? And why wasn't he able to hear the dead conversing in their graves, which was as "usual" or "normal" to Harry as real-life background conversation in a crowded room to a normal man?

But when he thought about it, at least that was something he could figure out for himself.

It wasn't his Ma, wasn't the Great Majority who had given up on him, it was Harry who had given up on them! It was this . . . this some-damn-thing inside him that didn't want him talking to them, and it was getting worse all the time. This need in him to protect his secret talents, his powers as a Necroscope and his use of the Möbius Continuum. He was like an addict obscuring his addiction, learning how *not* to give himself away. A difficult thing when using the Möbius Continuum, for his physical movements on entering into or exiting from the Continuum might easily be observed, but very much simpler in the case of his commerce with the teeming dead; for that was metaphysical, mental, invisible. He had simply erected barriers in his mind, shields that had always been there, which alone allowed him to lead a normal existence. Except now they were there permanently; for without even realizing that he had done it—and even now not sure—it was possible that he'd left those barriers in place and so cut himself off from the dead.

After a late breakfast, coffee and a bowl of cereal, the Necroscope had tested the theory, opened his mind and instinctively tuned in to that ethereal "waveband" to which he alone had access. Letting it flow through him, he had known at once that he was right. For they were there as always, the whispering dead, the Great Majority, talking to each other from their unseen, unknown graves across the world. But before they could sense him or feel the warmth of his lonely flame flickering in their long night, he had reinstated his barriers to shut them out.

But why? Why *do* that to them, when the teeming dead were the only real friends Harry had ever had? The answer was simplicity itself: the best way to keep a secret hidden forever is to lock it away where it can never be discovered. *This* secret was locked in the Necroscope's head, and if he threw away the only key . . . that was where it would stay.

Then for a while he had known regret, remorse, even something of surprise, at himself—that he was so ready, willing, and able to discard so much of what had been good in his life. But he knew that whatever else he did he must *not* risk anyone else finding out about his talents.

He couldn't tell anyone about them, display them, or—

—Or use them? Yes, and it might even come down to that, eventually. And what hope would he have then of finding Brenda and his boy? None, he supposed. So maybe he should get on with the search for them—involve himself personally in it again—while he still could. Which seemed like another good reason (a *valid* one, anyway) for getting himself out of this old house.

As for Bonnie Jean's reasons: Harry didn't even know what they were, exactly. Something she feared? Something he should fear . . . ?

At which moment, as he'd pushed his plate away and stood up, the telephone had jangled in his study. And *that* was maybe something he should fear. Or something he should fight, whichever.

Harry had breakfasted in his kitchen. At first the sound of the phone had frozen him rigid; then he had taken a moment or two to unfreeze, decide what to do and get mobile, and several seconds more to make his way to his study. And all of the time the telephone had kept on ringing.

After that . . . he'd found himself snatching at the thing, no longer giving himself time to wonder or worry about it but doing it. And even in full daylight, or as full as it ever got to be this time of year, still Harry had felt the short hairs rising at the back of his neck, and the creep of his flesh as he anticipated the Unknown . . .

. . . Feelings which were still with him when he'd heard:

"Harry, is that you?" Darcy Clarke, his voice made tinny by the two or three inches Harry held the phone away from his ear, his face. At first he had failed to recognize his caller, partly because it had been so long, and also because he'd been expecting . . . well, almost anything else! But then:

"Darcy," he had answered, almost gasping his relief as he flopped into his chair. "It's . . . it's *good* to hear from you!" And that was something he really hadn't expected to say again, not and really mean it.

Darcy was quick on the uptake, as usual. "Harry, is anything wrong?"

"Wrong?"

"You sound—I don't know—sort of tense?"

"I was expecting a call from, oh, someone else. So what's on your mind?" He had tried to sound as much at ease as possible, but at the same time had realized that he wasn't the only one who sounded "sort of tense." And his heart—and his guts—had given a lurch as he asked: "Is it Brenda?"

"Brenda?" As if nothing could have been further from Darcy's mind— which after all this time might well be the case. "Oh, Brenda! No, no it's not your wife. Harry, it's something else. And we have to talk—I mean face to face. And I do mean we *have* to talk!"

Well, and Harry had wanted to get out of the house, hadn't he? "A talk? You want to talk to me?" But his voice had turned sour in a moment. *"Just* a talk?"

"For the moment, yes."

"Not about Brenda and my son?"

"No . . . and if I may say so, it's bigger than that. Don't give me a hard time over this, Harry. I mean, considering what I've just said, you have to know now that it really *is* big."

"What if I tell you I don't much care?"

"And what if I tell you that you'd *better* care? This time it's not just the Branch, Harry. It could be everything . . ."

Everything was a lot, especially if Darcy Clarke said so. "And it's something you need my help with?"

"Maybe," Darcy sounded uncertain. "But on the other hand, it could be that you need ours . . ."

Harry had thought about that, briefly, before answering, "There's a train out of Waverly Station about midday. I'll be on it." It wasn't that he had simply accepted Darcy's argument, or given in to the veiled threat, but . . . who could say? Maybe the Branch had the answers to some of his many questions.

"A train?" Darcy had seemed surprised and Harry knew why. But his *thing*, his obsession, was really starting to take control now.

"A train, yes," he had snapped. "What, and did you think I would walk it?" With which he'd put the phone down . . .

His train had got into King's Cross a little before 5:00 in the evening, but there'd been E-Branch or Special Branch men aboard from Darlington on down the line. Harry had seen them and known who they were, but said nothing. They had sat close but not too close, just keeping their eyes on him. Only a handful of people would have noticed, but the Necroscope had had plenty of experience of just such people. So, were they escorting, protecting him? Obviously the first, probably the second. But from what? "Something big," as Darcy Clarke would have it.

Darcy himself, Head of Branch, had met him at King's Cross, driven him to headquarters in the heart of the city. Which was where they were now . . .

Despite all of Darcy's efforts to the contrary, he was nervous as a cat. He had problems aplenty, all of which were or seemed connected to the Necroscope to one extent or another. He could have had him watched at home, of course, but he had long since promised Harry that he wouldn't interfere with him or his son, if ever they should find him, and he wasn't about to break his word. So since Harry was a "friend" of the Branch, this seemed the best way: a face to face confrontation.

In fact there had been no other route. Or there *had* been, but that was a route Darcy would avoid at all costs. The other way would have been to tell the Minister Responsible about Harry's possible involvement in certain matters, sit back and let him make the decisions.

But in the past Darcy's dealings with that specific government body had taught him a number of valuable lessons: not least that it could be . . . well, heavy-handed to say the least. He was well aware that "in the best interests of the country," even innocent men were occasionally expendable. But the Necroscope Harry Keogh wouldn't be one of them, not while Darcy was Head of E-Branch.

The Branch was housed in, or on, a hotel; the elevator at the rear stopped on an extra floor, the top floor, E-Branch HQ. Ben Trask was pacing the long corridor when the elevator doors hissed open and Harry and Darcy stepped out. Trask fell in with them in a moment, his gruff greeting, "Hi, Darcy, Harry!" echoing in a place whose offices were more than half-empty. It was after five and most of Darcy's staff had gone to their homes; which was just as well, because the business in hand was on a strictly need-to-know basis. And:

"Ops room," Darcy said, leading the way. Enroute from the station he had said very little. When he'd spoken at all it was to ask Harry how his search was going, which the Necroscope had answered with a shake of his head. Darcy had desperately wanted to ask, "Why the train?" but had held it in. That was what they were going to find out. That . . . and hopefully one or two other things. Or hopefully not.

The ops room was empty, gloomy, sterile-looking. Darcy put on the lights, dragged three steel chairs around a table, threw his coat on another chair and sat down. Harry and Ben Trask followed suit. And when they were seated:

"So what's going on?" Harry looked from to face, taking in the little tell-tale changes. Not that Darcy Clarke ever changed a lot, not that you'd notice. He was still the world's most nondescript man, middling in every way except for his weird talent, that "guardian angel" that kept him out of trouble and made him the ideal man for the job. As for Trask: if anything, he looked younger! A human lie-detector, the last three or four years had tightened him up a little, sharpened him, taken away his jaded, lugubrious look. Or perhaps it was the job . . . or maybe it was whatever this was now.

"You mean *you* can't tell *us?*" Darcy leaned forward, looked him straight in the eye. "See, the fact is we don't know what's going on. We were hoping you would, and that you'd want to tell us about it."

Ben reached out and let his hand fall on Darcy's arm. "You said you were going to tell him straight," he said.

And Harry said: "So that you could judge my reaction, eh, Ben? What is this, good-cop, bad-cop? Or is it *just* inquisitor and adjudicator? He asks the questions and you tell him if I'm lying or not?"

They said nothing and Harry began to stand up. But Darcy said, "Harry, don't. Please don't. If you walk out on us, then it's out of my hands . . . " The way he said it—so cold, yet at the same time brokenly, as if he had to force the words out—made Harry sit down again.

"And whose hands will it be in, whatever it is?"

"Harry, we're covering for you," Ben took the opportunity to put in. "For a long time now you haven't been straight with us." But his voice, too, was shaky, because he knew that for a long time now they hadn't been straight with Harry. Which went against Trask's grain. It wasn't just that you couldn't lie to him, but also that he didn't like telling lies. Not even white lies or half-truths. And to him *not* telling something—hiding something, especially from a friend—was tantamount to lying about it.

"Covering for me?" Harry said, uncertainly. And again he looked from one to the other. Then, shaking his head, "Well I'm sorry but you've lost me right from square one!" And angry now: "I mean, what the hell am I supposed to have done?"

Ben Trask was staring right at him; he blinked and looked at Darcy. "I can't read a thing. There isn't one lying hair on Harry's head, not where we're concerned. A lot of uncertainty, soul-searching, but no deliberate mendacity." And to Harry: "It could be you kept something back that time four years ago, but you certainly aren't doing it now." Then he frowned. "Not that you're aware of, anyway . . . " Then back to Darcy again, "So do it the way you said you would, and tell it to him straight."

And Darcy sighed (gladly, Harry thought), and said, "Very well." And to the Necroscope: "Harry, all sorts of things are going down, and we don't have a clue what it's all about. When we've told you about it, then you'll understand why we thought you might be involved. And then, too, you might be able to suggest something. Or maybe we can work it out together."

Before they could begin the Duty Officer looked in, asking if they would like coffee. Darcy said yes, and they sat in silence until he had brought it in. Then Darcy told him to see to it they weren't disturbed, and after he'd left they got down to it . . .

Leaving everything else out for the moment, Darcy went straight to the story of the bomb in Hyde Park. And Ben Trask, of course, monitored Harry's reaction: blank astonishment at first—then something quite different.

The Necroscope's universe reeled and he knew what was coming. He had just commenced saying: "What? A nuclear device? In Hyde . . . " when it happened.

His face went pale; he clutched the rim of the table and groaned, "Oh, no!"

Darcy and Ben flanked him in a moment, their hands on his shoulders. "Harry?"

"Leave it," he gasped. "I know what it is and it'll pass." Well maybe, but not right now. For instead the room, the operations room, "passed" right out of existence! And:

Everything was white! So white, so blinding white, that he gasped with the hurt of it, closed his eyes and turned his face away—and a moment later felt a slap. The hard slap of a cold, gritty hand, or a handful of ice—like a snowball with a rock in it, such as the colliery kids had used to make when he was a boy—on his face, stinging it. And then a punch, or rather a body-blow, full body, as if someone had slammed a giant door on him. It picked him up, spun him head over heels like a leaf in a gale, hurled him down in a deep snowdrift, so that he left a man-shaped depression where he broke through the thin crust and crunched down deep into the snow.

And overhead, suddenly, there was a wind! A gale! A hurricane, as the white light turned red and sound, momentarily suspended, returned—with a vengeance!

A crackling of electricity; a tracery of electrical fires racing across the sky; a rumbling born out of nothing that grew louder and louder until it was deafening! And then the debris, dirt, snow and ice, chunks of rock, a horizontal avalanche passing over Harry where he hugged himself down and tried to disappear into his hole in the snowdrift.

It went on for long seconds, and when it was done and the ground stopped shuddering . . .

Harry got to his knees, looked out of the trench he'd compressed into the snow . . . looked out on an awesome scene. Near-distant, some two or three miles across a dirty grey desolation a low, squat mushroom cloud bulged upwards, still expanding. At its base, ground zero was hidden in the boiling flame-shot stem where rocks and rubble were still tumbling from the sky. And as a backdrop, gaunt grey mountains capped with white marched into a familiar distance.

"What . . . ?" he said. And:

"What?" Darcy Clarke echoed him. "Are you OK, Harry?"

And the ops room was there all around him.

For a while he couldn't speak, licked his lips, was glad, (a hell of an understatement!) to be back. Not that he'd been anywhere; not his body, anyway. Another of Alec Kyle's bloody indecipherable precognitions, it must have been. Brought on by all the talk of an atomic bomb in Hyde Park. And he spoke the thought out loud even as it came to him: "One of Alec's glimpses into the future."

Trask knew the truth when he heard it. "You've retained a part of Alec?"

"We thought that had left you by now," Darcy put in. "How would we know any different? We're never in touch these days."

Still disoriented, Harry reeled, clutched at the desk. He looked at their concerned faces where they flanked him, realized that what Darcy had said was true: that these were friends, real friends, and he'd been too long out of touch. And steadying himself, he blurted, "The fact is I'm a total fuck-up! Alec Kyle? He's only a small part of it. But yes, I still have something of him in me—which I don't understand any more than he did! That was an example of it: a bomb blast—a nuclear blast, was how it seemed to me—out of some unknown future . . . "

. . . Future! Future! Future!

And the world reeled again!

"Jesus!" Harry gasped, as the room started to rotate, and Darcy and Ben grabbed his shoulders, holding him still.

Then they were gone, and a kindly, learned, face—a long face, with grey eyes whose inner orbits curved into the bridge of a straight, even nose, over drooping moustaches that touched the corners of his small but by no means mean mouth—peered into Harry's. The man's forehead was large and open; his cheeks were ruddy; his ears protruded slightly, with sideburns that flowed down into a full golden-brown beard. But his eyes were his most remarkable feature, for at one and the same time they were severe and smiling! And as well as discipline, a great humanity—an inexplicable mysticism—seemed to blaze outwards from them.

Then:

"Ah, son of my visions!" he said. "Or are you in fact the father? But away with you now, for I am assured that as yet it is not your time."

And that was all. The ops room swam back into focus again and Harry felt like he was about to throw up.

"What the hell . . . ?" Ben Trask's eyes were staring. "Where *were* you, just then?" For he had been unable to read the truth of a mind that was elsewhere.

And Darcy wanted to know: "Harry, how long has this been going on?"

They stared so hard at him—they tried so very hard to pierce the veil of the Necroscope's metaphysical mind—that he felt their gaze was almost hypnotic.

Hypnotic! Hypnotic! Hypnotic!

He couldn't stop it. His every thought conjured new, even stranger visions. "Just hang onto me!" he croaked, as yet again the universe stood on its head.

This time it was a mere moment, a displacement, a genuine "glimpse," such as the precog Alec Kyle had used to experience. A frozen picture like a single celluloid frame that gets jammed too long under the hot glare of the projector's lamp, until it browns, crisps, and blisters out of existence.

Harry stood at a crossroads. On the one hand beyond a low wall, the mainly un-tended plots and leaning headstones of some unknown graveyard were half-obscured by long grasses. While on the other a signpost said "Meersburg" along with a distance in kilometres. None of which had any relevance to Harry—not yet at least.

But then the picture browned, crisped, distorted all out of shape and vanished—

—And Darcy and Ben were holding on to him for dear life.

Then:

It hurt! Something in the Necroscope's head hurt like all hell! And just *ex-actly* like the single frame under the burning glare of the projector's lamp, he felt or sensed the something being burned of him, too.

Those unique connections, near-magical synaptic triggers, in what had once been Alec Kyle's brain, finally disconnecting themselves, re-aligning, con-forming to Harry's mental patterns. For he had overburdened the old system, channelled too great a current along its circuits. And at last the "fuses" had blown.

It went out of him like a sigh, *with* a sigh, as he stopped straining and fell back in his chair, where for a long time his face gradually, tentatively unscrewed itself as the pain ebbed until it, too, went out of him. And:

"Done," he said. And Ben Trask knew that it was so.

"The last of him, gone," he said.

Darcy looked from one to the other and back again. "What?" was all he could say. "What?"

And eventually Harry was able to tell him: "You know, I've never been too sure of God—that there is one, I mean. And I'm still not. But if there is, well, I thank Him for this at least, that at last Alec is out of my system for good."

Which was all he was willing to say by way of explanation. But at the same time he knew that there'd been much of value in Kyle's talent. In the begin-ning it had warned of an IRA bomb in Oxford Street and saved lives, a great many. And at the last—or almost at the last—it had warned of another, greater bomb. The meaning of the first was now academic: it had worked itself out. But as for the last?

"Where is it now?" Harry asked out of the blue, after Ben had replenished their coffees. "That bomb, I mean."

"Made safe," Darcy told him. "And in a very safe place."

"I'd like to see it."

"Tonight?"

"As soon as possible, yes."

"I'll make the arrangements," Darcy said. "But it's quite a distance. Just how do you propose to, er, get there?"

Harry looked at him almost in surprise. "Don't you have a duty vehicle?"

"Of course," Darcy nodded at once. "Silly of me . . ." Then he left Ben and Harry on their own for a few minutes, while he went to "make the arrange-ments."

* * *

Darcy made several calls from an office next door to the Operations Room, then turned to the saturnine figure who was seated before a one-way window looking in on Ben and their guest. And despite that the walls were soundproofed, still Darcy kept his voice low as he asked, "Well, have you formed any opinions?"

Doctor James Anderson, hypnotist, turned and looked at him with eyes deep as space. "Several," he said, in that sepulchral voice of his. "Even some about our Mr. Keogh! But tell me, this bomb story. Is it true?"

Darcy sighed. "Look, we're short on time. As for anything you've learned: I know I don't have to remind that you're still subject to the Official Secrets Act."

"It is true, then? My God, but . . . !"

". . . But that's the kind of thing we're up against here in E-Branch," Darcy's voice was cold now, even harsh. "Now forget it and tell me about Harry."

Anderson nodded, took a deep breath. "Maybe we should reconsider. It could be I went . . . what, too deep? Going on what you've told me, and on what I've seen, it seems to me he's developed an obsession; he's now denying these skills of his as if even *he* no longer believes in them! And that's a kind of schizophrenia. And it could get worse, manifest itself in a variety of ways."

At which Darcy knew what he must do. "I want it reversed. But will he know? I mean, will he suspect what we did to him?"

"Not if we do it the same way. In fact you can be certain he'll only feel a great relief—because that's what I'll *tell* him he'll feel."

"I'll convince him to sleep here tonight," Darcy said.

And again Anderson nodded. "That will give me time to prepare myself," he said.

"And you'll be here when we get back?"

"You can be sure of it," Anderson answered, because he had no way of knowing that he'd be somewhere else entirely . . .

II

ANDERSON, THE BOMB, AND R.L.'S OBI

James Anderson, Harry Keogh," Darcy Clarke "introduced" the two men as all four of them, including Ben Trask, entered the elevator. But he deliberately left Anderson's "Doctor" prefix unstated. The hypnotist and the Necroscope shook hands, and Harry showed never a sign that he recognized or remotely remembered the other. "James," Darcy went on, feeling as treacherous as a dog who turns on his own master, "Harry was once with E-Branch and still helps us out occasionally." And to Harry: "James is a specialist who also gives us a hand now and then. Nothing to do with the current situation; we're just dropping him off at his home, that's all."

The conversation terminated there and then, which was what Darcy had intended. The least said by both parties the better. And twenty minutes later, as Trask stopped the car at a junction in upper-class Knightsbridge where James Anderson got out just a short walk from his home, no one gave a second thought to the vehicle that pulled up close behind, or the two passengers who alighted at the same junction. The streets were full of people going home.

Following which Trask set out in earnest to drive west to Greenham Common near Newbury, Berkshire, the US Air Force base that housed NATO's American-owned Cruise missiles . . .

And when at last they were on the west-bound motorway:

"How long?" Darcy leaned forward to ask Ben Trask.

"An hour and a half, maybe two," Trask answered. "Depends on the traffic. But now that the rush hour is over, it's looking good."

"So then," Darcy turned to Harry where they sat together in the back of the car. "Plenty of time to talk. And with luck that gaggle of CND harridans at the Common will have quietened down for the night and we won't have to run the gauntlet. Can you hear us back here OK, Ben?"

The driver glanced at them in his interior mirror, gave a thumbs-up sign.

"Very well," Darcy said. And to Harry: "So, if you've got any questions for me . . . ?"

"Bomb questions, yes," said Harry at once, with the white heat of his incendiary vision still burning on the eye of memory. "Like, whose bomb is it?"

Darcy understood and nodded. "Its design? Chinese. Dirty as the 'rough' technology that produced it. But miles ahead of anything the West might have suspected of them. In other words, they're catching up on us fast."

"And if there was one bomb—?" Harry said, or questioned.

"—There could be more?" Darcy cocked his head. "No, not anywhere in the UK, anyway." He looked uncomfortable. "But . . . we do know that there was one more bomb, at least."

"Where?"

"Would you believe . . . Russia, Moscow?"

Harry's jaw fell open. "What? But how do you know?"

"Even harder to believe," Darcy grinned, however humourlessly. "Yuri Andropov told us. He's the Big Chief over there now, you know. He also told us about the bomb in Hyde Park!"

Now the Necroscope shook his head in astonishment. "Well it beats me!" he said. "Gregor Borowitz established The Opposition under Brezhnev, but Borowitz was anti-KGB from head to toe. And the Russian outfit, before we wrecked it, was just as covert, esoteric, as E-Branch itself, and hated by the KGB even as much as Borowitz hated them. And God only knows they have to hate *us*, or you—or me—even more! Yet now Andropov, ex-head of the KGB, is taking time out to warn you of nuclear sabotage? A bomb that the Chinese have buried in a London park? It doesn't make sense!"

"It makes perfect sense," Darcy told him. "Because while the Cold War was one thing, World War Three would be something else entirely. Can't you just see it? These bombs going off at some time in the near future—let's say at a time when East-West relationships are at a low ebb—and the utter chaos that would ensure?"

Harry frowned and shook his head. "It still doesn't work out. What, China? The agent provocateur? But surely they'd get dragged in. Don't nuclear weapons have their own signatures?"

"China would get dragged in, certainly," Darcy answered. "She'd be answerable eventually, but much too late. What, with London and Moscow in ruins, and all the world's big guns targeting and firing on each other? And because the West is still way ahead, you can bet we'd obliterate China, too."

"Then how can China profit by planting these bombs?"

"Who said she did?" And Darcy grinned his mirthless grin again—more a grimace, really—and as the Necroscope fell silent told the rest of the story.

"So that's it," he said at last. "Tibet. The bombs were planted by a bunch of Tibetan extremists, the crazy devotees of some kind of sect. Which leads us to your involvement . . . "

"Eh?" Harry jerked upright. "Me? You think I'm involved? But how? In what way?" And his indignation was a hundred percent genuine, Darcy knew, else Ben would have spoken up about it. Yet while Trask remained silent, he was in fact conscious of something strange; he had definitely "felt" the Necroscope go on the defensive at first mention of Tibetan involvement, and again when Darcy had spoken of "red-robed monks."

"We were hoping you could tell us," Darcy said.

And now Trask came in with: "Like I said back at HQ, you haven't been straight with us for quite some time, Harry. And you're not being entirely straight even now."

"I haven't told you any lies!" the Necroscope snapped.

"Maybe not," Ben said. "But neither have you told us the whole truth. It goes right back to that 'werewolf' job you did in London. That's where it started: the night you—well, did your thing—in that garage."

"Where what started?" Harry demanded. But in fact he already had an inkling of what they were talking about. And they were right: he hadn't told them everything about that night.

Darcy answered his blustered question anyway: "Where you began to deviate from the true facts a bit . . . ?"

Then, after a long, thoughtful pause, Harry sighed, sank back into his seat. "The night Brenda and my boy vanished," he said, his voice subdued, his thoughts going off at a different tangent entirely.

"But that's not what we're on about—" Darcy told him, and at once shut up as he realized that his tone wasn't as sympathetic as it might be. "I'm sorry," he said then. "That's not how I meant to put it."

"Harry," said Ben Trask from the driver's seat, "it isn't fair of us to be grilling you when you can't see the whole picture. I mean, we're not interrogating you. We're not trying to make you trip over your own tongue. So it's only right we tell you what's bothering us and let you take it from there. OK?"

"So tell me," Harry said.

And Darcy took it up again. "Do you remember when I called you about those Tibetan sect members who got killed in a mobile shoot-out? It was in your neck of the woods—the Spey Valley?"

"I remember," Harry said, frowning again. "I wasn't involved . . . " (*Was I? Bloody was I?*) "So what of it?"

And in the front of the car, Ben Trask likewise wondered, *Was he involved? Was he?* What the fuck was wrong with his talent? He couldn't make any sense of it. For to him things were either black or white, but never, *never* grey! Until now.

"One of those monks in that burned-out wreck was shot with a crossbow," Darcy said. "There was another bolt in the door of the car, and both of them had the same silvered heads that were found in the bodies of those thugs you dealt with in the garage that night in the East End. You told us you shot those two. And if so, doesn't it follow that you might also have had something to do with the Spey killings? Or that you'd know about them, at least?"

Harry's head reeled in sudden conflict—of identity, forbidden knowledge, and loyalty—but he quickly brought it under control. It wasn't him they were after but Bonnie Jean, and she was innocent. Definitely innocent of whatever Darcy was talking about, because she had been with Harry that day. The day she'd called off their climbing and hunting expedition. He remembered it well . . . didn't he? Of course he did.

They had stayed at Auld John's place overnight, setting off early the next morning to go climbing in the Cairngorms. Except B.J. had called it off at the last moment. Maybe she'd reckoned he wasn't up to it. And then they had driven back to Edinburgh. That was all there was to it.

. . . *Yellow men in red robes!*

. . . *A burning car!*

. . . *And B.J.—with a crossbow in her hand!*

"Harry?" Darcy pulled him out of it, offering him a target for his frustration. And:

"I don't know anything about any shoot-out!" Harry snapped. "As for the garage job . . . no, I didn't do it." (There, it was out. But it was all they'd get. He wasn't about to betray B.J.)

Darcy nodded. "You never did actually tell us you were responsible that time. So, you were covering for someone else."

"Someone who helped me, yes," Harry said under his breath. "Someone who saved my life, stopped that lunatic 'Skippy' from splitting my head with a machete—or would you rather have me dead? Look, you said you'd been covering for me. Well, is it so hard to understand that I might want to cover for someone else? Surely it's a question of loyalty. As for *my* loyalties: they've always been in the right place."

Darcy pulled at his lower lip, looked for comment from Ben Trask. Trask saw Darcy's querying look in his mirror and gave a puzzled, irritated shrug. Damn it to hell, he wasn't sure!

"So we have to assume," Darcy said, "that if you didn't take out those red-robes in Scotland, whoever you're protecting did."

"No way!" said Harry with conviction. "For she was with me . . . " And in the next moment he saw Darcy's trap, except it really hadn't been intended that way. And:

"We didn't hear that," Darcy said at once. "So it makes no difference. And anyway, that makes two favours we owe him, or her, or whoever. One for pulling your fat out of the fire, and two for getting rid of a couple of saboteurs. But—" (and he couldn't hold it back,) "she must be one hell of a girl!"

And something clicked into place in Harry's mind—incorrectly as it happened, but to the Necroscope it seemed to fit just exactly right.

For he had in fact *seen* those red-robed priests when he and B.J. had stopped at the tea-shop in the Forest of Atholl. He'd seen and remembered them; and since the sighting hadn't been part of the action, B.J. hadn't thought to erase it.

But now, to Harry, it seemed that if B.J. had had reason to fear the Tibetans, it might be why she had called off their trip so suddenly. It might also explain why she'd suggested he should vacate the old house for a while: if the four remaining monks were a threat to her, they might also be a threat to him. But as to her connection with them—or to the bolts that had killed one of them—he didn't have the foggiest idea!

Did he?

And what about the tele-Tibetan? That bloody awful visitation in the old house, when his phone gave birth to a yellow *Thing* that turned to so much slop, but not before it cried for help? Obviously there was a connection, but what was it?

From the driver's seat, Trask half-looked back over his shoulder and said, "So you see, Harry, we've been more than a little concerned about you ever since the werewolf thing. And before you ask: no, I wasn't checking on you at the time. And if I had been I'd have asked you for the truth there and then. But your back-up on that job was Trev Jordan, a damn fine telepath. His report details how he detected someone else in that garage but couldn't get a clear reading. The same someone who you're protecting, obviously."

"Which leaves only one question unanswered," Darcy said. "That of the silvered boltheads. Maybe that's something you'll look into some time, eh, Harry? I mean, surely you can see why we're interested? When it comes down to people depositing nuclear weapons left, right and centre, we can't afford to leave any loose ends dangling. There *is* no lead that we, or others, wouldn't follow up. So someone shot those two red-robes, fine. But *why* were they shot? And where have the other four gone to? And who is it that seems to be protecting our interests here?"

"I'll . . . give it some thought," Harry told him, knowing—or hoping—that he wouldn't . . .

Meanwhile the Necroscope had other things to think about: such as the last three precognitive "glimpses" bequeathed to him by some revenant of Alec Kyle's talent.

First the bomb blast. A true vision out of future time or simply a connection, a glimpse, brought about by Darcy's story of a nuclear device discovered in Hyde Park? Harry wasn't sure he'd been told enough about that as yet, and like it or not he suspected he'd have to "give it some thought" after all. Or if not thought, some conversation at least.

But turning to Darcy, he saw that his head was down where he slumped in the corner of the seat. looking back, Trask said, "He's had a tough day. Let him sleep. Did you want something?"

"Did Darcy tell me the whole story about the bomb?" Harry had always felt easy talking to Trask. You couldn't lie to him, no, but at the same time he wasn't likely to lie back. "I mean, how did Andropov find out about it? How can we be sure this was the work of the Tibetans, or 'our' Tibetans, these monks?"

Trask understood his query and answered, "The Soviets have always been interested in parapsychology, as witness The Opposition, the Russian version of E-Branch. Brezhnev was very keen on his mindspy organization. So when the Chateau Bronnitsy fell and the best of the Russian espers were taken out, he wanted it built up again—not the chateau but the organization. He fixed it for a convention of espers in Moscow, perhaps to see what he was up against. We sent along a pair of our lesser lights; they wouldn't glean a hell of a lot, but they wouldn't give too much away either. The Chinese had a delegation, too, from their outfit on Kwijiang Avenue, Chungking. The Tibetans got into Moscow with them. We presume that what's left of the Soviet ESP-organization was in on the convention, and that they found out what was going down."

"Chinese bombs, planted by the members of a Tibetan sect," Harry mused. "So in fact—since the devices are Chinese, and the Tibetans were part of China's delegation—the Chinese are responsible after all, and the Tibetans were only their dupes. Probably because the Chinese knew that they'd be the ones the Russians were watching, not the monks. But Darcy said the Chinese weren't to blame."

"They aren't," Trask answered. "The bombs were stolen. And something Darcy didn't tell you: there's a *third* bomb in Chungking! Andropov's using it as a bargaining chip in the Sino-Soviet border disputes. He isn't saying where it is or who planted it, just that it's there . . . and that there's this little strip of dirt in yak-land that belongs to Mother Russia, and he would very much like the little yellow soldiers out, thank you."

"Blackmail?"

"And of the worst sort. Political, nuclear, nasty. But our locators have found the bomb; or rather, they know where it is, approximately. And now we've given Andropov a deadline: he has two weeks to tell the Chinese what he really must—what he's simply *got* to tell them: the location of the bomb, which city, where—or our government will. Which will take any kudos away from him. Now Harry, this is all highly classified, obviously, on a top secret, need-to-know basis. Which is why Darcy didn't mention it. On the other hand, since you do 'need to know' . . . "

And when Harry failed to reply: "Is there anything else?"

But the Necroscope shook his head, sat back again, and was soon lost deep in thought . . .

He considered his other visions, or "visitations."

After the devastation of the imagined nuclear bomb blast, he had tried to tell Darcy and Ben what he'd seen: a glimpse of some future cataclysm, or an oblique warning that such a calamity was likely to occur. All of which seemed to find an explanation in what Ben had just told him. But the word "future" had been like an invocation or trigger, and again he had been whirled away to some unknown place . . . or rather, an unknown face!

Those eyes that were simultaneously severe and smiling—blazing with humanity and mysticism both—and blazing full on Harry. "Ah, son of my visions!" *the owner of the face had said* "Or are you in fact the father?" *(But the father of what, this mystic's visions?) And then:* "Away with you now, for I am assured that as yet it is not your time."

Not the Necroscope's time? So did that mean that his time was coming? But *what* time?

For a *long* time Harry pondered it, and got nowhere except to accept that the mystic had not posed a threat. If anything, he had seemed to offer shelter against some unknown storm . . .

And then there had been the final visitation, or perhaps visit was a better word, for certainly Harry had been transported somewhere:

A crossroads with a low wall to one side, sheltering the untended plots and leaning headstones of a graveyard. While on the other side a signpost pointed to Meersburg . . .

None of which made any sense, had any meaning (he'd never heard of Meersburg), or seemed in any way menacing to the Necroscope; for graveyards and lichen-covered slabs were familiar motifs in his world, by no means frightening. Yet this glimpse had ushered out the last trace of Alec Kyle's talent, had been its last throw. It was gone forever now, burned out of Harry's identity. And if only because it *was* the last throw . . . surely it must have meant something?

"**H**arry?" Ben Trask's voice. Harry looked up, shook his head to clear it, wondered, *Have I been sleeping, too?*

Darcy Clarke was stretching, yawning, and Ben was looking in his mirror at both of them. "We'll be there in four or five minutes," he said. Then he switched on the car's police radio, tuned in and identified himself, spoke into the handset. And:

"Uh-oh!" he said. "The Greenham crones—sans knitting—are gathering for the execution!"

"Problems?" Darcy was alert in a moment.

"Shouldn't think so. A couple of CND bigwigs, along with the usual tribe of retards."

"You have no tolerance," Darcy tut-tutted.

"I know the difference between the truth and a lie," Ben told him. "Nukes are a bad thing: true. But without them we'd have been into World War Three years ago: also true. The organizers of this sort of thing know it, yet still use the terrorism of lies for their own political ends: *definitely* true. Biased? Sure I am. How can I be otherwise with a talent like mine? It's the old question: are espers blessed or cursed?"

They drove along a country road, turned into a lane leading to a huge wire-fenced enclosure. And a sign told them that this was the US Air Force Base at Greenham Common.

Darcy held up his ID, and a uniformed police officer saluted and waved them on. On both sides, walls of policemen held back a crowd composed mainly of angry women. The striped guardroom gate went up, and Ben drove through. But as the car began to cross the threshold a fat, red-faced young woman broke free of the cordon and threw a clod of wet earth at the windscreen. Ben avoided her, used his wipers to twitch the muck aside.

"A hairy one," he grunted, as the clod fell away.

"The mudball?" Darcy said.

"No, the silly cow who threw it!" Ben replied. "What, ban the bomb? That one could fall on a bloody bomb and smother it!" Then they were into the base and all the ballyhoo left behind.

Harry wanted to know: "How did they know we were coming?"

Darcy shrugged. "When the police come out in force, someone is coming. Doesn't matter who it is, it's always the same reception."

Then a huge black American Air Force officer flagged them down, got in the car, and took them where they wanted to go . . .

* * *

Trask drove down a ramp into a "hangar" that wasn't, switched off his lights in the floodlit interior. Their passenger directed him into an elevator that could have taken a tank, and Ben drove in and stopped when red lights blinked on. A warning bell clanged, and the cage descended three levels. And as the doors opened:

"Roll her forward six or so feet," the officer said.

Ben did so, and applied the brake.

"Leave yo ve-hicle half-in, half-out the cage," the American, a Colonel, told them as they got out of the car. "The door works on electric eyes and won't close on the ve-hicle. And the elevator can't move with the door open. That traps the elevator down heah and ensures some privacy. And incident'ly, yo'all are trapped down heah too, until I see some ID." He took out an automatic pistol from his belt and cocked it.

Darcy showed him his ID, and the Colonel goggled. "Man, yo has more right bein' heah than I do!" He put away his gun, took them out of the elevator and down a vast, arched-over, and apparently endless corridor, over echoing expanses of empty, flood-lit concrete, and past a dozen steel-panelled doors to one that was hung with a red-stencilled sign on a white board:

NO ENTRY!

Unlocking the door, shoving it open with a massive, muscular shoulder, the Colonel said, "I takes it yo'all knows what yo's doin'? Look all yo want but don't touch the glass cos it's alarmed. Yo'll have the whole damn camp down heah—and they's every one crazy as me! It's the job." He grinned, saluted, and left them to it. His footsteps moved away from the door—but not too far.

Darcy Clarke had been here before. He led the others to a dais in the centre of the floor, climbed steel steps and leaned on the side of a tank-like container to look down on the contents. "And here's our bomb," he said, "all nice and tidy—and safe—under glass."

Harry moved to one side of him, Ben to the other. The Necroscope was fascinated. "This is an atomic bomb? It looks more like the engine of an experimental, medium-sized motorbike!"

"Just a bit more powerful," Darcy said, with typical British phlegm. Darcy's casual attitude spoke volumes for the safety of the device.

"How much does it weigh?" Harry looked down through plate glass at twin metal cylinders—like a pair of elongated dumbbells, joined in the middle by an eight-inch diameter stainless steel pipe, with the entire surface machine-routed into grooves that were packed with wiring and sealed over with plastic laminate. The whole thing had been set on a rubber-wheeled trolley for ease of movement.

"Two large suitcases worth," Darcy answered. "About a hundred and ten pounds."

"And they could smuggle this into Moscow?" It seemed unbelievable.

Darcy shrugged. *And* through Gatwick—don't ask me how! But take it from me, there's all hell going on right now. Airport security will never be the same again."

Darcy took three paces along the dais to a second container. Harry joined him, looked down through the glass cover at a small safe with a combination lock, and said, "What?"

"The trigger," Darcy told him. "The firing mechanism. It's locked in the safe. Which is supposed to make the bomb safe, or safer." He shrugged again, uncomfortably this time. "And so it does—but to my mind there are enough of the homegrown and far more deadly variety of nuclear devices in this complex already, without they should worry too much about this one. That's what all those women at the gates are up in arms about: nukes—of which this is just one more."

"The trigger?" Harry looked for clarification.

"Basically, it's a radio receiver with an electrical lead that plugs into a socket in the middle section of the bomb. The bomb would be armed remotely, by radio signal, and set off the same way. The people here have rigged a duplicate receiver in an operations room where the only thing it will activate is an alarm. There's a twenty-four hour watch, so that they'll known if or when the signals come in. That'll be the moment that London would have gone sky high."

"But the bomb *is* totally safe?"

"Absolutely. It's leaking a little radiation, that's all, which is why they've isolated it down here in a lead-lined container. But if you take the trigger out of that safe, which you can't, plug it in and extend the antenna a little: bingo! It's all set up again, just waiting for those special signals out of Tibet. Which right now it can't receive . . . else I wouldn't be here."

Harry took a pace to the right, looked at the bomb again. Somehow it had changed: it was now obscene. And the Necroscope shivered. "Sudden death," he said, in a small voice.

"For millions, yes," Darcy agreed. "But the bomb itself—this bomb—would only be the trigger. I mean the *real* trigger. The starting pistol for a nuclear holocaust, and a nuclear winter to follow. Not just World War Three but probably the beginning of a new Dark Ages . . ."

And in a little while Trask came in with: "Well, and have we interested you, Harry?"

Harry looked at him. "I . . . don't any longer work for the Branch," he said. "But on the other hand, this is something we all should be interested in. Any madman who is capable of this could try to do it again."

Darcy said, "Exactly. So you will help us out, if you can? I mean, we know most of it, except why and who. The reason, and the mad mind that reasoned it. But finding the answers to those things will take a very special kind of investigator." He knew he was taking something of a chance here but risked it anyway.

. . . But when he saw the sick *look* that the Necroscope gave him then, he wished he hadn't.

It was as if Harry wanted to say something, as if he wanted to help but didn't know how. For the fact was that he was no longer willing—nor *able*—to admit what he was and what he alone could do. And such was his obsession he wouldn't accept that there were others who already knew about him.

And though Darcy had had doubts before, now he was happy with the arrangements he'd made with Dr. James Anderson. For he knew that Harry *must* be put back to rights. So taking the Necroscope's arm, he said, "Anyway, it's late and we have to be on our way. So don't worry about any of this now. You asked to see the bomb, and now you've seen it."

By now, too, Anderson would be waiting for them back at E-Branch HQ in London—

—Except he wasn't.

And despite that later that night, until the small hours, Darcy called, and called, he got no answer. And after he'd sent a car round to find out what was going on, still no answer. For Doctor James Anderson wasn't at home. By which time Harry Keogh Necroscope, was fast asleep, and E-Branch HQ was very still and quiet. And yet unquiet, too.

Which was always the way of it, at E-Branch HQ . . .

James Anderson had never made it in through his front door. He had made it through the wrought-iron gate, and two of the three short paces through the terracotta-potted shrubbery of the narrow strip of frontage, but at the arched-over porch to the door itself he had paused, blinked and frowned, and wondered why the pair of yellow globe timer-lights flanking the entrance on ornate stands were out. A blown fuse? Probably.

At which he'd gasped and taken a pace backwards, as a pair of lithe dark figures stepped from the darkness behind the last of the potted plants and reached for him. And he had known that whatever this was it wasn't a friendly reception. Then, turning to run, he'd bumped into two more dark figures right behind him and inside the gate.

A grin was all the doctor had seen and all he would later remember—feral eyes that seemed to glow yellow in the dark, and a gaping mouth full of pointed white teeth—as the men in front of him pinioned him, and one of the pair from the bushes put an arm round his neck to cut off any shouting.

Then he had struggled briefly, frantically, and started to kick as he began to run out of air. At once the pressure on his windpipe had been relieved, but as he'd inhaled massively something had been clamped over his nose and mouth. Something that smelled of . . .

. . . Chloroform!

Darkly quiet voices woke Anderson up. They came to him faintly at first as his aching mind surfaced through the slowly fading reek of chloroform fumes, and his dry mouth cracked open as if his lips had been sealed with sugar-sweet crusts of the stuff. He might well have vomited then, but daren't because he didn't know where he was, or why, or who the sounds of sickness would alert. And so he kept it in, swallowed hard and painfully, and listened to the voices.

". . . all yours," one voice was saying. "Big Joe owed your bosses a favour, and this was it. But now we're out of it and the rest of it—whatever's going down here—is your business. Just understand this: anything goes wrong . . . *that's* your business, too! Joe's legitimate now; he's all paid-up; he owes no money, no allegiance to any pot-bellied pigs in Palermo. No offence, you understand. But this is England, and Sicily is a long way off. So you boys are on our turf now. Just fine—as long as you don't go staking any long-term claims in it."

"Hey—it was a favour, you're right," a second, far more coarse and sinister voice hissed, rising and falling in timbre and heavy with unmistakable Italian accents. "A little favour. But you've been well paid for it, OK? Well, who can say when Big Joe might need a favour, too, eh? So what's this with all the threats? We don't need it and we don't scare any too easy, you know? Just be sure to tell Joe we appreciate his help. And remember to say thanks, from Tony and Francesco Francezci."

"Huh!" the first voice grunted, followed by the sounds of footsteps moving away, and a door closing.

And as full consciousness returned to Anderson there were other sounds, too: along with an evenly spaced, echoing drip, a steady rushing sound or sensation, as of vast amounts of water, even a river, sluicing along directly beneath him. But *beneath* him?

He was upright, seated in (no, bound to) a chair. Underfoot, rough wooden boards creaked as he shifted his weight to ease the cramp starting up in his legs. And gradually, experimentally, he tried to force open eyelids that felt gummed down as from sleeping too long or deeply. Then, before he could open them all the way, he froze on hearing what could only be a boat or ferry, the haunted *phoom!—phooom!* of its foghorn.

Somewhere on the river, then? A cold, damp foggy night on the river. What, a houseboat, maybe? Or a pier? And—and what the hell?—*Someone had to be making a terrible mistake here!* Whatever this was all about, they'd got the wrong man!

Finally his eyelids came unstuck, and Anderson lifted his head from his chest. That was painful, too, sending brilliant, jagged flashes of lightning through his skull. He hadn't been hit, had he? Hit on the head? No, it was the chloroform, which he'd received in what must have been close to an overdose.

Chloroform? Kidnapped? James Anderson, who didn't have an enemy in the world? Who would want to do anything like this to him? And why?

He drew a huge draft of air to yell for help, and . . .

. . . A door opened behind him, and a light came on. It was dim, that light— a single unshaded bulb hanging from twisted flex—but it came so abruptly and unexpectedly that he jerked back in his chair, gave an involuntary yelp of terror, and tried to turn his head. Which only caused him more pain.

"No, no," came that same, hoarse, sandpapered voice—the one with the Italian accent—"just save your strength and sit still." And the owner of the voice stepped into view from somewhere behind Anderson and continued: "You can save your breath, too, because no one is going to hear you. And even if you were able to shout that loud . . . well, we're not about to let you."

In fact there were two of them, but not the sort of heavies Anderson might have expected from the texture and tone of the voice. Tall, slender, dark in their long overcoats, their hats set to shade their eyes, they seemed more *clinically* sinister than the thugs his aching mind would have pictured. And he knew that these were the ones who had followed him through his gate, and that one of them at least had feral eyes and a sick, toothy grin.

They pulled up ricketty chairs, sat down facing him with the light behind them, so that only the glimmer of their eyes told him there were faces there at all in the shadows cast by the pulled-down brims of their fedoras. Their eyes, and maybe the white glint of grinning teeth, too. For long seconds nothing was said, until Anderson could stand it no longer. Then:

"What is this?" he gasped. "What the *fuck's* it all about?" And he strained against the industrial tape binding his wrists, ankles, and head to the high-backed chair.

The pair looked at each other, then back at Anderson. And as he continued to curse and babble, one of them reached out a slender, almost female hand to grab his throat. But the incredible *strength* in that hand, the almost casual way the pressure was oh so slowly increased, the deliberate and effortless constriction of the fingers. So that Anderson knew—knew with an absolute certainty—that this brute could crush his windpipe to a pulp! But even as the knowledge dawned, so the steel claw of a hand released him and withdrew.

He gulped air, desperately wanted to massage his throat, swallow, but couldn't, and could no longer hold back the vomit boiling up from his stomach. His captors quickly stood up, got well out of the way as he gagged, managed to turn his head an inch or two to the right, and threw up on the floor.

They let him get it out of his system, and as he sat there rigid, coughing, spitting out the last of the unutterable debris, came forward again. And the one with the voice said, "Now see what you did! It must have been all that abuse—all of the unnecessary vitriol, eh? But the next time you want to be sick, just tell me, OK? I can make you sick faster than you'd ever believe."

"What . . . what is it you want?" Anderson tried to turn his face away from the smell of his own vomit but could only manage a few inches. Swathes of tape across his forehead held his head firmly in place.

"We want to know about E-Branch. In fact, everything about E-Branch." The second of the two, whose voice was soft and sibilant as a hiss, leaned closer. And this was also the one with hands like steel claws.

"E-Branch?" Anderson, blinked his watering eyes. And Darcy Clarke's words came back to him . . . some stupid fucking warning about the Official Secrets Act? Well, *fuck* the Official Secrets Act! And in any case Anderson didn't know anything about bloody E-Branch, except that it was part . . . part of the security services?

He said as much, and the one with the gravelly voice said, "Oh, but you do—you know a great deal about it. Today we saw you with a Mr. Clarke, Darcy. And a Mr. Trask, Ben. Also with a Mr. Kyle, Alec. And we find him—Mr. Kyle—especially interesting. I mean we find all of them interesting, but *especially* him. So we can start there. Tell us about Mr. Kyle."

"But I don't know anyone with that name," Anderson gulped. "I wasn't *with* anyone of that name. Darcy Clarke, yes. And Ben Trask, too. But no . . . what, Kyle? No Alec Kyle, no." He tried to shake his head, moved it too and fro, barely sufficiently to emphasize his point.

"You don't know anyone called Kyle?" the hissing one said. "But we saw you in the car with him."

Anderson tried to nod. "Trask, Clarke, and Keogh. The one you're talking about is called Harry Keogh. So you see, you're making a big mistake here."

As the two looked at each other, Anderson saw their faces in silhouette: gaunt, angular outlines, expressionless now and somehow lifeless. Or if not lifeless, then a different kind of life . . .

They turned back to him. And: "Harry Keogh," said the one with the snake's hiss. "Tell us about him." And as if anticipating the doctor's answer, he reached into his pocket and took something out. A knife—a Stanley knife—with a knob on the handle that he slid forward.

Anderson tried not to see the blade but couldn't take his eyes off it. "I . . . I don't know anything about him," he said. And, as the hissing one shuffled his chair closer: "Oh, God! I . . . I mean . . . I don't know very *much* about him!"

And the one with the knife turned his head to look back a little at the one with the gravelly voice, as if he were waiting for him to make a decision. Which, a moment later, he did. "You know," he growled, "but if we let you, you could waste an awful lot of time. So maybe we can afford the time—and maybe not. But our patience has its limits. So let's simply take . . . a shortcut? A short *cut*, yes. That sounds right. Now listen:

"When my friend here has finished with you, we'll go away and let you think it over. Then, when we come back, there'll be no more questions and answers. You will simply tell us all that you know in one long stream, one long gush, until everything is out. Because you'll know that if you don't . . . well, there are nine—or even nineteen?—more shortcuts."

The whisperer stood up, stepped forward . . . and Anderson tried to cringe down into himself. The knife went down, down to his left side—sliced through the tape binding his hand to the leg of the chair. Then the whisperer took that hand and gave it a sudden jerk, dragging it upright, so that Anderson yelped his agony as his cramped elbow joint was forced through an angle of one hundred and eighty degrees. Finally the whisperer used more tape to bind his wrist again, this time to the chair's backrest alongside his shoulder, with the palm facing forward. And:

"No heckling, please," his tormentor grinned, as he shoved a gag in Anderson's mouth and taped it in place, and showed him the knife again.

The blade was one of those special things. It was curved, almost hooked, shiny and sharp as a surgical tool. Using it, a skilled man would be able to cut the most intricate shapes out of the toughest timber. A wood-carver's tool, yes—or maybe a surgeon's?

"A-a-about K-Keogh—" Anderson somehow managed to mumble, around the rag and the tape where it had come unstuck from his bottom lip. But:

"Ah, no," The gravelly one's voice was deep now, and dark as a dungeon. "Later, save it for later. You see, we have to be sure we get it all. And this way we *know* we'll get it all. For it's a small example of what's in store if we don't."

With which the whispering one trapped Anderson's wriggling hand and smallest finger, applied the blade of his knife to it, and commenced to work on the smallest knuckle. He made his incision just half an inch back from the quick of the pink fingernail, at the permanent crease where the finger bends, and with appalling speed and dexterity worked through the thin layer of flesh and cartilage to the bone and around it, and between the interface of the ball-and-socket junction. So that as the fingertip came loose, the stump had only just commenced to spurt.

It was so quick that Anderson barely felt the pain, not at first; rather, he *sensed* it, through goggling eyes that barely believed what they were seeing. And as the whisperer—or butcher—took his spurting finger into his mouth and began sucking on it, like a baby on a finger of chocolate, the one with the gravel voice said:

"So there you go. Nineteen shortcuts left, or maybe even a few more? It all depends on your appetite for pain."

At which the *actual* pain, not to mention the true horror, finally came. Then, as Anderson fainted, the same man or monster took a thimble from his pocket, lined it with cotton wool, and taped it over the mutilated finger.

And his sibilant companion sucked a dribble of Anderson's blood from his lower lip and whispered, "Waste not want not," then popped the severed section, fingernail and all, into his mouth.

"A tidbit," the other nodded. "But after he's told us all he knows, the main course is still to come."

The Necroscope—the reluctant Necroscope—stayed in London for a further week. It seemed to him the ideal time and opportunity to work a few things out. Bonnie Jean had said he should get out of the house in Bonnyrig for a while, so that was OK. But she had also said he shouldn't wander too far afield. Well, what was far afield to him? He could come and go as he wished, provided no one knew how he did it . . .

Couldn't he?

Coming to London, he'd taken the train because Darcy Clarke had *known* he was coming; he hadn't wanted to arrive too quickly—or weirdly—despite that Darcy knew him for what he was, and what he could do.

Oh yes, he *could* still do it, certainly—

—But reluctantly.

Harry just didn't *want* to use the Möbius Continuum, that was all, not if he could avoid it. As for his other thing: he wouldn't even let himself *think* about that! For the Great Majority knew; all of them knew what he was and what he could do. It made no difference that they couldn't possibly tell anyone, that the Necroscope's secrets were absolutely safe *with* them, for the danger—whatever it was—lay in the fact that his talents weren't secret *from* them.

So he stayed in London a while, seven days, and tried to work a few things out.

Darcy Clarke was happy to have him stay at E-Branch HQ, less than happy with the fact that James Anderson had disappeared and the Branch's locators couldn't find him. In itself, their failure wasn't that odd: the hypnotist wasn't an operative—wasn't an esper as such—just someone they'd used from time to time. Therefore he wasn't much known to the rank and file, and his habits were very much *un*known. He had left very little of an "aura" with the locators, which meant they didn't have much to go on. It was that he'd vanished *now* that worried Darcy most. And that he was probably the only one in the world who could switch Harry back onto the right track.

But having Harry here was a good thing, even if he wasn't seen too much in and around the HQ itself, and Darcy even dared hope that one day his presence might be permanent. For the Necroscope was still the most powerful tool for good that E-Branch had ever known and used. Which was of course the problem: that they'd used him and then discarded him—but not without first making sure he'd be of no further use to anyone else. Not even to himself, apparently . . .

So the Necroscope wandered the streets of London, but in fact got very little sorted out. And semi-detached as it were, from his own world of strange metaphysical powers, the more he looked out on the real world the less he felt a part of it, or of any world. London, which had never seemed familiar, was totally alien to him now, utterly strange. *He* was a stranger here, adrift in a strange world, but he suspected he'd feel the same almost anywhere. Except perhaps in his own place in Edinburgh, or in the arms of B.J. Mirlu.

He was adrift, yes. Because his anchor had come loose.

Which was why he called the wine-bar at least three times a day every day, only to get the same message from B.J.'s answering machine:

"Ah'm sorry, but due tae circumstances beyond mah control, the bar has been closed indefinitely." Bonnie Jean's voice, her phony Edinburghian burr, but sounding oh-so-distant and seeming more dispassionate every time, as if she too were slipping away from him. That would be the real breaking point, he knew. That would be when the world really fell apart. If he were about to let it happen.

But he wasn't.

Harry's last night at E-Branch was a restless one. He did sleep, but derived little benefit from it. He was accommodated in his old room (or "Harry's Room," as it was now known) which opened directly into the main corridor; and about three in the morning his foggy but somehow desperate dreams finally crystalized into something that was more than a dream.

Awake, the Necroscope no longer had contact with the dead; he had all but shut them out of his life. Asleep . . . he was far more receptive.

And as for R.L. Stevenson Jamieson: well, *he* was very determined. And no way he was going to be ignored.

Harry? Necroscope? Man, you is hard *to reach! What's with you, Harry? I mean, you gots to know I wouldn't bother you if it wasn't real improtant?*

"R.L.? Is it you?" Harry mumbled and muttered, tossing in his bed. "God, can't a man get any sleep around here?" At first irritated—which showed in his attitude and apparent disinterest—still there had been that in the black man's dead "voice" which went several degrees beyond urgency; so that despite the barriers that the Necroscope was tempted to erect, he nevertheless felt inclined to pay attention. Sensing this, R.L. said:

Necroscope, me and my obi has been lookin' out for you for a long time now. And I's tellin' you: man, you has enemies! *You has enemies in London, and you has 'em in Scotland, too. They's been watchin' you, Harry! Just bidin' their time, watchin', and waitin'!*

"Yellow men," Harry answered, because in sleep the borders between the various levels of knowledge and being are far less clearly defined; also because "yellow men" were on his mind in connection with the bomb.

Don't know what colour or creed they is, only that they's there, R.L. answered, and sighed his relief that the Necroscope was listening. Then, quickly continuing: *Also, that maybe what they was waitin' for has come.*

"Come? What are you talking about, R.L.? Maybe *you'd* better come again!" But Harry's attention was fully centered now.

Not what but who, R.L. told him. *Him, Necroscope: the one they was waitin' for. And he's just 'bout the worst! Not just a watcher but a . . . a doer, a boss. And he's here, close and gettin' closer all the time. He came quick, tonight, right out o' the blue. And I can feel him like a fog over a swamp, reachin' out for you.*

Harry felt the alien cold in R.L.'s dead voice, and said, "Out of the blue?" He clung to that. "He came by airplane?"

Is that what I said? R.L. thought about it. *I suppose it be! Anyway, he's here, and the others is clustered to him. But like I said: they was watchers: kinda small fry, you know? And this one's a doer. What's more . . . he knows where you is, Necroscope!*

"So, there's danger everywhere," Harry answered. "In Edinburgh, and here too." But the real nature of the threat continued to elude him. And R.L. dared not enlighten him.

In all three places, the dead man said, stepping a little outside the parameters of his mission.

"What?" Harry hadn't failed to notice a certain emphasis. "Did you say *three* places? Where else, then?"

Buried, Harry. Buried deep. Buried . . . real . . . deep . . .

"What is?" The Necroscope was definitely interested now. But he was anxious, too, for he could sense the dead man slipping away from him, perhaps deliberately. "What's buried deep, R.L.?"

Can't say no more, Harry. Believe me, I'd really like to, but it gots to break in its own sweet time. Or, might could be you'd end up broken, too, right . . . along . . . with . . . it . . .

With which he was gone.

III

VICTIMS

A FEW HOURS EARLIER, SOME THREE HUNDRED AND FIFTY MILES AWAY, IN
Scotland: Zahanine had been watching Harry Keogh's place for a week,
which had to be the most frustrating, unrewarding job that Bonnie Jean
had ever given her. And in this cold wet weather, the dreariest. Keep an eye on
Harry? Follow him? Oh, really?

That time a week ago, he had been in the house. She knew that for sure.
Then—no *longer* in the house—gone! And she hadn't seen him go. Since when,
never a sign of him. No smoke from the chimney, or lights of an evening; no
answer when finally she'd lost patience and gone knocking at the door.

The man was some kind of ghost! A very attractive, mysterious ghost, but
just as spooky as the rest of them. Which, from someone like Zahanine, was a
compliment. But to be here in the third week in February, at midnight, on a
night like this . . . she supposed she should consider herself lucky it wasn't snowing! Anyway, she would stick it out for another hour, and then she'd be out of
here . . .

. . . But she knew she would have to be back again at seven in the morning. That was the routine Bonnie Jean had set until *he* was back. For Harry Keogh
was very important to her. And to them, and to everything. And B.J. had spared
no effort in making her point:

"He *is* everything," she'd told the girls before they quit the wine-bar and
went into hiding. "Without him there's no me, no you, no tomorrow. I mean
that quite literally: let anything happen to him, it's all over, done, finished. He's
the one and only one. In whatever shape or form, Harry Keogh *is* the future—
mine, and yours."

That was why she had told him to go missing for a while: because of all the
trouble that was brewing. Well, fine, except he was *still* missing! A week had gone

by and Zahanine was sick to death of these seemingly interminable six-hour shifts spent watching his place. But it was one of only two places B.J. had known to look. The second was her wine-bar in town, where even now one of the other girls would be keeping watch for him.

Distracted by her own thought processes, bored by tedium, and no longer concentrating on the job, Zahanine almost failed to notice the flickering head-light beams sweeping briefly over the night's faintly glowing horizon and paint-ing the stonework of the old bridge across the river yellow. The bridge was half a mile down the road. And by the time she'd used her sleeve to clear a patch in the lightly misted windscreen, there was only a tell-tale splash of yellow on the far side of the water, rapidly fading to darkness. So that even now she wasn't one hundred per cent sure that a vehicle had crossed the bridge. But at least it had served to waken her up a little.

Zahanine got out of her car and trained her glasses on the black silhou-ette of the old house. Was that a yellow glow over the rooftops—suddenly switched off—leaving the ridge and chimney even darker against the velvet sheen of the night? And now she felt a certain elation, that perhaps her vigil wasn't in vain after all.

Seconds, then minutes ticked by, and a light came on downstairs. Then another, upstairs, in the bedroom. Harry was back!

Zahanine started up the car, drove a mile into Bonnyrig—a public tele-phone box—and calling B.J. told her what she'd seen. Then she suggested: "I could put a note in his letterbox, let him know where you are?"

"No, nothing like that!" B.J. cautioned. "No notes or letters. Nothing that might tell someone *else* where we are! First let me speak to him. Call me again in five minutes."

And five minutes later Zahanine did just that. But on the other end of the line B.J. was furious. "His phone is off the hook!" she said. "Either he's using it—or he's still afraid of the damn thing! But time is wasting, so don't ask me about that . . . " And after a moment's thoughtful silence:

"Maybe he just doesn't want to be disturbed, doesn't want to have to iden-tify himself," she said. "It's possible he went back to pick up a few things. I don't know—but you can find out. Zahanine, he knows you. Go to the house and *tell* him where I am. No written messages, but a spoken one. After that he can make his own way here or come with you, whichever. But if he's going to be in the house any length of time, tell him to be on his guard. And tell him to put the phone on the hook so I can speak to him. And you can give him my phone number—but make him remember it. *Don't* write it down! Now tell me, did you get all that?"

"Yes," Zahanine answered, breathlessly. "I'm to go to him, tell him where you are, give him your number—but in his head. I'm to tell him to be careful if he's going to be in the house for a while. If he's not, then he can come with me or make his own way to you. That's it."

"Good! Go now . . ."

Two or three minutes to get back to Harry's place. There was a car parked on the rutted track behind the house. Zahanine parked a hundred yards away, approached as quietly as she could on foot. This was simply so as not to alarm Harry. Then she was up the path and knocking on the door. From inside, no response, utter silence—but the upstairs lights went out!

Zahanine waited a minute or so, then knocked again, calling softly, "Harry, it's me, Zahanine, one of B.J.'s girls . . ."

And as the door oh-so-swiftly opened, an oddly-accented voice *behind* her said, "Why, so it is!" But it wasn't Harry's voice.

Zahanine was feral-eyed in the dark, night-sighted as all B.J.'s moon-children. The man in the doorway was medium height, had slightly tilted eyes—and was yellow. Asiatic! As for the one behind her: he'd be cut of much the same cloth. Drakuls!

Twisting her supple body, Zahanine let fly with a foot to the groin of the one before her, at the same time striking with the edge of her hand at the one behind. Her foot found its soft target, but the one behind leaned backwards out of range—and fired his silenced handgun from no more than four feet away. It made a sound like a big cat spitting.

The bullet hit her on the inside of her left breast, went deep, lodged beside her heart. And it was a silver bullet. The assassin had slow-healing sores on his fingers, cracked flesh, from filling his weapon's magazine with silver bullets.

Zahanine was lifted from her feet and tossed back into the crouched, moaning form of the man in the doorway where he cradled his aching testicles. Her sudden weight knocked him off his feet, bowling him over in the narrow corridor. The pair of them went sprawling. The one outside looked back into the darkness—glanced this way and that furtively, and sniffed the air with a flattened nose—then pointed his gun straight ahead and moved inside. Closing the door, he dropped the catch on the security lock.

Zahanine was on her feet, her hands pressed to her chest. Wild, wolfish, she bared sharp white teeth, turned, and kicked again at the one crumpled on the floor as she stepped over him. Then she fled, stumbled, went bouncing from wall to wall along the corridor, and finally lurched headlong into Harry's study. But the one with the gun was right behind her, and as she made for the patio doors he fired again.

The first bullet was a white-hot agony, as if someone had slid a poker into her chest. And it was a pain that would kill her, Zahanine knew, even without the second shot. But at least that one put an end to the pain.

Caught up again in the same massive fist, her spine shattered, she was driven through the patio doors in a tearing of glass and a splintering of narrow mullions.

Face down in the garden she lay, bloodied and dying. And her killer put his gun away, caught up her ankles, and yanked her backwards through broken glass into the room. Barely conscious, she didn't even feel it . . .

When the killer's companion was able to come from the corridor, he found him between her legs, tearing her flimsy underclothes away. And: "Eh?" he groaned in their own tongue. "What are you doing? Is the bitch dead?" He continued to gentle his sore testicles.

"She's dying," the other grunted. "And much too soon. But let's face it, she wasn't going to be taken alive."

"You should take care," the other cautioned. "She could be a lieutenant!"

"No," the one on the floor gasped as he entered the girl, at the same time sucking at the scarlet hole in her breast. But he paused to explain, "If she was . . . right now there'd be hell to pay! We'd have to burn the house down. It would attract attention, and perhaps alert Mr. Kyle or his werewolf bitch! That is something we can't—*uh!*—afford."

"But what you're doing . . . would Drakesh approve?"

The killer looked back over his shoulder, said, "I don't know, and I can't ask him. But compared to those docile, flat-chested cows in the walled city, this one is just *ripe* for it! And she's a member of the pack. The last Drakul told us to get the job done, not how to do it. Myself, I've gone without long enough. And you—you're putting me off. So go and search her car, find her handbag, anything. But let me get done—*uh!*—fucking her."

His partner turned away, and over his shoulder said, "In that case you can fuck her for me, too!" And he went achingly back down the corridor.

Grinding away in the girl, the vampire on the floor felt her body begin to shudder, vibrate. Looking directly into her face, he saw her eyes open and blaze up yellow! He sensed her enormous effort; he *felt* the contraction of exhausted muscles, and gaped his disbelief as Zahanine's arms bent at the elbows and her hands came off the floor. Her nails were long . . . and they were bleeding.

Bleeding, as they elongated from the quick and thickened into hooked claws. He felt their trembling—those shivering, shuddering claws—jerked back his face as they oh-so-gently touched him. A mere touch, that left five scarlet tracks down each side, from the orbits of his eyes to his quivering chin, as he wrenched himself free!

Zahanine's first—and final—attempt at metamorphism, the true lycanthropy.

But it was over. Her claws shrank back into fingers; her arms flopped to the floor; her eyes glazed and slowly closed, as she breathed a wolf's last breath. Breathed it out and out . . . until it was gone.

Her killer cursed, adjusted his clothing, headed for the kitchen to see if he could find a meat cleaver. And on Harry Keogh's desk the telephone went *purrrrrrrr* where it had been lifted from its cradle . . .

Francesco Francezci had flown in from Sicily around midnight. Three of his own people—a youngish, good-looking lieutenant called Vincent Ragusa, a senior thrall, Guy Tanziano (or "Dancer"), and the Francezci pilot Luigi Manoza—had accompanied him. Staying at the airport hotel overnight, the four men had tidied up before meeting in Francesco's suite.

"This is how it is," he told the others. "Tomorrow, first light, Vincent flies up to Edinburgh and joins up with a long-time 'friend' of ours, Angus McGowan. McGowan has been in Scotland—oh, just about forever! He knows his way around. Knows the country, the people and their customs—*and* he knows where Radu is. Close enough, anyway. Radu's actual location, his den or lair— that won't be known until the last minute. Unless we get lucky. But somewhere in a little village in the Spey Valley there's a thrall, a moon-child: a man or maybe a woman with too much fucking wolf in him! And this thrall of the dog-Lord *does* know where Radu is, definitely.

"So that's where you and Angus McGowan are going, Vincent: looking for Radu's friend or friends in the Cairngorms. In the event you find them, Mc-Gowan knows what to do. You'll take your orders from him. Remember, McGowan has been one of ours, a lieutenant, for a very long time—longer than you've lived. He'll know you, and he'll pick you up at Edinburgh airport. So those are the arrangements. Any questions?"

The others around the table were at ease; Vincent Ragusa, less so. Waiting for him to speak up, if he intended to, Tanziano and Manoza looked at him, then at Francesco or "the Francezci," as they thought of him.

Wamphyri, Francesco was adaptable. In "high" Sicilian society he would be, and was, eminently acceptable. On a rainy day at Ascot in the Royal Enclosure, he would seem, and had seemed, perfectly at home. But when in Rome—or in London in the company of lieutenants and common thralls—he could just as easily do and say as they did. And think that way, too.

Ragusa was maybe five-nine, slender, and handsome with an Italian vampire's good looks. Of old Mafiosi stock, he dressed expensively but tastelessly. Shrugging, and managing to look a little disappointed, he said, "You know, I was hoping to join up with Jimmy and Frank? They're my boys. I mean, you and Anthony put me in charge of them, back at Le Manse Madonie."

"Your boys, yes . . ." Francesco nodded understandingly—or perhaps not—and after a moment's thought said: "The thing is, you're *all* our boys. And this isn't Le Manse Madonie. It's England, and later Scotland. And we didn't plan ahead for the fun of it, and we aren't *here* for the fun of it. You and McGowan up in Scotland: two strong lieutenants looking out for each other, eh? And a little later Luigi, too? Three of you? That gives you real strength. And myself, Dancer, Jimmy and Frank down here in London? That makes us a strong team, too. Then, finally, we all join up, and we're unbeatable . . . Now, have you got that?"

Ragusa nodded his understanding, but said, "It's like—I don't know—a lot of guys to waste just one lousy dog!"

Francesco sighed and narrowed his eyes. His jet-black nostrils gaped a little. But then he grinned—which would be fine except that his grin widened, and widened. Until finally: "Vincent," he husked. "Your grandfather was a Don; he is dead. Your father was a Don; he's dead, too. So who knows, maybe it's something that runs in the family? All that power—and they still wind up dead! And now you. More power coming your way than your ancestors would ever believe. More to live for, a lot more. And longer, *much* longer to live and enjoy it. Yet now and then, the way you talk . . ." He shook his now terrible head. A bad sign.

"Hey, Francesco, I'm sorry," Ragusa saw his error. "Like, no offence, right? I mean, I know this Radu is something big, but . . . "

Francesco stopped grinning, stuck his face forward across the small table where they sat, snarled, "Vincent, let me tell you something. This Radu could drive a hand through your navel, grab your liver and pick you up by it, and before you had time to start screaming *bite your fucking face off!*" His jaws gaped wide and his eyes were the colour of blood. "Yes, and for that matter—" he said, his voice dying to a hoarse whisper, "—so could I."

"I . . . I didn't mean . . . !" Ragusa's face, always pale, was now white as chalk.

"You don't *mean* fuck!" Francesco said. "So, that's it—it's dealt with." He slapped his hands together in a slicing, dismissive motion. "You'll do exactly as I tell you. But just to be absolutely sure: are there any *more* questions?"

"Nothing," Ragusa shook his head, held up his hands placatingly, palms facing outwards. "No questions, no—nothing—uh-uh!"

Francesco scowled, sat back, and as if Vincent Ragusa no longer existed said: "Luigi, you know what your job is. What's this problem with the, the . . . what are they called?"

"The CAA," Manoza answered. "Civil Aviation Authority. I have to register with them, that's all. They'll issue a temporary licence. Anyway, we have a contact on their exec. I can buy him if we're pushed for time. No problem."

"Sort it out," Francesco told him. "We're going to need a chopper and soon. And it has to be able to carry more than our machine back in Sicily.

"Now listen everyone, I want you to remember our 'reason' for being here. We're scouting a location for a movie. A climbing movie, probably in the Scottish Highlands. The British will stand to make lots of money from it—and the British authorities are worse than Americans when it comes to money. Likewise the Scots, and not only by reputation. So, if you want co-operation, try flashing some high-denomination dollars! It'll work here like anywhere else." Grinning a normal grin this time, he turned again to Manoza.

"When you've got a plane—and if I'm still in London—we'll fly up to Scotland. The rest of us, that is. But first I have a little business here. It's possible we have a real line on the intruder. We may finally find out who he is and why and how he hit our vault at Le Manse Madonie. And then I'll make sure he can't do it—can't do anything—ever again."

And lastly, to Guy Tanziano: "Dancer, you stay with me."

Tanziano—bullet-headed, six foot tall and sixteen stone, yet light as a dancer on his feet—a common thrall with an uncommon appetite and reputation for brutality, merely nodded.

The meeting was over . . .

Darcy Clarke took Harry to King's Cross in the greyest, ghostliest hours of morning when the ragged ones are out: discarded pages from yesterday's newsprint, drifting aloft on the draughts from canyon street-junctions. Those ragged ones, *and* the other sort: the stumbling kind, with their bottles of nameless stuff in paper bags. Both sorts were thinning out, however, and disappearing wherever they disappear to. London was coming awake, however slowly, and the station already noisy, thronging with people. The Necroscope caught the first train north.

He had seemed irritable, and Darcy himself wasn't entirely awake yet, or he might have simply dropped Harry at the station and returned to E-Branch HQ. Finally, on his way back, suddenly he realized what the problem had been—and felt like kicking himself. The Necroscope would have preferred to go home by his own route, maybe, but he hadn't been able to because Darcy was in the way. Oh, well, too late now.

But in fact it wasn't.

The train was barely fifteen minutes out of the station before Harry bought himself a paper cup of vile coffee in the buffet car. Then, swaying right on through the cramped buffet area into the first-class coach, he checked the passengers.

There were only a handful of them, reading newspapers and magazines, all facing forward and away from him. And no one in the buffet car behind him. Perfect.

Without thinking about it (because he knew that if he did he wouldn't), he conjured a Möbius door and stepped through it, and out again into his study in Edinburgh . . .

. . . Where he dropped his coffee from nerveless fingers! And before he was capable of *rational* thought, he thought: *This has to be my punishment for using the Continuum!*

His coffee had splashed the naked thigh of the black girl, the black and red girl, where he had stumbled over her. Zahanine! . . . One of B.J.'s girls! . . . Dead! . . . Here!

Still without thinking what he was doing, numb, he went to the kitchen and came back with paper towels, got down and wiped the cold coffee from her thigh—then slowly balled the towels, tossed them aside, and jerked spastically to his feet.

Coffee? Jesus God in heaven—*coffee?* A black bullet hole gaped in the girl's left breast; her skirt was bunched up round her waist, and her blouse was stuck to the throw rug with dried blood! Indeed, the rug was *drenched* in blood! Worse, Zahanine's head lay under Harry's desk where it had been kicked, three or four feet from her body. A bloody meat cleaver lay there, too.

And this charnel house was his study.

The Necroscope stumbled back from the girl's body—from everything—and fell into his chair; and sprang out of it at once as he heard a car pull up out front.

In the corridor, still not knowing what he was doing, but trying desperately hard to pull it all together, Harry went to the door and found it shut but unlocked. As he reached to engage the security catch, he heard footsteps that paused beyond the door, a double knock, and a breathless: "Harry?"

B.J.! He yanked open the door, fell back against the wall of the corridor. She stepped inside, took one look at him . . . and his expression must have said it all. Then:

"B.J.," he sighed and wrapped his arms around her. But as he hugged her, so she felt him tense up again, felt the relief, the tenderness, the welcome, turning to something else.

"Harry, what is it?" Her eyes were as wide and staring as his had been just a moment earlier. But now, as he pushed her away, held her at arm's length, and looked at her as if he were trying to look right through her, those oh-so-deep eyes of his had narrowed to become part of a frown, or even an accusation.

"What is it?" he repeated her. "Maybe you can tell me. And B.J., this time

I do mean *tell* me!" Catching her wrist, he half dragged her along the corridor, past the front room, stairwell, and kitchen, to his study—where she saw what it was.

"Zahanine!" It came out of her as a wail, a very small cry, a gasp. "Oh, Zahanine!" Then she was down on her knees, fluttering her hands inches over the body—wanting to touch it here, there, everywhere—and touching it nowhere.

"I got in fifteen minutes ago," the Necroscope lied. "This is what I found." He got down beside B.J., and at last was able to look at the body and see more than blood. "She was shot, and—I don't know, tortured, raped?—before she was beheaded. But why, B.J.? Why? And I *know* you know! Oh, I'm sure you're an innocent, wrong-headed but innocent, but you *do* know what's going on here. And you have to tell me."

"Harry, I—"

"This is why you wanted me out of the way, right? Because something like this could have happened to me?"

"Harry—"

"Yellow men," he stood up, pulled B.J. up with him. "What about the Asiatics? Tell me about them." (For if she could, it might also explain how those red-robed "monks" fitted into his future: some connection with the device they'd planted in Hyde Park? It seemed more than likely. But if they were also responsible for what had happened here, then they most *certainly* had a place in his future . . . or would have when he caught up with them!)

But why this aching sensation deep inside? This burgeoning feeling of something waiting to cut loose, like a word on the tip of his tongue that try as he might he couldn't remember. Was it simply the need for action, revenge, justice? . . . Or something else?

"Harry!" B.J. snapped, trying to pull him out of it. But:

"No!" he snapped back. "Tell me *now*, B.J.!" He was angry; angry and impatient; his lips were tight, showing a narrow bar of gritted teeth.

B.J. saw the warning signals, reading them like a threat in his eyes, his voice and attitude. Tilting her head a little—perhaps warningly in her own right, maybe even threateningly—*"Haaarry,"* she began to growl . . .

. . . And he gasped, reached to cover her mouth with a hand. But too late, as B.J. finished in something of panic: "Mah wee man!"

The moon . . . the wolf's head . . . the howling! And at last the calm, descending like a blanket over his troubled mind.

Harry blinked, and the anger, the questions, and the fear went out of him. For B.J. was here to put things back in order again. And she did, by telling him, "It's OK," Harry," and by hugging him to stop him reeling and maybe falling. "Sit down."

He blinked again, shook his head, waited for her to go on as he obeyed her and sat in his chair by the desk. "It will be . . . OK," she said again, trying to believe it herself. "But, oh, where've you been?" And before he could answer: "No, never mind that now. Just let me think." She had come within an inch of learning the truth, his truth at least, and by her own command had thrown it away.

B.J. looked at the body on the floor, its head beneath the desk at Harry's feet, and grimaced. And almost or wholly to herself: "They were making sure," she said.

He wondered, *Of what?* But inside knew of what. Except that couldn't be because B.J. and her girls were innocent. How could they be . . . what she was suggesting they were, when she herself wasn't? He reeled again, swaying in his chair, and B.J. saw her mistake.

"Making sure she was dead," she told him. "That she wasn't going to be able to talk to anyone about . . . about this."

Oh, really? Well, the Necroscope knew someone who Zahanine could talk to about it. But he couldn't or wouldn't—and certainly not while B.J. was here. And still he said nothing.

B.J. looked at him and it was as if she were here on her own, or at best with a zombie. But that was all her own doing, too. "You can talk," she said. "Talk normally. Tell me what I should do!"

A new twist. He should tell her what to do! But it was a genuine appeal, to Harry and not to what she'd made him. "Turn me loose," he said, with that certain something in his voice.

She looked at him, and he was no longer the zombie. He had that look: like the first time she had seen him, or in the Spey Valley when they had killed those Drakuls. The Mysterious One — Radu's Man-With-Two-Faces. Mysterious because he'd been trained to be that way, by these people he'd worked for, this E-Branch. A man with two faces, yes. The one face a mask, to obscure the true nature of the one underneath. The face of a killer in the name of justice.

And now Harry was asking to be turned loose in the name of Bonnie Jean, or more properly in the name of Radu. And why not? For she had told him it might come to this, hadn't she? But no, she would not, *dare* not put him in that kind of danger, not her Harry. And not when there were so many greater dangers ahead—for both of them.

"You don't know what you're saying," she told him.

(But he did! Oh, he did! *Only ask me!* he screamed, however silently. For he couldn't tell her what he knew *until* she asked him! And even then he could never tell her *how* he knew, because that would be to endanger his secrets.)

B.J. saw the sweat break out on Harry's face and actually heard his teeth grating. It was something she'd noticed before in times of stress, and she thought: *His mind is stuck in neutral where I've jammed the gears! He knows we must do something, but can only act on my command.*

"Zahanine," she said. "We can't let her be found here like this. The Drakuls did this. They could be on a phone somewhere speaking to the police even now. They could be trying to corner me—or you, or us—and startle us to flight, cut down on our options. Then, when we run, they'll be right on our heels knowing where we're running to. Do you understand?"

"To Radu," he nodded.

"We have to get rid of Zahanine!" B.J.'s hand flew to her mouth. "I mean, we have to get her out of here. But I can't—damn it—can't *think!* Zahanine thought it was you last night, but it was them. And I sent her here—she *came* here—of her own free will . . . " She was rambling; for one of only a very few times in her too-long life, B. J. knew she was actually panicking. "Harry, I don't know what to do with Zahanine! And her car is parked down the service road near the bridge! What can we do with her, and the car? Do you know of anywhere we can . . . *dump* them? I mean—do you know *any* fucking thing?" She grabbed hold of his collar, shook his head to and fro. "Do you have a single fucking suggestion?"

These were direct questions and he could answer them normally. And yes, he did know somewhere, and he did have some suggestions. "You get out of here," he said. "Right now, and leave this to me. But first tell me where to find you. Then, when I'm done, I'll join you."

Just like that, delivered like a right to the jaw so that she jerked back from him, her eyes wide, wild and disbelieving. There were depths here she still hadn't explored, still didn't understand. Harry got to his feet. "Where are you staying?"

She told him: the place where he and she had breakfasted, the first time they had gone climbing together, a roadside pub this side of Falkirk. "They have rooms. The girls and I, we're supposed to be doing a local survey, a census of people living in the area. But most of the time they've been out looking for you. You're a hard man to find, Harry Keogh. And a hard one to follow. A hard *act* to follow, too."

Yes he was, and he'd said he could handle this. Which was just as well because right now B.J. didn't feel she could handle much of anything. "Will you need help?" She could at least make the effort. For him. For them.

He shook his head. "You go. I'll follow as soon as I can."

"I'm going to turn you off now, Harry," she said. "But you will remember what you have to do—the things you do so well—and where to find me when they're done."

"B.J.," he said, and held her tightly while she whispered in his ear:
"Harry, mah wee man . . . "

It was like waking up from a bad dream to a worse one. But B.J. had gone and the Necroscope knew what he had to do.

He placed Zahanine's head and the cleaver on the throw rug with her body, rolled the rug up and tied its ends with string, finally rolled the whole bundle again in a sheet of clear plastic packaging from the new carpeting in his bedroom. There was a place he knew where Zahanine would never be found. Or if she was, it wouldn't much matter.

Then he brought a carpet from the front room to cover the dark spot on the floor, and made a final check of the house to see if there was anything he'd missed. But no, the place would seem absolutely normal to anyone who didn't know better.

But Harry did know better, and there was a certain smell that the draught from the broken patio windows was having difficulty dispersing. Or maybe it was only in his mind. In any case, he used a deodorant spray which seemed to help a little.

Then he called a handyman he knew in Bonnyrig and told him about the damage to the window. "I won't be here," he said. "So I'll leave the front door locked. You'll have to go to the back of the house on the river's side, and get in through the garden gate. When you're done, leave the patio doors secured." As simple as that. And then the difficult bit.

Harry went to Zahanine's car; the keys were in the ignition and he was able to drive it back to the house. Back indoors he put a penknife in his pocket, hoisted the rolled-up rug and its contents to his shoulder, (it seemed to weigh half a ton!) took it out to the car and placed it as gently as possible in the boot.

All done, he checked that no one was about, which wasn't likely for in this place no one ever was about. And the "highway"—which was in fact a country road, and the only vantage point—was on the other side of the river on the far side of the house.

Finally, satisfied that he was alone, unobserved, he got back in the car and drove it very slowly forward in first gear. And as he drove, he set familiar Möbius equations rolling down the screen of his metaphysical mind, to conjure a broad, squat door directly in front of the car—

—And drove through it!

Moments later he vacated the Continuum on the Roof of the World, the Tingri Plateau, Tibet . . . In a snowstorm!

The car stalled at once, sank through a frozen crust into a deep drift, gradually settled on compacting snow. Harry wound down his window, slid out backwards onto the crust of snow, and flailed through the drift and the blizzard to the boot. Already feeling the intense cold, he dragged the bundle out and cut it open, then propped Zahanine against the back of the car.

It was cold, so terribly cold, but the Necroscope knew she couldn't feel it. And he hadn't wanted to leave her locked away like that, in the stifling dark. The darkness of death, when at last she had accepted it, would be bad enough.

But just looking at her he knew it wasn't right. Zahanine wasn't complete. And shuddering—also from the cold—he took her head and placed it on the neck. In another minute it would be frozen there.

And he would be frozen here, if he didn't get moving!

But first—

—There was something he must do. And somehow the sheer desolation, the utter isolation of the place, helped him to do it. Not a conversation with Zahanine, no (Harry doubted if she would be ready for that a while, and he certainly wasn't), but he did know what would be on her mind. And here in this place—this icy, windswept, nowhere place—he dropped his mental barriers to let a different kind of cold come creeping in.

She would feel his warmth and know it for life. She would huddle to it, a frightened mouse. And in that moment the darkness would recede a little and Zahanine would remember. Cruel? Perhaps, but not as cruel as what had happened to her. For the Necroscope didn't know (or wouldn't accept) what she had been, only what she was now—a lonely, frightened dead thing, foresaken of life.

And he was right. Her whimper came to him and the feel of her wraith's arms around him, like the Little Match Girl crushing to the tiny bonfire of her own worthless matches to draw a last ounce of warmth from it. But he wasn't afraid, not of the girl. This was what he was, after all, and what he had used to do; and with the exception of his lost son he was the only one who could do it. He *was* life and she knew it, which caused her to remember her own life and how it had ended. And the Necroscope was witness to it:

The slant-eyed, lustful yellow face leering down on her, and the feel of his cold member in her. Then his eyes widening and the look on his face changing, as she reached up trembling hands to it; the feel of his skin caught up under her scraping fingernails, and torn away in ten red stripes!

And then this: the endless darkness that Harry had woken her up to. So that now Zahanine knew for sure. That beyond any shadow of a doubt, she was—

—But no! The Necroscope didn't want to hear it, what he had heard so often before. That sudden tortured shriek of denial. And he brought the barriers crashing down on his mind so fast that it unbalanced him, sent him staggering back from the half-buried car, stumbling on frozen legs.

But he had seen what he'd needed to see: confirmation of her murderer, and now all he wanted was to be out of here . . .

It was still only 8:50 A.M. in London, in the disused dockside warehouse with its loading bay that jutted out over the river, where Dr. James Anderson had spent the last terrified, agonized week of his life and slow death. But his torment was over now, and his vampire torturers were still baffled.

"You should have left it to me," the Francezci told his thralls, Jimmy Nicosia and Frank Potenza. "What, did you think you were still under orders from Vincent? Did you think you were the Mob? You're *mine*, mine and Anthony's. You're Francezcis! And this . . . isn't us." Shaking his head, he gloomed over the mess that had been a man. "It's simple butchery. And worse, it served no purpose. You got nothing out of him."

"Er, something. We got something, Francesco," Jimmy Nicosia tried hard not to grovel. "And we didn't have much choice. We couldn't be here twenty-four hours a day, not and keep an eye on these E-Branch types. And that in itself is a problem. You follow those guys—you look at some of them for too long—sooner or later they turn and look right back at you! These people are something else, Francesco. Not the kind you'd want to mess with."

"There isn't any *kind* I can't mess with!" the Francesci snarled. "But . . . I take your point. I've heard the same sort of thing before, and from people who are supposed to *know* what they're doing! That's why we picked this Anderson." He glanced again at the remains of a man. "He isn't—wasn't—part of their organization, just someone they used."

"But not any more," Frank Potenza whispered, smiling his wide-mouthed, emotionless yet oddly girlish smile. All of the Francezci's displeasure had been wasted on him.

Francesco scowled at him, but knew it was useless to do more than that. Despite (or maybe because of) Potenza's androgynous nature, he was muscle with very little of mind. He was simply weird; he knew how to whittle flesh but nothing of terror's true subtleties. Therefore pointless to punish him; you might as well kick a pet cat. He wouldn't understand but would simply lash out at you, claw you—and then you'd have to kill him. It was best to ignore him, which Francesco did by turning again to Nicosia.

"OK, I accept that this was an accident. You sought to slow Anderson down—to stop him trying to escape, and weaken his mental resistance—by weakening him physically. But you went too far. Still, as you say, you did get something. So go over it again, everything he told you."

"Four years ago," Nicosia began, "E-Branch called him in to hypnotize this Harry Keogh character—or the one they *call* Harry Keogh. He was to restrict Keogh's 'talents'—don't ask me what talents—so that when Keogh left the Branch he couldn't be put to use by any other organization. All Anderson knew was that Keogh was hot stuff. Darcy Clarke, Head of Branch, and all the other weird fucks thought very highly of him. But they didn't want him doing whatever it was he did for anyone else." He gave a shrug, fell silent.

"And that's it?" Francesco was baffled, or maybe not.

"Until a week ago. Then Clarke contacted Anderson again, told him to come on in, take a look at Keogh. It was then that we saw them all together for the first time—Anderson, Clarke, Trask, and Keogh. And when they split up we took our chance and got a hold of Anderson. It seemed the right thing to do . . . not just because we'd been told to do it but because plainly Anderson and Keogh knew each other, or why would they be in company with each other?"

The Francezci nodded. "You were told to pick him up—not to kill him! Anyway, what about Anderson taking a look at this Keogh? What was that all about? What was he looking for?"

Nicosia shrugged. "Clarke was worried that Anderson's hypnosis—what he'd done to Keogh the first time, four years ago—had gone too deep. He wanted Anderson's opinion, and also to know if it was reversible. Anderson told him it was, and that he would go back that night and fix it."

"Give him back these special talents?"

"Yeah, I suppose. But he didn't, because we had him."

"But still no mention of what these skills were?"

"Francesco, we tried!" Nicosia threw up his hands. "Hell, you can *see* how we tried! But Anderson didn't know. I swear it. He'd never known in the first place!"

And Francesco growled, "That's the bit that kills it. He didn't fucking know! Well maybe he *did* know, but it was so big he would go through all of this to hide it!" And again he glanced at the debris of a man. But in fact he suspected that Nicosia was right. No man would be capable of suffering a fraction of this without talking his head off . . . if he had anything to talk about. As for Kyle's or Keogh's talents: maybe Francesco already knew what they'd been and what they still might be.

The man had to be some kind of living ghost; he came and went and left no tracks. Steel doors, labyrinthine tunnel systems, and combination locks couldn't stop him, and his obvious contempt for all such was . . . destructive. And expensive. Naturally E-Branch would want him intact, especially if they were going to try that stuff again. Or if they knew about Radu and planned to use him against the dog-Lord . . .

"Francesco, what more can I tell you?" Nicosia was down-cast. "That's it, everything . . . " He looked this way and that as if wishing there were more to say but knowing that the Francezci wouldn't buy any pretty packaging. He was only interested in facts. And Francesco thought: *Yes, he'd make a good, loyal lieutenant.* But Frank Potenza spoiled the moment by grinning in a gauntly girlish, what-the-hell fashion and whispering:

"Anyways, it wasn't all waste."

And Francesco knew what he meant: that not too much blood had been spilled here. Not *spilled,* anyway.

But Potenza . . . was an irritation, a big itch. And sooner or later Francesco knew he would have to scratch. But not while there was a job to be done. Later, when all of this was over—time enough then to take care of that.

As for Potenza's immediate superior in the Francezci chain of command, Vincent Ragusa . . . it might also be time to rethink *his* position in the grand scheme of things. Jimmy Nicosia would make a better lieutenant for sure. And without complaint, without trying to be an "original thinker."

But for now:

The Francezci relaxed, smiled and said, "Very well, let it go. Later I have to call Anthony, tell him what's gone down and find out what's next. He's our contact with the Old Man, who we hope will give us his best co-operation."

The pair of thralls knew who he was referring to: Angelo Francezci, in his pit at Le Manse Madonie. They blanched a little—even Potenza—and instinctively backed off a pace. But Francesco merely smiled, changed the subject and said:

"I don't think we'll be in London too long. Luigi is sorting out a helicopter, Vincent is on his way to Edinburgh, and Dancer's at the Dorchester getting rooms. You two . . . do nothing; just wait for me to get in touch with you."

But as he made to leave he glanced back at them and said, "Oh, yes. And before you get out of here make sure that *that,*" he looked for the last time on Anderson's remains, "goes into the river."

After he had left they did just that—opened a trapdoor in the floor and disposed of the evidence. There were several splashes in the morning mist on the Thames; some loud, others faint. The last thing to go was an arm blanched to alabaster. Its hand had a thumb and index finger, and three stumps.

The other arm, already bobbing its way to the sea—nibbled on by small fishes and fresh-water shrimp—had no fingers at all . . .

IV

ANTHONY AND ANGELO: AFRAID.
RADU: AWAKE.
BONNIE JEAN: INNOCENT?

TWO HOURS EARLIER, AND MORE THAN A THOUSAND MILES AWAY—
It was the first hour of a dim grey dawn under a lowering ceiling of cloud.
Slowly churning, the sky released banks of spume-like moisture, not quite
rain, to sprawl on the high plateau, pile up against the outer walls of Le Manse
Madonie, and roll over them in queasy waves into the courtyard . . .

Anthony Francezci had been about his business most of the night; with
Francesco out of the way—indeed, from the moment Anthony's brother had
left Sicily for England—their grotesque father, Angelo, had been more volu-
ble, more forthcoming. He had more "in common" with Anthony and found
him easier to talk to than Francesco, who had always been something of a
thorn in his side. As to what they had spent time in the early hours of the morning talking about . . . *just* such subjects, and one especially, had served to
prompt the nightmares which would later plague Anthony's dreams.

"Called" by his loathsome father within an hour or so of Francesco's departure,
Anthony had been unable to attend him immediately. But as evening turned
to night he had sensed an increase in the mental babble, the telepathic confusion, emanating from below, and in the small hours of the morning he had
visited the pit. Then, from an awkward beginning, their "talk" had finally
evolved into an hour or so of conversation, broken only by the occasional in-
terruptions of Angelo's multi-minds . . .

After that:

Not long before dawn, Anthony had gone to a female thrall for sex, blood—
comfort?—then to his own bed intending to sleep until late evening when he was
due a call from Francesco. With a little luck his brother would have good or at
least promising news from London; and certainly Anthony had news for him:

Namely, the substance of his "conversation" with the Thing in the pit. Or some of it . . .

Now, with the dawn, he nightmared, by no means an uncommon thing among vampires. For the dawn is not their time; indeed it is the one time when the otherwise mainly *in*vulnerable are *most* vulnerable—when the worst fears in the subconscious minds of such monsters take on the shapes of reality, and their memories conjure once more the terrors of *their* youths.

"Tony" Francezci was no exception, though in his case memories out of time were not especially horrific . . . not to him. He was what he was by birth, and as such had developed free of any lingering impressions of Wamphyri conversion. Therefore he didn't dream any common thrall's or lieutenant's nightmares of what he had been and what he was now, but of what he *might yet become!* Which was a horror without peer—unless it lay in the hideous shape and substance of his father Angelo, the devolved and ever-devolving Thing in the pit under Le Manse Madonie.

First, before the actual horror, he relived his conversation with the Old Ferenczy more or less as it had taken place; except he was vaguely aware that somewhere behind the "spoken" words something darker was building, as in the atmosphere of a well-lit room that gradually glooms over with the slow but irresistible approach of a storm:

"Father," he whispered into the mouth of the echoing pit. "Francesco has gone to England. He has men with him; they will seek out Radu's thralls and follow them to the dog-Lord in the hour of his resurgence. And we have heeded your words: already our advance party is . . . *interrogating* a man believed to be in league with the one who raided our vault, this 'Harry' of whom you spoke. Also, we'll soon have men in Scotland who will seek out Radu's thralls there, discover their weaknesses, and eventually destroy them. But now we need your help, too. For only you can see afar and know what's in the minds of men . . ." Anthony paused, and in a while continued:

"And father, I know that you have been spending more and more time looking outwards, for I have felt it. Even Francesco has felt it, and he is . . . well, far less sensitive than I am. So, anything you have learned could be of great benefit . . . "

The mouth of the pit was open; its electrified grille was switched off and Anthony had raised one flap of the cover. The spotlights in the cavern walls blazed down, lighting the pit's surroundings in overlapping circles of stark white light. Outside that central glare was blackness, and Anthony's shadow an elongated inkblot poured on the cold stone floor behind him.

The reason the power was off and the shaft half-open was simple: it was a precaution the Francezci brothers used to insure against inadvertent self-electrocution. The old well was after all a deep one, and Angelo no longer capable of attempting an escape. His disorder, the rampant metamorphism that had altered him to a protoplasmic Thing, was such that he no longer had any control over his bulk. It controlled itself, albeit mindlessly, and therefore was mainly without menace. The current procedures existed from a time when Angelo had retained a small measure of control; that they were still in use . . . was simply another precaution. It was never a good idea to second-guess the Old Ferenczy.

Anthony leaned on the low stone wall to look down into the silent, sentient throat of hell. Within the shaft, light penetrated maybe nine or ten feet; below that the darkness increased commensurate with the depth, until it seemed absolute. And this was a darkness that seethed . . .

But while Anthony could *feel* Angelo's hidden intelligence (or madness), and while he knew that he had his father's attention, still the telepathic aether carried no message but merely conveyed an awareness of Angelo's vast mental presence; this in addition to that almost physical foreboding on the rim of Anthony's subconscious perceptions, warning him that *something* was coming.

Then, losing patience, unwilling to remain in this place any longer conversing with himself (and even more unwilling to meet the unknown *something* when it chose to arrive) he tried a threat, however subtle:

"Father, always remember: it is still true that whatever endangers me endangers you. Should the Francezcis come to harm and Le Manse Madonie fall, then we all fall with it. Including the Old Ferenczy. For who would suffer such as you to live except myself and my brother?" Perhaps during the actual conversation he had not been so forthright, but these were the words he would have *liked* to use, and so he used them in his dream.

The pit seemed to cling to one word, and threw it back at him as an echo: *Suffer, suffer, suffer* . . .

But it was in fact Anthony's father, goaded into "speech" at last. And:

Suffer? Angelo's telepathic voice—but a definite voice now, gurgling in Anthony's head—took over where the echo had left off. *And you know all about suffering, do you? And you can tell me something about suffering, eh?* Hah! *The worst thing you have ever suffered was being born. But what* I *have suffered . . . is worse than death!*

Argumentative. But it was better than nothing. And Anthony was skilled at word-games in his own right. If he could involve his father—inveigle or even challenge him—then with luck he might also be able to lead him in a more cooperative direction. Wherefore: "What?" he said. "But if your fate is so disenchanting—if what you are suffering really is worse than death, the true death—am I to understand you would *prefer* death? If so, then speak up! For as you are probably aware your other son, my brother Francesco, has been counselling just such a solution to your problem for many a long year!" Again the words were harder than those he had actually used. But in any case:

Suddenly the psychic aether was ripped apart in a demented telepathic storm!

DO IT!—Like a great roar of joy!—subsiding at once to a hoarse, crazed gurgle of anticipation: *Do it! Kill the Ferenczy! Kill the old bastard! Kill all of us!*

Kill us, yesss!—A woman's voice this time, and one that Anthony recognized immediately. It was Julietta Sclafani, vampirized by Francesco before the brothers had sent her to hell, bubbling now with an evil that could never know release except in the death of the Thing in the pit. *Kill Angelo. And kill us with him—kill all of us, now—and put an end to our hell!*

And: *Oh, ho-ho-ho! Oh, ha-ha-haaarrr!* A mad voice, almost entirely insane—

yet knowing and willing enough to shriek at the end of its burst of crazed laughter, *Kill, kill, kill him! Kill Angelo Ferenczy!*

And a host of others—all of the brothers' and Angelo's victims, who had gone to feed him in his pit—all joining in the blast from the gross mad brain that was the nucleus of the mutant Thing. All of these identities imprinted upon or absorbed within his mind, much as his protoplasm had absorbed their flesh. And just exactly like that metamorphic flesh, they were no longer under Angelo's control. Anthony knew it at once: his father had lost control of the imprisoned multi-minds!

"But how . . . ?" he wanted to know as the babble subsided to a background rumble.

Because of "this Harry," as you see fit to call him, the Thing in the pit answered at once. *This Englishman, this Harry whose second name is Keogh, and whose dead friends—and they are legion!—call "the Necroscope." Do you know what a Necroscope is, Anthony, my dear Anthony?*

Anthony was not an ignorant man; no one with the weight of years, the guile of the Wamphyri could be entirely ignorant. "A . . . a viewer on the dead?" he answered, wonderingly.

Indeed! his father answered. *And more, a speaker with the dead! But didn't I say so right from the beginning? The man who broke into your treasure vault, your intruder, this Harry is—*

—NO! An angry voice shouted him down. *DON'T LET HIM TALK! THROUGH HIS VAMPIRE SONS, HE PUTS HARRY IN DANGER!* And the rest of them joined in—a tidal wave of mental emanations from the pit.

But Angelo, whose psychic maelstrom had sucked them in in the first place, could not be shouted down. Aiming his sending directly into Anthony's reeling mind, he said: *Me, they feared, which was my only hold on them. They didn't know what I could—what I might—do to them, or what I was capable of doing. They feared me because they were my prisoners, trapped in me as I am trapped in this pit, and no hope of rescue. But him, this Harry, they love. Because he would set them free . . . by destroying me! And Anthony, ah, my Anthony, despite everything you've learned and think you know about the passions of the world, human love is stronger far than fear.*

"Father," Anthony said then, trying to aim his thoughts as Angelo had done, to break through the telepathic tumult thrown up against him, "this Harry is as good as dead. If he's really the man who broke into our vault, then he has *always* been dead, and it was just a matter of time. But tomorrow I'm speaking to Francesco, and we shall make Keogh's death a priority. You say he's a Necroscope—what, *the* Necroscope?—and talks to dead people? Well, take it from me: soon he'll be in the best possible place to practice his skills!"

You don't understand, do you? his father said then. *Do you even believe me? Doubtful. But powers such as this one possesses . . . you have no idea what you're up against! Until he came along, Radu Lykan was the greatest possible threat, the greatest threat imaginable. But this man . . .*

Anthony could picture him shaking his head, as if in disbelief.

"But doesn't that say it all, father?" he asked. "I mean, haven't *you* said it all? 'This man,' you said. Well that's all he is, a man. While we are Wamphyri!"

He talks to dead people . . . talks to dead people . . . dead people! Angelo started to babble—to echo himself—and immediately reined back. It was the multi-minds interfering with his thought processes. *He talks to people in their graves,* he began again. *And all the world's knowledge is down there with them!*

"But even if what you say were possible," Anthony argued, in an attempt to steer his father in a useful direction, "what good is dead knowledge? How may anyone harness such knowledge, to make it work for him?"

Angelo gave a snort of derision, frustration. *Huh! And I had thought only one of my sons was a fool!* Then, before Anthony could protest or make any further comment, *Now listen:*

The dead converse, in their graves, with each other. The first time I took a victim, absorbed into myself, I suspected it was so. Don't you understand? The mind went on, in me! And what of those buried in the earth, or gone up into the air in smoke? It is the same: their thoughts—spirits if you will—live on. And now, through the Necroscope Harry Keogh, they've learned to converse in their perpetual darkness. Love him? Of course they love him, and they'll do anything for him!

Even against his better judgement, Anthony was beginning to believe. His father was making more "sense" than he'd ever known him to make; his words and ideas, however wild, grotesque, seemed based in some sort of logic. Turning the concept over in his mind, he said, "But . . . but a Necroscope?"

THE Necroscope! his father snapped, startling him. *There is only one. Which is why they can't let him come to harm!*

"They?"

The dead, fool! The teeming dead! The Great Majority!

At which Anthony believed he had him. And: "Only one Necroscope, who talks to the dead, eh?" He smiled into the mouth of the pit, but mirthlessly. "And all of this a waste of time, eh, father? Of my valuable time. For if it was true, how would *you* know? How *do* you know, father? Or are you perhaps the second Necroscope? Is that it? That you, too, talk to the dead?"

In the long silence that followed, the dark something at the back of Anthony's mind crept closer, and the light seemed to dim a little in the cavern of the pit. But then:

No, his father told him. *I can't talk to the dead. But I can hear some of them!* My *dead, talking through me! They converse with each other, Anthony, my faithful—or faithless—Anthony. And, since the Necroscope Harry Keogh was here, they also converse with* others *outside of me! As to what they say: I hear the outgoing because it goes out from me, from all the minds that are my mind. But the incoming is secret, and known only to my multi-minds. Except they are no longer mine! But I do know that they accept Harry Keogh's talents. And also that you, and your brother—that we, the Ferenczys—are not safe from him, not even here. How can you doubt it? Didn't he come here, commit an impossible crime, and leave without leaving a trace?*

"Like a ghost, yes," Anthony whispered, thinking back on it. "But he did leave a trace; we have him on film."

He talks to them, (his father ignored him). *And all the world's mysteries lie buried in the earth, or aimlessly drifting in the sky. Who can say what he has learned from the dead? "Like a ghost," you say—but you don't know the half of it. This man moves through solid rock, through steel doors—and through doors of his own making!*

"What?"

Do you believe in telepathy, Anthony, my dear sweet Tony? (It was as if he had changed the subject entirely.)

"Telepathy? Of course. Among the Old Wamphyri, it was the prized skill of the thought-thief. So you've always instructed me, and your own mentalism proves it. As for Francesco and myself: we were born into this world, where such skills were not required."

I told you no lie, my Tony. Many of the Old Wamphyri were gifted in strange arts, but not all of them. I too was born in this world—it took me seven hundred years to develop my art! As for yourself and your brother . . . well, who can say? Perhaps it skipped a generation entirely. Or maybe there's still time. I would like to think so. But on the other hand, time has been known to bring about changes which are far less desirable. And sometimes the bloodlines hold true, passing things down to the next in line that . . . that should never be passed down to anyone.

With which another layer of gloom settled like a shroud on Anthony's dream. In an attempt to dispel it—or perhaps delay whatever it was he sensed coming—he made an effort to return to the previous subject:

"What point are you trying to make, father? Why this sudden leap from Harry Keogh to telepathy?"

The Old One seemed to grasp upon that. *A sudden leap? Ah, good!* So that Anthony feared it might signal the start of some new word-game. But no, for his father quickly went on: *Telepathy, then. It exists, we are agreed. But in that case, what of "sudden leaps?" What of . . . teleportation?*

Anthony shook his head. "No, I can't accept that. Even the Old Wamphyri had nothing of that order. At best it is theoretical. Telepaths, shape-changers—we know they exist. Evidence is immediately to hand. But teleports . . . ?"

And after a long moment: *Theoretical?* said his father, very quietly. *Oh, really? Well, I would have thought so, too, upon a time. But what about Harry Keogh?* And even the multi-minds were hushed, expectantly silent now.

Anthony, too, caught his breath. It was ridiculous—but it would explain the otherwise inexplicable: Keogh's entry into Le Manse Madonie, his escape, and the fact that but for an automatic camera, no one would ever have sighted him. So that he felt prompted to ask, "You learned this thing from the multi-minds?"

When they made inquiry about this Harry Keogh outside, in the dead void, yes.

"Even if it were true," Anthony said then, "what of it? I mean, he's still a man. Can he avoid high-velocity bullets? Is he impervious to steel, poison, a garrotte? Right now, father, Francesco is in England. And he *will* kill our Mr. Keogh, trust me."

And if he fails? And if Keogh strikes back? Tony, you said you would soon be speaking to Francesco. Good! Then tell him to leave Harry Keogh well alone.

"But Keogh has already robbed us once. And if what you say is true—why, he can do it again. Any time he likes!"

Which is why you must not try to kill him. Annoy, irritate him by all means, so that when this thing with Radu is over, if it is over, he might want to come here and seek you out, but do not try to kill him. Not yet.

"And if or when he does decide to return? Surely we should get rid of him now, so that he *can't* return, ever?"

But: *Where oh where has it gone?* Angelo gave a mock groan, his sarcasm dripping like acid. *The much-vaunted "guile" of the Wamphyri? Hah!* Then, with a snarl: *Set a trap for him, fool!*

"A trap? But how? Where?"

Where did he hit you the last time?

"The treasure vault!"

Exactly. He bombed your treasure vault. But this time you bomb him! Trip-wires, pressure points, electric eyes. Only let him materialize there—

"—And he dematerializes there, forever!"

Of course. But pursue him? Never! Rather than that, Francesco would be well advised to avoid him, and all who run with him.

"And if he 'runs' with Radu and the pack, what then?"

Then . . . it would seem unavoidable. Indeed, then you must *kill him! For if they are in league . . . together they would be unbeatable! Except it is hard to believe that Radu Lykan would be in league with anyone. Which is why I suggest you deal with the dog-Lord first, then Keogh, both in the manner prescribed.*

"But what of the treasure, our money, our power base? For such a plan to work, we'd first have to—"

—Move it, yes. Or what remains of it would be destroyed along with Keogh.

"Move it? But where to?"

Where would it be safest?

"Here," said Anthony, nodding. "Right here, in this cave. Where you can watch over it, and where there'll be less temptation for Francesco . . ."

. . . To destroy me, too? Indeed, said Angelo. *And temptation is sometimes contagious, eh? So be it.* Anthony could sense his awful, knowing smile . . .

And again, before he could deny the other's unspoken accusation: *So then, speak to Francesco, and tell him what I have advised. For the present that seems as much as you can do.* And in the next moment, changing the subject again:

Now then, tell me about . . . tell me about your dreams, my Tony, my little Anthony.

This *was* a dream, as Anthony was vaguely aware; albeit a "repeat performance" of a conversation that had actually taken place some hours earlier. But now, feeling that ominous something creeping closer still—beginning to understand or remember what it was—he shivered as he answered: "My dreams? What of my dreams?"

But his father only tut-tutted, and said: *Ah, Anthony, my dear, sweet boy! But I have listened to them. To yours, and to your brother's dreams. For years I have listened, even decades. Not merely to eavesdrop—though that was part of it—but because that was how . . . how it started in me. In dreams, yes . . .*

And now the something, no longer unknown—but definitely unspeakable—reared up large as monstrous life to come knocking on the doors of reality!

Thump! Thump! Thump! A timid, triple knock at first. But Anthony was ignoring it, gazing into the mouth of the pit even as he had gazed in real life. And he was asking the same question, too: "Father, that was how what started in you?"

I had thought . . . perhaps Francesco? his father answered, as if he mused to himself. *No, no, let's be honest: I had even hoped it would be your brother. But alas, I hoped in vain. For I have seen it in* your *dreams, my Tony, my poor dear boy. Even as it was in mine, so it is in yours.*

His dreams: those terrible dreams that he had hidden from everyone, even himself. The nightmare that he was—or that he was like, or that he *would be* like—the thing in the pit! But now Anthony knew, and horror reared up in the heart of him, in his mind, in his flesh and bones.

And creeping up from the pit—climbing the walls in sickening, seething rags, tendrils and groping limbs, staring up at him even as he stared bulge-eyed down upon it—Anthony saw his own mad future!

Then the *clang* of metal on stone as he lowered the grille, and the hum and crackle of electricity as he turned on the current, and his hammering heart and echoing, flying footsteps as he vacated that place, to renew himself with his female thrall.

But even blood and the comforts of the flesh are sometimes not enough . . .

Now it was dawn and another female thrall, but a very different one, made her patrol through Le Manse Madonie. It was the crone Katerin, who had been with the Francezcis since she was a girl, for at least seventy of her eighty-five years. Not a vampire as such—for she had never developed—Katerin was simply "of the blood" and no longer aspired. But despite that she was the lowest of the low in the Francezci household, she was trusted above all others. And because of her years of experience there was no secret however small to which Katerin wasn't privy.

But as she reached Anthony's door—

—*What was that?*

Some sort of worm-thing? A snake or similar injurious creature? For a moment it lay still on the marble floor of the high landing, and she saw that it seemed to be emerging from beneath her Master's door, from his room . . . Or entering it?

She stepped closer and the vibration of her footfall galvanized the thing. It wriggled, whipped to and fro; and she saw throbbing, purple veins in the vibrating length of its leprous flesh. Then, lightning-fast, it drew itself out of sight under Anthony's door. And because she feared for him—and for herself, if she did nothing—she knocked:

Thump! Thump! Thump! Timidly at first: the knock that Anthony had ignored in his dream. But when there was no answer she knocked again, louder, then turned the doorknob and went in.

For all that this side of the manse faced north-west away from the sun, the drapes at Anthony's windows were heavy, thick with folds. The entire room was shadowed, gloomy, where barely a chink of daylight found its way in. Katerin's eyes were feral, however; they saw in the dark as well as any cat's eyes. And what they saw . . .

Anthony's bed was of massive oak, an antique four-poster, with gauzy curtains tied back to the uprights on the side facing Katerin. He lay on his back, naked under the single black sheet that reached to his rib-cage and was his only covering. As yet he was still asleep, barely. Close to waking, he tossed and turned—and moaned to himself. Cold sweat gleamed on Anthony's forehead and limbs, forming sprays of fine grey pearls as he jerked his head this way and that.

Katerin started at some sudden movement on the floor by the bed, started again when the sheet over Anthony's agitated figure billowed with a weird, flowing motion. Her yellow eyes swivelled to and fro, unable or unwilling to accept what they were witnessing. For the snake-thing . . . wasn't a snake!

The harridan knew what the brothers kept in the pit deep under Le Manse Madonie. She knew that it was their father. And she knew that *this* was something like their father—except he himself was *completely* out of control and vaster far. And:

"Like father, like son!" Katerin breathed, stepping backwards, very quietly, towards the door. But not quietly enough.

There were a good many—extrusions? As they whipped and writhed, drew back under the black sheet and returned to their source and origin, Anthony came awake and saw, and perhaps *felt* the last of them: that rope of glistening matter, a chameleon's tongue of protoplasm, vanishing under his weirdly mobile covering. And yanking the sheet aside, eyes bugging, he saw it soak into him!

He wanted to scream but couldn't; there was no moisture in his throat. He had dreamed this before, all too frequently, and always worse than the dream before, but this was the first time that he'd actually seen it. Now he knew it for a fact. Except—

—He wasn't the only one who knew it. Anthony's panic passed, was replaced by his "natural" cold, calculating calm. The chilling logic of the Wamphyri.

Katerin was standing there, a bundle of dry sticks that he might oh-so-easily snap. And: "The door," he husked, sitting up in his bed. "Close the door, and come here."

She obeyed—what else could she do?—and stood beside his bed, shivering. Anthony nodded, and his eyes were flame as he said, "You saw?"

"A . . . a mouse!" the crone gasped, gagged, croaked. "Something very small, I think, that crept under your door . . ."

But he shook his head and smiled a ghastly smile. "No, you saw more than that—didn't you?"

"Yes, Master, yes . . ."

He sighed and reached out a hand on a long, an incredibly long arm, and grasped her throat even as she made to step back from him. "Katerin, I have fond memories of you. When you were a girl of fifteen I fucked you; we both did, my brother and I. Perhaps fortunately, you were barren. Your flesh had little of quality, and nothing seeded itself. Nothing at all. Since when you've known our protection, the safety of these strong walls, the sanctuary of Le Manse Madonie. It would be . . . oh, a *great* shame, if you were to turn traitor now . . ." His fingers tightened on her scrawny neck, and old Katerin knew their terrible strength.

"I would never betray you, Master," she wheezed.

His eyes were blood; his lips curled back from teeth that were long and salivating; his tongue was forked and scarlet in a red-ribbed throat. And as he drew her closer still: "You are less than refuse," he said. "And if I should hear so much as a whisper, then I would throw you like refuse—or you would be seen to fall, like refuse—from the great cliff. Do you understand?"

But Katerin could only gag and hang on to his wrist, and stick out her wriggling tongue at him.

Finally he released her, thrust her away, sent her stumbling across the marble floor. "Now go, and never come into my room again!" Clutching at her throat, she went.

Then, knowing there would be no more sleep for him this morning, shuddering, and trembling in every limb, Anthony got dressed. But as he finished he paused, lifted his head, listened intently as a voice came to him from far below:

I fought it for two hundred years, my son, my dear sweet Tony, before it won and you put me down here. But with help—with my help, my knowledge—why, your fight might last even longer. And as long as I remain safe, so do you. But ah! . . . Only see how our roles are reversed, eh, my dear, dear boy?

And then there was only silence . . .

Three days later:

In his lair in the high Cairngorms, the dog-Lord Radu was awake and aware as never before in six hundred long years. By now, Bonnie Jean Mirlu had contacted the surviving sons of the sons of his thralls throughout the land, calling them to Scotland to prepare for his coming, and to protect him in the hour of his resurgence. Indeed, he knew that it was so; at the full of the moon he had put out probes of his own to seek them out and reinforce B.J.'s instructions.

And moon-children that they were, they had answered him. Radu had sensed their response: the howling going up over the moors—over the Dartmoor tors, and in Bodmin—and the whimpering of Auld John in Inverdruie. But only three? Only three descendants of his Children of the Moon? Well, four if he included B.J. herself, and a handful more with her small pack.

But as for her girls: they were more dedicated to Bonnie Jean herself than to Radu. Which was only understandable, the dog-Lord supposed, for B.J. was Wamphyri in her own right—

—And becoming more so with every full moon.

Right now, the lunar orb was in the centre of its cycle, a crescent, but in a fortnight it would be full again. Radu's original schedule had been set to ensure Harry Keogh's audience with him at the full of the moon in May. And the dog-Lord's rebirth had been scheduled for the moon after that. Auld John, however—whom Radu had "taken into his confidence"—believed that he had brought these dates forward by two full months . . . and so he had, upon a time. But now the Old Wolf in his resin tomb had had second thoughts.

Auld John was a fool for his "wee mistress"; he had been in thrall to her for long and long, perhaps even too long. Who could say what she might or might not have winkled out of him? Which was one of the reasons why Radu had yet again rearranged his rebirth—to the end of February, just a few weeks away!

Another reason was that he could no longer wait to come face to face with B.J.'s mysterious Mr. Keogh, who might well prove to be Radu's Man-With-Two-Faces, so frequently glimpsed in prescient dreams; the one who would be there to greet, and perhaps even "succour" him, in his most needful hour.

Now, in just two weeks' time, the dog-Lord would see this Harry for himself, in the flesh, and know the truth of it. And then, one way or the other he would use him—and use him up! But however it went, in whichever eventuality, the meeting was now set to coincide with Radu's rising.

The final and perhaps most important reason for advancing the date of his return lay in Radu's constant state of nervous apprehension: his anxiety, the awareness of his own vulnerability while he lay here "in state." The knowledge that should his enemies find him here like this, they could do with him as they wished. And as to *what* they would do: the dog-Lord had no delusions about that.

For they were searching for him even now; and *by* now, but for B.J.'s vigilance, her diligence, they might even have found him. This wouldn't save her, however, for Radu knew why she was so "diligent": because she could not hope to stand against them on her own. What, the filthy Drakuls, and the loathsome Ferenczys? And both camps determined to destroy him and his? Not only were they vampire Lords, in command of unknown numbers of lieutenants and thralls, but they *were* Wamphyri, experienced in the arts and wiles of the Great Vampire! By comparison, Bonnie Jean was indeed innocent. Even as innocent as she'd fooled her Harry into believing.

And so she must have Radu up; to be her protection, and to learn what she could from him . . . before turning on him in earnest in the right place and at the right time. The dog-Lord *knew* this was her plan, as indeed it would be his, if he were in her place.

Ah, the Wamphyri! No two alike—not even twin brothers—yet in certain ways alike as peas in a pod.

Thus, being Wamphyri and a beguiler, B.J. had made a great fool of her thrall and lover Harry Keogh—because he, too, was a part of her plan. But Radu had plans of his own.

He was no female's fool like this Harry, to fall under the treacherous spell of any scheming witch or bitch however clever or buxom. No, he wasn't this mysterious Harry Keogh, not in any shape or form . . .

. . . Well, not yet anyway.

It was midday and the moon was a pale sickle hanging low in the wintry grey sky. The dog-Lord Radu couldn't see it, but he felt it there—its influence on him—tugging at the fluids of his brain. It wasn't strong, indeed it was at its weakest, much as he was at his; for this was ever an inauspicious time for him, midway between his mistress moon's cycle. But with just a fortnight of waiting left (a mere fourteen days!) there were still things he must do, precautions to take. He couldn't allow himself simply to lie here like this in a gluey semi-torpor, with the resin weighing on him like lead and only his mind free.

But since it was so . . . very well, he would use his mind.

Radu knew the danger in using his mentalism, his telepathy. But he had been taking risks with it for six hundred years now, every time he'd reached out to some thrall or other to call him or her to his side when he needed sustenance. Recently, however—since his first true awakening—he'd used it that much more frequently: to call his few remaining thralls, or to see if the psychic aether was clear, and if not, to discover who else was probing it. And therefore the danger was that much greater.

For if anyone had sensed his sendings, or intercepted them, they too would know that his time was imminent. And if a really clever mentalist were in the vicinity (for example, some gifted vampire Lord) then Radu might easily reveal his location. These were the risks he took.

But vampires are vampires, children of the night, and this was midday. It wasn't the dog-Lord's time, no, but neither was it theirs. And so it was worth the risk.

He scanned far, wide and faint, fanning his probe over the far horizon, the curve of the world remembered from a time six hundred years in the past; but never lingering too long in any one spot. All those years ago, the world had been a vast place in which a man might easily lose himself. Now . . . it seemed so much smaller. But while the world had grown smaller—at least to the people in it— and while the dog-Lord's body must have lost something of its substance through the long, lonely centuries, still his mentalism was sharp as ever, perhaps even enhanced by his physical isolation. What Radu had denied himself of human sensation, he'd got back in psychic sensitivity, and in his telepathy.

And from due south, over a distance of more than six hundred miles—at the other end of the land mass, the moor districts of Devon and Cornwall—he sensed a faint response from his present-day thralls. Just two of them, yes. Moon-children, like Auld John, their long-awaited destiny was now clear.

. . . *Pausing in whatever they were doing, in their everyday pursuits as men, they lifted their heads, looked north, blinked suddenly feral eyes and held their breath. They were preparing to join him, yes.*

And: *Two weeks,* (he used the probe as a carrier). *Be sure to come to me then* . . . And despite that there were no alien emanations—no covert or inimical thoughts that he could detect in the psychic aether—still, without waiting for confirmation, Radu moved on . . .

. . . To Bonnie Jean and the pack. They were much closer and the risk that much greater. But even if some vampire mentalist were searching for Radu at this very moment, and even if there were more than one and they had worked out a system of triangulation, still they'd have to find a way to conquer the mountain heights, these Cairngorms, to get to him. And anyway, Radu *had* to know what was happening, if only to deaden the feelings of desertion and isolation building up in him.

Bonnie Jean's mind, her mental scent, was so familiar to the dog-Lord that he could find and converse with her—or at least make himself and his wishes known to her—anywhere in the world. She was no telepath, B.J., or at best a mere beginner, so that while she couldn't read Radu's mind without that he sent directly into hers, he could be *into* hers in a moment, even when she tried to keep him out. And she'd certainly done enough of *that* since discovering her Harry!

Right now, at this very moment, Radu's Man-With-Two-Faces was with her. Good! Also, at this moment . . . the dog-Lord Radu was the last thing on B.J.'s mind. *Not* good! Ah, but what they were doing—that was *very* much on her mind, leaving room for little else! Sex was on her mind, and the rest of her thoughts were clouded by a swirl of confused and contradictory emotions.

The gigantic emotions of the Wamphyri! She had definitely ascended, and was a Lady!

B.J. hated what she was doing to Harry. Not the love, for she loved that, but the lies. She feared for him, for herself, for the future. And the dog-Lord didn't come into it. Or if he did, it was only at the back of her mind, where she had pushed him. And this—the act of love—was her way of keeping Radu there, for she did not want to think of him. Not while she was with Harry.

She sat astride him, sucking him into her core. She wanted his seed, wanted to feel it spray her hot innards. She desired to see his face tighten up in that oh-so-sweet agony, the momentary "little death" reflecting the release of life, its genesis, when swarming minescule hordes leap to seek out the egg. Except they would not find it, for B.J.'s system was geared to their destruction.

Oh, she would bear him children if she could, if she dared, but what would be their future? And how would she care for him, for them, for herself, once she had littered? Perhaps, one day . . . who could say? And perhaps by then he would have an egg of his own: a vampire egg, spawned of her leech and vented in the passion, the burning lust of a moment such as this.

Radu saw through her eyes:

She looked down on him, on Harry Keogh, where his shoulders were propped on pillows and his hands gripped the fancy scrolling of the headboard. His feverish eyes were on her breasts and taut nipples where B.J. lowered them to his face, his lips. And as she rose and fell on him ever faster, so he panted, gritting his teeth and meeting thrust with thrust.

He was near his time—B.J. too—and as their bucking grew more frantic yet he released a hand that fluttered like a crippled bird, finding its way behind and beneath her to stroke her slippery anus. She crushed to him in a frenzy; her breasts flattening to his chest; her mouth kissing, sucking at his neck . . .

. . . And her teeth pausing, then poising there!

They came, together, their souls dislocating, bodies shuddering—and still B.J.'s teeth were brushing Harry's neck. And she thought: If I do it now, the dog-Lord will not want him!

It was only a thought, surely? She would not carry it out. But still:

NO! Radu sent, in a sudden panic. *DON'T EVEN THINK IT!* His mental howl, directly into B.J.'s mind.

Lost to the moment, spent, and giving in to her conscience and commonsense (for surely that was all the cry had been?) she collapsed, rolled onto her side and drew Harry with her, locked into her. But then—as the ringing went out of her ears—and the singing from her sex, she wondered:

What? Her conscience? Was it possible to have anything of conscience in moments as hot and fierce as those had been? But of course it was, else Harry were a vampire from the first.

Yet still—and still as a stone—she *listened*. But all she could hear was her lover's thudding heart, his panting, and finally her own as she, too, began to breathe again . . .

Radu had got out just in time. But still his probe lingered in the psychic aether, ready to stab down again, link-up with her, and act as a carrier as he berated her for her treachery. Upon a time he would have done it in a moment, but to threaten B.J. now . . . would be to threaten himself, his very existence. She was Wamphyri! In thrall to him now, yes, but for how much longer? If he were to let her know he'd found her out, what then? She would leave him to rot here, that was what then! Leave him, and run off with her Harry—except the bastard was not hers but his! And *she* was his, too, or would be. And:

So she "loves" him, does she? She ruts with him, eh? But I shall rut the bitch to death! the dog-Lord swore, if only to himself. And then—because suddenly he realized what his rage was about: damaged pride and jealousy, and because his need to strike out was so great—Radu opened his mind to the full and sent forth a howl of frustration into the psychic aether . . .

. . . And knew at once that he had made a serious mistake.

Bonnie Jean couldn't hear him, no, for his rage had been about her, not directed at her. B.J. *herself* hadn't heard him . . . but at least one other had.

It was like a taint to his metaphysical sixth sense. The touch of something slimy, or the smell of something rotten. A gurgle of sewage, or a bitter, poisonous taste. Worse, he recognized it at once and knew its name:

Ferenczy!

Francesco was aloft over the Cairngorms. It was late February and would soon be March, but the snow was holding off, perhaps finished for the season. The streams running off the mountains were black and swollen, foaming grey with slush where they fell sheer. And the scarred domes of snow-capped summits and jumbles of craggy plateaux were rounded as outlines on Christmas cards, modelled by the slow melt. From up here it all looked very serene, and very treacherous, too.

"Not the Madonie, is it?" Luigi Manoza, Francesco's pilot looked sidelong at him in the cockpit of their helicopter. They were alone; a reconnaissance flight sixty miles to the west from their base at a decommissioned North Sea gas facility in Aberdeen; the first of several such flights, planned to survey the mountains for a likely location. *Not* a film location, however, but the location of a lair.

Finally in answer to his pilot's wry question, Francesco gave a grunt and said, "No, it's not the Madonie. But wolf territory . . . yes, I think so. As it was six hundred years ago, so it is now, pretty much." He glanced at a map in his lap, and as Manoza brought them swooping about in a low turn from the north said: "That place down there with the skiers, that is Aviemore. Famous, so they say. They seem to be making the best of what's left of the snow. Across the river, that handful of cottages—there, you just flew over it—is Inverdruie, where this bastard dog-Lord has a thrall or thralls."

Manoza was climbing now, skimming the mountains that were rising ahead. "Well," he said, "there shouldn't be any problem sniffing them out. Not in a place as small as that."

"Correct," Francesco nodded. "Our people are on it right now. And through Radu's thralls, we get to him. But the thing is, we don't want to take him out too soon. If we can discover his approximate location, we'll know when he's set to make his comeback: the moment his thralls and the Drakuls all start heading in that direction. *Then* we go after them, and get him, his people, and the Drakuls too."

"And he's here, you think?"

"My father thinks so," Francesco frowned. "And my brother. But be quiet now and take it slowly, slowly over the mountains. I want to concentrate. It's not so much what I can see as what I may feel. Angelo, that damned Thing in his pit, says that we should know without seeing, without touching or smelling; says the Ferenczys and dog-Lords have been enemies for so long that it's bred in them, that the knowing is in our blood. And while I've always been suspicious of anything my father says, I have to admit that in this place . . . I do sense something. *Hah!* And I'm the one who is supposed to be insensitive! So maybe Angelo is right and at short range like this, I might even be able to . . . *Ah! Ahh! Ahhh!*"

"Wha—?" The squat Manoza, hunched over his controls, instinctively leaned away from him. "Francesco, what the fuck . . . ?"

The Ferenczy's eyes were suddenly red, bulging, staring out and down, this way and that, through the curved, clear plastic panel of his door. He clasped his ears; he seemed crushed down into himself, as by shock or astonishment, as if he'd seen the starburst of flak and heard the howl of shrapnel. But it was a different kind of howling he'd heard, while Luigi had seen and heard nothing at all. And:

"Again!" Francesco husked. "Turn her around, now. Fly over that same spot again. *Do it!*"

Manoza complied. And again, and again. But whatever it had been it was gone now . . .

Later, on their way back to Aberdeen, finally the bulky, toad-like Manoza's curiosity got the better of him. He had to know. "Well?" he queried. "I mean, do you want to talk about it? Was it him?"

Francesco had been silent, lost in his own thoughts ever since ordering their return. But now: "It's time we moved into Aviemore," he grunted, mainly to himself. "All of us—for the skiing, you know?" Then, as if he had only just heard Manoza's question: "Yes, it was him. Somewhere back there in those mountains, the dog-Lord hides in his lair. But not for much longer, Luigi, because he's awake. Radu is *awake*—and making ready!"

V
RIVAL FACTIONS.
THE DARKNESS CLOSES IN.

HARRY WASN'T "SWITCHED ON," NOT ANY LONGER. AFTER DEALING WITH THE
situation at his place, he had gone to B.J. full of anxious doubts, urgent questions and demands; "disturbed" simply didn't convey his condition. So that
she had immediately "down-loaded" him of the cause: she'd struck the most recent, most horrific events from memory. And what the Necroscope had been
left with was a series of "facts" that were so disjointed, disconnected, it felt as if
half of his life had gone missing.

He "remembered" in some detail, however blurred and unreal, his all but
abandoned search for his wife and infant son; even places he'd never visited
except in his mind, at B.J.'s hypnotic command. But he did know that he *had*
been there, definitely; for if not, then he was simply insane. He knew, too, all
of his early life—his time at E-Branch, the powers he had once mastered, and
how he had once used them—and, since quitting the Branch, his time with Bonnie Jean. But that last . . . was a huge jumble, a monster jigsaw puzzle with no
borders and most of the pieces missing or refusing to come together.

And thus his memory was as B.J. wanted it . . . more or less. But there were
things in there that she didn't know about, that she'd forgotten or hadn't had
time or inclination to ask about, which were Harry's alone. And because he was
restricted by previous instructions—the post-hypnotic commands of someone
who had been there before B.J., that he must not divulge his powers to anyone—
he wasn't able to tell her about them. For example: he couldn't tell her what
he had discovered about Le Manse Madonie—about the Thing in the pit—because in fact *he didn't know*, or "knew" on a lower level of consciousness. For
right at the beginning of their relationship she had ordered him to forget anything she told him or that he might learn about the Wamphyri, because it was
for her ears alone. Harry couldn't refamiliarize himself with this stored infor-

mation until she or the dog-Lord actually switched him on all the way and sent him out against their enemies, the Drakuls and Ferenczys.

Thus this was a level that was hidden even from the Necroscope himself—but on another level he couldn't even tell her that Le Manse Madonie existed! For then B.J. would want to know why—and far more importantly *how*—he'd gone there, and how he had got out again unscathed. Yet even now, if only she would say the right words and turn him on all the way, she could have instant access to much of this hidden information.

But she wouldn't, because she didn't know he had it.

Which was why he had gone to her begging her to switch him on and tell him everything; which in turn was why she had switched him *off* and taken most everything away! And the only thing about the current status quo that he had been allowed to retain was the fact that they were in hiding from their enemies while waiting for some kind of call. That and the entirely indisputable fact of Bonnie Jean's innocence. So that Harry no longer even bothered to ask himself: innocent of what?

It scarcely mattered at all that reality was a blurred and indistinct place somewhere outside himself, or that he was in a constant daze, little better than a zombie, confused in all his mental processes. What mattered most was that he was with B.J. And come what may, well, really that was *all* that mattered . . .

The first night they'd spent together at the inn, B.J. had made a mistake. Easily corrected, still it was the sort of thing she would have to watch in future. In their room she had started to ask him, "Harry, tell me about Zahanine? What did you—?"

—Until she remembered that he couldn't tell her anything, because she had cancelled it from his mind. By which time Harry had been frowning, asking: "Zahanine? Your black girl? I didn't notice her with the other girls. Is she OK?" *Was she . . . was she at my place?* He gave his head a small, worried shake.

And: "You're quite right," B.J. had quickly nodded. "My mind was wandering, that's all. So don't worry about it."

But maybe it had continued to make connections somewhere in Harry's head, because he'd still been frowning as he asked her, "Why can't we hide out at my place? I know the area like the back of my hand, and it's easily defended."

Oh really? From the Wamphyri? B.J. had smiled to herself, however bitterly. Oh, yes, easily defended—but isolated, too. And: "Hey, you!" Despite her gloom, and the fact that she felt chilly within, she'd forced a "real" smile, and sat on the bed hugging her knees. "Lighten up, OK, Harry? We'll be just fine right here. Why don't you come over here and love me?"

And he had smiled sort of lopsidedly and gone to her. But even as they'd been making love Harry had been frowning inside. *Something about Zahanine, and his house? . . . Something about a dark spot on the floor, in his study? . . . Something about that frozen plateau on the roof of the world?* It came and went, disappearing into limbo. For on his current level of consciousness he wasn't given to remember these things. They'd been erased—or should have been—and his reality reduced to a misty swirl far less coherent than a dream.

In fact he might as *well* be asleep and dreaming! And for all that B.J. had been real, hot, and vibrant in Harry's arms, still he had wondered if maybe it was so—that this was all a strange, jumbled dream. In which case it was way past the time when he should have woken up. Except . . . he was afraid of what he might wake up to.

That had been three days ago. Since when, among the rival vampire factions, there had been a deal of to-ing and fro-ing, a new arrival, meetings, much searching and surveillance, and a long overdue (and in its way "merciful") death.

. . . In London, a certain "political refugee" had arrived on a flight from India. Ostensibly a wealthy ex-guru whose estate in Patna had suffered from an ever-increasing incidence of sectarian violence, he was in the UK to find a suitable home with a long-term view to leaving his "religious career" behind and starting a business in oriental carpets.

Since his credentials were impeccable—and he appeared to have all of the "necessary qualifications," two hundred thousand of which he'd already transferred to a branch of Lloyds in London—he had been granted a business visa and made welcome.

In fact he was one of Daham Drakesh's lieutenants, a long-time sleeper—and long-distance telepath—who several years ago had established a bolthole and base for Drakesh in Lucknow. But as the dog-Lord's time loomed ever closer, the last Drakul was more in need of a lieutenant in the British Isles, or more specifically, Scotland, to contact and take control of his thralls there. Daham's bloodson and chief lieutenant, Mahag, along with a common thrall, had been killed by Radu's people; since when he'd had no contact with his four surviving "disciples."

Drakesh was hopeful that since the death of his bloodson the four had realized that their mission had now changed. With their cover blown they were no longer incognito; they could no longer play *agents provocateurs* but must abandon all such plans and let the dog-Lord and the Ferenczys get on with it. But for all that his thralls were expendable, the last Drakul couldn't simply leave it at that.

His people were vampires after all, and many miles outside of any reasonable means of communication and control. Moreover, he knew that the British authorities were looking for them, and he had problems enough with officialdom as it was. That fool in his office on Kwijiang Avenue, Chungking, for instance: Colonel Tsi-Hong, a regular Red Army officer seconded to China's paramilitary Department of Parapsychological Studies.

In the weeks since Drakesh had been obliged to murder the overly curious Major Chang Lun—the Officer in Command of the small garrison at Xigaze—he had found himself under increasing pressure from Tsi-Hong. Not that there was any way he could be connected with Chang Lun's "accident"; indeed, with the land all about deep in the grip of winter, and the terrain a mass of drifted snow under crusty ice, they hadn't even discovered the Major's body as yet. And when they did, what then?

There'd been a blizzard the night Chang Lun's driver nose-dived their snow-cat into a crevasse only a mile or so from the Xigaze garrison, and despite that Tsi-Hong acknowledged Drakesh as a man of rare talents, surely he wouldn't consider him capable of calling up a storm!?

Oh, really? Yet from his seat in the foreboding "Drakesh Monastery," the last Drakul, High Priest of his sect, had done just that! As Chang Lun had fled for Xigaze after a spying mission on the monastery and walled city, then, calling up a blizzard—and with the aid of his familiar albino bats—Drakesh had driven him to his doom. Following which:

A few days of silence . . . and then the messages, relayed from Chungking to the garrison, and delivered by hand to Daham Drakesh. He had known, of course, that Chang Lun was his enemy, and that the Major must have conveyed his concerns about him to Tsi-Hong; but he had believed that the Colonel's commitment to his "experiment"—to develop an army of supermen for the Red Chinese Army—would be sufficient to keep him secure from all but a minimum of supervision and interference. So he had *reasoned*, anyway. But apparently he'd been wrong.

Colonel Tsi-Hong knew about Drakesh's people in England. Having taken Drakesh at his word (that they were simply agents sent into the UK to initiate a low-profile investigation of the British mindspy organization) he had even sanctioned their visit. But now that the Chinese military intelligence services had picked up British press reports about their expulsion, and the Colonel himself was having to answer questions from *his* superiors, he wanted to know what the hell Drakesh was playing at?

What? Sectarian feuding? Firefights? Murders? Expulsions? And what if the British authorities took Drakesh's people into custody, and made a connection between the sect and Red China? Also, there was now this unfortunate thing with Chang Lun: his disappearance. That such a capable and *reliable* officer should simply vanish off the face of the earth—even in a region as treacherous as the Tingri Plateau—was a curious and perhaps even suspicious thing in its own right, without that the Major had made several damning eye-witness reports on certain activities at the Drakesh monastery and in the neighbouring walled city.

Wherefore Drakesh should take note that a new, very much more rigid Officer Commanding would be arriving shortly in Xigaze Garrison; and soon after that the High Priest could expect the first *thorough* inspections, both of the monastery and the facilities at the walled city . . .

At first, Daham Drakesh had read such messages with some concern, which in a while had turned to resolution. His course was set, and no turning back. So, a new Officer Commanding was coming to Xigaze, and then across the frozen waste to the monastery. Very well, but his first visit would be his last. What was in the monastery couldn't be hidden, not from a persistent inspection team. It was here to stay, until Drakesh was ready to send it—or them—out into the world. Therefore the inspection team could not be *allowed* to leave. And as for what was breeding in the old walled city . . . that was indeed the stuff of a new army, but in no way a Red Chinese army.

So then, Drakesh's course was set. And as for any sort of heavy-handed military threat from China: in two, three or four weeks' time, or whenever such a threat might have materialized—would China really have time to worry about some obscure sect in the cold waste of Tibet? Drakesh doubted it, not with Chungking, London and Moscow in ruins, and the whole world toppling over the brink into nuclear war!

Then, when the earth lay under the grey, windswept gloom of an unending winter, and Drakesh and his brood were the only kind who could profit from it . . . *then* his creatures and children, the spawn of his vats and loins, would go out from Tibet into the world, and the new order come into being.

On the roof of the monastery, where the vast skull façade sloped back into the face of the cliff, a radio antenna reared even now. And in a room near the dome of the rock, a crude but powerful radio transmitter wanted only Drakesh's finger on the button.

As for his lieutenant, recently sent into England:

He could rally the four surviving vampire thralls to him, assess the situation locally, and—in telepathic consultation with Drakesh—make his own decision as to the best course of action. After that, if the group continued to survive the cataclysm soon to follow, then it would form the tiny nucleus of a European cell.

And while the great nations of Earth devolved into a final chaos, and all their armies and their power came to nothing in the end, the master of their destiny—the last Drakul—would be secure here on the Roof of the World. For of all the places *in* the world, surely this was the safest of all. What country would think to target Tibet? What was there here that was even worth destroying? Nothing.

Nothing but the very seat of evil. But to Daham Drakesh's knowledge, of all living men he himself and his red-robed vampire "priests" were the only ones who knew about it.

To his knowledge, yes.

And of all *living* men . . .

Meanwhile two very disparate Ferenczy lieutenants, Vincent Ragusa and Angus McGowan had teamed up, journeyed north, and taken a suite of rooms at a hotel in Carrbridge north of Aviemore and a few cautious miles from Inverdruie. But right from square one things hadn't been much to the young Sicilian's liking.

Ragusa wasn't happy with the situation: that this little man, the tiny, wizened McGowan, was his superior, from whom he was supposed to take orders. He had typecast McGowan as a runt from the moment he laid eyes on him— an assessment he'd since revised, and radically. But at first . . . things had got off to a less than auspicious start.

And now, as the ugly little man drove his ugly little V.W. Beetle south along blackly glittering roads, between three-foot banks of snowplough-heaped slush and dirty ice, from Carrbridge to Aviemore, and on across the Spey where the road was signposted for Inverdruie and Coylumbridge, Ragusa's dark thoughts went back to their first meeting (a non-event if ever there'd been one), and to events since.

To start with, McGowan had failed to turn up to meet him at the airport in Edinburgh. That was the first let-down, when he had had to take a taxi into

the city and book himself into a hotel. Ragusa could speak English, a smatter-
ing anyway, but what the locals were speaking was scarcely English! And people said the Italians talked too fast! Then, in his room, he'd got a call from
McGowan:

"Saw ye come in," the gravelly voice told him on the wire. "But circumstances bein' what they are, well Ah could'nae meet ye. Yere room at the hotel:
was that an advance bookin'?"

"No. Spur of the moment. I was out on a limb. And what the fuck's all this
cloak and dagger shit about anyway?" Ragusa's tone of voice had said a lot for
his feelings.

"So, no one knows ye're there?" (The other might not even have heard
him!)

"No, of course not! What kind of dumb shit is this?"

For long moments there had been silence, then: "Oh? Upset, are ye?"
(That gruff, weaselly voice.) "Well, Ah'm sorry about that, laddie—but as Ah
said, it could'nae be helped. So meet me in thirty minutes, where the road leads
off Princess Street for Waverly Station."

"Eh? Laddie?" Ragusa had snarled his outrage. And: "What's that? Princes
Street? Waverly Station? What the—?"

But: "Aye, just so, ye've got it," that phlegmy voice had chuckled—just before the phone went dead.

And half an hour later:

That was the first time Ragusa had seen McGowan or his car, and he had
instantly disliked both of them. At the junction of roads the Beetle had pulled
over and McGowan had leaned across the front passenger seat to yank the catch
and push the door open. "Get in, will ye no?" Then, pulling out into a sluggish
stream of traffic: "McGowan," he had said, reaching across his small body to extend his right hand, while giving his passenger a cursory glance. And, when that
one deliberately ignored the proffered handshake, "No the best o' weather, is
it?" Followed by that phlegmy chuckle of his. "Which is all to the good, for it's
our kind o' weather, eh?"

Ragusa had looked at him then and scowled. "Vincent," he'd said. "Vincent Ragusa. You were supposed to meet me at the airport. Those were
Francesco's instructions—and the Francezcis like their instructions carried out
to the letter."

"Aye, so they do and always have," McGowan had immediately agreed. "Fifty
years ago they were much the same . . . and thirty before that when Ah was first
recruited, when Ah was about yere age. Since when Ah've been wherever they
had a mind tae send me, but mainly in the British Isles. Ah've been—ye ken—
sniffin' out big dogs, as it were? And other creatures, aye. While ye've been . . .
what? Learnin' the business in Sicily at Le Manse Madonie? Aye, Ah imagine
so. But it's no the same out here. It's a whole other world—laddie."

"Call me Vincent!" Ragusa had snapped then. "Or if that's too hard for you,
then it's Ragusa. Lieutenant Ragusa!"

But McGowan had at once made clucking noises. "Yere rank does'nae
come into it," he'd said then, but very quietly. "It will give ye away in a minute,
be sure. But Ah ken ye did'nae mean it. It was simply yere way o' expressin'

yere—what?—yere disappointment? Or displeasure? Ah'm no what ye expected, nor the cityation, eh?"

"The what?" (The accent had had Ragusa baffled.) "Did you say 'cityation?' "

"The way things stand," McGowan had explained. "Ah, well . . . it'll a' work out, Ah'm sure. Anyway, Ah could'nae meet ye at the airport. Things are no perfec', ye ken? Ah had a small to do wi' a polis friend—but ye'll be meeting that yin soon enough. We can even have lunch wi' him, if ye'd like? But see, Ah had tae be sure no one else knew ye were arrivin', that no one was watchin' tae see if ye'd be picked up. But it happens that no one was. So it seems we're a' in the clear."

"So what's this about the . . . the polis? The police?"

"Oh, a spot o' bother wi' an old friend. But dinnae fret, it's a' sorted out the noo—er, Vincent . . . "

And so it had gone.

They had talked about the job in hand: tomorrow they'd be travelling north to the Spey Valley—"sniffin' out big dogs"—and so on. But as they talked it had become clear to Ragusa that Francesco must have spoken in depth with McGowan; the ugly little man had a clear picture of the task in hand that left no room for argument or rearrangement. So that on the two or three occasions when Ragusa might have thought to question something, McGowan had always had the answer, or he'd got in first with a timely reminder: "But that's how Francesco *wants* it done—er, Vincent. And as ye're aware, the Franczecis like their instructions carried out tae the letter . . . "

And finally they had arrived at McGowan's address in that most dreary district of the city. On their way, the young Sicilian vampire had caught a glimpse of frothing wavecrests on a grey ocean mirroring desolate skies, and, in the darkly wintry distance, a bleak skyline of derelict-like monoliths that reminded him (oddly enough) of Palermo. Only the gelid slush was new to him—the way it ate like acid into his patent leather Italian shoes.

Ragusa had stepped from an icy pavement into the shadow of the dilapidated Victorian terraced property that was McGowan's home, and had followed the shabby little man through a wrought-iron gate, up wet stone steps to the drier cover of the arched-over entranceway, before even thinking to ask: "Er, Angus? Why are we here, anyway?"

"Are ye no hungry?" The other had cocked his head, raising a bushy, inquiring eyebrow, as he unlocked the stout oak door.

Ragusa had shrugged, stepped inside and smelled a familiar taint that he always associated with old buildings. Sicily was full of such. "We could have eaten at my hotel, or anywhere."

"Aye, true enough," McGowan had grinned. "But Ah fancy mah fare will be more to yere taste. Anyway, ye've entered of yere own free will . . . "

At which the Sicilian had paused half-way out of his coat to look curiously at his little host. The eyes of both men had been feral yellow in the gloom. And Ragusa had said, "You fancy yourself as quite the little comedian, don't you?"

But McGowan had only chuckled as he answered, "Well, er—Vincent? If a man cannae have a joke on himsel', then what *can* he laugh at, eh?" And he had switched on dim lights, taken his guest's coat, and ushered him along a narrow corridor.

"Now where?" Ragusa had queried, straightening his expensive tie and stretching his neck a little.

"Tae see mah big old polis pal," McGowan had laughed from low in his chest. "Down here." And he'd led the way to the cellar.

Ragusa hadn't been with it yet. "So, you bribed him, converted him—or what?"

"Or what," McGowan had answered. By which time they were in the cellar, and again the little man had put on dim lights.

And: *"Ahhhh!"* Ragusa had said—but by no means an expression of fear or detestation. More of surprise, even admiration. For Vincent Ragusa had served a long apprenticeship at Le Manse Madonie; but even there this would have seemed exceptional . . . well, if the setting had been a little more in keeping.

McGowan had sensed what he was thinking; in a voice that was deeper and more guttural than ever, he'd said, "D'ye remember, Vincent, how it used tae be . . . *before?* Why, o' course ye do! Mahsel', Ah certainly do—no that Ah'd go back tae it, ye understand. Still, some o' the best meals Ah've ever eaten were served up in the nastiest little places, aye."

A nasty little place, yes. Indeed Ragusa couldn't remember seeing one that was nastier. The brick walls were streaked with nitre; the floor was of stone flags, laid back in one corner to reveal a smelly hole, with rusting chains descending into darkness; there was a work-bench with assorted tools, a large fire-blackened stove with a hooded flue ascending, and—

—A dining table, in the centre of the floor! A table set for lunch with a white tablecloth, gleaming crockery and highly polished cutlery, glasses and a ship's decanter of red wine. It had been so incongruous that it was fetching; for a moment Ragusa hadn't been able to take his eyes from the almost hallucinatory scene. But with senses more than one, and all of them far more finely tuned than a normal human being's, he had detected the smell (or rather the *scent*) of food . . . or, as McGowan had put it, of "fare that was more to his taste."

Behind the stone stairway, the brick-arched entrance to a recessed passage or annex had been the source of the odour. Old McGowan, seeing Ragusa's eyes turn that way, his nostrils widening, had grinned, lit the stump of a candle and tossed the flaring match into the stove. And leading the way into the cramped space, he had warned: "Avoid brushin' against the walls. Dinnae get yeresel' hooked up—if ye see what Ah mean."

Ragusa had seen. Every two or three feet along the wall, meat hooks had been cemented into the brickwork. Most of them were stained, rusty, empty. But at the back of the alcove, the last one wasn't. The figure hanging there was human . . . it *had been* a human being. The arms were gone to the shoulders; a leg—the left one—was off at the knee; the right leg was missing half-way up the thigh, and all of the stumps had been cauterized. But the *neatness* of the mutilations was remarkable.

"You're a craftsman," the Sicilian had grunted, beginning to salivate.

"Huh!" McGowan's answering snort had been one of frustration from where he examined his victim. "Damn the man . . . he's gone and *done* it!"

"Oh?"

"Died on me! He was alive when Ah spoke tae him this morning—Ah had taken precautions tae preserve him, ye see. But now . . ."

Again Ragusa had been impressed. "He could still talk?"

"Oh, aye—but he was'nae strong enough tae scream. *Hah!* Ah had thought he would'nae be able tae do this, but damn the man, he has! Oh, he had a mind o' his own, did George Ianson! Still, he's verra fresh, as ye can see, and won't go entirely tae waste. Out o' here now, and sit yeresel' at mah table."

Back in the main cellar room, the little man had sprinkled olive oil into a large, shallow, blackened tray on top of the smoking stove. And selecting various tools from the bench, he'd inquired, "Name yere cut, Vincent—and tell me how ye'd like it prepared?"

"Oh, chef's choice," the other had grunted, with his version of an affable shrug. "But rare, of course—or maybe even bloody?" By which time his voice had been no less clotted than McGowan's. Then, as the deceptive little man disappeared again with his saw and knives into the annex behind the stairs, "But tell me, what was it you thought your 'policeman friend' would not be able to do? Kill himself?"

"Aye, kill himsel'," the answer had come back. "Still, it happens frae time tae time. Ye can drug 'em tae stop the pain and numb the shock, but if they've the will for it, there's no stoppin' 'em." And the whine of his saw had sprung into being.

At the table, Ragusa had nodded to himself, poured a glass of wine, then lifted his voice to answer: "I'd forgotten. Life isn't the fire in them that undeath is in us."

"No, it is'nae," McGowan's voice had come back to him. "No half the fire, nor half the heat. And Ah suppose that sometimes it's just no worth it tae keep it lit." But despite the "sentiment" in the words, there'd been no remorse, compassion or emotion at all.

Then the whine of the saw had changed to a biting *whirrr,* and Ragusa had sat at the table, thinking how despite the fact that he didn't much care for Mc-Gowan, still he had to acknowledge the little man's flair. And his generosity, of course . . .

So, then: in Ragusa's eyes, McGowan was still a runt but something less of a yokel. All those years working on his own had made him independent; perhaps when the Francezci met him again he would consider him *too* independent! There was this sense of authority, self-confidence, in him that would better befit the Wamphyri themselves.

And sitting in McGowan's old Beetle, the Sicilian thought maybe that was it. It was what he didn't like about the little man: his knowledge and his authority. Perhaps McGowan had been the Francezcis' "man" in these parts—left to his own resources—for far too long. Until (was it possible?) he'd begun to think of himself as a chief in his own right. No simple thrall this McGowan, nor even a simple lieutenant. But a wrinkled old man like this, Wamphyri? It seemed absurd. Did he aspire? Was it possible he might even ascend?

"This is Inverdruie," McGowan grunted, turning his rheumy eyes on his passenger. "Oh, and what are ye scowlin' about?"

"This car," Ragusa answered, but that was only part of it, of course. "How am I to fool anyone I'm a movie tycoon driving around in this wreck? In Sicily, we consign shit like this to the scrap heap!"

"This is a recce run," McGowan answered. " 'Recce'—that's reconnaisance. It's so Ah can show ye what Ah've learned, so's if anything shid happen tae me ye'll be fully in the know. But did Ah no tell ye that already? Or maybe ye did'nae understand me, eh?"

"It's a wonder I've understood any fucking thing!" Ragusa scowled again, then grinned sarcastically, and in what he patently considered a fair imitation of Rex Harrison, said, "Why can't the English learn how to speak?"

McGowan's turn to scowl. "Aye *laddie*, but Ah'm no English. And if wit was shit, ye'd have diarrhoea!"

It was early morning and as yet there was only light traffic: fit young fanatics who had struggled out of their holiday beds in neighbouring towns and hamlets, strapped their skis to their roof-racks, and were now making for Aviemore's slopes.

"This 'laddie' crap . . . !" Ragusa's lips drew back from eyeteeth as curved and sharp as fangs. "It stops right now!"

At which McGowan seemed to swell up in his seat, yanked on the wheel and aimed his Beetle straight at an oncoming car! It took very little effort; the second-class road was barely wide enough for two vehicles abreast, and heaped snow had frozen to solid walls on both sides. Ragusa's jaws flew open; he gasped, "What the fuck—?" and threw up a hand before his face.

But at the last moment McGowan yanked on the wheel again, swung left, and cut through an opening in the banked snow onto a service track. As he brought the Beetle to a halt, the other car went careering by on the far side of the snow wall. Ragusa caught a momentary glimpse of the driver shaking a furious fist through his open window. Then, leaving a settling cloud of blue exhaust smoke, the skiers were gone . . .

Ragusa found his voice at last, and said, "What in the—? Are you a complete, raving maniac!?"

But the little man wasn't listening to him or even looking at him. Instead he used his sleeve to clear the lightly misted windscreen, and stared ahead down the track. And his eyes were red as finally he glanced at Ragusa, a mere glance, and said: "D'ye see the smoke, the chimney behind they trees there? The wee house?"

"Uh?" Ragusa looked, scowled, and nodded his head. He was still a little shaken. "The house? Yes. So what?"

McGowan's eyes were rheumy again as he said, "The dweller is a man called John Guiney, or Auld John as he's known locally. He's a gillie, and he's been here forever."

"Eh? A gillie?"

"A tracker, gamekeeper, woodsman . . . and he's one o' Radu Lykan's thralls, Ah fancy."

Ragusa's attention now centred on the house in the trees. He was still angry—even furious—but this gave his anger a direction, a target. "What makes you think so?"

"That time Ah saw Bonnie Jean Mirlu and her man takin' out they Drakuls, it was Auld John's car she was drivin'. But later that same day, he had it back again. So if John Guiney's no the dog-Lord's thrall, he's certainly a friend o' B.J.'s."

"I don't see any car," Ragusa squinted ahead.

"Behind the house, Ah shid think."

"I want to see it. Then I'll know it, too."

"A quick look, then," the little man answered, slipping his car in gear. "But this is just a recce, remember? So don't you go forgettin' who's givin' the orders around here . . . " As if he deliberately calculated to irritate Ragusa more yet—which in fact he did.

As quietly as possible, in a low gear, McGowan drove over a thin layer of crunching, glistening snow, away from the main road to Aviemore, until he picked up a track through the naked trees that skirted the picture-postcard house. On the far side, mostly obscured by trees, he stopped the engine and wound down his window. There was only a wintry silence, and the sun a desultory grey blob in the sky far down the valley.

"There's Auld John's car," the little man grunted. "Back o' the house, as ye see."

"And does this guy know you?" Ragusa rasped. "And if not, why all this creeping around? I mean, what is he . . . some kind of threat? One old man, living alone, waiting for this fucking dog-Lord to come down off his mountain?" He started to get out of the car. But McGowan cautioned him:

"Where d'ye think ye're goin? Have'nae Ah told ye often enough a'ready that this is only a recce!"

"Fuck recce!" the other snapped. Opening his jacket, he showed McGowan his under-arm holster and gun. "Me, I check the old guy out. I can't recruit him if he's a—what?—a 'moon child?' In which case I ask him a question or two. He's just a thrall, after all. In fact he's less than a thrall, not even a vampire. This way we save a lot of time . . . for Francesco, you understand? So, if the old guy answers my questions—all well and good and we get to know something. If he doesn't, likewise good, except he gets dead sooner. We'll dump his body where it won't be found, and he's one less to worry about."

"And Vincent Ragusa gets all the credit, right?" McGowan hissed.

"Is that what's pissing you?" Ragusa snarled. "You shrivelled little fuck? So why don't you come and help out?"

But: "No!" McGowan scowled. "Go yeresel'—glory boy! Mah orders are clear enough tae me."

"Right," Ragusa grinned viciously. "It's why you're still a follower, Angus, and why you always will be. But give me ten minutes and I guarantee I'll know more about what's going down here than you've learned in ten years!"

He started away through the trees, a flowing grey shadow among lesser shadows. And McGowan thought: *Smooth as a badger's arse, that yin! More than Ah've learned in ten years, eh? Well, one thing Ah've learned in the last few months is the name o' a certain silversmith in Inverness—the one who makes the shot for John Guiney's cartridges, aye!*

Ragusa was skirting a hedge of dense holly bushes. In a moment he'd be at the door of the cottage. McGowan turned the key in the ignition, put her in gear and found a space to reverse, then turned about and headed for the open road. Drawing level with the rear of the cottage, he stopped again but left the engine running. He at least had some experience of Radu's allies. He'd seen them in action—the results of that action, certainly.

At the door Ragusa straightened his tie, took his automatic from its holster, tucked it in his trouser-band, where it was covered by the flap of his jacket. Then he knocked—and waited . . .

Inside, at the side of the house and upstairs, Auld John peered through a tiny window down on McGowan's car. An old V.W. Beetle, which was fairly rare up here. He wouldn't forget what it looked like, even if he couldn't read the number plate. And as for the driver: had he seen him before? Well perhaps he had at that. But from what he could see of him now . . . B.J.'s watcher? He fitted the description, anyway.

And again the knock at the back door, but more insistent now. "Ah'm comin', aye." Auld John called out, in a thin, trembly voice. "Gi' me a minute, can ye no?" And so down the stairs in an easy lope—pausing briefly in his front room—then on to the door. "Who is it?"

"Er, you don't know me," Ragusa's voice, his foreign accent. But having watched him coming through the trees, his furtive approach, Auld John knew exactly what he looked like. Knew it, and didn't like what he'd seen.

"Man Ah wiz on the toilet," he called out. "Ah surely hope this is *verra* important and no just someone wantin' directions? Let me just fix mahsel' up . . ."

"Sure, take your time. But you can bet it's important. I'm here to make you an offer. Big money, Mr. Guiney. I mean, it is John Guiney, isn't it?" Ragusa grinned viciously and tested his draw: thrust his hand under the flap of his jacket, gripped the butt of his gun. Yeah, it was fine.

"Aye, it is that," John answered, thinking: *And you know too damn much about me—mah oh so sharp-lookin' young friend!* Then he shrank down into himself, lowered one shoulder, became even more the old man. There! And now—

—He unlatched and half-opened the door.

Ragusa knew him at once; and face to face, Auld John knew Ragusa! Moonchild that John was, forewarned *and* forearmed, he let instinct take over. For if this yin was'nae Ferenczy, then he was'nae here! But he was, and he was.

"Mr. Guiney, we're . . . we're g-going to be sh-shooting a film . . . " Ragusa had commenced to stammer the first words that came to mind. But now—as his intended victim came from his hunched-up, rheumatic-old-man pose to the full, lean height of a sniffing, hound-eyed hunter, and growled:

"Oh? Shooting, is it?"—so Ragusa drew back a pack and reached for his gun! And: "Aye, so it is!" Auld John said, and brought his right arm and hand out from behind the door.

Twin barrels stared Ragusa in the face, and his hand still hadn't cleared the loosely flapping material of his jacket. But then, in the next moment, he found his gun . . . an entire moment too late. "Oh, dearie me!" said John, and squeezed one trigger.

The blast tore the cold silence, set birds fluttering and flapping in the trees, and at point-blank range blew all of the flesh off Ragusa's face and drove his ruined eyes deep into his skull. Performing an amazing backwards bound, the Sicilian formed a mid-air crucifix before his patent leather heels hit the ground and slammed him onto his back on the frozen earth.

Auld John loped after him, still aiming his shotgun at him but glancing left at McGowan in his car. Then, however briefly, their eyes met, exchanging looks that were sheer poison. But as John swung his shotgun to the left Mc-Gowan released the clutch, revved up, and rolled the car out of sight towards the front of the house. It was gone in a puff of exhaust smoke.

John loped to the corner of the house, saw the car accelerating towards the gap in the wall of snow. But the distance was too great; the spread of the shot would be too wide; John could only watch as the little man in his little car skidded out onto the road and drove away . . .

Then John went back to Ragusa's body—which was twitching and trying to sit up! A lieutenant, this one, aye! "Well, fuck ye!" Auld John said, and thrust the barrels of his gun into the gory hole that had been a mouth. "Cuttin' ye're head off is'nae the only way, eh? Ah can just as easily blow it off, right?"

And he proceeded to do just that.

Later, blue wood-smoke—and more than wood-smoke—rose up in a near-vertical column from behind John's house. He was burning all the dead wood come down from the trees in the autumn, stuff that wasn't big enough for firewood. As for the shots that he had fired off: his nearest neighbour lived a good quarter-mile away and wouldn't be bothered anyway. John was a gillie, after all . . . there were rabbits about, and pigeons for his table.

And Auld John himself warmed his hands by the blaze in a corner of the sprawling area he called his garden. There hadn't been much of a commotion, he thought; next to nothin', in fact. That yin had'nae been much o' a one tae send against the likes o' Radu and his folk! Well maybe it would warn the rest o' the bastards off. But as he inhaled heartily on the smoke from the fire, John doubted it.

Later still, in the house, he went through Ragusa's expensive clothing to see if he could find out just exactly who this Ferenczy had been. Information for B.J., who was still the "Wee Mistress . . ."

. . . For the time being, anyway.

That same afternoon McGowan moved from Carrbridge to Aviemore, and according to instructions received earlier booked rooms at the Ski Lodge for Francesco and his team. Then, in the evening, he spoke to the Francezci on the telephone in his room and told him of Vincent Ragusa's regrettable demise. He told it more or less as it had happened, leaving out only the fact that he was mainly responsible for goading the younger man to his death.

And when he was finished:

"Angus, listen—you can tell me," the Francezci had told him. "I mean, I warned you that you would have to keep an eye on Vincent, at least until I could find a fitting solution. So . . . did you perhaps take him out?"

"It was the way Ah told it, Francesco," McGowan answered. "The man was a bleddy hothead if ever Ah saw one!"

"You know, old friend, that it would make no difference?" The Francezci could be persuasive. But so could McGowan be obstinate. He had lied—to a degree—and now the lie must stand forever. But he could perhaps embellish it a little.

"Francesco, the man was intent on bein' boss," he insisted. "Mah boss, Ah mean. And one day—maybe everybody's boss? Orders meant nothin' tae that yin. Ah'm sorry tae have tae say it, but it's mah personal opinion ye're well rid o' him."

"Mine, too . . . " (The Francezci's softly grunted agreement.) "Just as long as nothing comes of it."

"Auld John Guiney is'nae about tae scream polis, if that's what ye mean," McGowan said. "And Ah certainly won't be reportin' Ragusa missin'!"

"Very well, then. What of our rooms?"

"All taken care of. Ye can move into Aviemore just as soon as ye like. They'll even mark out a helipad for Luigi. It'll be ready tomorrow mornin'. Oh, they quite like the idea that we're scoutin' locations for a film!"

"Good! I shall look forward to seeing you tomorrow, then," Francesco answered, and that was that . . .

At about the same time as McGowan was talking to the Francezci, Bonnie Jean Mirlu was talking to John Guiney. Some sixth sense, or female—or Wamphyri?—intuition had warned her that things weren't all they might be in Auld John's neck of the woods. And John had told her about his visitors.

Like Francesco Francezci, she was at first concerned that John's action might precipitate things, but he soon assured her that such wasn't the case. "It was'nae me but the dog-Lord they were after, lass," he said. (And B.J. wondered, Lass? What had got into John? He'd never called her that before!—perhaps it was just the excitement.) And, as if sensing her surprise, the fact that she'd been taken aback: "Beggin' yere pardon, Bonnie, but if Ah had'nae been the winner, why, we might all have ended up losers! The little man—yere watcher— was in charge. If he had got a hold o' me . . . maybe he could have made me guide them tae Radu himsel' in his high place!"

"They must know it won't be long now," she nodded, biting her lip with anxiety. "And yet—I don't know—they seem to be acting far in advance of anything I had expected. And John, they also know where you are now. They know for sure!"

"Aye," John's voice was stronger than she'd ever heard it. "And they know somethin' of what they're up against! Maybe they were—Ah dinnae ken—

testin' the water, as it were? Well if so, they would'nae find it much to their likin'. A wee bit too hot, if ye take mah meanin'.'"

"Ferenczys," she shivered. "And we don't know how many of them. In fact we don't know a damn thing about them!" B.J. sensed panic setting in again. Auld John was a brave old lad, but he was a brave old fool, too.

"Ah, but we *do* know somethin' about them!" He cut into her thoughts, actually seeming to relish this entire mess. "For Ah turned out this bleddy foreigner's pockets, and there were one or two verra interestin' items in them, be sure."

"Well, then—go on!" B.J. snapped. And immediately softened a little. "John, I'm sure you don't really understand the danger here."

"Oh, but Ah do, Bonnie Jean, Ah do. Verra well, now listen. There were cards in his wallet, credit cards and such. And even money. Mainly American dollars, but some small change, too—in lira!"

"Lira?"

"Aye. And the plastic is Italian, or rather Sicilian. Also, there's a wee personal card wi' names, an address, and a telephone number. The card's in Italian, but even an auld fool like me can read it easy enough. It says 'V. Ragusa: Personal Assistant to A. and F. Francezci, Le Manse Madonie.' "

"Le Manse Madonie!" B.J. gasped out loud as her mind began to whirl. A long time ago she had tracked the ancient Ferenczy bloodline to Sicily, where the trail had appeared to peter out. And now . . . now it seemed that they'd been there all the time!

Harry Keogh was at the window of their small room, looking out disinterestedly into the darkness of evening at the rear of their country inn hideaway. At least, B.J. hadn't suspected his interest. In fact with every passing moment, Harry seemed to be sinking deeper and deeper inside himself. Just what was happening in his head—if anything at all was happening in there—she wouldn't even hazard a guess. But now, startling her:

"Ferenczys," he said (simply repeating her?) And: "Le Manse Madonie. The Madonie is a range of mountains in Sicily. Is that Auld John on the phone? Some kind of problem?" And, continuing to stare blankly out of the window: "Margaret Macdowell's here. A taxi just dropped her off."

Margaret Macdowell: the police had finished with her now, and rightly so. For after all, she was the victim—or she had been the *intended* victim—of a rapist and murderer; and she'd told the police "all she knew" weeks ago. Weeks: was that all? But time had seemed to slow down. It felt like years to Bonnie Jean! Since the attack, B.J. had bided her time, keeping Margaret pretty much out of things in case the police should want to talk to her again. But that was then and this was now, and B.J. needed every ounce of help she could get.

Auld John was still on the phone. "Bonnie Jean?"

"Listen, John? I'm cutting this short. I think it's time you were out of that cottage. And I do mean tonight! Find yourself lodgings, but well away from Inverdruie and Aviemore. Then give me a call to let me know where you are. Do you understand? You're my mainstay, John. I can't let anything happen to you."

"Get out o' here?" He seemed bemused. "But it's mah home. Where would Ah go?"

"Anywhere that you'll be safe!" she snapped at him again, and meant it this time. "So do it! Now then, tell me you understand."

And in a moment: "Aye, Ah understand. But Radu . . . "

"When it's time, you'll hear his call. Until then . . . good luck, John."

She sensed his nod. "You, too, Bonnie Jean. Take care, mah bonnie wee lass." And the *click* as his handset went down. Then:

"B.J." Harry's voice again, a little more animated than it had been of late. She glanced at him; he continued to stare out of the window, but he was frowning now, blinking rapidly.

"Harry?" She made to go to him.

"That car," he said, without looking at her. "Its lights have gone out now, but it's there, where the hedgerow finishes at this end of the service lane. It drove in after Margaret's taxi, and now . . . it's just sitting there."

She stood beside him, staring hard through the gauze curtains and reaching to switch the lights out. From the corridor muted greetings sounded as the rest of the girls met Margaret. But B.J. wasn't interested in that; her attention was centred elsewhere. "A car?" she whispered, peering harder still.

"Where the hedgerow finishes," the Necroscope said again, in that not-quite-there voice that B.J. hated but was getting used to. And Harry could sense, could almost feel her concentration as he wondered however vaguely: *The people in that car: are they our enemies?* But his guard was down; his metaphysical thoughts went out . . . and a certain member of the Great Majority was out there waiting for them.

As for B.J.: she was no telepath, not yet, but she was on the verge of true ascension . . . Wamphyri! Scarcely knowing she was doing it, she found and probed the car, and the Necroscope heard her low, rumbling snarl, a growl that came and went deep inside her. She staggered a little in her passion, and grabbed his arm to steady herself. And:

"Drakuls!" The word, the name, left her lips like a poisonous sigh. Then, with a hiss—and a savage grin as her eyes glowed yellow in the dark—"Drakuls! Aye, as if I had wished it, and my wish had come true for Zahanine. For Zahanine!"

Without another word to Harry, B.J. made for the door. As she went, she called ahead—low-, husky-, dangerous-voiced—to one of the girls: "Keys! Sandra, I want your car keys!"

The girls were in the corridor talking to Margaret. Bonnie Jean swept upon them . . . there was a brief, astonished, shocked exchange, then small, fierce, raven-haired Sandra Mohrag seemed whirled along in B.J.'s wake, and went almost at a run with her down the stairs to the rear exit from the inn.

And Harry still at the window, looking out at the car in the shadows, and the dark silhouettes inside it; left abruptly to his own devices, and not knowing what to do or if he should do anything. So that when the voice came—in his head—it came almost as an electric shock:

Enemies, Harry! said that dead voice, urgently. *You was right first time, Necroscope—dead right!* It was R.L. Stevenson Jamieson, and the Necroscope's instinctive response was to erect his neglected mental barriers . . . Which he would do, except there was something he must know first:

"How many enemies, R.L.? And what kind of enemies?"

What? You knows *what kind, man!* R.L. answered. *Same ones you has had all along. Only there's five of 'em now, not six.*

Drakuls, Red-robes, Tibetans, but by no means priests. Not of any clean, healthy religion, anyway. But was something wrong here? *Five* of them? Not four?

I recognize four of 'em, (R.L. said). *Or at least, my obi does. But number five's a newcomer. Their new boss, maybe? Anyways, there be five of 'em for sure. Yeah!*

And Harry thought: *What do numbers matter anyhow?* The only thing that mattered was that they were enemies. That, and maybe something B.J. had said . . . something about Zahanine? And something else, about a dark spot on the floorboards in his study?

But Bonnie Jean had been in such a hurry, she hadn't left any instructions for Harry! B.J., in one hell of a hurry, yes. And that look on her face—

—The Necroscope knew what that look meant. And suddenly he felt himself galvanized to action.

Out there in the wintry evening darkness, there were five monstrous enemies. And hell-bent on revenge, Bonnie Jean Mirlu had gone rushing to meet them head on . . .

PART 4

Friends in Low Places

B.J.: STILL INNOCENT?— REALITY'S ENDING!—A GRAVE SOLUTION.

STILL AT THE WINDOW, ALONE IN HIS ROOM, THE NECROSCOPE FELT DIZZY, nauseous, and clung to the windowsill. His knees felt like water, as if they were trying to liquefy and topple him. He wanted to do something—any-thing—but he had no orders, didn't know what to do.

But he did, and he must! And the last thing he wanted was for B.J.'s girls to come into his room—not if he was going to have *to move!*

He *went* to the door of the room—seeming to drift there, scarcely of his own will—locked and latched the door, then drifted back to the window. Bon-nie Jean and Sandra Mohrag were out there, making for Sandra's car. So B.J. wasn't alone. Sandra would go with her. But go where? And the Drakuls were out there, too . . . those silhouettes in that sinister car.

Suddenly there was strength in Harry's legs, in his body, even in his mind. It was the strength of desperation. Even if what he was doing was making no sense (and what was sense anyway, in his senseless world, where even now his various levels were trying to interface, yet afraid of doing so?) at least he would be doing *something*, depending on what B.J. was doing.

Right now she and Sandra were walking, very nearly running, across the cold black surface of the service road to the inn's small car park, and Sandra seemed to be—what, laughing?—as she fumbled keys from her purse. They were dressed for indoors but the temperature outside was well below zero. And Harry saw that at all times B.J. kept her back to the avenue of leafless trees back there, where hedgerows cast long shadows. The suspect car was some forty or fifty yards away, as yet motionless, but the furtive, barely visible figures inside appeared to be leaning forward, intent on what was happening . . .

As to what *was* happening:

"Laugh!" B.J. told Sandra, grinding the words out as the smaller girl got her driver's door open. "Keep right on laughing, and make it look good. I don't want those bastards thinking I know they're there. I want them to follow us!"

Laughing, doing a twirl, and dancing even—and while she danced daring to scan the area around, but fleetingly—Sandra said, "What bastards, B.J.? I don't see anyone!" Then she slid into her seat, and reached across to release the far catch for B.J.

"Don't look for them," B.J. growled. "Don't even think about them. One of them's a telepath. I can feel his slimy fingers groping at the edge of my mind. And don't put your seat-belt on! We may want to be out of here fast. Now listen: start up and drive slowly and carefully out onto the main road in the direction of Edinburgh."

"For the open country? There's a lot of open space between here and Edinburgh, B.J."

"Yes!" (The *bite* of B.J.'s words—and the hundred per cent guarantee of her intentions.)

"You're . . . what, luring them?" Sandra had seen the headlights in her rearview now, where a black saloon car turned on to the road less than a hundred yards behind.

"Yes!" B.J. snarled. "For Zahanine. And for me. I'm tired of being a target. Now tell me—that shotgun, and the cartridges Auld John sent me: still in the boot?"

"Yes. Your crossbow, too."

"And is it loaded? And are there spare bolts?"

"One spare bolt, yes. But B.J., who are they? I mean, are they Drakuls? And will they have guns, too?"

"Oh, yes—but they'll be loath to use them. Open country, but plenty of farms, buildings, pubs, along the way. And we'll have the element of surprise."

"Where will they think we're going?" Sandra's fear was beginning to show. But she was a moon-child and when push came to shove there'd be no fear. She would be like Zahanine, fearless. But she wouldn't *be* Zahanine, dead—not if B.J. could help it.

"They won't know where we're going, because we don't know," B.J. answered. "But they're surely interested. If we've been under observation at the inn—if they've been following our every move—it's so they can know everything about us. Maybe they learned a lesson that time up north, or maybe their rules have changed. But mine haven't! I think perhaps they wanted to take Zahanine alive, and if so they may want us that way, too. That gives us a double advantage: surprise on the one hand . . . and I couldn't give a *fuck* on the other! So slow down a little. We're going too fast, and I don't want them to think we're running."

"They seem to be keeping an even distance," Sandra's breath was coming more easily now. B.J.'s, too, as she continued to do her thinking out loud:

"But suppose they've only just found us? Margaret Macdowell was the one who led them to us, because she was the one who got left out when we moved. When they found Margaret, they only had to watch her movements until she joined up with us. But *how* did they find her, mainly locked away in Sma' Auchterbecky?"

"But haven't you often said that the watcher has known most of our movements for years?" Sandra wasn't thinking straight . . . Or maybe she was.

"The little man, the watcher, is a Ferenczy!" B.J. snapped . . . and paused. "But according to Radu the Drakuls were always the most furtive of their kind. So maybe you're right and they have been watching the watcher!"

"So why are they following us now?" (Sandra's logic at work again.) "I mean, since they now know where we're hiding . . . ?"

"But they don't know for sure that we're all there," B.J. answered. And to herself: *And then there's Harry. Do they know about Harry? About his involvement up in the Spey Valley, when we took out their two colleagues?*

"B.J.—where are we going?" The fear was back in Sandra's voice. "The roads are treacherous and it's starting to snow. We can't just drive forever!"

B.J. glanced out of her window. There was a farm with outbuildings coming up on the left. "Slow down a little more," she said . . . then sighed her relief as the car behind them likewise slowed down. Another quarter-mile and they passed a long, open-ended, barn-like structure behind the high hedge that lined the road. Further yet, a four-barred gate stood open. And: "There," B.J. said. "Drive in there, turn left, go back to the barn."

"But they'll see us," Sandra gasped. "They're only a hundred yards behind us, and we're the only ones on the road." She slowed the car to a crawl, and the snow came down harder yet.

"I know," B.J. snapped. "I *want* them to see us! Do it."

And Sandra did it. Inside the field, a potholed metalled track led to the barn, in fact a large animal shelter and feeding station. Dipping the car's lights, Sandra drove inside and stopped, switched off the motor and lights, handed the keys to B.J.

B.J. was out of the car in a moment. Her night-vision served her well; she had taken the weapons from the boot, returned to Sandra's window, handed her the shotgun and the keys before the headlights of the saloon had cut their first swathe across the empty field. But as the headlights dimmed and scythed jerkily in B.J.'s direction:

"Stay there," she told Sandra. "Anyone comes to the window, don't hesitate but shoot the bastard! Move your body inside the car . . . pretend you're talking, laughing. My headrest will fool them into thinking we're both still in there. And Sandra, don't worry. I'll be right here."

Then, as the dipped beams from the black saloon reached for the feeding station, found it and blinked out, B.J. disappeared into the shadows—

—But she didn't go far.

The station was simply a large, open-ended, timber-built shelter. On both sides, bales of fodder were stacked almost to the low ceiling behind fencing so gapped that animals would be able to get their heads through. There was also a water trough, and stout wooden ladders that climbed to a loft so loaded with hay it sagged in the middle.

Then, as the sound of the Drakul saloon's engine died away, B.J. slipped between the bars of the fence into the musty-smelling darkness between aisles of stacked hay . . .

* * *

The saloon was a spacious five-seater. And the dead man, R.L. Stevenson Jamieson, had been right: all five seats were in use. Within the vehicle, as the hot engine cooled and slowly ticked into silence, and the wipers scratched a little as they arced to and fro, clearing wet snow from the cold, curved windscreen, four Drakul thralls waited for orders. The fifth member of the party—the new leader of the group—sat in the front passenger seat, staring forward through his arc of blurred glass.

One of the three in the back smoked a perfumed cigarette, a rare luxury. In the Drakesh Monastery, such was not allowed: inhuman vices took precedence over the merely human. But smoking was only one of this man's vices. His face bore testimony to that: sterile dressings, taped in place over hollow, badly scarred cheeks.

"So, they are waiting for someone." The leader—the lieutenant seconded by Drakesh from India and recently arrived in Scotland—turned to the thrall with the scars and said, "You . . . have some *experience* of Radu's people, yes? Did you recognize these women?"

"As his thralls?" the man answered. "Yes. One of them is called Sandra Mohrag. I didn't see the other's face. But what does it matter what they're called? They're his thralls, certainly. And all of them shapely, good-looking women. Or bitches!" His grin, twisted by the dressings, was sallow, shallow, and ugly.

"Their shapes and looks do not concern me," the leader's answer was cold, emotionless. "Only their knowledge. And this time we want at least one of them . . . alive?" His meaning was obvious. But the scarred man protested:

"That was an accident! We were waiting for the man, this Harry Keogh. It wasn't planned that the black girl—"

"—But," the leader cut him short, "this time there can be no accidents. And better still if there is no gunfire. Do try to remember that. And do not disappoint me, for if you do you also disappoint the last true Drakul. The 'accident' with the black girl was—what?—an opportunity wasted? Try not to waste this one. Now go, and hurry. For if they are waiting for someone, we do not want to be here when that someone arrives. Or, if it should be this Harry, then we *will* want to be here, most certainly. But until we may—question?—we may not know."

The thrall with the scarred face, and his companion from the Zahanine killing, left the car, melted into the shadows of the hedge, moved silently towards the animal shelter. As they went the scarfaced man took out his automatic and screwed its silencer in place on the muzzle. No gunfire? Oh, really? That was all very well, but he had seen how these bitches fought!

The shelter loomed close, a dark blot behind the diagonally slicing snow. Closer still, and there was movement, animation in the car. At the wheel a female figure moved, nodded her head, leaned this way and that, and laughed! Not for much longer, however.

Scarface took the passenger side. The other crouched low, crossed behind the car, inched his way to the driver's window. And as laughter sounded again from within, he wrenched at the handle, yanked the door open, and came to his feet all in one movement. In the next moment he was reaching inside with both arms, reaching for the girl where she sat at the wheel.

Sandra felt his hands touch her neck, shoved the shotgun cradled on her knees into his lower belly, pulled on one trigger. It was almost a repeat performance of the scene at Inverdruie, when Auld John killed Vincent Ragusa. The Drakul didn't know what had hit him. With rags of clothing flapping, and his lower intestines uncoiling from his blackened flesh, he lifted from his feet, sailed backwards, broke his spine on the fence as he crashed through it. The sound of the blast was deadened by walls of fodder all around, all but lost in the moaning of the wind and the hissing of the snow. While on the other side of the car:

Acting in perfect co-ordination with his number two, the thrall with the facial dressings had first tested, then likewise snatched his door open—in time to see the flash of the detonation, and hear its muffled *boom!*—as the figure of his comrade was hurled back out of sight. Then, moving with frenzied speed, he got his right arm and gun hand inside the car; but his target was already slipping out of the driver's door.

He instinctively reached after her, at the same time wondering: *But where is her passenger?*

The answer came with the three-inch claws that sank deep through the cloth of his jacket and shirt into his shoulder at the neck, yanking him backwards from the car, and in the fiery gaze of scarlet, luminous triangular eyes that stared unblinking at him from no more than twelve inches away, in the split-second before his weapon was batted aside, sent spinning from nerveless fingers.

Nerveless, yes, for he was merely a thrall. Oh, a vampire, but still only a thrall, not even a lieutenant. While *this* . . .

. . . This was Wamphyri!

B.J. Mirlu was only part-woman now, a very small part. But three-quarters of her was wolf, and not *just* wolf but werewolf. She had needed no full moon, only her rage, and the strength of her will. The rest had been reflex, automatic, and monstrously easy—as easy as that time a few weeks ago when Margaret Macdowell had been threatened. During daylight hours metamorphosis would have been highly improbable, if not impossible. At night, a time like this, when B.J. was so troubled and so furious . . . ? She *was* Wamphyri, and the puny man-thing she held oh-so-easily in one awful talon-like hand—while the other rested lightly on his jacket's breast pocket, feeling the pulse of his fluttering heart—knew it.

He looked at her (he could *only* look at her and do nothing else), at that forward-leaning, leering white beast. Looked at the shock of white, bristling ruff framing a face that somehow managed to retain something of B.J.'s humanity; at her figure, taller by inches than his own, like a rangy upright bitch-dog; at slavering jaws that cracked open, revealing teeth that made his own vampire fangs seem entirely insignificant. Looked, and shuddered, and might have screamed but was held breathless by those eyes. For Bonnie Jean Mirlu was a beguiler, and the fire in her eyes robbed him of all strength of will. Those eyes . . . intent upon the dressings on his face! And B.J.'s mind, remembering the bloody skin she had seen under poor dead Zahanine's nails.

White foam dripped from the corner of her terrible mouth as she lifted her free, nine-inch paw from his chest to strip away the dressings, and red fire seemed to drip from her eyes when she saw his scars. Then—

—Those eyes opened wider yet, became gateways to hell, and freed him of his paralysis as they smiled! But there are smiles and there are smiles, and B.J.'s entire face, her entire *being*, smiled . . . except this was a smile that the Drakul wouldn't have time to remember. Not in this world.

As her needle nails dug deeper yet into his shoulder and neck, his scream came bubbling up over a wriggling tongue but found no outlet. For B.J. had closed her mouth on his face! A gurgle was all he could manage, as the bones of his face *crunched* under those jaws. And lifting him off his feet—lifting him *by* the face—she shook him like a terrier shakes a rat, and tossed him aside . . .

Overhead, there was sudden movement. The hayloft creaked. A presence?

B.J.'s senses, more than the usual five now, went out and up . . . discovered nothing but a trickle of dust, and a handful of straw, spilling through gaps in the loft's floorboards. But it gave her an idea . . .

All of this action had taken mere moments. Back in the saloon, the three Drakuls had heard what might have been a dull explosion, but they had seen nothing. The wipers were having a hard time keeping the snow off the windscreen, and their breath was steaming up the inside of the car.

When the feeding station suddenly came bursting alive with light, however, they saw *that* clearly enough!

Then the leader gasped, "What the—?" For the light wasn't a car's side- or headlights. It was fire!

The shelter was on fire, and *well* on fire. Fire leapt from bale to tinder-dry bale in the fenced area, licked up the walls and was carried by the wind end to end of the loft. So that in a very few seconds the structure was lit up like day; brighter, as Sandra's car lights came on and she revved her engine, driving out of the far side of the blazing shelter.

The Drakul lieutenant could scarcely believe his eyes. The car swerved, U-turned, came skidding and fishtailing back past the burning outbuilding and onto the farm track. It came head on, apparently on a collision course! But the Drakul driver had had the presence of mind to switch on his engine; he was reversing along the track. Blinded by Sandra's oncoming headlights, he jerked his wheel and skidded backwards off the metalled surface. And Sandra's car howled by in a derisive wail of her horn, with Bonnie Jean's face—human now—laughing like a madwoman from her wound-down window.

Shaken up, bounced about inside their vehicle, which they were lucky hadn't rolled, the Drakuls weren't able to use their weapons and would be loath to do so anyway. But as Sandra's car left the field for the open road, the leader yelled: "Drive to the fire! Quickly!" And the driver bumped the saloon back onto the track and did as he'd been ordered.

The shelter was a furnace now, where impaled on opposing fence posts twin figures jerked, writhed and burned in the merciless heat. And the lieutenant knew that this wasn't the work of mere thralls, nor even of a creature of his own status.

"That woman," he hissed, throwing up a hand to shield his eyes from the glare. "The one who laughed at us . . . ?"

"B.J. Mirlu," his driver gasped. "But how did she—?"

"—Enough!" the lieutenant snapped, cutting him short. He believed he knew how, but had no desire to demoralize his men more yet. And so: "Away from here now," he said. "For there's no helping those two . . . No helping any of this mess, and that fire will soon attract attention. Now we have to put distance between. So head for the Highlands. Revenge comes later . . . "

Harry had seen it all. Dimly, through gaps in the loft's plank flooring, he'd seen it . . . and still couldn't believe his eyes. Following the cars had been easy: a series of Möbius jumps from his room along the hedgerow that paralleled the mainly deserted road. As for his plan: there hadn't been one. Only to make himself available if B.J. needed him. How he would have explained his presence in the event he had to show himself . . . Harry hadn't given it a thought. There'd been no time for thinking, only for worrying about B.J.

When her car had turned into the field and driven on into the ramshackle shelter of the feeding station, he'd made a last jump to the musty loft, got down on his stomach and waited. And with his eyes gradually adjusting to the gloom, he had managed to follow most of the action.

He had seen B.J. get out of the car and slip through the fence into the narrow spaces between the stacks of baled hay—and he had also seen what came out of there. Much worse, there was a name for it. Then, he'd seen what she did to the Drakuls. That hideous strength: to be able to lift a man, and drive him down onto a fence post with such force as to impale him.

But he had it wrong, surely? And now, along with his other senses, he couldn't trust his eyes either! *Oh, and what of his ears?* "For Zahanine." B.J. had said, before she ran out of the inn with Sandra.

For Zahanine?

The black girl, in his study. The stain on the floor, that he'd hidden under a piece of carpet from his front room . . .

Now he stood wet and miserable in the sleeting snow by the roadside. The tail lights of B.J.'s car were already disappearing in the direction of the inn, and the Drakul saloon was turning out of the field onto the road, heading the other way. The chase, or whatever it had been—B.J.'s lure, her trap?—was over and she had won. She'd won this round, anyway, but what of the rest of it?

Harry wasn't under orders. He'd been in such a bewildered, mentally confused condition that B.J. hadn't thought it necessary. Indeed, he had been like a child (no, he thought, not like a child; more like her "wee puppy," a little lapdog), following her around for so long now that she had almost forgotten he was ever anything else. And Harry had started—or wanted—to forget it, too. But he *had* been something else, and he was!

If only . . . if only the world would stand still a fucking minute and let him find his true orientation. He had to . . . to *stop* running from . . . from whatever it was.

Drakuls in their station-wagon, nose-diving off the road after he had bombed their car . . . The blazing wreck, and a lieutenant melting where he'd impaled himself on his steering column . . . His body fats slopping out from under the sprung door, flowing like candle wax around the shoulders of a dead vampire thrall . . . A thrall with one of B.J.'s silvered crossbow bolts buried in his heart!

Faster and faster the pictures came—a kaleidoscope of scenes flashing before his mind's eye—but all of them dreams and fancies, surely? The Necroscope couldn't control them. His computer-mind's limbo files were spilling over onto the screen of real life. It was what his mother and dead friends had most feared, and what B.J. had tried to eliminate from his life. It was the limbo interface, where Harry's various levels of consciousness were colliding and merging into chaos; but this time B.J. wasn't here to call him her wee man and put it right. And for the first time in a long time, he didn't want it put right. He wanted the truth, the whole truth and nothing but the truth, so help him . . .

". . . *G-God!*" He clutched at his head, sank to his knees in the slush at the side of the road.

He had seen B.J.—seen her *as she was!* Not as she pretended to be, but as she really was. *(But B.J. was innocent.)* Oh, really? No she fucking wasn't!

The truth and nothing but the truth. "Guilty, m'lud!"

"No, she *is* innocent!" (Harry shook his head, argued with himself.) "Everything else is fantasy, a dream, a nightmare—and I can prove it!"

A car went by, its headlights blazing. In passing, it sent twin waves of yellow slush over the Necroscope where he knelt in the snow on the dark verge of the road and the narrow rim of sanity. The sudden, freezing shock brought him upright and sent him stumbling—

—Stumbling through a hastily conjured Möbius door to the one place in the world where he could finally prove B.J.'s innocence. Or her guilt.

His house in Bonnyrig . . .

Now Harry slept, and slept "like a dead man."

For when, for the first time, he'd seen the work done on his patio windows—work he seemed to vaguely remember ordering—and after he'd rolled back the carpet on the study floor until the dark splotches of recent stains became visible, then the fatigue of uttermost confusion and panic had stepped in.

Then . . . it was his mental exhaustion that had saved him, at least for the time being. Not physical fatigue, for the Necroscope's *body* was in remarkably good shape, but mental.

The interface had worked against itself, draining Harry's teetering mind rather than toppling it over the edge. And he'd fallen deliriously asleep in his chair (or perhaps "lost consciousness" there) where gradually his whirling brain had settled into ordered patterns. And as the natural subconscious level of sleep had detached from the conscious, so his hypnotically manufactured levels had once again separated.

But the "floors" between the levels were fracturing, gradually sagging, and it was a very temporary reprieve . . .

Well into the night—vulnerable as never before but quite beyond caring—Harry slept dreamlessly, healingly. And as the mental fragmentation decreased, so his metaphysical mind became more receptive of outside influences. His barriers against the dead, normally enforced by strength of will, were down. And the Great Majority knew it, because Harry's lone flame flickered in their darkness as before, however weakly. So that when at last dreams came, they were more than just dreams.

First there was his beloved Ma, soothing, calming, careful. Her voice (neither chiding, or barely so, nor coddling) merely attempted to guide him, remind him of his teeming dead friends, and the fact that of all men he was not alone:

Harry, son. Have you foresaken us altogether, forever? It appears so. Where are you—where are your thoughts—that you no longer feel safe confiding in us? There was some pain in her voice, but far more of concern.

And just hearing her, the Necroscope knew what he had been missing for so long: his contact with the dead. But at last he had the oportunity to offer at least something of an explanation. "Ma, I can't, *daren't* talk to you," he said. "The talents I have—the things I can do, including *this* thing—have to remain my secret. And *only* mine, always. Even now, I shouldn't be speaking to you. But believe me, it isn't of my choosing."

In answer to which she asked the obvious question, and one that continued to baffle even Harry: *Not of your choosing? Then whose? Not the girl's—not that woman's, surely?—because she doesn't know about . . . your . . .* (And abruptly she broke off, so that he could sense her "biting her tongue." And even sleeping, Harry knew why: because *she* wasn't supposed to know about B.J. Mirlu!) But on the other hand, how long had he ever kept a secret safe from his Ma? What, when she could step into his dreams as readily as this? Why, he should have guessed that she knew a long time ago. Maybe he had at that. But he made no accusation; this was a time of reconciliation. And so:

"No, not Bonnie Jean!" he answered at once. "Because she . . . she's innocent?" His turn to pause abruptly, as yet again the facts and fictions of his existence gathered for conflict. For B.J.'s innocence wasn't proven yet, not entirely; nor yet her guilt, despite last night's evidence. But in any case his answer had been instinctive, an automatic response built into him through repetition. And now his Ma found herself treading very dangerous ground indeed. But at least she had recognized it, and the Necroscope's uncertainty.

And: *No, her innocence hasn't been proved yet, has it son?* she said. It wasn't a question that required an answer, just a statement of fact. But then—because she knew how close the interface had come to damaging him irreparably—she quickly changed the subject. *Your friends down here have really missed you, Harry; me especially. But we know how busy you've been.*

Busy? Had he been busy? It scarcely felt like it. Indeed his past, and his not so recent past at that, felt like years of nothing, like lost years.

Your search for Brenda and your son, his mother immediately explained, in perhaps too much of a hurry. *Which has taken up so much of your time!* Harry sensed the subterfuge, that she had meant something more. But it served to distract him anyway, leading him in a new direction:

"You've . . . had word of them?" (God, let it *not* be so!)

Oh, no! No, Harry. She was quick to reassure him. *Nothing like that. If they had come among us, we would know by now, be sure. We just, well, stay alert for them, that's all . . .*

And the Necroscope could breathe again . . . But still he felt that if this conversation was proving anything at all, it was that they shouldn't be having it! His weird talents seemed bent on leading him to more anxiety; every time he put them to use, or allowed their use, they took him into yet more tangled territory. And: "Ma," he said desperately, "please let it finish now . . . " She was his mother after all, and it went against the grain to simply erect his barriers and shut her out.

But: *Harry?* (It was a different, sterner voice that had taken over, but one that he knew almost as well—that of Sir Keenan Gormley, ex-Head of E-Branch.) And again the Necroscope was of two minds, and yet again his respect for a dead person was such that he couldn't ignore or turn away from him.

Sir Keenan knew it, of course, for Harry's thoughts were as good as spoken words to the dead. And: *Harry,* he said, *whatever this problem of yours is, it has to be pretty deep-rooted. I mean, who but the dead can ever know that you are the Necroscope? And even if it were possible, who among the teeming dead would ever betray you? All right, so you daren't display your knowledge and use of the Möbius Continuum. That's perhaps self-explanatory—the living could make use of such knowledge. But your ability to converse with the Great Majority? Your almost* unique *ability? Who among the living would believe it even if you told them? It sounds to me like an obsession, some kind of aversion, maybe a weird allergy. But if so, it has to have had a beginning. Why not try backtracking to the start of it?*

"You're right," Harry could see the logic of it. "It could be I'm becoming allergic to . . . to being me! And to doing what I do. But if that's true there are no pills that can help me—and no shrink. The nature of my problem would make it impossible to describe to him. And even if I could describe it, can't you just see me going to a psychiatrist and telling him that I don't like talking to my dead people any more? That would be a shortcut to the nearest madhouse, Keenan! And maybe . . . maybe that's where I'm headed anyway."

Don't talk like that, Harry! The other was angry now. *What, you, Harry Keogh, a defeatist? Huh! I don't think so. But maybe you're right and this is something you should work out for yourself, without help. In which case you've got to turn it over in your own mind, think back and try to find out where it began. It has to be worth a try, surely? For everything else in your life seems tied in to it, controlled by it. Why, it's alienating you from your own skills—and even from the dead . . .*

And now it was out in the open. Not only the Necroscope's Ma but all of the teeming dead seemed aware of his trouble. In a way it was reassuring: to know that they were there as ever, on his side. But in another way it was frightening: the spread of this forbidden knowledge abroad. The thing continued to go in circles, and Harry's head began to spin with it.

Sir Keenan felt his terrible confusion, the mental loop he was caught up in, and searched desperately for a way out of it. And the answer came to him like a bolt out of the blue.

Harry, my boy! he said, in a burst of excitement. *But why didn't I think of it before? That's it! And you really can do it! You can see a psychiatrist!*

"What!?" the Necroscope felt as if he had been banging his head against a wall. Didn't anyone ever listen to him any more? "But haven't I just explained that I—"

—*You can see someone who already knows your problems,* Sir Keenan cut him off. *Someone who believes in them totally—and in you!* And before he could finish:

"But there's no such . . . no such . . . *living* person," Harry almost shouted. Almost, but the last two words had come out in something of a whisper.

Exactly! said the other. *No such living person.*

And slowly Harry's head stopped whirling, because he knew what Sir Keenan meant: that some of the greatest minds who had ever lived *already* believed in him. Indeed a Great Majority of them! And as the idea took hold he said, "I'll try . . . try to keep that in mind," then gave a wry snort at his own unintentioned cleverness.

The fact that in his position he could still discover humour in any kind of situation or statement was hugely encouraging in itself. And as earnestly as ever, Sir Keenan said: *Yes, you do that, my boy. Keep it in mind. And we shall try to find the very best of help for you.*

But as the dead man's voice faded into the blown-leaf whispers and background static of tombs and tumuli, the Necroscope was suddenly very thoughtful. What he was thinking was this:

That maybe Sir Keenan wouldn't have to find anyone to help him. Maybe he had already found them for himself. Well, with a final bit of help from Alec Kyle, anyway . . .

In the morning, in that transitory period immediately prior to true waking, the Necroscope found himself pondering the previous night's traumatic experiences and wondering if, after all, they had only been part of some dreadful nightmare. More specifically, he wondered about Bonnie Jean.

What he had seen in the animal shelter had seemed so very real; but it had been dark during the period of B.J.'s metamorphosis (her "imagined" transition) so that even now he couldn't accept it for a fact. For surely he'd proved it to himself time and time again that she *was* innocent—of everything! In which case, why had he needed to prove it?

Or more properly, *what* had he needed to prove . . . ?

Currently, Harry wasn't "switched on"—which meant that his "reality" was in a state of flux. On various conscious and subconscious levels he knew something about everything that was real or that B.J. had initiated. He even remembered things that were unreal (about his search, for instance); but there was no single level on which he knew everything.

Last night, mental exhaustion had saved his sanity before the massed knowledge of all of his levels could interface, contradict, cancel each other out and leave him bereft. Today, his thoughts were "ordered" again, which meant that his reality was incomplete to the point of fragmentary.

But at least he *was* thinking about his condition, and not only thinking about it but considering a solution to one of its root causes. Which was the single salient possibility that had fixed itself in his mind since his conversation with Sir Keenan Gormley: that there could be a psychological—or metaphysical?—

solution to his problems, and that it might even be immediately available to him. As to why Harry had clung to this notion to the point of waking, when the rest of his "dream" was fading into obscurity . . . it was because it was all he had left.

And as that fact dawned, he sprang fully awake—

—Or groaned fully awake.

He felt like hell! Like that time he'd taken one of Darcy Clarke's sleeping pills at E-Branch HQ, just before he quit the Branch and headed north. Or the morning after he'd got drunk on B.J.'s wine. (And thank God he was out of *that* now!) But where in all the . . . ?

Then, as he opened his eyes, blinked them, ran his tongue over his furry teeth and looked around, he remembered and knew where. Bonnyrig. His house. His study.

And a piece of carpet, rolled back. And that stain on the floor. And his patio windows and frame, replaced, with the new wood still requiring staining.

Enemies, and they had been waiting for him. But Zahanine had been here, looking for him. On behalf of B.J.

It was part reasoning, part memory, but all come and gone in a flash. And only one word remaining: enemies.

But hadn't R.L. warned him that he had enemies? But what kind of enemies, and why? What had he ever done (no, what had he done *recently*, since leaving E-Branch) that had left him with such bad enemies?

You've got to be kidding! he told himself. *What have you done? What about Le Manse Madonie? What about all the millions that you've taken from drug barons and gang bosses and gun-runners all over the world?*

He went to the kitchen, made coffee, couldn't take it back to his study because deep inside he knew something terrible had happened the last time he had coffee in there. And so he drank it in the kitchen, and sat nursing his sore head.

Le Manse Madonie, Sicily. His raid on the treasure vault. That was quite some time ago. What else did he know about that place; why did he seem to remember hearing its name more recently? What was real and unreal here? *Did* he remember a conversation with B.J., when she'd mentioned Le Manse Madonie?

Her telephone conversation with Auld John, yes! When she'd told him to get out of his cottage in Inverdruie and find somewhere safe. Just like she'd told Harry to get out of his place. Shit, and here he was back again!

But he knew he had to be away from her, if only for a little while until he had sorted things out. And whatever else he did, he mustn't let his thoughts stray too far off course because he had some kind of pattern going here and didn't want to lose it.

What if . . . what if . . . what if . . .

What if B.J. wasn't the central figure here but Harry himself? What if *he* was the key, with everything revolving around him? What if he had tried—was trying—to transfer his guilt to her?

He gave a snort and thought: *Now I'm playing the amateur psychiatrist!* In his condition? Ridiculous! But what if . . . ?

What if those people at Le Manse Madonie (the Francezcis? That sounded wrong. Another name was sitting there on the tip of his tongue but he would not, dare not let it out), what if *they* had somehow managed to track him down? Darcy Clarke had warned him how dangerous they were. And poor Bonnie Jean had got herself involved through her involvement with him. It worked!

Oh, yes, it worked . . . but it had holes a mile wide. Like his head, his memory, and his whole fucking life since leaving E-Branch . . . !

. . . Sir Keenan had promised to find him the best possible help, but Harry had believed there might be a metaphysical solution available right here and now. He realized how close that idea had come to escaping him and slipping into limbo with the rest of his dream, and now clung to it anew.

When he'd been with Darcy and Ben down at E-Branch just a few days, a week, a fortnight ago—what, a fortnight? Really? Even time was completely fucked up!—he had experienced these weird visitations. He could only believe they were Alec Kyle's last shot before whatever was left of his precognitive talents followed him into eternity.

But "precog" was the key word: it was what Alec had been, and so far every one of Harry's "visions" of a like nature had turned out to be glimpses of the future. Which might mean that he was yet to meet the bearded mystic of the first vision, and yet to visit that graveyard near Meersburg, in real life. *Huh!* So far he didn't even know where Meersburg was—but it might prove interesting to find out. For the place had been a cemetery after all, and what else would the Necroscope Harry Keogh be doing in a cemetery if not talking to the dead?

Avoiding looking at the floor, he went to his study for a World Atlas, took it back to the kitchen. And in a little while—for the first time in a long while—he collapsed his barriers and deliberately contacted the dead. It wasn't easy, but he fought his psychosis and did it, and shortly:

Harry, were you looking for me? (Sir Keenan Gormley, from his Garden of Repose in Kensington, London.)

"Yes, sir, I was." (Harry, in his usual, most respectful mode once more.) "I believe we talked, last night? You gave me some good advice, and offered to help. And I promised to think it over. Now I'd like to take you up on it. You mentioned some of the best psychiatric minds that had ever lived, meaning of course that a good many are now dead. A bad deal for them—no disrespect— but useful to me, for they're the only ones I can talk to. So do you happen to know of anyone in Meersburg, Lake Constance, on the German-Swiss border?"

Meersburg? Harry, can I get back to you? I mean, will you be . . . receptive? Sir Keenan was almost embarrassingly eager.

"It's not that easy any more," Harry saw no point in pretending it was. "I mean, I don't like leaving myself open like this. But I'll try, yes."

Then give me a little time, Sir Keenan told him, "breathlessly," *for now I've some enquiries to make. I'll be quick as I possibly can about it . . .*

With which he was gone, and Harry was obliged to leave his barriers down.

And as he had expected might happen, the dead—or one of them—was quick to take advantage of that fact. He had thought it might be his mother, trying to reach him in his waking hours as she had "invaded" him in (how many?) dreams, but in fact the presence he felt was that of R.L. Stevenson

Jamieson. And again the Necroscope was loath to turn him away; R.L. had long since proved his worth and loyalty.

Er, you reckon you can spare me a little time, too, Necroscope? Sensing Harry's anxiety and vulnerability, R.L. was reticent in his approach.

"R.L.," Harry answered, "do I seem that ungrateful?"

Well, you ain't bin all that easy to reach, if that's what you mean, R.L. told him. And then, hurriedly: *But that's OK, man. I mean, it ain't everybody got your problems, right?*

"What can I do for you, R.L.? Only please make if quick, for I'm expecting some stuff that could be very important."

It's more what I'll do for you, Necroscope, R.L. answered. *Like, I can maybe relieve you o' some o' your worries, anyhow.*

"Worries?"

'Bout your enemies, man. You don't got a one right now—least, not in your neck o' the woods. They has all gone north.

"They what?"

You is in your house, right?

"That's right."

Well, your enemies is all up north. Not a one o' 'em left in your vicinity. Not the real bad serious ones, anyways . . .

Harry frowned. "Oh, and what other kind are there, R.L.?"

But R.L. had said enough, maybe even too much. And anyway his obi was as badly confused with regard to B.J. Mirlu and her girls as Harry himself. They had done the Necroscope no real or physical harm so far, but they had one hell of a bad aura about them. Harry's Ma had confirmed to R.L. just what that aura was, but he couldn't tell Harry about it. It was one of those things the Necroscope must find out for himself. And so:

Oh, you knows, he hedged. *There's always the bad folks out there, lookin' to make a mark. But if you aims to stay clear o' trouble, then just don't go into those mountains.*

And again Harry's frown, as he asked, "Oh? And what do you know about mountains, R.L.?"

Only what my obi tells me, R.L. lied, which was so out of character for a dead man that Harry didn't pick it up or question it. But he certainly sensed R.L.'s hasty withdrawal.

Or maybe that was only to make way for someone else. And:

Harry, you were right! Sir Keenan's excitement was infectious. *I won't ask you how, but you picked the very spot: Meersburg on Lake Constance, on the German-Swiss border. Do you have any idea who is buried there?*

Harry shook his head, which was as good as an answer.

Then I suggest you go there and find out, Sir Keenan told him. *Don't wait but do it today, the sooner the better.*

The Necroscope looked out of his kitchen window at a grey, gloomy dawn. "Well, not just yet," he said edgily. "I'm hungry, breakfast, one or two things to do first. But in an hour or so, when the world's had time to wake up . . . maybe then."

The other sensed his reticence. *Oh? Can it be that you're frightened, my boy? Of what you might discover?*

Harry shook his head. "No . . . Yes . . . Maybe. I don't know."

But you'll do it anyway?

Harry sighed. "It might help if I knew who I was going to see! Who do I ask for once I'm there: 'Hey, you?' What's the big mystery, Keenan? Look, you tell me who we're talking about, and I'll tell you if I'll go and see him." (He kept hidden the fact that his going was already a foregone conclusion.)

But you see, the other tried to explain, *what this man was famous for . . . it wasn't known as psychiatry. In his time psychiatry was in its infancy. But as to what he actually did . . . well, he was one of the best. So much so that his "science" took his name. And after all this time, well, maybe he's even better at it now.* Sir Keenan was talking about the fact that what men have done in life, they'll usually continue to do after death.

"But what did he do?" Harry wanted to know, and he was becoming impatient now.

He was one of the greats, Sir Keenan was uncomfortable. *He really was. But they cried him down—there was a great deal of ignorance—and it took away much of his faith in himself. You may have to rebuild it, Harry. See, it's not just a question of him helping you, but of you getting him to help you!*

"What?"

But you've done it before! Sir Keenan reminded him. *Möbius himself needed convincing, before he was able to help you.*

"Möbius was one of a kind," the Necroscope replied.

And so is Franz Anton, said the other.

"Franz Anton?"

Franz Anton Mesmer, Sir Keenan sighed at last. *That's who we're talking about, son. And that's where he is: in a cemetery in Meersburg, on the shore of Lake Constance . . .*

II

MESMERISM

A S HE HAD TOLD SIR KEENAN GORMLEY, THE NECROSCOPE HAD THINGS TO
do. But mainly, he wanted to think. Crunching his way through a bowl of
ancient cornflakes soaked in suspect milk, and drinking a second mug of
coffee, he tried ordering his thoughts. In fact, now that his mental hangover
was dissipating they were as clear as he could remember in a long time.

Of course his memory was shot to hell, for as well as the things he was forbidden to remember, there were those he didn't want to. And there were others that weren't his anyway. And the giant jigsaw puzzle that his life had become
seemed still to be missing at least seventy per cent of its pieces. So that he must
build it as a real jigsaw, starting on one corner first.

Oddly enough, he was fairly certain that B.J. Mirlu held the box that the
puzzle had come in . . . but he knew she wasn't going to show it to him. She
didn't want him to see the entire picture. For his own good? Maybe. Or maybe
not. But every time he thought things like that, the indisputable fact of her innocence would immediately spring to mind. And he suspected he'd be in serious trouble (or yet *more* serious trouble) if he were ever to prove himself wrong
in that respect.

Another paradox: he knew she could fix it, put everything right, but that
it would only be temporary. For whenever she'd "fixed things" in the past, it
had only ever led to periods of even greater confusion.

And so for the moment the Necroscope was pleased to stay away from her,
at least until he'd got this corner of the puzzle fitted together. But *staying* away
from her . . . would be a problem in itself. There was something about the
moon. At the moment it wasn't problematic, but in a week to ten days—

—It would be full again . . .

Then, he would have to contact her . . .

Deep inside, some inner contradictory voice corrected him: he even wanted to contact her now—if only to hear her voice—because her lure was twofold. The one that she had imposed, and the one that had grown in him. He didn't know about the first, but the second was probably love. And he suspected, hoped, that it had grown in her, too. Yet another reason why he didn't want to be proved wrong about her.

Harry closed his eyes and the frame of his kitchen window stayed frozen on his retinas: a blob of fuzzy light, gradually dissolving at the corners and rounding itself off . . . *Like the moon at its full, pale and featureless in a misted sky, with a wolf's head in silhouette thrown back in an ululant howl.*

He shook his head and the picture was gone, but B.J. was still there, like a magnet in his mind. And mazed, bewildered, he felt drawn to her, beguiled by her . . . hypnotized by her?

Hypnotism. Something about a graveyard in Meersburg? The connection was made and Harry was drawn back to earth, back to the present. Again he shook his head, blinked, and resolved to go and talk to Franz Anton Mesmer.

But before that there was still something he must do. B.J. would be worried about him; he could at least allay her fears.

Except he knew he mustn't talk to her. For then she would want to fix things. Just a few soothing words and he'd be back to square one. So . . . why not get someone else to speak to her on his behalf?

He went back to his study, to the telephone. The light on his answering machine was blinking. He instinctively wound the tape back and went to hit the play button . . . then paused. And shaking his head: *No, not this time,* he told himself. It could only be one person, and the end result would be the same.

He got out his telephone book, looked up the inn where he had been staying with B.J. and the girls, dialled the number.

The receptionist answered and he said, "Miss, my name is Harry Keogh. I was staying at your place until last night?"

"Oh?" the answer came back. "Miss Mirlu's party?"

"That's right," Harry said. "And now I have a message for her."

"Hold on and I'll put you through. In fact you're just in time, for in a little while she'll be booking out."

"No!" Harry said, perhaps a little too sharply. "Er, no, don't put me through. Just take a message, will you?"

"Whatever you say." (But she sounded puzzled.)

"We . . . had a little tiff," Harry lied. "So, I don't want to speak to her. But—"

"—But you do?" The receptionist gave a low, sympathetic laugh. "I think I understand. So what's the message?"

"Tell her I'm OK and she's not to worry about me," Harry said. "And tell her I'll know where to find her when the time's right. But I want you to warn her, too."

"Warn her?" There was a worried note in the receptionist's voice now. "Now just hold on a minute. I'm not going to pass on any threatening messages to a—"

"No, no threats," Harry cut her off. "Look, this is important. Just tell her that next time she goes north she's to keep her eyes peeled. There are people up there she would do well to avoid, OK?"

"Well, I don't know if . . . "

"Help a couple of lovers out, right?"

"Oh, all right then." And the smile was back in her voice again.

"Thanks," said Harry, and put the phone down.

Then he went upstairs and got his heavy overcoat. It would be cold on Lake Constance this time of year . . .

And it was. Normally, lacking a formal introduction, and therefore co-ordinates, the Necroscope would have had to find his way by trial and error, obliged to proceed in a series of cautious Möbius jumps. But in fact he *did* have the co-ordinates; they had been there in his metaphysical mind ever since he'd pre-visioned this visit during his stay at E-Branch HQ in London.

Therefore, in precisely the same way as he had been previously enabled to find Le Manse Madonie, and the Drakesh Monastery, he was able to make a single jump to Mesmer's last resting place. Or to the graveyard, at least. All he needed do was recall to mind the vision he'd had, let the location enter itself into his computer mind, and aim himself in that direction via a Möbius door.

Then, when he vacated the Continuum . . . he was there.

He stood at the crossroads of his vision. On the one hand, beyond a low stone wall, the mainly untended plots and leaning headstones of the cemetery were half-obscured by long grasses. While on the other a faded signpost said "Meersburg," pointing the way to a near-distant town whose silhouette shimmered on a backdrop of shining water.

But Harry wasn't here for the view.

Following the weed-grown wall until he found an iron gate standing half open, he went into the graveyard and for a minute or two wandered between the plots, letting his feet simply take him where they would. It was very peaceful, quiet, and not too bitterly cold; but south-west beyond the town and lake, seeming suspended in the clear clean air, he could make out blue, snow-capped, distantly-rising mountains. Then, if only for a moment, the *peace* of the moment seeped into him.

There was a spell on the place, which the Necroscope was loath to break. But he knew he must. And: "Franz Anton?" Harry spoke out loud, secure in his loneliness. "Sir, you don't know me, but I was told you were here."

Don't know you? The answer came at once. *Oh, but I do! I can even see you, in a fashion; I can see your flame, and feel its warmth. And I haven't seen or felt anything in a long time. Don't know you? But most of us know you by now, Necroscope. Or we've heard of you, anyway. And now . . . it's an honour to meet you personally.*

It came as no surprise to Harry to find himself standing at the foot of Mesmer's simple grave; his talent, or "natural" instinct, had led him here. But as usual, he didn't quite know how to deal with the praise and the compliments that the Great Majority were wont to offer him—especially hearing them from someone like Mesmer.

But he was mindful of what Sir Keenan had told him: that this great man had lost a lot of faith in himself, and how he might have to restore it before he in turn could benefit from his visit. And so:

"Sir," he said. "I won't beat about the bush. I'm here to ask a favour of you."

Yes, I know, said Mesmer in a little while, very quietly. *And Harry, I only wish I could help you. But I may not be able to.*

"Sir?"

You're not the only one with problems, Harry, Mesmer told him. *And I have had mine—oh, a lot longer than you have had yours!*

"Do you care to explain?" The Necroscope tucked his overcoat's tails under him and sat on the rim of Mesmer's slab. "I have the time if you do." And he sensed the other adjusting to and appreciating his living presence. Then:

Did you know, Harry, Mesmer began with a sigh, *that as a youngster I was much taken with Paracelsus's theories? Older, I mainly discarded them. But I remember when I was thirty-one, I passed my medical examinations—with honours, I may say—and my thesis was much influenced by Paracelsus. Horace supplied the heading or motto for that work of mine:*

> "Multa renascentur, quae jam cecidere cadentque,
> Quae nunc sunt in honore . . . "

Do you know Latin, Necroscope? Ah, no! A stupid question! For it's a "dead" language now, of course. But in any case the languages of the dead are all one to you.

"And they often convey more than is actually said," Harry pointed out. "You thought it in Latin, but I understood anyway:

" 'Much will rise again that has long been buried, and much become submerged which is held in honour today.' "

He sensed Mesmer's nod. *Especially relevant, it would now appear. Or perhaps not? The words seem applicable—applied to yourself, that is: your discoveries, your "friends" and mode of life?—but not in the sense intended. And never in connection with myself!* (Harry heard his sigh.) *Just another contradiction and my life was full of them! I was so . . . undoctorlike! So unprofessional. This constant searching for—this actual belief in—a metaphysical medium in which I might work entirely physical cures. Thus my work remains "buried," in no wise "held in honour," to this day. Plainly my reasoning was awry. But as has since been proved, my reasons for reasoning thus were very well founded. Small consolation. In any case, I see no cause to deny what I was never ashamed of. My beliefs and systems were in accord with the age, primitive, and my conclusions incorrect.*

"A great many thousands of people have benefited from your hypnosis," the Necroscope told him. "You were the first medical practitioner to recognize—or invent?—it."

(Mesmer's unseen shrug, by no means complacent, perhaps a little despondent?) *There were others who worked similar veins. But "inventor?"—scarcely! Why, the first true adepts weren't even men but creatures of nature! The snake, for example—*

"—And the octopus? I've heard how they 'mesmerize' crustacea, crabs and such—before eating them."

Really?

"So it would seem. Fascination, focused through the eyes or the mind behind them. A sort of living magnetism. But didn't you call it just that: 'Animal Magnetism'? Magnetisn, yes: beguilement or hypnotism. Mainly, it's your contribution we recognize: Mesmerism." It might be flattery, but it was largely the truth. While the sciences of the mind—and in Harry's case, mind over matter—had long since eroded and even obliterated Mesmer's contributions, still his work had been a landmark.

And you tell me it has been beneficial? D'you know, Harry, but in life, the last quarter century of my life at least—especially after I returned to Switzerland and semiretirement—I scarcely bothered to follow all the developments, the mutations taking place in my *science? I knew nothing of what went on outside myself. My theories had been so thoroughly and frequently ridiculed that even I had begun to lose faith! In 1814 Wolfart published my life work. But much too late. It was already out of date.*

Likewise in death: I have been too slow, too lax, too . . . disillusioned? And now you tell me my work is beneficial? Well, to tell the truth, I am not totally out of touch. Indeed, since you came along, the teeming dead have never been more in touch! But as I hinted, I haven't been taking notice. As in life, I've stuck to my own guns and ignored everyone else's. Now I am left alone with nothing more than my own theories. "Quack" theories, as I'm sure you'll appreciate. My "fluidum," indeed! I see how ridiculous it seems now. But I am a man of habit, as you see.

How was Harry to read that? Was Franz Anton Mesmer the odd man out? The only one of the teeming dead to refute the old law that in death a man will continue to do what he did in life? By continuing to isolate himself—at first from his contemporaries and detractors, and now from more recent practitioners—he may have done just that! And so the Necroscope was disappointed and frustrated. By now Mesmer should be one of the greatest, or even *the* greatest, hypnotist of all time. But not if he'd abandoned his art, or failed to follow it through. So perhaps Harry had come to the wrong man, the wrong place after all.

Beneficial, Mesmer mused again. *Well, I suppose so. In the reduction of pain, at least. But as the plaything of fakirs and stage magicians? What, to make men bark like dogs or quack like ducks?* His thoughts had turned sour; he was losing interest.

"What about psychiatry, psychoanalysis?" Harry challenged him. "Nothing bogus or theatrical about that. And your work is a foundation stone, perhaps *the* foundation stone!"

Do you think so? It's very kind of you to say so. And of course I have made advances . . . well, theoretical advances, at least, if only in my own mind. For down here there has been no one to practice on; I haven't—what, magnetized?—anyone in a long time. And being dead, incorporeal, sightless, is hardly conducive to practical experimentation! It has been, shall we say, something of a disadvantage? (It was the closest the dead man had come to humour, however dry.) *I have thought about it, certainly. But how may I exert my will to influence or "hypnotize" someone I can't even see?*

"I'm not sure, sir," Harry answered. "That's why I'm here: in order to find out."

You came here to consult me? In my . . . professional capacity? In death? Despite that I was discredited in life?

Obviously flattery wasn't going to suffice. The Necroscope saw now that indeed Mesmer no longer had faith in himself, and it was all-important that he should have. For if he was without faith, how could he expect his subject to have any? Harry understood how in large part it is the subject's belief in hypnotism that makes it work. But still:

"I need someone to examine me," he doggedly persisted. "To hypnotize me, look inside my head and tell me what's gone wrong in there. Since you have had a hundred and seventy years to perfect your art, I supposed you would be my best bet. That was my line of reasoning, and it's why I came here to see you."

Ah, but you're one hundred and seventy years too late! For I am dead, after all! How may someone who is ex-animate examine the living? And then, quickly, as if to change the subject:

But the way you came here—this miracle of instantaneous travel! What manner of new science is this?

For the moment—despite his frustration—the Necroscope allowed himself to be sidetracked from the main purpose of his visit . . . or perhaps not. For he had learned how to argue with the best (or worst) of them, and was quick to see how Mesmer's interest in *his* weird talents might provide a key to the door that the good doctor seemed to have locked on his own hypnotic skills. And so he said, "A science, sir?"

But if not magic, how else would you describe it? Mesmer couldn't understand Harry's hesitancy, the pause of a few seconds in which his mind worked overtime to develop his plan of campaign, his word game. And:

"A new science," he eventually mused . . . and denied it in a moment. "Well, scarcely! For as far as I'm aware and excluding my lost son, I'm its sole practitioner! It isn't something I can publish, for the math is alien, metaphysical. The equations don't equate, and the formulae mutate within themselves. And as you'll appreciate, if a formula isn't constant it isn't a formula."

Mesmer tried to understand him, gave up and said: *Myself, I was no great mathematician. Are you saying . . . you're so far ahead of your time you would be misunderstood?*

Harry nodded. "I suppose so. Much like yourself, in your time. Oh, I could 'prove' what I do, but even so I'd probably be called a charlatan, a fraud, a trickster or stage magician, as you were. We see men on our television screens who 'fly' or make massive monuments 'disappear,' or read the minds of their audiences. Sometimes they 'converse' with the dead, too! They are fakers, of course. Yet at the same time, I am living proof that the physical and metaphysical are definitely linked. You were ridiculed—worse, you now ridicule yourself!—for having sought or 'invented' a metaphysical medium or 'fluidum' in order to explain your physical cures. Yet even now we can't be sure that the fluidum doesn't in fact exist."

But of course we can be sure, because it hasn't been discovered! Mesmer was hooked . . . not only on their philosophical exchange but more probably, the Necroscope thought, on the notion, the forlorn hope, that perhaps in proposing his theories he hadn't been such a quack after all.

"I'm not sure I understand you," Harry answered, knowing full well Mesmer's meaning but feigning ignorance. "Not discovered? But neither have we explored the deepest ocean floor, yet we're sure it's there!"

I mean that in your modern age of radio waves, X-rays and gamma rays, and what have you—in the super-scientific world in which you live—there has not been discovered the tiniest, remotest germ of evidence to support the existence of any kind of fluidum! I mean that if it was there, your scientists would have found it. I am not that much out of touch, Necroscope!

Harry pounced:

"And yet there is an entirely physical, universal force, with universal laws that are universally accepted, whose influence within metaphysical or near-metaphysical spheres is extraordinary and entirely inexplicable! To give you a clue, it was 'discovered' by Sir Isaac Newton, who died seven years before you were born."

Gravity? Well, a fluidum of sorts, granted. But metaphysical? I have to say pish! We see its effects every day, and as you say, its laws are visible and universally accepted.

"Its physical laws," Harry nodded. "But can its other side be explained as easily?"

What other side?

"But didn't one of your 'quack' theories consider the motion of planetary bodies contributory to the ailments of *human* minds and bodies? Wasn't that what your fluidum theory was all about?" Harry sensed an incorporeal frown and quickly went on:

"The moon, sir! It lures the tides, you'll agree?"

Yes.

"And the fluid balance of the brain, to turn men and creatures into lunatics? So weren't you right after all?"

Gravity, my fluidum?

"Perhaps," Harry shrugged. "Who knows? And I've only given you one example of the moon's influence."

Eh?

"Isn't a woman's cycle governed by the phases of the moon? And what was unknown in your time, and probably unknown to you even now, a myriad ocean polyps and corals all around the world spawn together and turn the sea to milk, all in resonance with the moon."

But—

"—And sunspots?"

What?

"Disturbances on the surface of the sun. Whirlpools in its plasma. They interfere with our radio waves, television, communications in general. And the sun's rays cause cancers. So who can say about the other heavenly bodies?"

I was right then? (Mesmer was utterly fascinated now.) *As the spheres influence each other, the earth, its oceans, denizens, and all inanimate matter, so they also influence . . . men?*

"So it would appear. But haven't the astrologers been telling us that for ages?"

Bah! Mesmer was vastly disappointed. *You leap from science to fantasy in a breath!*

But: "No," the Necroscope denied it. "I *move* from the physical to the metaphysical. Do you know, I had an almost identical argument with Möbius?"

Eh? I don't know him.

"Well then, you two should get together some time. August Ferdinand would enjoy that, I'm sure. But he would have been a young man, only twenty-three or -four, when you died. He was a mathematician, an astronomer, and a very brilliant man. Unlike you, he continued to develop his sidereal math in death and so discovered his Möbius Continuum, without which I wouldn't have been able to visit you. For just as it applied to Möbius—an incorporeal, 'metaphysical' being—so it applied to me, or I was able to apply it to myself. He and I, we imposed the metaphysical upon the physical. But more to the point, what *is* the Möbius Continuum—if not another example of your fluidum?"

My fluidum . . . is several, even many things? Is that what you're saying?

"It could be," the Necroscope gave a shrug. "I don't know." (And in all truth he didn't.) "But just because it hasn't been discovered or isolated yet doesn't mean it doesn't exist. Why, it's a theory of *mine* that if men can imagine something, then sooner or later they'll discover, or make it, or prove it!"

I have heard something like that before, (Mesmer was far more animated now). *"I think, therefore I am!" It seems to me that what you propose is simply a new—and if I may say so, an egocentric—slant on an old theme: "I imagine it could be so, wherefore I shall make it so!"*

"Something like that, yes."

A many-layered fluidum, Mesmer mused. But a moment later, sharply, even suspiciously: *And I think that you are trying to inveigle me!*

"Well of course I am; I need your help! But that's not to say I've been talking rubbish."

All of this to make me attempt what can't be done? What I cannot do?

The Necroscope shook his head. "That runs contrary to our discussion," he said. "Not to mention the evidence."

What evidence?

"My evidence. I'm an entirely physical human being, yet I habitually impose myself on the metaphysical Möbius Continuum. Why shouldn't we simply reverse the process?"

But you are unique, Harry, (Mesmer sighed), *while I am one of a very Mundane Majority. You're of the air above, while I am of the earth below. Indeed, I have even passed into the earth! Mundane, aye. Why, I can't even see you! Not the physical you.*

"The Great Majority," Harry told him then, "men like yourself, sir, but not nearly as learned as you—not all of them—have helped me in so many ways, so many times, that without them I would be literally nothing, gone from the world forever; not even dead, not necessarily, but very likely *un*dead! As for sight: I believe you will see me as no other man saw me before. You'll even be able to see *into* me, if I open my mind to you."

Explain.

But Harry had no more time for arguments or explanations, philosophical or otherwise. He might have talked about the vampire Thibor Ferenczy, dead for hundreds of years, who in his own way had "hypnotized" and entered the mind of his necromancer protégé Boris Dragosani, in order to direct his thoughts and actions from a thousand miles away. He could have mentioned Thibor's vampire "father" Faethor, who from the grave had lured up liches from *their* graves to perform an act of vengeance. And as he had pointed out, he himself was living proof of the many ways in which the dead may have influence over the living. But if a picture is worth a thousand words, there were pictures in the Necroscope's mind that were worth millions. And:

"Let me show you something," he said. "Maybe that will be explanation enough."

He concentrated, and with Mesmer maintaining contact let Möbius mathematics commence their metaphysical mutation, their evolution, across the screen of his mind. "The numbers, symbols and formulae that govern the universe," he explained, and even his voice was hushed. "Now stay with me . . . *come with me.*" And he felt Mesmer's presence closing with his.

Come with you? Mesmer's dead voice was the merest whisper; his attention was riveted—mesmerized?—by the ever-changing display.

Before he could withdraw, even if he would, Harry formed a door and drew Mesmer across the threshold. *The Möbius Continuum,* the Necroscope switched his conversation to pure thought, for even thoughts have weight in Möbius spacetime. *From here I can go . . . anywhere! And take you with me.* (Mesmer could sense it was true, that this place was a great Universal Crossroads). *But I won't take you far because your place is here, or if not "here," then at a parallel point in space.*

And this—this place—is all *space?* Mesmer's awe was transmissible; Harry felt it, no less than the good doctor himself.

Yes, he answered, *the inside and outside both. A gateway to everywhere, containing everything that has been, is now, or will be.*

Has been? Will be? Time, too?

Let me show you, said Harry. He found a past-time door and drew Mesmer to the threshold. A million, million miles away, or so it seemed—but distant in time, not space—the faint blue haze of human creation, mankind's beginning, was like some vast long-exploded galaxy. Streaming out from this astonishing starburst, seeming to intensify and multiply as they rushed towards the time-door, a myriad neon-blue filaments traced the lives of people who had been and many who still were. Indeed, one of the threads crossed the threshold and connected with Harry himself, appearing to thrust him, the door, and Franz Anton Mesmer, too, before itself into the future.

The effect was dizzying. The time-door was the singularity men call NOW; to maintain the status quo, it must flee from the past into the future . . . as everything in creation does. Except with the past displayed beyond the immundane frame of the door, and Harry's blue-thread—the line of his life, his lifeline—*seeming* to thrust him ahead of it, he and Mesmer were actually witnessing time's unwinding! And all accompanied by an orchestrated one-note *ahhhhhhhhhh!* like a massed sighing of angels.

Mesmer was stunned. But before he could comment, or find words to try, the Necroscope drew back from the door and found its twin—but this time a doorway to the future. And no need to explain what this was, as he and the good doctor gazed away and out into every tomorrow. Those myriad neon threads sighing away into the ever-expanding future . . . And new lives blazing into being, scintillant sapphire threads separating from their parent lifelines to hurtle on alone, signifying birth and life . . . And others fading to amethyst and gradually expiring along with their weary sources, signifying old age and death . . . And the Necroscope's lifeline continually unwinding from him, luring him into the future, while the angelic chorus went on and on: *Ahhhhhhhhhh!*

Those lines of blue light, Mesmer said after a while, but very quietly. *I know what they are, and why I don't have one.*

But you did have one, Harry told him, *upon a time.* And he conjured a door at Mesmer's co-ordinates.

And did I sigh and soar, and burn as bright as they do?

"Brighter than most," the Necroscope answered, as he and Mesmer emerged from the Möbius Continuum together at the dead man's tomb.

Do you think so, Harry? Really? Mesmer sank down into his place, which he would never leave again.

"Yes, I really do. That's why I had to show you that which you yourself might well have imagined and sought after, without even knowing what it was."

My fluidum?

"I honestly don't know, but it could be. Even now scientists all over the world are seeking for a Grand Unification."

But if it is so, then it's so much greater than I might ever have imagined! An incredible aether—a Great Fluidum—*connecting the Earth, the moon, planets and stars, the sun and suns, the universe itself, past, present and future, and every creature in it. All in the mind . . . of a man?*

But Harry hastily shook his head. Being nominated as the All-Important Factor in something as big as this seemed like a great blasphemy. "No, I simply tap into it. It's there without me. But I wouldn't be here without it. Nothing would."

Mesmer's morale was boosted, uplifted; the Necroscope felt it in him: a sudden soaring of his spirits. *It isn't the way I imagined it, but it does exist!* he said.

"Well maybe," Harry was cautious. "I mean, I won't lie to you, sir. I use it and it works for me, but I don't pretend to understand what it is."

Much like myself, Mesmer nodded. *I used my—my hypnotism, yes—without understanding it.*

"But it worked. And it can work again, if just this once. Isn't that what matters?"

You're so very far ahead of me. Yet you've come to me for help . . .

"You were first in your field."

But I can perceive no outward sign of imbalance. And from what little I have seen inside . . . Necroscope, your mind seems very well-ordered to me!

"But it isn't. Someone is fooling with it—fooling with me—and it could well be a matter of life and death."

Do you say is fooling with it, or has fooled with it?

"I'm sorry?"

Who do you know—who are you in contact with—who might wish you harm or seek to control you?

"Are you taking the case?" Harry heard muted voices. Real, living voices. There were other people in the cemetery now and he would have to be careful. The sooner he could get finished here the better.

Taking the case? Mesmer answered, as if suprised at such a suggestion. *Why, so it would appear!*

Harry thought about it. Who was he in regular contact with who might seek to harm or control him? His enemies? R.L. Stevenson Jamieson said he had enemies, anyway. B.J. Mirlu? No, for she . . . was innocent. He backed off from the very thought. But:

AH! GREAT GOD IN HEAVEN! Mesmer cried then, so suddenly it shook Harry to his roots. And more quietly, in a sort of disbelieving whisper: *Show me . . . show me that again.*

"Show you what?" Harry was mystified.

That girl, that woman. She flickered over your mind's eye and was gone. But the picture was vivid. And she was the image—the living image—of someone I knew once, who I can never forget.

"B.J.?" In the Necroscope's mind, immediate conflict. His denial was instinctive: "But how could you possibly know B.J.?" And a moment later he realized that Mesmer had said nothing of the sort. He had only said that B.J. was "the image of someone he had known." And Harry began to sweat, because from deep inside—from a hidden place—something warned him that indeed Mesmer might have known her. And if the good doctor looked any deeper, he would *know* he had known her!

But B.J. was innocent.

Of what? (Harry argued with himself.)

Of anything, everything!

Innocent? An innocent with a killer's instinct? In London, I saw her kill one man and try to kill another!

They were my enemies. I owe her my life for that. She has *become* my life! And I have become . . . her wee man!

The full moon! A wolf-head in silhouette!

The Necroscope's mind was wide open, unguarded, and Mesmer witness to all that passed through it. And despite Harry's confusion—his sudden terror?—he *held* it open. Because this was what he'd wanted Mesmer to see . . . wasn't it? Or was there stuff in there that he couldn't let anyone see? Stuff that belonged to someone else?

Harry's mind began spinning in ever-decreasing circles, a mental vertigo he couldn't pull out of. But through the kaleidoscopic chaos of colliding ideas and conflicting knowledge, one thing stayed uppermost: the fact of B.J.'s innocence.

Oh, really? But the look on her face as she squeezed the trigger of that crossbow. And the Thing *in the animal shelter. Wamphyri! Wamphyri!*

I wasn't able to *see* her face in that dark garage! And in the animal shelter, the light was so very poor.

But what about the other time? When the red-robed priests—Drakuls?—attacked us in the valley of the Spey?

It was a dream, a nightmare like all the others I've been having.

Wamphyri!

Just fucking nightmares, all of them!

(His levels were interfacing, faster and faster.)

Radu! . . . the Ferenczys! . . . the Drakuls!—

—And B.J.?

"But B.J. is innocent!" he cried out loud—and collapsed there and then, crumpling sideways from his seat on the slab to the dirty gravel at the weedy foot of the grave.

But Mesmer was with him, in contact with the Necroscope's mind, witness to his torment. And knowing that he was responsible for—that he had somehow brought about—Harry's seizure, the good doctor was "galvanized" to instinctive action. He took charge; his hypnotic presence swelled enormous in the chaos of Harry's colliding realities; his power flowed back into him as if it had never been absent. And:

SLEEP! Mesmer commanded, demanded. *BE STILL, HARRY! SLEEP WELL, SLEEP DEEP, NECROSCOPE! HEAR MY VOICE AND ONLY MINE. AND OBEY IT. FOR MY VOICE IS A REFUGE. MY VOICE IS PEACE AND TRUTH. OBEY ME, HARRY, AND SLEEP. AND WHEN YOU AWAKEN, BE WELL . . .*

At which a vast and soothing darkness seemed to wash over the Necroscope's troubled mind. He sighed as his limbs stopped twitching, his heart slowed from pounding, and his wildly staring eyes blinked and grew calm, and finally closed as his head lolled back on the cold gravel chips.

Then there came the sound of running footsteps, and anxious voices raised in startled inquiry. But for a while these were the last real, physical sounds that Harry heard, and all that remained was Mesmer's voice telling him to:

BE STILL, BE QUIET AND REST, NECROSCOPE. LET ME WORK NOW, AND TRY TO FIND YOUR WOUND AND HEAL IT.

Harry did as he was told, opened his mind, felt Mesmer's powerful mental probe stirring in the wells of his memory. But that was all.

He certainly didn't feel the hands that gentled him onto a stretcher . . .

Voices, approaching and receding, coming and going, like a difficult radio station that won't hold still. And pleading? Harry recognized his beloved Ma's voice—pleading on his behalf? And Doctor Franz Anton Mesmer's, trying to reassure her. But it was all so very fuzzy, distant and delirious, as if he were in some kind of traumatized sleep. Or as if . . .

. . . As if he were under an hypnotic influence.

But this was only part *of it!* His Ma sounded close to hysteria. *And now you have to concede that I was right, Keenan. If we had told Harry—if my son had learned the entire truth, as we know it, all at one time—what then? And even now, if Mesmer wasn't there to see him through this, what would become of him? And all because of the merest hint, the merest* suggestion, *that this B.J. might be other than she appears!* (The Necroscope could picture his Ma wringing her hands.)

Then Sir Keenan Gormley: *Mary, Mary! But Mesmer is there! It's why we didn't interfere: because we knew that if anything were to go wrong, Harry would be in the best possible hands.*

And finally Mesmer himself: *Leave it to me,* the good doctor told them, and everyone else who was listening in, but with such an air of authority that it was plain his faith in himself was restored. *Leave it to me, please. For since it seems I initiated this attack, surely I should be the one to correct it? Ah, but if only you had come to me first . . .*

But we couldn't know he would come to you! (Keenan Gormley again.) *We simply advised, suggested, hinted, in our way, that Harry should see a specialist. We never for a moment guessed he would seek out the hypnotist! When he did—when we knew he was coming to Meersburg—we had so little time. And the last thing we wanted was that he should change his mind.*

Well, he didn't change his mind, Mesmer said, *and he did come. As for myself, I doubt if it was a coincidence. For I've seen inside his mind—and what I saw was amazing! It seems to me that the past and future are all one to Harry, and that his visit was preordained. Or previsioned?*

It's possible, Harry's Ma cut in. *He seems to have inherited at least a residuum of Alec Kyle's talent.*

Exactly! said Sir Keenan. *Perhaps that's why I don't seem to worry over him the way you do: because I have real faith in his talents. In the talents of E-Branch in general, I mean. In which I'm surely justified. They rarely let me down in my lifetime, and Harry hasn't let me down . . . since.*

His words, while spoken from the heart, might have been a little more diplomatic. The Necroscope's Ma, who seemed so much calmer now, was rather more so. *Despite your sincerity, Keenan,* she said, *still I won't stop worrying. For just as E-Branch was your baby, Harry is mine. That is why I worry over him!*

For a moment there was an awkward silence, until Mesmer said, *Well, and now that you've told me something of his problems, maybe I can work something out. He trusts me; his sleeping mind is open to me; I have his permission, and access. But there are things—or more properly times, memories—that are hidden, forbidden, where there is no access. Not to me, anyway. Harry's "injuries," the blockages in his mind, must have occurred at these times and are hiding in these forbidden memories.*

And you mustn't interfere with them. (Harry's Ma again.) *For that's what caused his collapse.*

But . . . it's why he came to me! (Mesmer's bewildered protest.) *Also, I may have the answer to his problem. That woman I saw in his mind. I don't know how, but unless I'm very much mistaken I've seen her before. Except I know it can't be, for that was close to one hundred and seventy years ago!*

Oh, it can be, Harry's Ma told him. *Believe me, it can be.*

And Sir Keenan corroborated it. *Don't ask us for explanations, Doctor, but just as Harry showed you incredible things, so could we tell you some. Such things as have been the Necroscope's life, and almost his death. And you're right, they are what we're up against, and that girl is part of it. What is it you know about her?*

When I was in Paris, Mesmer answered, *a gypsy woman foretold my death. Myself, I was never superstitious, but this time . . . there was something about this woman. She said I would die in 1814, and it preyed on my mind. Then, in the summer of 1813, back in Switzerland, I was visited by a girl who told me I had once spoken with her mother—a seer of the Szgany Mirlu! The girl's name, if memory serves, was Barbara Jane Mirlu; she preferred to be called by her initials. An odd preference for the period.*

Not necessarily, Sir Keenan told him. *A person may change her name to hide her true identity, but retain the initials as a fad or reminder, or as a constant. It would be easy for such a person to slip up in the use of a false name, but not if she simply used the initials.*

A criminal, perhaps? As yet, Mesmer had not entirely accepted or digested what they'd told him. But in the next moment: *Ah, no! I see! You mean, someone who has lived too long!*

Exactly, said Harry's Ma, grimly. *And well over a hundred years too long! This B.J. Mirlu is alive today, Doctor, and she has hypnotized my son. She's his problem. He's . . . in love with her! These blockages in his mind, she put them there to obscure her true purpose.*

Then surely they must be removed. (Mesmer's shrug.)

But he is like two people, two personalities! Mary Keogh cried. *Break down the barriers that this woman has constructed, and he'll fight himself to the death. My son's reality has been so undermined that . . . that you wouldn't believe the things he has been through.*

Things which he has survived, Sir Keenan pointed out.

But for how much longer? Harry's Ma rounded on him.

You do me no credit, Mesmer murmured, directing his words at Mary Keogh. *Are you forgetting that your son—a living man—has spoken to me, or that he has shown me certain things? I might have doubted or disbelieved before I met the Necroscope, but no longer. Moreover, I no longer doubt myself, for which I have him to thank. And I tell you that despite all your fears, still I may be able to do something for him.*

Sir Keenan spoke up again. *It seems we've digressed. You were telling us about your meeting with B.J. Mirlu, in 1813?*

Ah, yes! Mesmer answered. *She reminded me that all those years earlier, in Paris, I had succeeded in putting her mother into a trance. Now she wanted me to* try *to do the same to her. Except B.J. would allow no apparatus, no special setting, only the power of the eyes, the mind. I sensed that in fact* she *intended to hypnotize* me—*she used the term "beguile"—but I went ahead anyway. It was like a challenge, but a challenge I lost, for she completely defeated me! Which is to say, she put me to sleep quite effortlessly. Her skill was in every way superior to mine. But she did me no harm, and before leaving she told me it had been a matter of pride: what I had done to her mother, she had now done to me.*

And the curse? Sir Keenan pressed him. *That you would die in 1814?*

Well I did, of course. But as B.J. explained, it wasn't a Gypsy curse. Her mother had simply looked into the future and seen my death. Telling me had been spiteful, however: her way of paying me back.

For what? (This from Mary Keogh.)

For failing to beat me at her own game—hypnotism, as you call it now.

(Sir Keenan's incorporeal nod of understanding.) *She was a vampire thrall, testing out her powers. You are to be congratulated, Doctor. Even an "expert" in metaphysical skills would expect to be beaten by someone touched by vampirism. And B.J.'s forebears . . . well, they've been more than merely "touched," and for a very long time!*

But that was the mother, Mesmer answered. *While the daughter, this B.J., was different again. Indeed a beguiler!*

And this is the woman who has my son so completely in her spell, (Harry's Ma spoke up). *And you are proposing to go into his mind to try and correct or expunge her influence? How will you go about it?*

I shall discover what I can of the Necroscope's problem. (Again Mesmer's shrug.) *After that, since I may not reveal to him the actual cause of his—what, lesions?—perhaps I can suggest when they occurred? Surely if he knows when the damage was done, he'll be able to work it out for himself who is responsible?*

Good! said Harry's Ma.

And Keenan Gormley put in: *I suggested something of the sort myself.*

While on second thought, Harry's Ma said, *But a lot better if you could break this creature's spell on Harry without his knowing there is one! If you could do that, then he would be his own man again.*

But you said he loved her, Mesmer pointed out. *And as you yourself are proof, that is the strongest spell of all . . .*

Mary Keogh had no answer to that. But Sir Keenan said, *Do what you can. We'll be grateful for anything of benefit.*

But please be careful! With which the voice of Harry's Ma—and all of their "voices," their dead thoughts—faded slowly away, drifting as the Necroscope drifted in his sleep . . .

Harry didn't remember anything of his dream, only that he *had* dreamed of dead voices locked in some obscure argument. But in any case his sleep must have been beneficial; he *felt* relaxed, rested and quite well. Post-hypnotic suggestion—Mesmer's implants, of course—but the Necroscope didn't know that. Instead he would consider his mission to Mesmer a failure, and wouldn't know what the dead doctor had achieved until much later.

Time to wake up, Harry! (Mesmer's last words to him.)

Drifting in a place between sleep and waking, the Necroscope began to stir. He felt air from an open window, and sunlight on his face; he smelled crisp, clean sheets covering his shift-clad body, and idly wondered how much of his life was a dream.

And then he wondered at a certain antiseptic smell . . .

Crisp linen? A shift? And voices speaking . . . in German?

Switzerland! And Mesmer!

Harry's eyes snapped open; he clutched at his bedclothes and swung his legs to one side; he sat up. And his weakness at once belied any feelings of well-being. (Mind has only so much say over matter, after all.) He tried to stand up, swayed, was at once grasped and gently lowered back to his hospital bed.

"How long?" he asked then, looking at the doctor and two nurses who stood by his bed. Their concerned expressions immediately turned to smiles. And:

"Three days," the Swiss doctor told him, in excellent English. "And four to go before you can be up. Exposure, we think. Despite that you seem in good condition, it has left you quite weak. But from now on, I think you should recover very nicely. Except—"

Harry looked at him inquiringly. "Yes?"

"Oh, there are one or two questions. You carried no documents. We don't know who you are, or where you are staying. We think people might be worried about you. You are a tourist, am I right? You can perhaps help us with these enquiries?"

No, he couldn't. But then, he didn't have to. "Tired," he mumbled, letting himself sink into his pillows. "Can't we talk later?"

"Of course, of course!" The doctor ushered the nurses out of the room, and at the door turned and said, "I will come and talk to you later, Mr. . . . ?"

"Smith," Harry told him. "John Smith."

"Smith," said the other smiling. "Yes, a good old English name. Rest now, eat later, and perhaps then we'll talk."

But a moment after he left—

—The Necroscope was scrabbling his clothes together from a wardrobe beside the window. And when he was sure he was leaving nothing behind . . . then he, too, left.

III

NOSTRAMADNESS!

THE DEAD IN THEIR GRAVES CONVERSED—NOT WITH THE NECROSCOPE, BUT about him—with each other, across all the miles between, as they had learned to do through him.

How did it turn out? Harry's Ma was fearful still.

As well, and perhaps better, than I expected, Franz Anton Mesmer told her. *For one thing, possibly the main thing, you were worried about the grip that this woman had on him?*

Yes? Her anxiety was obvious.

Well, no more, said Mesmer. And then, more cautiously, *At least, I think not.*

And Sir Keenan Gormley, unable to control his excitement, joined in: *You mean you've broken her spell?*

One of them, Mesmer answered. *I don't think I'm qualified—that is, I shouldn't have any legitimate, professional concern—about the other. That isn't for physicians or friends, nor even for a mother, but for Harry himself. And after all, a subject's will is still the most important factor. Harry* wanted *someone to help him find himself again. But as for his love for B.J. Mirlu—whether he should* love her or not—*surely that's for him to decide? Should I have weakened the post-hypnotic commands which he has accepted by giving him others that he can't possibly accept? I think not. And he* does *love her.*

So what real good have you done? (Mary Keogh again, still worried "to death.")

I discovered two blockages or lesions in the Necroscope's subconscious psyche, Mesmer answered. *Two areas where, through the interference of outside agencies—through hypnotism or beguilement—his will has been subverted. But unlike me, whichever persons did this to him were utterly unscrupulous and powerful beyond reason! Marvellous hypnotists, both of them. And yes, I recognized the work of one at once.*

B.J.! said Mary Keogh, bitterly.

Of course. The same girl who defeated me all those years ago. Ah, but this time the shoe is on the other foot! Your son has been taken in and out of trance so frequently that the connection has been weakened to breaking point. And yes, you were quite right: he might well have been driven out of his mind by the truth, causing an abrupt interfacing of his several states. Indeed, I was witness to just such an interface! Fortunately I was on hand, in mental contact with him, and was able to take some of the strain. But it is precisely because *the balance is so delicate that I was able to do something more than that.*

And Sir Keenan wanted to know: *What, exactly?*

There are . . . triggers, Mesmer explained. *Key words that trip when Harry hears them spoken by B.J. Or at least they did, but not any longer. Now when B.J. tells him things that are not so, he will know it. And when she orders that which he wouldn't normally do, he won't obey; or if he does it will be of his own volition.*

He'll be his own man? Mary Keogh's dead voice was lighter by several degrees.

Yes, and no . . . Mesmer sounded uncertain. And before they could question him: *I said that more than one person had interfered with Harry's mind—*

—I knew that! I've known it all along! Harry's Ma cried.

But Mesmer continued: *And whoever the other person was . . .* (The baffled shake of an incorporeal head.) *His commands are so deep-rooted that I simply can't reach them. They are locked in; they've never been relaxed; they've fused in position to become almost a part of Harry.*

Do you know what they are? Sir Keenan sounded suspicious; the others sensed a frown, despite that his face was long gone into ashes. *Do you have any idea what it is that's so restricting him?*

I don't know. I couldn't get in, Mesmer admitted defeat. *When I probed . . . why, the seal locked itself tighter still!*

Anyway, Harry's Ma said after a moment, *you did what you could, for which I'm thankful.*

And one other thing, Mesmer continued. *I also planted an idea in his mind, one that we talked about previously: that he look back into his past and try to remember where things started to go wrong. That way it's possible he might yet discover for himself the identity of whoever is responsible. It should at least provide him with a clue, or maybe even a suspect.*

But as for now? (Sir Keenan again.)

(Mesmer's shrug.) *As for now—we can only wait and see.*

And as their conversation terminated and their metaphysical thoughts were drawn back to their own places, Mary Keogh wondered why Sir Keenan Gormley, ex-Head of E-Branch, was suddenly so quiet, so thoughtful, but no longer willing to share what he was thinking . . .

Three days? It felt more like three weeks to Harry! His legs were like rubber, as if he'd fought an enormous battle, been knocked down, and was just getting back up on them again. He remembered his visit to Franz Anton Mesmer, their conversation in the graveyard in Meersburg, up to a certain point . . . and then nothing. Or perhaps snatches of a dream in the hospital, but that was all.

Maybe his visit had been a failure, maybe not. His head felt messed-up as ever—certainly his memory—but his concentration seemed a little sharper, like someone had taken a wire brush and scrubbed some of the rust off his brain. Mesmer? Well, possibly.

In Scotland it was mid-morning. But three days! Ye gods! And Harry was hungry to the point of ravenous. He dumped the hospital shift, also the bundle of stained, crumpled clothing he'd brought back with him, showered and got dressed in fresh things. Then, still shy of using his talents too openly—and despite his shakes, probably from hunger—he rode his bicycle into Bonnyrig and bought food . . . then visited a hardware store to purchase a gallon of heavy-duty wood-stain and a new broom. He knew what the last items were for, but wasn't about to dwell on it.

Back home again, still shaking, he made a huge breakfast of bacon, eggs, sausages, and fried bread, washed down with a mug of sweet coffee. He had some ideas that surfaced while he was eating; they seemed to stick to his mind the way the varnish-like wood stain stuck to the floor in his study.

That was what he was doing when the ideas finally crystalized: moving the few items of furniture, clearing the floor, pouring the stain straight from the can, and brushing it into position with the broom. It worked like a charm, stank to high heaven—and he wouldn't be striking any matches in here for a while! Nor living in here.

Finished, he closed the door on the smell, clambered over piles of furniture and books in the corridor, went back to the kitchen for more coffee. And sipping it in his front room, he concentrated on his ideas; or rather on *the idea,* which wasn't his after all but had two sources that he actually remembered.

Sir Keenan Gormley, and Franz Anton Mesmer. The former had definitely suggested that Harry should backtrack, and try to remember where things had started to go wrong for him. And as for the latter . . . but things were only very vague in connection with Mesmer. *Had* he also suggested something similar? The Necroscope seemed to remember something of the sort . . .

Now, in his own home (and however shadowy certain of its memories had become), Harry felt relatively at ease. Well fed and safe for the time being from whatever "enemies" he shared with B.J.—free of her presence and influence—he decided on one final attempt at going back into his past to see if he could find a clue to his condition.

But first there was something that was even more important. His mission to Mesmer had failed—well, probably—but there was still that other visitation experienced at E-Branch HQ. And since it was now part of his past, he began by recalling that oh-so-enigmatic face to memory:

That kindly, learned face—a man's face, and long—with grey eyes whose inner orbits curved into the bridge of an even nose, over drooping moustaches that touched the corners of his small but by no means mean mouth. The forehead, large and open; the ruddy cheeks; the slightly protruding ears, with sideburns flowing into a full golden-brown beard. And those *eyes*—at one and the same time severe *and* smiling—with discipline, humanity, and a consuming mysticism blazing outwards from them.

Harry remembered his voice, too, full of learning, and in that moment it struck him that it had been a "dead" voice from beyond the grave; and who better than the Necroscope to recognize that fact and know the difference? Then there had been an abrupt dismissal: "Away with you now, for as yet it is not your time."

Well, perhaps now it *was* his time. The Necroscope's mental barriers were once again in place; risking what he still saw as a fraught procedure, he lowered them, inviting contact. And:

So, finally you would seek the source of your troubles in your past? (It was the self-same voice, but seemed full of a wry humour now.) *What do you hope to find there, Necroscope? What's done is done, after all. Ah, but if you would know the future—come speak to me in Salon. But do not wait too long, for I have other times to scry upon.*

"Salon?" Harry repeated the as yet unknown other out loud. "I'll come, of course,"—well, as soon as he knew where Salon was!—"But who should I ask for?"

Michel de Nostredame, came the mind-boggling answer immediately. *Find me in the church, no later than tonight . . .*

It meant another frantic bike trip into town, this time to the small but well-stocked library. The bicycle was necessary, for unless he could use the Möbius Continuum with an absolute guarantee that he wouldn't be seen, Harry was determined to avoid it. And so into the afternoon he read all he could on Nostradamus.

Then an early dinner at a Bonnyrig café, following which, and conscious of the hour—eager to be home again—he found a deserted alley and risked riding through a hurriedly, fearfully conjured door directly into his back garden. And finally a series of equally sweaty jumps to Salon-de-Provence, in the south of France.

The Church of St. Laurent was a landmark and easy to find; its doors stood open; though he heard muffled voices from somewhere within, no one challenged Harry as he approached Nostradamus's grave in an alcove, where his portrait hung on the wall. And staring up at that portrait . . . Harry saw that indeed this was the man who had "visited" him at E-Branch HQ.

There was no one around. Only the echoing old church, and from somewhere a scurrying of mice. Harry lowered his barriers, and under his breath said: "Sir, I'm here."

And: *So you are!* Nostradamus answered at once. *And you're welcome, Harry Keogh, Necroscope. I've waited long and long for this day.*

"You knew we were to meet?"

Oh, yes. Nostradamus answered. *For am I not a—what, a "precog"—after all? And isn't that why you came to see me?*

"That's exactly why," Harry supposed he shouldn't be surprised, really. "But if you know—or if you've seen this much of things, sir, that I would come to see you—perhaps you've seen much more? And I do need to know my future. But I need to see it clearly defined, not in fragments or cloaked in mystery. I mean no disrespect, but your writings are at best confusing."

Oh? You've researched me, then. And did you find some reference to yourself, that you would now clarify?

"To myself?" Now Harry really was surprised. "In your Centuries? Why, no! I hadn't the time to read them all."

That were as well. Perhaps you would be yet more confused. I myself am confused, and amused, by certain interpretations.

"But you've been dead quite a while. How can you possibly know of these interpretations?" The Necroscope was fascinated.

A good many of them that interpreted me are likewise dead. And as you of all men are aware, we have intercourse of sorts.

Of course. And now Harry felt stupid. Nostradamus sensed it and chuckled, but not maliciously. *What, you? Stupid? Lazy, perhaps. But never stupid!*

"Lazy?"

You have access to all the great libraries of the dead—all knowledge!—and yet you stumble.

"The books of the future aren't written yet," Harry retaliated. "And those that are are sketchy, couched in cyphers."

As to why I wrote in brief, it was because I saw in brief. A lightning flash upon the mind, a picture come and gone. Revelations—or distillations?—of future things. Harry, do you remember your dreams? Not all of them, I am sure; and of those you do remember, not in every detail. So were—so are—my visions of tomorrow. I must record them quickly, lest they are lost. Why, I even thought *that way! In quatrains obscure. Even now, because I have trained myself to it, my words and even my reasoning seem obscure. In my day there were other reasons. I had my detractors as well as my champions. Both were powerful. If a tongue spoke wrong, in the fantasies of certain sects, it could be cut out—the Inquisition! Ah, so easy to talk of the past, for it is done and gone. But the future? Ever a devious discourse. Mercifully I am strengthened in the knowledge that I may no longer suffer harm. Yet in my day I suffered witches. Henry's Queen, Catherine de Medici, was one such. Fleeing pain, I embraced scandal. The Catherine is a wheel, did you know? As is time. Even as the stars and planets wheel in their celestial orbits, so does time. And what will be . . .*

" . . . Has been!" Harry cut in. "Time is relative."

Indeed! A good word: relative. *Do you like word games?*

This was such a departure from Nostradamus's previous theme that Harry was momentarily lost for an answer. But in any case, and before he *could* answer:

I know you do. For you have heard them, and perhaps even played them, in *the mouths of experts! And will again. Ah, take heed! Anyway, I have some word games for you. Are you game? Or, am I? What's in a game, or in a name for that matter?*

Harry thought about it, for he'd been told several things and asked several things—all in a few dozen words! And as in all of Nostradamus's writings, and his conversation so far, his meaning was obscure, hidden.

Word games, *"in* the mouths of experts." Spoken with dire inflection. But the emphasis was on "in," and Harry believed he knew why. Nostradamus's experts could only be the Wamphyri. To play word games with them—as the Necroscope had done—was an invitation to disaster! Thus the great prophet was simply indicating that Harry had risked his all, and would do again. With the Wamphyri? But they were dead and gone, surely? And yet deep inside he knew that they weren't. Not yet. Not all of them. The idea came and went, much like Nostradamus's visions, or like the dreams to which he had referred . . .

Harry blinked his eyes, continued to divine the great prophet's meaning:

He desired to play a word game or games with the Necroscope. Was he game? And was Nostradamus game? Well of course he was, else he wouldn't have proposed it. Or was he stating that he was a different *kind* of game? A game that was *in* his name!

"In your life you were . . . Michel de Nostradame?" He made an opening stab at it.

And in your era, "Nostradamus." You refer to me in Latin, a dead language. Appropriate! And thus we are one in more ways than one. Do you know these ways? First, try my true name . . .

"Nostredame? It has ten letters—as does my whole name, Harry Keogh."

And your assumed name: Necroscope! Indeed, it strikes me—I have been stricken— that Nostradamus and Necroscopus share much of a feel, a certain ambience *or* stimmung; *a relationship? And so we return to that word again: relative. Are* we related, do *you suppose? If so, then I am ancestral, patently. For I am old and dead and gone, while you are new. But time, as stated, is relative. What came first, the chicken or the egg?*

Frustrated, Harry said: "If your riddle was in numbers, I might hope to match you!"

Names and numbers, they are the same. Nostradamus replied enigmatically.

"As in the Biblical sense," Harry answered, neither agreeing nor questioning but equally mysterious.

Precisely! The number of a man is the man. And do you know your number?

Because of his interest in—and his mastery of—sidereal or lateral mathematics, Harry understood something of the theories of numerology, and instinctively referred to the following table:

1	2	3	4	5	6	7	8
A	B	C	D	E	U	O	F
I	K	G	M	H	V	Z	P
Q	R	L	T	N	W		
J	S		X				
Y							

Nostradamus saw it in his mind and said: *The Hebrew system! I know it. I speak it! It was the tongue of my Grandfather, who taught it to me. The letters of your name, Harry Keogh. Why see, they total eleven, and twenty-two! The first is the number of the visionary, the martyr, and the second of the* Master *Magician! Small wonder you are a dead-speaker, and move through secret places!*

A dead-speaker? That rang a bell, but one that immediately tolled into silence. As for the rest, the sum total of the numbers of his names: Harry knew and accepted the coincidence, but he had little faith in numerology as yet. "And you're a seven," he said. "A seer, clairvoyant or prophet—or all three. Either way, as Michel de Nostredame, *or* Nostradamus, you have the same number, for *both* of your surnames total forty!" (Another coincidence?)

Would you expect any less? So much for numbers, but what of names?

"To know a man's name is to know his number," the Necroscope answered, "but how may we divine a name *from* a number? Or do you mean the *meaning* of names?"

We get to it! Nostradamus was excited now. But in the next moment a cry, almost of pain: *Ah, a vision—and a quatrain—but quickly, before it is gone!*

Their minds were linked through Harry's talent. The Necroscope saw what Nostradamus saw:

Time unwinding—no, devolving! A figure falling through past time, through the neon-blue (and scarlet, and *green?*) bars or life-threads of men, vampires . . . and of what else? But vampires? Was this the past or the future? Whichever, it was unmistakably Möbius-time. And the tumbling figure: a dead man, burned and blackened, spreadeagled as on a cross, spiralling into the past.

The vision was ghastly enough in itself but there was something yet more horrible about it. The Necroscope had seen this before, surely? His skin began to prickle. But then:

A blinding flash, a disintegration, a bomb-burst of golden fragments, like darts, hurtling outwards in all directions from the space where that smoking shell of a body had been. The way they moved: angling this way and that, *sentient* as they sought exits from their **NOW** into other places, other times . . .

It was over, and Nostradamus groaned: *Did you see? Do you have it? A quatrain, quickly!*

And Harry said:

> "A man of weird times and places falls in reverse
> towards some new beginning, some multiple fruition.
> Seeming like death, it is in fact a multiple birth.
> His pieces are enabled by golden transmutation . . . "

And it was as if Nostradamus sighed, *Exactly!* In the Necroscope's mind. *My thoughts exactly. Do you have children?*

"Eh? Only one."

Ah, no—a great many, I think.

"Who knows the future?" Harry answered with a shrug, and thoughtlessly.

I do—did—do! For in death I continue as in life.

"You'll help me, then?"

I am helping you! Had you seen it before, my vision? that one of many visions? For a moment there you thought so, for I read it in your mind.

"Yes . . . no . . . I'm not sure. Maybe it was a dream.

But you cannot remember, cannot be sure. And didn't I say it was like that? The future guards its secrets well. Which is one of the reasons why I guarded my secrets. Note, if you will: Nostradamus is speaking plainly. It is difficult after all this time, but I am trying. For your sake. Therefore for ours.

"But still a word game to me. Great prophet, I have to ask you this: have you played with *Them*, too?"

A shudder. No, but I have seen . . .

"In your visions? There's no record in your quatrains."

Ah, but there is! But mainly since dying. Since knowing. There are those with whom the Great Majority will have no commerce. Their minds have illumined mine. They impinge. But knowing a little, I saw or remembered a lot. What will be has been.

Riddles were all very well, but the Necroscope's frustration was mounting. He didn't want this opportunity to be wasted. "Sir, tell me my future. I know I shouldn't ask—I understand the dangers—but you've seen so very much of the future in the stars, in your dreams, and in your bowls of water on their tripods . . . " He seated himself on the corner of Nostradamus's slab.

In the stars? I believe it is written, yes. For the stars are a million years ago, therefore a million years to come. And what are our dreams but extensions of the **NOW**? *But my bowls of water? Like a crystal ball, do you mean? Ah, no. All in my time had a device, and so I must have mine. Better to be seen to consort with "science" of a sort than with demons who have gained entry to the mind. For the rack has power even over demons!*

"It was a trickery?"

The water? My safety net! But the visions were instinct. Now tell me, do you need *a crystal ball? And your visions: can* you *remember in detail, or explain what you have seen?*

"No, they are outside my control. I inherited my visions, from a precog like yourself. But a lesser talent, of course. I have no control over them."

Nor I mine. And I too inherited them. All in verse, in reverse.

"Your meanings are hidden!" (Harry's frustration was showing through now; he shuffled on Nostradamus's sarcophagus.)

They must be. Forgive me. It is my way—and your protection! What of the golden darts? (Again a change of direction, a return to a previous theme.)

"The darts? In your vision? They seemed sentient . . . "

Ah! They knew . . .

"Knew what?"

What, indeed. What's in a name?

"If I were the Master Magician you named me—"

—Not I, but numbers. And where numbers are concerned, you are *a magician!*

"—*If* I were a Master Magician, I might fathom these riddles. They twist and turn, like—"

—Your Biomus loop?

Biomus? Möbius, of course! "You know about that?"

It, too, goes back to its beginnings. Start at the end and work forwards. What of the golden darts?

"What's in a name . . . ?" Harry frowned, felt his head beginning to spin with the other's riddles. "This has to do . . . with your name?" It was a wild guess, but a starting place at least.

Bravo!

"In your quatrains, you employ various tongues to further confuse your work. *You* were fond of word games, anagrams . . . "

Have I not said so? Verses and reverses, Harry.

"Reverses? Start at the end and work forwards? Michel de Nostredame: Emadertson ed Lehcim?"

Try the Latin, as I am named in your time.

"Pardon? Nostradamus: Sumadartson. But I don't see—"

—Because you are not looking. Try sum.

"Sum? An addition? The result of an addition? Or to be the epitome of, or exemplify, as in 'the sum of a man'? Or 'in sum'—in short? Or . . . I exist, I am, as in Descartes's philosophy. Cogito ergo sum?" (He remembered that from Mesmer.)

I exist! said the other. *I am! Which leaves us with . . . ?*

"Sum, adartson? I am . . . adartson?" The Necroscope frowned again, but his frown slowly turned to a gape as his jaw—or at least his mind—fell open. Nostradamus in reverse. Sum, a dart son. "I am . . . a . . . dart . . . son!"

Or a dart's son, yes! A golden dart. A shaft of great wisdom:

> *Which speared me in that fatal year,*
> *I cured the pustule-riddled sick.*
> *Alas, the ones I held most dear . . .*
> *. . . God's mercy, it was quick.*

"It was . . . 1537, perhaps?" said Harry. "The bubonic. You were a doctor and cured many, but it took your wife and children."

Misery! I would take my own life! But then I viewed this wonder: a man like one fallen from a stake or cross of the Inquisition, all smoking from the fire, tumbling through time. I was given to know it! I knew! And in Scaliger's house in Agen, where I wept in a room of mourning, a brilliant flash of gold! Lightning on a cloudless day, which struck me in my temple, as the dart from time struck home! I was not dead. I lived. And I — could see! Harry, you eleven, you martyr, I could see . . .

"More than other men. More than me, for sure!"

More than "sum," from that time on. Six years I wandered, wondered what to do with it. Write it down, and offend the powers that be? For many of the things I foresaw would not be allowed; they went against those who would not be gainsaid. Was I to burn like the one who empowered me? Yet I knew this knowledge must be known, be shown!

> *Wherefore,*
> *in cryptic verse,*
> *the things I saw*
> *were made perverse.*

And after six long years of wandering in the wilderness, I began writing my quatrains for other men to fathom. In death, I continue, on the pages of my mind. It has become a habit . . .

"But it doesn't spell out my future," the Necroscope shook his head.

Oh? Doesn't it? (Was that a note of sadness in Nostradamus's voice?) And quickly:

> *Some son of yours.*
> *Hannat will read the stars,*
> *and in them read his course.*
> *But ours are not his stars . . .*

"I have no son of that name. Is that an anagram, too? And the stars are unchanging. They're the same for everyone."

In this world they are the same, aye. As for "Hannat": was "Hister" the King of the Germans? What's in a name? But it came so brief! I almost got it right.

"You could drive a man mad," said Harry with feeling. "And with me not far to drive, for I'm half way there! Hannat? I see no name in that. Hannah is closest, and that's a woman's name!"

> You *shall not name him,*
> *nor even know his time.*
> *He dwells beyond the rim,*
> *in a far and alien clime . . .*
>
> *Yet a third son is better, or worse!*
> *Take my first six and reform his name.*
> *Himself, he is beyond reform, perverse!*
> *His father's opposite,* never *the same!*

"Your first six? 'Nostre'? There's a name in that?" Harry shook his head. "I'm lost. Two unknown sons, Hannat and Nostre, or derivations of those letters? Why can't you just tell me *my* future?"

But I'm doing it. And your future's future! Except nothing is simple. The future is not to be known. It resists. Very well then. Your *future. Except you may not see it. Can I trust you?*

"Not to see it? We're in contact; I'll see what you see."

Hear my voice, my quatrains, and remember; but close your mind to my visions. Else, it cannot be.

"More puzzles for me to work out?"

It is the only way. And what difference any-*way? It never works out exactly as foreseen. But I am here for you. Perhaps I was* put *here for you! To remind you of a course that will bring me into being. What came first—*

"—The chicken or the egg? Very well, I won't see. Guard your mind, and tell me your quatrains—or mine."

But see—you begin to think as I think! Or did I always think like you? Whichever, our maziness is catching.

"I have a feeling this can't last much longer," Harry felt a terrible urgency. "If you would enlighten me, do it now."

And I feel you here, seated before me for my knowledge. I see you, see into you, and beyond you! Ahhhh . . . !

> *South-east of where you sit,*
> *a great mind seethes and shudders.*
> *Transmuted but not muted, in his pit,*
> *he is the father of blood brothers.*
>
> *They are found six hundred miles in space.*
> *In time their names are distant, indistinct.*
> *Seeking some* Other *in his resting place,*
> *they have discovered you—they think!*

She is her Master's kennel-maid.
His castle is a hollow place and high;
His bed is yellow, glowing where he laid
himself to rest who would not die.

Her name is Pretty, but her thoughts are dark.
Hers is to choose where no choice fits her role
in His survival. Six hundred, since the mark
of pestilence entered his soulless soul.

The face looks out across a frozen waste.
Red the thoughts and robes of him who dwells
within the labyrinth of that dire place,
within the 'fluence of the golden bells.

They are of one blood, one and all,
composed of blood, inheritors of life,
which was not theirs to take. Their fall
is possible: the stake, the fire, the knife!

But there are stakes and stakes,
fires and fires, knives and knives.
Success accepts of no mistakes . . .
Would-be avenger of a thousand lives.

The means is in the sun, as it transpires,
where such as these are loth and loth to stand.
For fires that warm mere men are funeral pyres
to them, to be directed by his mind and hand.

With numbers and with solar heat and grave-cold,
with mordant acids, and his friends in low society,
and alchemical thunder; with all of these, behold!
He may transmute impurity to peace and piety!

He knows!—yet may not know, until set free
by the kennel-maid; he sees, yet may not understand,
until this Pretty's eyes search out the treachery,
in the Dog that would bite its keeper's hand . . .

Six hundred north, and west unto the Zero,
the men of magic are his friends, but chained.
They may not help the one who is their hero,
or tell him that which may not be explained . . .

And: *All done,* said Nostradamus.

"But . . . can I remember all of that?" It seemed impossible to Harry. "And even if I do, can I fathom it?"

Perhaps you'll know it when you see it. Please understand, I don't myself understand it. The future is a devious place.

"Time I was gone," said the Necroscope, hearing footsteps approaching. "I can't be discovered doing this."

I could tell you more, but may not! Nostradamus, too, was anxious, frustrated. He knew how important was the moment: his last opportunity to say anything at all. *You might attempt to avoid the unavoidable, and all of this were for nothing. Also, the Great Majority have expressly forbidden it. I am* forbidden *to say more! For your friends in low places know the dangers. It is for me to know and you to discover.*

Harry was desperate to hang on to him; he knew that if he let him go, Nostradamus would return to his dreams of the future. But the echoing footsteps were ringing closer. "Nostradamus," he whispered. "You hinted that at least one of your quatrains pertains to me."

In the Second of the "C"s:
find it under my name.
For tree read trees.
pride may be read as shame.

"Under your name?"

What's in a name? Oh, you'll find it . . .

"What, by trial and error?"

Use your numbers—and mine!

"Wait!" Harry cried. But Nostradamus and the Necroscope's chance for enlightenment were going, going, gone!

"Sir?"

Frustrated beyond measure, the Necroscope mumbled, "Names and fucking numbers!"—then realized that someone had spoken to him and jerked his head from his chest where it had lolled. He saw a tall young man in black clerical garb. The priest put a hand on his shoulder, placatingly.

"English?" He smiled uncertainly. "I did not mean to disturb you, sir, but there is a service tonight and it is getting late. You should find a seat if you intend to stay."

Harry didn't intend to stay.

The church had smelled musty, as churches do. But outside it was evening in Provence and the air was sweet. While it was still light, Harry found a street lamp and made some quick jottings in a pocket notebook. He tried desperately hard to remember everything but knew that a lot would be lost.

Of course, for the future is good at covering its tracks. The number six hundred was recurrent. A distance, or a measurement of time, or both? As for Hannat and Nostre: who were they? And one called "Pretty": Bonnie Jean? Sum a dart son. That was easy: a reversal of Nostradamus. But what did it mean? Eleven: a martyr. And twenty-two: a Master Magician. Simple numerology.

Even the remnants of the conversation were fading now!

Frantic, Harry searched his mind. Numbers, solar heat, and grave-cold. Mordant acids, dead friends, and alchemical thunder. Stakes, and fires, and knives. Only one possible meaning there! Or was all of this simply a dream

within a dream, the echo of a nightmare from the past? Or were his problems—
the *worst* sort of problems?

A dire place with golden bells? Did he know such a place? A mutant Thing
in a pit, the father of blood brothers. Or brothers of blood?

Hell and damnation! It was all slipping away!

He ran back to the church. Songs of praise echoed within. "Nostradamus!"
he called. And twice more: "Nostradamus! Nostradamus!" But the great prophet
wasn't listening. Perhaps he was singing, too. Or perhaps his mind was already
winging far into future times . . .

Back in the old house near Edinburgh, Harry sweated like a man in a fever trying to remember what he'd been told. Could it be he wasn't supposed to remember? So why had he been allowed to retain any of it? Maybe it would come
back to him as it occurred. But wouldn't that be too late?

Too late for what?

"Shit!" he exploded, and sweated some more. For there was something desperately wrong here. No, just about *everything* was desperately wrong here!
Somebody—and maybe more than just one somebody—was *still* fucking with
his mind! But how? And why? Or was he simply insane?

Six hundred. He knew about *that*, definitely . . . except he still didn't know
what he knew! The mental rambling of a crazy man, or lunatic. "Lunatic"—
someone made mad by the moon. And now he really was starting to think like
Nostradamus—in riddles and word games.

Six hundred. Six *fucking* hundred!

A measurement in space or time or both.

Try space. *"They are found six hundred miles in space . . ."* It came and went,
but the Necroscope clung to it like the proverbial drowning man to his straw.
Distance! Six hundred miles from Salon—*"south-east of where you sit."*

The World Atlas was still in the kitchen where he'd left it; it seemed to leap
from the table into his hands; he scrambled feverishly for the huge double-pages
showing Europe. A set of compasses, his kingdom for a set of compasses! Fuck
the compasses, he'd make a set of his own!

He took a strip of paper and marked off six hundred miles on the scale of
the map, and pinned the strip over France with the pin through Salon. Then
he described a circle, and saw that the mark he'd made crossed through Sicily,
the mountains of Le Madonie . . .

> *"A great mind seethes and shudders,*
> *the father of blood brothers . . ."*

What did it mean? The Francezci brothers, who he'd robbed? But what if
it was all *only* a dream? What if he was making this up himself?

Six hundred. What *else* about six hundred?

Harry's lips were dry. He was so tired. Those three days he'd spent in hospital had only seemed to refresh him; but the reason he'd been there had been

more mental than physical. And it was the same now: a mental weariness. His eyes and mind were hot, heavy hurting. He remembered some idiot character in Monty Python whose brain had hurt. Harry's brain hurt, too!

Six hundred. Three times that number had come up. Triple sixes? The Beast in Revelations? No, no, they were distances in space and time. But one thing for sure: all of *this* was a beast—and a bastard!

> *"Six hundred north, and west unto the Zero."*

He laughed hysterically and swung his strip of paper into the vertical: north. Then west until the mark hit . . . zero degrees! At the Greenwich meridian! London!

> *"The men of magic are his friends, but chained.*
> *They may not help the one who is their hero,*
> *or tell him that which may not be explained."*

Men of magic? In London? *E-Branch!* Harry's intuitive maths—and his knowledge of numerology—leaped to the rescue. Darcy Clarke:

D=4, A=1, R=2, C=3, and Y=1. Darcy, an eleven, a magician! Damn right he was! and Clarke:

C=3, L=3, A=1, R=2, K=2, and E=5. A seven: a mystic, occultist, and dedicated delver!

So, E-Branch—or Darcy—knew something but couldn't tell him. It couldn't be explained. Or perhaps they daren't even *try* to explain it. E-Branch? The dirty tricks brigade?

Harry heard a growl—and it was himself. He was growling deep in his throat! *Quit it!* He told himself. *Quit it now!*

And one six hundred to go.

Six hundred . . . *"since the mark of pestilence, entered his soulless soul."*

But whose soulless soul? And six hundred what? Days, weeks or years? Surely not years? *Oh, really?* A pestilence, six hundred years ago . . . the Black Death!

And something stirred at the back of Harry's mind, or in the secret mind he wasn't given to know. It stirred, and reached to make connections with the rest of him. He felt it like a small flame burning in him, waiting to catch hold and become a roaring fire, a conflagration.

The sweat was dripping from him now, and his mind felt as if it were in a vise, being slowly crushed. And yet he felt he knew.

"I . . . Christ, I *know* these fucking things!" Harry cried to no one. "There's a part of me that *knows* them!"

> *"He knows, yet may not know until set free*
> *by the kennel-maid; sees, yet may not understand,*
> *until this Pretty's eyes search out the treachery*
> *in the dog that bites its keeper's hand . . ."*

This Pretty? This Bonnie? This Bonnie Jean? *Oh, God!*

"Stop it now." A voice warned from deep inside. The Necroscope's voice, he knew. "Stop it, or you're going to push yourself right over the edge." But Harry couldn't stop. No way. He *had* to know. Had to know who Bonnie Jean was. Had to know *what* she was.

> *"She is her Master's kennel-maid.*
> *His castle is a hollow place and high . . . "*

Harry? His Ma called out to him from the river, dark now under non-reflective clouds. *Harry, come to me now! Come to the riverbank and talk to me this minute!* Her voice was filled with a tangible terror, brimming with the need to distract or divert him. But Harry wasn't about to be diverted. Shielding his mind, specifically against her, he shut her out. Other channels were still open, however, and:

Harry? (It was Sir Keenan Gormley, in no less of a state than the Necroscope's Ma.) *What the hell are you trying to do, son? Destroy yourself?*

"No," he answered, "I'm trying to *find* myself!" He closed his mind to Sir Keenan.

> *"Her name is Pretty, but her thoughts are dark.*
> *Hers is to choose where no choice fits her role*
> *in his survival . . . "*

Necroscope, man, you has some bad *enemies!* (It was R.L. Stevenson Jamieson.) *But right now your worst enemy is you! Can't you see we is only tryin' to help out here?*

"OK," Harry went for it. "OK, so help me out. Do you know where they are, R.L.? My enemies? Like the Madonie Mountains of Sicily? And what about Tibet? Or how about up there in the Highlands? Am I getting warm, R.L.?"

All those places, Necroscope! And they knows *you, man!*

"Which means I daren't stop, because I have to know *them*. And now, before they're all over me!"

But there's bigger dangers in you knowing, Harry! Big dangers, Necroscope! 'Cording to your Ma at least.

"And there's more in my not knowing. You're out of here, R.L." And he shut him out.

> *"They are of one blood, one and all,*
> *composed of blood, inheritors of life,*
> *which was not theirs to take. Their fall*
> *is possible: the stake, the fire, the knife!"*

Wamphyri!

> *"She is her Master's kennel-maid.*
> *His castle is a hollow place and high;*
> *his bed is yellow, glowing where he laid*
> *himself to rest who would not die."*

Radu! Radu Lykan! A wolf's head laid back in a protracted howl, against the bloated yellow disc of the full moon . . .

Harry's barriers were firmly in place, his mind closed. He had shut out the frantic voices of his teeming dead friends and was alone with his reasoning, or unreasoning. The two halves of his psyche were merging again. Nostradamus's quatrains, and some which were the Necroscope's, swept in disarray across the narrowing screen of his crumbling mind, until—

> —where once his formulae held sway,
> worlds in weird collision were left.
> With his magic numbers blown away,
> the Magician was . . . bereft!

And he knew it, or thought he knew it: that he was mad. He had no reality. What was real was unreal, maybe his whole life! Too many people had fucked with his mind—and together they'd fucked it up completely.

"All done," said Harry in the voice of a little boy, with an almost glad sigh. Now all he wanted was a safe place that he could go to, where he might do and think . . . nothing at all.

At Oakdeene Sanatorium, a white-clad orderly with a disbelieving, worried expression rapped urgently on the door of the Director's office. Then, entering—bursting in before Dr. Quant could so much as look up from the paperwork on his desk—this previously unflappable orderly blurted, "Sir . . . !" But that was all. He seemed lost for words.

"Willis?" Quant, squat and balding, brushed a few strands of red hair back behind his small ears and stared at the least of his subordinates through thick-lensed spectacles. "I take it there's a reason for this abrupt intrusion?"

"Intrusion," the other nodded, his Adam's apple bobbing. "An inmate . . . an intruder, anway. And you're the Duty Officer on call, sir."

"Well," Quant sighed and stood up, all five foot three of him. "And aparently a good thing, too! Trouble with an inmate, did you say? Or an intruder? An uninvited guest? Surely not."

The place was quiet. No alarms going off, no telephones ringing, none of the controlled hustle and bustle of daylight hours. No distance- or insulation-muted cries of rage, frustration, or simple madness; and everything seemed quite literally "sedate." And most things were.

The Director was here tonight to kill two birds with one stone. It had become neccessary to review some of the asylum's administrative procedures, its many SOPs and security regulations. Oakdeene housed a good many extremely dangerous men and women; it made sense to check occasionally on their security, and ensure that they really were secure.

So tonight Dr. Quant had put himself on duty to spend the evening with rules and regulations—sufficient to satisfy himself that unless something was radically wrong here, this simian orderly or so-called "male nurse," Dave Willis, was in fact in error. Oakdeene's physical barriers were sufficient guarantee in themselves that no unauthorized person could ever gain entry. And yet:

"In D-Ward," Willis gulped again. At which Quant's interest picked up apace. D-Ward? ("D" for Dangerous!)

"What about D-Ward?" the director queried, frowning. "Are you supposed to be on D-Ward tonight? And if so why aren't you down there?"

But Willis wasn't about to be intimidated. "You'd better see for yourself," he said. "I couldn't get you on the phone."

"I took it off the hook. Busy with the books, Willis. Now what *is* going on? An intruder? In D-Ward? But how could anyone get past you . . . *if* you were there, that is?"

"I was there, all right—and no one got by me." Was that a sneer on the orderly's face, in reaction to Quant's insinuation? "Three security doors between me and the cells, and cameras and alarms on all of them." He pointed at the book of SOPs on Quant's desk. "But what am I telling you for?"

"And someone was in there, you say?" The Director shrugged into his jacket.

"Is," Willis answered. "*Still* in there. In a locked cell! Of course he is. With all those doors and electronic gear, how would he get out?"

"The question must surely be," Quant answered, and slammed his office door behind him and the orderly, "how did he get in? And how did you find him? Who is he, anyway?"

They went quickly down the rubber-carpeted corridor, took an elevator down through the three storeys to the ground floor, from where Willis must use a special key to command their descent to D-Ward. And as the cage lowered them silently into the realms of madness, Willis said: "I've no idea how anyone could get in. He must have been left in there by the day shift. Someone playing some kind of crazy joke? You tell me—sir. As to how I found him: I was doing the periodic scan of the cells on the monitor. I hit the number of an empty cell by mistake and got a picture. The list said 'empty'—but the camera doesn't lie. This man was in there, sitting in a corner. I checked the computer and it said the door was locked. I checked admissions and no one had been booked in. The SOP says . . . "

" . . . Any extraordinary event—or any occurrence that may indicate a breach of security—is to be reported to the Duty Officer immediately. Yes, I know," Quant nodded. "But a joke? An error? Someone is in trouble for this. *Deep* trouble!"

They were down into D-Ward; the elevator hissed to a halt and the doors slid silently open. At this end of the corridor, in the security cell, two more orderlies from the less sensitive wards were waiting for them. "I called them down," Willis explained. "I couldn't leave the place without they were here. The SOPs, sir."

All four men looked through an unbreakable window down D-Ward's corridor to the first security door. None of the fail-safe indicators showed anything wrong. But to one side of the window, from the monitor screen above the security console—and from an allegedly empty cell—the face of a stranger stared back at them. An utterly vacant face, for the moment at least. The face of someone who might well warrant being where he was.

"Cell number?" The Director snapped.

"We'll have to go all the way to get to him," Willis answered. "Three doors, three sets of keys. He's in C-Section, the very last cell."

"Whoever he is," one of the other orderlies grinned, then saw the look on Quant's face and dropped it, "he's, er, taking no chances. I mean, er, you can't get any more secure than the very last cell in C-Section. Right . . . ?"

IV

IN THE MADHOUSE. THE OTHER HARRY.

B.J. HAD GOT HARRY'S MESSAGE. HE HAD SAID HE WOULD KNOW WHEN AND where to find her. Of course he would; as the moon neared its full, he would be *obliged* to find her and would know where to look. As for the rest of his message: how did he know where their enemies were? Had he interfaced, working it out for himself that things were coming to a head, and where the ultimate venue must be? In which case he was even stronger and stranger than she'd thought. But then, who could know it all about that one? Her mysterious Harry Keogh—or Radu's. But that remained to be seen . . .

And meanwhile, she had had to move on. If Harry was wrong and the Drakuls hadn't gone north, she couldn't have them knowing her location. And then there were the Watcher and the Ferenczys: she knew for certain that they *were* in the Highlands, in the Spey Valley, for they had tried to kill Auld John in Inverdruie. So either way Harry was half-right: *some* of her enemies, at least, were up north, which in turn meant that B.J. couldn't be—not yet. And trapped between two possible perils, B.J. had moved. But not too far, and not into the Highlands.

If she had—with all three rival vampire factions concentrated in one location, a narrow valley with a handful of towns and villages—sooner or later they must clash. And with Radu's resurgence so close, B.J. wasn't about to risk any further confrontations. Anyway, both the Drakuls and the Ferenczys were probably just as leery of her now as she was of them. In three clashes so far, they had come off the worst. As for the fourth: well, poor Zahanine's death could scarcely be reckoned as part of any legitimate war. No, for that had been sheer murder! And so:

It was a stand-off, and they were biding their time. Having divined Radu's approximate location—and knowing that B.J. must travel north eventually, to attend him in the hour of his rising—they would lie in wait for her. Then, if they couldn't take her out before she went to Radu, they would simply follow her and catch both of them at their most vulnerable.

Now B.J. and the pack were back in Edinburgh, in a small, backstreet hotel, never leaving the place except for absolute necessities . . . one of which had caused B.J. her biggest headache to date.

On the off-chance that Harry had tried to contact her at the wine-bar (despite that he'd apparently chosen to stay away from her until the hour as yet to be appointed), B.J. had ventured out one night and followed a circuitous route to the bar. There she had found some unimportant messages on her answering machine, and two that were very important.

Of the latter: one was from a local police station in respect of Inspector George Ianson and requested that she contact the police at her earliest opportunity, and the other was from someone she had never expected to hear from. Or if not "never," then certainly not as soon as this.

Radu had thralls in the country, moon-children, the sons of the sons of his people from six hundred years ago. Dwellers in lonely places, only two remained, but still they were aware of him. B.J. had visited them on occasion, when it was safe to do so, advising them of their duties at the time of His return. Her instructions between times had been simple to the point of elementary: they were *never* to contact her until the time appointed, and even then the probability was that she would contact them first. Yet now—

—One of them, Alan Goresci, from his home on the edge of Bodmin Moor, had contacted her and left this message:

"Bonnie Jean. This is Alan-on-the-Moor." (His accent was pure Cornish.) "I've spoken with young Garth, who is close by as you know. Both of us, we've heard the call. And we're restless. It's the high ground we're heading for. We'll be on the way by the time you hear this. I wouldn't have contacted you, but if you were to do it, you've left it a bit late. So maybe there's a problem? And Auld John's no to house that I can see. We'll look him up; doubtless through him we'll find you. Till then, we're hoping that all is well under the moon . . . " End of message.

What was she to make of it? Alan Goresci and Garth Trevalin had heard the call? All the way back to her hiding place in the small hotel, B.J. had worried about it. *They* had heard the call—Radu's call, obviously—and she hadn't? What was going on here? She had tried calling both men, but their telephones had just rung and rung. And the dog-Lord's return not scheduled for another two months. Oh, really? So why were the Ferenczys, possibly the Drakuls, too, up in the Cairngorms so early? What did they know, and Radu's other thralls, that B.J. Mirlu didn't?

But her course was set and no changing it now. She, too, must wait for Radu's call. Until then there was nothing to do except worry over why she was the last to hear it, and to wonder what was on the dog-Lord's mind . . .

And in Sicily, in Le Manse Madonie:

Anthony Francezci had never felt more alone in his life; never in his long, his too-long life.

Despite that he and his brother were rarely in complete accord, still he missed Francesco. Without him, Le Manse felt like some great stone tomb. A house of vampires, and the oldest of them all seething in his pit in the very bowels of the place. And the daily horror, when Anthony took to his bed, of never knowing what his dreams would be; but knowing quite definitely that when they came they would be nightmares, even to a monster. And knowing, too, what they would bring with them.

It had been only nine or ten days since the morning when Katerin had stumbled from his room clutching at her throat and vowing to tell no one what she had seen. Nor would she for her life's sake, he was sure. But what difference did it make that no one else knew of his condition, the onset of his mutation? None at all, for Anthony himself knew. Knew that however long it took, the day would dawn when he was as his father was now. And that fact alone—its certainty—paled every other eventuality to insignificance, bringing him ever closer to the living, frothing horror that was Angelo Ferenczy.

Ten days, yes, in which short period of time, out of all the *centuries* of his time, Anthony had become as a ghost. Now he wafted through Le Manse Madonie much as a vampire thrall in the early days of conversion, spending most of his time in the cavern of the pit. And those of his men who saw him—hardened vampires who yet feared him for what *he* was, Wamphyri—could only marvel at the change in Anthony: his sunken cheeks, slumped shoulders, and fevered eyes. But only old Katerin and his father knew what troubled him.

Ah, my son, Angelo told him one time, where he leaned on the wall of the pit. *It puts all other problems to flight, eh? As it was for me, so it is for you. Terrible! Terrible! But can you possibly believe that your brother will be as accommodating to you as you were to me that time all those years ago? Did you think I did not know? Oh, I knew. If not for you—your vision, your foresight—I would have been a dead thing, a truly dead thing, a long time ago. And who can say, perhaps that were for the best.* The Old Ferenczy was at his most lucid, and his most tantalizing.

"How do you mean?" But Anthony was listless, enervated; he was sleeping badly, as from now on he always would.

In these latter centuries, without my guidance, my advice—without me as your "oracle"—you would have been more like an original. You would have had *to be Wamphyri! But now . . . ?*

Anthony had offered a shrug. "It's a modern world. In order to live in it, we had to be modern, too."

And sacrifice your vampire powers? I have thought long and long on it. Perhaps it was because I no longer had any real use for my powers that they started to overtake me. I was a dam and they were the water piling up within. When the pressure was too great, and they could no longer be contained, they burst forth. First the cracks, then the flood.

"Are you saying our passions were pent? Too constrained?"

Yours especially, the other answered. *Francesco gave vent to his desires. As a child I had to curb him. He and I . . . were never close. Nothing strange in that: we are Wamphyri! But when opportunity presented, he went out into the world—perhaps to be away from me? And you were the home bird. You learned wisdom while he . . . learned! He was ever the more lustful, avaricious, bloody! Which was why, in this "modern" world, I must curb him. But the truth is that he was more the original, too. Even now.*

"So, because Francesco 'gave vent,' as you have it," Anthony replied, "and still gives it, he has probably saved himself from this? But I had thought the opposite was true: that a muscle atrophies through *disuse*."

In human terms, according to the physicians of this world, yes. But the skills of the Wamphyri are only ours by virtue of the creature beneath *the skin. The leech is our strength, Tony, my Tony! We are each two creatures; and we, the external creatures, believe that we hold the power. In this we are mistaken.* We *are the muscle that will atrophy, if our vampire leeches are not allowed to use us! But when the balance tilts too far, even the leech loses control.*

"And when Francesco sees what is become or becoming of me?" Anthony tried to peer through the miasma rising from the shaft. "You hinted that he'd be less accommodating than I was."

I could be wrong, (and Anthony sensed a shrug). *But even if I am, what is this for "accommodation?" Is this what you want, my Tony? To be a thing in a pit?*

"I would rather be dead, even truly dead!"

My sentiments exactly, said the other. *And I have seen . . . I have seen . . .* (He fell silent.)

"You've seen—what?"

Nothing! Nothing beyond the fact of the dog-Lord's return. Oh, and his coming here, of course! But nothing else, no.

"His coming here!" Anthony hissed. "You've made no mention of this before?"

But I did, I did! Those years ago, before this Harry stole into your vault, and stole off with your money. I told you then that Radu would seek us out.

"When?" Anthony gripped the wall, leaned out a little more over the black gulf of the pit. "When will he come?"

He is awake even now.

"I know that," Anthony barked, "for I've spoken with Francesco. He sensed him in the mountains, in Scotland. Radu's return will be soon now. But . . . you say he'll come here? How can that be? Francesco will stop him, surely?"

I think not. Oh, your brother is more like *an original, be sure. But Radu* is *an original!*

"Then I've got to get out of this place!" Anthony was beginning to panic. He felt the oppression of Le Manse Madonie as surely as any previous prisoner.

He would find you, wherever you go. Commonsense says stay here, defend what you've got. Have you strayed so far from your origins that even your territorialism has deserted you?

"I see right through you!" Anthony snarled. Finally galvanized, he shook off his mood of morbid depression—or his terror did it for him. "You want me to stay here to defend you!"

No, for I see no future for myself. Now be calm, my Tony, my Anthony. Think what you have here: a veritable fortress, and men, your vampire thralls, to defend it. How may Radu come upon you without that you see him? From the rim of the plateau, from the walls of Le Manse Madonie; vampire eyes at night, searching for the great wolf! How can he come but across the plateau jumbles, or along your roads? Have you no watchmen? Also, you know when *he will come: when it is his time. One night when the moon is full.*

"He will take Francesco—who by your own words is closer far to your damned 'original' than me—yet fall before me and mine? Also, if Francesco is on the verge of destruction, as you have hinted, then why should I concern myself with how he might 'accommodate' me?" Anthony's normally pale face had grown livid now and his eyes blazed red. "You trip on your own tongue, Angelo Ferenczy. The things you say don't add up. You are playing a game with me, which sooner or later will come to light!"

No games, my son, my dear sweet Tony, Angelo replied. *The future was ever devious; how may we be sure of anything? Also, these matters are much too serious for games, and I am far too old for them . . . not to mention too hungry! Deprived, I cannot even think straight. You have not fed me in a while. Some tidbit, perhaps? Something sweet? Someone young?*

"No!" Anthony snapped. Then changed his mind—apparently. "Yes!—when you have told me all you know. For I am *sure* that you have foreseen the end of all this. As for now . . . " He stumbled back from the rim. "Now I'm weary. I can't get enough of—can't get *any*—sleep, not with this thing in me, changing me. I'll leave you to consider *your* future!"

Staggering to the gears, he lowered the half-grid over the mouth of the shaft and switched on the current. But then, as he made to leave the cavern:

ANGELO LIES! HE LIES, LIES, LIES! The Old Ferenczy's multi-minds, over which he no longer had total control, were suddenly screaming in Anthony's head, rocking him on his heels.

"What?" His trembling hands flew to his temples.

ANTHONY, YOUR FATHER IS LYING TO YOU! . . . YOU ARE RIGHT: HE KNOWS THE OUTCOME AND PREPARES FOR IT EVEN NOW. THE TENACITY OF THE WAMPHYRI! . . . ANGELO NEITHER WELCOMES NOR FEARS DEATH. WHY, A PART OF HIM IS DEAD EVEN NOW, IN WHICH HE IS BREEDING . . .

Be quiet! (Angelo would try to shout them down. And Anthony knew that the Old Ferenczy could will himself comatose, and the minds of all his victims with him, if he so desired.)

"How has he lied? Tell me, quickly!" He turned back to the pit, hoping they would "hear" him through his father. "What is he breeding?"

MYRIADS . . .

Be quiet! (Angelo's bullfrog grunt, a threat in itself, as he strained to shut himself, and them, down.)

"Myriads of what?" But Anthony saw that already the exhalations from the pit—the vapours that were the "breath" of his father—were thinning.

MYRIADS! That word again. And finally:

Myriads, in a fading whisper, which died away entirely.

Then silence . . .

Climbing towards the saner, upper regions of Le Manse Madonie, Anthony fumed. His loathsome father could blame who or whatever he desired for his condition, but Anthony saw it as hereditary. And if Angelo hadn't contracted it, or if it hadn't been in his blood in the first place, then it wouldn't be in Anthony. Well, and now the ancient Thing was hungry again, was he? Nothing new in that. And he wanted something young, something sweet. For he liked them fresh and clean, the Old Ferenczy.

And now Anthony grinned to himself, however viciously. He would satisfy the monster's lusts—but in his own way. And not until he was satisfied himself:

that Angelo had told him all he knew. And until then he could starve. Not that he would starve. No, he would simply *shrink*, dry out, eventually fossilize! Destroy him with fire? Ah, no—Francesco had it quite wrong. But to seal him in his pit, and let him rot and scream forever down there in the dark . . . that would be much more in keeping.

Then, because he suspected that his father might be "listening," Anthony added: "Think on *that,* you old bastard! And be sure that it isn't an idle threat."

As for Angelo's "tidbit": Anthony had the very thing. But here he shielded his thoughts as best he might, for he desired that to come as a surprise. Young and sweet? *Hah!* But when finally his father gave in to his demands, then there *would* be a reward of sorts, certainly.

Her name was Katerin . . .

In fact the hideous anomaly that was the Old Ferenczy "heard" none of this. Shut down, his mass of metamorphic matter slept. While moist in a corner of the natural rock cyst that was his cell a deliberately extruded, excised part of him rotted down, vented warm gasses, and stirred with a "life" of its own. Purple strands of cryptogenetic mycelium were threading their way through it even now.

Soon, it would break open to the pressure of the first of many fungus domes. And beneath the black toadstool caps, myriad red spores would form like pollen on the gills of these obscene fruiting bodies . . .

Harry couldn't trust reality; indeed, from time to time he wondered if there was such a thing. But deep inside, as an all-too-human being, he was aware of the difference between what could and could not be. Or should not be. And some of the things that had been his life, before the times that he no longer wished to remember, were surely of the latter variety. But here there was no question of what was and wasn't, or what should and couldn't possibly be. No past and no future to worry about, only now.

Which was why he had incarcerated himself in this place of safety, this refuge. Since when he really hadn't bothered thinking much about anything. Yet now he seemed to be conscious, and wondered *why* he was thinking again—and knew why. Because soon it would be feeding time, when the refuge wasn't nearly so safe after all.

He went to stretch—and couldn't. Couldn't? But he could move his head, to look and see why he was immobilized. And then he remembered, or had this vague, shadowy recollection, of men bringing a heavy, padded armchair into his small, padded room. That had been after a very bad nightmare, when he'd started to scream and couldn't stop. And he remembered the jacket they'd put him in, before sitting him down in his chair and strapping his wrists to the padded arms.

But these were only very small irritations; they were as nothing compared to the other thing, when he heard dead people talking to him. And it happened all the time: awake and sleeping alike! Awake it wasn't so bad; he could handle it; he knew how to shut them out. But asleep it brought on the nightmares, when he must struggle and fight and *kick* to be rid of all that! Hence the . . . straitjacket? For the people here didn't seem to understand that if they would only keep him awake he wouldn't need to be tied down. And they wouldn't let him explain—probably because he wasn't very articulate, or because he kept mentioning things they didn't want to hear—which only frustrated him and made him angry. And then, when he began to yell, they would give him a needle and the teeming dead would start in on him again.

It was a cycle he couldn't break out of—despite that he had broken in!—and it detracted from his security. It wasn't the refuge he'd envisaged. Perhaps we would leave and find some safer place, but that would mean going through those doors that didn't exist . . . and he'd done *that* for the last time, too! And anyway, he couldn't move, not tied down like this. But that was OK; the solitude and silence and stillness were good, weren't they? Except, he didn't know what to do about the feeding.

He sat in his chair, itched and couldn't scratch, ran his tongue over the roughened areas of his gums above and below his front teeth; the rough, raw areas of torn skin where Willis had forced the sharp spoon into his mouth. And he felt the crusted rims of dried food clinging to his nostrils and ears, where the sadistic intern had stuffed the mush when Harry wouldn't accept it driven savagely into his mouth. The next time Willis came—which would be soon now—he'd bring a wet sponge with him and clean Harry up a little, before starting again. And while Harry wasn't sure what he could do about it exactly, still he knew he must do something about the feeding . . .

. . . But right now someone was speaking to him, a live someone, and Harry realized he'd been answering out loud. Well, not necessarily *answering*, but speaking at least; voicing his complaints, probably.

"You see," said the voice, "I just don't know what we are dealing with here. If I knew who you were it would help. And it would be even better if I knew how you got in here. But all you had on you was a notebook with a lot of scribble, none of which made any sense, and the only person you've spoken about is this Harry. Is that you? No second name? And no desire to . . . communicate?"

"Second name," Harry said, trying desperately hard to focus his eyes, his mind. "Snaith . . . or Keogh . . . or Kyle." And finally he got his bearings, brought the room out of blur.

Director Cyril Quant saw Harry's eyes swim into focus and sat still in the lightweight folding chair he had brought with him to Harry's cell. Willis was outside in the corridor, where Quant had told him to wait. But doubtless he'd heard this mysterious inmate's—this "illegal" inmate's—mumbled, incoherent accusations. And Quant could see for himself the litter of dried-out slop on Harry's face.

"But if you fight your feeding," he said reasonably, "you must expect to be made to eat. We can't have you dying on us—er, Harry?—and not even know who you are! Now can we?"

Harry hung on to his vision, clung to the idea that somehow this man might be able to help him with this food problem. What he saw was weird; his eyes weren't right; they hadn't focused properly for—oh, for however long he'd been here. But Quant would look funny, if he didn't look so grotesque! It was some sort of weird telescopic effect. Quant's body was tiny on an even smaller chair, swelling up into round humped shoulders supporting a hugely bloated head. Balding, with a few strands of red hair slicked back behind smallish ears, and peering at Harry through thick-lensed spectacles that made his eyes look bigger yet, the man was batrachian, some kind of super-frog!

"Are you smiling?" Quant said. "Do you understand any of this at all?"

"No, do you?" Harry tried to ask him—which came out of his dry throat as a croak, a mumble. But in any case it was all too much. Only let it continue, they'd lure him back into their world, which no longer had any meaning for him. Best to simply let it slip.

And Quant snorted his disappointment as Harry's eyes slid out of focus again and his head lolled from side to side . . .

Out in the corridor, Quant spoke to Willis. "He doesn't seem to like you, Mr. Willis."

"It cuts both ways," Willis answered. "I heard what he was on about. Feeding time? It's like feeding a rabid dog! I try to get something into him—he spits it right back at me! How am I supposed to feed him if he won't keep his . . . *head* still?" Just for a moment he'd almost said "his *fucking* head," and Quant was looking at him curiously. "I mean," Willis continued hurriedly, "can't we put him on a drip, feed him intravenously? And what's he still doing here, anyway? He's not ours; he isn't a legitimate inmate. Shouldn't we—I don't know— give him to the authorities or something?"

Leading the way out of the ward through its system of security doors, Quant answered, "That's just the problem. Until we know who he is and how he got in here, how do we explain him?"

"Why bother trying to 'explain' him?" Willis said. "Maybe we simply found him wandering in the grounds, inside the security fence. No one's going to argue the fact that he's a mental case! Maybe someone couldn't look after him any longer, dumped him on us."

"And what if that someone is the inspectorate?" The director rounded on him. "We're a hospital, a mental institution. Do you think that puts us beyond scrutiny? On the contrary, people care about our inmates. And we are supposed to care *for* them!"

"And if he is a plant?" Willis argued. "I mean, how do you know they're not waiting and wondering right now why we've done nothing about him?"

"Not we, me!" Quant snapped.

And Willis shrugged. "Your problem—sir," he said, with a narrow-eyed, sideways look.

"Tomorrow," Quant nodded, entering the elevator. "I'll report what has happened here tomorrow. There are higher authorities, after all. Meanwhile . . . tidy him up, will you? And ensure that he stays tidied up? If it means handing him over, which it probably will, I would want him in the best possible condition. And that goes for *all* of the inmates, got it? If there's to be an inspection of the facility, we need to be beyond criticism."

As the elevator took Quant aloft, Willis stormed back to the control room. It was swill time for all these crazy pigs—but he knew who he was going to attend to first. *We're supposed to care for them, are we?* He grumbled to himself. *And there's a problem with the feeding, is there? Oh really?* Well, Dave Willis knew how to give this mysterious whoever-he-fucking-was lunatic a problem or two! And whichever—come what may—the *next* can of slop was going down and staying down!

Harry failed to hear Willis enter his cell, didn't even know he was there, until he felt the hot baby-food stew on his lips and the sharp rim of the spoon thrusting in his mouth. Then, shaken from his torpor, his immediate reaction was to choke and cough, and spit the muck out. Following which—

—It got much, much worse. But when it was over and everything was quiet again, Harry stayed focused. Because now there was something definite to focus upon. At which the Great Majority, his friends in low society, saw their best opportunity yet and took it.

And for once Harry listened to them—gave them his whole-hearted attention, or what was left of it—because almost anything had to be better than this . . .

He's not crazy, a man who in life had been a top-level psychiatrist reported to Sir Keenan Gormley. *He simply opted out of a world that* was *crazy, from his point of view. The problem will lie in getting him to opt back in. But right now he's very confused. His mind is full of a dislike bordering on hatred for a man called Willis. By no means unnatural: the man is an intern who is abusing and literally torturing Harry! But on the other hand, Willis is also the reason we have access. Harry is looking for a way to escape from the mess he's in. Which means he can reason well enough, if we can supply him with a* reason *to.*

Franz Anton Mesmer joined in. *I feel I have something of a stake in this,* he said. *Harry was my patient first, after all. Or rather, he was my* therapist *first! He gave me back my self-confidence, and now I would like to do the same for him.*

Through hypnotism? (Harry's Ma was at once fearful.)

Not really, Mesmer answered. *My hypnotism only allowed me a degree of access to his mind. Now I intend to work with what I found there—with knowledge, yes. And I'll need your help, Mary Keogh.*

My help? What do you mean?

Your promise not to interfere, Mesmer told her, bluntly.

I don't understand. (The shake of an incorporeal head.)

His love for B.J. Mirlu, Mesmer explained. *I still know the way into his head. And I remember that he feared for her. Right now she is in danger; we all know that from the men—and some monsters—who have come among us. It may be the one thing that can bring him out of this: to know that this girl is in danger.*

Two things, then, the psychiatrist put in. *His love of this woman, and his fear of this man Willis, therefore his desire to be out of it.*

Three, said Nostradamus, surprising them with his presence. *For as yet he hasn't worked through all the riddles I gave him. And I know how reluctant the Necroscope is to leave unfinished business!*

What else do you know? Sir Keenan asked him. *What did you see, in his future?*

Don't ask it, Nostradamus answered. *It's not for you, nor even for me to know. Not in its entirety.*

So, said Mesmer. *What's it to be? Shall I enter him then? Shall I remind him that*

B.J. Mirlu is relying upon him, that as yet he has not unriddled Nostradamus's clues—which may provide the only viable solution—and that his one "safe place" is really a place of torture and peril?

But Harry's Ma wanted to know: *What lies will you tell him about B.J.?*

Only that she loves him—which we can't be sure is a lie anyway. And also that the case against her remains unproven. If he loves her . . . that should be enough.

"Should" be enough? Sir Keenan queried Mesmer's use of the word. *Where's the risk?*

Mesmer was cautious as he answered, *The interface between the Necroscope's reality and unreality has been so weakened by use that it has stretched taut as a tightrope. When next he is challenged to choose between what is and what isn't, it's possible he could fall the wrong way.*

And is that likely to happen? (Harry's Ma again.) *I mean, will his levels interface one last time?*

Franz Anton's reluctant, incorporeal nod. *Oh, yes. And the trigger is in B.J. Mirlu's hands . . .*

For long moments there was utter silence in the metaphysical aether, until Mary Keogh "sighed" and asked: *And is there no way round it?*

Oh, yes, said Mesmer again. *There's always an alternative. To let things be—to let a horror befall the living world, and everyone in it—and then to explain to the multitude when they come among us why we let it happen! I know what I choose, but I can't make that choice alone. And meanwhile, time is wasting.*

At which a new voice said: *You has my vote, Mr. Mesmer.* It was R.L. Stevenson Jamieson. *Least ways I can watch out for the Necroscope, and use my obi to do whatever I can for him.* He was his usual, humble, selfless self.

My vote, too, said Nostradamus. *For without that the Necroscope goes forward, he can't go back! And I . . . can't go! It is a paradox as old as time. What came first . . . ?*

I love him like a son . . . excuse me, Mary, said Sir Keenan. *God knows I wouldn't place him in jeopardy. But to have him as he is now is to have nothing. And it is also for him to have nothing. Doctor,* (now he spoke to Mesmer), *I believe I can help with Harry's motivation. So if I may, I'll go in with you.*

Which left only Harry's Ma herself, with whom no one would dispute the final decision.

And time ticking inexorably into the future, and NOW continually sliding into the past . . .

Harry was conscious. *Suddenly* conscious. And just as suddenly he knew what he had done, and what he hadn't.

He had quit. He had given up the ghost with the job half-done and less than half understood. He had let someone or someones do this to him without even knowing who or what they were. For even the fear of finding out had been too much for him. But it had proved to be the classic case of out of the frying pan into the fire. And now he wanted out of the fire, too. And back into the frying pan?

But from out of the blue (or out of his dreams, or the insistence of the *inhabitants* of those dreams) sanity had flowed back into him. Or rather, the emptiness—the vacuum—which he had self-created had been filled again, and he wasn't about to let it drain away a second time. For if nature abhors a vacumm, then how much greater the abhorrence of the dead when the space in question was one previously filled by the Necroscope?

And so he was suddenly conscious, and sane, and his body-clock told him it was close to morning. And despite that from the moment he opened his eyes he began to feel stiff, he knew that this was only an illusion, a natural result of being confined to this chair. For his sleep had been deep and (paradoxically?) restful, so that even now there was this fading inner voice reminding him: *You'll sleep deep and soundly, Harry, and wake up feeling quite well and rested . . . wake up feeling well and rested . . . well and rested.*

There had been other voices, too, but while they were gone now their messages remained. Or were the messages simply ideas, stuff his computer mind had been working on before it crashed? Whichever, they were there, surfacing with Harry from his deep and restful sleep.

The idea that one of his basic problems stemmed from his time with E-Branch. That was an old one, developed from Nostradamus's quatrains. But what else was locked in those quatrains that he hadn't released yet? He had work to do!

And the idea—or more correctly the fact—that Bonnie Jean hadn't yet definitely been proved guilty of fouling up his life. Not one hundred per cent guilty; fifty-fifty at worst, if in fact E-Branch had had a hand in it, too.

And the idea, again a fact, that B.J. was in danger. Their enemies were abroad, probably searching for her even now, while Harry languished in here! And if indeed she loved him—and he was suddenly sure that who or whatever she was, she did—then her enemies were his. But he also knew that they were *big* enemies, not just little ones like the one he had here.

Willis! Morning! Breakfast!

No way! No fucking way!

Harry turned his head this way and that, stared wildly all about his cell, opened his channels to the dead. It was as good and better than a cry for help, a Mayday, an SOS.

Harry! said R.L. Stevenson Jamieson, in a hell of a hurry. *Is you listenin', Necroscope? There's this guy headin' your way right now, and he ain't exactly a friend!*

"How long do I have, R.L.?" Harry tugged uselessly at his bonds, the leather straps binding his hands to the arms of the chair. He dangled his legs, tried kicking them, couldn't bring any pressure to bear for his feet were off the floor.

How long? I don't deal in time, just distances, Harry! I only knows this guy is closing with you, lookin' to bein' with you. I sees your flame burnin', and this one's bent on snuffin' it!—well, a mite. He ain't got no good plans for you, that's for sure.

Harry quit fighting his wrist straps, strained against the broad belt across his chest. There was some give in it but nothing to use as a lever except his lungs! It was useless. Even if he got out of the chair, he'd still be in a straitjacket.

And panting now, he sent: "Is there anyone else out there? Is there a . . . a morgue in this place?" There wasn't, but even if there had been the thought had already crossed Harry's mind that it mightn't be such a good idea to call a madman back from the dead!

So, no physical help, not from a physical source, anyway. But there was someone else out there. *You have a lot of friends down among the dead men, Harry Keogh,* said an entirely new but definitely friendly voice, the voice of a total stranger. *And I have to admit I've been interested in you a long time, but they told me you were kind of busy.*

"Still am," the Necroscope grunted, shaking himself about like a *real* madman in his chair. And: "Friend," he let himself loll a while, tried to reserve his strength, "unless you've got some damn good suggestion, would you mind making room for someone who has? Who are you, anyway?"

Harry's my name, said the other, with a grin that only the Necroscope could ever hope to perceive. *Well, that was my stage name, anyway.*

"Some kind of joke?" Almost exhausted, defeated, the Necroscope gave a shake of his head. "If so, bad timing."

Amazing! said the other Harry. *I spent a lot of time—er, in my time—proving that you and your kind couldn't exist. And maybe at that time you couldn't. But then you came along. Since when I've been able to talk to my mother again just as you talk to yours! That's one great big debt I owe you, Harry Keogh. But it's also why I held off for so long: because I was afraid that you'd turn out to be a charlatan, too. Obviously you're not.*

"Er, Harry?" said Harry, "I'm sorry if I can't give you my full attention right now, but . . . "

. . . Harry Houdini, said the other. *I'm here to do a benefit on the behalf of the Great Majority—and I'm delighted to make your acquaintance.*

"Harry Houdi—!" Harry started to say, before his jaw fell open.

Houdini, yes, the dead showman said, from his plot in the Machpelah Cemetery, Cypress Hills, Queens. And out of the blue: *How much slack have you worked into those things?*

The Necroscope said. "What?" Then finally got himself together again and sighed his relief. "My straps, you mean? This straitjacket? Why not come on in and see for yourself?" And he opened his mind more yet.

May I? said Houdini, touching him mind-to-mind.

"Be my guest," the Necroscope sighed again, gladly. "Come right on in, Harry, and make yourself at home. But you'll have to excuse me if it's none too comfortable around here. In fact, even knowing who you are and something of what you've done, it still seems pretty hopeless to me." He felt some of the elation of a few seconds ago evaporating. "Time isn't on our side, and this jacket would be bad enough without the chair . . . "

The jacket's nothing, said the other Harry. *I made a study of such restraints. The reason you're still in it is to make it easier for your "keepers." When they want to move you, they'll simply release your arms from the chair, fold them across your chest and tie them. So your only real problem is the chair. And Harry, while I never tried it, I think I could probably get out of one of those things underwater! OK, so just let go and let me take it from here.*

The Necroscope did as instructed, relaxed as best he could, and let the expert take over. And a moment later he felt a new and different kind of magic in his life . . .

Fifteen minutes later Willis arrived with Harry's breakfast. In the control cell, the CCTV screen had been down, which meant he hadn't been able to do a remote check on the ward's inmates. It didn't matter; the padded cells had safety-glass windows; Harry was sitting in a corner, like little Jack Horner, and he'd soon be eating his curds and whey—or was that little Miss Muffet? Whichever, he'd eat it or get it stuffed into him!

A single glance into the dim cell had been sufficient—no change since last night. Just the nutter with his arms strapped down and his head on his chest. Asleep? Well, he'd soon be wide awake.

Willis put the tray on a rounded shelf surface built into the padded wall, turned and closed the door, then turned again to face Harry—who was facing him!

"Good morning, Mr. Willis," said Harry from where he stood not two feet away. And then, to someone Willis couldn't see and wouldn't have believed in anyway:

Sergeant, he's all yours!

And as Willis's thick-lipped mouth formed its incredulous "O," "Sergeant" Graham Lane—an *ex*-ex-army physical training instructor—did the rest . . .

Director Cyril Quant got in to work just half an hour later, in time for all hell to break loose. It broke as he finished reading the note on his desk for the second time:

> To Whoever Probably Isn't Much Concerned—
> You have an ape called Willis on your staff. I wouldn't let this man clean out the monkey house in Edinburgh Zoo. He's brutal and sadistic and has just had his arse kicked. When I get the time, I'll be sending a full report to the proper authorities. Or, you can investigate yourself and save us both a lot of trouble.
>
> Harry
>
> P.S.
> Leave me out of your investigations—unless you want to end up in one of your own straitjackets.

It was the name that did it. Director Quant tore open his desk drawer, ripped out a handful of the paper contents, tilted the rest onto the floor. But the only evidence that "Harry" had ever been here—his scribbled, meaningless notebook—was no longer there.

And ten minutes later, down in C-Section of D-Ward, Quant saw that indeed Dave Willis had had his arse kicked. The other orderlies were in the process of freeing the unconscious, simian Willis from the chair. He had a broken nose and collarbone, a black eye and fat lip—and his hair was matted with congealing porridge . . .

Back home, the Necroscope could scarcely believe the change in himself. After a shower, some decent food, a sleep lasting well into the afternoon, he felt . . . well, not *quite* as good as new, but better than he'd been for a long time. His memory was still at fault, (the post-hypnotic commands that governed many of his thoughts, actions and mental processes were still in place, however shakily), but there was this newfound sense of freedom in him that wasn't just the result of his actual freedom. In fact he felt uplifted and reasoned that it was because he now had a sense of direction, a course to follow, and things to do. Just how those things would work out . . . remained to be seen.

But it was more than just that. In the madhouse Harry had regained a little of his faith in the teeming dead—therefore in himself. He was no longer so shy of them; he knew that when he needed them, they'd be there for him. Without knowing what it signified, he felt a weakening of James Anderson's original commands, brought about by Mesmer's probing. And he no longer felt so restricted, so fearful in his use of the Möbius Continuum. These things had been major shackles but were now falling away from him.

Likewise his doubts about B.J. Mirlu. Harry no longer wondered if he was only her dupe; if it was so then it was so; but nothing was proven, and until it was Harry would love her as he desperately wanted to believe she loved him. Should unknown dangers lie ahead, they would face them together—but at the same time he wasn't about to face anything blindfold, or even blinkered.

Nostradamus had given him clues galore, only a handful of which had sufficed to drive him over the edge, or close enough to it that he didn't care to be reminded. Yet in a way he felt strengthened by the experience; he knew the dangers now of trying to learn too much too soon. From this time forward he would proceed step by step, adjusting as he went.

But Bonnie Jean was constantly on his mind. Her weird attraction continued to lure him, and he felt his recent (but how recent? Just how *long* had he languished in the asylum?) resolve to stay away from her dissolving to nothing as the monthly cycle neared its full.

The monthly cycle? Its full? The full moon!

A Möbius trip into town, to the newsagent's, told him how right he was.

Tomorrow! The moon would be full tomorrow! Little wonder he could smell the musk of her perfume . . . or simply her musk? He knew where she was even now and must cling desperately hard to his crumbling will in order not to go to her immediately—this very minute!

But no, for there was work to do, and he still had a full day in which to do it before he could no longer resist.

Nostradamus's riddles.

The incoherent ramblings, scribbled quatrains, and "meaningless" jottings in his notebook. Dangerous work. He had been trying to decipher them—read something into them—when he . . . But that was all over now and he must begin again.

And sitting in his kitchen, he opened the notebook on the table before him . . .

V

HARRY: WORKING IT OUT.
MOON-CHILDREN: ANSWERING
THE CALL.

HARRY'S SEVERAL LEVELS OF BEING AND KNOWLEDGE WERE ONCE MORE IN place, however insecurely. On his conscious level—in his real world—he knew that his future was somehow tied to a place in the cold waste of Tibet. Or perhaps not; for he had incontrovertible evidence that he had *already* returned to that place once, to hide Zahanine's body there, so maybe that fulfilled not only his vision but also Alec Kyle's weird forecast of nuclear devastation. Certainly the Necroscope had experienced enormous *emotional* devastation on discovering Zahanine's decapitated corpse in his study.

Or perhaps the vision's purpose had been simply to make a connection: to show him that the device at Greenham Common was of Tibetan origin? A fact which Darcy Clarke had corroborated. Harry had felt uneasy about those red-robed monks from the beginning; but again, that could have been a revenant of Kyle's intuitive precognitive powers.

So then: that the monks were enemies of the country—and indeed of the civilized world!—seemed self-evident. But why were they B.J.'s enemies? Who *was* B.J., that she could call up such allies to her aid as he had seen (or thought he had seen) in that animal shelter in the snowstorm?

But no, that line of investigation was forbidden. The Necroscope had been there before; it was one of the reasons he had gone over the edge, shutting himself down almost beyond recall. And anyway, every time he found himself casting doubts on B.J., a little voice from the back of his head would immediately deny it and cry her innocence. Actually, Harry had certain reservations about that voice, for sometimes it sounded a hell of a lot like B.J. herself! But—

—There it was again, that immediate denial! And perhaps a warning, too. So he went back to thinking about the red-robes.

Some scribbled lines in his notebook took his attention:

"The face staring over the frozen waste. Red thoughts, red robes. Labyrinth. Golden bells."

And the quatrain fell into place:

> The face looks out across a frozen waste,
> Red the thoughts and robes of him who dwells
> Within the labyrinth of that dire place,
> Within the fluence of the golden bells.

A face over a dire, labyrinthine place, looking out across a frozen waste-land. The monastery? It could only be. "Red the thoughts and robes of *him* who dwells . . . "

Him, and not them? The master of the monastery, then. So, whoever *he* was, he would be the one to look out for. And there was a line in the notebook containing the word "master." Harry turned a page and found it:

" . . . Her master's kennel-maid." (Harry felt he was skating on thin ice again, but went on anyway.) "A castle, hollow and high. Glowing yellow bed. Resting place . . . "

Did that make sense? Did he know something about it? Fuck it! Why did simply *thinking* about it make him sweat? (Maybe he wasn't supposed to think about it—not yet.)

And so he moved on.

"Of one blood, composed of it. Takers of life. The stake, the fire, the knife!" And again the quatrain:

> They are of one blood, one and all,
> *composed* of blood, inheritors of life,
> which was not theirs to take. Their fall
> is possible: the stake, the fire, the knife!

And yet again he must stop, for at this juncture the ice was just too thin to support him. He let that one ominous word cross his mind again—Wamphyri!—and quickly moved on.

Nostradamus had told him that one of his actual, published quatrains pertained directly to the Necroscope. And sure enough when he checked his notebook: "Second 'C,' under Nostra's name. Tree(s). Pride = shame."

Whatever it meant it was a couplet in itself:

> Second 'C,' under Nostra's name,
> Tree is trees, and pride is shame.

Outside, it was already dark. The moon was low, almost at its full where it limned the rims of scudding clouds in flowing silver. Harry shivered, closed the curtains, made a Möbius jump to a back street near the library in Bonnyrig. The library was closed—good! Another jump took him inside, to the shelf with the books on Nostradamus. He chose an armful at random and took them home with him.

Beginning with a volume containing the complete quatrains, he turned the pages to the second "Century," the second set of one hundred four-liners, still without knowing what he was looking for. All he knew was that it had something to do with Nostradamus's name. What's in a name? Names and numbers . . .

That was what Nostradamus had said to him: "Find it under my name—use your numbers, and mine." But he hadn't meant the Necroscope's intuitive grasp of maths; no, his meaning had been more esoteric. Indeed he had *meant* esoteric numerology!

And so Harry used numbers. The Hebrew system:

M	I	C	H	E	L	D	E	N	O	S	T	R	E	D	A	M	E
4	1	3	5	5	3	4	5	5	7	3	4	2	5	4	1	4	5

The total of Nostradamus's name was seventy, which Harry remembered from his conversation with the dead seer. Likewise, if he were called Michel de Nostradamus, the modern version of his name, the total came out the same. In both cases the Necroscope had added the seven and the zero to make Seven: the number of the bookworm, mystic, occultist, and magician.

But the actual number of his name or names was seventy in both cases. And now Harry turned to the page with quatrain number 70 of the second Century.

> Le dard du ciel fera son estendu,
> Mors en parlant: grand execution:
> La pierre en l'arbre la fiere gent rendue,
> Bruit humain monstre purge expiation.

Damnation! It was in the original French. They all were, with translations "according to the author," doubtless to suit the author's opinions. Beginning to feel like a fool on a wild-goose chase, the Necroscope delved into his pile searching for a book with direct translations. But the only one he had didn't contain this specific quatrain.

He opened metaphysical channels, spoke to "friends" in the local graveyard. "I need someone who speaks—spoke—French." The teeming dead had never heard him so blunt and to the point. They knew his urgency and quickly responded, finding him an ex-linguist who had once taught French at a school in Edinburgh.

Following brief introductions, Harry quickly took down the translation in his notebook:

> "The dart from heaven makes its journey.
> Death in speaking . . . A great execution.
> The stone in the tree(s); the toppling of a proud (shameful) nation.
> Suspicion or rumour of human monsters, which shall be purged and
>   expiated."

But Nostradamus had "seen in brief," in flashes or momentary visions, and he wrote his quatrains accordingly. Also, he had probably jumbled the sequences to get the things to rhyme. But all done very quickly so that the meaning would be lost on anyone except Nostradamus.

Therefore Harry must use what he knew, remembered, guessed or sensed, to restructure the thing into a meaningful observation or clue.

"The dart (of knowledge?) completes its cycle, to one who speaks from (or to?) the dead. There are rumours of human monsters, where the stone rises from the tree(s). But following a purge and expiation, a proud (and/or shameful?) race shall be toppled . . . "

Harry remembered the telepathic vision he had been privileged to see in Nostradamus's mind: of a figure falling into the past (therefore *out* of the future). Spreadeagled as on a cross, the figure had been male, burned, blackened, smoking, which had been ghastly enough in itself; but yet there had been something even more horrible about it. And Harry had known that he'd seen or experienced this thing before. Or perhaps that he was *yet* to experience it . . . ?

Then:

That blinding flash, that disintegration, that bomb-burst of golden fragments, "darts," that hurtled outwards in all directions from the space where that crucified shell of a body had been! The way they had moved, full of intent, sentient, as they sought exits from their NOW into other places, other times.

And one of them had found Nostradamus in time to lift him from the debris of a wrecked life, when the physician had been unable to save his wife and family from the bubonic plague. He had been the recipient of knowledge from the future; he'd been gifted with a means to change that future! With a means to ensure that eventually a golden dart *would* come back to him! And Harry heard himself as in a dream repeating: "What came first, the chicken or the egg?"

As for the line about human monsters: the Necroscope had purged a few of those in his time! But did this mean he was yet to purge more? What had happened that time up in the Cairngorms when B.J. cancelled their climbing trips? And what else—other than a treasure vault—had he discovered at Le Manse Madonie? Thin ice again, and time to skate away from it. He did so, and moved on . . .

. . . Or tried to. But a certain word had stuck in his mind.

Cairngorms. Harry knew that a cairngorm is a stone, a variety of smoky-yellow or brown quartz found mainly in the Cairngorm Mountains, of course. So that now he thought:

Is it "the stone in the trees," or the stone rising from the trees? Is it in fact the granite massif of the Cairngorms, rising up from the fertile tree-clad valley of the Spey!?

The Cairngorms, where B.J. climbed and lived off the land. And Auld John's cottage at Inverdruie. And memories that simply would *not* come however hard the Necroscope tried to recall them to mind.

Bonnie Jean. "Bonnie" meaning lovely, or at the very least pretty. And the quatrains sprang at once to mind:

> Her name is Pretty, but her thoughts are dark.
> Hers is to choose where no choice fits her role

in His survival. Six hundred since the mark
of pestilence entered his soulless soul.

She is her master's kennel-maid.
His castle is a hollow place and high;
his bed is yellow, glowing where he laid
himself to rest who would not die.

He knows!—yet may *not* know, until set free
by the kennel-maid; he sees, yet may not understand,
until this Pretty's eyes search out the treachery,
in the dog that would bite its keeper's hand . . .

The interface was very close now and the Necroscope knew it. Beads of
sweat formed on his brow; tremors shook his body. There was knowledge here,
there was truth, and there was great danger. The meaning of Nostradamus's
lines, burning now in his memory, couldn't be mistaken. But the great seer,
Nostradamus himself, could be. Hadn't he admitted that forecasting the future
was at best a dubious art?

Harry knew the danger of arguing with himself, forced himself to close the
books, sit back and relax as best he was able. Until the trembling in his limbs
subsided and the kaleidoscopic but indistinct pictures on the flickering screens
of his memory and mind's eyes gradually faded away . . .

Something was very wrong and Daham Drakesh knew it. The scenario in England—more properly Scotland—was wrong to start with; it was working out
other than the last Drakul had intended. But that was secondary to the main
threat. The main threat had been reported by Colonel Tsi-Hong from
Chungking.

Just a week ago Drakesh had received another ominous message from the
garrison at Xigaze; the messenger had been a non-commissioned officer (indeed, a lowly Corporal), the commander of a snow-cat driven by another NCO
from the rank and file. But Drakesh wasn't overly concerned with his apparent
loss of face, the fact that he no longer warranted liaison with a senior officer.
More importantly, the messenger had not even waited on an answer. Therefore the contents of the sealed envelope could be one of only two things: ex-
ecutive commands (in other words orders), or matters of an advisory or
instructional nature.

In fact they had been the latter, but that hadn't relieved the pressure.

Drakesh understood the Communist Chinese psyche only too well. As an
asset, their agent in a remote region—and especially "under the wing," as it
were, of Tsi-Hong—he had been left largely to his own devices. He had even
been empowered to argue or "state his case," make demands and requisitions
almost as a puppet dictator, though on a much smaller scale. His "empire" was
after all no greater than a monastery and walled city, and his value as yet con-
jectural. But only let his loyalty fall suspect, or his usefulness wane; only let him

fall from favour . . . his standing would suffer, and indeed *was* suffering, accordingly.

As to what had brought about this reversal, Daham Drakesh believed he knew that well enough: the disappearance and "presumed" death of Chang Lun, and the deceased Major's unfavourable reports before Drakesh had dealt with him. And the letter had appeared to corroborate this conclusion. It was private (genuinely private this time, for the seal wasn't broken; of course not, for Chang Lun was no more) and bore the signature of Tsi-Hong himself. Also, it was to the point:

The Red Army's security services were "dissatisfied" with the situation at the Drakesh Monastery. Drakesh's spies—his so-called "emissaries abroad"—had brought the sect into disrepute; there could be repercussions on an international scale. At least one foreign agency had discovered connections between Drakesh's "monks" and certain Chinese military authorities. In the very highest places behind closed doors, awkward questions were being asked and trouble was brewing even now . . .

Basically, that was the substance of it. It would be more than Tsi-Hong's rank and position were worth to clarify the situation any further. But because he had been Drakesh's sponsor, and therefore might somehow be considered "involved," in effect the letter was a further warning, additional to the one already received. And now, if there was *anything* at the Monastery or in the walled city that Drakesh (or Tsi-Hong) would not wish to be discovered there—anything that lay outside the parameters of Drakesh's approved experimental mandate—now was the time to be rid of it . . .

Following which Tsi-Hong had appended an apparently innocuous note:

Because of the increasing incidence of Tibetan insurrection in a handful of border towns and villages, the replacement Officer Commanding of Xigaze Garrison was now scheduled to take up his appointment in only nine or ten days time. Also in respect of the hostilities, he would be supported by a half-Company of Special Forces—storm-troopers! Armoured transportation for the group was forming up at the air-bridgehead in Golmud on the Sino-Tibetan border even now. It might be prudent to anticipate a meeting with the Major just as soon as he was in situ . . .

And the last Drakul had greatly appreciated this fool Colonel's warning. Since the letter had arrived a week ago, surely an inspection of his "facilities" was now imminent? Indeed Drakesh knew it was so, for in the last forty-eight hours his familiar albino bats had reported the arrival of several armoured convoys at Xigaze, and flurries of activity within that previously sluggish garrison. His aerial observers—unseen against the stark white backdrop of winter—would likewise make report to Drakesh at the first sign of any massed movement in his direction. Which would come, he was sure.

A shame, for if he'd been faced with a merely token force, Drakesh might have taken them on and gained himself a few extra weeks. But a half-Company of trained commandoes? His monks were vampires, true, but even they were only flesh and blood. And as for his warrior creatures: they were waxing, but not yet formed enough to be brought out of their vats and unleashed. Like his many children in the walled city, they were immature, and despite that they were created in his image it would be a while yet before any of them—men and monsters alike—took on the true aspect of their father.

Except the last Drakul wasn't about to wait that long. His plans must be brought forward; tomorrow would be remembered (by its survivors) as the first day in a last long winter of death. The death of civilization as humanity knew it, but the birth of the new order. He had hoped to avoid it until his vat creatures were fully waxed, until his brood in the walled city had sucked their mothers dry and gnawed on their bones; but alas there was no avoiding it, not any longer. For he needed a diversion, something to draw the attention of the soldiers at Xigaze away from himself, and then to draw *them* away from Xigaze, back to Peking and whichever front lines would soon be opening. For this would be a diversion of the first magnitude!

What Daham Drakesh did not know (nor even Tsi-Hong, else he would never have dared send a warning of any kind) was that his stolen weapons of mass destruction were no longer a secret, no longer in place, no longer a threat. For two weeks ago Yuri Andropov had informed his counterpart in Peking of the Chungking bomb, and had supplied the intelligence necessary to make the final connection with Drakesh. This in response to a British ultimatum that if he didn't tell the Chinese authorities, they would.

And as in England, and as in Russia, the Chinese were now waiting for that radio signal out of Tibet, which would inform them of the date and time that the High Priest of Drakesh Monastery was to have commenced Armageddon. The military force at Xigaze would also receive that signal, triggering an overwhelming response. And at the Red Chinese air-bridgehead in Golmud, a fighter-bomber force was waiting even now. So that whether or not this was an act of rebellion by the Tibetan nation, or the crazed scheme of one mad mind, its author would cease to exist at its source, and there was no authority on the entire planet that could condemn China for its action.

None of which was known to Drakesh—and certainly not to Colonel Tsi-Hong, who was after all only a civilian in uniform, an adviser on the possible military applications of ESP-ionage and parapsychology in general. Without his knowing, his superiors had already cleared him. But such had been their attitude during a brief period of covert investigation that he had sensed something in the air, hence his warning to Drakesh. He had simply been covering his back.

Meanwhile, in a secret room only a block or two away from Tsi-Hong's headquarters on Kwijiang Avenue, a team of watchful scientists smoked brown cigarettes while waiting for a motionless needle on an indicator panel to spring into sudden life. Triangulation systems were already in place; even if the task force at Xigaze Garrison found no conclusive evidence at Drakesh Monastery, these men would know precisely where the signal had its origin.

And their response would be just as precise, and far more effective . . .

Ten o'clock in Sicily that night, the moon almost at its full, when Anthony Francezci took the call from his brother at Aviemore. Anthony was alone in his private rooms, the heavy drapes thrown back and glass doors open to his balcony. When he heard his brother's voice he picked up the telephone's cradle, carried it onto the balcony, and sat down at a wrought-iron table. And with a cold breeze blowing off the moon-silvered Tyrrhenian, to cool both his fever and his fear, he said:

"How goes it, brother?"

On the other end of the line, Francesco frowned at something in his twin's tone, shrugged it off and at once came to the point. "The time limit is almost up, or it will be in the next twenty-four hours. Have you spoken to Angelo? And if so, did you get anything out of him? One of my assistants has, er, gone sick— you understand? Vincent came down with something, ignored the symptoms, paid the price. I do not think I'll miss him much, but it means I'm a man short and the job might prove a little harder than I anticipated. And after all, I'm not the only one who is after this contract. That's one reason I would appreciate a little advance knowledge. Forewarned is forearmed, I know you would agree."

Anthony said, "Give me just a moment." Putting the phone down, he stood up and went to the balcony, leaned over, looked down onto the patterned mosaic of courtyard flags, then lifted his eyes to scan across the broad courtyard to the outer wall. Angelo was right: except to an assault squad, this place could be made impregnable. If—and in the light of what Angelo had said, it was a *big* if—but *if* Francesco should be successful in Scotland, it could be made just as difficult for him to get back into Le Manse Madonie as for Radu if Francesco were unsuccessful. Convoluted thinking, but Anthony was good at it.

Moreover, the old Thing in the pit was probably also right about Francesco's reaction when he discovered Anthony's secret. He wasn't at all likely to be "accommodating." Since Francesco was very definitely a throwback to his Starside origins, mercy wasn't one of his virtues. And the very thought caused Anthony to offer up a mirthless grin to the landscape beyond the outer wall. Ridiculous! For unless tenacity could be considered virtuous, the Wamphyri (including Francesco and obviously himself) had never had any virtues in the first place! Just love of self and a sense of perpetuity, timelessness; and now, for Anthony, this new and awful awareness that in fact it was all coming to an end.

Oh, years to go, and possibly even centuries, but no longer years without limit, and certainly not without . . . certain restrictions. (He thought of his father's confinement and shuddered.) And the bitter knowledge, too, that when he was gone—"put out of the way," if he was lucky—his brother Francesco would go on. *If* the dog-Lord Radu were defeated in the hour of his resurgence, and *if* Francesco returned to Le Manse Madonie, and to a position of power, unopposed.

Angelo believed that Francesco was heading for a fall. So why not make sure of it? "Forewarned is forearmed," true. But in this case *not* to give ample warning—indeed to reverse the process—would be treachery. Again Anthony's grim, mirthless grin, as he thought: *So there you have it! And am I not a true "original" after all?*

He sat down again, picked up the telephone. "Brother, are you there?"

"Where else would I be?" came Francesco's impatient growl. "What took you so long?"

"I'm on my balcony and wanted to close the door," Anthony lied. "We should keep our conversations private. Why advertise the fact of Vincent's, er, incapacity? It would only alarm our people needlessly. And I'm conscious of my insularity. Divided like this we're that much weaker, brother."

"Speak for yourself," the other's voice was a sneer. "What, are you lonely, then? Is the place getting you down? Or can it be that you crave something other than the company of the bastard Thing we call—"

"Francesco!" Anthony snarled a caution . . . *and watched the fingers of his free hand where they gripped the stem of a wineglass elongating like wrinkled boneless worms! Against his will they wrapped themselves round the glass and crushed it, whipped in their own—in* his *own—blood, until they encountered empty space, then slipped from the table's rim and went slithering to the floor!*

And: "Ah! Ahhh!" he cried, his eyes staring in their dark, shadowed sockets.

"Tony?" (Francesco's squeak, from the telephone that Anthony had let fall to the table.) He jumped up, grabbed his wild hand, gritted his teeth and demanded obedience from his wilful flesh. His entire left arm felt like jelly; it writhed and bulged at the elbow, tried to put out another arm—or *something*—from the joint, then gradually, mercifully stiffened as his will won and the rampant metamorphic process reversed itself.

And very slowly—and reluctantly, Anthony thought—his pulsing bloodied tendrils shrank, drew back and reshaped themselves into a hand, as his arm solidified again . . .

"Tony?" (From the phone.)

Trembling, he picked it up, said, "On the telephone, where business is concerned, we are always so careful. You might have compromised things. You got me worked up, I'm afraid." (To say the very least!) "I . . . I broke a glass and, uh, cut myself."

And again there was that something in Anthony's voice that his brother had never heard before. Or perhaps he had. Ah, yes! And Francesco could see Anthony's face even now: his morbid expression. And that awed tone he always got in his voice—that catch in his throat—whenever they visited Bagheria, the Villa Palagonia with its lunatic array of carved stone monsters. Perhaps Anthony had been there, to stand in awe of those loathsome statues yet again. At which, in a way, Francesco came closer to the truth than he could ever have imagined.

"Are you . . . all *right*, Tony?" Francesco's voice was curious now, and Anthony knew he must bring himself yet more firmly under control.

"Yes—yes, of course I am!" he said, fighting a terrible thing within—an inner voice crying that he wasn't all right, and far from it. "Now be . . . be *civil*, will you, and I'll tell you what Angelo told me."

"Get on with it, then."

"The hound is finished. The contract is yours. You'll win, hands down. The opposition will collapse. As for the rival outfit: you may encounter some token resistance from them . . . but it will provide the ideal opportunity to put them out of business for good. Costs to you: minimal . . ." Treachery, but it scarcely registered. No sick feeling in Anthony now, just pleasure.

"That's it?" Francesco sounded puzzled. "Angelo didn't go into details?"

"You are to do what you'll do. Your plans will suffice. No details, no."

"As easy as that?" (Surprise, now.) "After all the . . . the 'shaggy dog' sto-ries he's told us? Listen, I've got Angus with me—local liaison, you know?—and he says it won't be easy at all! He's been here a long time, Tony, and he's wise to the way of things in these parts."

"I can only tell you what Angelo told me," Anthony replied, with a typical shrug in his voice. "He says you'll have it easy. What more can I say?" (But then, in order to display at least a semblance of concern, participation): "How are things locally? Are you all set up?"

"Nothing can get past us unseen," Francesco answered. "For the last day and a half we've been on standby. The final stages of the contract are crucial, of course. But we have the chopper—er, for 'aerial surveillance'?—in order to cover the high ground, you know? And we've picked up a lot of quality hard-ware from Italian friends in Newcastle. Then there are gut feelings, and mine tell me it's going down on schedule. So Angelo is probably correct. Let's face it, he'd fucking better be!"

"Nothing more to say, then," said Anthony. "Except you'll keep me in-formed?"

"I'll be in touch as soon as there's anything definite to report. Take care, brother."

"You too," said Anthony, and put the phone down—

—To sit there feeling his face doing things that weren't entirely his idea, and listening in the back of his mind to his father's distant, lunatic laughter . . .

Radu had called to them, and Alan-on-the-Moor—Alan Goresci, the *real* Beast of Bodmin, itinerant farmhand, footloose odd-job man and ravaging slaugh-terer of livestock, but so far *only* livestock—and young Garth Trevalin had an-swered his call. Moon-children, descendants of thralls out of the past, they had come to Radu's aid, but not without the assistance of Auld John. And in find-ing their way to him they had proved Francesco Francezci quite wrong: they could get past him unseen. But what were they after all but a pair of skiers from the south-west out to enjoy the last decent snows of the season? By no means fully-fledged thralls, the musk, the *aura* of the Great Wolf was not attendant to them; their thoughts were neither guarded nor searching, and except for an ancient taint their blood was human.

They had met in Edinburgh and hired a car and gear, then driven up to the Spey Valley and found lodgings in Newtonmore well to the south of Aviemore and the Cairngorms. Sensing them there, sniffing out their location, the dog-Lord had passed it to Auld John, who had taken a circuitous route to them, avoiding Aviemore and the surrounding countryside. Thus the Ferenczys had been avoided, too.

As for the remaining Drakuls: their new lieutenant commander out of India was a powerful telepath. It would be difficult for anyone to avoid such as him. Especially since in the night, last night, he had received his final orders from his Master in Tibet. From now on he was to engage his enemies at every opportunity, and while keeping it covert as possible, he was to take out as many as he was able. Radu Lykan was still the main target, of course, but secrecy was no longer the top priority. Not in a world on the verge of nuclear war . . .

* * *

And so, while Anthony and Francesco Francezci conversed by telephone between Scotland and Sicily, and in Tibet Daham Drakesh pondered his Doomsday scenario, the dog-Lord's three remaining moon-children (who, with the exception of B.J. Mirlu, were the last descendants of many hundreds he had once enthralled) came together quietly in Newtonmore, where Auld John told the others how it was to be:

"Lads," he began, "ye'll understand ah'm no too happy tae be the bearer of bad tidings. But hear me out and ah'll tell ye true. And if Him in his high place has spoken tae ye, ye'll ken mah words are frae His own mouth. The wee mistress, Bonnie Jean Mirlu . . . she is 'nae up tae it. She has taken a lover and cares more for him than for the Master! Oh, she'll hear His call and go tae Him, but no wi' a guid heart. And the dog-Lord cannae be sure she'll no try tae do Him harm! Aye, it's that bad. B.J.'s that smitten wi' this . . . this bleddy man!"

The three were at a table in a quiet corner of the smokeroom of a small pub. Beyond bull's-eye windows, a few scattered flakes of snow drifted on the cold, still air. And Alan Goresci, a man as wiry and lean—and wolfish—as John himself, whispered, "But why haven't you put paid to this man, John? This— what, 'Harry,' did you say? If you know him, and if you've met him . . . I mean, where's the problem?"

"Aye, Ah wiz comin' tae it," John answered. "But it's no that easy. See, this yin's *verra* important! Tae the Master himsel'! Why, it could even be that this Harry is the 'Mysterious One' that Radu has been waiting on a' these years! His 'Man-Wi'-Two-Faces,' one o' which could even be the dog-Lord's own!"

"Eh?" Young Garth Trevalin put in. He looked a youth but was in fact thirty-five years old to Alan Goresci's fifty and John Guiney's more than sixty. For the blood, and even a taint in the blood, is the life. "What's that you say? He has Radu's face?"

"Ah!" John grinned in his fashion. "But ye see, mah meanin' was more that Radu could have his!"

At which Garth frowned and shook his head. "I still don't understand."

"Well maybe it's not for common men to understand," Alan-on-the-Moor elbowed Garth none too gently in the ribs. "Maybe we aren't *supposed* to understand. Eh, John?"

"Oh, but ye are!" Auld John assured them. "Then, when we go up tae Him tomorrow, ye'll know what it's a' about. See, he fears he may have lain too long, fears the disease might be in him despite the long centuries he's waited it out. Or if no the Black Death, his body may have surrendered tae time itsel'. But Radu, this wolf of wolves—why, he was a god! He'd no want tae come back tae us like some auld, rusty hinge that'll break the first time ye bend it. He would be young again, romp among the lassies, get bloodsons and be the true Lord and leader his kith and kin across the world have a'wiz waited for."

"Huh!" Alan scowled. "His kith and kin? What, a handful of nobodies like us?"

But Auld John only gave his head a shake and muttered, "Oh ye o' little faith! Do ye no ken what a wee bite can do, Alan-on-the-Moor? And you a Goresci at that, whose forefathers come not only out o' olden times but frae a far strange world, too! It's the full o' the moon, man! And Ah ken how the likes o' ye can feel it pulling like a tide in yere blood. How long, d'ye reckon, for Radu tae make himsel' a pack? And wouldn't ye just love tae run wi' him under the moon? The two o' ye, aye, young Garth too: his lieutenants in the woods and wilds o' tomorrow? Gods, ye'd be, tae all the yobs and ex-politicians and lawyers and *shite* o' today's so-called 'society!' "

By which time the two had been leaning forward across the table, eager for John's every word. And: "When he's up there'll be no stopping him," John continued. "But *getting* up's the problem. If he's been wasted by time or the plague he'll need a new body. And dinnae ask me how, but he can do it. He can take this Harry Keogh and transfer intae him! Radu's mind and powers, in this young man's body. It'll be like starting anew—but never frae scratch. For this time he'll take men and women o' power. And just like the plague in its time, he too will rage across the world tae make it his."

"When do we climb?" Seduced by the fever in John's words, young Garth's voice was husky, trembling.

And glancing from face to face, seeing the fire in their half-feral eyes, Auld John grinned and nodded his head to make his knotted mane bob. "Have ye kept it up? Have ye been practicing yere climbing? The way's hard, Ah'll make no bones o' it. Even the easy route can be treacherous tae them as dinnae ken it. It'll be a trial in itsel'! But we have tae go, tae bring the great auld wolf up out o' his sleeping place. And we must be there first, Radu's allies when Bonnie Jean arrives."

"Oh?" Alan-on-the-Moor frowned. "Is B.J. so far gone then, that he can't trust her in any degree?"

"But did Ah no say so?" John answered. "Why else would he call tae such as you and me, leaving his wee mistress out? Aye, Ah've spoken tae him and Radu knows his business. He fears that B.J. will try tae keep this Harry to hersel'. And if bad comes tae worst, that could be the end o' Radu."

"But she was so true!" Young Garth was mystified. "I mean, after all these years, why would she change?"

"Perhaps ye've hit on it," John told him. "Change, ye said . . . and aye, Ah've seen it for mahsel'. She's no the lassie she was. What, B.J. Mirlu, a lassie? Man, she can triple mah years and still manage tae look like—like a . . . "

" . . . Like a girl?" Young Garth prompted him.

"Aye, but she is 'nae. But she *is* more like the Master than we are. Too like him, and he will'nae have it!"

"Wamphyri?" (This from Alan, so low they could barely make him out.) And Auld John blinked yellow eyes in the smoky light, and nodded.

"Ah've seen it for mahsel'," he repeated. "Often. Cut her, she heals, but *so* quickly! And when she's mad . . . oh, ye would'nae want tae make Bonnie Jean Mirlu mad . . . " He shook his head.

"Then what's to choose between them?" Garth, in his "innocence," asked the logical question.

"She has'nae the power," Auld John answered. "Oh, she has the blood all right, inherited. She's a true-blooded throwback, aye. But inherited frae him! He knows it a', while B.J. has it a' tae learn. But she has'nae the time, not wi' a' they Ferenczys and Drakuls bent on destruction. The dog-Lord . . . he sends his very thoughts—ye *ken* it's so, for ye've heard him!—but she does'nae have that, no yet. And anyway, he has proved himsel', has he no? He's back! He's up there the noo, in the high places. And he's waitin' on us!"

"So then," Alan nodded, "that's one question answered, but one other remains: when do we climb? And don't go worrying yourself that we can't make it. If you can, we can. Let me tell you, John, there are crags on the moors so steep and high you wouldn't believe. Also, we've got you to show us the way."

"First light," John answered. "Crack o' dawn. Ah have gear enough for a' three o' us in mah car. As for when we start out: is the noo soon enough?"

"Now?" (From both of the others.)

"Aye, so's tae be at the start o' the easy route by daybreak. We camp out the nicht, under the glorious moon. And oh, she'll inspire us, be sure."

"But why camp out?" (From Garth.)

"Because our enemies will have men on the roads, and more by daylight. So the nicht we drive up by Tromie Bridge, on the Badenoch side o' the river, maybe as far as Insh. Yere vehicle is hired, so we take mine. Then after we ditch it, if it's discovered—so what? Ah'm a local gillie after a'. It'll be just me, out in the wild. But you two . . . they'd think ye were lost and send out a search party. We dinnae want that."

"And is Insh where we start to climb?" (Garth again.)

"Ah no, laddie," John told him. "Frae Insh it's a wee trek in the woods, some five or six miles or so—just in case some damn fool is following—to where we camp the nicht. That will be our starting point tomorrow morning."

"And if some damn fool or fools *is* following us?" Alan-on-the-Moor inquired.

And John narrowed his eyes grimly. "Ah've a'ready had some dealings wi' the like," he said. "They're no so hard. One thing for sure: they're no moors- and woodsmen like us. It'll mean one or two less o' they for Radu tae worry over, that's a'."

And that had been that . . .

And now, first light it was—crack o' dawn, or even pre-dawn—but it felt like the middle of the night to Alan-on-the-Moor and Garth. Shaken awake, half-dragged from their sleeping-bags by John, they were cautioned to silence by his narrowed yellow eyes, his finger to his lips and hoarsely whispered, "Some damn fool, aye! Up and away, lads. Up and away . . . "

Then deeper into the woods where the snow hadn't reached, and the grey light filtered itself through an evergreen canopy of branches. All three men treading lightly, never a twig snapped or bird disturbed; and whoever followed just as quiet, even eerily so, so that Auld John had to admit: "They're like—ah dinnae ken—*ghosts*, these yins! It was Ferenczys called on me, modern types. But these yins have tae be Drakuls! Probably patrollin' the roads and found mah car."

And he was right, but they wouldn't know for certain for a while yet.

After less than a mile, where the ground rose steeply into the first craggy ramparts of the Cairngorms, the trails petered out. But the way was as familiar as his own handwriting to Auld John, and soon the three came to a sheer cliff rearing some two hundred feet or more to a green-clad rim.

"Up there, a broad ledge like a wee false plateau," John whispered. "Some mile and a half long by a quarter-mile broad. There's bonnie fat deer runnin' wild, and no man alive today who ever saw them except mahsel' . . . And one woman. Now quiet as ye go. There's a chimney just along here."

At which Alan-on-the-Moor paused, held up a finger, sniffed the air. And: "Something . . . " he grunted.

Auld John's nod. "Ye're pretty guid, Alan. It's that same damn something— or someone—who has been on our trail since first light. But man, yere senses are alive! And we both know why. It's the full moon, Alan! Yere blood answers tae it, and yere senses, too."

Moments later found them at the chimney, a vertical fault in the face that climbed through creeper, hanging foliage and dusty cavelets into the heights. "Easy as pie," Alan-on-the-Moor grunted, squinting upwards, while young Garth nodded his agreement.

"The first half, for sure," John told them. "After that, there are pitons where the face tends tae overhang a mite. As yere fingers feel the cold, so yere grip weakens. We're lucky the weather has let up some. We'll rope-up on a ledge Ah ken frae a dozen climbs. Then Ah hope tae show ye a wee trick."

"They're close now," Alan glanced sharp-eyed back through the under-growth. "If they have guns, they could pick us off."

"But if they're wanting tae find the dog-Lord," Auld John reminded him, "they will'nae *want* tae pick us off. Anyway, we have nae choice. So the faster we go the better."

They climbed to his ledge, one hundred and thirty feet up the cliff face, where they quickly roped-up. Looking down, the foot of the cliff was lost below dangling creepers, crevice-grown shrubs and the canopy of the forest. "So, they'll no be shooting at us after a'," John commented. "And now, hush!"

He took a coil of rope from his shoulder, let out a good length, lobbed a smaller coil out into the dim light and down into the woods. And: "There," he said. "It'll fall a'most tae the bottom." And he tied it off on a rusty piton.

The two newcomers glanced at each other with puzzled expressions but said nothing. And then they waited, until Alan tried to whisper: "They're clos-ing in!" But John stopped him with a grip of steel from fingers that dug deep in the flesh of his shoulder.

"Still now," he muttered. "Dinnae shake the rope. They'll think we were in such a hurry we left it a-dangle. Nice o' us, eh?" (His wolfish grin. And a minute or so later): "See! What did ah tell ye?" The rope went taut, vibrating very slightly as someone tested its strength.

Down below, under the forest's canopy, three men dressed in ex-Army, camouflage-green combat suits examined disturbed undergrowth in the wake of Auld John's party. And Singra Singh Drakesh looked up into the tangle, nar-rowed his eyes, frowned and hauled on the rope.

Flanking Singh, the two remaining Tibetan thralls seemed eager to climb; containing themselves, they waited on his word. Drakesh's lieutenant out of India was cautious, however. He had been taught something of a lesson by this

Bonnie Jean Mirlu and her people, and he was still stinging from it. But up there in the heights, three of them were making for the lair of the dog-Lord Radu even now, and this could be his chance for revenge—*and* his chance to discover Radu, still weak from his centuries of sleep.

He sent his greedy, avidly writhing thoughts up into the gloom. The telepathic aether was heavy with wolf-taint—from which his probes recoiled! Probably just their stinking trail. But no thoughts at all to mention, or at best only the fading echoes of thoughts.

Which was correct, for John and the others weren't thinking at all, just holding their breath and waiting. And:

"Go, then!" Singra Singh Drakesh hissed, watching his men slide upwards out of sight, one after the other. Vampires—or vampire thralls at least—they seemed to flow up the rope; the chimney's vegetation was barely stirred by their passing. Below them, Singh followed their progress for a moment or two; then, as they disappeared, he sent out another probe.

Was there . . . something there? A feeling of . . . anticipation? At his place in India Singh kept Venus Flytraps. Their *unconscious* voraciousness—their subsistence on lesser lives—had always fascinated him. Plants, they had no thoughts as such, but there was this same aura about them. Like the trapdoor spider, lying in wait.

Lying in wait . . . ?

At which Singh sprang alert, calling out to his men where they'd reached Auld John's ledge. And his trap!

The three men on the ledge heard Singh's cry of warning simultaneous with the emergence of arms and a shaved head rising into sight at the rim of the ledge. Then Auld John stepped forward, grunting: "And it's good morning to ye—ye slit-eyed yellow bastard!"—as he drove the toe of a climbing boot deep into the Drakul's gaping, sharp-toothed maw. Teeth splintered, blood spurted, in the moment before the Drakul fell; and below him the second Tibetan clung tight to the crack in the rock as his colleague's body hurtled by.

Then the second man was frantically wedging his foot in a crevice, and trapping the rope under one arm as he tried to unsling an automatic weapon from his shoulder. And he had somehow managed it, had even started to bring the muzzle of the machine pistol to bear on the trio of faces looking down on him—when Auld John casually drew his razor-sharp clasp knife across the taut rope.

Wedged in a crevice, the Drakul's ankle snapped before his foot came loose. One sharp and weirdly alien cry, as he fell in a tangle of rope and leafy debris; and one short burst of machine-gun fire that buzzed harmlessly off into empty air and only served to accelerate his fall. And Auld John nodded his approval, wagged the sliced end of the rope at his friends, and said: "So then. A wee trick. And now let's get on . . . "

Down below, spreadeagled to the cliff face, wide-eyed and trembling in rage and disbelief, Singra Singh cursed under his breath as the last of his thralls smashed down into rocks long since fallen from on high, and was broken by them. Even Singh himself would have been broken by such a fall; if not fatally, then most sorely. But these Tibetans were mere thralls; their bones were splintered and their flesh pulped. And Singh was on his own.

Orders were orders, however, and at the Drakesh Monastery the last true Drakul would expect them to be carried out—to the last. Singra Singh *was* the last, of this group anyway. And he was not a man to be confounded or ridiculed by mere thralls . . . and *dog*-thralls at that!

And there and then he vowed it: that his Master would be proud of him yet. He would have to be, if Singh was ever again to meet him face to face. But for now—there were other ways up this cliff, he was sure. A lieutenant for long and long, he would find one. For him the climb would be as easy as taking a walk through the woods.

After that, well, the rest might not be so easy—but it was definitely preferable to explaining to his Master the many fine details of his several failures . . .

PART 5

Revivals and Devolutions

I
RADU: RESURGENT.
THE SIEGE AT AULD JOHN'S.

ATOP THE CLIFF, ON THE FALSE PLATEAU BEFORE THE MIGHTY BULK OF THE Cairngorms commenced their true assault on the sky, John's party jog-trotted through woods mainly undisturbed for centuries. They headed north-west to the foot of a higher, much more difficult climb. But again John knew a route up the apparently sheer face, following which they would make easy going across a gradually climbing terrain of weathered rock, crevice-clinging heathers, crusted, snow-filled depressions, and rare, slanting, wind-blasted pines.

It was ten-thirty in the morning before they reached that higher elevation, the severe, undulating, boulder-littered but mainly open dome of the rock—the Cairngorm "stone rising in or from the woods"—but they'd covered the ground in half the time it would take the best of ordinary men.

"Six miles, now," said John, getting his second wind as he paused to adjust the small pack on his back. "Rough ground and uphill a' the way, but no more than an hour and a bit tae such as we three. Last time Ah was here, the place was a' under the snow; white over, and cold tae freeze yere bones! A hell o' a climb, and going down even worse. Ah had . . . injured mahsel—a wee cut, ye ken?—Ah'd lost a little blood. Anyway, this is much easier. But avoid the iced-over snow in they hollows, and watch for cracks in this auld rock. Where we're going the rock gets more rotten the farther we go, and some o' they crevasses go down forever!"

He led the way, and the stony ground—and as often naked rock—flew under their booted feet. There was no recognizable track that John's companions could see, but he was the tracker, not them. And to Auld John's eyes there was a track as clear as day. Made by a light, fleet foot it headed north-east, and John knew that in following it he'd find the best possible route. Of course he would; the trail had been tried and tested times without number.

Aye, fleet o' foot and fair o' face—but a cheat for a' that, who would even cheat on the greatest o' them a'! Bonnie by name, but no by design. Oh, it was a great shame. Ah, well. Move over, wee lassie, for there's a man here the noo, and the wolf's no much longer in his lair . . .

One minute the air was clear and clean, only the whistle of the wind through leaning crags and the scratch of blown heather . . . and the next—

—The helicopter seemed to come out of nowhere, rising up over the rim of rock only a half-mile away, and the *whup, whup, whup* of its rotors reached out to them on a rising scale. "Hell and damnation!" Auld John cursed, as he flung himself down in a scoop of rock. And: "To me, ye fucking eejits!" he yelled. "Eh? Dinnae just stand there gawping!"

Alan-on-the-Moor and young Garth joined him, as John ripped a great swath of heather from its roots to cover and camouflage his body. They quickly followed suit, huddled together, lay still. And the helicopter buzzed closer across the roof of the mountain, and seemed to descend directly towards them.

"Ah might o' known," John moaned. "A bleddy whirlybird, o' course! How else were such as they tae get up here, eh?"

"Do you think they saw us?" Alan gasped.

"Ah dinnae ken. We'd be like ants to they, for sure. Aye, but the only ants tae be seen! We'd stick out like sore thumbs if they were looking in the right direction. But we were down pretty damn quick. Ah simply dinnae ken . . . "
And:

"Here they come!" said Garth.

They came . . . and went. The helicopter passed almost directly overhead, flew on uninterrupted in the direction of Montrose. Auld John sighed his relief—then cursed again, "Bleddy *hell!*"—as he stood, tossed heather aside and brushed himself down. His companions followed suit.

"But a helicopter, here?" Alan looked angry, suspicious, afraid.

"Aye," said John. "Mah thoughts exactly—at first sight. But now: it looks like she was frae Aviemore: some poor sod who could'nae ski straight. On his way tae have his bones fixed in Montrose or Aberdeen. But man, mah heart was in mah mouth!"

While in the helicopter:

Disgusted, Frank Potenza stuffed binoculars into a padded container in the cabin wall, picked up and lovingly fingered a high-velocity rifle with a sniper-scope, and whispered in Italian, "What an opportunity! Hey, Luigi. Did you see them lying there? I could have taken them out before they even knew I was firing on them. And you know something? I'm probably going to hate myself forever that I didn't, if only for Vincent's sake." Tall, gaunt, vicious, yet paradoxically feminine in his mannerisms and movements, Potenza spoke to the pilot, Luigi Manoza.

"I saw them," Manoza answered. "But you know as well as I do what Francesco told us to do if we sighted anyone. Unless it was the woman, let it be. Let them go where they're going. Sure it's important that we saw them, but their direction of travel is more important yet. Francesco thinks he knows where the dog-Lord is, approximately. *You* saw them, fine . . . but *I* saw where they were heading before they got down. And it looks like Francesco's right. It's the same area, some four, five miles northeast of here. That's where he picked up Radu's scent the first time we were out."

"So," Potenza whispered, "if we're sure we know the location of this dog-bastard's lair, why can't we knock his people over? I mean, why wait? Vincent is dead—I mean, he's *really* dead! If it was up to me, I'd take these fuckers out here and now. It would be like swatting flies."

"You worry too much over Vincent Ragusa," Manoza told him. "And I don't think Francesco worries about him at all! Vincent was your boss, OK—your immediate superior—but he was also a pain in the ass. That's why he's dead. He didn't listen. The moral of my story is, stop being a pain in the ass. The Francezci is pretty good at swatting flies, too. Know what I mean?"

"*Huh!*" said the other, as Manoza lost altitude, swung the helicopter over and headed north. "Now what?"

"Now we're going where I think they're going," the stubby Manoza grunted. "I'll stay low, you'll see if you can spot any suspicious or identifying features or landmarks, anything that looks like an entrance. Wolves hole up in caves, you know? And you can also try to spot a decent, level landing place."

"We're going down?"

Manoza sighed, shook his head in mock despair. "No, we're not going down! Not yet, anyway. When we do it'll be in force. I just want to know where I'm going to land at that time."

"*Huh!*" Potenza said again. "Why all this muscle? Against these people? I mean, they're just *people!* Not even thralls!"

"They're thralls of a sort," Manoza answered. "Francesco calls them 'moon-children,' dedicated to Radu, and their blood has the wolf-taint. Also, they're not 'just' people. Certainly not the woman. We can't push them around like it's a big night out in Palermo. They push back—hard! They sure pushed Vincent, anyway."

There was no answer to that, so Potenza kept quiet.

Skirting higher ground, putting it between his machine and the dog-Lord's people, Manoza followed the crack of a ravine in the area where Francesco had sensed . . . something. And: "OK," he told Potenza. "Keep your eyes peeled. This is it—or close enough it makes no difference."

As Manoza laid the chopper over on its side and circled the ravine with its ribbon of water foaming at the bottom, Potenza looked down. "Crevasses," he whispered in that way of his. "And potholes, too. On the roof, some hollows full of water; others that look bottomless. In the ravine, the face of that cliff is riddled. The whole place looks rotten, ready to cave in."

"Cave?" Manoza grinned knowingly. "That's exactly the kind of word I wanted to hear. The kind of place Francesco's looking for." He straightened the chopper up, leaned her the other way, took a good look for himself. And: "This has to be it!" he nodded excitedly. "Almost inaccessible, and who would want to come here anyway? High as hell, and cold and hollow as old Katerin's tits. But it's granite; it isn't about to cave in just yet." He marked a map taped to his control panel, straightened his machine up again and followed the course of the ravine back towards Aviemore.

"That's it?" Potenza sounded disappointed, petulant.

"For now," Manoza told him. "But be patient, Frank. I've a feeling we'll be seeing action soon enough. Between now and nightfall, for sure . . . "

Two hours earlier:

At his old house in Bonnyrig, the Necroscope Harry Keogh had slept well despite last night's sense of urgency, the feeling that he stood upon the brink of something vast, awesome and dangerous; slept well despite all feelings of breathless expectancy and weird anticipation; despite all of those things, and last but not least his inexplicable terror of tomorrow.

But now it was tomorrow. The light of day, of morning, had brought him awake from a dreamless state where all his mind had wanted to do—and all it had done—was rest. But in the final moments of awakening, as had been so often the case, that restless urgency reasserted itself. And floating up from subconscious wells of mind, the lines of what could only be three especially relevant quatrains stood out as clear in his memory as if freshly planted there:

> She is her master's kennel-maid.
> His castle is a hollow place and high;
> his bed is yellow, glowing where he laid
> himself to rest who would not die.

> With numbers and with solar heat and grave-cold,
> with mordant acids, and his friends in low society,
> and alchemical thunder; with *all* of these, behold!
> He may transmute impurity to peace and piety!

> He knows!—yet may *not* know, until set free
> by the kennel-maid; he sees, yet may not understand,
> until this Pretty's eyes search out the treachery,
> in the dog that would bite its keeper's hand . . .

And the Necroscope knew that he *did* know, yet didn't and couldn't know, until set free by this Pretty, this Bonnie Jean Mirlu. But set free of what? In what *way*, set free? Free in his body? That wasn't going to be easy. Oh, he had had his doubts, but what had they come to in the end? Only the realization that he loved her. Set free of that? No, he didn't want that kind of freedom, would much rather stay a prisoner. Or . . . set free in his mind, to be his own man again? Now that was something else.

While breakfasting but not tasting anything, he remembered something else. Or rather, he knew it without knowing how: that today was the day. He felt it, could feel it even now, over . . . there! And he looked at a blank wall. But that's where it was, whatever it was that was tugging at him.

And the feeling was so strong—the urge, the compulsion—to go to B.J., right now, that after washing his meal down with the dregs of a pot of strong black coffee, he went out into the garden to look for it. The sign.

And there it was, low on the horizon where Harry had known he would find it: the full moon, hanging pale in the wintry sky. And yes, of course this was the day. And tonight was most certainly the night. The night of the full moon . . .

Harry knew where B.J. and her girls would be, and he *must* go to her. God, he wanted desperately to go to her, right now! But (and he clenched his teeth, forcing his mind away from that), first there were preparations he must attend to.

Certain words from the quatrains repeated in his head:

Numbers, solar heat, grave-cold, mordant acids, friends in low society, and *alchemical thunder.* Using all of these things, he could put right what was wrong.

Numbers: not numerology this time but metaphysics, Möbius maths, of course. Solar heat: the ultimate weapon against whatever it was that was waiting for him . . . which was something he still didn't dare concentrate on. Friends in low society, and grave cold? Well they were one and the same thing, and what they were was obvious. As for "mordant acids," that had him baffled; but at least he had some knowledge of alchemical thunder. He'd seen plenty of that on the night the Chateau Bronnitsy fell. He *knew* how to make alchemical thunder, or the *chemical* sort anyway . . . but alchemical to Nostradamus in his day and age. And if Harry didn't know, he had plenty of friends in low society who did.

Harry knew where to go and what to "borrow." He was familiar with the interior of several ammunition dumps and magazines And if there was something new that he might take a fancy to—something he might have difficulty figuring out—well, there were plenty of bomb-disposal people among the Great Majority to help him out. Or ex-people, anyway.

By midday he had everything he needed, except maybe a little extra time. But time to do what? Worry about what had to be done, and what he was going to do anyway, come what may? And at last, kitted out in much the same rig as he'd worn for that job at Le Manse Madonie—black track-suit and black canvas shoes, black T-shirt and an ex-Army web belt with canvas pouch attachments—he was ready. The only additions he had made, in deference to the weather, were thick black socks and a heavy, black woollen commando-style pullover. Finally he thought about a gun, then decided against it. Go up against armed killers with a gun (if that's what he was going up against, and it could well be), and they weren't going to try to take him prisoner . . .

And at last it was time for the "wee puppy" to go and see the kennel-maid.

He took the Möbius route into the undergrowth at the edge of a copse to one side of Auld John's cottage in Inverdruie. It was sheer guesswork; not the co-ordinates—for he still remembered those from that time when he and B.J. had visited the old gillie—but that she would be there. But obviously B.J. would have to have a starting place, and she was probably relying on Auld John, so his cottage in Inverdruie seemed the best bet.

And Harry was right, it was his best bet—and his worst—and he'd landed right in the middle of it!

A big black Mercedes saloon was parked on the service road with its nose pointing in the direction of the main road and Aviemore. From what the Necroscope could see, no one was in it. In the cottage: downstairs, the curtains were drawn. Upstairs, faces and figures—female, he thought—flitted before small windows. Occasionally, and cautiously, a figure would pause to look out, but briefly and always from the side. The reason was simple: the place was under siege.

Outside, a man splashed petrol from a heavy plastic container all around the perimeter of the house, but especially on wooden fixtures such as doors, windows, the timbered frame and a lean-to firewood store. Covered by a second man with a machine-pistol, who crouched not twenty paces from Harry behind the boles of a clump of silver birches, the would-be arsonist kept low; he seemed eager to get done. And he, too, had an automatic weapon slung from his shoulder.

Harry gave a moment's study to the house. In the wall facing him, a single-paned kitchen window. He could of course make a Möbius jump directly into the house, but that would mean he'd probably be seen "materializing" by those inside—B.J. and the girls, he presumed—or at least raise awkward questions. That wouldn't do; he couldn't display his talents to anyone; and the man with the petrol was moving now round a corner of the front-facing wall of the house, slopping fuel as he went.

And suddenly B.J. was there at an open window almost directly over the arsonist's head. Twisting her body, leaning far out of the narrow space, she aimed her crossbow—at which the Necroscope heard the dull but vicious *phut! phut!* of a silenced weapon. The man in the birches had taken out a pistol, was aiming and firing across his arm. His bullets spanged off the wall close to B.J.'s head, spoiling her aim as she squeezed the trigger of her weapon and causing her to duck inside. And now Harry wished he'd given more thought to carrying a gun.

But B.J.'s aim hadn't been entirely spoiled. Her bolt had flown home, transfixing the arsonist's right shoulder. Any ordinary man would probably have fainted in agony; this one let go the container of petrol, slumped against the wall for a moment, then straightened up and picked up the container left-handed!

Harry had seen more than enough; he knew what he must do; and in the brief moment of time that he would be visible to the sniper . . . well, he would sooner face single shots from a hastily aimed pistol than a burst from a machine-gun! And conjuring a door, he entered the Möbius Continuum . . .

. . . And exited on the far side of the Mercedes. From this angle he could see the bonnet of Sandra's car sticking out from behind the house. So the Merc was theirs—the people who held B.J. in siege—and the driver's door was open. It took just a second or so to set the timer on a small but deadly item no bigger than a packet of cigarettes, and deposit it under the driver's seat. Then Harry used the Continuum again . . .

. . . And emerged running, not five paces from the house and its kitchen window. Diving forward and up in a curving trajectory, he rolled, curled himself into a ball, hit the window with his shoulder and went through the glass onto the kitchen table, which gave under his weight. In the moment it took to disengage from the mess of torn curtains and wreckage, hurried footsteps sounded on the stairs, and also from a corridor leading to the back of the house. And: "B.J.!" he yelled. "It's me, Harry!"

Three seconds later and the kitchen door flew open; B.J. stood there, hair awry and slanted eyes blazing a furious yellow in the unlit, winter gloom of the house. Her crossbow was pointing into the room, aimed directly at Harry, until she saw that it really was him and applied the safety. Then she was in his arms and her breathing a sob—of relief, he knew, but for him, not for herself—as she crushed to him, her face in the crook of his neck and her body straining against his . . . for a moment.

Then she pulled away and, as Harry's eyes adjusted to the light, she even *turned* away, as if to hide something. The Necroscope was fairly sure he knew what she was hiding . . . but he dared not let himself dwell on that. He stepped forward and was right behind B.J. when she started to say, "Harry, mah—" until he slapped his hand over her mouth.

"No!" he said. "I'm already switched on, B.J.—as far as I want to be, anyway. And, believe me, I can work better without it. Trust me." He gave her a little shake. "Trust me, OK?"

For a moment he felt her furious strength; it was in her, live—like the contained hum of a giant dam's dynamos—the only sign of the power raging within, and B.J.'s hand where it grasped his wrist felt like an iron band. But then she relaxed, pulled his fingers free, said: "All right—all *right*, Harry!" Then, turning to him, she was B.J. again. "But where have you *been?* You, and John, too. I don't know where John is!"

He shook his head, licked his dry lips. "B.J., there's no time for any of that, not now. Do you have any other weapons?" He took the crossbow from her.

"Upstairs, a shotgun," she said.

"Then go . . . go now! Cover me, from upstairs."

Her eyes went wide in fear, for him. "Harry, I—"

"—It's what I do, remember?"

She bit her lip, nodded, and went.

As soon as she was out of the room he smashed some loose glass from the window, simulating an exit, and departed via a Möbius door back to the copse. The entire episode in the house had taken only half a minute at most. And the man with the petrol was just finishing up. Tossing the container to the ground, he fumbled in his pockets left-handed for a cigarette lighter.

Harry saw a glint of metal in the man's hand, thumbed the safety off the crossbow, pointed it, and let fly. The bolt flew true—or as true as it had been aimed—struck home in almost the same place as B.J.'s bolt. It jerked its target upright and pinned his shoulder to the wall of the house. And the cigarette lighter went flying. This time the man yelped his agony . . . yet a moment later he was jerking his body from side to side, snapping the hard-wood bolt, and staggering away from the cottage towards the Mercedes! He'd had enough, but he was still on his feet.

And now Harry was indeed "switched on"—he knew exactly what he was dealing with here. Vampires!

But suddenly lead wasps were buzzing to left and right of him, followed by the tell-tale *phut! phut!* of silenced fire. The man in the birches had stepped clear of the trees; in a crouch, he was firing at Harry. Then, from the open upstairs window, a single shotgun blast, which did the trick. The distance was too great to do permanent damage, but still the man with the pistol leaped and cavorted as his long overcoat was blown open. And a moment later he, too, was running for the Mercedes.

Harry stepped deeper into the copse, where unseen he conjured a Möbius door. It took him to the road, where he crouched down behind snow-clad bushes and took a transmitter from one of the ammunition pouches on his belt. The Mercedes went rocketing by, and Harry let it go a half-mile before jumping ahead of it. Why he didn't simply extend the transmitter's antenna and press the button he couldn't say. But so far his actions in this business—whatever it was about—had been covert, and he wanted to keep them that way. Maybe that was it. As for his powers . . . well, these creatures were hardly going to be talking to anyone about his use of the Möbius Continuum, were they? Not when they were *in* the Continuum. And not when they were deep in the shit!

The Merc came blazing, and Harry stepped out into the road in front of it. They saw him and maybe even recognized him, and the driver grinned and kept right on coming. Harry had set the timer on his bomb for just three seconds, time enough to prepare himself and turn his face from the blast. But that had been when he was thinking in mundane terms, and now he wasn't. This wasn't going to happen in mundane space and time.

He had learned a new trick when Zahanine was murdered—or terminated?—in his house at Bonnyrig. He knew about Zahanine now and accepted it: that it hadn't been a dream. The stains on his floor hadn't been a dream, anyway. And he knew where he had taken her body, and how. A new trick, yes.

The car bore down on him, and the driver's mouth was open in a ghastly, gaping laugh of pure pleasure. So Harry laughed, too, and conjured a door big enough to take the whole car. And a split-second before the car disappeared, he pressed the button on his transmitter. Then—throwing up an arm and turning away, even the Necroscope, unable to accept that a ton of hurtling metal was simply going to vanish at his command—he gritted his teeth and half-closed his eyes. And in so doing, omitted to collapse the door.

One-hundred . . . two-hundred . . . three-hundred—

—There was a muffled roar, and an explosion as if from far, far away; a sound or feeling more in the mind than in the real world. And then a very real sound: a clanging, clattering, skittering, metallic sort of sound.

Harry opened his eyes. Above the road, a red lick of fire that burned itself out as it rose through a ring of smoke. And in the air—spinning end over end, bounding one last time as it hit the road and flew sideways to scythe among the roadside trees—the twisted, smouldering rear fender of the Mercedes. Nothing more than that.

And the Necroscope gave a small shudder as he pictured it: in the Möbius Continuum, a meteorite shooting through the endless night, its fireball winking out, and a cloud of shattered debris—plastic and metal and flesh and blood—going nowhere, and taking forever to do it . . .

* * *

Half an hour earlier:

Auld John Guiney, Alan-on-the-Moor, and Garth Trevalin had arrived on the crumbling, striated and wind-scarred dome of the rock over the cavern system of Radu's redoubt. Rusty pitons hidden under shards of stone had told a tale, pointed the way, and were still usable. Ropes had been lowered into the throat of a black, echoing pothole, down which the men had slithered, descending into the hollow, unhallowed skull of the mountain.

And in the gloomy, cavern-riddled world below, John had led the others deeper still into the secret heart of the rock—to Radu Lykan's resting place.

At the dog-Lord's sarcophagus on its platform of stony rubble, John and the others had climbed to the rim and looked down on Him. His outline had been dim, vague, blurred by his bath of glutinous resin and the cracked, dusty yellow crust on its surface. But where the blot of his head was situated, the darkness glowed with twin areas of red light. And:

"It's like some kind o' weird womb," John had explained in a throaty whisper. "Surrounding our Master, a thin envelope of fluids that replenishes itsel' by drawing off the essence, the preservative powers, o' the resin."

"And he lives?" Young Garth had been awed by the wonder of it. "After all these years?"

"Are his eyes no open?" John had answered reverently. "Has he no spoken tae ye, tae a' o' us, calling tae us wi' his mind? Oh, he lives, laddie, aye. The nicht . . . we'll see him up, and be his loyal subjects for a' time: immortals among common men! But time's wasting. So let's be at it the noo."

Then he'd freshened and set fire to the flambeaux in their sockets about the base of Radu's stone coffin, and warned young Garth: "Yere task now, Garth. Tae keep yere eye on they torches there. And when the warm resin starts tae drip frae the outlets, tae ensure the flame does'nae jump. This resin's the stuff that blazes up in auld pine logs . . . It does'nae take verra much tae set it afire. But it's a comfortable wee job. Ye can have yeresel' a snack from yere pack, and Ah've something here that will warm ye up no end. A drop o' red wine. Aye, guid for the blood, so it is . . . "

From his own pack John had taken a bottle of wine, popped the cork, poured the thick, resinous stuff into their drinking mugs. Then a toast as they'd drained it away: "Here's to Radu! Long has He waited, and long may He reign!"

"To Radu!" they'd echoed him, not noticing or used now to the gleam of fervour in John's yellow eyes. But he'd poured himself the merest drop, and then scarcely touched it . . .

And Alan, smacking his lips, had questioned, "But if this is Garth's task, what about us?"

"A *great* task, ours!" Auld John had answered. "What Garth does here, we do elsewhere. For Radu is'nae the only one who'll be up the nicht, and we must ease the way for his creature too. So come on with me now, Alan-on-the-Moor, for it's a'most noon. Ah, but this yin will take some melting out, be sure!"

Then, before leaving Garth to his vigil, John had poured him a further measure of wine, winked and asked him, "Ye'll no be, well, a-feared? Tae stay here on yere own, Ah mean?"

"What's to fear?" Garth had narrowed his eyes. "I've some food and water, light and warmth from the torches, plenty more torches if these burn low. How long will you be, anyway?"

"As long as it takes," John had answered. "But when we're gone ye'll find it awfy quiet. Guid! No yin can come upon ye or take ye by surprise! And remember: if there's some problem, ye only need tae yell. These caverns will carry yere cry like the echo o' a howling wolf—as they will soon be echoing, aye."

And he and Alan had gone off into the mazy interior, their footsteps rapidly fading, as the silence of forgotten centuries had come crowding in.

Ten minutes and Garth had felt drowsy. Shaking himself, he had climbed again to the rim of the sarcophagus, looked down on Radu. But by then the dog-Lord's outline had become very indistinct, distorted by the slow circulation of resin at the bottom of the great vat. And a froth of bubbles had begun rising oh-so-slowly, gathering under the crust and seeking a way through.

Garth had sat with his back against the base of the sarcophagus a while, until again he'd felt himself nodding. It must be the warmth of the torches, he had supposed. And after checking them he'd climbed down to the rubble-strewn floor to eat a bite from a sandwich. Sitting there in the gloom, in the rhythmic, flickering torchlight, his nerves had slowly relaxed, his muscles softened, and his head had fallen onto his chest.

Just once Garth had started, at what he imagined was some far-away cry. But it was nothing, and the torches were burning steadily, and there was this slow drip, drip, drip, hypnotic in the regularity of its pacing. Or regular to Garth, at least, as the effect of John's or Radu's wine worked steadily on his system. Except the drip wasn't regular but speeding up.

And on the dais, slow puddles of yellow resin forming; and in the stone sarcophagus, an original Lord of the Wamphyri sending out telepathic probes which at this range couldn't help but find their target . . .

Auld John and Alan-on-the-Moor came to the vat of Radu's creature. "My God!" said Alan, looking at the massive stone "staves" of the container, bolstered at the bottom with boulders, in the light of John's torch. "What the hell . . . ?"

And John looked at him strangely. "God, did ye say? Do ye have faith then, Alan? I mean other than faith in Him?"

The other shook his head. "You mix with men, and talk with men, you end up thinking and speaking like them. That's why you are so lucky up here on your own, John. But I worked in a brewery a while, and I've seen ten thousand gallons of beer brewed in smaller vats than this!"

"Ah!" said John. "But it's no beer brewing here. Listen!" And he placed his ear to the cold stone.

Alan followed suit—and at once reacted, and sprang away. "What!?" he said. "A heartbeat? But what kind of heart?"

"A big yin, aye!" John grinned, and continued listening. But after a moment the smile fell from his face, replaced by a frown of strange concern. The heavy, thudding beat was far more frequent than on previous occasions, but it was also very irregular. If the thing in the great womb (and more literally a womb this time) were a human sleeper, he would either be nightmaring or very, very sick . . . Or perhaps simply weak? Well, maybe John had the cure for his weakness. Which was why he was here, after all. And why Alan-on-the-Moor was here, too . . .

"Up ye go," John grunted, lighting the way with his torch. "And now ye're *really* going tae see something!"

To one side, a stairway of stacked stone slabs lay against the vat. Suddenly tired, depleted, Alan clambered to the eight-foot high rim with Auld John right behind him . . . and failed to see the old gillie reaching into a deep crack under a slab, or what he brought out. At the top, Alan crept forward on hands and knees until a sickly sweet resin-reek wafted up to him. A sweetness—and the smell of something other than resin, and other than sweet.

John planted the torch in a crack well back from the rim, and said, "Well? What d'ye make o' that?"

Shaking his dizzy head, Alan-on-the-Moor gazed down into the semi-solid murk of a mainly opaque, luminous resin reservoir, and as his eyes adjusted peered through the crusted surface into the looser liquids beneath . . . at the *Thing* that lay half-curled there, no longer entirely foetal, just waiting to be born.

The massive head, triangular in profile; dog jaws two and a half feet long; the yellow glow of an eye as big as a saucer that opened and turned in its socket to glare up at Alan, even as he gave a strangled cry and lurched back from the rim—

—Driving his spine onto the sharp metal point that Auld John rammed forward to transfix and hold him shuddering like a hapless slug on a nail! The beast's feeding funnel, which made as good a weapon as any.

As for the rest: John didn't make a meal of it. His knife across Alan's throat, and the tube withdrawn, thrust deep into the resin to catch his spurting blood. Then, the fluids of the sac-like inner egg turning red as Alan's life drained into it. No, John didn't make a meal of it . . . but he hoped that Radu's warrior-creature would.

Down the stone steps Auld John went, to set light to the row of great torches around the base of the vat. And watching them flare up—*feeling* them warming the feeding beast and the liquids that had preserved it through six long centuries—he congratulated himself on a task well done. And only Alan's single strangled cry when the sharp feeder chopped into his spine to give the game away. Except young Garth would be so far gone by now, he probably hadn't heard it . . .

In fact Garth had heard it, but it had made no impression. And now he was lost to his stupor, and to the dog-Lord's hypnotic, telepathic voice in his stumbling, staggering mind:

Garth. Oh, you faithful one, you child of my children, you moon-child! You heard and you came . . . you are here! Here to be my protection, my guide. To . . . to sustain me in the hour of my resurgence. And you shall be one with me, Garth; and when lesser men speak to me, they shall also speak to you, for we shall be inseparable, you and I. You shall be named Raduesuvia: *"who came out of Radu"—yet you will forever be a part of me.*

Except . . . why do you sit so far apart, who will sit upon my right hand forever? I need you here—to feel my strengthening heartbeat, the stirring of these stiffened limbs of mine—to help me up from my cold stone coffin. Come, Garth, come, and be my strong right hand . . .

It seemed an invitation, which was in fact an irresistible command. And with his eyes full of moonlight, and a cold sweat upon his brow, Garth stood up, swaying as he clambered awkwardly up the tangle of stone that held aloft the dais and sarcophagus, until he crouched at the rim. The resin bubbled, not from the heat of the torches—or only partly—but mainly from the commotion beneath the surface. And:

Ah! Ahhh! It was a cry of pain—almost a birthpang—in Garth's mind. *I would breathe, Garth! I would be up. See, see—I reach for you, for the light, for the full moon where soon my olden mistress will ride the sky! But I have not the strength.*

The surface of the resin bulged, split, sent out a jet of gas and a spurt of yellow liquid like pus, that slopped Garth's face. Beguiled, he felt nothing, saw nothing but the heaving of a glorious womb, heard only Radu's telepathic voice:

Now, child of my children, now *Garth! See, I breathe—I would be born—so bring me up, bring me forth from these ugly juices! Now, Garth! Now!*

Pink and purple tubeworms broke the surface of the liquid where its crust had split. Resin bubbled up as the worms developed pouting mouths that sucked greedily at the air. A hand—or more properly a great dog's black, leathery paw with three-inch claws—reached upwards in an agonized spasm and clutched at thin air. But Garth saw only a hand and, washed by the bubbling resin, a face floating just beneath the surface—

—The kindly, beneficent but agonized face of a god suffering all the pain of the world. And he clasped the hand that the dog-Lord offered.

But on the instant, everything changed. Garth was Garth again—in the full knowledge of where he was and what he was about—and Radu was Radu. And as the dog-Lord's soft, trembling hand firmed up, grew hard and drew Garth inexorably into the sarcophagus:

"Ahhhhhh!" said Radu . . .

Auld John heard the cry—that rising shriek, that echoing, ear-piercing scream that climbed the scales to the whistle of a boiler about to burst—and his eyes went up to the shimmering, vibrating air of the cavern complex. And when the scream stopped, and the air stopped trembling, he smiled his wolfish smile.

And: "Aye," he said after a moment, and returned to lighting more torches, to warm the vat of Radu's creature, "that'll be Him the noo. Bless ye, Alan-on-the-Moor, and especially ye, Garth Trevalin. For we shall long remember ye."

Then, as the first low howl ululated in distant darkness, John's feral eyes widened and lit like yellow lamps. And shaking his fists at the world, he cried: "Oh, Ah'm coming, dinnae fear," as he went loping off into the cavern labyrinth to greet his reborn Master . . .

B.J.'s girls were dousing the lower walls and woodwork of Auld John's house with water when Harry came striding down the service road. B.J. saw him, went running, held him close for a moment, then pushed him away. "Cover you?"

she said. "Cover you? I didn't even see you leave! But I saw you put a bolt right next to mine in that . . . that man's shoulder, and—"

"That *vampire's* shoulder," Harry said. "Don't worry about those two— they're finished. But B.J., it's time you levelled with me. I already know most of it, and I don't think it makes any difference to my feelings. It's the half I *don't* know that worries me, because that might make a difference. But I'm here, for what that's worth, and you know you have me. Now I want to know if I have you. I want to know that and everything else. I mean . . . everything. And you're the only one who can tell me." He unclipped her crossbow from his belt, gave it back to her.

"Come back to the house," she said. "We're making ready to leave, but we've a few minutes. And then you can decide whether or not you want to come with us."

"Into the mountain?" he said, walking with her towards the cottage. "And if I decide not to?"

"You won't," she shook her head.

"You don't intend to . . . *accept* my refusal?"

"Can't. I *can't* accept it, Harry. You have to come."

"Tell me everything and let me decide for myself," he answered. "You said you loved me. And if that's true—"

"It is."

"—Then you wouldn't place me in jeopardy. And if I climb that mountain with you . . ." He came to a halt, caught her arm.

She turned to face him, and he could see how torn she was. "If you don't climb it, I'm dead," she said, quite simply. "And if I do tell you everything— now, all at once—you could be dead, too. A different kind of dead, but close enough it makes no difference."

They started to walk again, and Harry said, "A part of my life, maybe several parts, have been a lie. And you're the one who told it." It wasn't an accusation, just a statement.

"That was before I loved you."

"But you've kept the lie going." Now it was an accusation.

"No," she answered. And to herself: *Yes—for two hundred years—until I saw the truth. But I can't show it to you.*

"No?" Suddenly he looked haggard. "B.J., you're lying even now!"

At the door of the cottage, it was B.J.'s turn to catch at his arm. "Only on the surface!" she blurted. "They're only lies on the surface. Underneath, you *already* know the truth!"

"I know the . . . ? But I . . . I don't understand." Or did he?

> He knows!—yet may *not* know, until set free
> by the kennel-maid; he sees, yet may not understand . . .

"You know most of it, yes. Except for the *real* lies. If I tell you about the real lies, then I'll really lose you." *I'll lose you, Harry—if I tell you that your search for your wife and child was the biggest lie of all. And if I tell you it was for me, not for Radu.*

"You've always known," she went on, "but you can't remember. Not until I switch you on. I mean, all the way on."

"Then do it," Harry said, as they entered the cottage. "Do it now, switch me on all the way and let's see what happens. I mean, let's face it—it's got to be better than being a half-person! See, I'm trying hard to hang on, but I think I'm losing it, B.J." He tried to grin but only twisted his face; and suddenly she looked just as haggard as he felt. Which made him feel better, because he knew this must be equally hard for her. Love was like that: it was only real when it hurt.

Inside the house, gloomy now that they were out of the daylight, even the winter daylight, B.J. put her arms round Harry and held him close. "Do you remember that time we came here? I asked you about life? What it was all about? About growing old, and watching your partner grow old, and wondering where it had all gone? You gave me your philosophy of life, said that when we are young we know everything, but the older we get the more we realize we don't know any fucking thing! And I said what if it didn't have to be that way?"

"I remember, yes," he frowned. "But not how the conversation ended."

"We were . . . interrupted," she told him. "But this time we won't be. Harry, what if you could love me always? I mean, what if we could always be the same, and never have to change. Or at least, not for a very long time?"

"What?" he said, feeling her pressing against him and loving it. "Is that a mountain up there, or Shangri-la? Is this an invitation to a nightmare, or the fountain of youth?" His questions were serious. And now she understood that in fact he did half know.

"I believed in something—worked towards something—oh, for a very long time," she said. "And then you came along and changed my mind. But are you right? Is love really the way? Or are you a false prophet?"

"Switch me on," he urged her, holding her away from him.

"You may hate me . . . " There was fear in her face, and enormous inner pain, and emotions beyond Harry's or any mere man's understanding. And yet she looked more—human?—than he had ever seen her. And he knew, too, why that thought had occurred, but daren't admit it.

And when he made no reply: "It *will* hurt you," she said.

"You know something?" said Harry. "I don't think I care."

"What, that I'm a liar? That I'm not . . . innocent?" There, it was half out.

His mind reeled, but a very little. For he'd been expecting it. "What's done is done. From now on let's be straight."

And B.J. thought: *If I tell him, and if it breaks him, damages his mind, then he'll be lost to me; but he'll also be lost to Radu . . . which would be good, except Radu will exact payment from me! And if I don't tell him, he'll never be himself. Mentally, he will vegetate; he'll only be what I tell him to be; he won't be the real Harry Keogh, the man I fell in love with. But he'd never get that far anyway, for Radu would have him. And so it boils down to this: do I love him enough to risk his sanity, to believe that he will still love me, and that together we can defeat and destroy the dog-Lord, my so-called fucking "Master?"*

But right at the end of the question, she knew she'd answered it herself.

And looking at her face, the Necroscope knew it, too.

Her name is Pretty, but her thoughts are dark.

Hers is to choose where no choice fits her role in His survival . . .

My fucking Master, yes. (B.J.'s eyes were more slanted, more golden-yellow, more feral than ever; a low growl escaped her throbbing throat.) *Yes, she did have a choice, and she had made it. For Radu Lykan was treacherous and the worst possible liar, compared to whom B.J. was in fact an innocent. Auld John: missing. Alan-on-the-Moor, and young Garth Trevalin: nowhere to be found. Oh, really? But B.J. knew where they were, all right! That bastard Thing in the resin had called them to his redoubt. He knew B.J.'s destiny and was taking no chances, wouldn't let her reach it. She had discovered his Mysterious One and was no longer of any use; none that B.J. could contemplate, anyway!*

"B.J.," Harry said, taking a pace backwards, away from her. And his strange eyes had a look in them that she had never seen before; not fear or fascination but an odd mixture of both, and a great sadness, too. And B.J. knew now for certain that he had spoken the truth: he did know half of it, at least. And now he must know it all.

Controlling the beast within, she said, "You win, Harry, mah wee man!"

The Necroscope jerked his head, took a second step backwards, and the backs of his knees hit John's old rocking chair, tipping him into it. The full moon blazed down on him, with the silhouette of a great wolf's head black against the yellow. And the rocking chair rocked back, and forwards . . .

. . . And Harry said: "You're his kennel-maid. His castle is a hollow place, and high."

"Do you remember what I told you about the Wamphyri Lords of Starside, Harry?" she said, stepping forward and bending to loosen the belt around his waist, the strap over his shoulder. "And about Radu, the Drakuls and Ferenczys?" She took the belt and his explosive devices from him, dropping them to the floor behind her. "No, you don't . . . because I told you to forget it all, until we were ready to go up against Radu's enemies. Well, and now we're ready. Except the dog-Lord is one of them, one of our enemies, one of *my* enemies! So now if you haven't worked it out already, you can remember what the Drakuls did to Zahanine at your place in Bonnyrig: revenge for the two we killed in the Spey Valley, probably. And you can remember that, too: how they died in their blazing car. Also what I told you about Ferenczy, Lykan, and Drakul history. And Brenda: your search for her? But it never happened, Harry. All the places you remember going to, well, you didn't. Those were memories that *I* put there, that I suggested to you, because I wanted you for myself. And now I'm admitting it and so losing you. So whatever else you do, don't you ever dare ask me again if I fucking love you!"

From outside, Sandra was shouting: "B.J. We're ready."

"There, and now you have it," B.J. continued. "So remember it all, Harry. Every damn thing. Put it all together, tie it up in one big bundle. And when you know what you're running from—and if you're still capable of running—then when you wake up, run, run, *run!*"

He rocked back and forward, back and forward, and his eyes were huge and round, and his face was pale and blank.

B.J. sobbed, got behind him, and took up her shotgun from where it leaned against the wall. For she had made another decision and must act now before she changed her mind. Radu's Mysterious One, his "Man-With-Two-Faces," Harry Keogh? Well, *fuck* Radu, the two-faced treacherous bastard! And whether Harry wanted to be in on this or not—whether he would or wouldn't be able to be in on it—it was too damn late now. He wouldn't be going anywhere, not for a couple of hours at least. But when he did wake up, at least he'd know that she had loved him.

And as the chair rocked forward she gritted her teeth and smacked the butt of the shotgun up against the back of Harry's head, so that he kept right on going off the chair and crumpled to the floor . . .

II

RESTRAINTS REMOVED.
THE *REAL* HARRY KEOGH.

AULD JOHN WAS HEADING BACK NOW, ALONE ALONG THE EASY ROUTE, NO longer held back by his role of guide and watchdog for inexperienced companions. As for the two he had guided: well, they had been found worthy and accepted. So best to forget them now. And because on this occasion John had not been weakened by any sacrifice of his own blood, he was able to make even better speed; which was very necessary, for he had a job to do.

Loping along the near-invisible but well-known trail that led down to the secret plateau and forest, and on to the final cliff descent, he thought back on what Radu Lykan had told him when he'd returned to the sarcophagus . . .

The torches at the base of that high altar had been flickering low by then, and no sign of Garth Trevalin. For a moment that had worried John—until he'd heard his Master's voice in his mind . . .

. . . Just a second or so before realizing that it wasn't in his mind at all but in his ears!

"John—ah, John, you faithful one!" That low growl, that rumble of sound, the *power* in that voice! And yet—was there something else in it? Some pain, secret knowledge, recognition and acceptance of some doom-fraught intuition? Concerned, John had turned in a circle at the foot of the jumbled slab pyramid, looked all around in the gloom as he searched for the source of that voice. On the floor, the imprints of feet—or great paws, or a cross between the two, laid down in resin on the cracked slabs and fallen lintels—had directed his eyes towards a crevice in the rotted stone of an inner wall. And from the deeper gloom within that crack a pair of triangular eyes like crimson lanterns had stared out at him.

John would have gone to Him at once, but Radu's voice had held him at bay:

"No, John, not now! I would not have you see me now. I am . . . basic; I am risen but yet laid low, not the man I would be. But it's not too late and I *can* be that man even now! So listen to me. Listen and obey me." From out of the darkness, the fire of his eyes had burned into John's wolf soul, searing his words there.

"Go down from here and find the Mysterious One. He is here, I know it. I found him in Bonnie Jean's mind. He came to her as she must come to me—which is a confrontation I no longer relish. And B.J. is no longer the 'wee mistress' whom we trusted, John. She will not bring this man, my Man-With-Two-Faces, to me. And without him all this is for nothing. Wherefore *you* must bring him here. Do you understand?"

"Master!" John had stumbled a pace closer to the crack in the wall.

"No! Be still!" That rumble had come again, not only the physical sound of it, but the *feel* of it, too, like a tightening of telepathic jaws on John's brain. For Radu had made contact—waking contact—at close range and was now firmly established in John's mind.

"Yes, Master," Auld John had come to a halt, stood stock still.

"Do you understand what must be done?"

"I'm tae find Harry Keogh, and bring him here."

"And without delay, John, if I'm not to suffer." (A movement of the eyes in the darkness, signifying a nod.) "For it's not only Bonnie Jean but others I fear now."

"Aye, and Ah have dealt with some o' they," John had answered. "A Ferenczy, and Drakuls, too."

And the dog-Lord had seen the truth of it in John's mind. "Good! Good!—but still others *will* come. I sense them close to me, sniffing me out. I may have to hide from them—when I would so love to ravage *among* them!—but I will not hide from you, when you return with my Mysterious One. Very well, go now, my faithful. But hurry, for the time is nigh . . . "

Then the red-glowing eyes had dimmed a little, backed off and turned away, and John had heard the receding sound of slow-padding footsteps. And when at last he had ventured to stand in the mouth of the crevice, it had been dark, deep, and empty.

Time had been of the essence, but still John had stolen a little of it to climb the jumble to the foot of Radu's sarcophagus and snuff the failing torches; following which he must get on his way. And there on the dais platform he'd seen the resin slopped from Radu's emergence—and something else to stop him momentarily in his tracks:

A white alabaster hand hanging loose over the rim of the huge stone coffin; a hand so white it looked carved from snow. Young Garth's hand, obviously, for it wore his gold ring on the index finger. But no longer young. The arm was shrivelled, that of an old, old man, and John remembered the rising scream shut off at its zenith.

Well, and there you had it, and John could find nothing to fault it. What was the dog-Lord's to give was his to take away, and he had. And after all, wasn't it only to be expected after a fast such as his?

After that: time *was* of the essence, and John had wasted no more of it. Retracing his tracks through the labyrinth, and climbing up his rope through a vertical pothole, he had exited from the lair onto the rotten roof of the promontory—and at the moment he emerged thought to see some hasty movement among a clump of boulders! But there were only clouds scudding west in a lowering sky, the wind in the signpost branches of a leaning, stunted pine, and the hammering of his own heart. The perhaps imagined motion could only be his nerves, or a rabbit, or maybe an eagle settling to its nest beyond the rim.

And without more ado John had set off south-west along the well-known trail—

—Never knowing that Singra Singh Drakesh was his rabbit, or eagle settling to its nest. And in *his* nest of boulders, the Drakul lieutenant composed himself in a meditative trance, completely ignored the cold, and settled down to wait for whatever would be. Oh, he could have ventured down into this wolf's lair there and then, but Singra Singh was an exceptional telepath in his own right and had "overheard" Radu's conversation with Auld John.

Radu was weak; perhaps from his years of hibernation, perhaps from something else. What use to catch and kill one ailing Lord of the Wamphyri when others might soon be presenting themselves as unsuspecting targets? And then there was the woman—and her girls, too—and this was now Singh's vendetta no less than that of his Tibetan Master. And last but by no means least there was this Harry Keogh. The Last Drakul's instructions with regard to Keogh, the destroyer of his bloodson, had been especially explicit.

And so, with his eyes closed and palms flattened together on his chest, Singra Singh sat amidst the boulders of the mountain, composed himself in a discipline learned as a boy, sixty years ago at the Drakesh Monastery, felt the comforting weight of the machine-pistol in his lap, and waited . . .

At Aviemore, Francesco Francezci was furious. But the resort wasn't Le Manse Madonie; he couldn't display his displeasure too openly; the dark genie of the Wamphyri must be contained, bottled up inside for now.

In the iced-over tennis court that served as a makeshift helipad, he spoke, whispered, spat at Luigi Manoza and Angus McGowan where none of the resort staff could see them. "Where the *fuck* are they? Where's Jimmy Nicosia, and that idiot Potenza?"

"You sent them out in the car, Francesco, to that game-keeper's place," the stubby Manoza nervously answered. "You said they were to check if the woman was there. But . . . that was all of an hour ago."

"It was *more* than an hour," Francesco continued to spit his words. "What, for a job that should have taken twenty minutes?"

"Aye, it was a mistake, that," Angus McGowan nodded . . . and at once stepped back a pace as he realized his own mistake. The Francezci rounded on him, his dark eyes bloodshot in their corners. "Ah mean," McGowan hurriedly added, "a mistake for ye tae place yere trust in they two. Split up, they're OK. But put 'em taegether—a pair o' fuckin' hotheads! No worthy o' ye, Francesco."

"Damn them to every hell!" Francesco hissed from between clenched teeth. "Are all of my people idiots?"

"They were too long under Vincent," Manoza tried to calm him down, find excuses for the missing men, and for everyone. "Maybe they found what they were looking for but weren't satisfied to leave it at that. Maybe they did it for Vincent."

"Did what, got themselves killed?" Francesco snarled, not yet knowing that he had guessed the truth of it. "I told them to *observe* and report back! And I told them when to *be* back."

"Aye," McGowan took another chance. "But maybe they found what they *weren't* lookin' for, or weren't expectin'. And maybe *they* were observed, eh?"

"I should have sent you," Francesco said, "and maybe Guy. Dancer's a dummy, too—but at least he does as he's fucking told!"

"Here he comes now," Manoza said, glad of the diversion, as Tanziano tooled the second of their saloons into the court. As they reached him he was opening the boot. Dancer was a six-foot wedge of bullet-headed muscle; his piggy eyes met theirs, redirecting their gaze into the boot of the big car.

"What?" said the Francezci, his jaw falling open. "What the—?"

"It was caught up in a bush about a kilometre from that old guy's house," Dancer grunted. "I recognized it. It was me hired the car in Aberdeen. But I used fake ID, so there'll be no trouble with the hire company . . . "

"No trouble with the—?" Francesco looked at him disbelievingly. *"Fuck* the hire company! Where are Jimmy and Frank?"

But Dancer could only shrug, as Manoza picked up one end of the buckled fender and sniffed it. "I thought so," he said. "This is hi-tech stuff. Ordinary plastic's about as deadly as toothpaste by comparison."

"And this . . . is *all* that's left?" Francesco still couldn't believe it.

"And a few nuts and bolts," Dancer told him, shrugging in a way that only increased his master's irritation. "I checked out the whole area but there was nothing. Just scorch marks on the road."

"Scorch marks?" Francesco was trembling now, barely able to contain his rage. "Fucking scorch marks?"

"Harry Keogh," said McGowan, his ugly face as thin as a greyhound's, eyes silvery-yellow under the brim of his hat.

Francesco whirled on him again, but eagerly now, no longer in anger. "Do you think so?"

"I saw the mess that yin made o' the Drakuls that time," McGowan answered. "Their car was a wreck, too. And Keogh did'nae fuck about wi' them, either!"

Francesco actually grinned, but it was mirthless: a grin full of malice and the promise of an agonizing death. "And you think he could be with the woman at the cottage? Personally, I want that one more than I want the dog-Lord. Angus, you found fault with my sending Jimmy and Frank to do a simple job. Well, the job's still available but it's not so simple now. If Keogh and the woman are there, they'll be alert for us. So this time you're going. You and Dancer. I'll be here with Luigi when you get back. But *do* try to get back, won't you?"

"It'll take maybe half an hour," McGowan called after him, as Francesco and Manoza strode off towards the ski lodge.

"But no longer," Francesco called back. "In something less than four hours it will be dark. And we still have to load the . . . the cameras." He was talking about a box of heavy weapons.

Left on their own on the tennis court, McGowan and Tanziano looked at each other. Then the latter turned up the collar of his overcoat and got back into the driver's seat, while McGowan sniffed at the cold air for a moment or two before joining him. And: "Guy, laddie," he said, "this is where it really begins. Ah can feel it in the air, so Ah can. Tomorrow it'll a' be over, and we'll be able tae take it easy and sit down tae a guid breakfast."

But as Tanziano headed back for the road, the little man quietly added, "Or we won't . . . "

Francesco was watching from a table in the lodge bar's panoramic window when the saloon returned; it drew up under the helicopter's rotors and a moment later McGowan and Dancer unloaded something from the boot of the car into the aircraft's passenger cabin. Then:

"Let's go," said Francesco. He and Manoza carried a heavy wooden box marked "cameras" out of the bar to the tennis court, where Tanziano had lowered steps from the aircraft's interior. Hoisting the box between them, Francesco and Manoza passed it up to Dancer and McGowan. And looking up at McGowan, Francesco saw that he was wearing a grin as broad as his narrow face.

"So what have you got?" he said, climbing the steps.

"Except for one item," McGowan answered, assisting Francesco up, "the cottage was deserted." He pointed to a corner of the cabin.

Francesco looked, said, "What, a sleeping bag?"

"And what's in it!" McGowan stooped, unzipped the top of the bag. And Harry Keogh's pale face lolled out. "Someone has given him a bump on the head he'll no forget in a while. He's out cold. Oh, and one other thing. There was a lot of makin's—explosive makin's—tossed under a bush outside the house. Keogh's gear, Ah reckon. It'll have his prints a' over it but none o' ours, so Ah left it there. It looks like Ah was right and he's the one who got Frank and Jimmy."

Manoza had joined them inside the cabin. Closing the door behind him, he said, "So, what have we here?" Then he saw what they had here, and gave a low whistle.

Francesco was smiling. It would pass for a smile, anyway. And: "The best prize of all!" he grunted. "Well done, Angus."

"Also," the little man told him, "if ye're interested, we spotted two o' B.J. Mirlu's girls in the woods on the mountain side o' the road. At least one o' them was armed wi' a shotgun. They'll be coverin' B.J.'s tracks, Ah reckon. An ambush for anyone who might try tae follow her."

Francesco's smile grew broader yet. "Oh, indeed I am interested," he said, and he visibly relaxed. For suddenly he was in no great hurry. "B.J.'s girls in the woods?" he repeated Angus. "That's means she's not long flown. And how long, do you think, to climb that mountain, Angus?"

"For me? I would'nae even try. For her: she's been doin' it since she was a girl. And that was a long, long time ago. Still and a', she could'nae make it in daylight. It'll be late in the evening by the time she's up."

"And we can do it in fifteen minutes," Francesco was almost ecstatic now.

"And meanwhile . . . from this one, I want answers. We can wait for him to wake up. And from those girls, more answers. About B.J.'s and maybe even Radu's plans. The more we can find out the better, before we fly up to the dome of that mountain and finish this thing." He turned to Manoza.

"Luigi, you stay and look after this one. Tie him up, throw the sleeping bag over him, and watch him. I mean stay *here* with him. This is one slippery fish. Later, I'll want to know why he fell out with the woman. And there are also a few things I want to know about his visit to Le Manse Madonie that time. *Hah!* But one thing is certain—however he did it, he won't be doing it again! Myself: I'm going with Dancer and Angus to see if I can get hold of one of these girls. Any questions?"

There were none, and Manoza was left alone in the helicopter, guarding the unconscious Necroscope . . .

B.J.'s rearguard was made up of Moreen Lowrie and Margaret Macdowell, which was all she could afford. They were moon-children—which is to say would-be werewolves and blood-takers, naturally—but they were up against Francesco Francezci, a Lord of the Wamphyri, Angus McGowan, a lieutenant of long-standing, and Guy "Dancer" Tanziano, a brutal thug of a vampire thrall.

Trapped in a pincer manoeuvre, they didn't stand a chance. Separating, trying to lead their pursuers off through the woods in different directions, away from the foothills route taken by B.J. and Sandra, Margaret was the first to be caught and killed by Dancer—broken like a stick over his knee, when she fought back with such ferocity as to demonstrate to him that there was no other way. Dumping her body in a deep ditch, he rolled rocks and earth on top to bury and hide it.

By then Francesco and McGowan had taken Moreen; when she ran out of shotgun shells, they'd jumped her and Francesco had knocked her unconscious. Then back to the car where Dancer had parked it at the edge of the woods, and so on to John Guiney's place. In this Francesco took a chance, but he didn't have too much choice. Unable to take the girl live and kicking (or soon to be) back to the lodge at Aviemore, the old gamekeeper's cottage had seemed the next best bet. And with the big saloon hidden behind the cottage, invisible from the road, the Francezci did what he liked best, working on the girl to get the information he wanted.

Left outside to keep watch, Tanziano felt a little out of things, but McGowan soon came to him, grinning, and told him it would be their turn before too long.

"She's talking?" Dancer's pale blank oval of a face showed signs of animation. He knew that when the Francezci was through with the girl, she'd be his and McGowan's.

"Oh, aye," McGowan told him. "With Francesco's hand up her muff, she's talkin' all right—and so would ye. Imagine havin' a wee umbrella wi' sharp spokes up yere dick, and if ye're difficult somebody puts the brolly up and yanks on the handle, eh? It's a verra weird thing, a woman's muff. Outside, it's no such a sensitive part as ye might think. But inside . . . there's organs up there that's *verra* sensitive! And those hands o' Francesco's; man, they're like so many snakes . . ."

Twenty minutes later Francesco came to them, said: "She's all yours. I've gagged her—I don't want any screaming. Also, when you've done, her body goes with us. We can dump it in the heights. I have this feeling there's too much rubbish been left lying around already. None of this was as tidy as it might have been."

"You first," McGowan told Dancer, who was grateful. "Only dinnae kill her or knock too much life out o' her. Ah'll enjoy doin' that mahsel, OK? Oh, and make sure that gag is secure. For now, anyway." And Dancer went off to the house.

Francesco said nothing. It was as well to keep one's lieutenants and thralls satisfied in however small a measure. And it was of old repute that Angus had a "thing" for tongues. Not for languages so much as *real* tongues, and especially women's tongues. As for this one screaming: she'd have no strength for that when Dancer was done, and no capacity for it after McGowan. Out of curiosity, he asked, "Are you *hungry* then, Angus?"

"Oh, ye ken yere people well, Francesco," McGowan answered with a grin. "Ah cannae help but wonder how many throats she's had that slippery tongue o' hers down. But when Ah take it off at the roots, mine will be the last! As for her heart: when Ah call a girl 'sweetheart,' it has a different meanin' entirely. Aye . . . "

While his men shared the girl, Francesco thought over what she had told him. First, that B.J. Mirlu had ascended and *was* Wamphyri! Perhaps after all this time that was only to be expected. No ordinary thrall could have lived her years without at least a dash of "superior" blood—or in the case of a dog-Lady, "inferior" blood—but Wamphyri blood in any case. And so Radu's watchdog, or bitch, had ascended, but only very recently. This made her a Lykan, of course, an immemorial enemy to Drakul and Ferenczy. In that respect nothing had changed, but in another everything had changed; for in the "grand" tradition of the Old Wamphyri B.J. was now opposed to her old Master, *his* enemy. All of B.J.'s life—through all the years she had served the dog-Lord during his "absence"— she had been the mistress of these territories, if only in her own mind. And now she was reluctant to give them up. Also, she had fallen for this man, this Harry Keogh. And if there was one thing about the werewolf Radu that was certain, it would have to be that he wasn't about to entertain the notion of a human rival . . .

When McGowan and Dancer were done with Moreen—after they'd bundled her body into the boot of the car, and on the way back to Aviemore—Francesco told them what he had learned from her and outlined his plan for tonight:

B.J. Mirlu was climbing to Radu's lair with another girl called Sandra, the last of her pack. B.J. suspected that Auld John Guiney and two others of Radu's thralls had sided with the dog-Lord and were already in the mountain. It fitted with Luigi Manoza's sighting of three men up there and probably meant that the woman would have a fight on her hands before she'd had time to recover from her climb. Since the dog-Lord must be active by now, she couldn't possibly win— but she might take out one or two of his people. Which was all to the good.

As for the Drakuls who were known to be in the vicinity: if they were in the mountain, that was better still. Let them all fight it out between them, and then the Francezcis—more properly the Ferenczys—would pick off any survivors! And so it appeared that old Angelo and Francesco's "dear" brother had been right: it was going to be that easy.

"But," Francesco concluded, "Anthony also said our losses would be light. His exact words, or as near as I can remember, were, 'The hound is finished. You'll win hands down. The opposition'—which I took to mean the Drakuls and B.J. Mirlu and her people—'will collapse. They'll offer only token resistance, and costs to you will be minimal . . .' " Francesco paused, narrowed his eyes a little, then shrugged.

"Well, and so far our 'costs'—our losses—have been minimal. Ragusa and Potenza? What were they for a loss? Nothing. As for Jimmy Nicosia: well, that was unfortunate. But no one can expect to win all the time."

Then they were back at Aviemore, where Francesco told the others, including Luigi Manoza: "Now we wait for nightfall. We have a couple of hours yet. You three take it in turn to watch that one," he aimed a thumb at the helicopter, "and we can all relax and eat in the bar . . . that's if you're *still* hungry. If or when this Keogh wakes up—no matter what we get out of him or don't— we're taking him with us into the mountain. *Up* into the mountain, and *down* from it. Or more properly down from the chopper. He flew like a ghost into and out of Le Manse Madonie that time, so now he can fly again—into thin air! I'm going to enjoy watching that bastard step or get tossed into space a couple of thousand feet up!"

Which the others found a very agreeable sentiment . . .

B.J. had hit Harry very hard, perhaps even too hard. But she'd wanted to be sure he wasn't going anywhere, that he was definitely out of the real trouble. It had never occurred to her that leaving him at John's house might place him in yet more jeopardy; surely, after the fighting there, and this close to Radu's rising, her enemies wouldn't go back there? They must know she would no longer be there. So she'd reckoned, but reckoned without the tenacity of the Wamphyri.

By now the Necroscope had been out for almost four hours, it was the twilight before true night, and a full moon was coming up over the Cairngorms. Wrapped in a blanket, Moreen's body had been transferred to the helicopter; her killers were aboard and Luigi Manoza was warming up the engine, waiting for Francesco's order to get aloft.

"The moon is on the roof of the mountains even now," Francesco said. "Are we all ready? . . . Then I'll tell you what you can expect. By now there may well have been fighting up there, between Drakuls and Lykan thralls, and maybe including the dog-Lord Radu himself. It could be going on right now, and from the moment we touch down we could be in the thick of it. So what do we have against Radu, who is Wamphyri? First there's me, for I, too, am Wamphyri! I can be hurt—I *can* be killed—but that's not an easy thing to do, and we have it on very good authority, advance information courtesy of Angelo, that we are on the winning side.

"Then we have superior weapons. You've seen what the woman had: a shot-gun? *Hah!* But on the other hand the Drakuls could be heavily armed, though not as heavily as us, I fancy. You've all got red armbands, and you can all see in the dark. There can be no errors: if it moves and it isn't wearing red, shoot it! And shoot to kill!

"Radu: the odds are he'll be weak physically. But if he's still the legendary wolf, we can tame him. Every third round in your magazines is a silver bullet. Deadly to all of us, I know, but even more so to him. If you see him, if you get him in your sights—*don't fuck with him!* Give him all you've got. And when he's down get up close and keep hosing it to him. I want him in pieces, and then I want to burn each piece!"

He looked at the faces of McGowan and Tanziano, where they were seated with him in the passenger cabin, and at the back of Luigi Manoza's head at the controls. "That's it, then. Now, are there any questions?"

There were none, and Francesco leaned forward to give Manoza a tap on the shoulder. "Luigi? Can you put her down OK?"

"I got a good look at the place," Manoza shouted over the rising clamour of the rotors. "Most of it is fairly flat where I'll put down. The weather forecast gives us a clear night, no wind to mention and the temperature several degrees above zero. It couldn't be better. And then there's the dog-Lord's big silver friend in the sky." He meant the full moon. "It'll be like daylight."

Francesco nodded. "Yes, this time his silver mistress has really let him down. Very well, let's get on our way . . . "

Harry heard none of this, or if he did it was as a fuzzy background static to the gradual transition he was making from true unconsciousness to healing sleep. The sleeping bag tossed over him had kept him relatively warm, and his good physical condition overall had guaranteed that apart from a headache he would come out of this intact—for however long or short a time.

He was aware, however dimly, dreamily, that someone else was with him, close to him; he could feel a cold marble thigh against his, and a cold arm across his body. But then again it could be part of his dream. Except he dreamed of flight . . . of motion through the air. It would be soothing—like rocking in a chair or drowsing in a hammock—except someone seemed to be trying to tip him *out* of the hammock. "Whoever you are, please piss off!" he tried to say. But if he said anything at all it was lost in the rumbling of the helicopter's rotors.

The Necroscope's mental barriers were down; the disturbance he experi-enced wasn't anyone trying to tip him out of anything, but rather *into* some-thing; in fact, into a response. It was Sir Keenan Gormley, who was insisting:

Harry, for God's sake accept me, can't you? Listen to me! I thought we'd lost you. We all did—for suddenly you weren't there! Your light had gone out and there was noth-ing but darkness out there. But just a moment ago it flared up again, so I know you're still there. And Harry my boy, I must *talk to you!*

Keenan? (Harry dreamed on, but at least the dead man had got his atten-tion.) *Can't it keep? I don't feel too good, need to take it easy.* It was a weak response—as weak as and weaker than Sir Keenan had ever had from the Necroscope—but knowing him of old, the ex-Head of E-Branch read him like a book. And:

You've been hurt? Well, that doesn't surprise me. For without your full range of talents, without being able to use them to maximum effect, what are you but a man after all? But Harry, I can give them back to you! Or if I can't, I know someone who can.

Now Sir Keenan had his full attention, even if it hurt, and Harry said, *Give something back? What are we talking about?*

The Möbius Continuum! Sir Keenan told him. *Its unrestricted use! Harry, you've been robbed, and you don't even know it.*

"I was robbed?" he spoke out loud—or rather in a croaky whisper, unheard over the throb of the helicopter's engine and the *whup, whup, whup* of rotors— as one of his legs jerked in a semi-conscious, reflex manner, striking against a naked figure lying beside him. Harry was waking up, and Francesco Francezci had noticed his twitching.

"Keogh moved," he said to Angus McGowan and Dancer, seated opposite him. Tanziano at once reached down, flicked aside the blanket covering the girl's body. But when he went to yank the sleeping bag from the Necroscope's crumpled figure, Francesco stopped him. "Let it be," he said. "I can't really talk to him here anyway, and who cares? He's a dead man; our mission is as good as accomplished; we have my father's guarantee that we're coming out on top. And if this one is, or was, as dangerous as Angelo thought he was—why keep him around any longer than we have to, eh?" He reached out, touched Manoza's shoulder. "Luigi, let's have a little altitude. There's someone back here wants to go sky-diving."

Meanwhile Sir Keenan Gormley had introduced Harry to a new "voice" in the metaphysical aether. But whoever it belonged to, he was so faint, distant, damaged that the connection was like a long-distance call to another planet.

We met once, Harry, the disembodied, dislocated voice told him. *Maybe you'll remember? It wasn't long ago, at E-Branch HQ, in London. You, Darcy Clarke, and Ben Trask, you gave me a lift home one night. But I didn't make it. Since then . . . it's taken me a long time to get it together. And me . . . well, I don't suppose I'll ever get myself together! My name is—or was—James Anderson. I was a self-styled "Doctor," and my business . . . was hypnotism. I did the occasional work for E-Branch, and you—*

"And I was one of your subjects?" Even half-asleep (and the Necroscope had never known the sleep or dreams of ordinary men) Harry's voice was hard. He caught on fast and things were dropping into place. And the more they dropped, the closer he came to waking.

Anderson told him everything and, however faintly, his message got through. And because intercourse with the dead is more akin to telepathy than physical speech, more an experience than a conversation, Harry absorbed it all in double-quick time. But when he knew how Anderson had died, and why he was so faint . . . then there was nothing for it but to accept his apology and forgive him. For Anderson hadn't known what it was all about, after all, only that he was doing a job for E-Branch. And:

"Bloody E-Branch!" Harry said, disgustedly. "They dropped you right in it, didn't they? Oh, they're good at that! Well, I don't know if this will help any, but I can tell you—or show you—what happened to the two who . . . who did it to you." And he pictured again the explosion in the Möbius Continuum, a fire-ball expanding, then shrinking, as the wreckage of the Mercedes sped on forever. And the death-shrieks of the men inside going on forever, too.

Forever? Anderson queried, his voice even smaller.

"I can't say," Harry answered. "I don't know. I don't want to think about it . . . " And a moment later, explosively: "Fucking E-Branch!" he spat, as one of Nostradamus's quatrains leaped to mind:

> Six hundred north, and west unto the Zero,
> the men of magic are his friends, but chained.
> They may not help the one who is their hero,
> or tell him that which may not be explained . . .

Chained by their own rules, yes—by the Minister Responsible, bureaucracy, governmental "expediency," by the Department of Dirty Tricks—but mainly by their fear: that someone else might try to recruit him after he'd quit! Harry saw it all now. He'd always suspected that there was something Darcy desperately wanted to tell him but didn't know how to explain it.

E-Branch, the bastards!

But Harry, Anderson told him, *I can put it right. I'm the only one who* can *put it right! Why, it's as easy as this:* (The snap of mental fingers—Anderson's oh-so-talented fingers—in Harry's mind, as he came a little more fully awake . . . then sprang *fully* awake, in knowledge at least.) And this time there was no conflict; Harry's various levels of conscious awareness, his several realities interfaced perfectly, because the man who had been responsible for creating the first of his mind-blocks was also the one who removed it.

And Dancer said: "Francesco, this guy's talking to himself and starting to move. He's coming out of it."

But not quite, for the dead were still talking to the Necroscope, and they still had his attention. Indeed, they had his attention more fully than at any time since Anderson had placed his post-hypnotic manacles on Harry's mind and behaviour, constraints which now were lifted.

Harry? said a new voice, male, with a slight Scottish accent; a voice of once-authority, but shaky now and with nothing of its former confidence. *I just wanted to warn you about who—or what—you're up against.* Ex-Inspector George Ianson paused to introduce himself, and then quickly told his story . . . which was as bad or worse than Anderson's. *So, there you have it,* he finished with a mental shudder. *That little man, McGowan, a man I called my friend, has to be the devil incarnate! And while he is alive, I . . . can never rest. Literally . . . *

"One devil," Harry answered. "Just one of many. So thanks for the warning but it really wasn't necessary. I *know* they've got to go. It's them or me, and I don't intend it to be me . . . "

I was a man of law and justice, Ianson told him, *but there can be no sane or civilized "trial" for such as them, just revenge—or maybe a "just" revenge? I'm only one, Harry, but how many other victims have there been?* And his voice slowly faded into the background static of the grave—or in Ianson's case, a place even darker than the grave.

The Necroscope's anger was making him restless now; it was a cold anger, that bit into his soul like an icy blast. All the way down the line he had been everybody's fool, and he'd placed all of the blame on himself. He had actually believed himself a drunk, or an amnesiac, or a madman; he had *committed* himself to an asylum! And only now, when it might well be too late, did he have the complete story; only now the missing pieces of the puzzle had fallen into place. And the bitter chill of realization, of knowledge, was eating deeper and deeper into him.

Harry? said a female voice from close, very close at hand. *Can I—I mean, would you mind—if I talked to you, too? You are human, but you were our friend. My friend, briefly. But you should know: I can't, couldn't help what I was, and neither can B.J. It was in the blood, that's all. In her more than in me or any of the girls. That's not an excuse, it's simply a fact. And Harry, if you don't already know, then you should know that she really does love you.*

The Necroscope knew the voice: it was Moreen, one of B.J.'s girls. But dead?

By the Watcher's hand, McGowan's hand, yes, she said. *But I won't go into details. Anyway, who am I to say what should or shouldn't be? What, with my background? But that policeman you were talking to . . . he's so right, Harry. For no matter what I was, that little man* is *the devil incarnate!*

The helicopter rolled a little, and Moreen's arm flopped across Harry's face. He felt it there, and knew it for what it was. Then the icy blast hit him again, and not only in his soul but physically. A blast from the open door, and the *whup, whup, whup!* of the chopper's rotors finally getting through to him.

Harry gave a single spastic kick, yelled out loud, jerked awake! He scrambled half-way to his feet, fell to his knees as whip-crack lightning flashes from the back of his head threatened to engulf him again.

McGowan and Dancer flanked him, grabbed his arms, yanked him moaning upright. In the red glow of the cabin lights, hanging onto a ceiling strap, Francesco Francezci grinned directly into his face and said, "Hallo, whoever you fucking are—and goodbye!" He jerked his head to indicate the open door and the end of Harry's life.

Disoriented, the Necroscope let himself be dragged to the door. Then, seeing what had been planned for him, he might have fought, but it was too late. As they catapulted him into space, McGowan leaned his devil's face out after him a little way and grinned from ear to ear—for a moment.

Then he stopped grinning, gave a wild shriek—and came tumbling after!

While in the aircraft, Francesco took the safety off the machine-pistol slung over his shoulder, cursed and brought the weapon up into the firing position, and let fly point-blank with a spray of bullets . . . directly into the naked back of an entirely dead Moreen! Dead, with her tongue and heart ripped out, her blood stolen, and her body ravaged, but "alive" enough to have clawed herself up off the floor and to have pushed Angus McGowan out into thin air! And Harry hadn't even asked.

Devastated by the spray of bullets—almost cut in half, hurled forward, projected out of the door—she was only a rag doll again fluttering in the downblast. And her last words to the Necroscope were:

It seems I left it too long. Sorry, Harry . . .

But: *Don't be,* he told her, falling. *And don't worry, you won't be alone. The dead may take their time, but they'll talk to you eventually. And so will I when I get the chance.*

His first thought was to conjure a Möbius door, but then he saw McGowan angling towards him. The little man was falling like a genuine sky-diver, with arms and legs forming something of an aerofoil. And Harry remembered from what Ianson had told him that this one had been a lieutenant for a long time. Even as he watched, McGowan's body was flattening, more surely gliding. And his arms were stretching, reaching. Extending towards Harry!

And his *face!* His mad eyes blazing, triumphant! His jaws gaping, wider and wider! And his teeth elongating, curving up out of riven, bleeding gums. His hands were hooked into claws, and they were only inches away . . .

. . . When Harry mouthed, "So you're the devil himself, are you? Well then, welcome to hell, Watcher!"

And opening a door directly beneath his falling body, the Necroscope plunged through it. But only McGowan's arms, sliced through above the elbows, went with him. Hot blood sprayed and Harry held up an arm to deflect its red jet. Then it was over, and he was hanging there as limp as a rag, cold, damp, motionless, but safe now in the nothingness of the Möbius Continuum.

While in the universe he'd just left, McGowan howled his agony and his helplessness, waved his scarlet stumps, and went plummeting into a rocky gorge a thousand feet below.

If someone were cruel enough to hurl a garden snail onto a concrete slab, he would get much the same result.

George Ianson could rest easier now, Moreen, too, and many another with them . . .

And in the helicopter:

Shocked rigid, astonished, Guy Tanziano stood frozen beside the open door. And even more ashen than usual, Francesco slumped back into his seat and said, "Shut the fucking thing!" And: "Did you see that? Or am I going mad? That girl . . . "

"What happened?" At the controls, Luigi Manoza had caught very little of the action.

"She was alive," Dancer mumbled stupidly, sliding the cabin door shut and turning the locking handle.

"No," Francesco got a grip on himself, snarled low in his throat. "She was dead meat. But . . . I don't know. He—they?—had seemed to be talking to each other!" And to himself: *Didn't Angelo tell us that he talks to dead people?*

"Maybe . . . " said Dancer. "Er, maybe . . . "

"Maybe what?" The Francezci spoke as if to himself; he was scarcely able to believe what had happened.

"Maybe she'd been a thrall, even a lieutenant, longer than we thought."

"What?" But suddenly Francesco was seeing Dancer in a new light. For "maybe" he was right at that! No maybe about it; he *had* to be right. The girl had been a fully-fledged vampire, and this had been her last shot at metamorphism. Nothing to do with life or intelligence, just the vampire stuff inside her hanging on to dear life. But no longer. By now she'd be so much slop.

"What? I mean, *what?*" Luigi Manoza's chubby white face was still staring back into the passenger cabin.

The Francezci looked at him and said, "McGowan's gone. An accident. Now there are just the three of us . . . "

It had been the fastest climb of B.J.'s life, as if everything else she had done, every moment of practice on a hundred cliff faces, but especially on this one, had been trial runs for the one big effort. Like an athlete who holds himself in reserve for the big race, B.J. had held herself back for this one.

Even handicapped by climbing with Sandra—to whom, for the last thirteen years, B.J. had been teaching everything she knew—still she had outdone herself. For the last hour or so, however, Sandra had been flagging; B.J. had more or less dragged her through the final stages of the ascent. But where she had been Sandra's life-support system on the inhospitable, often vertical granite faces, Sandra would be hers when at last she stood face to face with her terrible Master—or her ex-Master, as she kept reminding herself.

For where B.J. was expert with her naked hands—as well as with the despised ropes and pitons of the climber—Sandra was a crack shot. And in her small pack she carried a pistol loaded with very special ammunition: silver bullets that B.J. had never believed she would use except against her mortal or near-immortal enemies. But what the hell . . . the dog-Lord *was* her enemy now, else he would surely have contacted her before this! But here the full moon lit their way and Radu's redoubt no more than a slight overhang and a narrow rocky ledge away, and *still* the psychic aether was as empty of living thoughts as a crumbling ruin.

Or perhaps not. For every now and then—briefly, as a ripple on water, or a riffle through the pages of her mind—B.J. would feel an observer where there could not possibly be one. But it wasn't Radu, no. For she would know his mind, his feral *feel*, his mental musk, anywhere.

If Radu was up—if Auld John and the others had had any success in raising him from the resin—then the dog-Lord was keeping very quiet about it. And so B.J. must be mistaken. It had to be the proximity of the redoubt, preying on her mind.

She took a small grapple from her belt, sprang its tines and swung it up into the riven rock some twelve feet overhead. It caught at once, and she tried her weight on it while still clinging tight to the cliff face. No problem; she'd done this a hundred times before. She braced her feet, climbed hand over hand to the overhang, reached across it and drew herself up on to the ledge. Eight feet overhead, the grapple was still firmly wedged. And:

"Sandra," she called down softly. "You climb, I'll pull."

The girl at once obeyed. And she was on the rope, bracing her legs, leaning back into space and looking up at B.J. when it happened.

Sandra's eyes went wide; she saw beyond B.J., and uttered a small gasp that had nothing at all to do with her exertions. B.J. rolled on her side and looked up. Above her ledge, a hole or cave in the honeycombed rock—it, too, must penetrate into the mountain, but on a slightly higher level. And looking down on her out of the mouth of the cave, over the rim of the rock, the vicious visage of an Asiatic—a Drakul! And:

Revenge! Singra Singh Drakesh thought, directly into B.J.'s mind, as he sliced through the rope. *Revenge for mine that your people broke on the rocks of this selfsame mountain!*

B.J. had the rope in her hands, but Sandra had panicked. Now she dangled there, with all of her weight on the rope that slid ever faster through B.J.'s fingers. And she couldn't trap it! Blood spurted where the rope cut, lubricating its passage, until the sliced end whipped between her fingers and was gone. And Sandra gone with it, a small frightened figure twirling in darkness, down to the black river where it frothed at the bottom of the gorge. As quick as that . . .

B.J. stuck her legs deep into the narrow slit of the rubble-littered natural "window" at the back of her ledge, looked up again, and panted: "You, you bastard—you're a dead man!"

On his belly, Singra Singh looked down on her, and said, "I think not." His knife had been put away but now he dragged something else into view.

Seeing the blued-steel muzzle of an ugly machine-pistol, B.J. scrambled to turn her body out of the line of fire, draw herself under the lip of rock into the labyrinthine system of caves that she knew lay within. But her gear snagged on something, trapping her, and Singh's thin lips formed a grinning gash in his face where they drew back from needle teeth. Taking his time, he lined up his sights . . .

. . . And a growling voice in *both* of their minds, that yet spoke to Singra Singh, said: *You are by far the lesser of two evils, true, but you are closer to hand. And by preference, I would kill a Drakul every time before a Lykan. Even a treacherous bitch like that one!*

Then . . . something crunched. It crunched so loud and clear that B.J. could almost feel it: the snapping of bones. And the agonized, tortured look on Singra Singh's face said it all, as he dropped his weapon and flopped like a beached fish . . . then began to slide backwards, dragged effortlessly into his cave!

B.J. knew what had him, but had to see it for herself:

That monstrous paw that reached out over his head to catch it in the raking hooks of three-inch talons, and snatch it out of view. And the Drakul's death-cry rising up and up, *"Ah! Ah! Ahhh!"* before it shuddered into an awful silence.

Then, galvanized by her terror, B.J. struggled free of the opening and into the redoubt. And slipping into the darkness of mazy caverns and corridors that no other person had ever known so well, she took her crossbow from her belt, opened its wings and nocked it, slid a bolt into place on the tiller. With Sandra gone, the crossbow was her only weapon against all the pent-up horror and lust of six centuries.

And her single advantage, for what it was worth, was that now she had only herself to worry about . . .

III

IN RADU'S REDOUBT.
HARRY AND THE DOG-LORD.

T HAT WAS OUR BIGGEST FEAR, SIR KEENAN TOLD HARRY, SHORTLY AFTER THE
Necroscope emerged from the Möbius Continuum at Auld John's place.
That the interface would cause a complete and final mental breakdown. Thank God
we were wrong!

But Harry had never been too sure about God, and so answered, "I prefer
to thank Nostradamus, and maybe Mesmer. I'm not sure what Mesmer did, but
I think he eased the way for me. Nostradamus took a chance—and again I'm
not too sure about a lot of the stuff he told me—but in making me work some
of it out for myself he provided the cure. The way I see it, it's easy to be scared
of the unknown. But once you begin to understand what you are dealing with,
then it gets easier."

Your mother said as much, Sir Keenan told him.

And Harry nodded. "If I had been hit with the whole thing, all at one time,
I'm pretty sure I would have lost it, totally. But bit by bit I could take it. And
not only that, but I'm mad as hell! I mean, angry mad."

And this time it was me who said as much, Sir Keenan said, worriedly. *But not*
so mad that you'll start taking chances?

"I'll do what I have to," Harry answered. "And now I have to make myself
useful. Please excuse me . . . "

He found his belt and munitions where B.J. had tossed them under a bush
close to the house, and re-equipped himself. Also, he looked for and pocketed
the cigarette lighter dropped by the Ferenczy thrall when he had shot him. After
that there was only one thing left to do, one place to go, and he believed he
knew the exact location. For when B.J. had told him—or re-told him—about
the Wamphyri, she had awakened certain memories, too.

One of them was about a dream he'd had, or a premonition; or, since it had been a long time, even years ago, when the Necroscope had been new to Alec Kyle's body, maybe it had been one of Kyle's glimpses out of the future. Whichever, he had visited Radu's redoubt and stood by the dog-Lord's sarcophagus. And now he need only recall that specific scene to mind and the coordinates were there, rock solid in his renewed, repaired and even refreshed memory.

Climb to the lair? He had no doubt that he could, but that was for people who knew no other way. Harry's way was simply to go there.

And taking a deep breath, he prepared to do just that . . .

Francesco Francezci, Guy Tanziano and Luigi Manoza found Auld John's rope still dangling into the pothole where he had left it, and clambered down into darkness. Vampires, they found no great difficulty in the climb; the lack of daylight was hardly problematic; the light of the full moon and the coldly enigmatic stars lit their way through the first stage, and when they were down into the labyrinth their eyes quickly adjusted. The Francezci's eyes flared red, and those of the others were the sulphur yellow of vampire thralls.

They went carefully, soundlessly at first. Radu's redoubt wasn't what they had expected. It seemed rough, uninhabitable, deserted—it *seemed* deserted, at least. Its many levels were hollow and echoing; the deeper they penetrated, the more constant and life-sustaining the temperature, which was typical of cavern complexes world-wide. Overall, the silence, both physical and psychic, was utter.

"The three we saw," Tanziano whispered hoarsely, "the old tracker and his friends: they were definitely headed this way. And then there's that rope. Somebody came down here."

"Obviously," said Francesco. "But that was hours ago, and they could just as easily have left. On the other hand . . . perhaps something stopped them from leaving. Radu has been down a long time, with little or no sustenance to see him through the centuries. Personally, I shall be interested to see how he did it. But now, waking, he would have his needs—*immediate* needs, I mean. And while you may not smell it, to me this place *stinks* of wolf! So, it could be that he's resting—after taking food? Anyway, let's keep it quiet. Sound will travel a long way down here, and thoughts go further and faster yet. So as of now you would be wise to guard your thoughts, and if you feel or sense anything at all . . . " He looked at his thralls, nodded meaningfully, and left the rest unspoken.

They followed footprints, occasionally mere scuff marks in places where the dust of centuries lay thin on the naked stone. After a while, descending a steep passage to a floor of broken flags laid in a rough crazy-paving fashion, Tanziano pointed a blunt finger, grunted, "Two sets of tracks, going in both directions."

Francesco nodded, and whispered, "But the majority go this way." He eased back the cocking handle on his machine-pistol so that the distinctive ch-*ching* as it engaged was kept to a minimum of noise. And the others followed suit.

They were down now onto the floor of the main cavern, into the lair itself, and every one of Francesco's vampire instincts told him it was so. But he still couldn't detect the dog-Lord himself. He was here, certainly—wolf-musk lay thick in Francesco's mind, almost as if he felt it on his skin—but Radu's actual location remained unknown.

Anthony Francezci (had he been here) would not have found this surprising. Through greater contact with his father, Anthony had learned far more of Wamphyri history than his brother; he knew that two thousand years ago in Starside, the dog-Lord was *already* a powerful telepath. He could control his thoughts—disappear from the mental aether—as surely as Angelo Ferenczy himself. But Tony Francezci wasn't here . . . and this was the last place he would *want* to be despite that he had assured his brother of his coming triumph . . .

Following the major trail of prints and scuffs, eventually the trio came to Radu's sarcophagus atop its dais of piled debris. Here the wolf-taint was thick, if only to Francesco. But something of the eeriness of the place—its pregnant silence perhaps, or distant, monotonous, almost musical drip of water—had got through to Guy Tanziano.

Tugging on Francesco's sleeve where the Francezci looked up at the great stone coffin, he whispered, "This place makes the pit back at Le Manse Madonie feel downright friendly!"

Francesco shrugged him off, scowled at his obvious reluctance. "Stay here then, and watch our backs," he said. And with a twitch of his head he indicated that Manoza should accompany him up to the sarcophagus. Leaving Tanziano at the foot of the pile, the two climbed to the dais's platform and lit the stubs of several torches in their sconces. Then, stepping across the pooled resin, they carried on up to the rim of Radu's coffin.

"Shit!" said Manoza then, gazing down on what the bath of gluey yellow fluids contained. But Francesco only grinned, and used the folded butt of his weapon to prod the pair of corpses where they lay half-submerged in the resin.

"I was right," he said. "He's not only awake but he's up, and he's hungry. He *was* hungry, anyway . . . "

One of the corpses was that of a young man; nothing extraordinary about him, except the wolf-taint. "Moon-child," Francesco commented. "Drained to the last drop, and drowned in the resin just to be sure that Radu's bite wouldn't take. The dog-Lord isn't making lieutenants—not just yet, anyway. And this other one—a Drakul, definitely. Asiatic, a full-fledged lieutenant and leader of his group. Which tells me that his group is probably no more. He would be the last to go."

And Manoza murmured, in something of awe, "His back's like a 'Z.' And those knife marks go right through to his skull. *And* he's missing his heart! It's like he went through the cogs of a big machine!"

"Not knife marks," Francesco shook his head. "Claw marks."

While down at the foot of the stack Tanziano gave a start and turned in a jerky circle, his eyes swivelling this way and that as they tried to follow a shadow that seemed to leap from wall to wall and surface to surface in the flickering light of the torches. Until finally his gaze rested on a vertical crack in the cavern's wall, where for a moment the torchlight seemed reflected by twin points of red.

And gritting his teeth, nodding his bullet head and unnoticed by his companions, Dancer pointed his weapon ahead of him, moved in that direction . . .

. . . While the Francezci said to Manoza: "It's like I told you it would be: the bloodwar is on and they've already engaged each other. Somewhere in this maze, we'll find the rest of them—those you observed on their way here, the woman and the last of her girls, and of course the dog-Lord Radu—if they haven't killed each other off already! We can always hope, eh?" He turned, glanced down to the foot of the pile, and started to say: "Guy, now we're going to follow that other set of—

"—Tracks? Guy? Dancer?" His voice came echoing back, but that was all. Tanziano wasn't there.

The Francezci and Manoza scrambled down to the floor, and Francesco called: "Dancer? Where the hell . . . ?" And it was as if the cavern had been waiting for just such a question.

"Where the hell . . . ? Where the . . . ? Where . . . ?" it echoed.

And then something that wasn't an echo, but a hoarse whisper—yet sharp and clear as a shout to their enhanced hearing. And not only in Francesco's ears, but in his mind: *"Oh, indeed! Where the hell. But the hell is here, Ferenczy scum!"*

"Wolf!" Francesco snarled, as that cough, bark, rumble of sound faded in his head. He and Manoza stood back to back and stared into shadows left and right. Nothing moved—for a moment. Until suddenly something was lobbed out from behind a massive, natural column of rock. It spun lazily in the smoky air, landed soggily on the rough-hewn flags, slid a little way, and left a red trail. It was an arm, torn off at the shoulder like a chicken joint, with all of the ligaments, the flesh and tendons of the right shoulder and breast attached. And it was still clad in the sleeves of Guy "Dancer" Tanziano's parka, jacket, and shirt!

The howling, when it came, was an anticlimax. But more than howling, Francesco knew it was also laughter. And reverberating in his mind as well as through the maze of caverns, it bounced from wall to wall and nerve-ending to nerve-ending like an out-of-kilter dervish.

"Howling!" Manoza said, unnecessarily.

"And laughter!" Francesco snarled. "The bastard's laughing at us!"

"I only heard the howling," said Manoza, visibly shaken. He looked at the Francezci wide- and wild-eyed. "Francesco, are we nuts or something? What the *fuck* are we doing here?"

Francesco indicated the massive column of rock. "I'll take this side, you take the other. Circle the column, stay close to the rock, and fire at anything that moves."

But as they came together on the other side without seeing anything: *Far too late, too slow,* came that deep dark rumble of a voice in Francesco's mind. *Three of you came down here—came of your own free will—but now there are only two. Soon, only you and I, Ferenczy. Are you afraid?*

For a moment it was as if Francesco had been slapped in the face. Then he snarled out loud, "What, afraid of a halfling? Of a dog-thing? If you're such a menace, such a threat, Radu, then why not do it here, now, face to face?" It was part-bravado and part something else. For he had sensed—what, frustration? Or desperation?—*something,* in the dog-Lord's bluster. Something behind it that he was trying to cover up.

And Radu *knew* that he had sensed it. The telepathic contact he'd established had conveyed far more than he had wanted Francesco to know. And the dog-Lord's growl became a furious whine as he withdrew his probe.

Francesco turned to Manoza, who was looking at him as if he were mad. "Oh? What now?" the Francezci scowled.

"You were . . . you were *talking* to him!" Manoza said. "You were challenging him. But he's not here."

Francesco grinned his humourless grin. "Of course he has moved on, Luigi—gone from here because he's afraid—but he heard me well enough. And I challenged him because he is weak. Radu is ill! He's sick from his hibernation, from the waking, from disease, and from time itself. This is one sick old wolf, and his only advantage is his familiarity with this damn labyrinth. But his thoughts give him away. They're like a beacon to me. Come on, follow the trail . . . "

It was a trail of blood: Dancer's blood—which after a handful of paces came to an abrupt end at his body, where his legs stuck out from behind a slab of rock. His fat tongue had been ripped half from its roots, dragged forward to block his mouth and stop him crying out. His back was broken; his heart had been torn out through a gaping hole in his chest and shattered ribs.

"Holy . . . !" said Luigi Manoza, his throat bobbing with the effort of gathering saliva to get the one word out.

"Holy?" Francesco glared at him. *"Holy?"*

"Holy shit!" Manoza finally gasped. He was a vampire, but he was only a thrall. And this was the work of something else. Wamphyri, but different again from Francesco.

Ahead, an interior rock wall was split into twin tunnels. Tracks went into both of them. "You can see in the dark," the Francezci reminded the badly shaken Manoza. "You have a superior weapon. You can pump twenty-five rounds a second into this bastard! Get into that tunnel. If the trail peters out, come back to this point. And I shall do likewise. Now move!"

Manoza moved. But only a few stumbling paces into the tunnel he saw an irregular patch of light far overhead, and to one side blocks of stone piled into steps, with more steps cut into the wall leading to what looked like the arch of a natural rock causeway. Everything led upwards and out of here, which seemed to Manoza a very good place to be.

The Francezci would kill him, if he didn't get killed himself. But right now, not knowing what Francesco knew or *thought* he knew, Manoza considered that a distinct possibility. And the chopper was up there. And light, and air, and freedom. And down here: the true death, in the shape of a terror out of time. Not much of a choice—especially with that growling voice in his mind, urging him: *Run, little man, run! Save yourself, for your master is as good as dead!*

And with a hammering heart Manoza ran, or rather climbed, and a gibbering horror seemed right behind him all the way . . .

In the Continuum, Harry had thought twice about it. And in the end he hadn't taken the Möbius route directly into Radu's lair. For one thing his olden dream or preview forbade it. More than a dream, that had been a nightmare! And for another, he wanted to see what was going on up there on the mountain. With

Drakul and Ferenczy involvement it could and most probably would be a mine-field. And so he had gone in stages, from false plateau to ledge to rocky butte, and finally to the dome of the mountain.

There he had found the helicopter deserted on flat ground close to a huge fissure in the pitted rock. A rope dangled into another, smaller pothole close by, and he rightly supposed that this had been the Ferenczy gang's route into the lair. But knowing they were equipped with high-powered weapons, and likewise their advantage in the dark, he hadn't followed them or tried jumping ahead of them. And despite that the Necroscope's heart was in his mouth for Bonnie Jean—though in truth he couldn't say why—still he'd sat it out for more than half an hour to see what would happen.

Now he was more cold and anxious than ever, and the moonlit scene was as still as when he'd first arrived here. Still, and quiet—or maybe unquiet—except for the low moaning of a steady breeze that swept across the mountain's dome. Quiet, yes . . . Or perhaps not.

He was close to the pothole entrance when he saw the rope go taut and heard a distant panting. Then the vibration of the rope as someone climbed into view. By then Harry had moved back into the cover of a clump of rocks, but when the stubby man who climbed out of the pothole headed for the helicopter he stepped into view. The man was in a hurry and failed to see him. Reaching the airplane, he yanked open a door in the machine's side.

Harry couldn't see him too well, didn't recognize him and wanted to be sure of who he was and what was going on here. So he called out: "Hey, you!"

Luigi Manoza's answer might easily have cut him in pieces. Whirling, the thug opened up with his machine-pistol, and lead—and a little silver—buzzed like a cloud of angry wasps all around. Most of the rounds were wasted, trapped by the Möbius door that Harry erected as Manoza spun and went into a crouch. The ones that went wide of the door were the ones that buzzed. And now Harry could be sure of what he was dealing with.

But Manoza couldn't. He had fired on someone, had used up half a magazine on him from a distance of some forty or forty-five feet away—and that someone, or thing, was still on its feet and hadn't even moved! That was more than enough for Manoza. Scrambling aboard the airplane, he slammed the door shut after him and threw himself into the pilot's chair. The flick of a handful of switches, the pressure of the thug's thumb on the starter button, and the engine coughed into life. Then the vanes began their *whup . . . whuup . . . whuuup* air-slicing revolutions, quickly blurring into a shining fan whose draught bounced the machine on its pontoons.

Taking out a transmitter from one of his pouches, extending the aerial, Harry waited for the helicopter to drift just an inch or two off the ground, then pressed the button. At the chopper's tail-end just below the lateral fan, a magnetic mine consisting of a detonator and four ounces of plastic exploded, blew the fan off, and sent the airplane crazy. She keeled over and snapped a pontoon, rolled the other way and forwards until the vanes hit the deck and snapped off in razor-sharp sections. One such section shot in through the windscreen and pinned Manoza to his seat, holding him there while the chopper skittered like a singed moth to the edge of the fissure. It tilted for a moment, stood in a ballet-dancer pose on one pontoon, and fell. A count of four and the fuel tanks blew, and seventy gallons of avgas made a blast that shook the rock under the Necroscope's feet, and a smoke-ring that went up and up, following a tongue of fire that licked fifty feet into the night sky.

Harry nodded grimly to himself. Another Ferenczy down and just two to go, of this mob anyway. Moreover, he had destroyed their escape route. Maybe now it was time he had a look inside Radu's lair.

As he conjured a Möbius door, another explosion shook the mountain from deep within. And the great fissure vented streamers of black smoke.

Now more than ever the Necroscope was conscious of his error—the fact that he didn't have a sidearm. His bombs, devastating as they were, and even his grenades weren't designed for close-quarter combat. On the other hand, what good was a conventional handgun against the Wamphyri? Instead, he palmed a heavy little fragmentation grenade before making his jump.

In his dream, remembered as clearly now as if he'd experienced it just last night, he had seen ragged natural "windows" in the crumbling outer wall of the lair, located at a seemingly "safe" distance from Radu's sarcophagus. The co-ordinates were clear in his mind as he conjured a door . . .

. . . And his dream came to life as he stepped from the Möbius Continuum at one of those precise co-ordinates—barely in time to witness an astonishing occurrence, and one that he had set in motion.

The place was reverberating with distant and not-so-distant echoes, creakings, and groanings; dust settled in rivulets from a ceiling lost in height and darkness, also from various ledges and levels. Even a handful of stony splinters and one or two geometrically shaped slabs of granite came hurtling from on high. But all of this mainly in the unsupported central section of the cavern, not on the perimeter where Harry stood.

Nor was this disturbance finished. There was a continuous metallic grinding, a nerve-shattering screech of tortured metal, which seemed if anything to be getting louder; and, from a huge borehole-like aperture or cave where the dim ceiling curved out of the heights to form an inner wall, an intermittent stream of stony rubble and smoke. But when fire gushed from the hole like a giant's blowtorch, Harry believed he knew what he was seeing.

Through unknown caverns, stony chutes and rock-slides, the wrecked helicopter had found its way down to this level. And as the blowtorch blaze turned to black smoke and a twisted mass of hot, blistered metal erupted from the hole and smashed down in the cavern's debris, Harry saw that he was right.

But the glare of the fireball had lit up the whole cavern, and the Necroscope had taken the opportunity to note his position, the best route to Radu's dais and sarcophagus, and especially the fact that the place seemed void of life. But certainly life had been here. For just a few short paces ahead of him, he had also seen B.J.'s crossbow, still loaded, lying on the floor where she had tossed it—or where it had fallen. Stepping forward he put away his grenade, retrieved the crossbow, refused to dwell on what its discovery meant.

The guttering torches at the base of Radu's coffin served as his guide, and in a little while he was there. A few moments more, and he would know if the dog-Lord was up and about in the world. But if he wasn't, then he never would be.

And holding the crossbow waist-high, aiming it ahead, determined to see this thing through to the end, Harry climbed the jumble to its level dais, avoided the slopped resin, and resolutely continued on up to the rim of the great sarcophagus . . .

The dog-Lord Radu Lykan was finished. He knew it, and had known it even before rising from the resin. It was only *since* rising that he had come to accept it: that in his current shape he was finished. In his *current* shape and form, aye. Which was why he had sent Auld John to bring the Mysterious One—his Man-With-Two-Faces—to him in his lair. For the man called Harry Keogh was his one way out of a fix that had stayed with him, stalking him through six long centuries.

But to think of it at any length, to even consider it, was simply too much. That one of the greatest predators of all time, a Lord of the Wamphyri out of Olden Starside—indeed a primal werewolf—should have been brought low by one of the very smallest predators: by the bite of a flea, carried on the back of a rat out of Asia! The Black Death, which had defied even his vampire leech to combat the poison in his otherwise all-conquering system.

He had known it from the moment he crawled from the resin and loped to groom himself in the waterfall near the great vat that contained his warrior creature. Oh, he could still run—especially after feeding (and oh so *deliciously*) on the blood of a strong man, and the heart and vampire leech of a Drakul!— but even then he had felt the poison coursing in his veins, and had suspected that it was more than just the ache of centuries that gnawed at his bones.

And at the waterfall . . . he had proved it. The black pustules in his armpits and groin, the texture of his flesh, which no longer answered when he called for metamorphosis but seemed stuck in his wolf shape, and the fire inside called lust—the lust for life, a life that could last forever—which he felt burning low to match the flow of energy.

Energy: he had none. Oh, sufficient to enter the mind of a mere moon-child, and beguile him to suicide, certainly. And then, bolstered by that one's blood, to pluck the life of some piddling Drakul lieutenant, and tear loose the arm of a trembling Ferenczy thrall. But how much energy did that take? None at all, not to the Wamphyri! Not to a vampire Lord in all the strength of his youth!

Except, where was his youth now? Left behind in a different world, a different time. And his strength? All eaten up by a flea. And his lust for life? But how may one lust with great black lumps in his groin, poison in his piss, and a sure knowledge of his bones crumbling under the ancient leather of his hide?

Yet even now it seemed a scurrilous accusation, to blame all this on a poor flea. For while black-rat fleas had carried the plague, it was a different "bite" entirely that had transferred it into Radu's system. Until now it seemed there was no way of getting it out. For the resin hadn't worked . . . it had merely preserved him, to die later, to die now. And his leech hadn't worked, for it was dying, too.

For a little while Radu had felt a surge of power as his system converted Garth Trevalin's life-blood, but every action since then had only served to drain him like a leaking bucket: six drops spilled for every five put in. It couldn't go on. He was dying, and the rate of his decline was accelerating. Moreover, along with his physical strength, his mental powers were likewise diminished. That was how the Ferenczy, this weak, so-called "sophisticated" modern version of a Lord of the Wamphyri, had seen through his bluster.

But wouldn't it be the irony of all time—or of six hundred years of time, at least—if Radu were to be destroyed by a Ferenczy? For it was doubtless an ancestor of this Francesco who, all those years ago, first stabbed a plague-ridden corpse, then plunged his sword into Radu. In which case it were better he had died then, than to let a member of the same cursed clan kill him now!

His one chance: Harry Keogh. Metempsychosis into the body and mind of a new or newer man. And then Keogh's physical conversion into Radu.

And thus Auld John Guiney, sent out upon his most important mission: to bring Keogh here, for Bonnie Jean would not—

—Could not, not in her present condition, position . . .

But Auld John:

Radu had found him with a weak probe, discovered him nursing an arm broken in a fall in the final stage of his descent. Which had made it appear that that avenue, too, was now closed. Yet during all the years of Radu's oneiromantic dreaming he had frequently *scried* this selfsame Harry Keogh and had *known* that his Mysterious One would be here to sustain him, in one way or another, at the time of his resurgence.

Ah, but how often in his waking years had it been proved to the dog-Lord that the future is a devious thing? Oh, the future will always *be;* of course, for what force can ever stop it? But it will seldom *be* as foreseen.

And yet . . . perhaps there was still a chance, albeit a slim one. For B.J. Mirlu was a beguiler second only to Radu himself: a hypnotist with her eyes and mind, and a seducer with her body. If she had followed Radu's good advice— which he knew she had—then by now this Harry was far more her thrall than any mere bite might ever decree! And if he knew she was here, surely he would want to know what was become of her?

. . . For which reason Radu would cling to life to the bitter end, in the hope that his Man-With-Two-Faces would yet put in a late appearance. And meanwhile, there was this Ferenczy scum to deal with, who might yet deal with him! For Radu had "seen" in the Ferenczy's mind the devastation he held in his eager hands: a technology lost on the dog-Lord, which he scorned as much as he misunderstood it. He, too, could have control of just such a weapon, yet he had taken Guy Tanziano's machine-pistol and broken it in pieces against a granite wall! And all that remained to him now were the wiles of a wolf, with which to combat this ancient enemy. Which was why he had doubled back to the lair's main cavern, in the hope of eluding him.

But just as surely as Radu's mistress moon blazed high in the night sky, his immemorial enemy was returning for him even now. And Radu knew it . . .

* * *

The dog-Lord was right. Alerted by a shuddering underfoot and in the walls, and an uproar of inexplicable sounds from behind him, the Francezci had abandoned the trail and returned to the main cavern in time to witness the wrecked helicopter's plunge. Then, working out what had happened had scarcely taxed his intelligence, and while he waited for the rockfall to subside and the dust to settle, he roundly cursed the coward Manoza—for whatever good that would do him. What good to curse the dead, who were beyond it? Oh, but if only he had the little fat bastard here, now!

Instead . . . he had someone else here! For in the cavern's smoky light Francesco had seen a slim male figure climbing the jumbled rock pile to Radu's great coffin. Just who it might be . . . he couldn't say, wouldn't hazard a guess, though certainly he seemed familiar. But then again, what odds? If he was here, he was an enemy, and all of Francesco's passions were incensed to murder.

So he went from shadow to shadow—flowing in the manner of the Wamphyri, soundlessly, across the rubble-strewn floor—in the direction of the dais and its massive sarcophagus. While at the coffin itself:

Harry remembered *his* dream. In it, no less than in Radu's, he and the dog-Lord had come face to face—which was the part that had been the nightmare. So that now, in real life, he was taking no chances. With the crossbow at arm's length, he gradually raised himself up to look in at an angle on the contents of the coffin. And he saw what Francesco had seen. But no sign of Radu—

—Until claws like the tines of a garden fork, set in a paw eight inches across, sank into his clothing—but not into his skin, for the dog-Lord wasn't about to pass on his ancient disease to his future-self and so perpetuate it—at the shoulder, turning him about! Radu had emerged from *behind* his sarcophagus and was crouching on the uneven tangle of granite slabs at the head of the coffin like some grotesque gargoyle. Inches from the Necroscope's astonished face, a pair of great triangular yellow eyes with crimson cores bored searchingly into his own, and Radu's breath was as hot and rank as molten copper in a forge. And:

"*Ahhhh!* The Mysterious One," that vast mouth cracked open in wonder, in something of disbelief, and finally in a twisted, drooling smile. "*My* Mysterious One . . . "

Harry couldn't get the crossbow between them. Crushed to the side of the sarcophagus, he tried, was rewarded by a glancing buffet from the monster's free paw that nearly broke his wrist and sent the crossbow flying free. Then . . . Harry knew he was a dead man. Held like a child in Radu's grip, he could conjure a Möbius door but couldn't move to step through it. He *knew* he was dead, but the dog-Lord only knew he was alive! And his eyes continued to hold him.

To hold him, yes, with a grip as powerful as his great paw. Harry *felt* himself held, felt his muscles relax, his breathing slow from its hoarse panting. And finally he felt Radu's mind, groping to be inside his!

Dr. James Anderson's post-hypnotic restraints had been lifted; to such a telepathic power as Radu, Harry's very soul was laid bare. Radu saw and absorbed all, almost in as little time as it takes to tell:

Necroscope . . .

He talks to the dead, and can call them from their graves!

He moves in the spaces between *the spaces—goes from place to place as quick as thought!*

He is a man of the modern world, and understands all of its technology, its scientific wonders. Yet not one of its wonders, or all of them together, can explain or understand him!

He knows about the Wamphyri . . . has even removed, destroyed *members of our species, Drakuls and Ferenczys!*

He knows the locations of all my enemies out of time, their power-bases, their seats in this modern world!

He is my Mysterious One!!!

But mysterious no longer . . .

And: "Now, Necroscope, now," Radu growled, a low rumble in his great throat, as his eyes grew large as lanterns in Harry's trapped perspective. "Tell me: is there room in that marvellous mind of yours for both of us? Well, for however brief a time?"

"Radu!" The shout snapped like the crack of a whip in the great cavern, snatching the dog-Lord upright from his gargoyle crouch—all seven feet of him—and jerking him to face the one who shouted. But his great paw remained fastened on Harry's shoulder, and the Necroscope could only hang there, like a rabbit snapped up by a hunter, dazed in Radu's grasp; dazed mainly by his telepathic encounter, which had had the effect of draining him.

And at the foot of the dais Francesco Francezci—or more properly, the Ferenczy—aimed his machine-pistol and grinned as he squeezed the trigger. Radu read the other's mind, whined:

"Ah! No! Not now! *Nooooo!*" But the bullets paid no attention whatever.

The staccato coughing and spanging of that stream of lead and silver would have been an obscenity in itself, without the amplifying, echoing qualities of the labyrinth; but the liquid *spattering* that accompanied it was far worse, for it signified hits on Radu's flesh. Not that Harry felt any sympathy for the dog-Lord, but the huge, hairy, twitching, shuddering body that gave him cover had only so much resistance, and any one of the bullets might find its way right through!

Radu was hit a dozen or more times as the Ferenczy hosed him down, waving his clamouring weapon to and fro in a criss-cross over his half-human target. Harry saw bright splashes of red against the side of the sarcophagus, and gobs of red sent flying during the frantic seconds of the machine-pistol's mad chattering, and he wondered if in fact he, too, had been hit. But then it was over and the dog-Lord's weight—Radu's dead weight—came down on him. Trapped as the werewolf was thrown back against him, jammed down into the ragged jaws of a broken slab, between Radu's quivering, slumping frame and the side of the sarcophagus, Harry was still trying to recover his orientation following Radu's invasion and near-occupation of his mind. Indeed the roots of that contact were still there and the pain he imagined he felt was the dog-Lord's death agony, but it was ebbing very quickly now.

And realizing he *was* still alive and apparently unharmed, the Necroscope began struggling to free himself, all the time aware that a scarlet-eyed vampire Lord was climbing the rocky jumble towards him.

Francesco, however, was taking his time. For Radu was Wamphyri, too, and there might yet be a few surprises . . . as there doubtless *would* be, when he set fire to his body! But no great ruckus as yet, so maybe he'd got Radu's leech, too, crippled by a silver bullet. Or perhaps he'd been right to suspect that the dog-Lord was on his last legs, and his vampire leech with him. *Hah!* But after six hundred years in a bath of resin, wasn't it only to be expected?

Thus Francesco rationalized, as he climbed warily towards Harry and the monster pinning him. But in the Necroscope's metaphysical mind:

Dead! (Radu couldn't believe it.) *Murdered by a Ferenczy!*

Killed, Harry corrected him silently. *Executed. Not murdered, but put down— like a mad dog.*

So close, Radu whined. *So very close. We could have been great together, Necroscope.*

No, Harry answered, *it doesn't work that way. No partnerships, not with your sort. And well you know it!*

But in death the old wolf's mind was as agile as in life, and he saw a way to prolong his existence even now. Obscuring his true thoughts, he said: *You are eager to insinuate, quick to accuse, Necroscope. But did you ever see me do wrong? What evil act, pray, have I performed against* you—*how have I mistreated you*—*that you should so misjudge me? No, don't tell me what you* think *I have done, but what you* know *I have done, which you have seen with your own eyes.*

How to answer him? Harry had forced himself half-way out from beneath the dog-Lord's body, but the pouches on his belt were caught up on sharp edges of rock. "I only know what B.J. Mirlu told me," he finally gasped out loud. "But I also know that she . . . that she's a *liar* just like the rest of you! All of your 'glorious' bloody history: a handful of truths, a few half-truths, but mainly damned lies!"

"What?" Francesco Francezci, his head and shoulders level with the dais's platform now, looked to see who the Necroscope was talking to. Harry's top half was sticking out from beneath the dog-Lord's carcass, and he made the mistake of looking directly at Francesco—who could no longer doubt the evidence of his own excellent eyesight.

Before, the Ferenczy hadn't even considered the possibility. But now:

"What the . . . ?" he said. And, "How . . . ?" For the man trapped under Radu's riddled body was the same one he'd had thrown out of the helicopter! For a moment it stopped him dead in his tracks.

The dog-Lord read the fact of it right out of the Necroscope's mind, also the absolute certainty that Francesco wouldn't miss this second opportunity to kill Harry. And: *What?* he growled. *Do you give in that easily? But you can stop him even now, and permanently. Or . . . we* can?

"The dead come up of their own accord," Harry told him. "I suppose I'm the focus, but their love is the true catalyst."

"What?" Francesco said again, frowning as he climbed on up to the dais. "Are you a madman? Not that it matters, for you're certainly a dead one! But first I want to know how you did it."

Love? Radu growled. *Human love? Hah! But that is something I left behind along with my "humanity." Hate I understand, and greed, and lust. Maybe I can use them in-stead? No? I thought not. So now it is up to you. If you would live, call me up . . . or don't you ever want to see B.J. again?* With which he played his one trump card.

Harry dragged the upper half of his body to one side, out of Francesco's immediate line of fire, clawed his way just two or three inches to the edge of a tilted slab, and glanced over between his clutching fingers. And the Ferenczy rose up to face him, grinning from ear to ear, and pointing the ugly muzzle of his weapon directly into Harry's face.

"On the other hand," Francesco grunted, "don't bother telling me how, for it no longer matters. Maybe there were two of you, eh? Twins? Well—since my father has assured me you talk to dead men—give your twin my regards when next you see him, OK?" And:

"Radu," said Harry. "I . . . I think I may need you!" Which seemed to be quite enough. The dog-Lord's weight lifted off him and he at once rolled to one side, through a Möbius door—but not before he saw a massive, monstrous paw reach out in a dark blur of motion to swat Francesco's weapon aside.

Then, materializing a third of the way across the floor of the great cavern, the Necroscope breathed his relief and looked back on what he'd left behind. He saw, and *heard* it all . . . and then for a while wished that he hadn't:

The Ferenczy's sobbing at first, then his pleading as Radu dragged him writhing and kicking up the last of the stone steps to his sarcophagus, finally his shrieking, and the sharp *snap!* of his arms as Radu broke them across his knee one after the other at the elbows. Upended, Francesco's cries were re-duced to guttural gulps and gurgles as the great wolf plunged him headlong into the warm resin that remained in his coffin, only to drag him out again. And:

"But—you're *dead!*" A final explosion of disbelief from the doomed Francesco, his words coughed out in resin slops and yellow bubbles from gap-ing jaws. "You're only a f-fucking *dead* thing!"

Radu picked him up by the broken arms, whip-lashed him in an arc over his head and down onto the stone steps, and growlingly, joyfully answered: "Ap-parently—but not nearly as dead as you are about to be!" And planting his feet on Francesco's shoulders—catching him under the chin and at the back of his skull, with several expert twists and turns of his hugely corded arms, and straight-ening his back in one smooth movement—he very quickly pulled his head off!

The pulpy sound as living flesh was literally torn apart would have been sickening in itself, but the sight of it was worse. The Necroscope had seen many horrific things in his time, but this ranked among the worst of them. That in-credible *elongation* of Francesco's neck, until his metamorphic flesh could take no more of it and came apart. And the upper part of his backbone, dragged out in a red spray like the spine of a gutted fish—

—Except fish don't have leprous, corrugated, living flesh twined about their spines! Francesco's leech—which Radu tore free with a howl of delight, and dangled into the red cave of his throat. It was gone in two bites, two mas-sive swallows. And only then the *real* commotion!

One smoky torch still flared and sputtered at the base of the coffin. In a bound the dog-Lord leaped free of the lashing nest of grey and purple tentacles sprouting from the Ferenczy's shattered, erupting body, tossed his head up into the sarcophagus, and followed it with the torch.

Twirling end over end, the torch flared up with the rush of air, and came down on the warm resin. And blue fire lit the cavern as the semi-liquid surface was patterned with whooshing streamers of flame like some fine, fiery Greek brandy. Following the trail of resin that spattered the rim, the fire leaped to Francesco's soaked, broken body. And mindless vampire protoplasm with neither the will nor the intelligence to escape the flames began to roast.

It went on for quite some time . . .

. . . Until the dog-Lord came loping in Harry's direction, calling: "Necroscope, a proposal."

"I don't think so," Harry backed off, hastily conjured a door. "It's time you rested from all this, Radu. For that one was right, you are a dead thing."

"Wait!" The other skidded to a halt some thirty feet away. "I've rested long enough! And what about Bonnie Jean? Don't do it, Harry—not if you would see her again."

Harry hesitated; he more than hesitated; for the fact was that he didn't know if he could put Radu down again! When members of the teeming dead came up it was out of love or fear for him, as he had stated. And when they went back down it was because they were no longer needed. But Radu wasn't here out of love or fear but hatred, and the Necroscope wasn't sure he had any control over that. His shields were up again, however, and Radu read nothing of his uncertainty.

The dog-Lord took a loping, tentative step closer, prompting Harry to warn him: "Stay right there, Radu!" And, because he didn't know what else to do: "So, what do you propose?"

"Help me and I'll help you," Radu barked. "Refuse me, and B.J. rots in hell forever!"

Harry avoided his eyes. "Help you? But you're beyond help. You're dead."

"Would you destroy an entire species?"

"Yes." (Without hesitation.)

"And B.J., too?"

"Is she Wamphyri?"

"A fledgling Lady, yes—but *only* a fledgling! I can stop it. She can be wholly human again. What is in her can be taken out of her."

"I've heard such lies from the like of you before," Harry answered, even as he felt his heart leap within him.

"No," the dog-Lord laughed, coughed, barked, "not so. For there never has *been* the like of me before. And I promise you, I *can* give the woman back to you clean of this contagion."

"You see it as a contagion?"

"Perhaps—upon a time—oh, a very long time ago. But no longer. Now I see it as life. *You* see it as a contagion. Don't bandy terms. Will you hear my proposal?"

"Where is B.J.? Is she safe?"

But Radu knew that the Necroscope was hooked. He laid back his head and howled to set the cavern echoing, then fell to all fours and pointed his terrible muzzle in Harry's direction. And his lantern eyes blazed as he said, "For the last time. Hear me out or put me down—and kill that bitch Bonnie Jean, too, all in one fell stroke! What's it to be? One more bound will force your hand, Necroscope. No more arguing then, for it will all be over. For me, at least—and for B.J." His muscles seemed bunched to spring.

"Very well," Harry licked his dry lips, nodded his agreement. "Let's hear it."

Radu relaxed a little, sat back on his haunches and growled, "In one way at least, our aims are much of a sort. For the last six centuries I have dreamed a dream whose source lies two thousand years ago in Olden Starside in another world. But now, in this world, there is only one way my dream can come true."

Without more ado, he told Harry what he wanted.

And he was right: their aims *were* much of a sort, for the Necroscope wanted it, too . . .

IV
DEAD RECKONINGS

IKE SOME STRANGE GAUNT BIRD OF PREY, HUNCH-SHOULDERED AND SUNKEN-eyed, the once-handsome Anthony Francezci stood alone—for the first time truly alone—beside the pit under Le Manse Madonie.

The current was off, and the wire-mesh cover stood open on its hinges; the heavy chain hung stationary on its pulleys, its load delivered into the unknown; the sounds of furious seething—sounds like hard acid biting into bone—had died down and faded to nothing.

But there had been no sounds of rending, no screaming from the crone Katerin—or at best, only a brief period of gasping, an "Ah! Ah! A-*ahhh!*" sound, almost of pleasure, then silence—and, strangest of all, no cries of outrage from the Old Ferenczy, Angelo himself, the nightmarish inhabitant of the pit. Then again, there had been nothing from him for quite some time now.

Which was why Anthony had come down here: because something less than an hour ago, at eight-thirty, he had received some sort of communication, a message, from his twin brother. Or not a message as such, but . . . knowledge? Pain, momentary; there had been a brief aching in his arms, his back, his neck. A burning in his blood, and since then nothing. Except a dawning awareness that it was dark out there, and darker still in his mind. An awareness that indeed he *was* quite alone. Except for Angelo.

For Francesco was dead.

And so Anthony had brought Katerin down here as an offering to his father, in the hope of soliciting a corroboration or explanation of his suspicion. For of course the mutant thing in the pit would know. Old Katerin, yes—but he hadn't told Angelo what he had for him, only that she was "a tidbit." *Hah!*

The pit had been silent, just as silent as it was now, so that no amount of cajoling, threatening, or bribing could solicit an answer, and in the end Anthony had given in and lowered a mildly-anaesthetized Katerin down the throat of the pit. The pain would bring her out of it, of course, and that was important. For not only did Anthony want his father to know what he was getting, but Katerin to know who was getting her! And when she was down, he had waited for her screaming, and for the Old Ferenczy's cursing.

But no, there had been only the unknown creeping (and the creeping of his flesh), and the seething, and at the end Katerin's "Ah! Ah! A-*ahhh!*" cry or sigh, in response to what? Some weird sexual pleasure, or perhaps exquisite pain?

And now this unbearable silence . . .

. . . Of which, Anthony had had quite enough. And:

"*Fuck* you, Angelo!" he cried out, beating on the old well wall with his fist. "Are you beyond all this? Is that what you have become, what *I* shall become: a pile of slop in a stinking pit, not knowing the difference between a juicy young girl and a smelly old hag? Very well, then *rot* down there, if you will. But whether Francesco is dead or not, *I* live on!"

HE IS DEAD, came the gale in Anthony's mind, so sudden it drove him back from the rim. **HE IS DEAD, AND I . . . PREPARE!**

Anthony came forward again, stabbed at the button to work the hoist, to bring it up. Then, as the motor throbbed and the gears engaged, and the chain quivered as it wound on its pulleys, he said, "Prepare? Oh really?" His voice dripped its sarcasm. "And do you have something to prepare for, father? Death, maybe, the true death, when I plug this stinking hole?"

Life, said the other, the volume of his telepathic sending more nearly bearable now. *Lives! And death, yes. But Anthony, ah, my Tony. Haven't you learned anything? Don't you know that there is life in death? Especially for such as you and I? Rot down here? But I've been doing that for long and long, and I tell you that life may spring even from corruption.*

"Life in death? Undeath, you mean?" But Anthony was feeling very uncertain now; his father's tone was so doom-fraught, so mournful.

Undeath is one thing, the pit-dweller said. *But there are others. I prepare for one of the others. While you . . . you have your own problems.*

The platform was coming up into view—but old Katerin was still on it! "What?" Anthony's eyes bugged.

Several problems, his father went on. *For one,* he *is coming, as he came once before. Only this time he isn't coming to steal from you. And he isn't coming alone . . .*

"What?" Anthony said again, bringing the hoist to a jerky halt, and, in his confusion, switching on the electric current. The chain swung against the open cover, made contact—

—Sparks skittered down the chain. And ten feet down the shaft, on the dangling platform, old Katerin's body swelled up like a grotesque balloon—and burst. Burst open, revealing a *part* of Angelo! The old bastard would have tried to escape. Or something of him at least. But escaped to where, to whom? Anthony believed he knew well enough to whom.

Not now, however, for Katerin's gutted body had collapsed back to the dried-out husk, or less than the husk, that it had been. And a corrugated nucleus of purple-grey protoplasm ten to twelve inches in diameter, with dozens of flickering cilia-like tentacles propelling it, was skittering down the sheer wall of the shaft like a crazed, alien spider!

"Damn you!" Anthony snarled. "Was that your . . . your 'preparation?' Did you intend that for me? To go on in me? A mutant leech from your own mutant body, to continue in *me?*"

Bringing up Katerin's remains, he switched off the electricity and swept the debris from the platform, to flutter in rags and tatters back into the pit. Then, with the current on again, he let the wire-mesh cover fall with a clang, and watched the "breath" of the pit-thing steaming and sputtering where it drifted up and made contact with the grid.

Tenacious, his father told him, and Anthony sensed the Old Ferenczy's irritation, his impatient mental shrug, but nothing more than that; as if this were some minor setback. *It's in our nature and we can't help it, in you just as it's in me. And oh, I'm not finished yet, my Tony—not yet. But you are. For he's here.* They *are here!*

"Madman!" Anthony hissed. "Mad *thing!* Who is here?"

You grow more like your brother every day, said the other. *For he never listened, either . . .*

An alarm went off high in the wall; and from up above, the concerted clamouring of more alarms. Anthony stared at the silvery blur of the bell's hammer striking its dome, and back down into the pit. "He? They?" he mouthed. "Do you mean that fucking thief—and Radu? But that can't be. It *can't* be!"

BUT IT CAN BE! Angelo's multi-minds screamed in unison, in wild excitement. **HE COMES TO DESTROY YOU, AND LE MANSE MADONIE, AND ALL OF US—FOR WHICH WE HAVE PRAYED!**

At which Anthony was gone from there, rushing like a wind through the subterranean system, up into Le Manse Madonie where he was met in the great hall by the cadaverous Mario. "What is it?" He grabbed Mario's shirt front in claw hands. "What in the name of *hell* is it? And where is everyone?"

"They're all at their posts," Mario told him. "On the walls or in the courtyard, or outside the walls. I sent them out. And I set off the alarms, because I didn't know where you were." He led the way up the great staircase to Anthony's private rooms.

"But why? What's happening?" Anthony swept along behind his first lieutenant.

"A man on the wall thought he saw something," Mario answered, as Anthony let them into his rooms.

"Thought?" Anthony was less panicked now. "On a clear night like this, someone *thought* he saw something? What, is he going blind or someth—?" But there he paused, choking on the words.

They were through his rooms to the balcony. Out there, the courtyard; armed men scattering left and right, taking up defensive positions on the walls or hurrying out under the wide arch of the main entrance. And in through that entrance, a mist came creeping. But *such* a mist! In the valleys and coastal villages, it wouldn't be too extraordinary. But up here in the high mountains?

Rolling in off the plateau, the mist seemed concentrated in front of Le

Manse Madonie; a dense white bank of mist, writhing at the high wall. And as Anthony gasped his astonishment . . .

. . . An eerie howl came echoing out of the mist. The inhuman, ululating cry of a beast, but in no way mournful, and in every way threatening!

"*Radu!*" Anthony whispered.

"A dog?" Mario shrugged.

"No," Anthony turned on him, grabbed him again. "A wolf!"

"A wolf? Up here on the Madonie?"

"*The* wolf!" Anthony gasped. And quickly pulled himself together. "You," he snapped. "You stay with me. And if you're not already armed, do it now. Orders to the rest of them: anything that moves—and I do mean *anything*—shoot it! Especially if they see . . . a big dog. Go, tell them, then come back here. And Mario, is the chopper fuelled?"

"Yes," the other answered.

But as he left, "Radu!" Anthony breathed again. Then, leaning on his balcony—feeling suddenly weak in all his limbs—he anxiously scanned the courtyard and the ocean of mist beyond. And his eyes were like crimson marbles rolling in the orbits of his skull . . .

Out on the plateau, in Radu's mist, Harry and the dog-Lord were on the far side of a clump of boulders. "Your mist has its disadvantages, Radu," the Necroscope said. "They can't see us, but neither can we see them."

"Sunside of the barrier mountains, in my own world, I used it as cover," the dog-Lord coughed. "Here I use it differently, to inspire fear! When the Ferenczy sees it—and when he hears this—" He laid back his head and howled at the full moon hanging low on the horizon, and Harry stepped back a pace. "—Then he will know what is what. But I have discovered a weird thing: that what I did in life, I do with greater efficiency in death! Because in life there were the limitations of the flesh: air to be breathed, and a body to be fuelled lest it fail through exhaustion. But in death there are no limits . . . except that you impose them, Necroscope. *Hah!*" Cocking his head on one side, he let his lantern gaze light on Harry. "Ah, but without you there would be nothing at all. I suppose I must be thankful. Well, so be it. Now I drive my mist in through that archway . . . "

He called the mist up from the dry earth, let it roll from his body's pores, and loping towards the vague white blur of Le Manse Madonie's lights drove it before him. The men outside the walls were engulfed in it; it rolled over them, into the courtyard, piled in a swirling drift against the manse itself.

"And now," said Radu, quivering and leaning forward as if drawn by a magnet, "I go to ravage among them!" He dumped heavy sausage bags, one from each shoulder. "Ferenczys," the dog-Lord snarled. "The first and worst of my enemies!"

"Wait," Harry told him. "We have things to do. You can . . . ravage later, if you must. And be careful with those bags! That stuff is dangerous."

Dangerous? That wasn't the half of it. The Necroscope had stolen it right out of the Czechoslovakian plant that manufactured it. A single stray shot could set it off—a thought that the werewolf read clearly in Harry's mind. "So for now," Harry continued, "first things first. That's if we don't want anyone to walk away from this."

"I agree," Radu barked, straightening from his crouch. "No one is to walk away from it. And any who run, I shall be behind them!"

"How's the mist coming?" The Necroscope heard himself say it, thought about it, blinked and shook his head as if to clear it. Good grief: he wasn't only accepting all this, he was actually getting *used* to it!

"The courtyard is filled with my mist," Radu growled.

"Then let's go," said Harry. He made to pick up the sausage bags, but Radu beat him to them.

"You do your part, Necroscope, and I shall do mine."

They emerged from the Möbius Continuum in a corner of the courtyard, and Radu quickly sniffed out what Harry was looking for. As he was finishing up the job, two armed thralls came at a run, calling to each other through the mist—and ran right into Radu. The speed, the savage efficiency of the dog-Lord as he dealt with them was incredible and terrifying to watch. But Harry quickly turned away. The *sound* of it was enough . . .

Mercifully they were sounds that were lost in the general confusion. And finally:

"That's it," said the Necroscope. "Their transport is useless to them. They're stuck here, trapped. By now most of them will be out here, and the interior of Le Manse Madonie will be empty. That's how it was last time, anyway. Give me the bags."

Radu read what was in his mind, said: "What about me?"

"Stay clear of the place," Harry answered. "There's a rocky outcrop in that direction," he pointed. "Wait for me there. And take this with you." He handed him a transmitter. "If you see a vehicle or vehicles on the move, press the buttons till you get the right one."

"Another of your modern toys? I hate them!"

Harry showed him a mental picture of what this "modern toy" would do, and Radu grunted his reluctant appreciation.

"And if something happens to you?"

"Then it happens to you, too . . . " (Harry hoped he was right, but he kept that thought to himself.)

He conjured a door and took Radu back out onto the plateau, watched him lope away into the thinning mist, and without pause returned to Le Manse Madonie—

—To the co-ordinates of a forbidden location in the very bowels of the place. The cavern of the pit.

The spotlights lanced down, illuminating the throat of that ominous shaft; the electrified exit was barred; the alarm clamoured high on the wall. Except for a cloud of red vapour drifting over the pit, nothing moved. The cavern seemed still, safe. Harry checked again, then made an exit through his door, which he hadn't collapsed. He had another use for some of his plastic that he hadn't wanted the dog-Lord to know about.

But on a count of ten he was back again, carrying just one of the sausage bags.

The weird red cloud over the pit was denser now; lured by the ventilation system, it was drifting towards the air-ducts. Whatever the stuff was, Harry was well away from it. But as he moulded plastic—twenty *pounds* of plastic—into a wide crack in the wall:

Necroscope!

And Harry gave a massive start. "R.L.? Is that you? Damn, you nearly scared the life out of me!"

You mean, like you is scaring me, Necroscope? R.L. Stevenson Jamieson came back.

"What? I'm scaring you?" Harry didn't understand.

Man, you has enemies all around you! A million of 'em!

"I what?" Harry fell into a crouch, scanned the cavern all around. Nothing. "R.L., your obi must be playing tricks on you. There's no one here."

Hell, no, R.L. insisted. *My obi's just fine, Harry—and there's more'n I can even calc'late. But . . . but they's all the same one!*

It was quite beyond Harry. But: "OK, R.L., I'll be looking out for them—whatever they are!" And he finished packing the plastic into the wall. But as he stuck the timer and detonator into the explosive mass:

Harry? said another voice. *Is that what I think it is? And if so, do you know what it will do down there?* It was J. Humphrey Jackson Jr.—"Humph" to his friends, the American who had built the Francezci treasure vault in another part of the underground system. A man they had murdered for his efforts.

"I know what it will do, Humph," Harry said. "I shouldn't think you'd have any complaints about that."

Not as long as you're out of there when it happens, Necroscope, Humph said. *But do you really know what you're doing?*

"How do you mean?"

I mean this is Sicily, and these mountains are as shaky as a lightning-struck tree! Hell, I even warned the Francezci brothers they shouldn't do any blasting down there. But in my day, well, we had nothing like that *stuff!*

"I want to reduce this place to rubble, and destroy what's in that pit," Harry said, dispassionately.

I am with you, Humph said. *I just thought maybe I should, you know, point out that we're on a fault-line here? This part of the Med is volcanic. From here across to Etna, and due north into Italy, then west through the Peloponnese to the Greek islands: one big lightning-flash of a fault. Oh, you won't be setting anything really big off, but I think you'll do a lot more damage than just filling in a hole . . .*

"Good!" Harry said, and set the timer for two minutes. "Now I have to be out of here. Have fun, Humph."

You too, said the other, as Harry conjured a door and left.

But he and Humph didn't know the half of it; couldn't know, for instance, that Anthony Francezci had also booby-trapped the treasure vault and other rooms and junctions in the tunnel system. And now, from the balcony of his private rooms, he and the corpse-like Mario were watching the madness that was going on at the arched entrance to the courtyard and on the plateau.

Searchlight beams were sweeping the plateau; diffused by Radu's dispersing mist, they found nothing. Yet when Anthony had ordered a Land Rover out onto the rough terrain just a minute ago . . . the vehicle had travelled maybe forty yards beyond the archway before it blew itself to pieces in a searing flash of light that was still fading on his retinas. And now the men on and outside the walls were firing at nothing—blazing away with fire and steel—cutting holes in the swirling mist.

"Did something hit the Land Rover—or was it sabotaged?" Mario's slit of a mouth hung open.

"Sabotage?" Anthony face was a mad white mask. "Sabotage? The last time this bastard was here, *that* was sabotage!"

He is here! came a desperate cry in Anthony's mind. *He is down here,* under *Le Manse Madonie! Or he was just a moment ago.*

"Angelo! Angelo, are you sure?"

Yes, yes, I am sure. And I know what he did. Goodbye, my Anthony. Goodbye, my dear sweet Tooonnnnnyyyyy . . . !

Two more vehicles went speeding out under the archway—but they got no further than the Land Rover. Hot twisted metal shot aloft, and fire lanced the night.

"We can't fight this," Anthony snarled. "Fuck—there's nothing to fight!" Hunched over, he ran inside, yanked open a drawer in his desk, and pressed a button.

In six different locations—some deep and others not so deep—under his feet, under Le Manse Madonie, timers started counting off the seconds. "Two minutes," Anthony's face cracked open in an uncontrollable grin, snarl, something; his gums spurted blood as teeth like knifes sliced up through them; his tongue seemed to unwind endlessly from his throat. "Do you think," he choked on that fantastic snake of a tongue, ". . . I mean, do you *think* that we can . . . that we can make the chopper in just . . . in just two minutes, Mario?"

Mario ran—for the helicopter, of course, but also away from Anthony—out of his rooms, down the great staircase, and out into the courtyard. And his master came flowing and floating, collapsing and reforming, laughing and loping behind him.

Harry emerged from the Möbius Continuum near the rocky outcrop, where Radu came running to meet him. "All done, Necroscope?"

"I think so," Harry nodded. "But we'll see better from up there." They ran back to the rocks, and Radu sprang to the summit in two bounds. Harry climbed, looked up, saw the dog-Lord's great paw reaching down for him, and his lantern eyes watching his every move.

"Allies, for the moment, Harry?" Radu growled. Harry took the proferred paw, and the dog-Lord pulled him up.

All the lights blazed in Le Manse Madonie; weapons blazed, too, uselessly. Headlights swept the plateau as another vehicle—the Francezci's stretch limo—glided out under the archway. The dog-Lord grunted and pressed the last but one button on the Necroscope's remote. And the car's roof blew off, and its sides ruptured, as the blast expanded into a red and yellow fireball. Then: a lone wheel went bounding, and a bent axle turned lazily in the updraught. It was a scene in slow-motion—which suddenly speeded up. Scarred metal rained to earth, leaving other scraps burning where they drifted on high.

Harry nodded and glanced at his watch. "I don't know how much we'll see of this," he said. "Maybe nothing of the actual bang. But it's due just about . . . now."

Then, very faintly, the ground trembled underfoot. A section of Le Manse Madonie's courtyard wall buckled and fell. Dust fountained up from a jagged crack that suddenly appeared in the earth, zig-zagging like a bite from rim to rim of the high promontory and encompassing the sprawling villa and its walls.

Lights dimmed, went out, and cries of alarm came drifting from antlike figures staggering atop the walls. And:

"Damn!" Harry said. "It looks like Humph was wrong."

But then the dust jets geysered higher yet, and the crack widened as yet more detonations—mysterious this time—were felt underfoot . . .

"Get her up!" Anthony mouthed as Mario gunned the helicopter's engine, willing her to lift off. The machine twitched, bumped, skittered, and began to lift as the engine's whine climbed up and up. And Anthony frothed and foamed where his rubbery tentacle fingers couldn't fasten his seat-belt. Then the walls of Le Manse Madonie were falling away—but they were falling faster than the chopper was lifting! *Literally* falling, and the entire Francezci-Ferenczy empire going with them—crumbling from the face of the great cliff.

Anthony laughed and laughed, his flesh *rippling*, his face transforming, and Mario leaned away from him, choking where he fought to control the aircraft. But she was lifting, yes, gaining elevation even as Le Manse Madonie lost it and slid groaning into the ravine.

And a quarter-mile away on the roof of the rocky outcrop, Radu and Harry saw the chopper's lights and heard the accelerating *whup, whup, whup* of its rotors. "The other brother," Harry said, grimly. "You can bet your life—or you can't—that it's him. The last button, Radu. Time to press it."

The effect was extraordinarily dramatic. Like a giant fan cut loose, the complete rotor assembly blew off, shot into the night sky trailing sparks. And the body of the machine was gutted, a black shape disintegrating in the fireball that consumed it and the blast that reduced it and its vampire passengers to the basic elements of plastic and metal and flesh, indistinguishable one from the other.

Where Le Manse Madonie had stood there was now the rim of a cliff, fresh and raw, and scraps of debris still floating on the billowing air. Of the Ferenczy dynasty, nothing remained—except a few antlike figures, thralls and a lieutenant or two, stumbling in their dazed panic-flight across the plateau.

"And *now* I ravage!" Radu growled.

Harry thought: who better? And said, "While I have other things to do."

"The Drakuls? I should be there . . . " Radu was uncertain.

"No," Harry answered. "Best if you . . . clean up here."

Radu nodded his great shaggy head. "I have faith in you—of a sort." And he urged, "Do it for me, Necroscope!"

"I'm afraid not," Harry told him. "I'm doing it for someone else. A whole lot of someone elses."

"Don't forget to come back for me," said Radu. And then, the inevitable threat: "Remember, there's always Bonnie Jean."

"Oh, I haven't forgotten," said Harry, in a certain way, with a certain look.

Then he was gone, and Radu went to ravage . . .

Midnight was two hours past in the so-called Drakesh Monastery on the Tingri Plateau, yet still Daham Drakesh held back. Despite that he had read the death-cries of his lieutenant Singra Singh across all the miles between, and despite knowledge of a new regime at the Xigaze Garrison—and the fact that he could be visited and investigated at any time—*still* he held back. His creatures were not yet waxed; his many children in the old walled city were as yet infants, drawing blood from flame-eyed, vampirized mothers; his monastery was still the safest place in the world, especially a world primed to burst into flame at the touch of a button.

Drakesh had planned to press that button—still planned to do so—but yet hoped that the task force at Xigaze would hold off a little longer. If he was forced to flee this place on his own, to leave his children and waxing warriors behind, he could not doubt but that they would be destroyed, all laid to waste; and he would have to start again without advantage, in a world likewise laid to waste.

Also, it could be true that the special forces at Xigaze were in fact there to put down Tibetan insurrection, and that Drakesh and his project had little or nothing to do with their current deployment. And what a folly *that* would be: to abandon his works and initiate Armageddon, out of an ill-founded sense of insecurity! On the other hand, he could always pre-empt matters, press the button anyway, and blow Central London, Moscow, and Chungking to hell! Which might do the trick at that: China would doubtless discover new priorities, and deploy her forces elsewhere.

Thus the "High Priest" of the sect was torn two ways where he paced the floors of his apartment, pondered his options, and waited on word from his familiar albino bats . . .

. . . But for the Necroscope Harry Keogh there was only one option, one objective, as he exited from the Möbius Continuum at the only co-ordinate he was absolutely certain of: Zahanine's snowed-in car where he had left it in the lee of a cluster of rocks on the frozen plateau a mile from the Drakesh Monastery.

Almost entirely buried in a drift now, with only its rear-end free where it stood at an angle with its trunk to the leaning boulders, the car formed a hump of snow entirely in keeping with the terrain. But knowing what was under the hump—a modern motor vehicle, where never such a thing was seen before—and knowing who sat with her back to the fender—a black girl in modern Western clothing, equally alien to these parts—the Necroscope felt the strangeness of it. Like a scene from some weird fantasy.

The large trunk was open; a soft bed of snow lay within; Harry picked the girl up and put her inside. She was solid in his arms, like an ice-sculpture. Then he got in with her, and yanked down on the cover from the inside until the frozen hinges gave way and the cover crunched most of the way shut. And now for the real miracle.

Scrambling over the seats to the front, Harry found the keys in the ignition where he'd left them. Using the cigarette lighter salvaged from Auld John's place to warm the frozen barrel, finally he tried turning the key. And even Harry was surprised when the engine gave a muffled cough, caught, and began to tick over. The car's nose was way under the snow but it was soft, fluffy stuff; there'd be plenty of air down there. Also, the radiator was very likely full of—

—*Antifreeze,* said Zahanine, startling him. *In the winter in Edinburgh, I never took chances, always used twice the recommended dose!* And then straight to the point. *What's on your mind, Necroscope?*

Getting the accelerator pedal working—jamming it in a fast tick-over and turning on the heater—Harry told her. And as the car and the dead girl warmed up a little, Zahanine told him one or two things, too. For she had been here a while now, and she'd talked to the local dead, of which the Drakesh Monastery was responsible for more than its fair share.

Now the Necroscope could talk to them, too. And he did:

Talked to the *original* inhabitants of the forbidden city, about the "plague" that had taken them a hundred years ago and how Drakesh had used them—and used them up—in building his monastery. Talked to a certain would-have-been initiate, a boy the Necroscope had once seen in a precognitive vision tramping the white waste to the monastery, in the company of six of the sect's bell-jingling acolytes; a mere youth—crushed like an orange for its juice, to fuel the vampire appetite of the high priest, Daham Drakesh. And talked to others who knew the innermost secrets of that nightmarish "temple," until he knew those secrets, too. And until he knew their co-ordinates.

And even when he thought he was through there were others waiting to talk to him. Major Chang Lun, for instance, speaking from the bottom of a ravine near Xigaze, where he and his mangled driver were friends now forever, lying frozen and broken in the tangle of wreckage that had been their snow-cat.

So that finally all the pieces of this last corner of the jigsaw puzzle came together, and Harry could see the whole picture. Except for one detail. One last piece, which would remain missing until he fixed it in place. And: "I'll need your help," he told Zahanine and Major Chang Lun.

Against the Drakuls? Zahanine was eager.

"Against their master," the Necroscope answered. "Against him and his charnel house, that entire temple of blood!"

Then you've got it, Harry! she told him. *Let me know what you want, and it's yours.* And Chang Lun was in complete agreement.

Harry explained what he would do, and finished by saying: "I want to drive him to the limit, panic him into action."

He is a madman, Chang Lun said. *Or teetering on the edge, at least. A megalomaniac, yes—but even so, how can you make him do a thing like that?*

"I probably can't, but you can." And again Harry explained his meaning. "He's on the edge, you said—so why not push him right over? I would very much like him to do it himself—do it *to* himself—but if not, then you'll be there to finish it."

And if I should fail, or something should go wrong?

"Nothing will go wrong. And I *know* it's going to work, for I've seen it. It's just waiting to happen, there in my future—or as it now seems, in all our futures. What will be has been."

Except we don't have futures, said Zahanine of herself and Chang Lun, *and so nothing to lose. So let's do it.*

And as coincidence would have it:

At the vampire monastery, Daham Drakesh's albino familiars reported back to him that a large contingent of military vehicles at Xigaze had commenced forming up in his direction. They were coming by night, doubtless to surprise him. Well, surprise was on his side. They would be in radio contact with each other and with the garrison, of course, and the garrison with Red China; and if anything were to happen in the outside world, more specifically Chungking, they might yet be diverted. If they weren't . . . then Drakesh would let the soldiers into the monastery, but of necessity their vehicles, and most of their firepower, must stay outside. And in the monastery:

His bats would fight, of course; likewise his "priests"—fight with the strength of vampires—and win. But even if they lost, Drakesh would not lose. There were refuges in the outside world where he would be welcome, where he could start again as the planet devolved into chaos.

And if he won, then he would stay here and finish his work with little or no threat of outside interference. Indeed, Tibet would be the last bastion of mainly radiation-free, air-breathing man, and the first whole nation with a new ideology: vampirism. Enough! They had forced his hand.

Hurrying through the monastery, issuing orders as he went, Drakesh climbed to the transmitter room in the hollowed dome of the skull—*and found Major Chang Lun, his old enemy, waiting for him there, where Harry Keogh had left him . . .*

At a little after 8:20 P.M. GMT, the American Air Force Base at Greenham Common was a quiet place. It was a weekday and people had to work in the morning. Security and other duty posts were filled, of course, but the bomb-proof underground storage facilities might just as well have been tombs. Which would make the Necroscope a ghost where he emerged from the Möbius Continuum at a co-ordinate remembered from his one previous visit.

A short Möbius jump took him into the container with the combination safe. He kneeled, frowned at the knurled, numbered knob, and said, "Harry, this is it." But he wasn't talking to himself. And Harry Houdini answered:

OK, I see it. But now I need to feel it—through your fingers.

The Necroscope blanked his mind, let the *other* Harry take over, felt his fingers thrill to the weird magic of Houdini's entirely different talent. The knob twirled this way and that, spinning through a seemingly endless sequence of combinations. But to the dead magician it was as easy as turning a key in a lock. When a final sharp *click!* sounded, Harry's hand left the knob to yank on the safe's handle—and the door sprang open.

"Damn, you're good!" the Necroscope said.

But Houdini only chuckled. *Tell that to my agent the next time you stop by his way,* he answered.

Harry took the harmless-looking receiver and antenna from the safe, made a second short jump into the container with the bomb on its trolley. But the floor of the container was wired, and as it took his weight alarms were triggered. As the first distant sirens started to sound, he placed the receiver on the trolley, conjured another door, and wheeled the entire contraption through it and right out of there. And out of this universe.

Taking his deadly cargo with him, he followed the instantaneous Möbius route to Zahanine . . .

While in Daham Drakesh's transmitter room:

Chang Lun was a lumpish, broken, scarecrow caricature of the man Drakesh had known and killed, but he was unmistakably Chang Lun. Splintered bones stuck out of his torn, dishevelled uniform; sagging to the right from a crushed spine, he threatened to crumple to the floor. His left shoulder hung awkwardly askew, but his right arm and hand seemed to be in good working order—especially the hand, and the pistol that followed Drakesh's every move.

Not that the last Drakul was moving much; spreadeagled to the wall, his blood-red eyes bugged and his split tongue wriggled like a crippled snake, uselessly in his gaping mouth. But Chang Lun stood between Drakesh and the transmitter's console, and as Drakesh gradually recovered from his shock, he knew he would have to move the Major in order to finalize his plan.

But what would he be moving? A corpse? A figment of his imagination, his conscience? Ridiculous! He had no conscience. And whatever this thing was, it was real, it was happening.

Facing him, Chang Lun faced a dilemma of his own. He was here to "drive Drakesh over the edge"—but the master of the monastery was already past that point; he *wanted* to press the button, to press it twice. Once to arm his bombs (as he imagined), and once again to detonate them. But Chang Lun couldn't let him, not until the Necroscope gave him the word.

Harry, where are you? Chang Lun's dead thoughts went out; and the Great Majority were "breathless," keeping the psychic aether clear.

Right here, Harry answered, where at that very moment he and Zahanine wheeled the trolley out through a Möbius door into the bowels of the monastery; indeed, into the "temple" of self-flagellation with its bloody trough and terrible sluices. None of Drakesh's people were there now, but from his conversations with ex-priests and initiates the Necroscope knew well enough where he was. And it was as good, or bad, a place as any.

Drakesh was a hugely talented telepath; while he couldn't intercept or read the incorporeal thoughts of the dead, or the Necroscope's thoughts while he was using that medium, still he sensed that something—some form of communication—was happening here. And putting out a vampire probe, he at once found a second intruder, Harry Keogh, in the guts of the monastery. And his crazed mind immediately flew to the wrong conclusion, or a conclusion that was only part-right.

He was under attack! His plan was known! They would stop him, destroy the monastery, his works, even Daham Drakesh himself! He couldn't be sure who "they" were, but it was definitely time to give them something else to worry about. Advancing on the dead man, his clawlike hands and arms elongated towards him. And the pistol in Major Chang Lun's dead hand went *click! Click! Click!* The weapon was empty.

Drakesh swept Chang Lun aside like a tailor's manikin. The Major's broken spine collapsed, his legs gave way and he crumpled to the cold stone floor. And Drakesh stabbed at the button once . . . and paused, blinked, reconsidered, as he saw—what? A smile?—transforming Chang Lun's face. Alive, the Chinese Major would be in agony. Dead, he wouldn't be feeling anything—but he was. It was a smile of satisfaction, yes. Of triumph!

And again Drakesh's probe went out to the Necroscope, and read, and *saw*, what was on his mind! Instantly, he snatched his skeletal hand from the console, staggered, turned and ran—out of the room, up the last flight of stone steps to the bald dome of the skull carved in the mountainside—ran like the grotesque parasite he was from a terror beyond anything he could ever dream to conjure. From a man who called up dead men from their graves, to enact their own vengeance!

And high on the moonlit dome of the skull he threw up his spindly arms to the night and willed metamorphosis. That greatest of all the skills of the vampire Lords, at which every Drakul before him had been past-master.

While in the room of the transmitter, Chang Lun still had a job to do. And dragging himself inch by inch back across the floor, he somehow managed to heave his wreck of a body upright at the console. And:

Necroscope, he said. *I'm too badly broken. I can't keep it together. I can still do it, but don't wait too long.*

That's OK, Harry answered, for by now he had told Zahanine what she must do. *On a count of five, Major. And thanks.*

And he conjured a door and stepped through it . . . and immediately removed himself far from the monastery, a little over two miles, to a spot close to Zahanine's car. Then:

Harry knew what was coming. With no time to spare, he dug through the crusty snow and buried himself in the softer stuff beneath. And in the monastery Zahanine extended the aerial and made the connection; and buckling at the knees, Chang Lun fell face-down on the fatal button.

Daham Drakesh flew! Like some monstrous man-lizard—like primal pteranodon—he spiraled up, up into the night sky above the monastery. And his retinue of pink-eyed familiars with him. Or more properly he flew like an ill-fated moth, and only for a single instant recognized his fate when the biggest candle in the world burst into flame directly beneath him. A candle brilliant as the solar orb itself, made of the same deadly energy.

It was a mighty, merciful singeing . . .

At first, the Necroscope was surprised; it seemed such a small thing, a small beginning—a *shudder* felt or sensed deep down under the snow, in the earth, and then a moment of stunned silence—following which it became something else. The crust of snow overhead was ripped away, then the softer stuff, peeling in layers, and finally Harry himself: snatched up and whirled head over heels like a leaf in a gale, and hurled down in the drift that had piled against Zahanine's car.

And overhead, a wind, a storm, a hurricane! The crackling of massive bursts of electricity; a tracery of electrical fires racing across the sky; the sky itself turning dirty-red, and an awesome rumbling that grew louder and louder until it was deafening. In short, it was his vision all over again.

And briefly, snatches from Nostradamus's quatrains passed before his mind's eye: "The means is in the sun, as it transpires . . . With numbers and with *solar heat* and grave-cold, with mordant acids, and his friends in low society." Most of it had meaning, but the mordant acids were yet to be explained . . .

When the ground stopped shaking, Harry sat up in the hole his hurtling body had made in the snow. He looked across a dirty-grey desolation at a low, flat-topped mushroom cloud bulging upwards and still expanding. He looked at it for long moments, and then no more. Because for all that the Necroscope had seen in his short life, still there were some things that were just too terrible to contemplate. And this was one of them.

Another was the squadron of Red Chinese bombers that was passing overhead, releasing their napalm payload some distance away on the forbidden walled city. Which was one job, at least, that Harry wouldn't have to deal with.

Napalm . . . Was this the "mordant acid?" he wondered.

Shaken, Harry conjured a door and almost fell through it. And in the eternal peace and quiet of the Möbius Continuum, in his own time, he went back to Sicily, the Madonie, and the dog-Lord Radu Lykan . . .

Radu had done with ravaging—there was nothing *left* to ravage—and he gave his assurance that the plateau of the Madonie was clean. "I've played my part," Harry told him. "Time now to fulfil your end of our agreement."

"Bonnie Jean?" the dog-Lord growled. "She is a treacherous bitch. We don't need her."

" 'We' doesn't come into it," Harry said. "There is no 'you' and 'I.' There never can be. The way I remember it, you gave your word." He was standing close to Radu—would have to be, if he wanted to convey him via the Möbius Continuum.

"And you trust the word of a Lord of the Wamphyri?" Radu caught Harry's jacket, his shoulder, and drew him closer still.

"Do I have a choice?"

"You could try searching my lair for her on your own. And with luck you might even find her in time."

"Before what?"

"Before my creature is up and about. I left her as a tidbit, to break his long, long fast!"

Harry took a gasping breath. "In which case, it could be too late even now!"

"Oh, ha-ha-ha!" The dog-Lord's barking laugh. And then his snarled: "No, for my warrior needs me to bring him forth."

"In the Möbius Continuum," Harry said, gritting his teeth, "I could transport you instantaneously to the other side of the world, into brilliant sunlight."

"And if I thought you would," Radu answered, "I could grip your scrawny neck and squeeze your head off!"

Harry looked into his lantern gaze, then looked away, let himself cool off. And finally: "You'll take me to Bonnie Jean?"

"Such was my word," Radu nodded his grinning wolf's head. "But first you must take *me* to my redoubt."

And there was nothing else for it . . .

Harry knew the precise co-ordinates—but so did Radu. As they emerged at the foot of his dais, the dog-Lord beat Harry to it, reached down and took up B.J.'s crossbow, bent it out of shape and tossed it aside. "One of us might be tempted to cheat," he explained, knowingly.

And then they went to B.J.

Radu led the way, loping like a wolf, but upright, leaning forward. "Once long ago," he said, blinking his feral eyes, "oh centuries ago, I had just such a hollow place, a crag in Moldavia. I built it so as to be able to destroy it utterly, in the event I must evacuate. This place is very much the same. A bonfire down here would crack these columns, bring down the rotten walls, floors, ceilings, destroy all evidence of my ever having been here. My plan for continuity. Longevity is synonymous with anonymity."

"What continuity?" said Harry, hard on Radu's heels through the labyrinth. "I see no continuity. Not any longer. You've fulfilled your ambition: to outlive all your enemies."

Radu paused a moment to look back at him. "All but one, as it now appears," he said. And before Harry could answer he turned and loped on . . .

Closer to their destination, in a very dark place, Radu paused again. His eyes lit the walls of the narrow passage. "Time you were rid of your belt and munitions, Necroscope," he said. "My trust goes only so far."

Harry released the belt, let it fall. "Mine, too," he said.

And in a little while they were there, at the place of the huge stone vat that housed Radu's warrior. There was the sound of rushing water; the dim sheen of water, falling from on high. Also, from somewhere far below, the splash and gurgle of a subterranean sump. Apart from that it was a dim, smoky place. The torches in the base of the stone vat had long since burned out, but one last torch stood fresh and unlit in its sconce on the wall of the cave facing the massive stone "staves" of the vat.

"We could use a little light," Harry said, uncertainly.

"By all means," Radu growled low in his wolf's throat. "I gave my word that you would see her at least one more time. Or one *last* time."

And with his heart thudding, Harry fumbled the cigarette lighter from his pocket and brought the torch flaring to light.

And sure enough, B.J. was there, and alive, but only just. She was hanging by her feet, which were caught fast in a noose. The rope was wrapped around a knob of rock and tied off. B.J.'s head hung level with the rim of a broad, zig-zagging crevasse, a crack in the floor that might go down forever, for all Harry knew, but at least as far as the underground lake.

B.J. was naked, unconscious. Blood had dried on her arms, which were hanging limply into the chasm, and more blood caked her hair. As she turned slowly on the rope, Harry saw the gash in her back where the dog-Lord had torn her leech right out of her spine. His legs numb, he stumbled towards her, went to his knees—from which position he saw another rope around her neck. A long length of rope, its other end was tied around a boulder that must weigh at least two hundredweights. The tenth part of a ton, balanced at the edge of the crevice. Radu stood grinning beside the boulder, and Harry knew what he would do and when he would do it. Right now!

"No!" he choked the word out.

"Didn't I tell you that what was in her could be taken out?" Radu growled. "So it has been. And now, say goodbye to her!" And as the Necroscope's jaw fell open—as he reached out his arms uselessly, spastically towards B.J.—Radu gave a grunt and a heave, and rolled the great rock from the rim. It fell; the rope uncoiled; thirty-odd feet of rope, and the boulder hurtling faster and faster . . .

. . . And then that *sound* that Harry knew he would hear for ever and ever. But not the sight of it, for he had closed his eyes. But the dog-Lord only laughed and said, "Well, *now* you can say goodbye to her. Indeed, you're the only one who can."

"Bastard thing," Harry gasped, whispered, choked, his face a frozen grimace, eyes tightly closed. "You lousy bastard wolf-thing! Why? Why did you have to . . . to . . . ?"

Radu came close, caught him by the shoulder, drew him up. "You would have killed her anyway, because she was Wamphyri. I did it because it was my right, and she was treacherous. In my world—in *our* world—there will be no room for traitors. Especially Ladies of the Wamphyri!"

"Bastard thing!" Harry said again, limp in Radu's grasp.

"I remember how it was," the other told him, "when I was a man and lost loved ones. For a little while it made me weak—but then it made me strong. Right now you are weak, but *I* shall make you strong!"

"You are a dead thing," Harry told him. "A dead, soulless thing. Go back down into death, Radu."

"Ah, no, I think not," said the other, holding the Necroscope closer still. "You guarded your mind well, Harry, but little by little I prised it open. I have seen your greatest fear. You don't know if you can put me down. Apparently you can't."

"Then you'll rot," Harry told him, "because you're a dead thing. Yours is just a semblance of life. Cling to it while you may, until your flesh is seething and all your bones separating at the joints. But it would be easier to go down now, Radu."

"Look at me," said Radu, and his voice was hypnotic now.

Harry must open his eyes, must look into the feral yellow gaze with its twin scarlet cores. Must swim in the fires burning in the centre of Radu's mind. And the dog-Lord said:

"I dreamed of a man with two faces, one who would be with me when I triumphed over death."

"You merely dreamed of metempsychosis," the Necroscope's voice was faint now, faltering. "I . . . I have already known it. I've *had* two faces. I don't want a third."

"But you have no choice," Radu said, as his eyes expanded in Harry's sight, and in his mind. "I stand on your threshold, and I *will* enter. Of my own free will . . . "

No way! James Anderson told him, his mental gaze a furnace to match Radu's own. And:

To heel, great dog! said Franz Anton Mesmer. The Necroscope's friends in low society, who were far more adept in death than ever they had been in life. Their *combined* hypnotic power sliced into the dog-Lord's like hot knives through butter.

Radu pushed Harry away to arm's length, snarled, "What?"

And there was sudden movement—a surging of liquids—a mewling of some vast thing in terrible agony, from behind him. One of the stone staves of the great vat cracked, buckled outwards, slopped resin. Others followed suit and a wave of resin came gurgling over the high rim, its stench sickening where it flooded the cave and flowed sluggishly over the jagged lip of the chasm. Radu's warrior creature had waxed at last.

"What!?" the dog-Lord said again, and was knocked from his feet as more staves collapsed and a second wave of resin drenched him, threatening to carry him into the depths. Releasing Harry in order to save himself, Radu pushed him away.

Shaking his head to clear it, Harry backed off, got to his feet, stumblingly retreated to the wall of the cave. And when Radu's feral glare had faded in his eyes and his mind, he took in the entire scene at a glance:

That black lumpish misshapen wolf-thing emerging, flopping in agony through the shattering staves from its womb of stinking liquids! Living corruption in a shape from a madman's worst dreams! Vast, and vastly diseased— even as its maker himself, with a plague six hundred years old—its sick red saucer eyes pleaded with the dog-Lord. But it was the Necroscope who put it out of its agony, the creature and its "father" both.

The blazing torch was to hand, hissing, spitting and flaring brilliantly in the flow of gases from the vat. Harry need only wrench it from its sconce, and toss it in a lazy arc . . .

. . . He conjured a door, and was thrust through it by a huge hot hand. A jump took him to the far end of the tunnel—only to witness a roaring yellow fireball expanding along it in his direction. Another jump to Radu's sarcophagus, behind which he had deposited his second sausage bag of high explosives.

Which now he would use.

But not until he had seen to Bonnie Jean—if that were at all possible.

And one last long howl ringing in Harry's mind, and a picture of the dog-Lord blazing bright as a star, "gloriously," as indeed he had seen himself in his visions of the future. Except as he remembered now too late and only too well, the future was ever an unknown quantity, ever a devious thing . . .

* * *

Certain members of the teeming dead talked, made their points, argued their arguments. But it was Nostradamus who won. *I could not know,* he said. *I could only say as I saw, and saw only what I was allowed to see. But it appears that I showed too much. If the Necroscope works it all out—which he will, given time—maybe he won't want to go on. And we're all agreed he must! And if he tries to change what will be, he can only damage himself. Wherefore you must limit the damage now. Harder still, you must eliminate it from your own minds, too. For from now on, you can never so much as hint of it.*

And the ones he spoke to—B.J., Mary Keogh, Franz Anton Mesmer, Keenan Gormley, James Anderson, and any and all of the Great Majority who had played their parts in the thing—they all agreed . . .

Epilogue

THERE WAS NO SIGN OF ANY COMMOTION. B.J. WAS — OR HAD BEEN — AFTER ALL a fledgling Lady; with her leech gone, her flesh had simply succumbed. And the dog-Lord: he was a smoking, cindered black thing, still dumbstruck from the realization of his true, his final death. Crumbling underfoot like charcoal, he made no protest when Harry separated his dust and brushed him into diverse corners and crevices in the burned-out cave of the warrior creature. That *thing* had been burning still, and its stench was terrible. Doomed from the day of its "conception" in this place six hundred years ago, it was no threat.

B.J. still hung there. Miraculously, though the rope was charred it hadn't burned right through. And after several hazardous trial-and-error Möbius jumps into mainly unknown depths, the Necroscope found her head. Oddly—or perhaps not—from the one glance he was able to give her face without completely breaking down, she looked at peace. Something B.J. could never be if she'd survived. For then she would be Wamphyri!

Harry took her remains, wrapped in a blanket, up onto the roof of the mountain, under the moon and stars. Where she surprised him by saying:

So what they told me is true! And didn't I always know you were the strange one? Strange and deep. Oh, it was in your eyes right from the beginning. And I thought I was the beguiler . . .

"You were," he told her. "But I loved you for you, not for your lying eyes."

Do you forgive me for that? For in the end, as you see, I went against Radu— for you.

Harry guarded his thoughts, because now in his turn he too must lie. But a white lie. For there was no way of telling even now whether she spoke the truth or not. Had she in fact turned against the dog-Lord *for* Harry, or to *possess* Harry? She would have been a Lady, after all, terrible and possessive and territorial. These mountains had been hers for two hundred years. It would be hard to turn them over to Radu. And as for turning the Necroscope over . . . who could say?

But he wanted to believe her anyway, and so said, "There's nothing to forgive."

I feel your warmth, she said, thoughtfully. *Little wonder they love you, too. Strange that such warmth lies behind those cold, cold eyes, and in that cold, cold mind. Or maybe not so strange. You walk with death, which has to be a cold path. And like a fool, I once asked you for your thoughts on life!*

Harry was choked now, but he didn't want B.J. to see him like that. And so he changed the subject. "You're a brave one," he said. "Sometimes it takes a *long* time to . . . to get used to the idea."

But they welcomed me, she explained. *The teeming dead; for now they've welcomed me, anyway. Though I fancy the—what, the novelty?—may soon wear off. Your mother welcomed me, and your friends. You have a great many, Harry, a Great Majority. So for the moment I'm at peace with them.*

"I'm glad," said Harry.

But if I want to keep it that way, I can't stay here, B.J. continued. *So tell me . . . have you thought what to do with me?*

"Do with you?" Harry's emotions were on the boil now. They threatened to spill over.

Don't! she told him tremulously. *You'll only set me going, too . . .*

He fought it down, said, "Where do you want to go?"

And she showed him: a far cold golden place, but one that was entirely in keeping. He took her there, but alive he could only accompany her so far. And at the end, he spilled her body gently through his door and let it drift to earth—but not to Earth . . .

. . . Then, suddenly furious, Harry returned to Radu's lair, where he separated his deadly plastic, set fuses, and stood off across the gorge to watch the rotten rock of the uppermost dome of the mountain crumple down into itself. And it was done.

Now he could look up at the moon again, see B.J. there and say his last goodbye.

I was ever a moon-child, she told him from afar. *And so in a way I've returned to my beginnings. You, too, Harry. You must return to yours, and forget me.*

"But how could I ever forget you?" he husked, and couldn't stop the tears that came and kept coming.

Ah, see! B.J. said. *That was how you beat me, and how you beat Radu. And I was right: the cold in you is only the way you are destined to walk, along a cold, cold path. But you, inside, you're burning. And those tears are like some mordant acid that burns more on the inside than out! . . . Which we can't allow.*

"What?" Harry said. But he knew what.

> With numbers and with solar heat and grave-cold,
> with mordant acids, and his friends in low society . . .

Go home, Harry, B.J. told him. *None of this ever happened. Only your search for Brenda and your child was real. Yet at the same time nothing has been lost—only your wife and child! And whether you find them or not, you will recover, and you will go on.*

"B.J., don't do it," said Harry. But she, they, had to.

And before he could erect his shields, together all three of them—B.J., James Anderson, and Franz Anton Mesmer—snapped their magical fingers in the Necroscope's mind . . .

Returning from Edinburgh, Ben Trask reported directly to Darcy Clarke. Seating himself tiredly in front of Darcy's desk in his office, Trask shrugged his shoulders and said, "Nothing. He had nothing to do with any of it. That unholy mess at Greenham Common? Nothing. Events in Tibet, Sicily? Forget it, Harry wasn't involved. Reports of explosions in the Cairngorms, and missing people left, right and centre? A complete blank. I approached it all obliquely, of course, but he never even twitched. The only thing he was interested in— and then not too interested, not any longer—was to ask me if we'd heard anything of his wife and child. I told him no, nothing. In other words, it was nothing all round."

But on second thought: "Oh," Ben straightened up a little. "There is one thing."

Darcy looked at him. "Something good?"

Ben grinned. "It rather depends on how you look at it," he said. "At the time, I didn't think so. But when it was time for me to leave, he asked me if I'd like a lift."

"A lift?" Darcy frowned, then sat up straighter himself, and laughed out loud. "What, along the Möbius route?"

Ben nodded. "It looks like you're off the hook," he said. "He's not afraid to talk about it any more—or even to do it. But I was. I came back by train!"

It was a weight off Darcy's mind. "So what do you think?" he said. "Could we perhaps ask him if . . . ?"

"The Branch?" Trask shook his head, sighed. "I didn't get the warmest possible reception. No, I suggest you leave it out for now. He won't be coming back in a while."

And they would leave it out, for almost four more years.

But at the next full moon:

Harry was on the riverbank talking to his Ma. *Spring,* she said. *I can feel it in the air. Spring, when a young man's fancy . . .*

". . . Turns to spring-cleaning," said Harry. "There's still a lot I can do to the house. God, more than four years! And it doesn't feel like I've done anything much."

You'd be surprised, she said.

"Hmmm?"

I said I'm always surprised, she corrected herself. *At the way time flies, I mean, even down here.*

And: "Tempus fuck-it!" thought Harry, perverting the Latin but keeping the thought to himself. Four years, yes. It was . . . it was like they were lost years.

But of course they weren't.

And in a little while—when his Ma started pestering him about catching a cold again—he walked back to the house under the moon.

* * *

In Inverdruie, Auld John nursed an arm that didn't seem to want to heal, and stood under that same moon looking up at the high Cairngorms. For the first time in his life he felt old, and he really was old. Time had caught up with John, as if some deadly catalyst had been added to his blood, to make it congeal. Or as if something had gone out of him, out of his life.

And he believed he knew what it was. It was the howling he would never again hear in his mind, the fever that was fled out of his veins.

For the Auld Wolf was gone as if he'd never been, and that barking was only a dog out with his master, running for the joy of it in the streaming moonlight . . .

AUTHOR'S END NOTE

In Part Four, Chapter III, the seventieth Quatrain from Nostradamus's Second Century is authentic—and coincidental, naturally. In the same Chapter, the Hebrew cryptogram as used by numerologists is also authentic, and the results of the Necroscope's, Nostradamus's, and Darcy Clarke's numbers are likewise coincidental, of course.

My own lifelong interest in numbers, the macabre, and magical things in general is . . . yet another happy coincidence!

Brian Lumley
22115 364351